THE GREEK TREASURE

Books by Irving Stone

BIOGRAPHICAL NOVELS

LUST FOR LIFE
(Vincent Van Gogh)
IMMORTAL WIFE
(Jessie Benton Fremont)
ADVERSARY IN THE HOUSE
(Eugene V. Debs)
THE PASSIONATE JOURNEY
(John Noble)
THE PRESIDENT'S LADY
(Rachel Jackson)

LOVE IS ETERNAL
(Mary Todd Lincoln)
THE AGONY AND THE ECSTASY
(Michelangelo)
THOSE WHO LOVE
(Abigail Adams)
THE PASSIONS OF THE MIND
(Sigmund Freud)
THE GREEK TREASURE
(Henry and Sophia Schliemann)

BIOGRAPHIES

SAILOR ON HORSEBACK
(Jack London)
THEY ALSO RAN
(Defeated Presidential Candidates)

CLARENCE DARROW FOR THE
DEFENSE
EARL WARREN

HISTORY

MEN TO MATCH MY MOUNTAINS

NOVELS

PAGEANT OF YOUTH

FALSE WITNESS

BELLES-LETTRES

WE SPEAK FOR OURSELVES
(A Self-Portrait of America)

THE STORY OF MICHELANGELO'S
PIETÀ

WITH JEAN STONE

DEAR THEO
(Vincent Van Gogh)

I, MICHELANGELO, SCULPTOR
(Autobiographies through letters)

COLLECTED

THE IRVING STONE READER

EDITOR

THERE WAS LIGHT
Autobiography of a University
Berkeley: 1888–1968

LINCOLN: A CONTEMPORARY
PORTRAIT
(with Allan Nevins)

BOOKS FOR YOUNG READERS

THE GREAT ADVENTURE OF MICHELANGELO

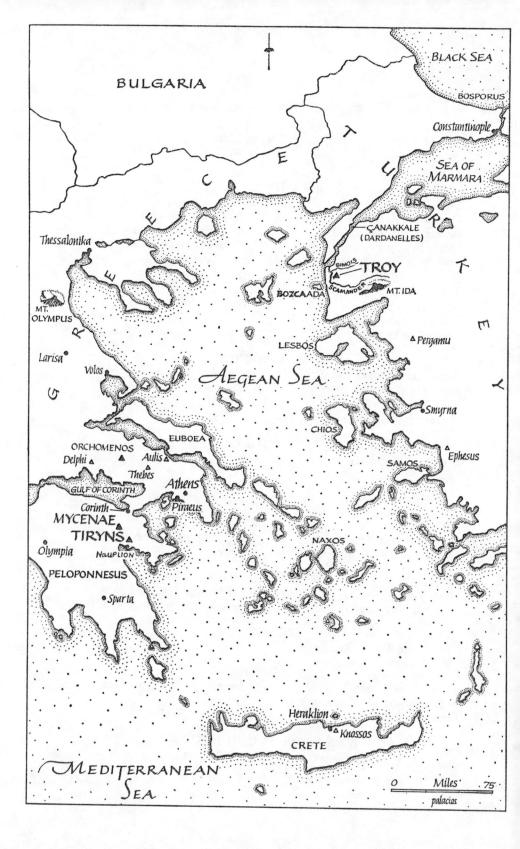

BLACK SEA

BULGARIA

BOSPORUS

Constantinople

SEA OF
MARMARA

ÇANAKKALE
(DARDANELLES)

Thessalonika

SIMOIS
TROY
SCAMANDER
BOZCAADA
MT. IDA

MT.
OLYMPUS

LESBOS

Pergamu

Larisa

AEGEAN SEA

Volos

Smyrna

CHIOS

EUBOEA

ORCHOMENOS
Delphi   Aulis
Thebes
Athens
GULF OF CORINTH
Corinth   Piraeus
MYCENAE
TIRYNS
Olympia
NAUPLION
PELOPONNESUS
Sparta

SAMOS

Ephesus

NAXOS

MEDITERRANEAN
SEA

Heraklion
Knossos
CRETE

0   Miles   75

palacias

For Carol Belliston:
a good friend to books.
Fraternally

The Greek Treasure

A BIOGRAPHICAL NOVEL OF
HENRY AND SOPHIA SCHLIEMANN

by Irving Stone

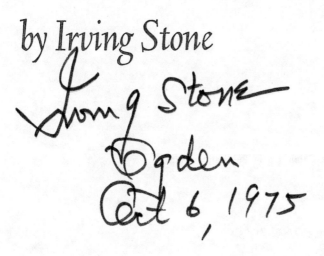

Irving Stone

Ogden

Oct 6, 1975

DOUBLEDAY & COMPANY, INC., GARDEN CITY, NEW YORK, 1975

Library of Congress Cataloging in Publication Data

Stone, Irving, 1903-
   The Greek treasure.

   Bibliography
PZ3.S87872Gr [PS3537.T669] 813'.5'2
ISBN 0-385-07309-7
ISBN 0-385-11170-3 lim. ed.
Library of Congress Catalog Card Number 74-33740

For Jean Stone

my own particular
Greek treasure

FOREWORD

I want to express my deepest gratitude to Dr. Francis R. Walton, Director, and his assistants at the Gennadius Library, American School of Classical Studies, Athens, Greece, for their unfailing kindness and helpfulness in my work on their Henry Schliemann archives, and for their permission to use and quote from those documents on which they hold the copyright.

I was privileged to be in Athens when the Gennadius Library purchased from the last of the Schliemann grandsons a large suitcase of the personal and intimate letters between Henry and Sophia Schliemann, and the Engastromenos family, all of which had been held out from the bulk of the literary estate already in the possession of the Gennadius Library. These letters reveal the full and true story of the relationship between Henry and Sophia from the day they met until his death twenty-one years later. The letters had never been seen by anyone outside of the family, not even by Ernst Meyer, who had the co-operation of the Schliemann descendants in publishing two volumes of Schliemann letters in 1953 and 1958.

I.S.

THE BOOKS

	FOREWORD	9
One	"YOU MUST HAVE FAITH!"	15
Two	GREECE IS GOD'S LOVE AFFAIR WITH THE PLANET EARTH	63
Three	THE WHEEL TURNS WITH TIME	117
Four	A SACRED LOCALITY	161
Five	TROY?	219
Six	A BRIDGE OF DAYS	275
Seven	MYCENAE!	331
Eight	IT TAKES TIME TO MATURE	395
Nine	WHAT IS BETWEEN MAN AND GOD?	455
	AUTHOR'S NOTE	473
	ACKNOWLEDGMENTS	474
	SELECT BIBLIOGRAPHY	475

"The long unmeasured pulse of time moves everything.
There is nothing hidden that it cannot bring to life,
Nothing once known that may not become unknown."

Sophocles, *Ajax*

EDITED BY JEAN STONE

BOOK ONE

"YOU MUST HAVE FAITH!"

1.

SHE was helping the other girls of the village decorate the icon of St. Meletios, putting daisies, end-of-August chrysanthemums and *skyllakia* around the shrine in the middle of the small church for the coming holiday. Her younger sister Marigo rushed in breathless, and cried:

"Sophia! The American has arrived. Your suitor, Mr. Schliemann!"

Startled, her slender arms still in the air where she had been festooning one of the walls, she could only murmur:

"Already? But he was not expected until Saturday."

"Maybe so, but he's sitting big as life in our garden, drinking a glass of lemonade. Uncle Vimpos brought him. Mother says to hurry."

"I'll be right there. Tell Mother I'm going to bathe first, and change my dress."

Marigo ran out the double wooden doors, already adorned with branches of myrtle and araceae. Sophia put the flowers down and stood on the small hand-woven carpets the girls had brought from home, new and beautiful, with many-colored geometrical designs, to replace for the day the used and poorer ones of the church. The other girls had also stopped work and were gazing at her with unabashed interest. Up to a year ago they had been her summer friends, the ones with whom she had associated when her family came out to Colonos, a mile from Athens, where the Engastromenos family owned a vacation house in the cool tree-shaded suburb. But that had been before her father suffered a financial blow. Now this summer house was their refuge. Sophia had been able to complete her last year at the expensive Arsakeion school for girls, the best in Greece, only through the most rigorous family self-sacrifice and the help of her already debt-ridden Uncle Vimpos.

"*Herete*," she murmured to her friends as she started for the door.

Outside, the dry beneficent heat of the late summer day still sat in St. Meletios Square as corporeally as the men who had drifted out to their favorite café under the palms and acacia trees for their cup of thick Turkish coffee. The accompanying glasses of water, small spoons laid across the top, sparkled in the clear air. Sophia's house was cater-corner from St. Meletios's church but instead of cutting diagonally across the warm pavement as she generally did she walked under the trees of the two sides of the square. She was in no hurry to meet the fate-laden moment; she needed a quiet interval to recall everything that had happened since that day in March, almost six months before, when her uncle, family cousin, really, had started what seventeen-year-old Sophia Engastromenos had thought was little more than a romantic prank; and was now just a few moments away from becoming a reality.

When Theokletos Vimpos was studying theology at the university in St. Petersburg in 1856, thirteen years before, he had taught ancient Greek to a native of Germany, though now a subject of the Czar, who had an insatiable appetite for languages as well as the talent to learn a new one in a few weeks. The man was without formal schooling, in fact had spent most of his thirty-four years as a wholesale merchant of indigo, olive oil and tea, accumulating a fortune by concentrating on the quality of his imports and the satisfaction of his customers. The twenty-four-year-old theology student and Heinrich Schliemann became friends.

Heinrich Schliemann had been born in a parsonage in Mecklenburg, Germany, on January 6, 1822. Because he had taught himself Russian, he was sent by the firm for which he worked in Amsterdam, B. H. Schröder & Company, to be their factor in St. Petersburg. Here he had served his principals well, had been given permission to open his own business, had become a citizen of the Czar. At the height of the gold rush, in 1850, he went to California, where he amassed a second fortune. Two years later he returned to St. Petersburg, married, had three children and accumulated a third fortune during the Crimean War.

The marriage was a total failure.

In the spring of 1869 he left for New York, got his United States citizenship papers, which were drawn in the name of Henry Schliemann, and moved to Indianapolis to secure a quick divorce. From here he had written importuning letters to his old friend, now Father Theokletos Vimpos, in Athens, urging Vimpos to find a young Greek wife for him. Father Vimpos immediately called on his cousins, Sophia's parents, suggesting that he recommend their young daughter Sophia. In drawing a character sketch of the man who now insisted upon his American name, Henry Schliemann, he told them of his visits to Schliemann's warehouse on the Neva River in St. Petersburg:

"His methods of doing business were thought by some to be fanatical, for he trusted only routine tasks to his clerks. He himself received every merchant who came to buy, learned what they required, checked the shipment before it left his warehouse. During the Crimean War he had a monopoly on the indigo trade, an indispensable item for the Russian army. By the end of 1863, at the age of forty-one, he was able to retire.

He told me that, although he admired money, it was for him only a means to an end: to finance the discovery of Homer's Troy."

And now he had arrived at Colonos, two months after Sophia's graduation from high school.

Sophia pirouetted at the far corner of the square, rising a little on her toes as she made the turn toward her house. She laughed a few bright, musical notes as she remembered the letter Mr. Schliemann had written to her Uncle Vimpos from Paris. Vimpos had given her the letter to keep. She had read it so many times she knew it by heart:

> Dear Friend, I cannot tell you how dearly I love your city and its inhabitants. . . . I swear to you, by the bones of my mother, that I will direct my whole mind and energies to making my future wife happy. I swear that she shall never have any grounds to complain, I will wait on her hand and foot, if she is good and amiable. . . .
>
> Therefore I beg you to enclose with your answer the portraits of several beautiful Greek women. But if you can send me the portrait of the girl whom *you* destine for me, so much the better. I entreat you: choose for me a wife of the same angelic character as your married sister. She should be poor, but well educated; she must be enthusiastic about Homer and about the rebirth of my beloved Greece. It does not matter whether she knows foreign languages or not. But she should be of the Greek type, with black hair and, if possible, beautiful. But my main requirement is a good and loving heart! Perhaps you know an orphan, the daughter of a scholar, who is obliged to earn her living as a governess, and who possesses the virtues I require.

Having reached her house, Sophia entered the rarely used front door, which would shield her from the view of her family and their honored guest sitting out in the garden. As she stood with her hand on the knob, a moment of uncertainty seized her: to go into the house? Or to begin the acquaintance of the man her family wanted her to marry? She could not decide.

"But for that matter, neither could Henry Schliemann decide," she thought. The second letter to Uncle Vimpos had almost prostrated her mother, known in Colonos as Madame Victoria because she copied the British Queen's outfits to the smallest detail.

Theokletos Vimpos, declaring that he was not going to get caught in a naked act of nepotism, had sent photographs of two other attractive young women as well as the one of Sophia. Schliemann had answered in early March, in modern Greek:

> As I am an old traveler and a good reader of faces, I can tell you right away the character of two of the girls from their pictures. Polyxene Gousti's surname shows that her ancestors were Italian. Her age is that which is suitable for my wife, but she is bossy, imperious, domineering, irritable and resentful. But I could be mistaken; perhaps if I saw her face to face, I might discover in her a treasure of all the virtues. As for Sophia Engastromenos, she is a splendid woman, affable, compassionate, generous, a good housekeeper, lively and well brought up. But, alas, she is too young for a man of forty-seven years.

She turned the knob and entered the Engastromenoses' modest though pleasant country villa, walked down a hall with the sittingroom on her right and the diningroom on her left. In the kitchen she picked up a round basin and poured hot water into it from an enormous pot Kyria Victoria Engastromenos kept bubbling on her coal stove.

She moved at an even pace up the narrow flight of stairs to her bedroom, careful not to spill the hot water. In her corner room, which faced the square, she set the basin on the washstand, stretched out a towel on the floor, took a washcloth from a chest of drawers, a square cake of Greek soap from its dish and dropped it in the water to soften its rigid contours. She took off her cotton dress, figured with tiny flowers, and made from a bolt of inexpensive material her father sold in his drapery shop on Romvis Square, something between organdy and muslin, first unbuttoning the buttons fitted close to each other from the neck to the waist on the side of the short jacket, then slipping out of the long voluminous skirt, which she hung behind a curtain in a corner of the room. She tossed her undergarments, piece by piece, onto the narrow bed with its bronze bars at head and foot, draping her stockings on the round knobs screwed onto the bars. She soaked the washcloth in the basin of water and scrubbed herself.

As she straightened up to dry herself she was reflected in the gold-bordered mirror which hung on the wall over the washstand. It was a lithe but sturdy figure, with beautifully rounded shoulders, firm, well-shaped breasts, a slender waist. She had surprisingly long legs for a Greek girl, and at seventeen had reached the height of five feet five inches, taller than most of her contemporaries at the Arsakeion. In her figure as well as her temperament she favored her father's side of the family.

With a start she realized that she was conscious of her body in a quite different way from any time before.

"Is it," she wondered, "because a suitor is here, in our very garden, and even now may be discussing marriage with my parents? Because this body of mine will be . . . shared . . . ? By a husband, by children growing inside me . . . ? What will love be like?" Would she be as happy as a married woman as she was as a girl?

She sat at the top of the bed, on a corner of the high bolster, while she slipped into fresh undergarments smelling of violets from the little bags of dried flowers her mother had put into her daughter's bureau; and drew stockings over her slim legs. This done, she looked across to the mirror, at eye-height now.

"My features are too . . ." she searched for the word, "too . . . positive." But at the Arsakeion she had been told that a woman's beauty lay in her character. She grimaced mockingly and turned away from the mirror. No one had ever said she was pretty; that word would not sit well upon her countenance. But there were those who saw in her features an emerging elegance: the patrician head held high with grace on the slender neck, the radiance of an inner light that reflected the combination of her strength and gentleness.

She remembered with a rush of emotion what her Uncle Vimpos had told her at her graduation exercises the previous June:

"Sophia, dear one, in your face today, sparkling with happiness, is all the serenity and beauty of the classical Greek woman: your raven-black hair combed behind your shell-pink ears, the slashing black eyebrows which both you and I inherited from your mother's side of the family; your enormous dark eyes, straight nose, your light complexion; your lovely mouth with its full red underlip, the chin that could have been carved by Phidias in his sculpture studio at Olympia. In spite of your cheerful good nature, there is a touch of gravity in your expression, and of dignity in the way you hold your head. That, too, is classical Greek."

"Uncle Theokletos," she had exclaimed in astonishment, for her family was not a demonstrative one, "you have just composed a romantic poem!"

"Alas, my first and last. I wanted to break the news to you today, Sophia. I am giving up my professorship at the university to become a bishop of our Church."

"A bishop! But that means you can never marry . . ."

". . . nor love. Sophia, I have never loved a woman. Only God and our Church. My investiture will be in November, when I become Bishop of Mantinia and Kynouria."

Sophia stepped out to the window in the hall, a sudden desire to see her suitor. Gazing down into the garden, she saw her mother and father. They were seated with their backs to her, on either side of a strange man. Doubtless that was Henry Schliemann, but she could see little. In the center of the group, facing the house, was Father Vimpos, a tall lean man in a black clerical robe which covered him from Adam's apple to shoetop. His big-boned frame was topped by an enormous head.

"It would have to be," her father had observed, "to carry around that quantity of brains. I wonder it doesn't make his neck ache."

Looking at the man with warm affection, Sophia heard his resonant voice, which originated deep within him and gained power in its upward march toward the soundbox in his throat. Theokletos Vimpos was thirty-seven now, twenty years older than Sophia, but his face was youthful and unlined. He had been born in the shadow of the Acropolis and graduated in theology from the University of Athens, gone on to study in Moscow and St. Petersburg, where he had tutored Henry Schliemann, then won a four-year scholarship to the University of Leipzig, where he studied under two of Europe's most renowned Hebraists, earning his doctorate of philosophy. Returning to the University of Athens at the age of twenty-eight, he had been named professor of theology, introduced the study of Hebrew into Greece, and published the country's first textbook on the subject, *Elements of Hebrew Grammar*. Six years later, without giving up his professorship, he was ordained a priest of the Orthodox Church, though without a congregation.

That winter he had come out to Colonos to counsel with Sophia's parents. As bishop he would have to live at Tripolis, the seat of his bishopric, in the rather poor and barren mountainous area in the central Peloponnesus. Because of his extensive travels and years of study, he suffered under a crushing debt, two thousand dollars, on which he was paying the local moneylenders two per cent interest a month. Handsome dowries were being offered to him by the best families in Athens. How then to become a bishop, when it paid no salary? How to get out from under his debts without marrying some unfortunate girl whom he did not love?

His friend Henry Schliemann had solved his problem by ordering his bank in Paris to send Vimpos a check which relieved him of the more crushing debts.

Henry Schliemann!

When Theokletos Vimpos received the first letter requesting that he find his friend a wife, his thoughts had immediately turned to Sophia. He and Sophia had been good friends as she grew up, sympathetic, particularly during her years at the Arsakeion when she had needed help with the more difficult courses in Euclidean geometry, experimental physics, the ancient Greek of Homer and Thucydides. Sophia had always been an energetic child who loved to laugh and enjoyed games.

She had also been serious in her studies, and at seventeen seemed more mature than her years.

"Seems . . ." Father Vimpos smiled. "What man can know what a young girl is really like?"

It was natural for him to think of marriage for Sophia. All Greek families with seventeen-year-old girls were beginning to look the field over, weigh the dowries demanded. The girls had little to say; no girl questioned the tradition. Theokletos Vimpos had broken the pattern by insisting that Sophia be present when he told her parents about Henry Schliemann's request. They had all agreed her name should be submitted.

Sophia studied her friend and relative, with the hollow cheeks of the ascetic who feasted on books and learning instead of *dolmadakia* and *moussaka*. He had already had a full beard as a professor, but his hair had been cut short. From the time he had been inducted into the priesthood, three years before, he had been obliged to let his hair grow, and it was now pulled back and tied in a knot on his neck, just below the round black clerical hat. Sophia was sure he did not want anything but a good life and happiness for her.

She took one fleeting glance at the back of Mr. Schliemann but avoided any speculation about him. Instead she slipped to her knees before her icon, an exquisite albeit solemn Virgin Mary in a deep purple robe and hood, and prayed for divine guidance.

2.

The white cambric dress her older sister Katingo had left behind when she married several years before had already been too small for Katingo, for she had her mother's figure, with heavily padded forearms, hips, stomach and backside. On Sophia it was too big, and she knew it as she buttoned the lace collar at her throat; but it was the best she had. There had been no new clothing in the Engastromenos family since her father had become involved in the financial catastrophe which cost him his prosperous drapery shop and their home above it in Romvis Square. It had overlooked the superb Byzantine church of St. Panaghitsa where Sophia and the other five Engastromenos children had been christened, and the busy Evanghelistrias Street with the magnificent Acropolis looming above.

The family had been able to afford Katingo a handsome dowry, which won her the clockmaker, Ioannes Synessios, as a husband; but shortly after the wedding a large loan which Georgios Engastromenos had co-signed came due. Georgios's associate fled the country, leaving him responsible for the debt. To fulfill his legal obligation Georgios had had to sell the handsome building bought with his wife's dowry, the spacious home which had been reached by a side entrance, with its many bedrooms, roof garden, penthouse in which the boys slept, the handsome double doors leading to a balcony enclosed by a carved wrought-iron balustrade, where the family could sit out after supper, enjoying the coolness of evening.

Now the house on Romvis Square, just off the fashionable Ermou, and Victoria Geladaki's dowry were gone. Georgios rented back the shop in which his older sons, Alexandros and Spyros, also worked, but at such a high rental that the three men could barely earn the day's necessities.

The failure had also injured the Engastromenos family's position in the social structure of Athens. Now there would be no dowries for Sophia or Marigo, which virtually ruled out marriage for them; no university education for the youngest boy, Panaghiotes, only ten, but already showing a flair for books and learning that earmarked him for the university.

Sophia's mother, Madame Victoria, short and plump, was a proud and poised woman who combed her glossy black hair down from a precise center part to cover her ears and tied it in a thick bun. She was always immaculately dressed, even in the kitchen. She was the descendant of a prominent family from Crete who had led one of the early uprisings against the Turks and had had to flee to Athens, a small dirt-paved town which had recently been made the capital of Greece, in 1834. Although the loss of their home and social position had been a severe blow to Madame Victoria, Sophia had never heard her mother reproach her easygoing father for this misfortune or complain about their reduced circumstances. Yet she had been honest with Sophia. She spoke quietly to her when the two were alone in the house after the move to Colonos.

"My dear Sophia, this affects you directly, for you are almost seventeen and will soon graduate from the Arsakeion. Neither your father nor I had any wish to hurry you, but we had already begun looking for the best possible husband for you. Now we cannot. There is no dowry, and no man you would want to have, who can give you your proper place in Greek society, would marry you without a dowry."

Sophia had jumped up and kissed her mother's firm, plump cheek.

"But, Mother, I have seven full years until I am twenty-four, before I will be judged an old maid and no longer fit to marry!"

Madame Victoria shuddered at the phrase "old maid."

"Oh, Sophia, our chances are so slim now. The best we could do for you is some poor parish priest or a young army officer in a remote military post. . . . Our best chance will be with an overseas Greek who has made his fortune in Egypt or Asia Minor or the United States and comes back to find a Greek bride. They are the only ones not interested in a dowry; they come seeking a well-raised girl who will be a good housekeeper. . . ."

Sophia had refused to take the matter seriously.

"I already made my application to be a schoolteacher. As a graduate of the Arsakeion, I don't even have to take the examinations."

Dressed now, her rich black hair brushed back from her brow until it gleamed and crackled, her pearl earrings secured in the lobes of her ears, she put away her linens, straightened the bed. She could procrastinate no longer. She walked through the hallway with its window overlooking the garden. Already the clan had gathered, for through the open window she heard the babble of some thirty relatives, all of whom had rushed from various corners of Colonos to have a first look at the mysterious, famous millionaire who had come to court their Sophia.

"Not really!" she thought with a little giggle. "He's now courting the whole of Greece."

The letter Uncle Vimpos had received late in April had been practically a proposal:

> My friend, already I have fallen in love with Sophia Engastromenos, so that I swear she is the only woman who shall be my wife. For two reasons I don't know whether I am in a position to marry: first, I am not yet sure that I shall get the divorce; second, because of my matrimonial difficulties I have had no relations with a woman for six years. . . . If I am convinced that I am fit, then I shall not hesitate to go to Athens and talk with Sophia, whom I shall marry if she consents. We are forced to wait until then, because if I am impotent . . . I should not marry. Yes, as much as a woman may love her husband before marriage, she will always despise him if he is unable to gratify her physical passion.
>
> How old is Sophia? What color is her hair? Does she play the piano? Does she speak any foreign languages? Is she a good housekeeper? Does she understand Homer and our other ancient authors? Would she agree to change her residence to Paris, and to accompany her husband on his journeys to Italy, Egypt and elsewhere? . . .

However Sophia knew that during the two days Henry Schliemann had been in Athens he had been interviewing other "prospects" in what Father Vimpos called "a combination of Teutonic thoroughness and American energy." He did not attempt to conceal these meetings from

Vimpos, in fact he had given him a full report. He had gone to visit a Miss Charikleia, "who did not make a good impression on me; she is too tall, sad and timid." From here he had gone by carriage to Kyria Cleopatra Lemoni, a widow.

"I expected to see an old woman bent under the weight of misfortune and sad looking. I found a young, beautiful and gay woman who did not look more than thirty years old. She attracted me very much. I think it would be better for me to marry a young widow of exemplary behavior, who already knows what marriage means. She would be less voluptuous and sensual, while young girls believe that heaven and paradise be in the fulfillment of their physical desires."

He had converted his suite at the Hotel d'Angleterre on Syntagma Square facing the royal palace into a self-serving matrimonial bureau: from the moment he arrived in Athens and it became known that he was there to find a Greek wife, he had been deluged by offers from the best families who had ideal but, alas! unwed daughters.

"As far as anybody can achieve accurate bookkeeping on a whirlwind, I would say he has already seen and talked to fifteen prospects in a couple of days!" her Uncle Vimpos told Sophia.

Sophia laughed, the musical laughter that lodged pleasantly in the middle register of the ear.

"Your Mr. Schliemann does sound extraordinary!" Then she turned serious, her dark eyes brooding. "But how do I handle a hurricane? Outside of the family I have hardly exchanged a dozen sentences with men."

If Sophia was amused at the idea of Mr. Schliemann trying to meet and interview every eligible young woman in Athens, her parents, to whom this marriage had all the aspects of a lifeboat miraculously dislodged from a sinking ship, were hurt and dismayed. Madame Victoria said to Theokletos Vimpos:

"But are we not suffering an indignity, a blow to our family pride, to have Mr. Schliemann scouring the town . . . ?"

"It's his way, Cousin Victoria. I watched him do business in St. Petersburg, where he made his fortune by these very methods. It will bring you even greater kudos that Mr. Schliemann did not choose blindly from a photograph, but only after testing every conceivable alternative."

The Engastromenoses had been mollified but there were lines of anxiety grooving downward from the corners of Madame Victoria's mouth. With Schliemann in the family there would be a handsome dowry for their youngest daughter Marigo; a university education for their youngest son. There would be a capital fund with which to restock the drapery shop which, since the calamitous sale of the building, was failing because of the disappearance of their credit.

Sophia knew all this; she had assented to the marriage without reservation.

"Arranged marriages are the best," said Greek tradition.

She stepped out into the garden to meet Henry Schliemann, to inspect and to be inspected.

It was cool in the garden now, in the late afternoon; the climbing vines still showed some grapes. There were fruit trees which Georgios Engastromenos had planted years before: pomegranate, almond, apricot and mulberry; the familiar *gazia*, a muskmelon with spongelike yellow flowers and a fine perfume. The table and chairs were simple wooden ones which had seen a lot of wear, for the Engastromenos aunts, uncles and cousins, as well as Madame Victoria's family, the Geladakis, also had summer homes in Colonos.

The family rose en masse as Sophia walked toward them. That had never happened to her before.

"I have suddenly become the reigning princess," she thought.

Her heart was beating in what seemed to her a noisy rhythm for a girl who had told herself she was not going to become excited over this first encounter, even though she knew that Mr. Schliemann would be examining her with all the thoroughness he had used in judging a shipment of indigo at the auctions in Amsterdam.

"How fast the news has traveled!" she observed. In less time than it took her to cross the square, bathe and dress, her relatives had donned their Sunday best and, with their children trailing them, had made their way to see this remarkable phenomenon: a multimillionaire who had retired at forty-four, had traveled the world and published two books; a German native who had become a citizen of the Czar, then an American citizen, and now wanted a Greek wife, and to become a Greek himself! Nothing quite so interesting had happened to Colonos since Sophocles had been born there, and later immortalized his birthplace by naming it "White Colonos, fed by heaven's dews, where the nightingales sing amidst the wine-dark ivy"; since Oedipus had disappeared close by. When the blind Oedipus was being led by his daughter Antigone toward Athens, and asked her, in the afternoon of a long day on the dusty roads, "What place is this? What people?" Antigone had answered:

> "Father, poor tired Oedipus, the towers
> That crown the city still seem far away.
> As for this place, it is clearly a holy one,

> Shady with vines and olive trees and laurel;
> Snug in their wings within, the nightingales
> Make a sweet music."

Sitting at the command post at the large garden table was her mother. Madame Victoria, head of her clan, was intensely proud of her Cretan heritage. Cretans were independent, fierce fighters, obstinate, hating the fact that they had been subjugated by the Turks, rising in revolt nearly every generation since the first Greeks on the mainland, led by their clergy, had secured independence. They stuck together; family loyalty was the first law of survival. Next came their dedication to the clan, a wider circle than the family because it included "blood brothers," those who had mingled their blood from knife cuts on the arm, to swear their undying fealty. An outstanding idiosyncrasy was that they were lavish and greedy at the same time: greedy so that they could afford to be lavish, to make the grand gesture. They were a lordly people, "and rightly so," Sophia's mother had taught her. As far back as 1600 B.C. Crete was the cultural center of the Western world, with great palaces, rich cities, talented architects, painters, sculptors, athletes, as well as being the commercial center of the Aegean, for her ships traded with every country bordering on the Mediterranean, her navy controlled the seas; and Crete dominated as much of mainland Greece as she had wanted to. Sophia had grown up on her mother's folk wisdom from the island:

Who has hope in God never goes to bed hungry; and if he does, sleep feeds him. . . . A good housewife can spin with a spoon. . . . Take the advice of old people and married people; they have eaten much bread and salt. . . .

Sitting next to her mother was Sophia's aunt, Kyria Lambridou, second in command of the clan; perhaps because of her inferior position she enjoyed sprinkling the condiment of controversy on other people's food.

On the other side of the visitor, Sophia saw her father, sitting in his garden chair as relaxed as Madame Victoria was tense. One of the valuables the family had rescued from the town flat was an oil portrait of Georgios Engastromenos painted two years before by a famous Greek painter, Kastriotes. The portrait now hung on the sittingroom wall of the Colonos house. When Sophia's thoughts conjured up her father's image she could not be sure which she was seeing, the oil portrait or the man of flesh. He was good-looking, approaching sixty, bald except for reminiscent gray thatches just above the ears. He wore a long well-proportioned mustache which dropped down to his chin. The eyes were wide-spaced; they observed but they did not judge. As a young man he had fought with his fellow Athenians in their war of liberation from the Turks and had been both exhilarated and decorated by the experience; but that had satisfied any need he may have felt for combat. His nature was a calming and conciliatory one. He was fond of food and drink. He had made his success by being hospitable and gregarious with his customers; he followed the same pattern with his children. Sophia loved him dearly; she could not remember his having raised his voice to her, although he occasionally had to quiet the boys.

He was wearing a small white bow tie tucked under a low white collar; his suit, of the best wool and tweed he could import from England, was well tailored; a big, broad-shouldered man, his only distinguishing mark was an angular cleft in his right eyebrow where, as a child, he had been bitten by a dog. There was nothing suspicious in his nature. A practical man rather than a theorist, he accepted life for what it was without rebutting or lamenting. Once he had become an independent Greek, he considered it folly for anyone to want to change or control the world.

The growing brood of six children had been dominated by Madame Victoria. There was nothing unusual about this; it was the centuries-old way of the Greek family. The father was the absolute master of the household, the mother the servant to his wishes and commands. No one would have dreamed of challenging his authority. Yet it was the mother who raised the children and tied herself to them with the knot developed by King Gordius of Phrygia, whose conquest of Asia Minor was remembered by the Trojans. Alexander the Great had managed to cut through the Gordian knot and take over possession of Asia, as the oracle had predicted; but Greek children had neither Alexander's strength nor his massive sword with which to sever their bonds to their mothers.

Sophia had fared best among the Engastromenos children; for once she started at the Arsakeion, and in particular during the last year of residence in the high school, Madame Victoria, who doted on her most attractive and gifted daughter, had substituted adoration for domination, giving Sophia freedoms denied to her brothers and sisters. Sophia had blossomed under these freedoms; they had increased her love for her mother rather than lessened it. She vowed that no one would ever be permitted to come between them, not even a beloved husband.

She had avoided a head-on look at the man who had traveled some seven thousand miles with the purpose of courting her. Only now in the silence around her did she realize how excited she was. She began to tremble as her father reached out a hand for hers. Looking back over the past few weeks, she saw for the first time that in spite of her resolution not to hope for a tall, handsome romantic figure she had been, in the back of her mind and without consciously willing it, indulging in fantasies about this sophisticated world personage who would surely be one of the most glamorous personalities she had ever seen.

"Sophia, this is Mr. Henry Schliemann, who has paid us the honor of calling upon us. Mr. Schliemann, may I present my daughter Sophia."

Schliemann murmured, "*Despossyne,* my young lady," picked up a book from the table and said in unaccented Greek:

"This is a little book I just published about my travels last year, *Ithaca, the Peloponnesus and Troy.* May I have the pleasure of presenting it to you? I brought the French translation thinking that might be more readable for you."

She bowed and took the book in her two outstretched hands. Although Schliemann had been right in saying that it was a slim volume, it felt as heavy as a block of lead, causing her insides to plummet; for the stranger she saw standing before her was short in stature, only an inch taller than she. He seemed a dull, lackluster man, partly bald, with a scraggly mustache, pale skin with dark hollows in his cheeks, his eyelids drooping as though in fatigue, the hair at the side of his head covering his ears untidily. The bow tie did not fit his collar; his dark suit with a heavy gold chain strung across it gave him the appearance of a bank clerk or grammar school teacher. In her young and inexperienced eyes he looked, at forty-seven, old, well past middle age; more like a used-up man who would be glad to be leaving an exhausting and meaningless world than one who considered he was just beginning his real and meaningful life.

Sophia felt sick at heart. The disappointment was too great. Blinking back her tears, she felt a new and strange emotion arising within her: a sense of rebellion. She believed that arranged marriages were good, the best for everyone concerned. She also knew that her marriage chances were poor without a dowry, and that she might do no better two, four or six years from now. But she had no way to gulp down, as she was gulping down her tears, the knowledge that this would be a difficult man to love, no matter how earnestly she tried. She felt a scream of "No!" form in her throat.

"But I can't say no," she told herself. "The future of my family depends on this marriage. My brothers can't marry until I am married. With my marriage to Mr. Schliemann, Marigo will have her dowry, my father's credit will be restored. We will be able to prepare Panaghiotes for the university . . ."

Not only her family but the entire village of Colonos as well expected this of her.

She braced her shoulders, raised her head, said in her normal robust voice:

"Thank you for the book, Mr. Schliemann. I have already read the

introduction in Greek. Uncle Theokletos brought me a copy of the
May issue of *Myria Osa*, with your excerpt."

Henry Schliemann smiled for the first time, a pleasant smile.

"Excellent! The magazine is published in Paris, but I did hope for
a good distribution in Greece."

She bowed courteously, walked to the empty chair next to Father
Vimpos which had been saved for her. At that moment Marigo came out
of the house carrying a large silver tray on which there were as many
glasses of water as there were guests in the garden. In the middle of the
tray was a bowl filled with cherries in a thick sugary syrup. Also on
the tray was a silver cup containing the right number of spoons. Marigo
started with the honored guest, then moved around the family circle.
Each person took a glass of water in one hand, a spoon in the other and
then a spoonful of the sweet fruit, holding the spoon over the glass to
catch in the water whatever syrup might drop from the spoon. Each
in turn ate the sweet, drank the water, and put the now empty spoon
into the empty glass. Marigo came around once again to collect the
glasses and take them into the house.

3.

With this ritual of the "sweet spoon" the ice was broken. Sophia saw
that, with the exception of herself and Henry Schliemann, everyone
around the table had started talking at once. To get her involved,
Father Vimpos said to Sophia:

"We will soon have to call our friend *Doctor* Schliemann. The University of Rostock, close to his birthplace, is about to confer on him the
title of Doctor of Philosophy for the very book you are holding in your
hand. That will prove its authenticity."

Sophia did not know what to reply. Before her silence could be noticed, Schliemann cried:

"Not *prove*, my dear Archbishop," thereby promoting the young
Bishop-to-be to one of the highest positions in the Orthodox Church;
"merely *suggest*. It is now up to me to prove my conclusions by action
rather than the printed word."

"Of what will this action consist?" one of Sophia's uncles asked courteously.

"The discovery of Troy! Excavating at Hissarlik, just across from the
mouth of the Hellespont! Until I have laid bare the entire city of Priam,
what Homer calls 'sacred Troy.' First I will locate the wall. What Poseidon describes in *The Iliad*: 'I verily built for the Trojans around their
city a wall, wide and exceeding fair, that the city might never be

broken.' And it wasn't. Not until the tenth year of the war, when the Achaeans fooled the Trojans by persuading them to allow the wooden horse to be taken into their city. At night the Achaean soldiers hidden in the horse got out and opened what Homer describes as the 'well-built gates.' Only by this stratagem could the Achaeans, who had pretended to sail home but had hidden their eleven hundred ships on the sandy coves behind the island of Tenedos, take Troy and burn her."

Henry Schliemann was leaning forward excitedly in his chair, his eyes aglow. Sophia was amazed by the change that had come over the man. She was also amazed at the seriousness in his voice.

Her beliefs about *The Iliad*, and consequently about Troy, had been formed by five years of training in the ancient Greek of Homer. Her teachers at the Arsakeion had had their opinions molded by the professors of the University of Athens, just across Panepistimiou Street. The Greek authority on Homer, Professor Vernardakis, had told his university class, when Sophia was in her second year at the Arsakeion:

"After the years of Turkish yoke, Homer's poetry with all of its unsurpassed art has been the ideal food for the Greek people. Homer achieves architectural unity. Everything looks true and natural. *But everything in Homer is false. All are lies.*"

Professor Vernardakis's *obiter dicta* had crossed the boulevard faster than the nimblest pushcart peddler. No Arsakeion teacher would have been so foolhardy as to question the judgment of a University of Athens authority. And so Sophia had been taught that Friedrich Wolf, in his weighty volume, *Prolegomena,* published in 1795, had proved once and for all time that there never had been a Homer, a Trojan War, or even a Troy. No reputable scholar or academician had wished to disagree with his arguments.

Sophia found herself in a mild state of shock at hearing this self-educated man, who had had to leave school at the age of fourteen to work in a grocery store where for five years he had labored eighteen hours a day and had never had a chance to open a book, disagreeing with her teachers and spouting a heresy believed in only by amateurs or misguided fools. Glancing about the garden at the family portraiture, she could see from the skepticism raising one corner of their collective mouths, that they all felt the same way.

Sophia also perceived that Henry Schliemann sensed the disbelief of her family, though they were doing their best to conceal it; she saw too that he was not upset by it. He said graciously:

"Forgive me for being so presumptuous as to tell Greeks about their own history. But you know how it is with converts; they're more ardent than those born into the faith. I don't mind doubt. I have come to live with it. People also doubted that the earth moves around the sun."

The Engastromenoses subscribed to the popular periodical *Pandora*, where rivers of ink had been spilled in what was up to the very moment of late summer, 1869, a burning debate on "The Homeric Question," with *Pandora*'s writers considering the Homeric works "a mere poetical emotion."

Georgios Engastromenos thought it incumbent upon him to encourage his guest.

"Please be so kind as to explain to us, Mr. Schliemann, just how you can uncover a city which was destroyed some . . ."

"Three thousand years ago," Schliemann replied quickly. "Somewhere between 1240 B.C. and 1190 B.C."

"Yes," said Sophia's father reflectively. "Won't that mean that everything that was burned and destroyed will have crumbled into dust?"

Henry Schliemann nodded his head appreciatively. Sophia saw color mounting in his cheeks.

"Hector, the great general of the Trojan forces, and Priam's heir apparent as king, tells us that 'of old, all mortal men were wont to tell of Priam's city, for its wealth of gold, its wealth of bronze.' That should still be there! We know from *The Iliad* of Priam's palace, which had rooms for his fifty sons and their wives; and of the adjoining palace where there lived his twelve daughters and their husbands. We know about Hector's well-built house with its open court where 'white-armed Andromache sat with her serving women, wearing lustrous robes of gold and wool.' When Hector goes to summon to battle his hated brother Paris, we are given a description of Paris's palace, 'the fair palace that himself had builded with the men that were in that day the best builders in deep-soiled Troy; these had made him a chamber and hall and court hard by the palaces of Priam and Hector in the citadel.' All these buildings were of stone, and stone does not burn.

"We know about the Scaean and Dardanian gates through which the Trojan armies marched out to do battle. They should still be there! As well as the 'well-paved streets' used by the charioteers; and the tall Watchtower from which Helen identified for Priam the Achaean leaders Ajax and Agamemnon. All of these and much, much more should still be standing, buried under later Troys, perhaps as many as three or four, but protected over the ages by a close-fitting coat of earth."

Sophia had been sitting demurely, eyes cast down; he heard with surprise the admiration in her voice:

"Mr. Schliemann, you quote from *The Iliad* so fluently one would think you had memorized the entire book. Is that possible?"

"Not only possible, Miss Sophia, but probable. I have read the lines so many times, in both ancient and modern Greek, that they have been burned on my memory. And why should I not be able to memorize the epic when hundreds of Homer's blood descendants and disciples passed it down from generation to generation in its entirety by listening to the bards sing the episodes?"

His manner was not boastful, just matter-of-fact. Sophia took a hard look at him; an astounding transformation had taken place. No longer did he appear lackluster, or even middle-aged. His expression sparkled, his clean-shaven face was flooded with color; he had shifted his shoulders about until his coat fitted him the way the tailor had meant it to; he bristled with a youthful zest and energy. A skillful forefinger had smoothed out the mustache, brushed back the hair behind close-fitting ears. But most important for her were his eyes, now bright, clear, knowledgeable, the lids opened wide to let in all the sights the world had to bestow upon an eager and penetrating mind.

Her sense of disappointment fled; in its place came an interested curiosity about this strange man.

Theokletos Vimpos knew Schliemann well enough to confront him.

"You keep referring to Troy. But there was no Troy! It is a figment of the poet's imagination. Nor was there a Trojan War, or a wooden horse, or a quarrel between Achilles and Agamemnon over a beautiful captured girl. It's all mythology!"

Schliemann laughed good-naturedly; he was accustomed to Vimpos's needling.

"I know. And there was no Homer either. Countless bards over the centuries each wrote some of the verses, and Pisistratus, the Tyrant of Athens, gathered all the bards together in the sixth century B.C. and had a benchful of scriveners write down their lines as they declaimed them, then had them all stitched together. . . . Even Grote says in his *History of Greece* that there is no conceivable way to prove that there was a Troy or that Homer actually wrote *The Iliad* and *The Odyssey*. Ah! But not the world's great poets, not Goethe, Schiller, Shelley, Pindar or Horace. They believe in the unity of Homer, because they recognize that the two books are organically whole, of a piece, created by a single mind of genius!"

Sophia, listening to his voice ring out, flooding the garden with passionate eloquence, found her insides strangely stirred by an emotion she had never known before. Without raising her eyes, she asked quietly:

"Mr. Schliemann, with respect, may I ask a question?"

"Most certainly, my young lady."

"We were taught in school that since the ancient gods play such an important role in both epics, and these gods have vanished from Mt. Olympus and Mt. Ida, obviously *The Iliad* and *The Odyssey* are myths."

Henry Schliemann smiled, his intense blue eyes alight with the love of contest.

"The answer is, once the gods have been removed, or shifted to mythology, what remains of both epics still can be humanly true almost to the last detail. But I don't agree that we have to 'remove' the gods. They were created by an ancient people, perhaps 4000 B.C., and they don't vary so strikingly from the gods of other ancient religions."

Madame Victoria cried:

"But the pagan religion of ancient Greece is looked upon by Christian Greeks as a childish one!"

Sophia wondered if Henry Schliemann would be offended. Instead, she saw, he was excited as he asked her mother to explain why. Her mother explained that the gods, with their human figures and conduct, were invented to fit the passions and deeds which people saw in their own nature, providing them with superhuman forces which would make them able to protect and help mortal man, also to harm or destroy his enemy.

"We never sought any other explanation to the ancient Greek religion, but accepted it as a rich, interesting and sometimes amusing tale."

Sophia watched Schliemann pull down his vest, straighten his black tie against his low white collar, then cross his knees while thinking out his most convincing answer.

"I am a Christian, of course, the son of a clergyman. But what was created by an earlier people and believed in by them becomes a fact of history rather than a myth. If the Trojans or Achaeans could come into your garden this evening and hear us expound on our religion, they would be as amused at what they would call our mythology as we are at theirs. I have a deep-seated admiration for pantheism, and I understand why people worshiped the god of the sun, of the fields, of the rivers. All natural forces have something of the godhead in them. I do hope I haven't shocked anyone?"

He had, as Sophia observed, but the Engastromenos family was too well bred to show it. Without raising her eyes to meet his, she said in a low tone, but sufficiently strong for her potential suitor to hear her:

"Mr. Schliemann, I have no way of knowing whether you are right or wrong, but I admire you for the strength of your convictions."

His eyes devoured the young girl before him.

It was dark in the garden. Quietly, several of the women had left with the younger children. The men had moved in closer, the better to hear.

"You believe that Homer was a single human being, like Dante or Shakespeare?" someone asked, her Uncle Lambridou, Sophia guessed.

"Beyond the trace of a doubt!" Henry Schliemann was on fire now.

"He was born in Smyrna, Izmir, not far from Troy, somewhere between 1000 and 900 B.C. The sons of Homer, either blood descendants or disciples, composed a guild of singers, centered on Chios, the nearest of the islands to Smyrna. These bards traveled from court to court around the Aegean, strumming their lyres and singing Homer's verses."

"When you say that Homer 'wrote' *The Iliad*, you mean that he created a great poem from the fragments that had come down from the war?"

It was Spyros, her eldest brother and closest friend, who had been observing Sophia's reaction to Mr. Schliemann. Schliemann smiled indulgently.

"Yes. We have no manuscript of Homer's, or any testimony that one existed. However he may very well have set everything down in writing, even as the Song of Solomon was written at almost the exact time as part of the Old Testament. When there is no written literary language, there is another force at work, equally powerful: *folk memory*. The stories of the Trojan War and the wanderings of Odysseus were repeated from parent to child and parent to child. Aside from their farm land, their sheep, goats, the heritage of these people, their history before there were written records, was their most valuable possession, and each generation handed down that birthright. There had been bards before Homer, and they composed songs about the great legends of Achilles, Hector, Helen, but it was Homer who went to Troy. He invented a Greek literary language in order to tell his story, gathering together all these earlier legends and ballads, to create singlehandedly *The Iliad* and *The Odyssey*. He studied and absorbed the Trojan terrain: the hill on which the original fortress, or Hissarlik, had been built, the two rivers, the Scamander, coming down from Mt. Ida on the south, and the Simois, coming from the north, forming a triangle of land lying between the walls of Troy and the sea, where the battles were fought. Troy has to be within a short distance of the Hellespont, where the Achaeans beached their 1140 ships, and made camp for their 120,000 men; because Homer tells us that the Greek foot soldiers sometimes went from their camp to the walls of Troy twice in one day."

Georgios Engastromenos struggled with the problem of credibility. Sophia knew her father well enough to see by his expression that at the back of his mind was the question, "Am I addressing a genius or a fool?" Aloud he said, "Hundreds of men have studied *The Iliad* without perceiving where Troy lies buried . . ."

Henry Schliemann started pacing within the family circle of black-suited gentlemen.

"I cannot speak for your hundreds, Mr. Engastromenos, only for myself. Perhaps for the same reason that hundreds of scholars have read

Pausanias's *Guide to Greece* and are still fumbling outside the cyclopean walls of Mycenae to find the royal tombs with their inestimable treasure of gold buried with the rulers."

By now Sophia too was shocked.

"And you know where these royal tombs are at Mycenae, Mr. Schliemann?"

"Miss Sophia, next time I come to Colonos perhaps you will allow me to bring my copy of Pausanias? Despite the fact that he wrote as late as the second century A.D. he says he saw the fountain Perseia and the treasuries of Atreus and his sons, which are indeed in the lower city, and perhaps some of the smaller treasuries in the suburb. But 'Clytemnestra and Aegisthus were buried at a little distance from the wall because they were thought unworthy to have their tombs inside of it, where Agamemnon reposed and those who were killed together with him.' There cannot be any doubt that he had solely in view the huge cyclopean walls of the citadel. I believe I know where this must be."

There was an embarrassed silence in the garden. Mr. Schliemann's claim that he knew where Troy was located, and that he was about to excavate it, had been hard to accept. With this second claim, that he knew where the royal tombs of Mycenae were, all faith in this mysterious millionaire sifted upward into the night air; the various Engastromenos and Geladaki relatives retreated into total doubt. Sophia said to herself:

"He simply can't be a lunatic. He has traveled the world, published two books, made fortunes from his own endeavors. He is egocentric, to be sure, but I doubt that he would expose himself to ridicule."

She asked quietly:

"Mr. Schliemann, the natural question we are all wondering about is: if you are convinced that you are right, why are you not excavating Troy this very moment?"

Schliemann returned to his chair and seated himself heavily, as though he had already done a day's digging.

"I would be, Miss Sophia. But in order to dig in Turkey one needs a *firman*, a written permit from the Grand Vizier in Constantinople. It is not easy to get. I have applied for permission. Once I have the official document in hand I shall quickly exchange it for a pick, a shovel and a wheelbarrow. Archaeology will not come of age until it ceases to be philology, until men get out of their libraries and begin digging in the earth. That is precisely what I intend to do. And that is why I am determined to find a Greek wife. She will be the hand of God on my shoulder. My Greek treasure!"

His voice was trembling. He mopped the perspiration off his brow with a fine cambric handkerchief.

"My, my," thought Sophia, "that is going to be quite a job for the Greek woman he marries. If he doesn't find Troy or the royal tombs of Mycenae, will it be his wife who has failed him?"

4.

Madame Victoria invited Mr. Schliemann for Sunday dinner, which he accepted with pleasure; she also suggested that he drop in whenever he might be free. His visits on Friday and Saturday afternoons were frustrating for him; the Engastromenos garden was now the most popular spot in Colonos. There was an ever growing demand for his tales of travel and adventure, but no way for him to achieve the intimate conversation with Sophia which he so ardently desired. She managed to murmur to him with a touch of amusement:

"It is never easy for a young Greek girl to be alone. In fact, it is impossible! The priest says, 'Until your children are twelve, never leave them out of your sight.' I was never allowed in front of my house in Romvis Square unless one of my brothers was there to watch me jump rope or play hopscotch, or just hold hands in a circle with the other girls, singing: 'My little bright moon, teach me how to walk, so that I can walk to school and learn how to read and write.'

"Right up to graduation I was never allowed to walk to the Arsakeion alone; one of my brothers or one of the older maids had to take me and bring me back. It's only a few months since I was a protected child in a white blouse with navy-blue skirt. There is no freedom for a Greek girl before marriage."

Mollified, Henry Schliemann began regaling the men of the family with tales of the Orient and Egypt. Young Panaghiotes asked:

"Mr. Schliemann, when you travel through so many countries how do you know what money they use?"

Schliemann smiled at the boy, reached into his inside coat pocket and took out a thick black leather wallet.

"I adopted this from the European waiters, who find it the easiest way to make change. You see, it has five compartments inside. In this first space I keep my American money, in the second French, the third German, the fourth Russian, and in the fifth bills from Egypt, India, Turkey, Japan. On the outside I keep my Greek money for convenience."

Sophia's brothers were fascinated by the currency, of which their guest gave them examples to read and feel. Alexandros, who loved money, any kind, asked:

"Mr. Schliemann, how can you tell what one currency is worth in relation to the others?"

"Here, do you see the white card on the inside cover of the wallet? It contains the exchange rates for all the countries in which I do business. I call it my *bourse*, and replace it once a month with the new rates. As of today five drachmas equal one American dollar. One drachma is worth one French franc. It takes four Reichsmarks to equal a dollar; the British pound is worth twenty-five French francs, while the Russian ruble is worth three French francs . . ."

To Panaghiotes he said with an amused gleam in his eyes, "I keep this wallet under my pillow at night because I dream a lot, and I never know which country my dreams will take me to."

Panaghiotes rewarded the man with shouts of glee.

"And when you wake up in the morning, do you find money missing?"

"Ah, yes, Panaghiotes. I dream in at least six languages every night, which means I practically circle the globe and spend all of my cash by morning."

Sophia watched the little exchange.

"How nice of him to entertain Panaghiotes. He has kindness in him, and humor too."

After early Sunday morning coffee, the Engastromenos family crossed the square to St. Meletios's. They did not go inside the little church; it could hold only the officiating priests and the elderly. The congregation gathered close to the two doors, talking and exchanging news of the week's events while at the same time participating in the prayers and chanting. Occasionally a priest would come out and bless the assemblage, everyone crossing himself three times.

The cooking began immediately after Mass. Sophia could remember mornings in their flat in Athens when a discussion would go on for a full hour between her mother and the maid in the kitchen about the recipe for a particular dish: a lamb casserole made with fresh tomatoes, small white beans or chopped parsley and white wine. Sophia had been brought up to have a profound reverence for food, and consequently for cooking. All Greeks shared this feeling, the little girls being trained by their mothers from the age of three, not as a game or something with which to occupy the child's time, but as a religious rite, for food was scarce in mountainous Greece and, except for the abundant fruits of the sea, hard to come by.

All Greeks had known hunger and even starvation; almost every generation had known so sharp a depression that even those few who had money to spend could find little or nothing in the markets to buy. There had never been a Greek born who did not subscribe to Euripides's lines:

> You see how lovely life can be
> Before a well-appointed board.

Grace was said before the two meals of the day, dinner and leftovers in the evening. On religious holidays Georgios Engastromenos made the sign of the cross over the bread, for bread was the symbol of Christ. If a piece was left over, Madame Victoria kissed it; it was sacred, as in the sacrament.

The diningroom table was the happiest place in the Greek house. The Greeks loved to eat, to have big meals together, or little bits of everything. The women grew plump around the hips. Yet oddly enough the men stayed thin. Except Georgios Engastromenos; perhaps it was his own laughter mixed in with the food that gave him his big belly.

It took Madame Victoria, Sophia, Marigo and the hired kitchen girl who scoured the pots behind them many hours to prepare the pans of aromatic deliciously blended food which they would then take to the communal ovens at the bakery. Here the housewives who had no adequate stoves, or did not wish to overheat their homes in summer, would pay a few cents a pan to have the food baked, after the baker had taken out his day's supply of breads and cakes on a long-handled shovel. He knew precisely how many minutes were needed for each dish.

This morning Madame Victoria commented:

"Enjoy these hours of cooking now, Sophia; you will be deprived of that great pleasure."

"Why will I be?"

"Because rich men don't allow their wives in the kitchen. They engage cooks."

"Wealthy Greek women cook. So will I! Greek men admire their wives' cooking."

"True. It's a central fact of life for them. But your husband-to-be is not a Greek, much as he would like to be."

For over an hour the family and their guest sat out in the garden, in the shade of the grapevines, the men drinking *ouzo*, a potent distillation of grape mash lightly flavored with anise, into which they poured a little cold water to turn the drink a milky color. With the *ouzo*, Sophia and Marigo served plates of *tiropetes*, flaky little hot triangular puffs of spinach and *feta* cheese; large marinated black olives; tomatoes stuffed with rice and spices; *dolmadakia*, miniature meat balls stuffed in grape leaves; *kalamaria*, wild pickled squid; golden fried octopus; mussels stuffed with rice, currants, spices, parsley; *taramosalata*, a dip of red fish roe and garlic; *iman baildi meze*, thin slices of eggplant sautéed in light olive oil, tomato and onion; and *loukanika*, slices of spicy Greek sausage.

Henry Schliemann complimented Madame Victoria on the delicious variety of *mezethakia*, appetizers.

"You must compliment my two daughters as well," Madame Victoria replied, "for while I was preparing the dinner Sophia prepared the puffs, the mussels and cooked the *dolmadakia.*"

Schliemann picked up one of the puffs and looked across the table directly at Sophia. She was particularly lovely this warm Sunday afternoon, still flushed from her work in the kitchen, but having stopped to bathe her face with an aromatic lotion, and brush her hair until it shone with a dark vibrance. Her big brown eyes danced with interest and excitement. She had put on a flattering blue silk dress, with gussets of pleats on either side; a frill of the same material started at her shoulders and met in a bowknot which created a décolletage somewhat lower than her weekday dresses. For all its simple charm, it was apparent that it was somewhat outgrown. Madame Victoria was unhappy that they had not had the money to make Sophia a new outfit.

When Sophia remonstrated with her mother: "Mr. Schliemann did not come all this way to look at a dress," Madame Victoria had countered, "We should always put on the best possible front."

Sophia twitted her scrupulously Victorian mother.

"Now, Mother, there is nothing wrong with my front. I am developing like a true Geladaki. This dress is not going to hide my light under a bushel."

"Hurrumph!" growled Madame Victoria. "That levity comes from your father's side of the family. Mr. Schliemann has traveled all these thousands of miles to look at your character."

Sophia laughed merrily.

"He never takes his eyes off my face or my figure."

To please her mother she wore a family heirloom, a gold brooch with a double intertwined cross.

Now it was time to go into the diningroom, which had been kept cool by its closed shutters. Sophia helped to serve and to remove the dishes; this was an argument she had won from her mother, who had wanted her to "sit at the table like a lady."

"Mother, there is no point in giving Mr. Schliemann a false impression. I think he would prefer to see me working as part of my family than sitting at the table like a queen. I think he wants a woman capable of working with him in the excavations."

"He is not here to hire a day laborer," exclaimed her mother.

Sophia and Marigo had gone in first to set out the plates of chicken soup with an *avgolemono* sauce. Next came a platter of small, crisp-fried *barbouni*, small fish with red stripes, a great favorite. When this had been cleared, Sophia brought in the roasted chicken parts; and after that, the leg of lamb with rice pilaf, string beans and tomatoes in oil and lemon. The salad was made of dandelion greens flavored with dill and orégano, olives and chunks of *feta,* the incomparable white goat cheese. For dessert there were walnuts in warm Hymettus honey, *loukoumades*, little fritters with rose petal jelly, oranges, small squares of *baklava*, and finally the tiny cups of Turkish coffee, proudly called Greek coffee since the War for Independence.

Back in the garden, Schliemann patted the gold chain hung low on his vest and remarked:

"It was a feast fit for a king! In Europe they do not yet know what great cooks the Greeks are."

Sophia watched him rise, start to come near her, and then show a look of keen disappointment: for at that moment, having finished their own Sunday dinners, relatives and friends began coming through the gate, and soon the garden was again filled with visitors.

Sophia was astonished at her change in status in Colonos. Before she had been the precocious child of the Engastromenos family, the one who had received the best education and was recently graduated from the patrician Arsakeion with high marks. Everyone had also known that the family had just barely been able to scrape together the tuition fees for the last semester.

But now! As she accompanied her mother to market in the early morning to buy the hot loaves of country bread straight out of the baker's oven, the older men took off their hats and bowed to her, the younger men gazed with wide-eyed admiration; the older women congratulated her profusely, the young girls did their best to hide their envy behind tight-lipped smiles. Sophia murmured to her mother:

"It's as though I have suddenly become the most important person in Colonos. Just because a wealthy foreigner has come to call on me. He has not proposed yet, and they all have me married already."

"He will," replied Madame Victoria laconically. "That's what he came for. And he was smitten by you, my little Sophidion, anyone could see that."

"To my eye and ear he seems passionately in love with Homer," replied Sophia with a laugh.

"Now, now, little one, you have grown too old to be irreverent."

"Irreverence is salt on a boiled egg."

The following morning she received a gift from Henry Schliemann, accompanied by a letter:

Athens, September 6, 1869

Dear Miss Sophia:

Please accept these corals from me. But please be careful because the ribbon is not solid enough, and should be changed for a silk one, otherwise you risk losing the corals.

Could you please ask your excellent parents and write to me if it is possible to see you without all those people around, but alone with you, and not once but more often, because I think we are seeing each other to get acquainted, and to see whether our characters can get along together. This is quite impossible in the presence of so many persons. Marriage is the most magnificent of all establishments if it is based on respect, love and virtue. Marriage is the heaviest bondage if it is based on material interests or sexual attraction.

Thank God I am not so crazy that I should go blindly into a second marriage; so if the fashion in Athens does not allow me to see you often alone with your parents, to know you well, then I beg you not to think any longer of me.

Please accept the assurance of my sincerest respect.

Henry Schliemann

She had hardly gotten over her astonishment at the first letter when a second messenger arrived with a shorter note:

Dear Miss Sophia:

Can you and your honorable mother come at a quarter to two P.M. today to the railway station? You will find there Mr. Lamprides and his excellent wife and we will all go to Piraeus together. There we will take a boat and will go sailing a little. Hoping that you will not deprive us of the joy to have you with us, I beg you to receive the expression of my respect.

Please answer me with one or two words.

H.S.

Sophia had never gone sailing; in fact, unlike her compatriots, she disliked the water. In all her seventeen years, even on their summer "going to nature" trips, when the family traveled to the nearby islands of Aegina or Andros in quite substantial steamers, she had become seasick. She exclaimed to her mother:

"What shall I do? The Aegean always seems to know the exact moment I get on a boat, and instantly kicks up a storm. But neither do I want to refuse Mr. Schliemann because that would offend him and he too would kick up a storm!"

"Send a note to Mr. Schliemann explaining that you'd love to go sailing, but if your father does not reach home in time to give his permission, then Mr. Schliemann must join us for supper here, and we will see that you have an opportunity to speak quietly, and alone."

She had no sooner sent off her message than Georgios Engastromenos arrived home for an early dinner, read Schliemann's two letters, and addressed himself to the two women.

"But of course you must go. Send Mr. Schliemann an acceptance immediately. And, Victoria," sternly to his wife, "see to it that Sophia and Mr. Schliemann have a little privacy at one end of the boat, while you engage Mr. and Mrs. Lamprides at the other. If you cannot turn your back on Sophia, then at least turn aside."

Victoria replied, "I will do this out of sympathy for Mr. Schliemann. A man living alone does more harm to himself than his enemies can do."

Henry Schliemann hired the largest sailboat available but it seemed pitifully small and frail to Sophia. The trip out of the harbor was calm, and she had hopes of coming through the afternoon without disgracing herself. But the moment the boat left the protected bay and entered the open sea the sun vanished behind a cloud, a wind sprang up and the sailboat began to pitch to and fro. Sophia became queasy. Her host did not notice the motion of the boat or the greenish tint to Sophia's usually rosy complexion, only that the other passengers had their backs turned to him.

"Miss Sophia," he began in an earnest, affectionate tone, "why do you want to marry me?"

"Oh no," thought Sophia, "not at this moment! When I'm about to lean over the railing."

There was no escaping his intense gaze, or the tense posture of his head on his neck as he awaited the all-important answer to his question. With a strong effort she gulped down her stomach, which had seemed to be rising steadily, crossed her arms tightly against her insides, and answered as honestly as she could:

". . . Because my parents have told me to."

She saw Henry Schliemann turn pale. For an instant she thought he was the one who was to be sick. Then anger thundered into his eyes; she had never seen them blazing this way before. Outraged color flooded upward on the lean cheeks. His voice was hoarse.

"I am deeply pained, Miss Sophia, at the answer you have given me, one worthy of a slave; and all the more strange because it comes from an educated young woman. I myself am a simple, honorable, home-loving man. If ever we were married, it would be so that we could excavate together and share our common love of Homer."

The sea had grown rougher. The sailboat was surrounded by white-caps. Sophia prayed, "Dear Lord, let me off this boat and I will never set foot on water again."

She licked her dry lips, smiled ruefully as she realized the incongruity of her promise to God, whose Son was the only one who walked on water; then decided that, nauseous as she was, she had better set this strange and unpredictable man straight.

"Mr. Henry, you should not be shocked by my answer. The marriage of every girl in Greece is arranged by her parents, who conscientiously try to find her the best possible husband. That is what my parents have done, and I accept their judgment. It is a quality you should value in me: if I am a good daughter, it means I will be a good wife."

Only partly appeased, Henry demanded in a quieter but still stern voice:

"Is there no other reason why you are willing to marry me? Surely there must be something in your decision besides blind obedience?"

Sophia's nausea was high in her throat; she had no idea how much longer she could control herself. Making a desperate effort to formulate her thoughts, she murmured to herself:

"But what other answer is he looking for? I have already said that I admire and respect him for the strength of his convictions about Homer. I have already indicated that I have faith in his writings. For what other quality does he want me to admire him, when he has told us that these pursuits are his whole life? That he wants a Greek wife to help him to fulfill his dreams. I have missed something. And how can I think when all I want to do is die?"

Then, as though the thought came from the sun, which had just emerged from behind the cloud, she said to herself:

"But of course! The quality for which all the world admires him, and because of which every family in Greece with a daughter to marry has been pursuing him. He is a millionaire! With more money than anyone we've ever heard of! And he achieved it all by himself, without formal education, without family or backing. He has a right to be proud of himself."

She looked up at Henry Schliemann once again, putting all the admiration and pride into her voice that she could muster, paying him the world's ultimate compliment:

"Because you are rich!"

Henry's face became stony.

"You want to marry me, not for my value as a human being, but because I am rich! I am no longer in a position to converse with you. I have decided not to think of you any more."

He turned away, calling curtly to the crew:

"Put back into port."

5.

Madame Victoria disappeared into the depths of the house. The proud woman, who held herself with the poise and assurance of a queen, was having trouble holding back her tears. Sophia could never remember having seen her mother cry, not even when she had learned the catastrophic news of the loss of their home. Now she would be humiliated in the eyes of everyone: for the Engastromenos family had been judged unworthy to have a daughter marry Mr. Schliemann. He would take another Greek girl.

Sophia locked herself in her room, her predominant emotion one of being rejected. When she thought of the damage she had done to her family, she began to weep. Through a sleepless night she came to the realization that, though her answers seemed to her forthright and honest, they were the precisely wrong answers to a man of Henry Schliemann's pride and sensitivity. He had quite rightly, she reproached herself, wanted to be admired and married for his clever accomplishments, and his bold plans for the second half of his life, for the earnest qualities of his character. She recalled how, on the train trip to Piraeus, Mr. Lamprides had spoken of Mr. Schliemann's unique method of acquiring new languages, by reading aloud, side by side, the same book in two languages, the one of which he knew, and the other which he had decided to master.

"Oh!" Schliemann replied. "We think and act differently in every tongue we speak. When I write or speak in German it seems harsh to me; in English I am polite and urbane; in French I tend toward irony. How do I sound in Greek, Miss Sophia?"

"When you speak Greek you are like the rest of us; generous in big things, stingy in the little ones. But when you write you are . . ." she searched for the proper word, "international."

He accepted this as a compliment, reached into his inside coat pocket and pulled out some printed sheets.

"This monograph just arrived from New York. I wrote it for the Convention of American Philologists last May."

He then asked, deferentially, if he might quote the opening lines. After he began to read, Sophia saw once again the magnificent transformation from the ordinary-looking, middle-aged man to the bright-eyed attractive young man, the shoulders squared, gesturing with the peculiar combination of intensity and grace that animated him when his mind was at work.

"To the question: 'How much time in a Collegiate course of study should be given to the study of languages?' I answer as Charles V justly observed to Francis I: 'With every new language one acquires a new life'; for by the knowledge of the language of a foreign country we are able to get acquainted with its literature, its manners and customs. . . .'"

It was clear to her now, as the powdery white light of a Greek sunrise flooded her bedroom and the square, that she had aged through the sleepless night of self-reproaches. She should have replied to Mr. Schliemann's question:

"Because you are a man whom I respect and admire. Though you were denied the advantages of a formal education, you have become an outstanding scholar and master of languages. I am thrilled at the opportunity to work by your side, as your wife, companion, and trusted friend, while you excavate at Troy and Mycenae, and bring to the world its rich treasures of the past. It is an honor and privilege that any young woman with vision could look forward to with joy. That is why I want to marry you."

"Ah," she thought, "how brilliant one can be the morning after!"

True, she had been very seasick.

Troubled as she was by the sense of her own loss of an opportunity which might never come to her again, she was overcome with sadness that her family would be crushed. Shortly after dawn she dressed, went downstairs for coffee and to recount to her father and two brothers before they left for their shop the trajectory of her first "private" conversation with Henry Schliemann. The family was sorely puzzled; they did not find her replies improper. Her father said:

"Mr. Schliemann is a well-traveled man. He must know that in this country all marriages of good families are arranged by the parents. Why should he protest if you tell him an obvious truth?"

"He wanted her to say she loved him," cried fourteen-year-old Marigo.

"He couldn't be that naïve!" exclaimed Madame Victoria, adjusting now to the loss, and aware of her young daughter's misery. "Sophia has seen him only a few times and then in the midst of our crowded garden. . . . Besides, she is seventeen. He is old enough to know that love comes after marriage."

"I don't think that's what he wanted," murmured Sophia; "besides, I couldn't say it. He would have known from the tone of my voice that it was an untruth."

Her father, bemused, sought to lighten the situation.

"Little Sophia, this was never anything serious. It was just a theater play of shadows, the kind I took you to see at the Karaghiozis. A very short show, a few hours, and now the curtain has come down. As with all make-believe, it vanishes like early morning fog."

Alexandros was the only angry one.

"It is said in Crete that 'God gives food to the birds but he does not put it into their nests.' We had a chance to be rescued. Would it have been such a terrible crime to say she was marrying for companionship and love? Couldn't my precious sister give an answer that would be truer for the future than it is for the present? What purpose has truth ever served except to curdle the soup? Ah, no, our petted Sophia thought herself too good to flatter a lonely man who came seeking a companion." He turned to Sophia. "Now you have made us all miserable, and Mr. Schliemann miserable; you sank the entire Engastromenos family in that sailboat."

The days of Henry Schliemann's silence were a sore trial. Sophia had never before experienced personal trouble. She had shared only vaguely in the family sorrow over their financial setback. This awkward situation was her fault alone. Her eyes flashed with anger as she tried to live with herself by silent dialogues.

"Why did he have to pounce that question on me while we were out on the rough Aegean? He could have seen, if he weren't so preoccupied with himself, that I was seasick. . . . Why was he so blunt . . . ?"

Then she relented.

"But it was his only time! Not for one moment had he had an opportunity to speak to me without a dozen people listening to every word. He had a right to ask the question. . . . Well, as they say in Crete, 'Wishing a scene away is like looking for a green horse.' . . . 'I lost my earrings, but I still have the holes in my ears. . . .'"

She had fallen from grace. The people of Colonos felt let down. The relatives stayed away in family groups; the women of the town seemed to sniff slightly in derision. The young men managed to look away; the older ones were polite but cold. Colonos had been about to become famous. Now it had returned to its former status, a small sleepy suburb of Athens, half deserted except in summertime.

Uncle Vimpos brought her the only encouragement. He had had a message from Henry Schliemann saying that he was taking a ship for Naples, perhaps never to see Sophia again. However, if she ever needed a friend, he hoped she would remember her devoted friend. Father Vimpos said gently:

"Don't take these hurt feelings too seriously. Mr. Henry is more depressed and frustrated, sitting in that lonely suite in the Hotel d'Angleterre, than all of you put together. He is yearning desperately for a way to effect a reconciliation. My dear one, you must realize that in addition to his great success Mr. Schliemann carries with him the scars of many failures, humiliations and deprivations. Those five years he spent as a slave in the grocery store, sleeping under the counter, without friends or family . . . The garret rooms in which he lived in Amsterdam, icy in winter, suffocating in summer, with only crusts of bread and stale cheese to eat so that he could use his small salary to buy books . . . Even after he made his fortune in Russia, during the years I knew him, the highest he could rise was 'Merchant of the First Guild'; he could find no entree to the intellectual and social levels for which he hungered, not even after his unfortunate marriage, which was a nightmare to him. A man who has suffered so much should be understood and forgiven."

Sophia studied her relative's long thin face under the black clerical hat. She was certain that he was counseling her to make the next move.

"Then you think I should write a note of apology?"

"If you feel you can."

"What shall I say to mollify him?"

"You are the best judge."

"Very well. I owe him that much."

Spyros brought her a sheet of writing paper. She took it up to her bedroom and wrote in a strong hand, quite different in manner from that in which she had written her graduation examinations the previous June:

> Dear Mr. Henry: I am so sorry you are going away. You must not be angry with what I said. I thought that was how young girls should speak. My parents and I will be very happy if you will come and see us again tomorrow.

She sealed the envelope, returned downstairs and handed it to her father. He said:

"I will deliver it to the hotel myself."

At noon the next day she received a reply:

> Wealth contributes to the happiness in marriage, but cannot build it by itself. The woman who will marry me only for my money, or to become a great lady in Paris, will regret very much to have left Athens, because she would make me and herself very unhappy. The woman who marries me must do it because she values me as a human being. . . .

He was still planning to leave.

Madame Victoria had paid her daughter the rare compliment of not opening the letter when it arrived, nor did she ask to see Sophia's reply. Sophia was grateful, but the thought also intruded: "She has been warned that this matter is best settled between Mr. Henry and myself. And so it shall be. But what shall I write now? He should be worldly enough to know that if he were a poor man he would not be in Greece courting a bride. How can I reassure this rich-poor vulnerable man that the last thing in the world I want is to become a great lady in Paris?":

> Dear Mr. Henry: With a great anxiety in my soul I awaited your reply to my letter to see whether your favorable attitude toward me in our first meetings could possibly return, since the explanation I gave to you during our excursion in Piraeus made you change your mind. But your respected letter of today caused me much sorrow.
>
> Reading in it how you felt, I prayed God to bring back to you the feelings that have fled. The same letter informs me that you are still planning to leave Athens next Saturday, and in that case, you take all hope away from me. This threw me into a very deep sorrow.
>
> If I can ask for nothing else, allow me at least to beg you to visit me at my house before your departure. In the hope that your gentle soul will not decline my request, I sign with deepest respect,

> Sophia G. Engastromenos

There was no reply that day, or the next, a most unexpected development from a man who took enormous joy in writing letters, as many as a dozen a day, he had told her. She became genuinely concerned, for it looked as though he would depart from Piraeus without giving her or her family an opportunity to save face. She felt a little sick at this turn of events, for the tension in the house was heavy. No one spoke about Henry Schliemann. In fact, no one spoke at all except in monosyllables. The family was saddened and hurt and perplexed, each in his individual way. She had no appetite and excused herself before supper, going to her room and throwing herself on the bed, her face in the pillow. She wept . . . but she did not know for whom. For her parents, whose hopes of returning to their good life in Athens had been dashed? For her brothers and sisters, who could have been helped by this marriage? For herself, because she had somehow failed in judgment and in doing her simple duty? Or for all three perhaps, and a crazy incomprehensible world she had never made?

She murmured half aloud, "I like Henry Schliemann. I admire him. I know I will come to love him after our marriage, as my mother came to love my father, and my sister Katingo has come to love her husband.

I want to marry him. And I have eyes to see that he loves me. But what more can I do?"

She passed a sleepless night, her pillowcase damp. In the morning, when her mother called her, her eyes were puffy and red. But there was a letter from Henry Schliemann. She went out into the garden, swinging a cane chair around to face the trunk of a tree, and tore open the envelope with trembling fingers. At first the handwriting, in precise but somewhat cramped Greek, was blurred. Then she read:

> . . . I am not flattering myself with illusions. I know perfectly well that a young and beautiful girl cannot fall in love with a forty-seven-year-old man who, in addition, does not have beauty himself. But I thought that a woman whose character completely agrees with mine, and has the same love and enthusiastic inclination for the sciences, could respect me. And because this student would be my student for all her life, I dare to hope that she would love me, first because love is born of respect, second because I would try to be a good teacher and would dedicate every free moment of my life to help the lover of science in her philological and archaeological interests.

She threw back her head and laughed heartily.

"Now I know what he wants; a marriage proposal from me! Then he will be reassured, he will know that I not only accept all of his conditions but that I am eager to become his wife, his student and fellow excavator at Troy! He shall have his proposal this very instant. I am no longer the naïve girl who went sailing with Henry Schliemann at Piraeus."

Father Vimpos arrived the following day to assure her that all was well, and to express his deepest regrets at being unable to perform the marriage ceremony, for he had to leave at once for Tripolis to prepare the church and congregation for his ordination as bishop.

"But I have not had a reply to my last letter. How can you be so sure about the marr . . . ?"

". . . he told me himself. This morning. He is now completely in love with you. He spent hours with a dozen or more young Athenian women in the past few days, but he told me, 'I could not find another Sophia.' He added, 'For this please accept the expression of my heartiest gratitude for such a benevolent choice of this rare Greek treasure for my wife.' A little on the literary side, wouldn't you say, Sophidion, but that is something you are going to have to remember: your husband will be half a man of action and half a *littérateur*."

"I must tell Mother the news. She is eating her heart out. Did Mr. Henry say when he was coming?"

"Yes. Tomorrow. Right now he is shopping for your ring."

"Did he mention a date?"

"Three of them: next Thursday, Friday or Saturday, depending on your choice, and when a ship leaves for Italy where he plans for you to honeymoon. I will stop at St. Meletios's to advise the priests about the wedding."

"Oh, Uncle Theokletos, we are going to miss each other's big day! You won't be in the church when I become a bride, and I won't be in the church when you become a bishop."

"Never mind, little one. We will always be close to each other, particularly in time of need. You will be back in a few months; Mr. Henry is certain that the permit from the Turkish government is about to be approved."

Father Vimpos made the sign of the cross over her three times with his right hand to protect her against all harm or evil, then touched her gently on the forehead with the three center fingers of his left as a parting gift of tenderness.

Sophia felt completely reassured, but her parents walked as though the floor were paved with eggs. Sophia pleasantly discouraged all talk about Mr. Schliemann, saying with more authority in her voice than had ever been there before:

"Let us wait until tomorrow. Then everything will be resolved."

Henry Schliemann arrived at midmorning, springing with a lively gait from the carriage, aglow with happiness, freshly shaven, his mustache impeccably trimmed to the curve of his upper lip, smelling of the after-shave cologne the barber at the Hotel d'Angleterre had applied. No mention was made of the fact that, aside from his cascade of letters, Mr. Schliemann had been perceivably absent for six full days. Sophia had put on Katingo's white dress, the one she had worn the first day he came to call. While the looseness of the dress made her seem younger than her seventeen years, her eyes were more mature as they sparkled with her sense of achievement.

Henry Schliemann visited cordially with her parents in the garden, regaling them with stories of being caught in San Francisco in the fire of 1851 which razed the city. He had also just received his doctorate of philosophy from the University of Rostock, and had brought the citation scroll along to show the family.

"It is a great honor bestowed upon you, Dr. Schliemann," said Georgios with added respect.

Schliemann's face was transfused with joy.

"That is the first time I have heard myself addressed with the title. How well it fits the ear." Then he turned serious. "But it is much more than the honor involved. I need the title in order to be taken seriously in my work; the universities look with contempt upon the self-educated man."

"But, Mr. Henry, won't your findings have to be judged on their own merits?" It was Sophia, wrinkling her brow at a center line. "If you discover Troy, no one can then deny it."

"Ah, they can and they will, Miss Sophia. You will see. But the title of doctor will lend me stature with the world public."

He asked Sophia if he might speak to her parents for a moment. She excused herself, went into the kitchen to put on coffee. She could hear quite clearly through the open window the voices of the three people in the garden, intense and charged with an underlying excitement.

"Mr. and Mrs. Engastromenos, I wish to ask for your parental approval of my marriage to Sophia."

Sophia knew her father would have liked to laugh at that point, for the question came so much after the fact. Instead he replied:

"Your proposition, my dear Dr. Schliemann, honors me and makes me happy and proud that a man of your worth is willing to marry my little Sophia. I trust she will be happy with a man like you. I give her to you with all my heart."

"There is no objection because of my recent divorce?"

"No. Cousin Vimpos told us that he accompanied you to the archbishop, who examined your divorce papers and declared them valid. As you know, our Orthodox Church allows three divorces."

Schliemann turned to Madame Victoria.

"I would also like the approval of Sophia's revered mother."

"Thank God we are not enemies of our daughter. It would be wicked for us to turn down such a great happiness, for which all of Greece envies us. If we waited ten thousand years it would never happen to us a second time that a Schliemann pays us the honor of marrying our daughter. The Erinyes, the Furies, would punish us if we committed such a sin."

While coffee was served, Sophia sat with her hands in her lap, studying the man she was going to marry. . . .

"He is thoughtful and kindly, with a terrible temper, which he manages to hold in check. . . ."

Feeling her gaze of judgment upon him, Henry Schliemann turned to her, took a black velvet box from his coat pocket, opened it, and said:

"Miss Sophia, in the presence of your revered mother and father, I ask permission to give you this pearl ring. The pearl, you will find, matches your earrings."

She fitted the ring onto her finger. The pearl was a beauty: creamy white with a pinkish tinge. It was obvious that he had shopped the jewelry stores of Athens with considerable care. She flashed him a smile of appreciation. Color mounted in his cheeks as it always did when he was under emotion.

"And with the ring, Miss Sophia, I hope you will also accept my proposal of marriage. I already have your parents' approval."

Sophia thought, "Our quarrel and separation have had a cauterizing effect on both of us. In a way I'm glad it happened. It has been only sixteen days since he first came to visit, and yet I feel years older. I know that this marriage is not going to be an easy one. I will have my problems. But I can face them with a sense of sympathy because I know how easily he is hurt."

She said, "Thank you, Mr. Henry. For the pearl and for the proposal. I accept them both with genuine pleasure."

Then Mr. Henry left, saying that he would return the next day. After kissing her hand in the gallant French fashion, she saw him slip an envelope into her mother's hand.

Sophia kissed her mother and father, both of whom clasped her in their arms. When they went inside the house Sophia asked:

"Mother, what is in the envelope Mr. Schliemann gave you?"

"I don't know, child. Let's take it to the diningroom table and open it."

The sun, streaming in through the windows, put their three faces, so alike in structure, into warm relief. Madame Victoria opened the envelope, took out a piece of stationery from the Hotel d'Angleterre, wrapped around a sizable batch of gold coins. She spread the money out on the table, then read aloud:

"My dear Madame Victoria, would you be so kind as to use
this little gift to buy Miss Sophia's underwear and stockings."

She exclaimed:

"What a generous but strange man! Why just underwear and stockings? As long as he had the impulse, why not money for an entire trousseau?"

Sophia's laughter rang through the house.

"But don't you see, Mother, that's exactly what it is. There's enough money here to buy me several trousseaux. . . ."

6.

She had six days to prepare for her wedding, but now that she was ready for marriage it did not seem too short a time. Greek girls, except those from the royal court or very rich families, did not have wedding gowns made for them. They were rented. Since her father's drapery shop

in the square was just off the fashionable Ermou, and Georgios Engastromenos had made friends with several of the owners of the well-
stocked "wedding shops" which rented out wedding gowns, Sophia
was able to find a gown which was newly sewn, of pure white Roman
satin, with a lace veil falling from a lace head crown. It was floor length,
with a train, widening a little at the hips and then flaring boldly from
the knees. Since the gown had never been worn, it was a simple matter
to adjust the seams, for Sophia was a little more robust in the bosom
and longer in the legs than the usual seventeen-year-old girl of Athens.

Henry had suggested that she buy only what she needed for her trousseau, since they would be spending only a few days each in Sicily, Naples,
Rome, Florence and Venice before they made their way to Paris, where
he had a spacious apartment at Place St. Michel 6, an entire floor in one
of the four apartment houses he owned in the French capital. Once
there, they would have her daytime outfits and evening gowns designed
by the best of the Parisian couturiers.

The days passed quickly, the family cleaning and decorating the
house and festooning the garden for the wedding feast. Sophia and
her mother shopped in Athens for a few hours each day, Henry insisting
that she have several pairs of proper shoes for walking the streets of
Italy, and in particular for the museums and cathedrals. He came to
the house for a daily visit, seeming to Sophia to grow younger with each
passing hour. He had reserved their suite on the S.S. *Aphrodite*, which
sailed from Piraeus after midnight of their wedding day.

Then an extraordinary thing happened. Henry Schliemann asked
Georgios Engastromenos to meet him at the office of a public notary
in Athens to sign an important document. When Georgios returned that
evening Sophia asked:

"What was it, Father, a marriage contract?"

Georgios, who rarely permitted himself a full-scale frown, said in a
puzzled tone:

"More like a renunciation contract."

Madame Victoria stared at her husband.

"What does that mean?"

"I know what it means, but I don't understand its purpose. I had to
agree, in this legal document, that Sophia could not have any claim on
his fortune during his lifetime or after his death, except if her conduct
toward him was such that it pleased him to leave something to her in
his testament."

The family chewed on this intelligence in silence; it was as tough
and nearly as indigestible as the thigh of a mountain goat. Madame
Victoria was the most upset.

"But that is outrageous! How can he disinherit the woman he is going to marry?"

Sophia answered in a soothing tone, "He's not disinheriting me, Mother, he's just keeping his hard-earned fortune securely in his own hands."

"He knows our plight," the ambitious Alexandros commented harshly. "Why would he not want to be generous to his new family?"

"He will, Alexandros. Give him time. Uncle Vimpos says he is a generous man, providing he is allowed to act on his own impulse. Once we are happily married, he will volunteer help for the shop, I'm sure. As the wife of a millionaire, how can I be content, or give him the help and companionship he wants, if he knows my dear parents are in difficulty? He will grasp that."

"I certainly hope so," cried Alexandros and Madame Victoria almost in one voice. Alexandros continued, "But I can't say it's a propitious beginning."

Georgios Engastromenos came to his daughter the day before the wedding to confess that he had no cash with which to pay the costs of the church or the priests.

". . . nothing, Father? Not even that small amount?"

Georgios gave a deprecating shrug of his left shoulder.

"No. . . . We have spent the last of our cash on necessities for the wedding. . . ."

Sophia was silent. She knew what was expected of her. Had her father been willing or able to borrow from relatives or friends he would not have troubled his daughter with his desperate situation.

"How much must you have?"

"Three hundred drachmas."

She did some figuring; the sum would come to sixty dollars in Henry's American money. Her father added, smiling weakly:

"It's not such a large sum to spend on the church services, and for a few other trifles. Some bridegrooms offer the costs voluntarily. . . ."

"Very well, Father, I will get the money for you."

She made the request matter-of-factly, determined to keep her poise and put down her sense of embarrassment. Perhaps that was why Henry did not seem surprised or troubled. He took out his wallet, turned to the Greek money in the outside compartment, handed her the gold coins.

"Perhaps, Sophia, I should have volunteered the church costs. It's little enough to pay for all the work that has been going on at St. Meletios's these past several days."

She thanked him with a smile but did not trust herself to speak.

The wedding of Sophia Engastromenos and Henry Schliemann was the greatest event to take place in the little suburb since Sophocles had written *Oedipus at Colonos*, which was produced just after his death in 406 B.C. The entire town was coming to the ceremony, as were the people from the surrounding countryside. Only the family and the closest friends would fit into the church, but that would not matter to the crowds outside, dressed in their national costumes, who would know exactly when to join the prayers, cross themselves, sing the hymns and give their blessing.

It would be a colorful assemblage, the men in red caps and long blue tassels, with embroidered blouses, long, ornamented sleeves, knee-length skirts and high socks to match the embroidery of the skirts; some in subtle reds, others in green with great shoulder straps coming down the back; older men wearing their swords. Women would be wearing long gold-embroidered dresses with a series of descending overvests and gossamer white shawls about their heads and shoulders; others would be in long flowing skirts, white with horizontal embroidery, the collar of lace, the blue bodice pinched tight at the waist, the little tan hat perched at one side of the head, with long tassels, and a string of large-cut beads below the throat.

Her wedding day dawned bright but with the beginning breeze of autumn in the air, for summer was about over. Sophia spent the better part of the day dressing and visiting with the female relatives who kept running in and out of her room proffering advice and help: her sisters Katingo and Marigo; her aunts Kyria Helmis and Kyria Lambridou; her cousins Eugenia, Helen and Marigo. There was no sign of her mother, who had been up all night preparing the foods which went into the bakery oven at dawn.

St. Meletios Square was decorated as though for a national holiday, with bunting strung between the trees, flags flying from the houses, the shopwindows dressed festively, the café tables set with water glasses full of flowers.

Sophia left her home at dusk with the wedding party, her youngest brother holding up the train of her gown as they walked to the church. She carried a bouquet of red roses with a ribbon of rosebuds cascading down one side of the long-sleeved dress which swayed gently over its ruffled petticoat. She was wearing the coral necklace Henry had given her because she knew he would be pleased. Inside the dress hung the silver cross which had been placed around her neck at her baptism.

The host of friends and relatives lining the square and awaiting the ceremony applauded softly as she passed, touching the fingertips of the right hand against the palm of the left. Sophia wore a small, fixed smile, looked neither to left nor right. She was extremely nervous.

Henry was waiting at the entrance of St. Meletios's, which the young girls of Colonos had again decorated with branches of laurel and myrtle. He had on a black frock coat with formal black trousers, a starched white shirt with a white tie and vest, white gloves, and carried a high silk hat. Sophia observed that he seemed pale.

She entered the exquisite little church, a gem of Byzantine architecture, and inhaled the first faint scent of incense as she gazed lovingly at the bishop's chair, the black marble walls, the front curtain closing in the *sanctum sanctorum*, the near life-sized panels of Mary on one side of the templum and Jesus on the other, the patron saints Meletios and John, their faces and hands painted in compassionate warm flesh tones, the rest of their figures encased in highly embossed superimposed robes of heavy silver. Once inside the sanctuary and the religion for which she felt such a tender and abiding love, all the knots in her nervous system came untied; she felt serene and secure.

The girls had brought to the church as many flowers as they could find, surrounding the shrine and the great icon of St. Meletios, standing by itself in the middle of the church. Wreaths of dahlias, yellow chrysanthemums, daisies, greenery, decorated all of the icons of the shrine which separated the main church from its sanctuary; there were vases of gladioli on the two steps which led to the Holy Door. Sophia's relatives had brought small hand-woven carpets, many-colored and beautiful, to replace the older ones on the floor.

An oblong table had been set before the templum, covered with a white cloth holding the Gospel, a glass of wine, and the two gold wedding rings which the bridegroom had provided, the name *Sophia* engraved in Henry's ring, *Henry* engraved inside Sophia's. The white coronet was beautiful on her black hair. On one side of her stood her young nephew Costaki, dressed in white, holding a tall, thick white candle; on the other side was her young cousin Eugenia, also in white and holding a candle.

The church had now filled. There were no chairs. Everyone stood. On Sophia's head and on Henry's were placed *stephanion* wreaths of fresh orange blossoms attached to each other by ribbon which Spyros, acting as best man, would reverse each of the three times the marrying couple was led around the table by the priest, who held them by the hand, while the cantor chanted and the congregation joined in the prayers. The priest read from the Epistles of St. Paul and the Gospel According to St. John, describing the wedding in Cana of Galilee. Only occasionally did Sophia hear the words over the thumping beat of her heart.

"God, the All Holy, and Builder of the Universe, who took Adam's rib and transformed it in your philanthropy to a woman, and blessed them both, and said: 'Increase and multiply yourselves and master the earth,' and gave them the opportunity of being one member through matrimony . . . ; because of this man will desert his father and mother and will adhere to his own wife, and the two will make one flesh; . . . and those that God united, no man should attempt to part . . ."

Sophia had steeled herself for the two hours of chanting, praying and reading of Scripture, for she had been taught that in the Greek Orthodox religion the most important event in a person's life, after the baptism, was the wedding. Without meaning to be irreverent in this sacred hour, the quip of the Athenian bachelors came to her mind:

"The marriage ceremony is so long that it takes a lifetime of living together to get over it!"

The double rings were blessed by the priest and exchanged. Sophia and Henry sipped from the same cup of wine to signify the joy and bitterness they would share. The wreaths of orange blossoms were crossed over their heads three times more, giving the blessings of the Holy Trinity to the new partners' lives. The congregation prayed. The priest turned the pages of the Gospel:

"O Lord, O Our Despot and God, send your grace from heaven on these your servants Henry Schliemann and Sophia Engastromenos. Make this girl be submissive to the man your servant who is at the head of the woman so that they may live on according to your will. Bless them, O God Our Lord, as you blessed Abraham and Sarah. Bless them as you blessed Jacob and Azineth. Bless them as you blessed Moses and Semphorah. Bless them as you blessed Zachary and Elisabeth. Protect them as you protected Noah in his ark; protect them as you did Jonah in the belly of the sea monster . . ."

The priest bade Sophia: ". . . go simply yourself as Rachel, enjoying your own husband and keeping the law, because this is the will of God . . ." and pronounced them man and wife.

There was a great deal of weepy embracing of Sophia by the women, and kissing on the cheek by the men; all the while her younger sister Marigo was handing each of the guests *koufeta*, shiny sugar-coated almonds wrapped in a bag of white tulle and tied with ribbons. Each guest murmured to Marigo:

"May it happen to you!"

In Greece a wedding feast is unabashedly joyous. Sophia's father had borrowed big metal cans and filled them with *ouzo*; there were barrels of *retsina* from the local vintners. Although Madame Victoria had the reputation of being the finest dessert maker in Attica, she had been relieved of this task by her relatives, each family bringing a large tray filled with apricot chocolate custard cake, cream torte, golden meringue cake, *ravani*, yogurt pie, honey-dipped cookies, pecan bars, almond pears, *baklava*, *trigona* with its pound of *phyllo* pastry sheets . . .

A long wooden table had been set out with appetizers to be relished with the *ouzo* and wine: salted smelts, fish roe patties, marinated lamb brains, giant beans, fresh mussels. At a center table there were deep bowls of salad; wild chicory, dill and mint had been thrown in to give fragrance to the lettuce, romaine and escarole.

From the oven at the bakery arrived the chicken, rabbit, shrimp, fish *plaki*, braised eggplant, okra, chick-peas, endive *avgolemono*, artichokes with butter sauce, zucchini, squash fritters, braised string beans and *shish kebab*. Yet not all the accumulated family pans would contain enough food to feed the wedding party celebrants, the men's appetites whetted by frequent incursions to the *ouzo* cans and to the casks of wine. At the back of the garden chickens roasted on grills, lambs and yard-long rolls of *kokoretzi* turned on borrowed spits, filling not only the garden but the whole square with delicious odors.

Standing by the window of the upstairs hall just before changing into her traveling clothes, Sophia was shocked to see the more than two hundred people assembled for the feast. In addition to their relatives and close friends there were now a large number of acquaintances from Colonos and Athens. She knew the cost of the food and drink, and she knew that the sixty dollars she had asked and received from Henry would not cover any part of the expense. It would be more like two hundred and sixty dollars!

Sick with anxiety, she asked herself:

"But where will Father get the money to pay the bills? If he could not spare the sixty dollars for the church costs, where can he possibly raise another two hundred? If he goes to a moneylender it will cost him two per cent a month, with no way of paying it off. My parents did this for me; they are proud people; they could turn no one down. And now, while I wake up in the sunshine of Messina, a married woman without a trouble in the world, they will wake up to the darkness of debt. I can't let that happen to them."

She took her father aside, squirmed the truth out of him. By actual count he had spent sixteen hundred drachmas, three hundred and twenty dollars.

"But, Father, you know that the merchants must be paid."

"That's tomorrow. This is tonight, my daughter's wedding feast. I could not let people think we were too poor to let them come and toast your happiness."

She sought out her husband, explained what had happened: the Engastromenos family simply could not lose face.

"My dear Henry, it kills my soul to have my first request as your wife be one concerned with money. But I have no alternative; I cannot steal away and leave my family bereft. Please help me this one time. I'll promise never to ask anything of you again."

"What did your father do with the sixty dollars I gave him?"

"Paid the priests, the church costs, the tradesmen who would not extend him credit."

He went white around the corners of the mouth.

"You are my wife, dearest Sophia, and you can ask for anything in the world you want . . . for yourself. But it galls me to think that I am to be exploited by your family without my knowledge or consent. Are you sure your father didn't spend so lavishly knowing that I would refuse you nothing on our wedding day?"

She held her head high, her somber eyes meeting his head on.

"I honestly don't think so. They're not like that. Pride, yes. The desire to make a big showing, yes. But deceit, no. My parents were simply putting off tomorrow's troubles until they arrived on their early morning doorstep."

Henry grimaced, took out his wallet, counted out sixteen hundred drachmas, put them into Sophia's hand. She leaned up and kissed him.

"Thank you. You are generous."

One corner of Henry's mouth moved upward in a quarter smile.

"Every other day!"

"You won't regret it."

He replied with a risqué gleam in his eye, the first he had permitted himself:

"My only regret will be if the Aegean kicks up. If it does, knowing what kind of sailor you are, Sophidion, I am going to have to postpone my honeymoon until we are on terra firma in Sicily."

BOOK TWO

GREECE IS GOD'S LOVE AFFAIR
WITH THE PLANET EARTH

BOOK TWO

1.

SHE dressed before the picture window in their room on the top floor of the Hotel d'Angleterre, making no sound. Syntagma Square was a dark green carpet running uphill before her, the center of Athens, the spot from which every Greek measures all other places in the world. Beyond the square, lighted by tall thin gas lamps, was the palace which the Greeks had built for King Otho when he was summoned from Bavaria to become titular head of the new and slowly cohering nation.

The lobby was deserted at this hour of four in the morning. She stepped out into the fresh night air, warming now that the January-February winter season was coming to a close. The purplish-black sky, close and vibrant, was lighted by stars so brilliant that they appeared to be bursting. A sense of peace and oneness overcame her. She thought:

"To live in Athens is to live at the heart of the universe. Just to take a deep breath of this fragrant night air, or to look at the bluest of all skies in the morning, is to know how beautiful the world is, and why it was created."

There was only a scimitar of a moon, a shape which had become familiar during the Turkish occupation. The high iron lamps, painted green and adorned with the head of Athena, created pockets of illumination among the palm trees, the acacias with their clusters of yellow and white flowers, the pepper trees and bitter orange, alive and glowing after the abundant winter rains. The chairs of the sidewalk cafés were piled somnolently in high stacks; cleaning men scrubbed down the sidewalks, sloshing water out of buckets and sweeping the refuse into the gutter with handmade brooms of broomcorn tied to sticks so short the sweepers had to bend over double.

Walking up toward the palace, she saw the *salèpe* vendor, his tall brass samovar full of the hot herb drink which he trundled through the dark streets in a cart. Sophia took a coin from her purse, the vendor took a cup off one of the dozen hooks studded on the front of the samovar, ladled it full. The scent of wild herbs assaulted her nostrils before the strong tea caressed her throat.

She walked quickly down Panepistimiou, passing the marble columns and covered arcade of the Arsakeion, which a Greek, coming back to his country of birth after amassing a foreign fortune, had presented to his city as a love letter. She then crossed the wide thoroughfare to gaze with joyful pride at the University of Athens and the National Library, built in the ancient Greek tradition of Pentelic marble and faced with majestic columns.

She entered a side street, now that the morning stars had become visible, to move into the residential district. The lamplighters in these secondary streets were turning down the wicks of the oil lamps attached by brackets to one house on each corner. It took her only two uphill blocks before she heard the vendors crying their wares.

"They wake every sleeping thing," she laughed.

Yet it was not a cacophony; each vendor had established for himself a distinctive and recognizable throat instrument, waking the housewives in Greek, Turkish, Italian, each one known by his cry. Just before sunrise she encountered the goatherds crying out, "*Galá, galá.*" The housewives came out with their pails, scrupulously choosing the one goat of many whose milk they wanted. The goatherd also sold curdled goat milk, which he carried in a tin box, calling out, "*Yo-wr-te!*" Sophia bought a small piece, the goatherd sprinkled it with powdered sugar. As she tasted the first pungent mouthful she murmured:

"Sharp as the bite of a dog."

The sun was making its overtures in the east. She felt an infusion of delight at the beauty of the pale rose sunrise. She climbed through a tree-studded park to the top of the hill. All of Athens lay below her, the Acropolis above. A mystical light like fine white powder seemed to sift down from the heavens, as though Zeus were sprinkling the firmament with some divine elixir to bring glory to the city. The thought came into her mind, born whole as a revelation:

"Greece is God's love affair with the planet Earth."

In Greece the light was not something external, that one looked at. It seeped through the pores of one's body and brain until it existed as a shining, pulsating force within the human citadel, an interior illumination, peculiar to each person, making life not only good but meaningful. The Greek sun did not heat the outside skin, it entered through every orifice to burn inside one's bosom as though it were a second palpitant heart, pumping the rich blood of vitality through one's veins. The Greek light and the Greek sun were indigenous to the islands, to the mainland, and the Aegean Sea, known to no other land on earth, part of the heritage that built the Parthenon. The Egyptians had been sun worshipers; the Greeks were inhabited by the sun.

The first daylight vendor carried hot rolls on a bakery counter on his head. Immediately behind him came a shepherd selling unsalted butter in a stone crock, to be melted inside the roll, which Sophia, hungry, gobbled down. She wondered:

"Where could I have found a sight like this in Paris: a shepherd in tight-fitting leggings, a bright shirt reaching halfway to his knees, a colored handkerchief tied around his head and knotted at the back?"

She had little time to wonder, for on came the contingent of bent women selling wild greens, crying out in aged voices, "*Radheekia!*" Behind them were the garlic vendors wearing the garlic heads on a long string over their shoulders. Sophia had been raised to believe that "garlic keeps away the evil eye." Filling the streets now was a typical Athenian sound, familiar and heart-warming: the creak of huge panniers on either side of tiny donkeys, obliterating them from sight; but not what was being carried: piles of fruits and vegetables, fresh-picked: cucumbers, tomatoes, potatoes, with the housewives in front of their doors carefully choosing the finest for their noon dinner, the most important judgments of the day.

For Sophia the most amusing sight was the turkey merchant. He came slowly up the hill, having been walking since midnight from his farm with a gaggle of two hundred turkeys, using a long pole to push them along faster and to break up pecking quarrels. Here the bargaining was long and hard, for each housewife wanted the best turkey on the march for the least price. Having made a sale, he moved on, crying in a shrill cackle:

"Turkey cock, little turkey, little hen turkey!"

In the now surging street the sweetest sight was the honey vendor, who carried a tree branch with a large triangle of honeycomb at its base, the honey made by bees from the wild thyme on the slope of Mt. Hymettus. Sophia had him cut off a small piece for her, and chewed on the waxy comb, letting the world's most delicious nectar slip down her throat. The honey vendor had started late, at sunrise, but his stock was soon exhausted.

Behind the food vendors there now came the pushcarts and high nasal tones of the handicrafters selling brooms, thread and spools, mousetraps made in the sheds behind their houses; then the repairmen who mended wooden or wicker chairs, sharpened the kitchen knives on emery grinders, hammered new soles on shoes. Last of all, pulled by two small ponies, and followed by the garbage men with shovels, came the garbage wagon, slim vertical poles around all four sides so that additional planks could be inserted when needed for added height, as the housemaids, hearing the wagon come down the street, dashed up from the basement to dump all of yesterday's garbage and dirty water into the gutter.

Walking back toward the main streets of Academias and Panepistimiou, Sophia heard the public crier with a strong voice heralding the new laws and orders passed by the police or the City Council the day before. The orders were not printed in the newspapers because the papers did not come out every day; besides, few people could read.

She turned back toward the hotel.

"A city's life should be lived on its streets," she thought. "There are always sights for the eye, sounds for the ear, smells for the nostrils. Italy was like that: Sicily, Naples, Rome . . . I loved Italy. Or was that because I had a beautiful honeymoon? Except that Henry walked my feet off in the museums."

She had felt at home in Italy, with its silver-green olive orchards, its dark blue sea. After all, Italy had been settled by the Trojan Aeneas and his son Ascanius. In spite of the fact that Henry had obliged her to learn the background of every painting, mosaic, vase, inscribed stone, ancient sculpture, weapon, tool and coin in the museums from Messina to Venice, she found time to write home every day. From Messina she confided:

"I really wonder how God has granted me such good fortune. I don't base my happiness on glory or wealth or the attentions showered on me, but on Henry's good attitude toward me. I am very pleased with my marriage, and I will always be. I pray that my revered mother does not worry about me."

From Naples she wrote, "We are all well, by the grace of God. All day long we went by carriage through the streets of the town. I am pleased here by the climate and the most glorious antiquities. We visited Pompeii, also Herculaneum. . . . Today we will go to Sorrento, where we will stay for the night."

From Rome, "If you ask about my health, we are very well, enjoying the earthly pleasures. We visited the biggest and most magnificent church in the world, St. Peter's, where I really marveled seeing the great luxury! We visited the Vatican Museum, the Sistine Chapel, the Raphael room, the Greek and Egyptian sculptures."

When Henry wrote to her parents he signed himself, "The happy husband of Sophia."

Sophia tried to entertain her family.

"In Venice I found it curious that throughout the city, except for a few narrow streets, there is sea. In place of carriages, they use boats that look like graves, black and half covered over. In Padua, when we visited the university, we saw a machine which goes on moving for thirty years. They call it perpetual motion. It reminded me of Henry. He does not merely visit a museum, he assaults and conquers it!"

He taught her to concentrate on the markings and decorations of the pottery, on the differing shapes, glazes, handles, bases, mouths.

"Pottery is our encyclopedia from prehistoric times," he said. "We can read it just as clearly as we do manuscripts on ancient papyrus. It has been said that man became man when he threw his first pot. Once you train yourself in reading pottery, you can tell, with each new discovery, precisely what age, culture and geographical area it comes from."

He had proved to be an ardent lover, yet he was tender with her, and solicitous, helping her to learn at her own pace. After she had become comfortable in her love-making, Henry revealed that he had suffered "six years' abstinence" because his wife had terminated their intimate relationship. Sophia, laughing as he told her this story, murmured:

"You are making up for those six lost years!"

She had liked Paris too, at first. The Rue de Rivoli with its smart shops, the wide tree-lined Champs Élysées, the flowering gardens in the Tuileries, the broad sculptured bridges over the Seine, the Île de la Cité with its great cathedral, and of course the Louvre, where Henry took her for full day excursions. She particularly loved the Venus de Milo. To her parents she wrote:

> What can I write about Paris; it is really an earthly paradise. Everything is pleasant to me; and still sweeter is the divine love between Henry and me. We are always careful so that each one makes the other happier. The only thing that worries me a little is the language. I am taking four one-hour lessons a day now. I have a woman instructor, and Henry teaches me too.

She did not add that Henry had also hired a German tutor, and was himself teaching her German from the Goethe and Schiller volumes in his library. He had also found a professor at the Sorbonne who taught French and Greek side by side, so that she could make better progress with her essays, which Henry insisted she write every day.

Not content with her ten-hour workday, he enrolled her in the University of Paris. She enjoyed most of it, particularly when Henry read aloud to her in the evenings in the quiet intimacy of their book-lined library. He was eager that, in preparation for the excavations at Hissarlik, she become acquainted with the beginnings of archaeology: Winckelmann's *History of Ancient Art*; Belzoni's opening of the tombs in Egypt; the discovery of the stone and bronze figures at Herculaneum, and the wall paintings found under the hard crust of lava at Pompeii, where they had been buried for seventeen hundred years.

Henry was a one-man university in his eagerness to educate her. She had no responsibilities in his elegant apartment. As Madame Victoria had warned, the French cook would not even let her set foot in the kitchen. She saw that the maids and the laundry woman were stealing, but she did not know how to stop them. Henry even hired a personal maid to take care of her clothing and other needs. He planned the dinners, set out the guest lists, entertained Ernst Renan and other intellectual rebels of Paris.

Her youth and lack of French set her apart, but her only problem was homesickness. The ever present need to see her family, Athens, Greece. Henry could not understand this.

"How can anyone *not* fall desperately in love with Paris?"

"Henry, I don't think any European can understand how close Greek families are. We long for each other if we are separated for only a few hours. Love of family is the deepest aspect of our lives. My homesickness is more painful than a broken leg."

To her brother Spyros she wrote, "You ask about my life here. It is very pleasant. I sit all day with a dictionary on my lap. But I am also starting to take gymnastic lessons. Sometimes I suffer from nostalgia. But my dear husband does not let this nostalgia last long; he takes me for a walk, or to the theater, or the circus, which I adore." To her sister Marigo, "The only thing that disturbs me emotionally is that I don't see you. God has given me all this happiness but I am deprived of my family." To Georgios Engastromenos, "My revered father, I received your beloved letter. I read it a thousand times, shedding tears of joy as I understood that you had not forgotten me."

Along with the deepening nostalgia she was troubled that, while she was living in luxury in Paris, affairs were not going well for her family at home. When they put her on the ship at Piraeus they had had hardly a drachma to their name. Her mother would have to buy her week's supplies out of the week's profits, and it would be thin gruel for everyone concerned. When no letter arrived she assumed it was because the family was too depressed to write.

She could think of no way to help them, though their need for help became more and more apparent. When she had asked Henry for sixteen hundred drachmas to pay for the wedding feast, she had promised that she would not ask again. She wanted to keep her word. Nor did she have any money of her own to send, for it never occurred to Henry to provide her with cash for her purse. What would she have wanted it for? He paid the servants, the merchants, the dressmakers, entering every check and receipt in his meticulously kept ledgers. He was generous with her, but since she had never handled money, why start now? No matter how often she set the roulette ball of her thoughts spinning around her head, it always stopped on zero. There was simply no way to ask for pocket money or a bank account when there was nothing she lacked.

It was particularly distressing that, from scraps of discussion and hints he let drop, she was beginning to get an idea of how much capital Henry Schliemann had amassed. His four apartment houses in Paris were valued at three hundred and sixty thousand dollars. He owned them outright, having paid for them with the sale of part of his imperial Russian bonds. They brought substantial rentals. From the Crimean War alone he had made a profit of two million rubles, roughly four hundred thousand dollars. He had bankers and agents in St. Petersburg, London, Hamburg, New York, Paris, owned blocks of railroad bonds in the United States and Cuba, industrial stocks in England . . . His annual income had to be considerable. There was no doubt in her mind that somehow, someday Henry would help her family. But he was certainly not thinking about that now, immersed as he was in Parisian life. What hardships would they have to undergo in the meantime?

As her concern for her family deepened she came to have little taste for the apartment full of servants, the elaborate cut velvet and gilt furniture, the box at the opera, the silk and satin gowns. At times, when she was low in her mind, she wished she were back in Greece, working as a schoolteacher, helping the family with her modest wage.

Then, in ample time for Christmas, Henry presented his wife with a charming watch which he had imported from England for her. He also sent Georgios Engastromenos one thousand francs, two hundred dollars. She saw the note that accompanied the bank draft, "To help you celebrate the holidays," little knowing, as Sophia did, that the two hundred dollars would help them *survive* the holidays! She was happy for her family; and happy with Henry because he had originated the gesture.

But if she breathed easier for a while when thinking of Greece and home, misfortune struck from a direction in which she had never permitted the weather eye of her mind to turn. Toward the middle of December, when they were sitting together in the library reading a pleasant letter from Henry's sister in Germany, a telegram was delivered. It had been sent by Henry's son, fourteen-year-old Serge, from St. Petersburg. The elder of Henry's daughters, Natalya, only twelve, had died of blood poisoning.

For three days and three nights Henry would not leave his bedroom, eat or take comfort. He wept. He had been a bad father. Had he remained in St. Petersburg he would have gotten the best doctors for Natalya, the best medicines, she would be alive today. . . .

Never having experienced this kind of grief, Sophia had no salve to apply to her husband's wounds except that of reason.

"Your agent in St. Petersburg, Mr. Günzburg, said in his letter that they summoned Dr. Kauzler and Dr. Eck. Are they good doctors?"

"The best."

"If you had been in St. Petersburg, would you have called them in?"
"Yes."
"Wouldn't her mother have given Natalya constant care and devotion?"
"Yes."
"Then what more could you possibly have done?"
"I should have been there. Natalya wouldn't have become sick."

Sophia summoned Ernst Renan and several other of Henry's men friends to console him, but consolation and sympathy were not the medicine he needed. She took another tack, and made a mistake in judgment. She sent messages to the older women who had been his earlier friends. They treated her coldly, as though the fault were hers: if she had not broken up Henry's marriage, Natalya would still be alive.

"What use to tell them that Henry had been separated from Ekaterina for six years before he came to Colonos?" she asked herself. "They act as though I am Henry's mistress."

Time paled Henry's emotions. But Paris was never the same for Sophia. Winter set in: rain, cold, sleet, snow, dark gray depressing skies. There was no more chance to go for walks. She caught cold. Henry came down with influenza.

Her mother sent her a box of little sweet cakes for Christmas. She limited herself to one each day, after breakfast, to prolong the endearing contact.

The weather became so bad that the ships from Piraeus to Marseilles were delayed, and with them her mail from home. Her longing for her family blossomed into a lush plant of acute homesickness and physical discomfort.

New Year's Day, her birthday, was a gloomy one, as was Henry's five days later. When the holidays had come and gone, and the passing days were invading 1870 with still no permit from the Turkish government allowing him to dig at Troy, Henry grew irascible. The eighteen-year-old girl had difficulty adjusting to a new land, without her own people, and the forty-eight-year-old man could not adjust to the fact that there was no way to hurry the Turkish government into issuing the permission. He had made his reputation as well as his fortune by being prompt, vigorous, efficient, straightforward, accomplished.

"It passes all understanding," he grumbled, "why the Turkish government, or the minister in charge, cannot write so simple a paper. They have everything to gain and nothing to lose. Why then the delays, the procrastinations, the putting off of a simple deed?"

She had learned which of his questions were rhetorical. Instead of consoling him by praising a virtue which he detested, patience, she talked to herself:

"My problem is that I am too young to begin. His problem is that he is too old to wait."

Since he could not take his unhappiness out on the Grand Vizier, he became angry at Sophia.

"You are not living in Paris at all! Night and day your thoughts are in Greece. Your only desire is to see and embrace your family, and to live under your blue Greek sky. Why don't you become an adult, and live in Paris with your husband who adores you? Your homesickness is spoiling our marriage."

Studying now gave her a headache. She could digest only a little food. Henry called in first a French doctor who diagnosed her trouble as stomach spasms; he then summoned a Greek doctor practicing in Paris, who felt that Sophia was suffering from an intestinal disorder. Henry asked him:

"Do you think I should take her to a German spa for the waters?"

"Why not take her home and let her bathe at Piraeus? You'll be astonished how quickly those waters will cure her!"

Though Henry was hard pressed to understand Sophia's desperate loneliness, his love for her asserted itself. He agreed to take her back to Athens and wait there for the *firman* to arrive from Constantinople. Sophia recognized that this involved a considerable sacrifice, leaving his spacious and well-staffed home for a hotel suite in Athens, deprived as well of his reference library and his sometimes distinguished friends.

By now she was too unhappy to refuse the sacrifice.

2.

At the dock in Piraeus the Engastromenos family engulfed Sophia in free-flowing tears of welcome. For a fleeting instant she had the feeling that they were standoffish with her husband, but the presentiment vanished in the joy of being reunited with her parents, brothers and sisters, the colorfully festive streets of Piraeus and Athens, for this was the last Saturday before the forty-eight days of Lent, and of rigorous fasting. Both the port town and the city were decorated, the streets and squares filled with people singing and dancing around the *romvia*, a hand organ hung with ribbons and flowers. Professional mummers were going about town disguised as Moors or women, dancing around a Maypole, or mounted on cardboard horses and camels, dressed in the traditional Greek white pleated skirt. Crowds of rollicking children followed the mummers who, after each performance, passed a tambourine into which the spectators tossed ten- or twenty-lepta coins of nickel and silver.

The next morning, Sunday, Sophia and Henry went early to spend the day with the family. St. Meletios Square too was gaily festooned; a spirit of fun permeated the village as young boys and girls dressed in masquerade. Sophia and her kinfolk chattered for hours, at midday in the garden, and then around the Sunday dinner table. Sophia told of her travels, of Paris; the family related news and gossip about relatives and friends, sometimes several of them talking at once with the vivacity of early awakened birds outside one's bedroom window.

Again Sophia had the feeling that Henry was being excluded. She turned to study her husband's face and saw that he was neither hurt nor withdrawn, but rather amused at the ebullient chatter. On their way back to the hotel later that evening, comfortable in the back seat of a carriage, Henry put his arm around her and hugged her in a possessive way, as though to suggest, "After all is said, you belong to me and not them." Aloud he remarked, not unkindly:

"Little one, how can you all talk so long and say so little?"

She gazed at him in astonishment.

"Why, Henry, talking is as important to life as breathing. It's not what my family and I say to each other that's important, it's the fact that we hear the music of each other's voices."

Henry chewed on that for a moment, then kissed her and replied:

"You are right, Sophidion; those who love don't need to make sense; they just have to feel each other's presence."

Monday morning, three days after their arrival at the Hotel d'Angleterre, she returned from her reunion with Athens to find Henry at his desk in his dressing gown, drinking coffee and writing letters in his cramped but precise hand. He looked up, said he had awakened at six o'clock to find her gone, and listened attentively to her tale of Athens awakening. He made room for her on the chair beside him, poured her a cup of coffee, hot and sweet.

"I am writing to Frank Calvert in Çanakkale. He is an Englishman who made millions provisioning the British navy during the Crimean War. One of the fields he owns includes half of the mound of Hissarlik. He has given me permission to dig there. He's also working conscientiously to secure my permit to excavate the whole of the mountain. He is an amateur scientist too; he has published several articles in the British *Archaeological Journal* on the ancient geography of the Troad."

Sophia's dark eyes seemed enormous with life after her happy time out of doors.

"Could I see the letter?"

She took the sheet and read half aloud, " 'I am intensely eager to commence the excavations at Hissarlik. If you have got the *firman*, please give me once more a list of the implements and instruments required, for in the hurry in which we left Paris I have forgotten to copy same from your letter of last winter. On receipt of your letter that you have got the *firman* I shall proceed at once to Smyrna, or Constantinople, if you think it better, to procure the articles in question.'"

She turned to her husband eagerly, moistening her lips with her tongue.

"Henry, do you think we can actually start digging later this spring?"

"I ardently hope so." His eyes were gleaming and the color had risen not only in his slender cheeks but on his balding pate, giving it a pleasantly rosy hue. "I'd like us to visit Aulis right away. It's where the Achaean fleet assembled prior to sailing for Troy. I've never been there. I think we should actually walk among the Achaean camps here in Greece before we reconstruct their camp on the Dardanelles below Troy."

Her breath caught at the thought of leaving her family so soon.

"Could we take Spyros and Marigo with us?" she asked. "The family would be delighted at the idea of your inviting them; they haven't been away from home since Father's setback."

She listened intently to his thoughts as they spilled one over the other, while he weighed the advantages and disadvantages of such an arrangement. His decision made, he smiled and nodded simultaneously; shifted his dressing gown over his shoulders so that it sat well.

"I'll find out when the boat sails for Chalkis. Then you can take a carriage out to Colonos and invite them."

There was an overnight boat from Piraeus to Chalkis, a trip which took fifteen hours. Henry engaged three cabins. Spyros, who had recently turned twenty-one, was a stolid character; short, stocky, with an olive complexion. He had no discernible enthusiasm except his devotion to Sophia, having been her protector during the years when she was growing up. He was an enigma to Henry because the young man had no ambitions or direction for his life. When Henry asked him what he wanted to become, Spyros answered shyly:

"I already am. I'll work in Father's drapery shop as long as we have it, then I'll work for Alexandros. He's the driven one. I am content just to be."

Sophia smiled, though barely perceptibly, as her husband shook his head in disbelief. She mused, "Henry thinks the purpose in everyone's life is to become rich or influential, that to be born without ambition is the equivalent of being born without an arm or leg."

Marigo, at fourteen, was a chirper rather than a talker, with a pleasant face, attractive except for the bony ridge of her nose, which gave her features a sharpened aspect. She chattered, albeit quietly, the way she breathed, unceasingly, although her sense of awe with Henry served to sew her lips together, something of a miracle.

They took the train to the port. The ship sailed from Piraeus at seven-fifteen in the evening. They had a pleasant supper in a little sitting-room off the main salon, then went on deck to watch the tiny islands glide by in the partial moonlight, each resembling a denizen of the sea: first a whale, then a porpoise, a shark, a seal; and afterward, animals of the forest: a giraffe because of a high-rising peak, a grizzly bear, an antelope. It was a game the Engastromenos children had played while traveling to Crete, Mykonos and the closer islands for their summer vacations.

The sea was calm, the night air still. They remained on deck until midnight, when the ship made its wide turn at Cape Sounion, and they could see the magnificent temple of Poseidon standing on the summit of the promontory, its fifteen columns of marble countable at least in fantasy from the prow of their ship.

When they awakened the next morning at seven and went on deck, Sophia saw that they had already passed Marathon and were about to enter the seventy-yard-wide channel leading to Chalkis. Henry took her arm and moved her to the port side so that he could point out the wide, deep beach where the Achaean ships had been pulled ashore around the necropolis of Aulis. Sophia gripped his arm tightly; he was trembling with excitement.

"What a fool I've been!" he exclaimed. "This is my third trip to Greece and only now have I come to the very start of my story."

"How could you have come to Aulis," she teased, "without the Greek wife who is going to help you find Troy?"

He turned her to him and kissed her robustly on the mouth, which astonished her.

"Why, he took me seriously," she thought; "I must be careful what I tease him about."

Henry hired a fisherman's caïque to take them across the channel to the Aulis shore, directing the owner to tack on an angle which would beach them directly in front of the little inn. Two small boys came running to collect their bags. From his own satchel Henry took his map of Greece on which he had marked in varying colors the exact location of every kingdom and area-tribe mentioned in Homer's *Catalogue of the Ships*, except for the few that had disappeared not only from the landscape but from folk memory as well. On a separate sheet he had made a sketch showing the layout of the Achaean camp on the beach of Aulis.

Sophia collected Spyros and Marigo. The four of them walked northward on the beach until Henry took a sighting of the port of Chalkis. Enclosing them, and this narrow womb of the sea, were bare rounded hills, denuded by the early Romans, who had cut down the trees to provide their ships with masts. The scene fitted Homer's description of "rocky Aulis." At the extreme northern end was a narrow gorge for the sea to move through, and ships as well, in a continuous line. This was the route by which the 1140 Achaean ships had left the channel to sail past the Sporades and into the open Aegean before cutting below the island of Lemnos for the Dardanelles.

Henry picked up a branch of driftwood, opened his pocket knife and whittled one end to a point. Then, consulting his map, he began making wide markings and trenches in the sand, setting forth the encampment. Sophia observed that his eyes, his moist lips, his quickly moving hands, his entire body were quivering with entrancement; again she realized that when Henry Schliemann plunged into the work he loved best in the world he became ageless. The thirty years' difference between them disappeared. He was darting up and down the beach with the movements of a gazelle, re-creating on the sands of Aulis the vast camp of the Achaeans.

"Here at the center of command was Agamemnon, king of Mycenae and of the entire Mycenaean Empire, which extended throughout most of Greece." He was speaking directly to Sophia, his associate and partner in this adventure; Spyros and Marigo were standing off to one side, eyes wide at Henry's performance. "His pavilion was set in the center of his hundred black-tar hulls and bronze-beaked ships. On either end—see, I will throw stones to indicate where—were the two strongest leaders, Ajax on the extreme north with his forty ships, Achilles on the south with his fifty ships and almost a thousand men. On Agamemnon's right was the aging but wise Nestor, 'king of sandy Pylos,' with his ninety ships; and on the other side was Menelaus, Agamemnon's brother, king of Sparta, with sixty. Next to him was the wily Odysseus, alongside the encampment altar, with twelve vermilion-prowed ships. Crete was here, a mighty contingent of eighty swift ships and eight hundred and sixty men; on the corresponding spot on the other side there were the Argives, also with eighty ships. Lined down toward the south were the Boeotian forces with fifty ships, the Phocians with forty, the Magnesians with forty. Extending upward to the north were the Euboeans with fifty ships, the Arcadians with sixty, the Epeians with forty.

"It was a vast encampment, some 120,000 men under forty commanders. Each flotilla built its own camp, provided its own meat, wine, barley. But the fleet could not sail for Troy because of lack of a directing wind, and the months wore on in idleness; the warriors began to drink, gamble, fight . . . Even the powerful Achilles could not control his men. Euripides had him say in *Iphigenia in Aulis*:

> "And here by the Euripus I must wait—
> Wait because here these light winds blow—
> And curb my own troops, my Myrmidons.
> They are forever urging me and saying:
> We are the army for Troy! How many months
> Must we drag out here? Act if you are going
> To act, if not, wait no longer upon
> Atreus's sons and on their dallyings
> But lead the army home."

His arm linked tightly through hers, Henry led Sophia from camp to camp.

"During the athletic contests, the boxing, wrestling, foot and chariot races, discus throwing, the men of the different tribes began quarreling among themselves; there must have been many a cracked skull. This, added to the fact that the white sails were decaying, the timber of the masts rotting, the food supplies vanishing, built to the climax where Agamemnon was forced to sacrifice his virgin daughter Iphigenia to the goddess Artemis so that she would create the winds that would enable them to sail at once, and save the expedition from dissolution."

Throwing his arms out in a widespread gesture, Henry cried to his wife:

"Can you see what a vast community would have been created here? It might have been the largest city any Achaean had ever known or heard about. There would be alleys, lanes, compounds, quarters for the merchants coming to sell their wares; women coming to sell theirs. Though there might not be more than forty spacious pavilions, there would be thousands of canvas tents, wooden shacks, lean-tos, improvised warrens for small game animals, open areas set aside for contests of jousting, mule breaking . . ."

Sophia had been thinking through a problem. She asked:

"Henry, these ships were only large enough to hold fifty men. I can see how they would dismantle the chariots and stow them in spare places. But where did they put the horses? When *The Iliad* opens during the tenth year of the siege of Troy, they seem to have all the horses they need, particularly from 'horse-breeding Argos' here in Greece. Did they dismember them too, and stow them forward and aft?"

Henry was amused, threw an arm roughly about her shoulder to protect her from the cool wind.

"Only the wooden horse, my irreverent Sophidion! Why could they not have gathered all the horses they needed when they made camp on the Plain of Troy? The Trojans and their twenty-plus allies had wonderful horses, particularly the Thracians, whose horses were stolen by Odysseus and Diomedes after they had killed the Trojan spy, Dolon, who had tried to capture Achilles's Thessalian horses."

"You see, Henry, you have proved my point. If Achilles had his horses from his home in Thessaly, so did the others. Maybe they had special horse-boats?"

"It's not in the folk memory, little one. I'm going to let you worry about how the Achaeans transported their horses from here to Troy."

She chuckled at having caught him out. Her eyes had a mischievous glint.

"As long as I'm worrying about horses, why don't I include years? Do you think Homer was right in saying that the Achaeans had been besieging Troy for nine years before *The Iliad* opens? If the masts and sails rotted in a few months here in Aulis, what would have happened to them in nine years on the Hellespont?"

"The mountains are full of timber," he replied patiently; "and the men knew how to weave sails."

"Henry, you once pointed out that the number nine was a sacred one to the Greeks. The Acropolis had *nine* gates. Homer uses the figure nine almost exclusively through *The Iliad*. I began to make a list last winter in Paris, when I was being unhappy.

"When Agamemnon refuses to return Chryses's daughter, whom he had taken in battle, Chryses appeals to Apollo to bring a curse down on all the Achaeans: 'For nine days' space did the missiles of the god fare throughout the host. . . .' When Patroclus's comrades wash his dead body, they 'Fill his wounds with ointment of nine years old.' When Hephaestus was creating a suit of armor for Achilles overnight, he sculpted 'nine dogs swift of foot.' When Priam reclaims the body of Hector from Achilles, Priam says, 'For nine days' space will we wail for him in our halls.' . . ."

"Enough! I congratulate you on this feat of memory," Henry said dryly.

She was too caught up in her argument to hear the warning signal.

"Doesn't it seem curious that after nine years of fighting on the plain below them Priam for the first time asks Helen while they are on top of the Watchtower to identify the Achaean warriors coming toward them? You remember that Helen identifies her husband Menelaus, and Ajax?"

"Yes, I seem to remember." Sarcastically.

"Wouldn't that give us the right to assume that Homer used the figure *nine years* symbolically?"

"No!" he replied sternly. "*We must have faith!*"

"But how could the Achaean forces have sustained themselves before Troy for nine years?"

"They raided for food . . ."

"I know," she interrupted, "but how could all of those kings, princes, fighting men have remained away so long from their land, their duties? There would have been usurpations of power, invasions by marauding neighbors, by barbarians. I believe that the figure nine means nine months of siege in that one year, rather than in the tenth year on the Plain of Troy! I think it means *for a long time. . . .*"

Henry grimaced.

"The student is now instructing her professor."

She stuck to her guns, head held high, lips compressed.

"Then you should be proud, rather than disgruntled, seeing how good a teacher you are."

He turned his back on her and stalked off to the inn. She thought:

"I guess another of Mother's Cretan proverbs is right, 'You can say anything you like, so long as you don't dispute my word.' "

She too turned toward the inn.

"Ah well, once started digging, there will be no energy left for theoretical discussion. Dear God, please soften the heart of the Grand Vizier so that he will issue a permit to Henry."

By the time they had had a nap and supper was announced, Henry's good nature had reasserted itself. He apologized to Sophia for his boorish conduct, took Spyros and Marigo each by an arm as he escorted them into the pleasant kitchen-diningroom of the inn. They were the only guests. Sophia chose one of the three tables in front of a tall wooden counter inlaid with colorful tiles which separated the workbench and the sink from the diners. However the stove in the corner was in full view, so that the girls could watch the owner's wife prepare lamb with celery and leeks, while Henry and Spyros sipped a chilled white *retsina* wine.

Sophia had asked Henry if he would read *Iphigenia in Aulis* aloud to them. He had the slim volume in his coat pocket. After supper they moved to the open fireplace. Henry held the book on his lap. The owner seized the occasion to dispatch his older son to the neighbors with the news.

Henry riffled through the pages of the drama, began in the middle of a sentence, as though his thoughts had decided to bespeak themselves. The owner and his wife, with their two sons, sat discreetly behind him.

". . . no human story exists solely on its own time level. Its antecedents go back generations, just as its ramifications extend into future generations. This is particularly true of the story of Troy."

Sophia was warmed by the crackling wood fire, which served as a tympany for Henry's low, mellow voice. His face was lighted from his inner glow at the joy of being cast in two of his favorite occupations: teacher and storyteller. She had learned on her honeymoon and in Paris that Henry was a fine storyteller because the stories he told were true for him: they were authentic history as well as literature. That was why he was able to weave a magic which moved his listeners out of their own skin, projected them backward in time to another age; they became participants in a drama that had been enacted millennia before.

"Let us start at the beginning of our tale," Henry said, "even though I realize that you were taught parts of it in school. We'll need the background to understand the story of Greece, Troy and the fall of Mycenae. One of the first kings of southern Greece was Pelops, after whom the Peloponnesus was named. Pelops had two sons, Atreus and Thyestes. The first-born son, Atreus, succeeded his father as king of Mycenae. However the younger brother, Thyestes, was jealous and vindictive. First he seduced his brother's wife; then he caused defections in Atreus's palace guard. Atreus crushed his brother's revolt and banished him, along with his sons. At the end of a year Thyestes returned to Atreus's court to supplicate Atreus for a pardon. Atreus pretended to forgive his younger brother, inviting him to a reconciliation feast. Atreus then killed Thyestes's older boys, had them cut up, cooked and served to Thyestes in a deep dish with a baked crust. When Atreus informed his brother of what he had just partaken, Thyestes importuned the gods to bring down a curse upon the house of Atreus, and fled with his only remaining son, Aegisthus . . ."

". . . who became Clytemnestra's paramour," Sophia interjected, "during Agamemnon's absence at Troy. He helped Clytemnestra murder Agamemnon the very night he returned."

Henry flashed her a schoolteacher's smile of approval.

". . . just so. But you are a little ahead of the story. When Atreus died, his sons inherited the empire; the older Agamemnon becoming king at the capital fortress, Mycenae; and the younger Menelaus the king of Sparta. Agamemnon found his wife and queen, Clytemnestra, in one of his raids. Clytemnestra tells the story. Let me read you the passage:

> ". . . This reproach I first hurl in your teeth
> That I married you against my will, after
> You murdered Tantalus, my first husband,
> And dashed my living babe upon the earth,

Brutally tearing him from my breasts,
And then, the two sons of Zeus, my brothers,
On horseback came and in white armor made
War upon you. Till you got upon your knees
To my old father, Tyndareus, and he
Rescued you. So you kept me for your bed.

"But after that I became reconciled
To you and to your house, and you will bear
Witness that I, as your wife, have been
Blameless, modest in passion, and in honor
Seeking to increase your house so that
Your coming-in had gladness and
Your going-out joy. A rare spoil for a man
Is the winning of a good wife; very
Plentiful are the worthless women."

When he had finished, Sophia leaned over and murmured to him:
"Look about you. You have an audience."

Henry turned around, was startled to see that one by one the people
from the scattered houses in Aulis had come in, silently, and seated
themselves behind the little family group before the fire. They were
still in their work clothes, but their faces had been scrubbed and were
gleaming in the firelight as they leaned forward on the hard chairs, intent to catch Henry's every word. They could neither read nor write,
nor had they ever seen a play performed; but they knew intuitively
that Henry Schliemann was bringing back to them a part of their
heritage.

Sophia could see that Henry was deeply moved. The people of Aulis
had paid him the highest of compliments. She slipped her hand into
his, said softly:

"Please go on, Henry."

"Yes, I shall. Menelaus found his bride in a more peaceful way, but
one which ultimately led the 1140 ships and the 120,000 Achaeans
here to Aulis, waiting for a fair wind to undertake the siege and destruction of Troy. Tyndareus, king of Lacedaemon and husband of
Leda, had a daughter of incredible beauty called Helen, sister of Clytemnestra. They had had a divine father, Zeus, the most powerful of
all gods, who, disguising himself as a swan, had seduced Leda. Since
Tyndareus was wary of picking any one king or prince to wed his
daughter, he invited them all to his palace to contend for her hand. The
young bloods arrived and were so ravished by Helen's beauty that a
civil war was on the verge of breaking out in the court. Tyndareus made
the supplicants pledge on their honor that they would abide by Helen's

choice and that if anyone ever wronged her husband all of those present would join forces and destroy him. Menelaus proved to be her choice."

Henry continued with the tale.

"Paris, son of King Priam of Troy, and the incarnation of male beauty, came to Sparta with rich gifts and was hospitably received by Menelaus. But when Menelaus left on a visit to Crete, Paris stole Helen. Helen claimed she went unwillingly, that it was the goddess Aphrodite who had bewitched her. Paris and Helen crossed the Aegean in three days to the Hellespont. Menelaus called in the pledge made by Helen's former suitors. Kings, princes and warriors assembled here in Aulis ready to cross the sea to Troy; to capture Helen, kill the men, burn down the city and take the women and children captive.

"But here in this safe harbor the vast fleet was stalled. First there were storms and high waves; later, the sea was becalmed for months. The armies of the kings began to revolt, demanding that they sail at once to sack and loot Troy, or return to their homes, fields and flocks.

"At this moment Calchas, prophet for the Achaean fleet and army, reported that the goddess of the hunt, Artemis, who controlled the winds, was angry at Agamemnon for killing one of her sacred stags, and demanded the ultimate sacrifice of his daughter Iphigenia. Agamemnon sent to Mycenae for his eldest child on the pretext of her marriage to Achilles of Thessaly. The father used his sword to cut the beauteous throat of his young daughter, letting her blood fall into a basin of 'lustral waters' as an offering of propitiation to Artemis.

"This is Iphigenia's plea to Agamemnon:

> "O Father,
> My body is a suppliant's, tight clinging
> To your knees. Do not take away this life
> Of mine before its dying time. Nor make me
> Go down under the earth to see the world
> Of darkness, for it is sweet to look on
> The day's light.
> I was first to call you father,
> You to call me child. And of your children
> First to sit upon your knees. We kissed
> Each other in our love. . . .

"At the end comes the heartrending farewell of Iphigenia to her mother, Clytemnestra:

> "Mother, now listen to my words. I see
> Your soul in anger against your husband.

This is a foolish and an evil rage.
Oh, I know when we stand before a helpless
Doom how hard it is to bear.

"Tell me if I speak well. All Greece turns
Her eyes to me, to me only, great Greece
In her might, for through me is the sailing
Of the fleet, through me the sack and overthrow
Of Troy. Because of me, never more will
Barbarians wrong and ravish Greek women,
Drag them from happiness and their homes
In Hellas. The penalty will be paid
Fully for the shame and seizure of Helen."

Henry turned to the beginning and read Euripides's entire play, softly, melodiously. Sophia watched the faces of the people of Aulis. The women were weeping, the men listening with their whole being, taken back to another age here in the farming and sheepherding village of Aulis, where they and their forebears had lived for centuries.

"They are all good Christians," Sophia mused, shifting her gaze from face to face; "but it would never occur to them that the goddess Artemis did not have the power to hold back the winds. Iphigenia was not sacrificed in another, remote age; her blood is flowing into the basin of lustral water this very moment on their own sandy shores."

Later, after the proprietors and their sons and neighbors had thanked Dr. Schliemann with an emotion almost too deep to express; after Marigo had kissed Henry on the cheek, with tears in her eyes; and the phlegmatic Spyros, acting out of character, had put a hand on Henry's shoulder and squeezed it, Sophia and Henry retired to their room.

Sophia put her arms around her husband's neck, kissed him warmly.

"You had us spellbound. You were living this tragic tale, and enabled us to live it."

Henry ducked his head toward his left shoulder.

"Henry, I am serious. Despite your persuasiveness over the past months, some part of my mind held out. But not any more! I know now that there was a Troy, and there was a war, and the Troy that was burned by the Achaeans is there waiting for us to uncover it."

3.

When they returned to the Hotel d'Angleterre there was a note for her from her mother:

Sophia Dear: Please come out to Colonos as soon as you return. Perhaps you could choose a time when Henry is busy.

Sophia knew her mother well enough to be able to translate the message. It meant, "Come alone!"

The lines had a foreboding ring. The boat had brought them from Chalkis to Piraeus at nine; it was now eleven in the morning. She saw that Henry had a stack of mail to answer.

"Still no letter from Frank Calvert," he grumbled. "I will have to write this very day to both the British and American ambassadors in Constantinople. They have considerable influence on the Sultan."

"Since you will be writing letters, do you mind if I ride out to Colonos? Mother wants to visit with me."

"I'll have my dinner brought up here so that I can work straight through. Send me a message if you want me to come out to Colonos for supper, and to bring you back. Otherwise I will expect you by dark."

Madame Victoria embraced her daughter, but it was a grim clasping, without warmth.

"Is something wrong, Mother?"

"Yes. Everything."

"Then let us go into the kitchen for a cup of coffee."

They sat across from each other at the rough wooden table ordinarily used to peel or slice vegetables and to hold pots just off the stove. It was one of the rare times that Sophia could remember the house being wholly quiet. No one else was at home. Weak yellow sunlight dripped into the kitchen like water from a leaky faucet. There was an onion stew boiling on the stove, and next to it a pot of okra.

Madame Victoria's wide strong face was unsmiling, her large lips held firmly together; her jet-black hair pulled down tightly from the center part looked like a close-fitting skullcap.

"Mother is a strong character," Sophia ruminated, "some have called her 'domineering.' She can't get used to the idea that I am a married woman now. Homesick as I was in Paris, her pain at having me away where she could not advise and guide me must have been even more excruciating."

She said:

"Mother, you're holding something back. Ever since I came home from Paris. Am I mistaken?"

Madame Victoria replied grimly, "You are not mistaken."

"I had a presentiment you were being cool to Henry."

"It *is* your husband. I'm afraid we made a mistake. We permitted you to marry a miser."

"Henry a miser! That simply isn't true. He doesn't give me sums of money to carry around, nor would I want to; but he takes me every place I want to go and buys me anything I want or need."

"Our relatives are saying that you have brought disgrace on the family."

Sophia was too shocked to do anything but stare at her mother with incredulity.

"When you married a millionaire, and lived for months in Paris, we expected you to come home wearing beautiful jewels, furs and expensive clothing."

Sophia looked down at the dress she was wearing. It was a brown wool, embroidered with small varicolored flowers. While it was true that it was on the plain side, it was not inexpensive; she had chosen the material herself and the dressmaker had done an expert job of fitting the high neck, the long sleeves, the bodice pinched in at the waist, and the full, flaring skirt. She smoothed the fabric over her hips, said quietly:

"Is there something wrong with this dress? I like it."

"I don't. Not for you . . . in your present position. And why have you worn nothing but that coral necklace ever since you returned?"

"Because it was Henry's first gift to me. I have a sentimental attachment to it."

"Sentiment is a luxury that poor people, as we are now, can't afford. That dress is too plain for the wife of a wealthy man. And you should have important jewels with it. Aunt Lambridou says you came home looking like a poor relation."

Sophia began stalking restlessly about the kitchen.

"Mother, you misjudge Henry. He took me to the best couturier in Paris. I have more gowns than I have use for. I am simply too young to be wearing diamonds. Furs are for cold climates."

"You should have them. You are entitled. Henry should have bought them for you."

"Henry gives me charming gifts. He even sent to England for a watch I admired."

"You should be more demanding." She shook her head in stern disapproval. "You always listened to me. Why are you being obstinate now?"

"I have always obeyed you, Mother. But I am a married woman . . ."

"You are eighteen. You should listen to older people and long-married people; they have eaten a lot of bread and salt. You are no more than a girl."

Sophia took a deep breath.

"Mother, what do you really want to say to me?"

"Your Mr. Schliemann has broken every promise he made to us. We gave you in good faith, but we've had nothing but bad faith in return."

Sophia's heart sank. "Oh, God, I'll get that stomachache again, the one that made me so wretched in Paris."

"Some people get stomachaches, others get heartache. I have a heartache."

Georgios, Spyros and Alexandros came home together for dinner but there was little food eaten in the Engastromenos home that day, nor was anyone in a mood for the ritualistic midday nap. Neither was Sophia able to refute their charges, as she had opposed her mother that morning.

The most serious one was that Henry Schliemann had promised before the wedding to buy the family a diamond necklace worth 150,000 French francs, thirty thousand dollars, as a bridal price. Madame Victoria was absolutely certain about this contract. Sophia's father, with less vehemence but no less certainty, declared that Henry had guaranteed him the sum of forty thousand francs with which to refurbish his shop and fill his shelves with imported fabrics. Marigo claimed that Henry had assured her a fund of twenty thousand francs for her dowry so that she could marry well . . .

"This is the first I've heard of any of this," Sophia cried in anguish. "Why have you not told me before?"

"Because we wanted to protect your feelings," her father said. "It is not proper for a prospective bride to be engaged in discussions of money."

She sat in silence for a long time, her stomach knotted, the clock in the airless livingroom ticking behind her. When she looked up her deep brown eyes were crackling with indignation.

"Mother, did Henry promise you the necklace in plain words?"

"No."

"Then who did he promise it to?"

"Your Uncle Vimpos."

She winced as though she had been struck a blow.

"Father, the money for the shop. To whom did he make his promise?"

"Your Uncle Vimpos."

"Marigo, you said not a word about a dowry on our trip to Aulis. When did Henry promise you a dowry?"

"He promised it to Bishop Vimpos."

Sophia turned to Spyros. His lips were clamped, he turned away. Tears came to Sophia's eyes.

"Uncle Vimpos doesn't lie. He is a man of God. Now, Mother, I can share with you your heartache; it is worse than anything I suffered in my most depressed days in Paris."

After a moment she added:

"There's only one thing to do: face my husband with his promises and oblige him to keep them. I'll write a note telling him that it is urgent that he come out with you, Father, when you close the shop this evening."

Henry did as she requested. There was a worried expression on his face when he entered the lamplighted parlor.

"Are you all right, my dear? Your note had an air of the frantic about it. Are you feeling well?"

"No." She stepped back from him. "I'm feeling the worst I've ever felt."

"But what is it? You were fine this morning."

"My family tells me that you made many promises before our marriage and that you've broken faith on every last one of them."

Henry's face went pale. He seemed to shrink in size, reminding her of her first impression of him, on the eve of St. Meletios's day, in their garden.

"Precisely what promises have I broken? I know of none."

Madame Victoria answered:

"Our cousin, Bishop Vimpos, said that you would present to us, or to your wife, a diamond necklace."

Sophia watched her husband. He tried on half a dozen emotions and discarded them all as he sometimes had changed cravats in Paris before going to the opera. What he came out with was an admixture of all the feelings that had flooded across his mind. His voice cut across the room like a knotted whip.

"My revered mother-in-law, the bishop is a distinguished and a most honest person. I'm sure you misunderstood him, all the more because I asked him fervently in every letter not to mention to anyone that I was rich."

He turned his attention to Georgios Engastromenos.

"My very honorable father-in-law, if it is true that the bishop made such a promise to you in my name, and even if it is not true, in any case you have committed a sin in selling your excellent daughter for diamonds. The disappointment of your hopes is the rightful punishment for such a deed. We are Christians and we do not sell our daughters."

Alexandros had been listening to Henry's outburst. He cried:

"The diamonds are between you and Sophia. What about the money you promised to put into our shop?"

"I made no such promise."

"And the dowry you promised Marigo?" Madame Victoria's cheeks were red with indignation.

Henry turned to Marigo:

"Did I offer you money for your dowry?"

"Uncle Vimpos said so."

Sophia thought:

"Never in my worst nightmares could I have imagined such a horrible scene."

At that moment Aunt Lambridou entered the room. She had a nose for trouble and could smell it faster than the pot of green beans beginning to burn on her stove. She rushed to the family's attack. Henry Schliemann had deceived them. He was stingy, spending only on sheer necessities. He refused his ex-wife money to live on, neglected his children's needs. He had forbidden Sophia to think of her parents, to do her simple duty to her family. . . .

By now Sophia's eyes were like hot coals in her head, and her brain on fire. Disgusted by everything that had happened, she gazed at her husband in disbelief, then said hoarsely:

"I do not want to live with such a man."

The rope of words seemed to fasten around Henry's throat and strangle him.

"Then you should not be obliged to do so." His eyes were bloodshot. "I will give you a divorce, and settle a large dowry on you so that you can find a Greek husband, one your own age."

When he turned to Aunt Lambridou, his tone was bitter.

"Where have you gotten all these nasty things you've said about me? From a Mr. Vretos, Greek consul in Livorno, who represents my wife? He was friendly when we met him there on our honeymoon, but he has now turned against Sophia and me. He has never been to St. Petersburg and never met my first wife, but he is spreading tales that all our trouble arose from my unfortunate character."

He turned to Sophia.

"You know these charges are untrue. I've adored you as few men have adored their wives. If you don't want to live with such a man as me, then the fault is mine for marrying too young a girl. But you should not allow my reputation to be blackened in public."

Sophia stood silent, her family in a phalanx around her. There was a storm raging in her head. When Henry started for the front door, Madame Victoria realized that things had gotten out of hand. She ran after him.

"My dear Henry, do not leave us in this fashion. Everything can be cleared up."

Georgios Engastromenos's genial nature reasserted itself. Sophia saw her father put his hand out to Henry.

"Dr. Henry, I think that the worst of my enemies would never offer me a drink of such poison as the one you are offering to me. I sold my

Sophia like a puppet for money! A Greek who brought himself during the resurrection of his nation to the altar of freedom and equality could never even think of such a cruel crime. How could you think that the parents and relatives of your wife could conspire to destroy your happiness? We never wished in the least to introduce the slightest obstacle to your happy life with Sophia. I never did ask jewels for Sophia; such a thought never went through my mind. I have told Sophia that she should not care about the financial condition of her father's home, but that she should care only about your home, its growth and prosperity; that her happiness lies in her affection and love for you. . . ."

Henry walked out of the room and the house.

He returned to the Hotel d'Angleterre and the next day packed a bag and left for a tour of the islands, giving as his reason for going alone that the Aegean was rough in the March winds, and Sophia would be seasick. The family gave out that Henry was traveling to see the archaeological digs. Yet it was impossible to keep such matters secret in so small a town as Colonos. The neighbors looked at Sophia with the furtive glance villagers bestow on trouble-bearers.

She tossed sleeplessly at night in the childhood bed she had left for a matrimonial bed. Her emotions fluctuated from deep shame that her husband was treating her family shabbily to guilt over what Henry called "miserable accusations." It was true that Advocate Vretos was spreading tales about Henry's first marriage. Though Henry had bought his family a palatial home in St. Petersburg, Vretos claimed that he had been withholding of cash, that people in Russia had considered him a miser. Yet Henry had been right when he expostulated:

"A miser! A man who has supported his parents for twenty years, supported his sisters until they married, financed his brother in a wine business . . ."

When in Paris she had accused him, in the depths of her homesickness, of ordering her not to think about her parents or her brothers, he had replied:

"On the contrary. I should detest you if you did not."

She was miserable and growing more so every day. Henry did not seem less so. Apparently he was not sightseeing on Syros, Delos or Santorini, but remained in his hotel room to pour out letters of reproach to her and abuse to her parents. To Sophia he wrote:

"I have never dreamed of such a horror, that I should marry a child who could be my granddaughter. Your horrible nostalgia in Paris was a sufficient proof that you do not love me at all, and that you married me against your will. . . ."

And again, "On our honeymoon and in Paris it was all respect and love between us. I idolize you, but when you make these accusations they freeze my heart. . . ."

To her father he wrote:

> You explain that in the family's letters to Paris you tried to make Sophia believe that she should not concern herself with the financial situation of her parental home, but only of her own. Yet when we sent you a gift of money, you wrote to Sophia that she should continue her efforts to get more help from me. . . .

Sophia grew pale. She could eat little. She lost weight. The days were difficult, the nights a terror. As the first week passed and the days dragged along in the second she felt a growing compassion for her husband. Yet she could see no way of reconciling with a man who had deceived her beloved family.

Her family was astonished that a grown man could take such a quarrel seriously. It came of Henry's not being a Greek! One said things and took them back! Victoria and Georgios Engastromenos harbored no hurt feelings . . . and no guilt.

What Sophia did not know was that Henry Schliemann, with habitual meticulousness, had written to Bishop Vimpos at his diocese immediately after the scene in the Engastromenos livingroom, restating every golden offer which he, Henry Schliemann, had supposedly made in order to win Sophia in marriage.

It was deep into the second week when Sophia, sitting alone in her bedroom overlooking St. Meletios Square, saw a carriage draw up before the front door. Out of it stepped Henry, well shaved, handsomely groomed, and radiating misery so palpable as to fill the square.

She ran down the stairs and opened the front door just as he dropped the clapper. They greeted each other formally.

"Uncle Vimpos is in Colonos," she informed him. "He sent word that he made the trip in response to your letter, and would only discuss our problem in your presence. Panaghiotes will go for him."

The family was sitting around the garden table in a tight, ritualistic circle. Sophia joined them. Henry paced at the lower end of the garden under the acacia trees. In a few minutes Theokletos Vimpos entered the garden in his billowing black gown, black hat with hair knotted up under it, and shining black shoes. His eyes were blacker than his gown, hat or shoes; Jeremiah storming straight out of the Old Testament! He gave his family a cool "Good day," then went to Henry and cried:

"My dear and erudite friend, I greet you out of all my heart and soul, and I bless you."

"My revered Archbishop, you are a true friend to come this far and on such short notice."

"I received your letter from Syros, and read its content with much sorrow. . . ."

Sophia said gently, "Uncle Vimpos, we are all sorrowing. . . ."

Bishop Vimpos looked only to Henry. "In the name of our Lord Jesus Christ, I tell you that I never promised Mrs. Engastromenos that you would present her or her daughter with diamonds worth thirty thousand dollars. Mrs. Engastromenos knelt before me and asked me to introduce her daughter to you. I said only about you that you are an honest and true person."

"That is all you said?" Henry asked.

"That is all I said. *Lies, lies!* You did not say one word about giving gifts, not the money they accuse you of having promised to put into the shop, nor the dowry for Marigo. Put your hope in God and your innocence will shine brighter than the sun."

There was an eerie silence in the garden. At first Sophia did not move, simply searched her husband's face. Then she rose, turned to look at her parents. Of Madame Victoria she demanded angrily:

"Mother, who told you that my husband had promised a necklace? Because obviously Uncle Vimpos did not!"

". . . well . . . I didn't say that he did. I learned it from Aunt Lambridou. She assured me that Cousin Vimpos had told her that."

Sophia wheeled about and faced Georgios Engastromenos.

"Father, who informed you that my husband was going to invest in your drapery shop?"

"I was also told that by Aunt Lambridou."

There was no need for Sophia to turn to Marigo, who said between her tears:

"I'm sorry, Sophia. I didn't mean to cause trouble. Aunt Lambridou told me that Uncle Vimpos had said Mr. Henry was going to put aside a dowry for me."

Bishop Vimpos turned to young Panaghiotes:

"Please summon Kyria Lambridou. Bring her here this moment. Tell her that I command it."

Kyria Lambridou did not look happy. Her efforts were going to be undone, and that would have wasted a good deal of her time and energy. Bishop Vimpos had no greeting for her.

"Madame, it is time to make it plain that you are no aunt in this family. You and your parents were long-time friends, but you are a friend no longer. No one in this family is to call you 'Aunt' again. Now, did you tell this family of promises that my friend Henry Schliemann made of great gifts?"

"Yes, Bishop Vimpos."

"And where did you get that information?"

"I thought I got it from you."

"How could you have gotten it from me when no such word was ever uttered by me?"

Kyria Lambridou smiled slyly.

"Then it was an honest mistake, Bishop. That was what I understood you to say, and that is why I repeated the good news to the Engastromenos family."

"You did no such thing. You planted the seeds of discord knowing that they would cause difficulties. Now I want you to apologize to Mr. Schliemann for the agony you have caused him; and to Sophia. Then you will remove yourself from this garden and I forbid you ever to come back. There is no way to tolerate a person who pours poison into the town well."

When she had gone, he turned to Sophia.

"I will not reprimand you, my child, you are young and have not yet learned to distinguish duty to your family from duty to your husband."

Sophia's face flushed a dark red. She clutched her family in the intensity of her gaze.

"This is a disgraceful thing that we have allowed to happen! And I've behaved most disgracefully of all. Why did no one check these promises with Uncle Vimpos from the beginning? Why didn't I, when my husband's love and my marriage were at stake? I have been stupid. More than that, we have all been ungracious to a man who has never done anything but good for us."

She walked over to Henry.

"Henry, please forgive us. I did not know better. I am still so childish that I thought even a married woman had to side with her family. I will never again take sides against you, and I will never again doubt the truthfulness of what you tell me. I love you and I want to live with you for the rest of my life."

A sob racked her chest. Henry put his arms around her.

"Yes, Sophidion. In the future we must defend ourselves and our marriage against all attack."

4.

The following weeks were a second honeymoon. Henry decided to take her on a tour of her own country. He engaged a spacious double carriage drawn by two horses and, because the mountain country was infested with brigands, hired two armed guards to ride with them, their Greek army rifles strapped behind their right shoulders, silver-mounted pistols in their belts.

For their first expedition they drove out to the fortress of Phyle, which had been built in the fourth century B.C. They left their carriage at the foot of the aqueduct and climbed the two-thousand-foot mountain, stopping frequently to drink in the panorama of mountains, gorges and valleys that unfolded awesomely the higher they went. They picnicked on a blanket spread beneath the ancient masonry of the fort.

Henry read her the story of Thrasybulos, who assembled a group of a hundred supporters in Thebes, started his march from this very fort and, because Athens had no army, overthrew the Thirty Tyrants and freed the city. However it was obvious to Sophia that he had something else on his mind. He slipped his book into the side pocket of his coat, took her hand.

"Sophidion, I know you are worried about your family. I was not looking for a victory, nor would I want them defeated. I have worked out a plan."

She waited quietly.

"I am going to make your father my business agent here in Athens, on a regular salary. Also I will guarantee the shop's credit up to a point, so that your father can get shipments from abroad. That should put the drapery business in running order."

"Oh, it will!"

"Nor am I going to forget little Marigo. I will put four thousand dollars in a special fund in the National Bank of Greece. When Marigo marries, you can hand over the dowry to the married couple."

She threw herself into his arms; her cheek was wet with tears. She thought:

"If people make demands on him, pressure him, he shuts that black waiter's wallet and locks it. What he thinks of for himself, he gives generously."

A few days later, again accompanied by armed guards, they set out for Marathon, taking the same road to the battlefield used by the Athenian hoplites in 490 B.C. when they had taken their stand on the plain waiting for the attack of the Persians under King Darius. It was a pleasant late March day, the air clear and pungent from the cherry and pear orchards through which they were driving. As they crossed the charming village of Kiphissia outside Athens, Sophia remarked:

"See how each house is surrounded by acres of pines and poplars. It's on higher ground than Athens, and in summer it is cooler here than in the city. Father used to bring us here for picnics."

At Marathon they climbed the tumulus where the hundred and ninety-two Athenians killed during the battle had been cremated and buried together. Henry read to her from Herodotus, the first historian's account of the defensive battle.

For a third expedition they rode south to Corinth. The isthmus was only four miles wide at this point. The Emperor Nero in the first century A.D. had attempted to dig a canal across it to save the ships coming from and headed toward Italy the long journey around the extreme southern end of the Peloponnesus. Uncompleted, the ditch had now lain dry for seventeen hundred years. From here they went on to ancient Corinth to visit the Agora and Temple of Apollo, with its seven monolithic Doric columns still standing in the peristyle. Henry's eyes swept the mount of the fortress-acropolis and the sea beyond.

"This will be a marvelous dig for someone. Below lie some of the richest archaeological fields in Greece."

She awakened one morning in Athens to find him in the livingroom of their suite writing furiously in his journal. When he heard her get out of bed he rose to greet her, a broad smile on his flushed face.

"Good morning, my lovely Sophia. This is our great moment. I just entered it in my journal: today, April 5, 1870, we leave for Hissarlik to begin our first experimental excavation."

She had not yet become accustomed to the suddenness of her husband's decisions.

". . . I don't understand. Have you received your *firman?*"

His smile faded perceptibly.

"No, no permit yet. Perhaps I can obtain it in Constantinople. But the *S.S. Menzaheh* leaves from Piraeus this afternoon. I made up my mind during the night."

She splashed cold water from the bowl over her face to hasten her awakening. Their morning coffee arrived.

"Henry, it's such a rash and hasty move. How can we go to Hissarlik when we've made no preparations? You have no Turkish permit, no equipment with which to excavate. Frank Calvert sent you a list of what we'll need to survive in the Troad as well as wheelbarrows, pick-axes, shovels . . . If this equipment in Athens is too poor to be used, will Constantinople's be better? You don't even have an agreement from Frank Calvert allowing you to dig on his half of the mound. I can't go along . . ."

He interrupted her stonily, eyes bright.

"You can't go along with my thinking, or you can't go along with me to Troy?"

He was furious.

"You promised with a thousand oaths never to contradict me, to be always obedient and to respect my will through all your life as a divine order. Because you vowed to keep your promises, I really thought I had discovered in you an angel sent to me from heaven as compensation for my past misfortunes."

Sophia waved aside his outburst.

"I like to obey you, Henry. But you promised that we would dig side by side in Troy as partners. If I am to be your 'God-sent grace,' then I am entitled to share in your decisions. No one expects you there. Among the dozen or more languages you have mastered, Turkish is missing."

"I can learn it in three weeks."

"Henry, this is an impulse. It comes of your excitement over those unexplored ruins at Corinth. If you begin to dig without a *firman* you'll be in trouble with the Turkish officials. Why antagonize them at the same time you're asking for a favor? I understand your impatience. I am impatient too. But I am trying to save us from embarrassment. Let us instead really begin to make our arrangements."

He stared at her, answered coldly:

"You consider I am confusing movement with direction?"

"Please think about it."

He said not another word, packed a bag, stuffed some papers into it, and left the apartment.

Sophia sat on a corner of the desk chair, crushed. She remained in the suite for two days, seeing no one. On the third day the manager approached her with the hotel bill. Henry had stormed out in such a fury that he had left no money with which to pay it, nor had he made any arrangements for her to remain. She had no idea how long he would be away. She packed their things, put her icon in a small case, and took a carriage to Colonos. As she stepped out in front of the family home, she thought:

"Dear Lord, is this what my marriage is going to be? Returning to my parents' home every few weeks, like an unwanted child?"

She had little time to suffer or feel sorry for herself. The Sunday before she had gone to their old family church, St. Panaghitsa's in Romvis Square, for the Palm Sunday ceremonies, the beginning of the Passion of Christ. Easter, for members of the Orthodoxy, was the religious ceremony closest to their spiritual life; for Sophia it was also a time of revival. As the days of Holy Week went by she became more and more receptive to the feeling of sorrow for his martyrdom. Christ's sacrifice brought to her soul a feeling of debt to the one who had suffered for her sake.

She was up before dawn on Maundy Thursday to watch her mother hang a red cloth from the bedroom, facing east, so that it would catch the first rays of the sun. She and Marigo boiled a dozen eggs and dyed them red. Sophia asked her mother if she might bake the Easter buns, with flour, water, olive oil and almonds.

In spite of the pleasure she took from the baking, however, Maundy

Thursday remained sacred and austere. She accompanied her mother and sister to St. Meletios's for the morning service, where they watched the children receive holy communion so that they might participate in the Lord's Supper. After a light dinner, the whole family returned to church to hear the priest read the passages from the Twelve Gospels describing the Passion.

Good Friday was a day of fasting. Sophia did not take so much as a spoonful of water. No fire was lighted in the kitchen. The men did not go into Athens. Sophia spent most of the day on the street outside St. Meletios's attending the Descent from the Cross. While the bells tolled funereally, the procession of the *Epitaphios*, Christ's funeral, began. She joined the villagers as they filed past the altar, the symbolic tomb decked with violets and lemon blossoms, some of which she had brought from the family garden.

When she attended the First Resurrection on the morning of Holy Saturday the church had changed its somber mood and was colorfully hung with laurel and bay leaves. At the end of the services Sophia returned home to bake the Easter bread, while her father and brother Alexandros slaughtered the paschal lamb they had bought and fattened in a pen at the end of the garden.

Her personal problems disappeared. Everything worldly seemed insignificant. The Resurrection encompassed her completely. It was not the festivities which raised her spirits, but joy for the end of Christ's suffering, the sublime hope of another life, the defeat of death; the perpetuation of her existence.

Shortly before midnight she attended the celebration of the Resurrection, holding a white candle in her hand and participating in the Ceremony of the Light. The church bells rang out exuberantly, guns were fired, fireworks brightened the sky. Priests and congregation surged into the square to exchange the "Kiss of Love." Serene, joyful, strong, Sophia crossed the square with her family. In the early dawn the clan gathered in the Engastromenos garden, each one picking up a red egg and tapping it against the egg held by another in an outgoing expression of good will. "*Christos anesti*, Christ is risen," one cried. "*Alithos anesti*, Indeed he is risen," another replied.

For Sophia the miracle of Christ's salvation was transferred to her own life, and she looked with faith to her future with Henry.

He was back in two weeks, contrite but not crestfallen.

"You were right on every count," he confessed. "There were no first-class accommodations on the ship going out, and I would not have let you stay in the airless, second-class cabin I had to put up with. The top Turkish officials would not see me in Constantinople; the stores had no wheelbarrows or pickaxes worth buying. The two Turks from Kum Kale

who own the other half of the Hissarlik mound used up several of my
days in fierce quarreling. They may have been afraid their goats would
fall into my trenches. I hired two men to dig, and at first the owners
were willing to settle for some big stones the men dug up; they needed
them for a bridge they were building across the Simois River. Then
they returned in a pugnacious mood and demanded an extortionate
sum for their land. I offered them twice what the land is worth, but
there was no dealing with them. To cap it all, a government official
came out from the Dardanelles to inform me that the pasha was highly
displeased with my digging there without a permit, and consequently
my official *firman* would be delayed.

"That's when I quit. But the important thing is that, with only a few
days and a few laborers, I managed to unearth the foundations of a
large building, some forty feet wide and sixty feet long. Now we know
for sure that there is a city buried in that mound."

He had brought her from the bazaar in Constantinople a silver filigree
bracelet about two inches wide, with strands of silver fine as hair
woven into a calligraphy of flowers. The long slender catch was made
of tiny gems outlined in bright blue mosaics. He must have spent hours
to find anything so lovely.

She was, she admitted to herself, genuinely glad to have him back.

5.

Henry had not cabled ahead to the Hotel d'Angleterre to reserve
them a suite. He had been under the impression that Sophia would
remain in their rooms and he would simply move back in. The management regretted that all it could offer the Schliemanns was an attic room.
Henry grumbled. When he received his first bill, three days later, he
was outraged at the price the hotel had charged.

"A hundred and seventy-six francs for this miserable attic room. And
they have the gall to charge us for full board though we have eaten
hardly anything from their kitchen. I am resolved never to set foot in
this *auberge* again!"

A plan Sophia had been hatching in her tranquillity and clearheaded-
ness after the Easter rejuvenescence had found its best possible moment to be launched.

"Henry, you've said that we must plan on digging at Hissarlik for at
least five seasons."

"Yes, I am convinced it will take that long to do the job."

"That means we'll be using Athens as our headquarters. Why don't we rent, or even buy, a proper house here? Then you'll have your own study, I'll have my own kitchen . . ."

". . . and our own comfortable bed in our own bedroom!"

"Then when you go away, on business . . . or whatever, I won't have to run home to Mama like a little girl. I don't think I'll feel properly married until I am mistress of my own home."

"And have a child or two." He held her against him, tenderly. "All of the doctors have said that your abdominal trouble will be cured when you become pregnant. In the past I have not been able to make a child with you because you have made me angry so often. People make children in love and not in anger." He kissed her on both cheeks. "You are right. When you are mistress of your own home, and happy in it, you will conceive. What part of the city do you think is best?"

"There is a little area a couple of blocks away from the Acropolis that is not built up yet. It is quiet, has a view of the city, and it's above the summer dust storms. We would live in the shadow of the Parthenon."

It did not take them long to find what they wanted: a newly constructed house on Mousson Street, neoclassic in architecture, two and a half stories high, with half windows at the ground level for the servants' quarters, a double wooden front door painted brown, large high windows in the livingroom and diningroom overlooking the wooded Hill of the Muses. The windows upstairs admitted light and air to the three bedrooms and small family parlor. Leading off this sittingroom was an unscreened veranda. Over the front door there was a balcony with a handsome grille; there was a simple roof line of baked clay akrokerami, upright shell-like decorations. From the garden in back they would be looking toward Piraeus and Old Phaleron; below them was the Kiphissos River that ran through Athens to the sea.

Sophia loved the house. The rooms were large, with high ceilings, the walls girdled with plaster floral designs and rosettes. In the downstairs rooms they were coated with marble stucco polished to give the effect of a light gray marble. The kitchen, family diningroom and corridors had square-tiled floors, the downstairs rooms wooden boards of random lengths. In the hallway there was a wide wooden staircase with a carved balustrade. In one corner was a water closet built in the Turkish fashion: a clay pan with a hole in the middle which led to a cesspool. On either side of the opening were raised pedals on which to place one's feet.

Mousson Street consisted of four blocks, with houses on one side of the street only; the other side was the rocky, heavily treed Hill of the Muses, with its Philopappos Monument. It was like living with a forest at one's front door. Just three short blocks away, on the side facing the theaters of Dionysus and Herodes Atticus, was the staggering marble pile of the Parthenon. Mousson Street came to a dead end; there was little traffic. To get into town by carriage they would have to drive past the Acropolis; Sophia could walk to its main entrance in a few minutes. It would become an intimate part of their lives.

Close by was the Areopagus, the hill on which the High Council had sat in classical times, to rule on both diplomatic and judicial affairs, and to try men accused of murder. It was here that Orestes was tried in Aeschylus's *Eumenides* for the murder of his mother, Clytemnestra, in revenge for her slaying of Agamemnon. Sophia climbed the steps cut into the side of the stone Areopagus to gaze over the agora to the town below and, in the distance, the silver-green olive orchards, the vineyards, the rounded Mt. Hymettus, covered with mint, sage, lavender, thyme, turpentine trees; home of the bees that made the world's most aromatic honey.

The corner lot next to the house, looking toward the Parthenon, was also for sale. Henry bought the land, and together they drew plans for a cool walled garden, with palm trees, pools of water, flowering shrubs, gravel walks, one wall of latticework for grapes, another for wisteria. Henry called in a carpenter to build an octagonal-shaped teahouse, similar to the one he had just seen in Frank Calvert's spacious gardens behind his mansion in Çanakkale.

It was not traditional in Greece for a husband to consult his wife about a home to be purchased, or to give her any say in its furnishing, but Henry included Sophia in both areas.

"I know very little about furniture," Sophia confessed. "Greek homes are sparsely furnished. We manufacture almost nothing because of our lack of wood; European furniture is very expensive for us. Most of our possessions in Romvis Square were accumulated slowly or came down from my grandparents."

"We'll remedy that. I have some expertise."

"Henry, your apartment in Paris is exquisite, but there were no open spaces in the rooms. I felt that I was on a narrow trail cutting through a forest."

"The French feel that any space not occupied by little upholstered chairs or elaborately carved tables is unused."

They searched out every piece of furniture available in Athens. For the bedroom they found a carved Italian *matrimoniale*, marriage bed, similar to the oversized ones they had enjoyed on their honeymoon: ample for tossing restlessly, sleeping peacefully, nestling or making love. Then they discovered a waist-high chest of drawers of walnut with satinwood inlays; this was for Sophia's lingerie and nightclothes. One of the antique shops had a French provincial armoire to hold her dresses and Henry's suits. They found a washstand they liked; the table top opened to reveal a small mirror and, in an enclosed area, a metal washbasin. On either side were drawers for their toilet articles.

The diningroom was a joy to furnish after they found the table they wanted, round, of English walnut, opening in the middle to admit extra boards and supported by a massive underpinning of wood carving. The chairs turned up quickly, of embossed leather with hand-carved wooden legs and backs. Against one wall they placed a semicircular china closet with glass panels to hold their highly hued ceramic tureens and Dresden china, and on the opposite wall a carved mahogany cabinet for storing crystal and silver. Suspended on bronze chains from the ceiling was a massive, bell-shaped porcelain lamp.

"The room is crowded," cried Sophia when the last of the ten chairs had been moved in; "with only space enough left to serve at table."

Henry chuckled.

Sophia groaned.

"Could we buy a little less for the parlor?"

In his own study Henry installed a tall secretary of dark wood, the upper half of which held books behind glass doors, the lower half of which could be locked, serving as a file for his private papers, business correspondence, bank accounts, journals. He also found a Regency mahogany horseshoe desk on which he could spread, profligately, his monographs, writing materials, books opened and annotated at strategic pages.

Sophia, for her part, now lavished her attention on the kitchen. It was at the rear of the house, spacious, with windows overlooking the back garden and the center of Athens. She purchased a wall stove with five burners, a copper hood high above, and a chimney pipe to draw off the smoke. A carpenter installed two wall brackets on which she stood chimney lamps. In one corner was a stone sink, and above it a water tank. High over an open fireplace was a wide mantel on which she placed her earthenware. On the rear wall she nailed a board, with hooks to hold her large stirring spoons, spatula, frying pans, ladle, measuring cups. On the wall to the left there was space for her pots to hang. She bought a small round table for the center of the room, and two cane-backed chairs. A door between the stove and the fireplace led out to the back garden; left open in warm weather, it would afford cross-ventilation.

"Henry thinks the bedroom is the most important room in the house," she thought, surveying the finished job; "but I think the kitchen is. It's used more."

"The house will be too small when we start bringing back our archaeological finds," he commented.

They passed a tranquil summer on Mousson Street. The house

being high above the city, there was a mild stirring of a breeze; the green forest of the Hill of the Muses in front of them absorbed the late afternoon heat and glare. Sophia spent much of the morning in the adjoining garden, where Henry had planted the most mature shrubs and largest trees they could transplant. Though she had resumed her hour's lesson in French and German, Henry decided that she must now begin to study English as well, since he intended for them to visit London during the winter months when they could not dig at Hissarlik. Her teacher was a genteel Greek woman who had lived in England for a number of years and had achieved a good accent.

He was up at dawn, writing letters in his library-office overlooking the town, working on his campaign to break down the resistance or indifference of the Turkish government to his pleas that he be allowed to excavate. At ten he walked briskly down the hill to the Fair Greece, a café for men only which subscribed to the important European and English newspapers, and where he kept abreast of international affairs.

Sophia had dinner ready promptly at 1:30 P.M., for her husband was a punctual man. After their nap a carriage arrived to take them to the newly opened bathing establishment at Phaleron, where they enjoyed a cool swim. By eight they were back at Syntagma Square, sitting outside at one of the two fashionable cafés, the Yannakis or the Dore, and Sophia had an ice cream. These two cafés, opposite the palace, occupying opposite corners on the main street coming out of the square, were called the Dardanelles because during the long summer days every Athenian passed between them. The sidewalks were broad, the tables three deep. The main occupation of the people in the chairs was to gossip, tell stories and spread rumors about those who passed. No one could escape this method of entertainment or get through the strait without being seen and discussed. The clients constituted the daily newspaper of the town.

The unique aspect of Athenian gossip was that it was intended to find its way back to the ear of the victim. In business, they said, Henry Schliemann was a genius. In his plans to unearth Troy he was a fool. The university professors thought so too; the professional men and educated ones believed that, even if he dug at Hissarlik for five times the five years he planned, he would come away empty-handed. A wealthy man had the right to indulge his eccentricities. But to take his ideas seriously . . . that was to join Henry Schliemann in his folly.

In August, when she missed her period, Sophia thought:

"Henry was right: people make children in love and not in anger."

Henry was longing for a Greek son. She did not want to raise his hopes falsely so she waited to tell him until October. When they were enjoying a companionable cup of coffee in their latticed teahouse, Sophia remarked with what she hoped was a casual air:

"Henry dear, I have certain symptoms . . . or rather I am lacking certain symptoms. I think you ought to take me to the doctor you consider best in Athens."

Henry paled; his brown eyes engulfed the rest of his face. He made no comment, except to say:

"That would be Dr. Venizelos. He is deservedly the most popular doctor in Athenian society. I'll send the boy down to make an appointment with him for early tomorrow morning."

The part of Dr. Miltiades Venizelos's face not covered with a full professional beard was dominated by an enormous pair of eyeglasses; behind the glasses were magnified, alert eyes. After his medical studies in Athens, he had gone to Berlin to be trained in obstetrics, and had been professor of obstetrics at the University of Athens for years. He had also founded Athens's new obstetrical hospital. He asked Sophia a series of questions: Have you been feeling tired? Has there been any lassitude? Morning sickness? Satisfied with the answers, he made no examination. He said:

"Congratulations, Mrs. Schliemann. You look to be in splendid condition. I see no reason why you should not bear a completely healthy child."

Henry had been holding himself in for fear of disappointment; now he threw his arms around Sophia and cried:

"It will be a son! We shall name him Odysseus. Remember what Achilles's mother, Thetis, said: 'A son he gave me to bear and nourish and he shot up like a young branch; like a plant in a very fruitful field I reared him.'"

Sophia smiled shyly.

"What will you name her if it's a girl?"

"No, Sophia, it's absolutely imperative that we have a male heir to carry on the Schliemann name."

Dr. Venizelos tipped Sophia an elaborate wink.

"Kyria Schliemann, inform your husband that a good vine bears many crops."

6.

They had achieved tranquillity in their marriage, but external forces were at work to trouble them. Henry had been concealing from her the fact that, as early as January 1870, when they had been married for little more than three months, Ekaterina had sent a lawyer from St.

Petersburg to Paris to file suit against him, claiming that his marriage was invalid because his divorce was illegal. The Paris court had refused to consider the suit because Henry Schliemann was an American citizen. Ekaterina made it known that she would request copies of the divorce proceedings through the International Bureau of Lawyers in New York, or the Russian ambassador in Washington. She was threatening to file suit to get the divorce annulled. Henry had written to one of his lawyers in Indianapolis, Mr. Naltner, to secure a full record of the legalities involved.

Everything came out in the open this October when Ekaterina announced that she was going to engage a lawyer to file a complaint against him in Athens. The story ran like a summer brush fire through the two cafés of the Dardanelles. Sophia remained calm. The archbishop had studied Henry's divorce papers, declared them legal, and approved her marriage. While it was not a question for the Church to decide, but rather the law courts, the bishops were empowered to testify before a judge. Bishop Vimpos would surely testify that he had taken Henry Schliemann and his divorce papers to the archbishop; and the archbishop would confirm that he had approved Sophia's marriage. The testimony of an archbishop bore considerable weight in Greek courts.

"Why didn't you tell me last January?" Sophia asked. "Perhaps this is why your women friends treated me as though I were your mistress."

Henry swore under his breath.

"Why is she doing this? Would it be revenge?"

"She's not vindictive."

"Could she still be in love with you?"

His eyebrows flared.

"She never loved me."

"Then why did she marry you?"

"I almost forced her to. She turned me down twice, over a period of years, but when I made my second fortune in California and returned to St. Petersburg, there was just too much money to resist."

"You had three children with her."

"Yes." Bitterly. "The first she gave me willingly. The second two I had to steal! Her real love, I have come to believe, was for a Madame Roller. They were inseparable."

In her growing anxiety she wrote to Bishop Vimpos. He replied that he had a number of affairs to take care of in the city but had been procrastinating. He would be there in a few days.

He stood in the hall of the new home, lifted his hand and made the sign of the cross.

"May God our Saviour, he who deigned to enter under the roof of

Zachhaios and save him and all who were in his home, keep safe from all harm those who come to live in this house."

He offered his hand to Sophia; she kissed it.

Then she told him of Ekaterina's threat to have the Greek courts declare her marriage to Henry illegal.

"Our Church and the Russian Orthodox Church are allied in many ways. If Henry's first wife charged him with being still married to her in a Russian court wouldn't our Church be influenced by their de‑cision?"

Bishop Vimpos was thoughtful.

"I doubt that such a case has ever come up. I will confer with the archbishop."

Sophia spent several gnawing hours before he returned.

"My dear, the archbishop says that as long as Henry was a legal citi‑zen of the United States in June 1869, and had renounced his allegiance to the Emperor of Russia, neither Russia nor any other country can overthrow his divorce. Henry secured his citizenship in California when the state was admitted to the Union, did he not?"

Sophia frowned.

"He claims that all males living in California in 1850 when the state was admitted automatically became citizens, but his diary says he did not arrive until 1851. He returned to Russia, maintained a home and business there for some fifteen years, and to the best of my knowledge never again alluded to himself as an American until it was time to se‑cure his divorce."

"Does he keep his naturalization papers in his desk?"

"Yes. Let us go up to the study."

Sophia took out the four longish sheets of legal papers. When Vimpos had finished reading them he turned to Sophia, his dark eyes troubled.

"He almost told the truth about his early citizenship, but not quite. He took out his first papers when he was in New York. Here they are. He announced his intention of becoming a citizen of the United States and renounced forever any allegiance or fidelity to any foreign power. It is dated February 17, 1851, signed Henry Schliemann, and stamped by the court. He signs his next paper in New York also, on March 29, 1869, more than eighteen years later, taking the identical oath. On this same date a man by the name of John Bolan swears that 'he is well acquainted with the above named applicant, Henry Schlie‑mann, and that the said applicant has resided within the United States for the continued term of five years at least, next preceding the present time, and in the state of New York one year at least preceding this ap‑

plication.' On the basis of Bolan's testimony Henry became a naturalized citizen of the United States."

"But that isn't true! He wrote in his diary that he arrived in New York on March 27, 1869, just two days before his appearance in court! There was only his stay in Sacramento in 1851, and a few days in San Francisco in 1851 and 1865, on his way back from the Orient."

Sophia blanched. The bishop stroked his beard as though he could find some solace in the texture of the silky hair.

"If he received his citizenship by someone swearing falsely . . ."

Tears came to Sophia's eyes. ". . . then his divorce is not legal either! Not if his wife's lawyer sees these dates. Oh, Uncle Vimpos, what am I going to do?"

"Henry must persuade his first wife to secure a divorce herself. In Russia. Can it be done?"

"Yes." Determinedly.

"How?"

"With money. Henry has always sent them more than ample funds to support them. Now he must offer her a part of his fortune."

"How is he behaving about money these days?"

"When he is unhappy it is sheer torture for him to part with a drachma. But this time he will. I give you my word as a Greek woman defending the legitimacy of her unborn child."

Her youthful shoulders squared, her eyes blazed.

Bishop Vimpos smiled.

"God will go with you."

So did Henry. He made a settlement satisfactory to Ekaterina. She secured a divorce in a Russian court. That trouble was over.

The second external force to upset their tranquillity was the outbreak of the Franco-Prussian War. Henry had strong loyalties to the land of his birth, but he had left the country at nineteen, had been a Russian citizen for many years, and had carried on a love affair with Paris equaled only by Sophia's love for Athens. Emotionally he found himself on the side of the French. This feeling deepened when he received a report that a German shell had razed the apartment house next door to his own on Place St. Michel. By September 19, 1870, Paris was in a German vise. Each day brought more bad news: The Bois de Boulogne had been cut down. So had the trees on the Champs Élysées and in the Tuileries. Under starvation conditions, all of Paris's horses had been eaten.

Then came the sad day when Henry heard that all four of his houses, which constituted a considerable portion of his fortune, had been destroyed by the bombardment. There was great loss of life when the shells hit the residential area. Henry was desolated. He spent weeks trying to get authentic information out of Paris . . . to no avail.

To take his mind off his worries he decided to dash off to Constantinople.

"Sophia, I simply am going to have to sit on Safvet Pasha's doorstep. I hate to leave you alone while you're pregnant, but I do believe I can bring the *firman* as your Epiphany present. That gives me about two months."

He was so upset that she did not have the heart to restrain him.

She had little opportunity to miss him: her family thronged the Mousson Street house the moment he left, happy to be reunited with Sophia and to be able to stay in Athens again. Her mother spent happy hours in the kitchen preparing the favorite Engastromenos recipes. Sophia was up at dawn to buy from the street merchants goat milk, fresh-baked buns and sweet butter, wild greens from the bent old women, fish caught during the night and weighed out of round baskets which the vendors carried on their heads and kept wet by frequent rinsings from a bucket of water carried in their hands. For Sundays she purchased a turkey cock chosen out of the driven flock.

"It's like old times!" Madame Victoria cried one Sunday when she glanced about the round English walnut table, every chair occupied by an Engastromenos bottom.

Henry's letters were infrequent though filled with hope. The Minister of Public Instruction had kindly offered to secure the land for Henry for the same two-hundred-dollar purchase price he had offered the owners from Kum Kale. The officers of both the American and British embassies had interceded personally for him. He was studying Turkish and already had a vocabulary of three thousand words.

He did not return for Christmas. Sophia was upset, yet held herself in control, reasoning:

"He does not want to return empty-handed. He would be not only furious but embarrassed by his failure. He'll be back by Epiphany, the permit in his pocket."

Madame Victoria decided that Christmas must be spent in the parental home. Sophia was now five months' pregnant and beginning to show. She was exhilarated at the early signs of life within her. The shops on Ermou Street had representations of the manger in their windows, surrounded by balloons, lanterns, cardboard bells and angels. The center of the city was filled with street merchants selling inexpensive toys from their carts.

She helped her mother bake the sweet *christopsomo*, Christ bread. Georgios made the sign of the cross over the bread with his knife, and cut the loaf. The first slice was for the Virgin Mary, the second slice for the poor, and then a slice for each member of the family.

On the New Year they celebrated the Feast of St. Basil and joined their neighbors in the square to hear the carols and sing the *Kalanda*.

Henry had not returned for her birthday and it became apparent that he was not going to be home for Epiphany, January 6. She felt abandoned.

He returned on January 24, empty-handed and sick at heart. There was no present for Sophia. He told her, wringing his hands, of his total frustration. Learning that a freighter was leaving within the hour for Piraeus, he had instantly bought a ticket for home.

"I would have brought you the whole bazaar, believe me, my dear, but I was in such anguish, so troubled . . . I couldn't think two consecutive thoughts."

Sophia held him to her and comforted him as best she could.

"The Turks think I am an adventurer searching only for precious metals, as the tomb robbers of Egypt have been doing for centuries. I am not able to persuade them that I am searching for a lost city, and not gold from which I can make another fortune. Unlike my business associates and customers all over the world, the Turkish government does not trust me."

"Henry, didn't you tell me that every foreigner who obtained a permit to excavate, and agreed to turn over half his finds, ignored the obligations and took out of the country everything he found?"

"Without exception."

"Then it's all foreigners they mistrust. Couldn't you find a way to put their fears to rest?"

"How?"

"Well, by leaving a substantial deposit with the Vizier as a gesture of good faith, for instance."

He put his head down and gazed at her, eyes raised, as though over the top of a pair of spectacles.

"Let's not go to extremes," he rejoined.

He took off his shoes, coat, vest and necktie, threw himself across the width of the wide bed.

"Oh, my God, to be back in my own bed again! And with my own wife, swollen-bellied as she may be. Come lie here in my arms, and let us enjoy an hour of friendship. Has Odysseus been behaving himself?"

"Quiet as a lamb."

He revealed the story of his final week's bad fortune in Constantinople. On January 1 he had been received by the Vizier, the chief minister to the Sultan, who had been cordial and invited him to return the next day. The next day the Vizier advised him to submit a complete statement of his archaeological plans to the director of the new Ottoman Museum. Henry wrote several pages and handed them personally to the director. He then received a note setting up an appointment with the Minister of Public Instruction, Safvet Pasha, for January 8. The minister was to make certain that the two Turks from Kum Kale who owned the second half of Hissarlik would, under orders from the Turkish government, sell their half of the mount to Henry Schliemann for five thousand piasters, two hundred dollars. As soon as he had purchased the land, Henry could commence his excavations, providing he turned over half of his finds to the Ottoman Empire. He had agreed.

He waited ten days before Safvet Pasha summoned him again, received him warmly, had coffee brought in, chatted amicably in Turkish, then announced:

"After our interview of January 8 I telegraphed the governor of the Dardanelles province instructing him to buy the second half of Hissarlik *on my account* for the Turkish government. We got the land for its true worth, three thousand piasters. You now have the permission of this office to begin your digging there."

Henry had burst into an uncontrollable rage, accused Safvet Pasha of deceiving him, of surreptitiously taking away land whose ownership he had promised to Henry Schliemann.

"My six thousand words of Turkish included a few obscenities. At one point I so lost my head that I almost exchanged blows with Safvet Pasha."

"Oh dear!" said Sophia, her eyes moist. "What about the permission to dig?"

"Rescinded. We're right back at the beginning of the labyrinth underneath the palace of Knossos, where the Minotaur devours everyone sent to destroy him."

"But the American minister, Wayne MacVeagh, will continue to plead your case to the Vizier?"

"Yes. Though in all honesty I must tell you that he thought I was wrong, not only in that outburst of anger but also in my interpretation of what Safvet Pasha had promised. It appears that my Turkish grammar is not as good as I had imagined. According to MacVeagh, Safvet Pasha could have said, 'We will purchase the land, and you may excavate,' which I interpreted as 'We will purchase the land *for you*, and then you may excavate.' A subtle distinction, but sufficient to send me into one of my finest temper tantrums."

She kissed his feverish forehead.

"Never mind, my dear, the birth of our child will bring us luck. You have only a few more months to wait, until April, Dr. Venizelos says. Then everything will fall into place."

When an armistice was finally signed between France and Germany, Henry left for Paris to see what he could salvage. Very soon he learned that the rumors about the devastation of Paris were as unfounded as those originated at the Dardanelles cafés. No one of Henry's four apartment houses had been damaged. The Bois de Boulogne had not been cut down. The trees were still standing on the Champs Élysées and in the Tuileries. Paris was as beautiful as ever! The only problem was that he was now prohibited, as were all landlords, from demanding any rent from the families living in his houses until the end of 1871, a ten-month lapse of income.

She became heavy-footed during March and April. The fact that she was carrying so comfortably reassured her about the well-being of the child. Her older sister Katingo, who already had two children, brought to Mousson Street a bolt of fine white cloth, laces and ribbons for the baby's lingerie. A dressmaker came in several times a week to cut and sew garments. Madame Victoria embroidered them with white thread. Sophia shopped with Katingo for a cradle. She prepared it herself, covering the straw all over with white satin, then added a tulle mosquito net.

Henry was elated to be having a Greek child; it somehow fitted into his mysticism about his Greek treasure. But when he did not know he was being observed, Sophia saw that his face was drawn, his eyes somber. One beautiful April day, with tiny fleece formations drifting across an azure sky, they were walking hand in hand on the gravel paths of the garden. Sophia asked solicitously:

"Henry, is something wrong?"

". . . well . . . yes. Money. I've lost thousands of dollars in rents during the past two years. The apartment houses have been neglected, there have been neither materials nor workmen to keep them up or to make repairs. My manager in Paris tells me it will cost a considerable sum to put them back in shape."

"I'm sorry, Henry dear." She sat down on a nearby bench. "Come sit down. The April sun will warm us."

He patted her belly with proud affection, then slipped a thin arm about her shoulder.

"Truth to tell, Sophidion, it's more than that. I suddenly find myself land poor."

". . . land poor? I don't understand."

"You see, my dear, like all converts, I am more zealous in my faith than those born into it. You adore Athens because you were born in the shadow of the Acropolis. Most people see it as a hot, dusty, waterless, provincial town, with less than 60,000 inhabitants, only a few paved streets, an impoverished city government, and no future. Barely six thousand men voted in the last municipal election! Yet I see it growing into one of the world's great capitals. The day I returned from Constantinople, angry and frustrated as I was, I found that, due to the money crisis and depression over the failure of the Laurium silver mines, the owners of that glorious plot of land I've been wanting on Panepistimiou, where we will build a palace one day, were willing to accept my long-standing offer of sixty-eight thousand drachmas."

"You paid cash?"

"I had to. But I didn't stop there. Let me get a topographical map from my office."

He returned with a map of Athens on which he had colored red a number of separate sections.

"These are the lots and parcels I bought. I reasoned that land values had reached rock bottom and would soon start an upward spiral as they have in all world capitals. There was little cash around, and even less credit. Owners were eager to sell. I had already searched the town meticulously, picking out the pieces I would buy when the right moment arrived."

Sophia was amazed at the extent of his purchases. He had a penchant for corner lots, and had bought the largest one available in the center of the city, just a block from the National Library, some 54,000 square feet. Directly across the street he had purchased two more large lots. Then he had staggered half a dozen purchases up the hill toward where the French Archaeological Institute was going to be constructed. Farther out, close to the Polytechnic School and the National Museum, he had been able to buy whole blocks of undeveloped land inexpensively.

"One day our children will inherit a considerable part of Athens. But right now we have to be what Ekaterina accused me of: stingy."

7.

The baby was born without much fuss or pain. Dr. Venizelos delivered the infant in the *matrimoniale*, slapped it sharply on the behind. It let out a cry typical of Henry Schliemann when he was angry. Henry, standing just outside the door, rushed in.

"What is it, Doctor, a boy?"

It was an affirmation rather than a query.

"I don't know yet. I haven't looked."

"Then for God's sake look!"

Dr. Venizelos turned the baby to him, a plump and rosy one, then murmured:

". . . a girl. Perfect. Beautiful. Congratulations!"

Henry swallowed his disappointment and his unshed tears, turned to his wife.

"How are you, my little Sophidion?"

"Just fine. Are you unhappy, Henry?"

He leaned over her pillow to kiss her on the forehead.

" 'A good vine bears many crops.' "

She was up and about in a few days and took a relaxed, sensual pleasure from suckling the infant. Her attitude toward Henry changed subtly now that he had fathered her child. There was a blood link between them; together they had created a life. Henry loved the baby and spent considerable time with her, his disappointment at not having a son all spent. He insisted that the little girl be named Andromache.

"Why Andromache?" she asked, puzzled. "Why not something simple like Maria or Loukia or Nausica?"

"Because Andromache is one of the noblest names in Greek prehistory."

Other affairs were not settled quite so easily. The Engastromenos family were elated with their grandchild and niece, and they were in the house on Mousson Street, her parents and sisters and brothers, for as many hours of the day and night as they could manage, deluging Sophia and the baby with love and admiration. Henry resented having so many Engastromenoses underfoot.

"I'm not a true Greek yet; I'm just not convivial on a twenty-four-hour basis. Please try to control the flow a little; get me some privacy."

Sophia had stood as godmother at the baptism of her sister Katingo's first child. Now Spyros insisted that he stand as godfather for the Schliemanns' child. Sophia called in extra help to prepare an elaborate dinner which would follow the baptism. Long wooden tables were set up in the garden with space to seat a hundred people. Henry bought cases of French champagne. Spyros sent her packets of the sugar-coated almonds and Sophia wrapped them in pink tulle.

Sunday morning they took a carriage down to St. Panaghitsa's. Mass was just over. The small church was a gracious Byzantine structure with an atmosphere of purity and a tiny interior encrusted with centuries of incense. It was divided by alcoves and columns into four parts, of which the central one was the largest and the highest. There were eleven-foot columns of unpolished marble, above which the walls and ceilings were decorated with murals. At the center was Christ in a golden aureole.

They went to the Assumption of the Virgin on its high shrine. It was carved out of wood and covered with gold rings, bracelets and crucifixes. Spyros lighted their candles. Each placed his on the candlestand near the Virgin. On the right-hand side of Christ were St. John and St. Charalambos and two archangels; on the other, Mary holding the infant Jesus, the Assumption of the Virgin, the Congregation of the Twelve Apostles, and two more archangels. To the right was the seat of the bishop. The pulpit was of white marble with lacework engraving.

The church filled rapidly, the standing guests, including the children, each holding a lighted candle. When the ceremony was ready to begin Sophia was obliged to leave, to stand in the portico outside the second door. The priest entered from the sanctuary wearing a long white satin cape edged with a light blue ribbon. Spyros had provided the bottle of olive oil, cake of soap, frankincense. He now stood before the altar with a tall candle wrapped in satin in his hands.

"Do you reject the Devil in the name of this child?" asked the priest.

"I do."

"What name is to be given to the baby?"

"Andromache."

The children rushed out to tell Sophia the name of her daughter. Sophia held a coin in her hand, which she gave to the first child to reach her. She could then re-enter the church.

The font was located at the steps of the sanctuary, a large bronze pot with a handle on each side. The sexton poured hot and cold water into the basin. Andromache was undressed, the priest removed his cape, raised the sleeves of his robe to the elbows and took the naked baby. The sexton opened the bottle of olive oil, poured some of it into Spyros's cupped hands. Spyros rubbed the oil over the baby's body. The priest then totally submerged the infant in the font three times, exclaiming:

"The slave of God, Andromache, is being baptized."

Andromache, frightened, cried with enough power to rattle the *lampions,* the silver and gold pots of olive oil with lighted wicks which hung from the ceiling by three chains. She was then taken to a far corner of the church and dressed. A gold cross on a thin gold chain was hung around her neck.

There was much kissing and well-wishing. Katingo passed the little bundles of *koufeta* to the guests. The largest one had been reserved for Spyros, who was being thanked and congratulated.

When they began to accept social engagements again, Sophia found that her figure was a bit more mature in the bust and hips. Her dresses were too tight. She asked Henry if he would accompany her to her fa-

ther's shop where they could pick out new fabrics for the dressmaker to
sew. Henry asked:

"Can't you let out your older dresses?"

"Why? They won't look right. You've always been so particular about
how I look in public."

"I want this to be a no-spending time."

"But, Henry, there is so little involved. . . ."

His cold stare shut her up.

She had said that the coming of the baby would turn their fortunes;
that the *firman* would arrive, the pieces of their preparations to leave
for Hissarlik fall into place. But the days moved ahead bringing no news
to lighten Henry's growing restlessness. Her father and brother Alexandros chose this time to ask for further financial assistance. They invited Henry to come to the shop, showed him that they had improved
their stock and position with his credit backing, and asked that a larger
sum be made available to them so that they could bring their business
up to its former level.

Henry refused: they had done well enough with his help to buy merchandise on their own credit.

Madame Victoria wanted to move back into Athens so that she could
be closer to Sophia and the baby. Would Henry buy them a house? The
Engastromenoses would pay rent like any other tenant.

Henry declined.

Sophia heard both sides of the arguments, first from her husband,
then from her family. She was caught in the middle.

There was no longer any peace in the house. Her stomach spasms
returned; Henry was in a state of despair, gripped by the fear that he
had mortally offended the Minister of Public Instruction, who undoubtedly had reported the violent scene to the Vizier. His chances of
digging had been ruined forever. That would be the end of him. Dis-
graced! With all his talk about how he was going to unearth Troy. He
had made a fool of himself. People would ridicule and despise him!
What would he do with the rest of his life? Run? From Greece? From
Sophia? To bury his shame in some obscure retreat where no one would
know of his folly?

By June, since he had to go to Constantinople anyway, they agreed
that sooner was the better. That night she fell to her knees before her
icon and prayed harder than she ever had before:

"Sweet Mother of God, listen to my pleas. I know that I am unworthy, but I need help from a source stronger than myself. In your
infinite wisdom and mercy, please help me, your loving child. Soften
the hearts of the Turkish officials and let them give Henry the permit
to dig. Then we can go to Troy together. I want more than anything

else in the world to work side by side with my husband and find Homer's Immortal City. That is why we married. That is what sustains our love. Without it we cannot survive, Andromache and I. I will leave my baby in Colonos where she will be safe. Henry and I will go at once to the Troad, which is the true home of our marriage. All this I ask in Christ's name. Amen."

In the morning Henry left for Piraeus.

The weeks passed quietly for Sophia and Andromache. She went back to her twice-a-day study of English.

Early in August she received a telegram from London:

> CONGRATULATIONS TO MY DEAREST SOPHIA.
> I HAVE THE OFFICIAL TURKISH PERMIT IN HAND,
> GRANTING US RIGHTS TO COMMENCE DIGGING AT
> ONCE. I THANK YOU AND LOVE YOU FOR YOUR
> PATIENCE AND HELP. WORKING TOGETHER WE
> WILL MAKE OUR CONTRIBUTION TO THE CIVILIZED
> WORLD.
>
> YOUR AFFECTIONATE HUSBAND
> HENRY

Tears came to her eyes. She picked up the baby, kissed her a dozen times.

"Everything will be all right now, Andromache."

Her mother arrived at noon.

Sophia announced: "Henry will be home in a few days. As soon as we have made the necessary purchases we will be leaving for the Dardanelles. I am leaving Andromache with you. The whole family loves her. She will be safe.

"We will excavate only until the heavy winter rains begin. . . ."

BOOK THREE

THE WHEEL TURNS WITH TIME

1.

SOPHIA was enchanted with Constantinople, its teeming waterfront with all manner of barque from tiny fishing caïques to colorful freighters in from the ports of the world. Turks, Arabs, Tatars, Mongols, Egyptians, Orientals, all in their native dress, thronged through the narrow streets. Their room at the Katlayan Hotel had a balcony from which she had a full view of the Bosporus, with Asia Minor only a water-mile away, and the muezzin calling the faithful to prayers from the tops of tall needlelike minarets piercing into the sky. Henry took her for a tour of the brilliantly domed mosques, the cobbled streets of the ancient quarter with their stone arches, family gardens behind tall fences, clusters of onion-shaped domes of the older churches, the incredibly vast arcaded bazaar with its hundreds of artisans working cross-legged in niches black as night, their small fires, copper and silver artifacts sparkling down the long tunnellike walkways.

As they neared their hotel late one afternoon they passed a Turkish bath. Henry asked if she would like to try it. Startled, she replied:

"If you'll come with me."

"I'll introduce you, and pay the twenty-two piasters. But I'm not allowed on the women's side, any more than you were admitted to the Blue Mosque during the noon prayers."

She was uncertain when Henry bade her good-by, but that quickly changed to a state of shock. She was only half undressed when two burly women, stark naked, came in to help her, undressing her the way one would peel a banana. They handed her a linen sheet, a pair of wooden sandals and led her to what appeared to be a ballroom of white marble, immaculately clean. Heat was coming from the furnace through holes in the walls, floor and ceiling. She began perspiring at once. Around the room were placed ten sinks, with hot and cold water running constantly, and a series of wooden benches.

By the time Sophia thought she was going to suffocate from the heat the two Amazons lifted her from her bench, laid her on her stomach on a sheet-covered wooden table, scrubbed her from top to bottom with a rough washrag, then turned her over and scrubbed the front of her, from the washing of her hair to the soaping of her toes. She felt as helpless as a child, wondering what was going to happen to her next. She was rinsed front and back, with hot and then cold water, stood up on the now sopping floor, wrapped in two sheets and led to an adjoining room, cool, with a comfortable cot.

She was emotionally drained from the experience, her body tingled. She fell asleep for a few minutes. When she awoke, her clothing was draped over a chair. She dressed and left the establishment with the owner's compliment ringing in her ears:

"Madame Schliemann looks so beautiful and healthy that she will live forever."

Henry was waiting for her in their room. He echoed the compliment, observing:

"For the next couple of months we'll have no place to bathe but the sea."

Sophia laughed, a trifle shortly.

Henry had his written *firman* in his hand, along with the good wishes of the Vizier and Safvet Pasha. Sophia acted as hostess for a "celebration dinner" at their prestigious hotel, to which they invited his friends from the American and British embassies, Wayne MacVeagh and John Porter Brown. It was the first time she had met these men about whom she had heard Henry speak so often. Her English had improved over the summer and they had an amusing time together as they ate a bounteous pilaf with their fingers.

Henry had reserved a stateroom on the *S.S. Schibin,* whose captain he knew, and whose wine closet he thought the best sailing those waters. It was an overnight trip through the Sea of Marmara. They retired early so that they could be up in time to watch the ship enter the Dardanelles, with the Gallipoli Peninsula on the European side and Asia Minor on the other. It was a crisp morning. The captain invited them onto the bridge, where they could watch the wonderful green mountainous landscapes on both sides appear in the distance and rapidly come close to hand.

About two thirds of the way down the strait, during which weather-beaten freighters from Greece and Italy passed them heading north for the Sea of Marmara, the *S.S. Schibin* put into a fair-sized port at the narrowest part of the strait, Çanakkale, the capital of this northern area of Turkey in Asia Minor. The captain assured them their crates of tools and supplies would be unloaded safely. Two boys carried their hand luggage to the small Hotel Nikolaides on the waterfront.

"We will walk over to the governor's offices immediately," said Henry, "show him our permit and get his signature added to it. The Minister of Public Instruction warned me that this must be done so that we are officially excavating in this province. After that we can rent our wagons and horses to take our equipment to Hissarlik."

It was only a few minutes' walk, but for Sophia a fascinating one. Çanakkale, though a busy Turkish port, was a mud village, the rutted streets filled with camel caravans, lines of heavily laden donkeys, large, creaking wagons bringing in timber from the interior mountains to be shipped to Europe; packs of roaming dogs. The shops were narrow caves, pitch-black, with little merchandise. There were Greek coffee-houses and restaurants with hand-painted signs in her own language.

"I thought we were in Turkey," she murmured.

"Other Greeks discovered it before us. The coastal area here is so similar in climate and character that the Greeks have been immigrating for centuries. There has always been plenty of fertile land for culti-vation."

The governor's house was on the main street, a short distance from the pier where they had disembarked. Sophia gazed down the narrow side streets and found that many of the homes were no more than twelve feet wide.

"Henry, why are they so narrow? Is the land expensive?"

"I think it's the icy winds that blow in from the Aegean during the winter. They glue their houses together to present the least possible front to the gales."

The governor, Achmed Pasha, a big-boned, swarthy, unsmiling gen-tleman, received them with the usual Turkish courtesy and coffee. He took a long time to study Henry's *firman*, then said, in a not unfriendly tone:

"I had already learned from the Minister of Public Instruction that you were coming to Çanakkale, and for what purpose. But from this *firman* I cannot give you permission to dig at Hissarlik."

Sophia blinked in incredulity. Henry's mouth fell open.

". . . but . . . but why? You have my official permit before you!"

"The position of the field in which you are to excavate is not accu-rately enough indicated in this document. I must receive a more defi-nite explanation from the Grand Vizier."

Sophia flashed Henry a warning signal. However his temper was un-der control.

"Excellency, my wife and I intend to work here for several years. We would hope to have your friendship and protection. If you need more clarity from Constantinople, would you do me the favor of cabling your needs, and ask that you be cabled in return? I will of course pay for both telegrams."

"Willingly, Dr. Schliemann, but that would do us no good."

"Why not?"

"Because I need a more detailed map, and maps cannot be sent by

wireless. Please be patient, sir, it will only be a few days and then everything will be in order."

Henry sent Sophia a distress plea over the top of his glasses. Women
were not expected to interfere in official business, but she felt she had
to try.

"Excellency, at any other time of the year a few days' delay would
not be important. But today is September 27. I understand your rains
start in November?"

"That is correct, Mrs. Schliemann. Heavy rains."

"Then you can see how valuable each hour is to us. Would you not
feel free to let us begin our excavating, and then sign the *firman* when
the new map arrives?"

"No, because you might dig in an unauthorized location. That would
go hard on me."

"Dear God," Sophia thought, looking about at the spacious, handsomely furnished second-story office, with its tall windows overlooking
the Dardanelles. "He's literally afraid for his job!" To Henry she said,
"We have to understand the governor's point of view. I'm sure he will
get his letter off to Constantinople this very day."

Henry grumbled, but for a man of his intemperance Sophia thought
he had not reacted badly.

"Let's go visit the Frank Calverts' Sea View. They're close by," he
suggested.

They entered a handsome wrought-iron gate, seven feet high, on the
main street, which ran along the seashore, then climbed a flight of stone
steps leading to a broad handsome arch and a curved door. Before entering they gazed at the five-acre garden opposite, fenced on three sides
by high shrubs and trees. From the stoop they could see a pool designed
after the geographical shape of England; a rose garden, fountains, areas
for cut flowers, a greenhouse, a little theater, walks shaded by flowering
bushes, a playhouse surrounded by porches; pagodas, teahouses, a ken-
nel, stable for horses. In all areas there was lush greenery.

"This park is the only place of beauty I've seen."

Henry chuckled.

"It was a bog several feet below the street level, filled with rain water
half the year. Frank Calvert bought it for a song, brought in thousands
of wagonloads of earth from the surrounding hills, and filled the
quagmire to street level. He built this park for his family."

They turned to the twenty-room stone mansion, which was Italian
Renaissance in style, with regal windows and above them carved stone
ledges and arches. At the second story, in the center, were three french
doors leading out to a balcony. A servant admitted them. The diningroom and library overlooked the park; the drawingroom and the bed-

rooms above looked out across the Dardanelles to the green hills of the Gallipoli Peninsula opposite.

"This is the kind of mansion I am going to build for us on our land on Panepistimiou. Only we'll have a view of Old Phaleron and Piraeus."

Frank Calvert welcomed them as they stood at the french doors of the music room overlooking the strait. A wind had sprung up and the waters were running high, depositing a layer of green sea grass on the stone-paved walkway used by the townspeople for Sunday promenading. Calvert was a tall, thin man with agate eyes, blond hair smartly brushed back, a thin-cropped blond mustache. He was dressed meticulously in a suit, cravat and polished boots, as though he were about to set out for his seat in the House of Lords. He scarcely looked his forty-three years. Yet for Sophia there seemed to lurk a bog of sadness behind the calm.

"Welcome at long last! Truly, Mrs. Calvert and I have been waiting a long time for you."

Frank and his two older brothers had been born in Malta where their father had served as Her Majesty's consul. Frank's oldest brother, Frederick, had come out to the Troad first, as British consul; then the middle brother, James, had come as the first United States consular agent. All three brothers owned large tracts of land in the Troad.

"How long do you think it will be before you leave for Hissarlik?"

"Several days. Until the governor gets a new map from Constantinople."

"Then you and Mrs. Schliemann must stay here with us. There is no adequate hotel. I'll send the carriage for your bags."

After a leisurely dinner Mrs. Calvert, a warmhearted mother of four, excused herself momentarily. Calvert invited the Schliemanns into his library, a replica of the libraries in the great country houses of England, solidly walled in leather-bound sets of Sir Walter Scott, Wordsworth, Tennyson, Dickens, Thackeray, stamped in gold, gray and red lettering. Frank lit a fire, settled back in a red leather chair. Henry asked solicitously:

"How are you progressing with your suit to Her Majesty's Government?"

Calvert was silent. His agate eyes darkened to the color of cold ash.

". . . nothing. I've tried, time and again." He glanced at Sophia. "Does your wife know my predicament?"

"I have not mentioned it."

"Then I would like to tell it before someone else poisons her ear." He switched the massive chair around so that he was face to face with Sophia. "I made my fortune during the Crimean War, some fifteen years ago, in 1854 and 1855. I was the only Englishman out here who spoke both Turkish and Greek—my brothers would have been excluded in any event because of their official positions—and so I was the only one who could have provisioned the British fleet. I did it extremely well, gathering in all the livestock and foodstuffs in this part of Asia Minor. Without me the fleet here in the Dardanelles would have gone hungry and we might have lost the war to the Russians.

"I paid the peasants a percentage more than they could expect in their own markets. Naturally, I passed on my higher costs to the British government. After the war they sent a commission here to investigate. They compiled records of how much I paid for things, and then said I had taken a four-hundred-per-cent profit. Called it profiteering. I was tried in London in absentia, convicted as a traitor and sentenced to death." He paused. "But they had thought the prices fair during the war, when their needs were desperate . . . !"

Sophia now understood the sadness behind his eyes. As a young man, only twenty-six, he had found an opportunity to make a kill and had seized it, becoming a millionaire. He had also become the Prince of the Troad, never having to work again because he had deposited his fortune in Swiss banks where the British government could not recover it.

When they retired to their high-ceilinged bedroom, Sophia asked:

"Isn't it ironic that Mr. Calvert is condemned to death by the English for the same kind of provisioning that earned you praise from the Russians?"

"It's a matter of ratio, Sophia. Frank took a four-hundred-per-cent profit on everything he sold the British fleet. When he paid a hundred dollars for a flock of sheep on the hoof, he charged the British five hundred for the flock, leaving himself a four-hundred-dollar profit."

"What rate of profit did you take?"

"A substantial one, but not out of line with the risks during a war. If a shipment cost me a hundred dollars, I charged the Russians about two hundred and fifty for it, delivered, which left me with a profit of about a hundred and fifty dollars. At the end of the war I had netted four hundred thousand dollars. Had I charged Frank's prices I could have come out with a million. However there is a factor to be considered before you congratulate me on my restraint: Frank had no competition; the British procurement officers could not get comparative prices. But there were a number of merchants in St. Petersburg who could have supplied indigo to the Czar's government. I had to bid competitively, not be so much higher that I would lose the contracts. Ergo, I am a hero in Russia, while poor Frank is a traitor in England."

"Henry, you are being modest. I hardly recognize you in the role."

"Don't misunderstand me. I have always been intent on profit. I made my first fortune out of the import business long before the Crimean War. I made a second one in Sacramento, California, where I went to put a proper monument on my brother's grave. He died of fever, but not before panning a considerable amount of gold dust. I went there to straighten out his estate, but his partner had absconded with the money."

"You've never told me about the gold fields. I know you were successful there."

"Yes, but not as a miner. By the time I reached San Francisco in 1851 after crossing the Isthmus of Panama, the gold fields were crowded. I found that most of the goldseekers were broke when they got to Sacramento. They needed a grubstake but had no collateral. The chances of their returning the loans were slim. Consequently the prevailing interest rate was twelve per cent a month. I established a connection with the House of Rothschild in London and opened my own bank. It flourished. When the Crimean War broke out I had large sums of money to invest. As you know, little one, nothing earns money like money. However, three fortunes seemed quite enough to excavate Troy. So here we are, overlooking the Dardanelles, on the eve of our great adventure."

Sophia settled herself deeper into the soft wool blankets, murmured sleepily:

"God works in mysterious ways His miracles to perform."

It took eleven excruciating days before the map arrived from Constantinople. The governor, having been haunted most of the time by Henry Schliemann's presence, was only too happy to receive it. Sophia had spent her days with Mrs. Calvert, reading or walking in their private park where they were served lunch and late afternoon tea in the English fashion: little tomato and cucumber sandwiches, buttered scones with jam, tea brewed dark enough to walk on. The Calverts lived like royalty, with a retinue of servants and a small army of caretakers and gardeners. Henry ran about the town pretending he had important chores to take care of. Sophia was grateful for his capacity to turn a little work into a lot, for this scratched the itch of his impatience. However he did find the stoutest wagon to transport his equipment; the most comfortable carriage for their own use; and hired a guard for the excavations whose duty it was to make sure that the Ottoman Museum got its half of everything the Schliemanns unearthed. The guard was an Armenian by the name of Georgios Sarkis, second secretary of the Chancellery of Justice for the region. Henry had agreed to pay his regular salary, twenty-three piasters a day, ninety-two cents.

The governor's signing ceremony was over by noon. Sophia and Henry had an early luncheon, embraced the Calverts and left by carriage a little past one, hoping to reach Ciplak before dark. The farm wagon carrying their wheelbarrows, shovels, bedding and other equipment had started earlier. The first stretch was level, along the Dardanelles, the sun warm overhead, the sky and sea a matching shade of cerulean blue. Then they were in the mountains, climbing perilous horseshoe turns as the horses strained at the pull. Henry got out and walked to lighten the load. Sophia was enchanted with the beauty of the deep green forests surrounding them, the tops of the trees bending toward each other as though to enclose them in a protected womb.

They stopped once for coffee at the village of Renkoi, Intepe, but at seven, with darkness about to fall, they ate their supper in the carriage: sausage, tomatoes, fruit, bread and honey out of a basket the Calverts' cook had prepared.

It was dark by the time they turned off the main road at Gölcali onto a narrow rutted peasants' path. Fortunately it was level land, and the driver knew the way. At a little before nine they pulled into the small stone village of Ciplak, dark and silent as the sleep of night. Ciplak was a community of ancient stone huts crosshatched by winding dirt trails barely wide enough for an oxcart to pass without scraping walls.

"Can you find our house in the dark?" Sophia asked.

"It's the only two-story in the village. Wait until the first dog hears our carriage wheels; the whole village will be awake."

The first barking came from the other end of the village.

"Must be an insomniac," Henry murmured.

The cacophony of barkings washed closer until a dozen emaciated mongrels surrounded their four wheels.

At Henry's command the driver turned into a stone-enclosed dirt yard. In one corner Sophia made out a bake oven, in the other a storehouse. In between was a long covered shed, its log roof upheld by forked tree branches, the enclosure for the family's animals. Dramali, the owner, dressed in an ankle-length nightshirt of striped wool and a nightcap to match, opened the door at the corner of the house, a saucer oil lamp in his hand.

"Fine time o' night to wake hard-working folk," he grumbled. "Couldn't you wait till first light?"

"Where?" Henry demanded. "With the sheep and goats? Light us up to our rooms, please."

Still complaining in inaudible syllables, the owner led them up a flight of wooden stairs to the two rooms Henry had engaged by messenger from Çanakkale. Sophia had brought the best lamps she could find in Athens, and a supply of oil, but they were behind in the wagon, as were their sheets, blankets, pillows and the supply of disinfectant. She tried to inspect the lumpy mattress on the bed but Henry cautioned her away.

"No use, Sophia, it will be crawling."

"Then we should have brought a new mattress as well."

"Fool that I am! Of course! That must be the wagon now. I'll bring up our lamps and linens."

They filled their oil lamps with olive oil, lit them and held them over the mattress. It was infested with bedbugs. Sophia took a separate container of illuminating oil, yellow-hued and of the thickness of water, found a brush in their tool kit, spread the oil evenly over the top and sides, then had Henry turn the mattress over for a further application. Henry in the meanwhile had been moistening the iron corners of the bed with a green pharmaceutical alcohol, to which he set fire by taking the glass chimney off a lamp and applying the flame. This done, Sophia gave the entire mattress a coat of the green alcohol, opened the windows overlooking the courtyard to let the oil and alcohol smells mingle with the sheep, goat and donkey manure. She set up her icon of the Virgin on a little table by the bed, took their nightclothes from a portmanteau, tucked her own sheets from Mousson Street very tightly under the mattress, put on two blankets, set down their own pillows in their soft linen cases, located the hooks on which to hang their clothes, extinguished the lamps and climbed exhausted into bed.

"May the bedbugs be as tired as we are," she supplicated. "Those roads have broken every bone in my body."

"I will wrap myself around you and serve as splints. You will be healed by cockcrow."

Henry woke her as the first gray-rose tint of day seeped over the eastern horizon.

"Dress quickly, *anghelaki mou*, my little angel, I want you to see your first sunrise from the top of Hissarlik."

She washed her hands and face in cold water in a basin they had brought from home, brushed her teeth, donned one of the dresses she had brought for work purposes, a brown calico which her family had considered too plain for the wife of a wealthy man, then the pair of thick-soled shoes she had bought for walking the cobbled streets of Palermo, Naples and Rome. Henry was trying to hurry her, but she refused to leave the room until she had stripped the bed, taken the linen and blankets downstairs, and in sign language conveyed to the wife of the household that she wanted them left out in the sun to air.

They had black coffee in the fire-warmed kitchen downstairs, but nothing to eat. Dramali remarked:

"We say in Turkish that in the morning our strength comes from sleep; for the rest of the day from food."

Henry measured out the four grains of quinine each of them would have to take every morning to avoid the malaria with which the Troad was infested in the summer and fall. They walked through the courtyard which served as a pen for the family's sheep, goats, pigs, cows, donkeys, horses, then set out diagonally one mile across the field that lay between Ciplak and Hissarlik. The field was uncultivated, used only for the sheep to crop and drop. Sophia could not believe her eyes, for even before sunrise the field gave an appearance of being covered by drifts of rusted snow. When she leaned down to examine the earth she found that it was a blanket layer of pottery shards, different parts of tens of thousands of vases and pots, some decorated with streaks of coloring. First she picked up the handle of a vase, then a pouring mouth, the bottoms they stood on, parts of the curving sides.

"Henry, I don't understand," she cried excitedly. "There must be millions of fragments all around us. Surely they weren't dumped here?"

"No." He was smiling at her puzzlement.

"Since they couldn't have fallen like manna from heaven, does it mean that they worked their way upward through layers of earth during the heavy rains or windstorms?"

"You are walking over the cadaver of a long-dead city."

Her dark eyes grew large with astonishment. Her cheeks were radiant in the early morning coolness.

"Then you already know what lies beneath our feet?"

"A large Roman city, second or third century A.D. If anyone excavated here he would find miles of streets, houses, shops, temples. But no one will ever bother to uncover these fields; it would be a gigantic task, and to no end, for the city would be too modern to be of interest."

Sophia, who was trying to match his vigorous strides as they made their way to the fortress-mountain straight ahead, said amusedly:

"That's what you describe as *nouveau arrivé* on the historical scene."

"Yes. We must work in the civilization that no one has found or documented. The first Trojan settlement may go back as far as 2000 B.C., though it did not reach its height until the time of Priam, around 1200 B.C. When you dig that far back, you can unearth temples to tell you what religion was practiced; tablets to teach you the language; records to identify the dynasties; armor to testify how they fought their enemies; coins to tell you how they traded; burial urns to show how they preserved their dead; foundations of houses to show how well or poorly they lived, how they cooked their food, what they ate; gold, silver and bronze works to show you the state of their art . . . and treasury . . ."

Sophia was shaking her head as she grasped her husband's concept. She turned glowing eyes to his.

"The best history books still lie buried, is that what you are saying? The materials are all here, and it is up to us to uncover them."

". . . day by day and page by page. You are a good student, Sophidion. I shall share my doctor's degree from the University of Rostock with you. In Germany you would be called Frau Professor Dr. Schliemann."

Sophia chuckled.

"What a long tail for so small a kite."

2.

It looked like a natural mount or hillock, though larger and higher than many others. A flock of goats, the devourers of everything that grows above ground, were grazing. The approach from the southeast was a mild slope, almost totally free of bushes and brambles. They climbed to the plateau of the hill, eighty feet above the Troad. To the northwest another mound rose before them, some twenty-six feet higher. They climbed to the very top. Sophia tried to grasp the size of the entire mount by the figures Henry was quoting to her from his notebook. It was close to a thousand feet long and a little over seven hundred feet wide. But even standing here, in the very presence of the mountain, she could not visualize its dimensions from the arithmetic of height, length, width. She had to make its size relevant to the world she knew and had grown up in.

"It's bigger than all of Syntagma Square, wouldn't you say, Henry? It looks to me as though it would stretch from the royal palace to the Arsakeion. As for its width, well, say as wide as the Acropolis."

Henry was amused at her "schoolgirl conception of geography," but allowed that her conceptions were roughly right.

The sun rose behind them, inching up tentatively as though not certain what season it was, throwing a pale yellow mist over the Troad, the triangle of the battlefield below them, and raising a silver sheen on the broad breast of the Scamander River flowing in from the south and the slimmer-waisted Simois River coming from the north. As the sun brightened, Sophia could see where the two streams emptied together into the waters of the Dardanelles where the Dardanelles merged with the Aegean Sea. It was an awe-inspiring vista.

In a straight line three miles to the west was the Aegean. Kum Kale, and the last protected cove of the Dardanelles where the Achaean fleet had spent ten years with the beached sterns of their hollow ships, were three miles to the north. Ahead lay several tumuli which Henry explained had long been considered the tombs of Achilles, Patroclus, Ajax and Priam. Frank Calvert had excavated Priam's tomb but found nothing.

In the foreground, moving along the high bank of the Scamander, was a caravan of seven camels, a rope around the neck of each attaching him in a line to the one in front, led by a man on horseback. To their left Henry identified the little village of Yeni-shehr on the crest of the hill overlooking ancient Sigeum. In the distance he identified the islands of Imbros, then Samothrace. Just emerging from the Hellespont into the Aegean Sea was a black freighter with a single smokestack belching a dark comet of smoke into the clear blue air.

Henry pointed out the island of Tenedos, Bozcaada, lying only a couple of miles offshore a short way to the south. Sophia remembered it as the island behind which the entire Achaean fleet had hidden, so vast were its beaches, on the day they pretended to have abandoned their siege of Troy and sailed home, leaving behind as a gift a huge wooden horse filled with Greek soldiers: Menelaus, Odysseus, Achilles's son, the pick of the Achaean warriors. The wiser Trojans, after hauling the heavy horse through their Scaean Gate, and up the paved road to the crest of the fortifications, had wanted to push it off the steep north ramparts and dash it to bits. Dissenters had prevailed. Troy had gone to sleep; the Achaean fleet had rowed back to its camp on the Dardanelles; during the night the Achaean soldiers, emerging from their wooden horse, unlocked the gates. The Achaeans poured into Troy, burning the "immortal city," killing most of the males, carrying off the females and the children to be sold as slaves; looting until there was nothing left but stone and ash.

"Henry, we Greeks are proud of the conquest of Troy. But what is there to be proud of in a conquest by trickery? When we had failed to capture Troy in ten years of siege? Wouldn't we have had to conquer them by our bravery and skill as warriors?"

Henry put an arm around her shoulder, warming her in the cool morning air.

"Troy had been invincible because it was under the protection of Zeus, the father of all the gods."

"What was the father of the gods doing when the Greeks played this clever but not entirely admirable trick on the Trojans?"

Henry thought for a moment, replied:

"It could be the same story that Homer tells about how Zeus was laid low by his sister-wife, Hera. Homer says, 'Then she took thought, the ox-eyed, queenly Hera, how she might beguile the mind of Zeus. And this plan seemed to her mind the best—to go to Mt. Ida, when she had beauteously adorned her person—if so be he might desire to lie by her side and embrace her body in love, and she might shed a warm and gentle sleep upon his eyelids and his cunning mind. . . .'

"When Zeus beheld his sister-bride he exclaimed: 'Come, let us take our joy couched together in love; for never yet did desire for goddess or mortal woman so shed itself about me and overmaster the heart within my breast.'"

Henry's face glowed. Sophia watched his expression: "This is the reality of life for him. Everything else is fantasy."

"With Zeus slumbering in the arms of Hera, the god of sleep flew to the camp of the beleaguered Achaeans and aroused Poseidon, the god of the seas. Poseidon assumed human form, led the Achaeans in an attack which drove the Trojans back to their city walls and killed a number of their noblest warriors. Thus do the gods intervene in the affairs of man. Perhaps the wily goddess Hera deceived Zeus again . . ."

". . . and put him into such a deep sleep that by the time he awoke in the morning Troy was destroyed and the Achaean fleet had sailed for home."

"Few of them ever reached their destination. Agamemnon got to Mycenae only to be murdered at a welcoming banquet. Menelaus reached Sparta safely with Helen; but it took Odysseus ten years of stormy voyaging to arrive in Ithaca and save Penelope from her predatory suitors. Most of the others perished at sea, and with them went the glory of prehistoric Greece. Soon came the Doric invasion from the north, then the Ionian, to conquer the Mycenaean civilization and create a new culture."

"It began here, where we are standing?"

"Yes, little one. And tomorrow we shall start digging it out."

At this moment the oldest Dramali son arrived on the lower plateau with the two horses for which Henry had arranged. They climbed down the mound. Henry helped Sophia up into the saddle.

"It's a good thing you took those riding lessons in Paris," he commented.

"I fell off more horses than I stayed on."

"This is a gentle mare. We'll go slowly."

First he showed her the two springs, just below the steepest incline, one hot, the other cold, where the Trojan women had washed their clothes. His next stop was at the oak tree which had been inside the Scaean Gate, near which Hector had made the resolution to fight Achilles hand to hand in hopes of ending the war.

"Now we must circle the mound three times. When Hector came out to fight Achilles, he was terrorized and ran three times around Troy before the goddess Athena stopped him and made him do battle. There are a few writers who believe in Troy but claim it was at Bounarbashi.

Hector never could have run around Bounarbashi three times. Besides it is eight miles and more from the mouth of the Hellespont. I dug there and found nothing."

Sophia, perched sidesaddle on the mare, asked:

"Could we ride out to Bounarbashi one day? I want to see with my own eyes why it could not have been Troy."

They were now at the base of Hissarlik. Henry turned the horses in a northwest direction. For a mile they moved along the level plain, then rode over a rise in the ground, after which the plain flowed toward the sea in a gentle descent. Soon they came to the Scamander, a majestic stream, child of a valley near the summit of Mt. Ida, summer home of the gods. Henry stopped their horses, tied them to a tree. The banks were thickly lined with elms, willows and tamarisks; lotus, rushes and cypress. Sophia had a flash of recognition.

"This is where Achilles killed the Trojan youths in revenge for the death of his friend Patroclus, and threw so many of their bodies down the bank that the river became clogged and could not flow to the sea. That's when the god of the river rose in his wrath, flooded the banks and chased Achilles with great waves of water, almost drowning him." Suddenly she sobered. "Is there really a god of the river? Could he flood this plain in pursuit of Achilles?"

"He does, every winter. You will see it happen in November."

They remounted their horses. Soon they were in marshy land within smell of the sea. Purple flowering weeds grew horse-belly high. Sophia tucked her legs up on the saddle and raised her long dress above her knees to keep it dry. They came onto higher land that led directly to a sheltered half-moon stretch of sand, the last cove of the Dardanelles, which was flowing at a rate of three miles an hour into the sea. Here the Scamander and the Simois joined their union to the Aegean. Close by was the village of Kum Kale; opposite was the lighthouse on the Gallipoli Peninsula.

He tethered their horses and cried:

"Here we are at last, at the ten-year camp of the Greeks. It is here that the Achaeans built their defensive wall when the Trojans were breaking through their lines. The Achaeans also dug a moat, studded with pointed timbers, too wide for the Trojan horses to clear. Nevertheless a few Trojans broke through the wall, crossed the moat and set fire to an Achaean ship."

Sophia knew the story but didn't want to spoil Henry's pleasure in retelling it.

"Before the wall and moat were completed the Trojans gained, by hard fighting, the upper hand. By nightfall they were encamped on the plain, confident they could storm the defenses of their enemies and sweep them into the sea. Agamemnon and his council were fearful. Before his assembled council Agamemnon acknowledged his own responsibility in the quarrel with Achilles which had dissipated the Achaean effort. When Agamemnon conquered Chryse, he had taken captive Chryseis, the beautiful daughter of the priest. When her father came to ransom his daughter Agamemnon treated him so harshly that the priest asked Apollo to bring down a plague upon the Achaean forces. After nine days Agamemnon was forced to return Chryseis to her father, but he took away from Achilles, instead, the exquisite young girl, Briseis, whom Achilles had taken captive in a town near Troy, and who had become his intimate and beloved companion. Achilles swore he would fight no more.

"Chosen as peacemakers were Odysseus and Ajax, who were to offer in Agamemnon's name 'seven tripods that the fire hath not touched, and ten talents of gold and twenty gleaming cauldrons, and twelve strong horses that have won prizes by their fleetness. And I will give seven women skilled in goodly handiwork, women of Lesbos, that in beauty surpass all womenfolk. Amid them shall be she that I took away. . . .'"

"*The Iliad* is sometimes called '*The Wrath of Achilles*,'" Sophia murmured, lying on the sand by her husband's side in the lee of a protected embankment. "Am I a hopeless romantic to be pleased that the first and finest novel ever written had to look for its plot to the love of a man for a woman?"

"We are both romantics," replied Henry softly. "It's the romantics who shape the world. The realists are content to fill their bellies."

They rode through the fishing village of Kum Kale, found the oxcart trail leading inland to the main road, coming out just a short ride from Renkoi, where they had stopped the day before for coffee. Renkoi was a good-sized town, its 3,500 Greeks making it as thoroughly Greek as Ciplak was Turkish. Henry had decided to hire his diggers here rather than in Ciplak because there would be a much larger labor pool from which to draw, and because his Greek was far better than his Turkish.

"Where do we go to hire help in Renkoi?" Sophia asked.

"In each village there is a head man, generally an older one, who owns the largest piece of land, or the best land and house, which has come down through his family. He will not be hard to find, for he is rarely more than a few feet away from any discussion."

After Alexander the Great's expedition starting in 334 B.C. the west coast of Asia Minor had become solidly Greek. Now it was a joint culture, with little if any intermarriage, and few differences in economic level. During the nineteenth century there had again been a heavy immigration from the mainland and Greek islands for the more abundant farm lands of Asia Minor. Completely Greek in customs and mores, these families were known as Turkophones. Smyrna, the large, prosperous port city about two hundred miles to the south, had ninety thousand Greeks and only two thousand Turks.

Since there was no school to teach the children Turkish, no hospital, government building, doctor, nurse or teacher, the Greeks were very much self-contained. Their life was as primitive as in biblical days; their few animals slept in the house in cold weather. The men raised only enough food to feed their families. Each man had his own small tobacco patch, to which he gave loving care. They had little clothing; the dress a girl married in lasted a lifetime. The men wore the same pants and coat for years, put leather patches on their shoes when holes developed. Cash was virtually unknown. If an urgent need developed, the father, or frequently the mother, would plow an extra patch behind a forked tree branch and an ox, so that later the family could make the journey into Çanakkale on muleback for the Friday fair, where they would barter their extra produce for a piece of cloth or a cooking utensil.

All Henry had to do was stop and talk to the first man they met on the road. The head man knew instantly that there were strangers in his village. He came as quickly as though the town had a fire bell.

He was not old, but aged. Sprinkled over his sucked-in cheeks and the top of his head was a white beard stubble; and there was rheum in his eyes. His clothes looked as though he had lived in them as long as he had in his skin. What few teeth he had left were brown crusts from a lifetime of chewing on his pipe. Yet, as Sophia observed, he bowed as courteously as any courtier. They dismounted.

"The gentleman is seeking something?" he asked in a high, hoarse voice.

"I need workmen to dig for me."

"Honored sir, the season is over, the fields lie fallow. There is nothing to dig until spring."

They had moved a few steps to a small coffeehouse, where a group of natives were sitting about a lone table with tiny, long-emptied coffee cups before them, playing cards with an old and begrimed deck. They rose to listen.

"I do not wish to plant. I wish to uncover."

"What is it the gentleman wishes to uncover?"

"A hill. Hissarlik."

"Ah, a fortress. But there is no fortress there now. Only sheep and goats."

Sophia said softly, so that none of the growing circle of curious men could overhear:

"These villagers are as Greek as any in Attica. Best not to tell them your purpose. It may confuse or frighten them. Suggest your daily wage, and you will have your crew."

Henry nodded agreement. An encircling gesture of his right hand brought the still wary group closer to him. He said:

"Each workman will receive nine piasters a day. We work from half past five in the morning until half past five in the evening. A half hour off for breakfast at nine, an hour and a half off in the afternoon for eating and smoking. No tools are necessary, I have my own. How many can come to work?"

The head man took off a battered hat, scratched the sparse turf of his scalp with black and broken fingernails. The men of the village talked to each other's eyes but said nothing.

"Why are they silent?" Henry asked Sophia. "Nine piasters a day is more than they have ever earned."

"Perhaps that's the reason. Greek villagers are suspicious of strangers. In our European dress we look foreign to them, particularly you in your business suit, vest and necktie. May I try? It will take some village vernacular."

The men were less perplexed when they heard Sophia's informal Greek. Eight of them volunteered to be at Hissarlik by first light.

"I need more," Henry persisted.

"How many more?" the head man asked.

"Perhaps fifty, seventy-five, depending on how the work goes."

"Eight will start," pronounced the elder; "you must leave half the first day's wages with me. After that you can pay at quitting time."

Henry took out his wallet, extracted the required number of piasters from the Turkish money compartment, handed it to the chief.

"If the men return satisfied tomorrow night, you will have more hands on Wednesday."

Sophia thanked him with a flavorsome salute from Crete. There were smiles and handshakes all around . . . except for one giant of a man, a full head taller than his fellows, built like a bull. He had a broad pair of mustaches drooping below his jowls, and a fierce scowl on his face. Sophia shuddered.

"I hope he's not one of the eight who shows up tomorrow."

As they started back to Ciplak, Henry reached across to her mare, took Sophia's hand.

"Thank you for the assist, little one. Why not teach me the Greek vernacular? Obviously I am going to need it. I'll teach you Turkish in return."

3.

She was awakened in the pitch-dark by Henry shaking her shoulder.
"What is it? What's wrong?"

"Nothing. Our horses are saddled. We're going to swim in the Hellespont."

"Henry! It must be the middle of the night."

"It's four in the morning. We can watch the sun come up while we're
in the water. It will be good for you."

"Sleep is even better."

"*Syzygaki mou*, my little wife, you know what your compatriots say:
thirty baths in the sea in any year will keep you from catching cold.
Sixty baths, and you'll never catch anything."

"I've never caught anything in my life . . . except from you. And
that turned out to be Andromache. Go for your swim and leave me be."

"Try it just this once."

Half asleep, jouncing hard on the horse beneath her, she rode to the
mouth of the Scamander where its fresh water joined the salt of the
Aegean. Henry disrobed, struck out vigorously for some hundred yards
into the dawning light over the sea. Sophia stood in an ankle-length,
long-sleeved, makeshift swimsuit, shivering as she put her toes into the
water. There was no help for it, she would have to get wet. She waded
out to just above her knees, sat down, splashed the cold water over
her chest and shoulders. Her duty done, she got out as fast as she
could, covered herself in a tentlike, concealing towel, shivered into her
underclothes, warm dress and shawl. Henry swam for a half hour, with
long, graceful strokes, going out so far she could barely see his head
bobbing in the mild ripples of the sea. But when he came out and had
rubbed his body with the rough towel, she saw that he was glowing
with health.

"No wonder you don't catch cold," she murmured. "Your blood
must be frozen in your veins."

The eight workmen arrived at five-thirty, riding their donkeys. They
had been on the road for two hours. Since their families originally came
from the nearby Greek islands of Samothrace, Lemnos and Lesbos, they
still looked like Greek islanders, wearing the *vraka*, large and baggy
trousers held tight at the middle of the leg, short straight pants underneath, and white stockings, white shirt, short loose waistcoat, large sash
around the waist, and small cap on the head. Only the shoes showed
Turkish influence, the toes turning upward.

Sophia was disappointed in her hope that the monstrous-sized one, with the fierce mustaches, would not be among them. She determined to keep a considerable distance from him.

The year before when Henry had dug for a few days and had laid bare a wall of stones some six feet thick, he had begun at the bottom of the northeast corner of the mountain. Going over the geography of the hill the morning before while riding with Sophia, he told her that he had made a mistake. This time he was going to dig his trench closer to the northwest end of the mount, where the terrain was the steepest, and where there was the greatest accumulation of debris, either thrown down or rolled down by natural forces over the millennia.

"Henry, there must be dozens of easier slopes."

"This is where the mound rises to its greatest height. From its imposing situation and natural fortifications, it would seem specially suited to be the acropolis of the town, as well as to contain the king's palace, the highest Watchtower and the strongest walls of the surrounding fortress."

Sophia, who was studying one of Henry's rough-drawn maps of Hissarlik, said:

"Please explain. I know that the battles and individual contests were fought in this triangle formed by the base of Hissarlik, which you show here as twenty-four feet above sea level, and the joining of the Scamander and the Simois. But why was all the fighting done on the north side, with the steepest slope rising . . ." she peered at the paper, ". . . at a forty-five-degree angle, with the most massive fortifications on top? The entrance to the east is fairly level, and on the south side there is a moderate grade. Why did the Achaeans always assault the north side when they had little chance of scaling the walls?"

Henry took some time before he answered.

"During the reign of the Trojan kings, coming down from Dardanus to Priam, they built up a formidable group of allies. Homer lists many of the tribes, among them the Mysians, Thracians, Phrygians, and the Amazon women, who were tremendous fighters. Individual warriors from these allies sometimes fought in their chariots, or hand to hand against the Achaeans on the battlefield. But mostly their task was to protect those easier approaches from an invading army: the Scaean and other gates, and all of the near-level land on the south. Besides, the Achaeans never wanted to be out of sight of their ships and camp so that they could get back quickly for extra weapons, chariots, horses, armor, provisions."

It was time to dig.

The equipment they had brought with them consisted of eight French wheelbarrows, five pickaxes, half a dozen wooden shovels, fifty-two tightly woven straw baskets. Because Henry maintained that it was

useless to start digging into the hill at ground level since Homer's Troy
was a fortress which had been built on top of a natural hill, he led his
men straight up the bank for forty feet. This northern side was covered
by a heavy undergrowth, much of it thorny, and by ancient trees, so
they made a narrow trail by cutting away the underbrush with knives
they carried in their sashes. Sophia moved up last, slowly, for her long
woolen dress was having its woven threads pulled by briars.

At the point where he wanted to start, sixty feet below the top of
the first plateau, Henry had the four men with the pickaxes, the ones
he deemed strongest of the group, including Sophia's giant, loosen a
shallow trench about fourteen feet wide. The two men with the shovels
lifted the earth into baskets which the other two workers carried away
and dumped down the hill. Henry drove stakes into the ground along
the fourteen-foot width, himself unwinding the rope he was carrying
to mark his bottom line of excavation. He then sent all eight men
straight up the hill, clearing the dense foliage as they went, hammering
down stakes to line up with the two he had set. Henry wound the rope
uphill, circling the stakes.

Sophia kept a time log of how long each chore took, and drew a map
of the northern slope, indicating precisely where and how far up on
the hillside they had begun their trench. Henry also asked her to keep
a written record of the nature of the material they were digging out.

"You mean whether it's debris or solid earth?"

"Yes. We're not likely to find anything but debris for many feet into
the hill."

"How far into the interior of the mound do you think you will have
to dig before you reach the soil on which the original Troy was built?"
she asked.

"That depends upon how thick the debris is. We started at forty feet
up the hill with our fourteen-foot-wide trench and we will carry that to
the top. While we are moving upward we will deepen the trench ten to
fifteen feet. My guess is that after we have dug inward some thirty feet
we should be on native soil."

"What a chilling thought!"

"Wait till we get there," he grumbled.

The enormous man, wearing a red Turkish fez with a black tassel
hanging from its crown, kept his distance. He was, Sophia had to admit, tremendous with a pickax, which he handled with the ease of a toy.
When in the course of his work he had to pass her, he not only lowered
his head but closed his eyes as well.

When they broke for dinner at eleven, the Renkoits selected a place
in the brittle sunlight to eat their meal, smoke and then sleep. Henry
and Sophia chose a level spot off to one side, spread the tarpaulin

Henry had bought in Constantinople, and started to eat the food Mrs. Dramali had sent with them. Sophia found the meat, which she guessed was goat, inedible. She concealed this from Henry but he too soon gave it up.

"I've eaten in China, Japan, Egypt, Mesopotamia, India and Java. Everything from fried ants to fish eyes; but I've never tasted anything like this. What do you suppose it is?"

"Better not to know. Put it aside. Here are some things I stocked up in Çanakkale; they won't fill you, but they won't give you a stomach-ache either."

She brought out a packet in which she had olives, *feta* cheese, salted sardines, dried figs. To this she added the fresh tomatoes she had bought in Renkoi the day before, and some of her mother's sweet cakes she had brought from Athens.

"A veritable feast!" Henry exclaimed. "Can I always rely on you to perform feats of magic?"

Suddenly the giant hovered above them like a mountain cliff. He took off his fez, bowed low, spoke in a diffident voice.

"Master, *doulos sas*, your slave. Name Yannakis. Tomorrow you have thirty-five workers. Who keep the book on them? You must pay cash each day. I read and write, Turkish and Greek. I know arithmetic. You name me hirer and paymaster?"

Surprised, but liking the odd combination of Yannakis's ferocious look and gentle manner, Henry asked:

"How do you propose to set up your system?"

"You give me notebook. I write each man's name. I write date of month. Man come to work, I put check after his name. I tell you total number men on hill. Sundown, give me that number times nine pias-ters. When I pay man I put check by his name. How we paid in Con-stantinople when I worked in shipyard."

Sophia said, "A bookkeeper and paymaster combined. Henry, that could relieve us of a lot of detail."

Yannakis pulled up to his significant height, squared his gigantic shoulders, bristled his Mongolian mustaches upward, and announced:

"I also cook!"

Yannakis had no concept of what the Schliemanns were doing on this hill but, unlike the other Renkoits, he did not consider them *palavos*, moon-struck.

Yannakis arrived before five-thirty the next morning with a group of thirty-five Renkoits who had been convinced that there was work avail-able at Hissarlik, and that they would be paid in cash by sundown. So-phia brought to the digs a ruled notebook, as well as a pen and ink.

Yannakis took it, bowed low with his red fez in his hand, murmured, "*Doulos sas*," jotted down the names of the men who had ridden in with him. A very few minutes later he was wielding a pickax and making the soft debris fly as he moved uphill with the agility of a mountain goat. Ahead of him were the Renkoits clearing brush and felling trees.

Henry wanted to dig only a foot or two deep until he had the sixty-yard trench to the plateau of the hill. When he approached the area where he believed the Trojan ramparts would commence, he said:

"Here is where we will begin to dig inward."

The major difficulty was that their eight wheelbarrows and half a dozen pickaxes and wooden shovels were inadequate for the thirty-five men scrambling over the mound. He assigned fifteen Renkoits to carrying the debris away in baskets but the going was slow and rough, the slope on either side of the trench thick with bushes, brambles, large stones and trees with down-swooping branches.

"Wouldn't it be faster just to clear the brush on both sides?"

"No, because once we get down below six feet it will be too laborious to raise all those baskets to the surface on ropes. Better to use the wheelbarrows on an inclining side cut and let the men dump downhill at the end of the cut."

At the nine o'clock breakfast break Georgios Sarkis appeared. He had apparently found a bed in Ciplak the night before, but little sleep to go with it. He was small of stature, with sallow skin and dark eyes which seemed to sop up the rest of his thin face. He was carrying a notebook similar to the one Yannakis was using, in which to list the Schliemanns' daily finds so that the Ottoman Museum would be certain to get its half. Henry commented:

"He is obviously unhappy at being yanked out of his comfortable life in Çanakkale and banished to an isolated peasant village."

"His expression is really wonderful. It says, 'What am I, an Armenian, doing here as a Turkish official, overseeing a German-Russian-American man and a Greek girl engaged in a folly that will turn up nothing!' "

Since they were not yet finding anything, Sarkis did not stand sentinel over them but wandered around, aimlessly, Sophia thought, in the conviction that a man in motion uses up time faster than one standing still. Sophia, checking by the thick gold watch in Henry's vest, saw that his rounds brought him to the trench about every half hour.

"I don't think we're going to have much trouble with him," she confided to her husband; "there's nothing on his mind except prayers for the heavy rains that will close us down."

"I don't see why I need a guardian. All I expect to find are stone palaces, the temple, watchtowers, the fortification walls. Surely the

Grand Vizier is not going to be interested in hauling those huge stones all the way back to Constantinople?"

"I hope not!" said Sophia with a grim laugh. "Under your *firman* you are obliged to pay the shipping costs from here to the museum."

Henry clapped the palm of his left hand with an upward stroke, hard.

"Idiot that I am! I translated that sentence for you, but I never recorded it in my own head."

"Anyway, you told me that stone walls are left *in situ*, where they are found."

It was late in the afternoon when they made their first find. Sophia was standing at the uphill end of the cut when she saw a glint of metal in a wooden shovelful of earth one of the workmen was about to drop into a nearly full basket. Her heart began to beat very fast; she let the workman raise the basket from the bottom of the trench and then, while the other carriers were working their way across the steep hill, baskets on their shoulders, ran her fingers through the top layer of debris. She came out with half a dozen coins, encrusted with dirt, but enough of the metal showed to tell her they were copper or bronze.

"Our first treasure!" she exclaimed. She was overcome with joy . . . and pride. . . .

Henry was halfway down the trench, directing his pickax men to dig deeper, four, five, six feet, and to follow that depth up the hill. When he caught her signal he joined her at the gray tarpaulin on the little knoll. She seemed a little faint.

"What is it, Sophidion? You look as though you just discovered Troy."

"I have my first unearthing as an archaeologist. I feel the way I did when I was handed my diploma at the Arsakeion."

She dropped the coins into his hand. He thumbed over one or two, moistened a rag with some water from their tin cup, wiped the coins clean. The first bore an image of Athena with a three-crested helmet; next he held up a round bronze depiction of the she-wolf suckling Romulus and Remus; the third was a bronze of Apollo dressed in a long chiton and holding a lyre in one hand; the fourth had a likeness of Hector standing with a sword in one hand and a lance in the other.

Sophia had seen similar coins in the museums of Naples, Rome and the library in Athens, where Henry had obliged her to stand for hours before the numismatic cases as he taught her what age and area they had come from, how the figures were designed in the molds or struck by hand. Her tired feet had not always appreciated her bridegroom's detailed instruction, but now she was grateful.

"Henry, I recognize two of these. This Apollo comes from New Ilium, doesn't it? From one of the Greek cities that existed about the time of Jesus, right on this hill?"

"Correct. This Athena coin is Greek too, I would guess from Alexandria Troas, the city which Alexander the Great's general, Antigonus, built about fifty miles south of here."

"How did this Roman Romulus and Remus coin get here?"

"Easy. The Romans founded the town of Sigeum, the one I showed you on the promontory across the Troad. They always took their money with them, or at least their molds, when they conquered another part of the world."

"When we discover coins from Troy will we have a way of knowing their worth?"

"Not really. Homer has both the Trojans and Achaeans using barter. For example, it took four oxen to buy a young girl."

Sophia frowned, causing wrinkles in her forehead.

"We know that the Achaeans had bars of gold . . ."

"That's not all. When Achilles offered prizes in the athletic contests to celebrate the funeral of his friend Patroclus, he gave for the horse races a tripod of gold, for the foot races a mixing bowl of silver, for the losing boxers a two-handled cup, probably of gold, for the archers dark iron: ten single and ten double axes. As for the Trojans, they were rich; the captured Adrastus clasps Menelaus by the knees and cries: 'Take me alive, thou son of Atreus, and accept a worthy ransom; treasures full many lie stored in the palace of my wealthy father, bronze and gold and iron wrought with toil.' Toward the end of *The Iliad*, before Priam sets out to ransom the body of Hector, 'he went down to the vaulted treasure chamber, fragrant of cedar wood and high of roof, that held jewels full many, gold talents, gold cups. . . .' "

"Henry, may I keep these coins? My first. We can give Sarkis an equal number that we find later."

"Of course. But you must record the exact place and depth at which they were found, then put them in an envelope and date it."

Henry had turned over to Yannakis a money belt he had bought in Constantinople. Each afternoon he gave him enough cash to pay the men. After a few days he came to Henry and said:

"*Doulos sas*. More men come tomorrow. How many I bring?"

"As many good workers as you can, Yannakis. Up to, say, eighty. The greatest difficulty we have is keeping this dirt out of our way."

That evening Sophia said:

"I have checked the money belt several nights against the book. He is not out by a piaster. Last night he took all our linen home in a big basket on his head, to be washed by his family in Renkoi."

"A rare find," agreed Henry. "Tomorrow I will raise his wage to thirty piasters a day. That will make him the Croesus of Renkoi. At the same time I shall make him foreman of a digging crew."

Yannakis declined to be a foreman.

"Master, I never give order. Who to? My parents? My brothers, sisters? My friends? Man I work with? Impossible. I never have wife or children, so I never learn make other people do what I want."

Henry was still getting up at four and riding horseback to the sea for his morning bath, but Sophia held him to his promise not to roust her out. She saw to it that coffee was ready for him and the four grains of quinine measured out when he returned at five. She also had her little package of food for their eleven o'clock dinner ready.

After work she bathed standing up, with her feet in the largest basin she had been able to find in Athens, using the second of their upstairs rooms, which they had converted into an office-study. It had a crude desk and bookshelf Henry had made from planks laid across piles of unfired Ciplak brick. Here, until midnight, they wrote their letters, the reports of the day's work, the progress they had made, with the precise number of men digging and how many piasters were going out.

Each night she put a drop or two of eau de cologne on her own pillow and Henry's to counteract the odors of the animal droppings in the yard below their windows. But that had to follow her ritual of brushing both sides of the mattress with her container of yellow-hued oil, then giving it its coat of green, pharmaceutical alcohol to kill or drive away the day's accumulation of bedbugs. There followed a considerable wait before she was willing to put her clean sheets and blankets on the bed.

They could eat little of Mrs. Dramali's food. The Dramali kitchen, with its earthen floor and open fireplace, was reasonably clean, but the decades of accumulated animal smells made it impossible for Sophia to swallow anything at the family board. They arranged to have their supper in their workroom. Nor did the village have anything but a hole-in-a-house which carried a few provisions they could tolerate. Sophia lived on the fresh fruit, tomatoes, cheese and bread which Yannakis brought to the digs each noon. Occasionally he would find a fresh chicken or baby lamb, which he would bake in the Dramali oven in the courtyard, and bring still warm to the Schliemanns at noon. These rare occasions became feast days.

Sophia was losing weight, getting back to her pre-Andromache figure. Henry remained at his same bone-and-muscle weight.

"It's not food from which he derives the strength to work for eighteen hours a day," she decided, "it's the excitement within him which keeps him going."

Henry made the next find, when the trench was down more than six feet, a Roman well covered by a large stone.

"How can you tell which period it belongs to?" Sophia demanded.

"By the cement holding the stones together. But we won't stop to clear it out."

They were making progress in digging the trench, groping into the side of the hill while at the same time moving upward to the crest of the mound. Yannakis kept bringing more workmen each day, until the count reached eighty and resembled an enormous anthill. There were insufficient tools for all.

Near the end of the first week Henry cried out to summon Sophia. He had come upon the ruins of buildings made of hand-hewn stones with and without cement. He was triumphant. He hoped this might be the ruins of a temple of Athena; if it was, there was a chance of a Trojan temple lying below it. The stones were immense.

"We're going to have to pry these stones out and remove them," he said unhappily; "they're blocking our progress."

"They're of no worth?"

"They're too recent. What a fool I am not to have brought some iron levers. We're going to have to move them by hand."

The men pickaxed around the foundations until the stones were completely exposed. Yannakis brought a team of oxen from Ciplak. Ropes were tied around each stone, then the Renkoits heaved and hauled until the stone came out of the hill. The ropes were taken off and the huge blocks allowed to crash down the hillside to the plain below. When the stone was ready to begin its descent a cry went up and all eighty of the workmen dropped their tools and hurried to the point where the stone was bouncing its erratic way down the steep slope, their exclamations and cackling laughter equaling the thundering noise of the blocks knocking out bushes and trees on their way to a resting spot on the Troad.

Henry was disconcerted by the work interruptions.

"You'd think they were watching the battle between Menelaus and Paris to settle the Trojan War," he groused to Sophia.

"To them it's equal." Sophia was also enjoying the spectacle. "They get the same kind of pleasure we do watching the changing of the guard at the palace in Athens."

Henry restrained himself until the scene recurred a third time, then he counted the minutes on his gold watch. From the time the cast-off cry went up until the stone had stopped rolling in the plain and the men returned to work, twelve minutes had elapsed. Henry said determinedly:

"Multiply twelve by eighty and you get nearly a thousand minutes. That comes out at sixteen hours of work we lose every time we roll down a big stone. I don't mind the wasted money as much as the wasted time. I'm going to put a stop to it or we won't get down to native soil before the rains."

Sophia kept her counsel. Henry issued his order sternly: no man was permitted to leave his work except at the regular rest and food time. The men gave abrupt nods of agreement but went right on rushing to the scene of action every time another performance was about to start. Henry was furious but there was no way of stopping them short of firing the entire crew.

4.

In the three-mile stretch between Hissarlik, Ciplak and the Aegean there were marshes inhabited by millions of frogs. The hot summer dried up the marshes and by the end of September the frogs had rotted in the sun. According to the people of the Troad, this caused *mal-aire* or malaria. Henry had learned about this on his earlier trips and had bought a sufficient supply of quinine at the Pharmacie Britannique in Constantinople to protect himself and Sophia during their stay. They had been in the Dramali house only a week when the family's seventeen-year-old daughter came down with malaria. When Henry and Sophia returned from the dig at dusk the mother was waiting at the door. She addressed herself to Henry.

"Daughter is down. Bad air from the swamp. Can you help?"

"I will try." To Sophia he said, "Please bring down our thermometer and our medicine bag."

The girl was huddled on a cot in the family's one bedroom. Sophia took her temperature; it was at the 102° mark. Henry said:

"We'll give her sixteen grains of quinine. I had the marsh fever in Nicaragua once, and was on the point of death when a German doctor traveling through gave me sixty-four grains in one dose. It cured me but it could be dangerous for a girl."

He asked for a cup of water; the girl swallowed the bitter-tasting powder.

"We'll repeat the dose in the morning and again tomorrow night, and the fourth time the following morning."

The quinine proved to be a miracle drug against the *mal-aire*. Within a few days the girl was up and around. That was the beginning of Dr. Schliemann's medical practice. Each morning there would be one or two peasants from Ciplak or the surrounding villages of Kum Kale or Yeni-shehr waiting to be treated. Since there was no doctor, nurse or medicine in the Troad, Henry and Sophia became the local clinic. Each morning as they arrived at the dig there would be a group of stricken ones, including women and children. Henry obliged them to come back for four doses. Sophia kept the record. By the fourth round of quinine the supplicants were well again.

"Dr. Schliemann, you haven't lost a patient yet."

"Thank you, nurse, but I'm running out of quinine. You'd better write to the Pharmacie Britannique to send us more posthaste."

Men who had been wounded, hurt or had cut themselves began coming from the length of the Troad. At dusk in the Dramali yard Sophia set up a big pot of boiling water with which she cleaned out the wound. Henry rubbed an ointment on the open sore and Sophia bandaged it. None of these strangers ever came back to report.

"I wonder if we killed them or cured them?" Henry mused.

Soon the villagers began bringing in their sick camels, horses, donkeys, sheep.

"Now I've become a veterinarian!" Henry groused. "What do I know about treating animals?"

"We have tincture of arnica in our medical box."

"I can use that for their sores or cuts, but I've never heard of giving arnica internally, have you?"

"Cure their outsides and leave their insides to God."

"Even that half is more than the Arabs will do. I once saw a camel at a camel market bleeding profusely from the nose. I pointed this out to his owner. He gave me a resigned smile and said, 'It is the will of Allah!'"

Yannakis brought reports that many of the animals had been made well.

"You know, Sophidion, of all the people we have treated, and the owners of the animals, not one of them has come back to thank us! Gratitude does not appear to be one of the virtues of the modern Trojan."

"Be content to know that you are considered a miracle man throughout the Troad. That will make our work here next year easier."

They found random medals, medals that seemed like commemorative objects cast to honor succeeding kings or emperors. Sophia took them home in the evening, scrubbed them and placed them in dated envelopes. Each day's depth surrendered up a different kind of object. They were now below six feet; the entire uphill trench was sixty feet long when they began finding an immense number of round articles of terra cotta, red, yellow, gray and black. Each piece had two holes at the top and was intact. Most of them had what appeared to be a potter's stamp on them. Sophia, who had charge of all the small objects they found, waited until Henry had recorded the depth and position of the finds, then carried them to their tarpaulin. Georgios Sarkis saw them, was disinterested, readily agreed to let Sophia take them home for cleaning and classifying.

Henry had built for her in their second room a separate plank table laid on Ciplak bricks. She handled the three- to four-inch terra cottas gingerly, washing them with a soft cloth and cold water. Beautiful decorations began to emerge. She called out in delight to Henry, who was writing in his journal.

"*Philtáte mou,* my dearest, here are our first works of art. Look at this one with a charming bird on it; and this one with a prancing horse. These would be deer, wouldn't they? And look at this one with the pretty young girl, her hands crossed demurely in front of her. What were they used for? How old are they?"

Henry took out his magnifying glass, distinguishing an altar with a bee with outspread wings above it, a bull, a swan, a child. They exchanged exclamations of surprise at the beauty.

"I simply don't know what they were used for. But those two holes at the top must mean something."

"They could be openings for thin strips of leather or wool thread. To wear or perhaps to hang on a wall, the way we hang our icons at home."

"Votive offerings, perhaps, to be hung in the temples as well as in the home? It could be. As to their age, these handmade shapes are too primitive to be Roman. After all, the Egyptians were using the pottery wheel as long ago as 4000 B.C., and everything the Egyptians knew, the Romans absorbed . . ."

". . . except how to build pyramids!"

Henry rewarded her with a one-note chuckle, said, "Put a string through a hole in each piece and attach to it the date of discovery, plus my note on the place of discovery."

After the first weeks of work, at which time they were down thirteen feet in the trench, they woke up to a heavy rain. The Renkoits would not come to the dig. Henry and Sophia were confined to their rooms. They used the day profitably, Henry writing a detailed report of his findings for the Greek Philological Society in Constantinople, which had agreed to publish anything he sent them in their society's journal. Sophia brought her diaries up to date and wrote letters home.

The Greeks would not work on Sundays or on Greek religious holidays, which were numerous.

"Even if I offered them a thousand francs an hour," he noted in his journal, "poor as the people are, and gladly as they would like to work, it is impossible to persuade them to do so on feast days, even if it be the day of some most unimportant saint. 'The saint will strike us' is their reply."

Yannakis scoured the countryside and found him twenty-five Turkish workmen. After watching them for a couple of days, Henry commented to Sophia:

"I would gladly increase their number if it were possible, for they work much better than the Asiatic Greeks, are more honest, and they work on Sundays and on the numerous saints' days. Since I can always be sure that they will work with unremitting zeal, I am going to pay the Turkish workmen proportionately higher wages than the Greeks."

Now on Sundays and Greek holidays there were eighty Turks scrambling over the hill. Yannakis had again fine-combed the countryside, this time to buy or rent any available tools he could find: shovels, picks, axes, long knives, metal bars. Henry rented four carts, each drawn by two oxen, to haul away the considerable tonnage of debris and earth, for the trench was now down twenty feet and up to the top of the mountain. It was no longer possible for him to supervise closely the several groups of men working in the different areas.

One night, after they had had a light supper of eggs, bread and tea, and had changed into their night robes, Henry began pacing their office room, obviously troubled.

"What's worrying you, Henry?"

"We can't wait any longer. We need to cut outside channels so we can carry off the dirt from the main trench and dump it at a distance. I must have an overseer to speed the work. Where can I turn? Perhaps in Çanakkale . . . ?"

"You'd have to be away from here for several days, and there is so little time until the winter rains. Hadn't we better cope for the next few weeks? Next year we can bring trained men with us from Athens."

"Yes, that's clearly indicated." Suddenly he twisted his head sideways, stared at her, and then chuckled. "We have our second foreman right in the bosom of our family."

"Henry, not me!"

"You!"

"You know what a low regard they have for women in this part of the world. In addition, they would never take orders from someone the age of their daughters. . . ."

"You'll think of something."

She shook her head in disbelief.

Henry located the relief lanes in both directions at right angles from the main trench. At five the next morning he marked off their dimension, chose ten men to work each channel, then said to them:

"Kyria Schliemann will direct this work. She knows precisely what I want and has been trained in science at the Arsakeion in Athens. In everything she says I want you to pay her the same respect you would pay to me. Anyone failing to do this will be discharged."

The workmen stared at him with sullen eyes. This outrage would cause them to lose face, not only with the other workers but with everyone in Renkoi when it was learned that they had been put in an inferior position to a woman. They would be laughed at; perhaps even lose control over their own families for having been publicly debased.

Sophia felt sorry for them. She knew something about Greek men and their fixed positions. But she could not let them quit, as they were threatening under their breath to do. Henry needed them. She decided that action, any action, was better than standing there on the side of the hill, flat-footed. She picked up a shovel, dug down hard, started loosening the topsoil inside Henry's markers. She neither looked at nor spoke to the Renkoits. They gathered in tight groups, rolling cigarettes from the tobacco each raised in his yard.

Sophia continued to dig, pitching each shovelful downhill. After some time she sensed a change in the atmosphere. Gradually the men had picked up their tools and begun to work behind her . . . but at a pace about half of that of the men in the main channel.

"It's all right," she thought, "they have to have a way to protest. I won't say anything today. Let them seethe themselves out."

That evening when they returned to Ciplak Henry was furious about the slowdown.

"I'll give them a tongue-lashing in the morning."

"No, Henry, you are not to speak to them. I am their foreman, and I have to win them over in a manner that will keep them won. Let me puzzle it out for myself."

The next morning she was relieved to find that all of her workers had returned. She greeted each of them with a pleasant albeit formal "Good morning" in Turkish. The men continued at their slow pace, pickaxes and baskets toted on one shoulder. She gave no sign. After an hour she noticed that one of the men was sweating profusely. She put the palm of her hand on his forehead and felt the fever. She exchanged a few words with Henry, then said to Yannakis:

"Put him on a mule. We'll take him to the house in Ciplak."

The Dramali family was not happy at the sight of Yannakis carrying the stricken man upstairs but, as Yannakis repeated their exchange to her:

"We cannot refuse the Drs. Schliemann. They cured our daughter."

Yannakis made a bed of blankets on the floor of the office. Sophia measured out sixteen grains of quinine, then held the cup of water to the man's lips. That night she gave him another dose, and a third one at dawn. He needed nothing more, silently walking over to the dig that afternoon to return home with his fellow Renkoits.

The next morning her two crews picked up their tools and settled into a normal stride. The slowdown was ended.

Toward the end of October living conditions in Ciplak became appalling. It began to rain every few days; the dirt roads of the village became ankle-deep mud bogs. The Dramali courtyard through which they passed to reach the entrance door was now crowded with the family's animals. After dusk, when the Schliemanns returned from work, it was impossible not to slip and founder in the various forms of droppings and manures, the stench of which penetrated their bedroom. The cold and rain seeped through the stone blocks of their rooms, leaving the insides so damp that oozing water flowed down the cracks, moving at right angles where the joints moved horizontally, and then downward again to form puddles on the warped wooden floors. Their clothes, hardy as they had been, became worn, never seemed dry. Physical exhaustion enabled them to get four or five hours' sleep a night.

Combined with the excitement of the day, it sufficed.

The pace of the work increased. There were rarely fewer than eighty Greek and Turkish workers on the hill. Henry was an efficient administrator in getting the masses of earth moved. But it was one of Sophia's crews which unearthed, close to the main trench, the first pots for which they had been searching: small earthen vessels of coarse workmanship, some intact, others broken. They were undoubtedly kitchen utensils. Sophia wrapped the intact pots in rough sacking to protect them, numbering them on the spot and adding the location of the find. The broken vessels presented a problem: in a group find, from what had apparently been the kitchen of a good-sized house, there was no way to tell which shards belonged together.

"You must gather them all," said Henry, "we will clean the pieces and lay them out on your worktable. Then we'll simply start matching the fragments and paste together the parts that fit."

They worked until past midnight, cleaning the intact pots and writing descriptions of them, then washing diligently all the shards before putting them on the wooden planks for assembly . . .

". . . on rainy days here," Henry suggested, "or back home in Athens where we can get a supply of plaster to fill in the missing spaces. We'll have to cook our own hot 'rabbit' or 'fishskin' glue."

Sophia was disappointed because there were no decorations of any kind.

"Made for use, not beauty," she murmured. "Without decorations, how do we learn what age they come from?"

"A very primitive one, if they're so bare. More disappointing still, I can't find the remains of any food clinging to the bottoms. It has evaporated or dissolved over the ages."

"Can we really find pots of food that are still in good condition?"

"The mound will tell us."

Their next finds were more puzzling than the "votive offerings": terra cottas hard as stone, some round as a ball, others "exactly the shape of the humming tops I played with in Ankershagen where my father had his parish," Henry observed.

They were in the form of cones, volcanoes, hemispheres, about an inch thick, each with a hole in the center. After Sophia had donned a work apron and had a pot of warm water brought up from the kitchen, she found that under the incrustations, though on one side only, there was a variety of marvelous linear decorations radiating out symmetrically from the center hole.

"Isn't it strange," she exclaimed, after she had laid out a batch of thirty of them for Henry's inspection, "no more birds, animals, or human figures such as we found only a few feet above these line carvings? Do you suppose they come from another culture?"

Henry held one of the pieces in his hand, the one on which there was a circle of *sauvastikas* inscribed, the double crosses running in an opposite direction from the swastika.

"I recognize this *sauvastika* from early Indian art, also Chinese art. Yes, they must come from a different age. The only question is, earlier or later? Which art did man practice first? These linear decorations, splendidly executed but still simple in design; or the faithful reproduction of birds, animals and people? We'll show both kinds to the professors at the University of Athens when we get back. They will know."

It was below the twenty-foot depth that they began uncovering calcined ruins of houses seemingly built in layers on top of each other. For Sophia this was the most interesting discovery; for the first time she was standing in the midst of a city, or a series of cities built one upon the other, in which people had been born, grown up, married, had children, shepherded their flocks and cultivated their fields for centuries on end. Then she came across several round vertebrae from the backbone of a huge animal or fish.

Henry studied the bone structure.

"Sharks' vertebrae, of which walking sticks are often made. The existence of these vertebrae seems to prove that in remote antiquity our Aegean Sea contained sharks."

"You must be careful when you swim."

He was amused. "No sharks now. Or in Homer's time, for that matter."

"How in the world does a shark get up almost a hundred feet above sea level? Can it be from the time when the whole world was covered with water?"

"Perhaps." He smiled gently at her as she stood with her feet deep in a trench, her hair tied in a knot on top of her head and wrapped in a Turkish *feredjé* to keep it free of dust. "Or perhaps the natives stripped off the flesh and cooked it over fires at the shore. The meat is generally unpalatable; but if people are hungry enough . . . They could have carried the skeletons up here to make tools or weapons out of the bones. Fire burned them out. Look here at these calcined ruins, the several layers we have laid bare on the side wall of the trench. At this depth all the buildings seem to have been destroyed by fire. I think we'll find only a few stone Troys, three or four at the most. The rest were built of wood, with thatch and straw roofs. One spark and the whole town is burned to the ground."

He directed her attention to an area three feet away.

"From these layers of ash it would appear that the people waited until the embers had cooled, then came in, leveled, spread fresh earth and built the town all over again. When the fires started the families could collect their spare food, tools, votive offerings and take off for the Scamander. It could not have been a serious blow because the people had so little to lose. With the woods close by, timber was readily available for new homes and hearths. They could make new cooking and storage pots in a few days."

The next day they came upon immense quantities of mussel shells and a smaller quantity of oyster shells.

"Just like good Greeks," Sophia murmured, her eyes twinkling, "the Trojans loved their shellfish. Homer speaks of them baking bread from wheat and having quantities of barley. We'll have to wait to find animal bones to know what kind of meat they ate."

"We know from *The Iliad* that they roasted lamb, oxen, geese, heifers, in addition to all the wild game they could capture: boar, deer, rabbit. . . . Between the fruit of the sea and the meat of the woods, our ancient friends ate well."

Each day evolved its own treasure and excitement, with stunning contrasts in the nature of the finds. Farther up the hill, lying at a depth of only five feet, in the ruins of the big building, they unearthed three marble slabs, from fifteen to twenty-five inches long, each of them containing a considerable inscription carved out with hammer and chisel. They washed off the slabs with water from their drinking can, then examined the writings. Henry paled a little.

"Sophia, how I have been hoping to find a written language! It would be a discovery of inestimable worth. Particularly if this was a temple!"

Sophia had been studying the letters and figuring out individual words. She put her hand sympathetically on his.

"I'm afraid not, *philtate mou*. It's ancient Greek, and probably not from a temple. Look here, at these individual words: council, citizenship, taxes, right to hold land . . ."

Henry's eyes drowned in pools of lost hope.

". . . yes . . . I see . . . then it must have been a city hall or council chamber."

"There's Sarkis. He's seen the slabs. Tell him we'll clean them and translate them tonight."

Sarkis agreed on condition that they show him the marbles in their workroom the following morning. Sophia and Henry were too stimulated to eat supper, contenting themselves with fresh fruit and honey. It took a thick brush and plenty of pressure to clean out the writing on all three slabs.

"You tackle the large one, since you have already deciphered some of the words," Henry suggested. "I'll rely on what Vimpos taught me of ancient Greek to get a reading on the smaller two."

It took her until one o'clock in the morning but she came out with a roughly readable translation of the three-hundred-pound marble, which had been brought to the house in an oxcart and carried upstairs by Yannakis:

> Since Diaphenes Polleos Temnites, being in the presence of the king, continues being friendly and well-minded toward the people, readily providing services to anyone who might call on him, it is to be resolved that he, the king, commends Temnites to the council and the people on these terms: to summons him and for all time to be grateful for the collection of the people's taxes, and to him is given citizenship. These rights having been given to him are to be registered on this slab and hung up in . . .

Henry emerged with a rougher translation of the two smaller slabs; they proved to be on a similar theme: the granting of civil or economic rights to specifically named individuals.

Sarkis was waiting at the house when Henry returned from his swim at five the next morning. He brought the quiet, patently disinterested overseer upstairs. Sophia served them coffee, then Henry read a capsule translation in Turkish of what the slabs said. Sophia noted that he made all three sound equally important. Sarkis was pleased to accept the two smaller slabs, as Henry suggested. It left the larger and more complete one in the Schliemanns' possession. When Sarkis had left, Sophia observed archly:

"Am I mistaken, or did you flimflam our Mr. Sarkis?"

Henry grinned impishly.

"Perhaps a little. But how often does an American get a chance to best an Armenian in a trade?"

Henry's first article, which was made up of a verbatim report from his day-by-day diary, was published by the *Journal of the Greek Philological Society* in Constantinople. It was well received. He had also submitted a report to the *Newspaper of the Debates* in Athens. He hoped it would find equal favor. Sophia, who was giving her hair a thorough brushing, said:

"I don't see why not. You've reported only what we have found, with scientific descriptions of the objects and the places they were excavated. You have not indulged in theories about Troy . . ."

"I expressed my conviction that it is here."

He decided to clean out the Roman well they had discovered. The lightest of the workmen was lowered into it on a rope. He dug, the baskets of earth were hauled up. They contained no interesting artifacts. Henry hung his head over the side of the well, called down:

"How far down do you think this well goes?"

"All the way to hell!"

"Then wrap the rope around you and come up. We're not ready to find and excavate the nether world."

The next day was a Sunday. The Greeks would not work. Yannakis announced that the Turks were sowing their crops. Henry said:

"Sophia, we've been here over a month, let's bring our journals up to date. Then we'll ride out to Frederick Calvert's house, near Bounarbashi. He said to come any Sunday. For dinner. He'll show you why his home is unquestionably located on top of Troy."

She clapped her hands with pleasure.

"It will be good to go out into society again. I'll have a bath and put on my best dress. But first I want to reread the last couple of letters from the family about Andromache. When I read the letters I see her before my eyes, and I know she is thriving."

Henry looked appraisingly at his wife: her soft dark hair parted in the middle, combed behind the ears; the slim, symmetrical oval of her face coming to rest securely on the characterful chin; the straight, aquiline nose and the full-lipped mouth, so joyous now.

After her bath she donned a two-piece green wool suit with a crimson blouse and gold buttons down the front of the long tailored jacket.

"You are an enigma, little Sophidion. In Paris, amid the luxuries of our apartment and all the pleasures of the most sophisticated city in the world, you were unhappy and frequently ill. Here, in the most prim-

itive surroundings possible, with no diversion but work, you are in-
destructible."

She gave him a broad smile.

"Look at you!" he persisted. "With little food and less sleep, you are
as beautiful as the Aphrodite sculpted by Praxiteles. Pliny called it the
finest statue not only by Praxiteles but in the whole world. It was
placed in an open shrine and was visible from all four sides, and from
all four sides, Pliny says, it was equally admired. Lucian speaks of 'the
smile playing gently over her parted lips' and 'the melting gaze of the
eyes with their bright and joyous expression.'"

"It's because I'm happy, Errikaki."

He blushed with pleasure; it was her pet name for him, "little Henry,"
and she used it only in moments of deep love.

5.

It was a crisp late October day, with sheer clarity for miles, both to
the mountains and the sea, and high banks of white clouds of the consistency of the snows on Mt. Ida moved northward as Sophia and Henry
rode down the ox trail to the main road and then turned south for the
five-mile ride to Thymbria, the two-story mansion which Frederick Calvert and his wealthy wife had built in the early sixties. Frederick Calvert
had been the British consul general at the Dardanelles for fifteen years
now; apparently Her Majesty's Government did not hold his brother
Frank's conviction for treason against him.

There was a long driveway leading to the house lined with pines and
raised banks of yellow flowers. A groom took their horses, they climbed
several steps to double golden doors and were admitted by a butler.
Frederick Calvert and his wife were as formally dressed for their Sunday dinner as though they had just returned from services in Canter-
bury Cathedral. Frederick was older than Frank, and more full-blown,
with red puffy cheeks, long sideburns and pale blue eyes. His wife was
older still, white-haired, wearing an English printed silk dress. They received the Schliemanns cordially, inviting them upstairs to sit on a balcony with an iron balustrade, where they sipped an apéritif overlooking
the olive groves Mrs. Calvert had had planted on the fertile farm lands
and the Roman barrel vaults she had built to serve as a reservoir for
trapping the mountain waters.

They were served a typically British dinner in the wood-paneled diningroom: a barley soup, rare roast beef, Yorkshire pudding, green beans,
a trifle, a white and then a red wine. Sophia was grateful for the English
she had learned that summer, for the Calverts had no other language.

The conversation was genial: stories of London, Paris, Athens, which the Calverts knew and admired; and wonderment that Sophia and Henry had so well tolerated life in the two rooms of the Dramalis' crude house in Ciplak, and the rugged stretch of work on the mound.

Mrs. Calvert asked Sophia how she was managing with the food.

"We've been on short rations," Sophia admitted.

"You intend to dig out here for six to eight months next year?"

"That's my husband's intention."

"Then surely you will have to bring a cook with you?"

"Mr. Schliemann intends to build us a house on the edge of our excavation this spring. Close by he will build a kitchen and storeroom. We'll either bring a cook from Athens or let our paymaster, Yannakis, cook for us."

"Is he English?"

"Turkophone. A monster in size and strength, with the soul of a kitten. He scours the countryside for food for us, vegetables, fruits, a wild rabbit—wild is best—or a lamb, and cooks our Sunday dinner. He is surprisingly good. When he fills the house with the smells of Greek cooking the Dramali family flees."

In the drawingroom, over a liqueur, Frederick Calvert asked Henry what he had been finding. Henry gave an account of the huge foundation stones, coins, medals, terra-cotta votive offerings, the variously decorated pots, the sharks' vertebrae. Calvert listened with good-natured indulgence.

"Nothing very startling." He turned to Sophia, said not unkindly, "I admire your husband, Mrs. Schliemann, but you know of course that he's completely wrong about the location of Troy."

"How is that, Mr. Calvert?"

"Because Troy is right here, on our five-thousand-acre farm. Come, we'll find you a pair of walking boots, and I'll show you all the proofs from *The Iliad*."

Henry rose, tipped her a wink, said:

"You said you wanted to see Bounarbashi. Frederick Calvert is the best possible guide."

Their host had the groom bring out the family carriage. They drove around a swamp which had resulted from plugged-up springs, then stopped at the ancient settlement of Thymbria, which Frank Calvert had excavated a few years earlier, and where he had located a temple of Apollo and several valuable inscriptions. Frederick Calvert then had the groom cross the southern end of the Troad plain and drive up the opposite bank until they came to another ancient town encompassed in several places by ramparts; shards of pottery were visible on the hillside. When they had descended from the carriage, Calvert bowed low to Sophia, said:

"Madame Schliemann, you are now standing on Bounarbashi, the site of ancient Troy."

"I'm enchanted, Mr. Calvert. But how can I tell?"

"I will show you. Come, walk a little distance with me. There! The two springs, one hot, one cold, where the Trojan women washed their clothing. Please feel the temperature of each."

She did. There was a slight difference in temperature. She straightened up and, as Frederick Calvert strode forward, Henry whispered in her ear:

"Don't ask him about the other forty-two springs close by."

Calvert turned, his cheeks red with victory.

"You know, of course, that I have two of the world's greatest scholars on my side. The first was Demetrius of Scepsis, who wrote that Bounarbashi was the site of Troy. This was confirmed by Strabo, who called Bounarbashi 'the village of the Trojans.' "

Henry said quietly at her side:

"Strabo was never here! But Alexander the Great hung up his armor in the Temple of Athena at Hissarlik in honor of the Trojans! And Xerxes sacrificed a thousand oxen on our mound in honor of Athena in 480 B.C. Herodotus is our authority."

As they walked over the ground and Calvert continued to extoll the historical virtues of his farm as the site of Troy, Henry finally became impatient.

"What about the distance to the Achaean camp at the mouth of the Dardanelles? You are a good eight miles away. It would take the Achaean army a full day just to march from here to the Hellespont and back, let alone fight a prolonged battle. Yet Homer specifically says that the Achaean army twice in one day went from their ships to the walls of Troy to fight, and then returned. Explain that."

"Easy!" retorted Calvert, unruffled. "All of the land between here and the Hellespont is alluvial. It was created by the overflowing of the old Scamander River beds. In the days of Troy the Hellespont was only three miles from here, and so was the camp of the Achaeans!"

Henry forbore. He had assembled evidence from geographers that none of this land, from Bounarbashi or from Troy, to the Hellespont, was alluvial. On the way home he told Sophia:

"The land between Troy and Kum Kale, which Frederick Calvert wipes out with his alluvial theory that it would all have been covered by the waters of the Hellespont, is original earth, the same as it was during the Trojan War. There are many deep tanks on the Plain of Troy, and one doesn't find deep pools and reservoirs on alluvial land.

But Frederick Calvert still convinces people; even the few who will concede that there was a Troy still want to place it at Bounarbashi, where Demetrius and Strabo said it was. God keep us from the mistakes and misjudgments which get into the flowing rivers of history and are perpetuated there."

They were riding their horses back to Hissarlik in the gloaming, for the Calverts had insisted that they stay for "a typical English tea, with toasted muffins and jam," before they started the journey back to the rigors of Ciplak. Sophia held the reins in her right hand, extended her left to take Henry's hand.

"No need to reassure me, Henry. It was good of you to take me to Bounarbashi; Frederick Calvert's arguments can't be all that pleasant to you."

"Ah, no! But that roast beef and Yorkshire pudding! Now they were pleasant, wouldn't you say?"

On Monday, October 30, his eighty workmen carried the trench to the top of the mound, a little over a hundred feet above the base of the hill. It was now fifteen feet deep, all the way up. At the very crest, where he had expected to find the noblest buildings of Troy, Henry was astonished to see the workmen unearth instead stone lances made of diorite, stone hammers, stone axes, weights of granite, hand mills for grinding made of lava rock, great numbers of flint knives, saws; needles and bodkins made of bone; primitive terra-cotta canoes which looked like salt and pepper holders; whetstones of green and black slate. Mixed in were pots of the crudest workmanship.

Sophia laid out their finds on the tarpaulin at the head of the trench. As the day progressed the workmen continued to hand up hundreds of stone objects, which threw Henry from sore puzzlement into consternation. A tic raised and lowered a muscle along his left cheekbone. He cried to Sophia:

"This is inexplicable to me! I don't understand how it is possible in the present stratum to find stone implements. I cannot explain why we are finding things which must have been used by uncivilized men of the stone period, but which could not have been made with the rude implements at their disposal. Why are we finding boars' tusks when it is inconceivable to me that men of the stone period, with their imperfect blunt weapons, were able to kill wild boars?"

Sophia did not know how to comfort him in his highly perturbed state. She said in as calming a tone as she could muster:

"Why don't we just take all the implements home with us this afternoon? Yannakis can carry them in panniers on a donkey. We'll wash and group them; write the detailed descriptions into your journals . . ."

He interrupted:

"I'll do more than that! I will state quite honestly everything that is inexplicable to me; that has astonished me and demolished all . . . all . . . my theories about where the Watchtower, the great defense wall, Priam's palace, Hector's palace . . . were located."

"A theory is only a tool. If one tool won't get the job done, you have to fashion another."

"Is that a Greek proverb?" he asked sarcastically.

He paced their workroom most of the night, taking into his hands, after Sophia had cleaned them, an ax, a saw, a lance, a knife, a hand mill, examining each minutely, either talking to them or to himself, or both, she could not decide. She heard him muttering over and over.

"How can the golden city of Troy lie below a Stone Age culture? It's impossible!"

She finally got him to bed by pleading her own exhaustion, cradled his head on her shoulder as she did Andromache's, and soothed him to sleep . . . but lay awake herself the rest of the night, worried about him and how he would accept this contradiction and defeat.

"Could it be, God forbid, that Henry has failed to find Homer's Troy where he thought it was, because *there is no Troy?* At least not here, on this mount!"

She eased her free arm under her head as though to bolster it.

"No, that cannot be true! *I must have faith.*"

The rest of the week was equally confounding. The rains and mud added to Henry's depression. They dug below the fifteen-foot level of the trench, the twenty-foot depth, and then twenty-five. The stone objects disappeared. They found a piece of silver wire, vases with elegant designs, and finally a lead plate with a raised "J" in its center. Henry was flabbergasted:

"A Stone Age on top of a highly advanced culture? History doesn't work that way."

"It could, Henry. Wars and invasions can upset the idea of progress."

His eyelids flared.

"Of course! An advanced culture overrun and destroyed by barbarians. It has happened many times!"

That night, cold in the damp of the workroom, wrapped in a blanket from the bed, he sat and wrote in his journal:

> My expectations are extremely modest. The single object of my excavations from the beginning was only to find Troy, whose site has been discussed by a hundred scholars in a hundred books, but which as yet no one has ever sought to bring to light by excavations. If I should not succeed in this, still I

shall be perfectly contented, if by my labors I succeed only in penetrating to the deepest darkness of prehistoric times, and enriching archaeology by the discovery of a few interesting features from the most ancient history of the great Hellenic race. The discovery of the stone period, instead of discouraging me, has therefore only made me the more desirous to penetrate to the place which was occupied by the first people that came here, and I still intend to reach it even if I should have to dig another fifty feet farther down.

"That sounds more like you, Henry. You had me frightened."

"The heart of Troy should be here. It is not. Then where is it? In which direction? It *has to* overlook the triangle between the two rivers and their nearly joining mouths on the Dardanelles. Next year we'll stay on this north side, but start fifty feet farther down the mount, moving westward to where the hill juts out into the Troad triangle. From there we can level out and make a platform of the entire northwest area. That is where the palaces, watchtowers, Scaean Gate must be."

Disappointment mingled with reaffirmation across his features, his face lean and weathered from the weeks on the mound.

"It was a good first try, and we have learned a great deal. After all, there are no textbooks to guide us."

Sophia picked up his journal, patted it, said:

"You are writing the textbook."

BOOK FOUR

A SACRED LOCALITY

1.

EVEN before they made for Mousson Street they rode out to Colonos to collect Andromache. Now seven months old, she was a husky, open-faced, good-natured baby, pulling herself upright on the legs of chairs, babbling for hours without uttering a word. Her face was almost a replica of Sophia's: dark hair, dark eyes, strong aquiline nose and chin, a bit plump at the moment since Madame Victoria considered that every bite a baby swallowed was a defense against the Devil. The chubby Andromache and the lean Schliemanns moved back happily into the comforts of Mousson Street. The slightly overcrowded aspect of the rooms was a sensual joy after the bareness of their two rooms at the Dramalis'. For Henry the single greatest deliverance appeared to be their *matrimoniale*, about which he declared, "What a joy not to have to wipe it down with oil and alcohol each night!" For Sophia it was the kitchen, the stove and cooking utensils, the clean air and fresh odors of a luscious zucchini soufflé and a chicken *kapama* made with cinnamon, tomatoes, onions, garlic, macaroni and cheese.

They moved in their boxes, unpacked their finds, hammered up new shelves, and within a week it was as though they had never been away. At the Austrian Embassy they purchased an exquisite chandelier for their livingroom and glassware for their table. The diningroom now became the center of their professional life. Greeks rarely asked outsiders into their homes, preferring to meet at the cafés for convivial visits. Henry, European bred, began inviting for midday dinner specialists in those fields in which he needed help: engineers who could teach them more efficient ways of digging and disposing of the debris, scholars who could identify the objects they had brought from Hissarlik, museum officials who knew how to clean and restore terra cotta.

Sophia welcomed the entertaining. She located a new young helper from a family the Engastromenoses had known in Romvis Square. When the girl returned from the early shopping at the Central Market, followed by a small boy with the basket of purchases on his head, Sophia spent the rest of the morning preparing the midday meal. Cooking became more than an agreeable pastime, it was a form of self-expression to prepare a roast suckling pig stuffed with cheese and parsley, and then add tart apples; after the deprivations of Hissarlik it was particularly gratifying. The baby banged on the tray of her high chair with a stout mixing spoon and then, tiring, fell asleep amidst the aroma of cooking spices, the sweet smell of baking pecan bars, her cheeks red from the heat given off by the five-lid coal stove.

Henry left early each morning with a sheaf of stationery in his hands for the Fair Greece and its imported newspapers from Europe, England and America fastened in layers to wooden poles. He read them over numerous coffees and broke into the reading to write letters in half a dozen languages to his associates. He returned home in time to dangle a new toy in front of his daughter's clutching fingers before she was put in her crib for the afternoon nap.

Prime Minister Koumoundouros's government had fallen just as Sophia and Henry left Athens for the Troad and now, upon their return, the government of Prime Minister Zaïmis was also ended, Parliament dissolved and new elections ordered for February 1872. Despite this political turmoil in Greece, the mayor of Athens, Panayis Kyriakos, was building the city into the world capital which Henry had foreseen. He had constructed a handsome town hall, improved the city's night lighting, paved more of its principal streets, begun work on a municipal theater in the square opposite the National Bank. There was a renewed feeling of optimism in the city; land values shot up. Henry was offered a substantial profit on two of the lots he had bought. He did not accept.

"One buys good land," he told Sophia; "one never sells. Instead of being land poor, we are now land rich!"

The economics of Henry's thinking was not clear to Sophia but she took his ebullient attitude as tacit permission to furnish the third bedroom for Andromache. She bought a bed for the child, a rug, bureau, curtains and draperies, and then a bed for the young nanny she brought in from Colonos. Henry seemed as pleased as though he had not forbidden her to furnish the room or hire a nanny only a few months before.

Relations with her family were congenial. Henry had left a substantial sum of money with Madame Victoria with which to purchase whatever the baby needed; he had continued Georgios on salary, and had guaranteed an extended credit for the shop so that Alexandros was now able to buy most of the foreign goods he needed. The Engastromenos family had a bit of spare cash with which to buy clothing and other necessities of which they had been deprived for two years. Madame Victoria began talking again of moving back into Athens.

It was a happy time for Sophia. Everyone was cared for.

On the eve of the New Year, 1872, St. Basil's Day, Sophia and Henry went out to Colonos to celebrate. At midnight the traditional pie, baked with a coin hidden inside it, was cut by Georgios into twelve parts. The one who found the coin in his slice would be the lucky person for the New Year. Even Madame Victoria, who had baked the pie, could not tell where it had lodged.

Panaghiotes had the coin. Everyone was pleased, for he would be entering the gymnasium in the fall.

Then the gifts were exchanged, simple tokens of affection. Sophia had shopped for gloves for her two sisters, Henry had bought neckties for Spyros and Katingo's husband Ioannes, books for Panaghiotes, a leather wallet for Alexandros. He had insisted that Sophia's parents receive something special for having watched over Andromache; they found a gold watch for Madame Victoria in Stephanou's jewelry shop, and a gold-headed cane for Georgios, who had been seen gazing longingly at it in the window of Katsimbalis's store. On the way to Colonos Henry had stopped the carriage at the Confiserie Lycabettus on Syntagma Square to buy a large box of chocolates for the Colonos house. When he returned to his seat beside Sophia he said:

"Did you know that houses have feelings just like people? If you treat a house shabbily your days in it will be troubled. If you treat a house well . . ."

". . . you will find happiness in it!"

She threw her arms about her husband's neck and kissed him.

"My dear Errikaki, New Year's Eve seems a proper time to tell you that I love you. My parents made a good choice for me."

He trembled as he held her against him in the dark of the carriage.

"As Bishop Vimpos made the best possible choice for me!"

In Paris, although Sophia had in title been the mistress of the household, she had in fact been little more than a silent guest at her husband's board. Here in Mousson Street that was changed. Her first Sunday party was a dinner for Stephanos Koumanoudes of the University of Athens, a professor of Latin philology, the Greek language and literature. He was renowned for his efforts to collect and preserve whatever remained of Greek antiquity from vases and ancient inscriptions to the Dionysus Theater on their side of the Acropolis. He was also the secretary of the Archaeological Society, had revived their *Archaeological Newspaper* and had read Henry's three reports from Hissarlik. Though he was only four years older than Henry, his achievements had already made him world famous.

After dinner, with the two men puffing contentedly on their cigars, the three went into Henry's office. Sophia had pasted labels beneath each vase, pot and stone tool placed on the new shelves, giving the depth and location at which it had been found.

"Yes, a good beginning," murmured Professor Koumanoudes in his mild voice; "now let us put our heads together and discuss the age and civilization of each piece."

Henry, humble in the presence of great minds, said:

"You understand, Professor, we make no claim of prehistory for any of these pieces. But we have high hopes that next year we can dig down to the native earth of the mount."

The following Sunday Dr. Émile Burnouf came for dinner. He had arrived in Athens in 1846, after taking his university degree in Paris, to become an assistant at the French Archaeological Institute on Syntagma Square. By the age of forty-six he had worked his way up to director, was having designs drawn for a superb new institute on Mt. Lycabettus and was planning for excavations at Delphi and in the Peloponnesus. Burnouf was short in stature, wore his hair down to his collar, as well as a mustache and a thin strip of beard along the cheekbones and chin. He was an intense man, with the small man's fastidious attention to every detail of his clothing: ruffled silk shirts, handsome cravats, wide-shouldered coats made for him by his tailor in Paris. He brought along his nineteen-year-old daughter Louise, who had grown up in Athens. She was a beauty in the French tradition, with looks the exact opposite of Sophia's: long silky blond hair, eyes as blue as delphiniums, a slender oval face, cupid-bow lips and just enough chin to hold up her bottom lip.

Henry was enchanted by Louise, speaking French to her during dinner. Sophia spoke Greek with Monsieur Burnouf but never quite found out where Madame Burnouf was, or why her place had been taken by her daughter.

Burnouf believed that a couple of the Hissarlik pots might be Trojan, particularly a round one with its handles extended upward like arms, but it was the large quantity of shards that excited him.

"My dear Dr. Schliemann, you may have many authentic Trojan pots lying here in pieces. They can teach us a great deal about the terra-cotta calligraphy of the time. You must reassemble them."

"My wife and I are most eager to do so."

"Two of my students are expert in the process. Why don't you and Mrs. Schliemann come to the institute on Tuesday morning? Bring along two or three of your baskets of shards. Louise and I will also help. It is a most amusing game, reassembling a vase that is in a dozen pieces. I hope you have some from tombs. If not, those from the kitchens or storehouses are second best."

When they arrived in Syntagma Square early Tuesday morning two tall, slender French students with scraggily blond beards came out to the carriage to carry in the baskets. They had cleared a long table in their assembly room, on which they had placed several rubber baskets called *zymbyli*, half filled with cold water. Director Burnouf and Louise came in to welcome them.

"The process is a simple, even primitive one, but it works. Let's take all the shards and place them in the *zymbyli*."

The students guided the earth-encrusted shards into the water to prevent breakage. When the water became muddied it was changed for fresh. When it remained clear, the shards were taken out and cleaned with a rag or brush or even a fingernail. They were then set out in long rows to dry. Then came the sorting of the clays; the coarse were separated from the fine, the figured, designed finishes from the plain, the differing colors divided into still other groups.

"Now comes the best part," exclaimed Louise.

Not to be outdone by the lithe beauty, Sophia said, "We learned in Hissarlik how best to start. We assembled the tops and bottoms of the pots first, they are the most easily recognized . . ."

". . . exactly," broke in Burnouf. "After that we can rebuild the walls."

They spent a couple of delightful hours among the dozens of shards, crying out with pleasure when a piece fitted into a pattern. All of them worked with equal zeal. Burnouf explained:

"The more experience you gain, the more quickly you will be able to tell by looking at a group of matching shards what the shape of the piece was originally. I think we have enough to start with now. Gentlemen, will you prepare the fish glue."

The students brought out several thin flat amber sheets and placed them in a pot which stood on a brazier. As the water came to a boil and the glue dissolved, the room became permeated with the stench of dead fish.

"Not in my kitchen," Sophia resolved, holding her nose. "Henry is going to have to build a shack at the back of the garden."

When the glue reached the required consistency it was taken off the fire and placed on the long table. The students then painted the glue onto the breaks with a small brush, holding each shard until the glue flowed into the pores of the clay. This done, the pieces were joined together and held over a flame until they became strongly attached. Moving upward from the bottom, they built a vase or pot as one builds a house of bricks.

They emerged with two complete pots and one vase with missing fragments. Burnouf told Sophia to use India ink and a fine-pointed pen first to give the whole pot its number for her notebook, and then a number written very small on each assembled shard to correspond with the number and location she already had for it.

"Now the final step," exclaimed Burnouf. "We prepare the plaster, mixed with water and fish glue, and model the shapes of our missing pieces. Louise is a trained artist; she is best at this task."

When the off-white plaster was of the right thickness, Louise with her long tapering fingers adroitly made patch-pieces the shape of the vacancies. When they had hardened the students applied the glue to the edges as well as to the assembled shards, let the glue be absorbed and then applied heat to fuse them.

"Voilà!" cried Burnouf. "We have just re-created your first incomplete vase. When you go back to Hissarlik, if you should find the missing parts, we will take out the plaster insertions and rejoin the original piece to its mother pot."

Henry insisted on taking everyone to the Eptanesos, the Ionian Islands restaurant above the Fair Greece on Ermou Street. At the dinner table he sat with the charming Louise beside him and launched into a long story in French. Sophia was amused. She said to herself:

"I may not be a trained artist but, alimono mou, I'll be damned if I can't make plaster patches as well as she can!"

Prior to the birth of Andromache, Henry had been a stranger to the family, an eccentric alien from a potpourri of foreign countries with whom they could have little in common. A thousand years before Christ the Greeks had called all peoples who spoke a different tongue "barbarians." Fortunately Henry had spoken Greek; but it was not his native language and a little of the opprobrium had hung on. Within the mystique of family, which was the most overriding of all Greek allegiances, Henry had joined his blood to theirs by siring a child with Sophia. Now, early in January, Sophia announced that she was carrying again . . . a child she had conceived in Hissarlik. Henry kissed her exuberantly, exclaimed:

"On the law of averages this one has to be my Greek son."

In Hissarlik Henry had put his worldly affairs completely out of mind, given instructions to her father that all checks be deposited, bills paid, correspondence about his many investments held for him unopened. He had never discussed matters of business while caught in the throes of digging, nor had they entered his mind. Now he attacked the piles of mail and telegrams on his desk, sorting them in methodical fashion, issuing orders, balancing books, buying and selling railroad stocks, sending monies to his brothers, his sisters, his children in Russia. He enjoyed the activity.

However, his converse preoccupation was as highly organized, as he made meticulous preparations for a major six-month assault on Hissarlik to begin the following April, establishing an equation between the largest number of men he could usefully employ, the number of foremen needed to direct and supervise them, the quantity of tools and implements required. During the latter weeks of their first dig they had averaged eighty workmen a day, with only himself and Sophia to supervise the crews. Now he wanted to take two experienced foremen with him from Athens.

"Experienced in what?" Sophia asked, a quizzical furrow between her eyebrows.

"Preferably mining. But I doubt there are any available in Greece. The next choice would be men who have built railroads."

"You're right. They have to dig through mountains. Do you know where to locate them?"

He grinned. "By going to the railroad. Your dinner guest tomorrow is an Englishman, Mr. John Latham from Folkestone, England. He managed a railroad running southeast from London to Dover and Folkestone. Now he directs, most profitably, the railroad from Athens to Piraeus. Don't let his formal exterior fool you; he is a man of warmth and humor."

Latham arrived on Sunday with flowers for Sophia. He was a clean-shaven Englishman of middle years who carried himself as stiffly as a rolled-up umbrella. Sophia unwound him with the dinner she had cooked after an inquiry at the British Embassy as to what dishes an expatriate Englishman might most enjoy. She had never before prepared roast beef, but she followed the strictures about keeping it rare; and attempted a Yorkshire pudding out of her leaflike phyllo pastry from which she made cheese puffs and cheese pies. The pudding was not a success but John Latham was amused and touched by her effort, and told her nostalgic stories of his mother's cooking.

"Everywhere I go on the Continent," he confided, "I am informed that the English are the worst cooks in the world. Yet I grew up thinking my mother's food was delicious."

By the time they reached the study Mr. Latham had agreed to lend them two of his best workers. Henry contracted to cover their travel expenses, find them lodgings, pay them a bonus for living in the Troad away from their families for half a year. He became excited.

"Now we can employ as high as one hundred and thirty workmen and have them well supervised." He turned to his wife. "But you know, Sophia, what we really need if we are going to level a work platform through the entire width of Hissarlik is an engineer. One who could make a detailed survey of the mountain so that we would have accurate figures on the width, length, height; an estimate of how many cubic yards of earth we will have to move; who could chart the dumping sites for the debris."

Henry addressed himself to his newly acquired friend.

"I don't mean to impose on your work staff, Mr. Latham, but do you have an engineer you can spare for, say, a month? I would pay him a top salary."

Latham tried to ease down the high starched collar eating into his jowl, a gesture, he explained, he had been making since his twenty-first birthday with no results whatever.

"Why can't someone invent a low, comfortable collar for a shirt?" he grumbled. "You'd think that with all of man's genius, building massive pyramids, the Acropolis, steamships that cross the Atlantic Ocean, he would be able to design a collar that does not choke a man half to death. . . . But no matter. I don't have an engineer on my staff to lend you but Eugène Piat, who is building the railroad from Athens to Lamia, does."

Monsieur Piat, trained in his native France, was that rare combination of administrator-engineer-architect-scientist who, with eight younger French engineers, had laid out a railroad from Athens a hundred and twenty miles north to Lamia and was now constructing it. He managed large numbers of workmen, kept the roadbed moving on schedule, and at the same time was designing the French Archaeological Institute. He was a cultivated man who spoke Greek well. He cared little about clothes, spent most of his life in a surveyor's outfit and high boots searching for the best way to wind a railroad around a mountain or span it over a gorge. He had a shock of gray hair which stubbornly resisted comb and brush.

"Ah, but what goes on *inside* his head," Henry commented, "that's not rumpled!"

Henry gave him a précis of the previous year's dig.

"I have to get out of my fourteen-foot-wide trench concept with its limited vision, its scarcity of finds and into our new concept: a working level which I want to cut straight across the mount about forty-six feet below its plateau, where I believe we will be on native soil. The platform would be over two hundred feet long, and I would want it about fifty feet wide. From this platform and the plateau above it we will work on the northwest corner, extending upward about twenty-five feet, which I am convinced contains the acropolis. We want to leave any of the buildings, temples, palaces, watchtowers, gates, free standing. From our platform we will excavate into the sides of the hill and when we find walls we will dig down and around on all sides until the structure is completely exposed."

Piat nodded his shaggy head in understanding.

"You will be moving *downward* to clear the structures whose tops you discover, and *upward* to expose whatever rises higher than the platform."

"Precisely. I figure that my platform will be midway between the top of the mount and the plain below, where the city of Troy was built. When I excavate the city itself and the higher hill of the acropolis, which should contain the actual fortress and watchtowers, I will have Homer's Troy complete."

"Monsieur Piat," Sophia asked, "can you spare us that engineer; one who could map every aspect of the very large mound?"

"Yes, Madame Schliemann. Adolphe Laurent is highly qualified, and youngish, so that he will enjoy the adventure."

Laurent came to dinner a few days later. His hair was cut short, like stubble in a hayfield, one eyelid drooped, and the rest of his features had a scrambled effect, as though they had been assembled haphazardly. He made frequent trips to the sideboard on which the bottle of *ouzo* rested, and quickly emptied his wineglass throughout dinner. He appeared unaffected by the large quantity of alcohol, continuing to eat hungrily and spin yarns from the countries where he had worked.

The two foremen chosen by John Latham called one evening after supper. Theodorus Makres came from Mytilene, the capital of Lesbos, a mountainous island lying off the coast of Asia Minor, with two magnificent bays. Makres had worked since he was a boy, carving roads out of his native island and building landing wharfs for incoming ships. He had a vocabulary of only two hundred words but John Latham assured them that he had eloquent communication with a shovel.

Spyridon Demetriou had been born in Athens, the son of a manual laborer. The boy had been put to work as soon as he could steer a loaded wheelbarrow in a straight line. Latham said he liked hard physical labor; it satisfied a basic need in him. Henry gave them a token advance and advised them that they would be sailing to Constantinople late in March.

An important visitor at Sophia's dining table was Professor Xavier-John Landerer, just past sixty, who had been trained in his native city of Munich in medicine and natural sciences. At the green age of twenty-three he had been invited to Athens by King Otho to become his personal druggist. The University of Athens appointed him their first professor of chemistry and pharmaceutics. Henry was interested in knowing whether Professor Landerer could explain the effect of oxidation on terra cotta and the chemical composition of the varying colors of clay: black, deep brown, red, yellow, ashy gray.

They were making more and more friends among the university professors. It meant the beginning of a scientific and academic base beneath their work. The professors from the various disciplines did not accept Henry's theories about Homer's Troy but neither did they scoff. They respected his attitude, his willingness to give the rest of his life and a large part of his personal fortune to achieve his goal.

Sophia noticed that, except when he was digging, Henry appeared happiest while working with the professors. It was clear that Academia was his idol in the same sense that Homer was his god. Even when he was a child it had been his assumption, as well as his family's, that he would complete his education at a university, perhaps in nearby Rostock, possibly in Munich or Berlin. The death of his mother when he was nine, and the discharge of his father from his pastorate in 1834 for getting his young housekeeper with child, had cruelly cast Henry's lot with a grocery store. The eighteen-hour day of physical chores had been hard to bear, but worse was the grim fact that he would emerge into manhood an ignoramus.

Now that they had engaged their foremen and an engineer, they set about the task of accumulating the needed equipment. Henry decided to deal through his long-time friends and business associates in London, Schröder & Company, the firm for which he worked in Amsterdam at the age of twenty-two, and which had sent him to Russia to handle their accounts because he had had the perspicacity to teach himself Russian. The company still had the highest regard for his talents and integrity. He was about to order sixty of the hardiest wheelbarrows shipped from London to Piraeus when Sophia uttered a word of caution.

"Couldn't you have them ship us a sample first? I don't think you would like to pick up a shipment of sixty wheelbarrows and find them inadequate."

"You're right. We'll apply the same reasoning to our iron shovels, pickaxes and crowbars. I'll get a cable off to London explaining our needs."

Then he changed his mind. He wanted to make a fast trip through Germany to study the terra cottas and other early finds in the big museums, then go on to London to inspect and buy the equipment.

He left at once.

2.

She was not carrying well. She began to bleed, to get backaches, to have a sense of heaviness all through her pelvis. There followed sciatic pains down both legs. When Henry returned after his trip of two weeks he was alarmed.

"You never had any of this with Andromache?"

"No."

"Then we must get you off your feet. You must spend most of your time in bed. That will keep the pressure off your back and legs."

"There is so much to do. How am I going to spend months in bed?"

He was adamant. Sophia asked, "Could we go to see Dr. Venizelos? He can give us good advice."

Dr. Venizelos listened attentively to her story. He minimized the symptoms, suggested that she not worry about little aches and pains.

"But I want her to worry, Doctor," cried Henry; "I want her to give full attention to taking care of herself."

Dr. Venizelos took off his glasses, calmly wiping them with a handkerchief.

"My dear Schliemann, your wife should go about her normal life. She is young and healthy. Plenty of movement and exercise will help keep her strong."

"I would prefer to do it that way, Henry," said Sophia. "You have said that a man who pays for the advice of an expert and then doesn't take it is a fool."

For several weeks she went along with Dr. Venizelos's assurance that there was nothing wrong. She insisted that she was going to the Troad with Henry in early April.

"My place is at your side. I'm happy and well in the Troad. You said you were going to build a little house for us on the edge of the dig . . ."

"Yes. I've already sent Yannakis money and told him to order the lumber."

But by the beginning of March she found herself gripping the small silver cross she wore around her neck. She knew that something was definitely wrong. She felt a tremendous weight on her back. The heaviness increased throughout her pelvic region; there was considerable bleeding. She took to her bed. Dr. Venizelos dropped by every day. To no purpose. By the middle of March she had a miscarriage.

Dr. Venizelos came quickly. Sophia asked:

"Why did it happen, Doctor?"

"It's one of those accidents of nature, Mrs. Schliemann."

"Did I do something to cause it?"

"Assuredly not. Nor could you have done anything to prevent it. The fetus was never properly attached to the womb. That would have happened almost at the moment of conception. Since the child could not grow properly within you, nature very wisely rejected it. When you recover your strength you can make a fresh start and have another normal, healthy child."

"Then I will have other children?"

"Assuredly so."

"Just so long as it wasn't my fault."

Dr. Venizelos brushed the hair back from her temples with his fingertips.

"No one is at fault. It happened. From my experience I would say that this kind of accident rarely happens twice. Take comfort from that. Also take a long sleep. You'll wake up feeling better."

Madame Victoria hovered over her daughter solicitously, bathing her face and hands in cool water. Sophia was anxious and frightened. In spite of the doctor's comforting words, she felt a sense of guilt, of having failed her husband. She hoped Henry would not blame her.

When she awakened some fifteen hours later she found him sitting by her bedside. His eyes were red from crying. She slipped her hand into his, comfortingly. She had known that Henry would miss the pregnancy even more than she; he had set his heart on a Greek son as part of the mystique that had led him to a Greek wife. She could tell by the way he kissed her hand and then held it to his burning cheek that he was attaching no part of the blame to her. But she was shocked at the intensity of his hatred for Dr. Venizelos. Although he kept his voice low, it was trembling with passion.

"He is the evil spirit of our house, that Venizelos! Do not take him as a doctor neither as long as I live nor after my death. Much richness would I have given if I had never listened to this accursed one who destroyed the best hopes of our lives."

"*Agapete mou,* loved one, don't anguish yourself," she pleaded. "I too want to find someone to blame for this loss. But it was an accident that nature contrived. The dear Lord giveth and He taketh away. Dr. Venizelos only advised me to lead my regular life. He says this won't happen again. When I give you a son it will be forgotten."

Henry was inconsolable. Yet his first consideration was for Sophia.

"I'll postpone my departure for the Troad."

"No, Henry, you need those days at the beginning of April to get the work started. After all, you're taking Laurent with you and the two foremen. Just as soon as I'm able I'll take a ship from Piraeus. The Calverts will meet me in Çanakkale and help me find a good carriage and driver to take me out to Hissarlik. If you could have our house ready by then . . ."

The first gleam of revived hope came into his eyes.

"By all means. I'll have Yannakis and the two foremen start building the day I get there. It won't be anything elegant, you know, just a buttress against the elements. . . ."

Henry's purchases arrived from London: sixty wheelbarrows, twenty-four large iron levers, one hundred and eight spades, one hundred and three pickaxes, screw jacks, chains, windlasses. About a week before he was to leave he brought her a new projection.

"Rather than ship all this equipment to Constantinople, then transship it to Çanakkale and then send it in wagons to Hissarlik, do you think I could find the owner and captain of a small boat who could ply under contract between Piraeus and Besika Bay, a few miles down the coast from Hissarlik? It would then take only a couple of hours to put the stuff on a wagon and have it brought to our site."

Sophia wrinkled her brow.

"It will be expensive, hiring a ship and a crew full time."

"No, only part time, say one round trip a month. In good weather they can make the crossing in three days. Paris did when he stole Helen and Menelaus's treasure from Sparta, and he didn't have steam, only oarsmen and sails. It will give us a way to keep provisioned. We would write home the lists of our needs, Spyros could make the purchases and deliver the merchandise to the ship."

"I understand. And on the return voyage they can take back our share of the finds."

"Yes, if we can get the guards to divide on a continuing basis rather than saving everything until the end."

"Guards? Are we to have more than one?"

"I had a note from the Minister of Public Instruction. He learned that I may hire up to one hundred and fifty workers this year and he says one man would be inadequate to watch everything dug up."

"What happened to Georgios Sarkis?"

"He's back in the Ministry of Justice, I would suppose. Getting back to our proposed ship and captain, I need only two things: a bottom that won't sink and a captain who won't talk. I want to keep the inner workings of our excavations entirely private. It's what we find that I want to make public."

It took him several days of searching along the waterfront before he found the combination he thought might do: the S.S. *Taxiarchis*, Captain Andreas Papaliolos, the crew of the black, weather-beaten ship consisting of family alone: a younger brother, his two grown sons and a nephew. Henry liked the feel of the gnarled, powerful old man who, like so many Greeks, had been at sea all his life, saving his wages for twenty-five years so that he could buy his own small ship and be independent.

When Henry returned the third day in time for dinner, Sophia saw that he was wearing a bemused expression.

"You've found our ship and captain."

"I've also found what a small world this is. When I asked Captain Papaliolos for a reference, he replied, 'Dr. Schliemann, the best reference I can give you is your honorable mother-in-law, Kyria Victoria Engastromenos.'"

"Mama! Why Mama?"

"I don't know. Why don't we go out to Colonos late this afternoon? Andromache enjoys the ride."

Madame Victoria exclaimed, "Captain Papaliolos? He is from Crete. Our families knew each other for a century or more. He comes to visit on my saint's day if he is in port. What is it you want to know about him?"

"Is he trustworthy?"

"To you? But of course. You are now part of our family and the Papalioloses have total loyalty to the Engastromenoses."

"Thank you, my esteemed mother-in-law. I shall take him into my service."

The parting was a considerable wrench for both of them.

"It will only be for a few weeks," Sophia said consolingly. "The sun is warm now and I'll be able to work in the garden. That will make me strong."

Henry knew that Sophia liked doves. Secretly he had a dovecote built in the corner of the big garden and stocked with several pairs of birds. The first day she went into the garden after his departure she discovered the little house with the doves on their roost. Her eyes filled with tears.

Bishop Vimpos came to visit. He had heard about her miscarriage and made the long trip into Athens to comfort her and renew her faith in God's will. The two years in Tripolis had brought a subtle change in the man. His gown and face seemed dusty and worn.

"He is the wrong choice for such a culturally impoverished diocese," she thought indignantly. "He has one of the best minds in the Church. They should be using him for creative purposes: researching, writing, teaching at a level where his learning would do the most good."

Instead he had been literally exiled. When Sophia asked about his duties he told her:

"Very little aside from the ceremonials. I oversee a number of priests in villages, make sure that enough money comes in to meet the expenses of the diocese . . ."

"Are you teaching?"

"Yes. Small children. There are so few schools for them. If I don't teach them to read and write they'll remain illiterate."

"The Church must bring you back to Athens."

He smiled wanly.

"I know you feel I should be teaching theology and Hebrew at the university. Sometimes I miss the university very sorely: the library, the scholars, the bright students one watches grow. Sometimes it's lonely with no one to talk to. . . ."

"You do have your books?"

Vimpos shook his head sadly.

"No, Sophia. I had to sell my library before I moved to Tripolis to get rid of the last of my debts."

Her indignation turned to sorrow.

"Surely there will be a reprieve?"

"My dear child, I asked you to accept God's will. How can I then not accept His will? If I love God and our Church I must accept with grace any task set before me."

Sophia took the carriage into town, the first time since Henry had left. She went directly to Koromelas's bookstore, which she had loved since childhood. It was one very large room with shelves on both sides, the rear partition rising to the ceiling, each section with its hand-printed sign: Poetry, History, Literature, Science; with sections devoted to books in French, German and English. Twice a year, for St. Basil's Day and her own saint's day, a member of the family had brought her here to breathe the flavorsome smell of print and bindings from all over the world. She had been allowed to pick any title she wanted. Now she was going to use a considerable part of the five hundred drachmas, one hundred dollars, Henry had left with her for use in an emergency to restock Uncle Vimpos's library. Not for an instant did she doubt that her husband would agree that this was an emergency: that Theokletos Vimpos, who had brought them together and then saved their marriage, should never be allowed to be lonesome, to be without his books to talk to him. She had told Henry in Paris, "Loneliness is more painful than a broken leg." Or had it been homesickness? They were the same. Theokletos Vimpos was homesick for the intellectual and scholarly life of Athens, and he was in pain. He too had suffered a miscarriage.

April was warm, the sky filled with a luminous white powder at dawn, then deepening shades of blue. She worked around the flower beds and budding bushes and fed the doves and was surprised at her continuing sense of loss and emptiness. She became impatient to get back to Hissarlik, the digs, the crews, the excitement of the finds.

Henry's first letters were discouraging.

"Life is hard," he wrote. "Except for the wonderful view, all is bad."

The house on the edge of the excavation was not yet up. He was sleeping in the little shack he had built to house their tools. For three nights in a row it had rained hard, the water leaking through the roof. The rain had been followed by intense cold. Yannakis was there and was assembling a reliable work crew, but he could not cook for Henry because they had neither stove nor cooking utensils. He was obliged to eat Ciplak food. There was so much mud, darkness and cold that he could not write his reports. "If it is possible for you, then in the name of God stay in Athens and strengthen your little body. . . ."

But if she was coming, she was to bring with her, on the ship, a stove, ten plates, knives, forks and spoons, a large and small mattress, blankets, towels, the oldest of her clothing and thick leather shoes, and several dozen wicker baskets of varying sizes in which they would send home their pots, vases, shards. She set out to make the purchases, her brother Spyros accompanying her in the carriage to make sure everything was crated in large hampers and wickerwork in which they could pack their archaeological finds and ship them back with Captain Papaliolos on the Taxiarchis.

Henry's next letter made it impossible for her to remain in Athens any longer. It was filled with his love for her, and his loneliness:

My dearest wife Sophia:

My master, my little angel, my life, sole subject of my thoughts and dreams, how are you? How are you enjoying yourself? How are you eating and sleeping? How are you recovering? How is our dear daughter Andromache? She should take at least a three-hour walk every day in her English cart. How is your garden? I hope that with your divine spirit you revived our poor palm tree. How are your doves? Undoubtedly your garden will be a delight to the eyes.

My love, go every day to the sea baths at Piraeus, and later to Phaleron when the railroad opens because I want you to recover completely. Send me good news and the sun will shine for me again.

That afternoon she reserved a stateroom for an early May sailing to Constantinople.

The day before her departure she received a fifteen-page article from Henry with the request that she give it to one of her cousins, who had been trained in Greek grammar, to correct before it was turned over to the Athens Newspaper of the Debates for publication. She was also to take the two enclosed drawings, one of a cross he had found, the other of a sauvastika, to an Athenian photographer to have plates made for the article.

She asked her father to carry out the orders, installed her parents in the Mousson Street house so that Andromache would remain in familiar surroundings, kissed her daughter and family good-by, and had Spyros take her and her European traveling cases down to the French ship at Piraeus.

Henry was at the dock to meet her in Çanakkale. Her heart sank when she saw him standing at the foot of the gangplank. He seemed to have shrunk two sizes inside the business suit. His face was sallow, with furrows gouged down his cheeks; he had not become this thin during the leanest days at Ciplak. Obviously he had had little sleep in the past weeks. Without her help he had also had the intolerable task of writing his Greek reports for the newspapers and learned societies three times over.

"Poor man," she thought, more in love than pity; "he's been having a bad time. It will be better now with me to take care of him."

He took her in his arms, murmured, "You're beautiful."

He had instructed her to bring her oldest clothes to work in but that did not include her traveling outfit, which she had had tailored during her last week in Athens: a twill jacket of a dark blue, its woven ribbing giving the fabric a sheen that threw a flattering light on her slender face, a wide blue skirt in a lighter hue and a silk blouse with a white lace collar. She had had every intention of being beautiful in the eyes of her husband.

He held her away from him.

"I've never been so glad to see anyone in my whole misspent life. Let me look at you. I've seen nothing for weeks but picks, shovels and Turkophones. You've gained weight. I'm glad. Your eyes are bright . . ."

". . . at seeing you, Errikaki. Yes, Mother prepared three meals a day for me, a thing unheard of in a Greek kitchen. Now you are the one who needs looking after. Here's a kiss that Andromache sent her father."

She leaned over and laid her cheek on his.

"That was sweet. Sweet and chaste. I trust her mother brought a few along on her own account."

"Oh yes. Is our house ready?"

"The kitchen and third building as well. Yannakis is waiting eagerly to install the stove. You *did* bring a stove?"

"Of course; with enough food to feed you sumptuously for six months."

They walked to where the baskets were beginning to come out of the hold. A big farm wagon was backed up to the ship so they could be loaded directly.

"Here's Demetriou," said Henry. "You remember him, the younger of our two foremen. If you'll give him your bill of lading he'll check off the crates and baskets as they reach the wagon."

They stood hand in hand overlooking the blue waters of the Dardanelles and the green Gallipoli hills beyond. The day was warm and clear.

"Sophidion, you brought the hot sunshine with you. We've lost seven days out of the last twenty because of rain and Greek festivals. Yet in spite of the intense cold we moved eleven thousand cubic yards of earth in the first seventeen days of April."

"I'm so eager to see it all. How is Laurent working out?"

"Gone. After his month. Drink. Came to the digs for only an hour or two a day."

"What about his engineering plans, the relief maps?"

"Good." Grudgingly. "I've brought them along to show Frank Calvert. Once we get our platform cut through the mountain I'm afraid there won't be much left of his half of the mound."

"He'd much rather own a part of Troy than a barren hill on which somebody else's sheep graze."

They were staying overnight with the Frank Calverts.

"I thought you might have had a rough trip and would need some rest before we started for Hissarlik."

He linked his arm through hers as they walked down the narrow sidewalks of Çanakkale's main street. She felt at home as she saw the caravans of camels, the strings of basket-laden little black ponies, the women in their *yashmaks*, the short veils covering their faces. Tradition obliged the Turkish women when in public to make shapeless bundles of themselves. Over their *shalvars*, large trousers, tightened to the ankle, they wore long skirts, and above these skirts brightly printed cotton *yeleks*, long coatlike garments that fitted snugly above the waist and buttoned from the bosom down. Over the *yelek* they wore coats with large sleeves. On their heads they had the *feredjé*, the long veil which covered the head and shoulders and came down to the waist. Sophia observed irreverently:

"Only God and her husband knows what the Turkish woman looks like under that massive tent of clothing."

The smile, the warmth and love, the eagerness of Sophia's presence brought the color back into Henry's cheeks. As they strode down the road he threw out his chest against the vest and gold watch chain and, chameleon-like, as he had in the Engastromenos garden in Colonos the evening she had met him for the first time, appeared to shed twenty years, to become a young man again. Glancing about him quickly to see that no one was looking, he clutched her to him and kissed her deeply.

He whispered:

"I still owe you a son."

She returned his kiss, happy that the past was behind them, where it belonged.

The Calverts greeted them as old friends, the matronly Mrs. Calvert bussing Sophia on each cheek as though she were still another daughter. All four of the Calvert children were at home: Edith, Alice, Laura and the young son. The children had sometimes accompanied their father while he was excavating the funeral mounds so numerous in the Troad. After dinner they went into the library and settled into the rich red leather chairs. Henry spread Laurent's drawings on the circular table.

"Let me show you where we have established our working platform through the mound. You see here, where I have the figure A, that is where we dug our fourteen-foot trench up the hill last year. It was sixty feet long when we reached the top. I had hoped to find noble buildings on my way up but had to be content with what we now assume was a third-century B.C. Hellenic council chamber and no part of the acropolis. This year we're going to start much closer to the northwest promontory, here at B, where I am now convinced I'll find the fortress walls and the palace of Priam."

The drawings now blueprinted that, starting from the steep northern slope, Henry intended to dig from north to south halfway across the width of the hill to level his earthen platform two hundred and thirty feet long and fifty feet wide. From here they would excavate in all directions, follow all leads with trenches and terraces into the remaining mound. When Frank Calvert saw the figures he whistled, then brushed down his blond mustache as though to smooth out his astonishment.

"That's a tremendous task, Henry. The very concept of it staggers me. How much earth will you have to move?"

"Laurent's estimate is one hundred thousand cubic yards. At the forty-six-foot depth I should be at the native-earth level. The important part of the mountain will be totally exposed and we'll be free to release the great buildings from their three-thousand-year imprisonment."

Sophia had been overwhelmed at the daring of Henry's approach to the excavation problem the first time he told her about it, but Frank Calvert was in a state of shock.

". . . I couldn't do it. I couldn't conceive of it. . . . I like little digs, like the mound of Ajax or the little temple at Thymbria on my brother Frederick's farm. It's a thing I like to do myself, perhaps with one or two helpers, work I can finish in a few days."

When Henry did not answer because he did not know what to reply, Sophia said softly:

"I understand, Mr. Calvert. If you were an author you would want to write short stories rather than novels. Henry wants to be Dostoevsky . . ."

". . . and write *Crime and Punishment*." Calvert blinked several times. "I've had my crime and punishment. . . ."

There was an awkward silence. Henry said:

"Frank, my digging may extend into your half of the mound. Do I have your permission?"

Frank Calvert's reply was instant.

"Indeed. Otherwise I would not have encouraged you to start when we first met several years ago, or have worked to get you your *firman*. But I would ask that you share the artifacts you find on my property half and half."

"Fair is fair, Frank. Will a handshake do or shall we draw up an agreement?"

"Your word is my bond."

They shook hands. Frank brought a brandy bottle out of a concealed bar. Even Sophia drained her glass to Frank Calvert's salute:

"To Homer's Troy! Send me a message when you make your first great discovery and I'll ride out to join you."

3.

She was amazed at the transition of Hissarlik; not only at the newly created trenches and terraces and exposed stonework, but at the stubble-covered mound which had the look of a tiny settlement with their three houses on the northwest corner, immediately in front of and overlooking the excavations, and farther off to the east on the level plain what appeared to be other small buildings. Henry had written her with pride that he had built the three buildings for only two hundred dollars, buying his ten-foot-long, ten-inch-wide planks for eight cents each, and so she had expected to find little more than contrived shacks. Instead, the structures were sturdy, the roofs covered with waterproof matting, the windows and doors hung by Turkophone carpenters.

Her own house had three rooms: their bedroom, an ample dining-room and a second room which Henry and Yannakis had made into a study-workroom with two walls of shelves partially filled by new finds which Henry had numbered but made no attempt to clean; and an old, battered desk he had come across in Çanakkale. Sophia was delighted with the desk despite its pock-marked surface because there was space enough for both of them to work at it. From her rear windows she could see the Aegean and the islands of Imbros and Samothrace.

She set her beloved icon on a crude nightstand Yannakis had built for her in the bedroom, and hung her dresses behind a curtained-off corner similar to the one in her bedroom in Colonos. There were three dresses she had outgrown, all with loose skirts which would allow her to climb over the digs with ease, a short-sleeved dress tight at the waist which she knew was too elegant for the digs but which she had never liked, a comfortable skirt and blouse. She had brought a wide-brimmed straw hat, and a felt hat, which would be more protection under the scalding sun of July and August than the scarf she had worn the year before, and two pairs of thick leather-soled shoes.

Henry then took her for a tour of the two other houses, one a bunkhouse for their foremen, Makres and Demetriou, the other the kitchen. Yannakis had already installed the stove, which had arrived in the wagon the night before, and was in process of cutting a hole in the roof for the long black exhaust pipe. When he saw Sophia the giant came gingerly down the rungs of his tree-trunk ladder, slipped to his knees before her, kissed her hand and murmured:

"*Doulos sas!* Welcome to Schliemannville. Master will be happier now."

"Yannakis," Henry asked, "did you find a girl for Kyria Schliemann?"

"A girl?" Sophia was taken by surprise. "For what purpose, Henry?"

"To serve as your companion and maid. Our situation is not the same as it was last year. The Renkoits only make the trip home on Saturday night, or on the eve of a religious holiday. They've built a camp where they sleep rolled up in blankets. I've set up water barrels for them and outhouses. A trader has also built a grocery shack to provision them, though they bring their staples from home on Monday mornings. We have the beginnings of a little village which we call Hissarlik. There are just too many men around to leave you alone in the house."

Suddenly they realized that Yannakis was beaming at them, a broad smile on his homely face.

"Master, I found a girl."

"Good. How long will she stay?"

"As long as you are here. I married her to make sure."

Sophia and Henry gazed at each other in incredulity. Yannakis, who was in his early forties, had implied the previous year that marriage was not for him: it was not in his nature to give orders. How could a man have a wife if he could not order her about? Particularly in Asia Minor? He had made the sacrifice for his master's sake.

"Where is she now, Yannakis?"

"I bring her."

He went into an adjoining room which he had added onto the kitchen wall under a large sloping roof, returning in a moment nudging his bride ahead of him.

"Master, this is Polyxene. My cousin. From Renkoi."

Polyxene stood with eyes cast down. She bowed low before Henry and Sophia, then murmured with Yannakis's identical inflection:

"Your slave."

She was an attractive little thing in a soap-scrubbed fashion, about sixteen years old, barely coming up to Yannakis's armpits. Unlike the Turkish women, the Greek girls were permitted to move about with their faces uncovered. Polyxene was wearing a white shirt with long sleeves, a long skirt, and a shawl over her head. In spite of her shyness it was apparent that the girl had poise and that she would be pleasant to have around.

Yannakis had stacked the hundred-pound sacks of coffee, sugar, white beans, lima beans, yellow and green peas, lentils, rice, dried figs, raisins, nuts, flour along the two free walls of the kitchen. Georgios Engastromenos had bought and paid for them at Henry's instructions and had had them delivered to Sophia's ship in Piraeus. There were also packages of macaroni, cinnamon, nutmeg, vanilla, pistachio and pignolia nuts, tomato paste, grated cheese and syrup. Still standing outside were barrels of pickles, herrings in brine, olives, sardines. The stout thread at the top of each sack had been cut, the sides rolled down slightly to reveal the contents.

"The aromas are delicious," Sophia commented, "like the big grocery stores in Athens when the bins are open."

Henry flashed her a happy smile.

"I've been hungry for six weeks. Now we're going to eat well."

"That is why you wanted me to come. You missed your cook."

Before Henry could answer, Yannakis cried in anguish:

"I cook! I the best cook in the Troad."

Polyxene spoke for the first time.

"Men do not cook. I cook!"

"No!" roared Yannakis. "I give orders in kitchen," and then almost fainted at his own audacity.

Sophia laughed. "We'll all cook. It will be the best entertainment in Schliemannville."

Henry took her for a tour of the excavations. The mountain was crawling with blue-trousered workmen in red fezzes. Sophia exclaimed:

"It does look for all the world like an anthill."

"It should. I have one hundred and thirty men working here. The new equipment is a great help, particularly the strong wheelbarrows and iron shovels."

He led her to the south side of the mound where a city called Novum Ilium had flourished until the middle of the fourth century A.D.

"From that day to this there have been no inhabitants on this hill."

A crew of forty-five men was cutting a channel from the plain up the easy slope. Directing them was a man she had not seen before, wearing a miner's hat and a pair of knee-high English boots.

"You remember in Athens I said I would like to find miners as my foremen?" explained Henry. "Well, a miner found us. Georgios Photides, a Greek from this area who went out to Australia and worked in the mines for seven years. Got homesick, returned and married a fifteen-year-old girl from a nearby village. No dowry, no work either. When I learned he had experience in tunneling, I hired him at once. He does a good job. Sleeps in the bunkhouse."

Henry took her by the arm, led her down to the channel and presented Photides. Photides took off his Australian miner's hat, put a hand over his heart and bowed low. Henry said:

"Photides, explain to Mrs. Schliemann what your task is."

"Gladly, Dr. Schliemann." He spoke an excellent Greek, one which indicated that he had had some education.

"Mrs. Schliemann, we are going to dig upward from the plain until we have reached the forty-six-foot level at which Dr. Schliemann expects we will be on primary soil. At that point we will cross the mound to meet the crews under Makres and Demetriou who are coming from the north. When we meet, our channel will go through the entire width of Hissarlik at the virgin-soil level. The soil of Homer's Troy. That's what the doctor wants."

"And that's what the doctor is going to get!" Henry replied grimly. "Come along, Sophia, I want to show you what progress we're making on the north side, working toward Photides."

They reached the area where another crew was loosening the earth crust of the twenty-six-foot-high hill which Henry was convinced contained the acropolis of Troy, carefully bringing down the centuries of accumulated earth to the natural crest of the hill. The outer half of this accumulation was the three- to four-thousand-year shell which had been built up by accretion. The inner half of the mountain was its kernel, the original rock mountain on which the first Troy had been built. It was the kernel of the nut that he wanted to digest; outer shells are for cracking.

Before starting across the plateau Sophia saw a sight that sent a chill down her spine. She cried out:

"*Panaghia mou,* Holy Mother of God, what a fantastic sight!"

Henry was exultant.

"Isn't that a beauty? I wouldn't let them be taken out of the earth until you had seen them *in situ.*"

It was indeed a stunning sight: ten huge, orange-colored *pithoi,* jars, seven feet tall and almost five feet at their widest point, standing out from the excavated cut in the hill, half released from their three-thousand-year-old prison but still firmly encased.

"Henry, what are they? What were they used for? And why are they standing almost in a row a dozen feet above our heads?"

Henry chuckled.

"I know it's hard to believe when you're gazing up at that immense earth wall, but you are looking at a street or a series of streets, and the remains of the houses on those streets. Those glorious *pithoi* were used as storage jars for oil, water, wheat, barley . . ."

"But, Henry, the people would have had to use a ladder to get to their supplies."

"On the contrary, my love, they would have had to get on their knees."

She stared at him, slightly openmouthed. Then light came into her eyes.

"You mean they were sunk in the ground?"

"They had to be. The ordinary house consisted of only one room. Put those *pithoi* on the floor and the inhabitants would have had to sleep in the outer court. So they buried them in a row in front of the fireplace where they did their cooking. The mouths of the jars would be level with the earthen floor."

Forty-six feet down from the plateau of the mound, where Sophia had stood gazing upward in admiration at the ten orange *pithoi* she saw something equally remarkable: the beginnings of Henry's great platform. Demetriou's crew had dug downward from the plateau; Makres's men had come up the steep north side in a direct line to join up with him. They had removed over fifteen thousand cubic yards of earth. The platform was already established for a hundred and fifty feet into the mountain, a solid workbench of earth from which Henry's men could scale down the earth walls rising above them and containing, in Henry's thinking, all the buildings inside the immense stone defense walls which the Achaeans had not been able to breach in ten years of siege. Here they would also find the broad roadway leading out to the plain.

"Henry, am I standing on the soil of Homer's Ilion?"

"I believe so."

He beamed at her.

"Our primary drive is to locate the walls. Come, sit with me on this little terrace."

He took his copy of *The Iliad* out of his coat pocket and read to her. It was Poseidon speaking to Apollo:

> " '. . . rememberest thou all the woes that we twain alone of all the gods endured at Troy, what time we came at the bidding of Zeus and served the lordly Laomedon for a year's space and he was our taskmaster and laid on us his commands? I verily built for the Trojans round about their city a wall, wide and exceeding fair, that the city might never be broken.'

"We are also looking for a double gate. See, it says here, a few pages farther on:

> " 'The old man Priam stood upon the heaven-built wall and was ware of monstrous Achilles, and how before him the Trojans were being driven in headlong rout, and help there was none. Then with a groan he gat him down to the ground from the wall, calling the while to the glorious keepers of the gate along the wall: "Wide open hold ye the gates with your hands until the folk shall come to the city in their rout, for lo, here at hand is Achilles as he driveth them on. . . . But whenso they have found respite, being gathered within the wall, then close ye again the double doors, close fitted; for I am adread lest yon baneful man leap within the wall." ' "

They returned to the house. Yannakis had a hot meal ready for them.

"The stove, it work," he announced proudly. "I cook a *moussaka*, rice pilaf, slices of pork in wine. The oven, it work. I bake first loaf of Greek bread."

Henry opened a bottle of his favorite Turkish wine.

"Let's drink to great and wondrous finds!" he cried.

"Yes, of course. That's why we're here. But first I would like to drink to happiness in this new home you built for us."

"We'll be happy," he replied soberly, "providing we free the Trojan acropolis for all people to see. That will put down the doubters."

"It's true," she thought, "our marriage depends for its success on whether or not we find Troy. But that's all right; I knew the conditions from the beginning."

After dinner he took her into the study to show her what they had dug out of the ground while she was in Athens. He had not broken down the artifacts into material groups: earthenware, stone, bone, ivory, but lumped together everything from a particular area.

"We found a buttress of shelly limestone which apparently was constructed for the purpose of consolidating the buildings on top of the hill. The debris behind the buttress was as hard as stone. We also found ruins of houses there, and this whole mass of diorite axes, lodestone sling bullets, flint knives, lava hand mills, fine marble idols, with and without the owl's head, clay weights in the form of pyramids, terra-cotta whorls."

"I'll start cleaning them in the morning, and set down their dimension and description. I brought plenty of fish glue and plaster."

"Good. There's a lot of work here for you."

"I want to work in the digs as well."

"Then we'll compromise. Work with me on the platform in the mornings and remain home after dinner to keep the records and copy my articles for the London *Times* and for the *Augsburger Allgemeine Zeitung.*"

She found on the shelves a silver dress pin, a mold for casting breast-pins and other ornaments, a broken water urn nicely decorated, rusted copper nails, a copper hunting lance; diorite hammers, a great deal of terra-cotta pottery of brilliant black, brown or yellow, plates turned on a potter's wheel, vases with men's faces, vases in forms they had not seen before; double cups that were shaped like champagne glasses, a black pitcher with the beak-shaped mouth bent backward; empty funeral urns, baskets of shards with vivid decorations, terra-cotta seals with inscriptions, and a three-footed jar apparently representing a woman, for it had breasts and a navel.

"It's too much to assimilate all at once. I wish I had been here during these past weeks, then I would have had a tactile sense of each piece as we took it out of the earth. That afforded me an intimate relationship with each vase and knife and marble."

"They'll become intimate enough once you start handling them."

"Have you any clues as to their age?"

"They're all mixed up, the way the several cities on our hill are. We'll learn more about them as we go along, and in Athens from our friends at the university. I thought we ought to go to bed now. It's been a long day for you."

Yannakis had opened the boxes of blankets Sophia had bought. Polyxene had put them on the bed.

Sophia laughed lightheartedly, threw her arms about her husband's neck.

"My darling Errikaki, wait until you lie under the soft lamb's wool blankets I bought in Athens. I had them bound in satin to give our house here a touch of elegance. You'll think you are in heaven."

"So I will be with you beside me."

She fell asleep in his arms but awoke sometime later to feel something crawling over her cheek. She screamed, brushed the creature off, then jumped out of bed to stare at it in horror.

"Henry, it's a centipede."

"No, not a hundred legs," he replied sheepishly; "only forty. That's what its Greek name says."

"Isn't its bite said to be fatal?"

"Nothing is fatal except death."

"I'm going to sleep with my head under the covers from now on."

By reflex she clutched the cross hanging from her neck beneath her nightgown. "May the saints preserve us!"

"They might take too long in coming. I'll have Yannakis sweep the ceiling each afternoon while it's still light."

Henry awoke at four in the morning; it was still dark. Sophia accompanied him for the brisk horseback ride down to a pool in the Simois River but she did not join him in the swim. On their return the sun broke over the ridge of the Ida Mountains, infusing the air with a rose light. She wheeled her horse about to watch the light touch the Dardanelles and bring the strait out of its darkness. Within a moment or two she could see the high peaks of Samothrace across the Aegean. Her first sunrise the year before from the top of Hissarlik had been breath-taking; this morning it was like returning to a beloved homeland, an integral part of Greece.

Yannakis had coffee waiting for them, and a noxious-looking fluid in a cup.

"What is this?" she asked. "Surely not a new form of quinine?"

"We won't need quinine until summer, when the marshes dry up," Henry replied. "This is the juice of the snakeweed. I want you to supervise the men who will be cutting out terraces. Among other things you are going to excavate are snakes: brown vipers about the thickness of rainworms, also poisonous snakes. The workmen drink this concoction of snakeweed every morning because it renders the bite harmless."

At five-thirty they left Polyxene to set their house in order and joined Yannakis at a point on the level ground to the east of the dig where Henry had had a fence and gate built. Each workman as he entered the gate had a check put after his name. Yannakis paid the men only when they left for home now, not each night. The grocer gave credit; all accounts were settled on Saturday night, or the eve of a religious holiday. Henry kept a large supply of coins on hand only on paydays. His agent, a Mr. Dokos in Çanakkale, sent the money out the day before.

As they reached the platform Henry pointed to the two Turkish soldiers who had been appointed guards. He did not introduce them.

"Unlike our former friend, Georgios Sarkis, these two are on top of us all the time. I manage to keep them at arm's length. I have put markers between the half of the mound which belongs to the Turkish government and the half which belongs to Frank Calvert. The guards are allowed to take half of what we find on the government property but I have imposed a new system, I don't permit them to enter our house. I oblige them to choose the museum's half as it comes out of the earth, either in the dinner recess or at twilight when all work stops. We are not going to permit them to see anything after it has been cleaned."

"How good is their judgment, Dr. Schliemann?"

"They don't have any artistic training or judgment. How could they? They are soldiers. On the law of averages they will choose as well from the unwashed as from the washed."

All Henry could spare for her was a crew of ten men. Some of them had worked with her the year before. She saw no resentment on the faces of the new workers. He had given her a sketch indicating that he wanted new terraces to be cut thirty feet on either side of the main platform, sixteen to nineteen feet higher in the hill. They were to be twenty feet wide and about one hundred feet in length. He had also drawn in the dozens of arterial channels he meant to dig in every direction from these terraces. Sophia exclaimed:

"You might as well have started at the peak and carried off the entire mound, wheelbarrow by wheelbarrow, resettling this pile of earth and debris somewhere else on the Troad."

"No, no, Sophidion, that would have defeated our purpose. What we have to do is carry off the debris after sifting it for finds, but we must leave free-standing all walls, embattlements, temples, palaces, streets, gates we uncover."

Photides came over from his channel building on the south side to help them mark out the boundary for the second terrace. She was delighted at how much more rapidly the work went now with the metal shovels, excellent pickaxes and stoutly built English wheelbarrows. She watched intently as the debris and earth were dumped into the baskets and wheelbarrows, rescuing the artifacts. She put them to one side, making no attempt to brush off the incrustations.

At the eleven o'clock break for dinner, after the two guards had collected, under Henry's careful eye, their portion of the finds of Photides, Makres and Demetriou, he brought the guards to Sophia's terrace. Sophia pointed to her baskets. They had no interest whatever in the shards, which she had kept separately. Henry and Sophia exchanged a meaningful glance; the shards, once put together in Athens, would provide them with some of the most beautiful vases, in both design and decoration.

Henry had established the dinner routine: the three foremen, Yannakis, Polyxene and the Schliemanns ate the same food prepared by Yannakis. Polyxene served Henry and Sophia in the diningroom, the other five ate together at a rough board table in the kitchen. Yannakis had done well. After finishing his job as checkmaster that morning, he had scoured the countryside and found four chickens which he brought home alive on his donkey.

4.

In late May Henry ordered a series of stone walls to be built to contain the debris, earth and rocks which the workmen, perched from ten to fifteen feet above him, sent down in a steady stream. He did not trust the first wall and ordered his men to stay away from it. He brought Photides over to build a higher wall out of the larger stones they had unearthed. When the work was done Photides exclaimed:

"This wall will stand for centuries."

"Maybe so," replied Henry, "but I think we had better buttress it."

Six of the workmen were directed to build the buttress. The wall collapsed with a totally dissolving crash. Sophia heard Henry's agonized cry, came running to his side. He was distraught. The six men had been working at the foot of the wall.

The entire work force, including those who had been shouted up from Photides's group on the south slope, was already feverishly pulling stone after stone off the tremendous pile. Henry joined them, working like a madman to move the stones onto the flat surface of the clearing. Sophia asked:

"Photides, are you certain the men are underneath?"

Photides, who knew himself responsible for the terrible accident, stared at her with a glazed look of horror on his face.

"Madame Schliemann, the last time I saw them . . ."

He stopped short, his eyelids popping open.

"Look! There they are! All working like demons to free themselves."

He crossed himself three times, quickly, as though he were brushing stone dust off his face and chest. Sophia called to Henry, who was working at the other end of the collapse.

"It's all right, Henry. The men are safe."

He came over, shaking his head, the tic in his left jaw bouncing the skin up and down. He shook the hand of each of the men as they emerged.

"It's a miracle. Nothing short of a miracle. They were all working under the stone ledge Photides built. God looks after fools and children. At the moment I feel eligible for both categories. Little one, I am undone. Let us go back to the house. Polyxene will make us a cup of coffee."

Once in their home sipping the thick sweet coffee, Henry leaned over, took both her hands in his.

"Sophidion, today was almost our last in our search for Troy. If those six men had been crushed by the wall no money and no promises could have saved us. The Troad women have this in common with their Greek sisters: the husband, be he old or young, rich or poor, is everything to them; heaven and earth have but a secondary interest."

"As it should be."

She went to her knees in front of the icon of the Virgin Mary and thanked her for saving the men.

"I will not rebuild the wall," said Henry. "The stones rolling down with the freshly dug debris are dangerous, they can injure feet and legs. But they are not fatal. Nevertheless we should hire a couple of boys from Ciplak as watchmen; when a stone comes rolling down they can cry out: 'To nou sas! Watch out,' and the workmen will move out of the way."

The passing weeks and months brought other crises, large and small; wonderments and disappointments. It seemed to Sophia that, with a crew of one hundred and fifty workmen tearing out its insides with ever new steps, terraces, canals, caverns, deep roadways, the mound changed its form and character every few days. She had never realized that mountains could grow or shrink, that they were not immutable but subject to other forces of nature, one of the most powerful of which was mankind. The descriptive phrases which formed in her mind, as she stood at the top and saw the gigantic gougings Henry was making into the vitals of the mountain, changed; at one time she saw it as a vast labyrinth, such as the one underneath the palace of Knossos on Crete where Theseus slew the Minotaur and, helped by Ariadne, who gave him the clue of thread, was able to find his way out. At another time, earlier in the morning or later in the afternoon, she saw it as a gigantic Mt. Hymettus honeycomb. Later, it was the inside of a long-dead volcano, the one tree still standing on the bottom, alive, an anachronism in the exposed cone of earth and lava.

With the coming of June and summer, the heat became intense. To provide his workmen with good water Henry hired the oldest Dramali boy to fill barrels from a cold spring four hundred yards to the east. A Dramali relative loaded the barrels on either side of a donkey and took them into the trenches. By late June there were ten barrels in use but barely enough water to go around.

When the winds swept down from the north with hurricane force Polyxene wrapped a diaphanous scarf around Sophia's hat and over her face in an attempt to keep the swirling dust out of her eyes, nostrils and mouth. But the snakes were gone; she no longer had to swallow the dose of snakeweed each morning.

On the warm spring and summer evenings they had their dinner out of doors, watching the sun sink into the Aegean Sea, changing its color moment by moment in a phantasmagoria of hues starting with shell pink, darkening to rose red, deepening into rich purples before the light faded and the stars came out. One soft evening, the air fragrant with the scents of nearby orange trees, Sophia commented:

"I've seen the Aegean take on every color from black, ash gray, deep green, morning-sky blue, down to that riot of purple we've just seen fade. But I don't ever recall seeing it the color Homer ascribes to it: 'the wine-red sea.' "

Henry took a cigar from his upper vest pocket, clipped the end off with the little gold knife at the other end of his watch chain, blew smoke into the air contentedly.

"It's like the 'golden apple of discord' that Eris threw among the gods and goddesses at the wedding of Achilles's parents; or the three golden apples which Melanion dropped in his foot race with Atalanta, tricking her into stopping to pick them up and thus obliging her to marry him instead of murdering him, as she had her former suitors. . . ."

"You're trying to make a point, *philtate mou;* what about the golden apples?"

"They weren't apples at all!" He rubbed his hands in glee. "There never were any golden apples in Greece. But they always had the most golden oranges in the world. Isn't it a frolic when the golden apples of mythology turn out to be golden oranges of reality? Anyway I have a heretical theory about that phrase, wine-red sea. I don't think Homer was referring to color at all, but rather to the consistency of the sea. But please don't tell that to our professorial friends; they would blow me right out of the water, wine-red water at that."

Each day brought a fresh excitement. On the south side, where Photides was excavating about three hundred yards from an ancient wall they had discovered the year before, they discovered the original quarry of shelly limestone from which all the stone cities on the mound, from Priam's Troy down to the very last settlement of the Christian Era, had been built. The entrance was through a large tunnel which had been covered over by bushes and brambles. Henry and Sophia stood in the midst of the hollowed-out quarry.

"One more reason why the Trojans built on this spot rather than elsewhere in the Troad, Bounarbashi, for example," Henry proclaimed; "they had the best possible building materials immediately at hand."

The following day they uncovered the walls of a house, hewn blocks of limestone joined with clay. The stones were of uniform size, the walls had been constructed by such skilled artisans that the surface, which Henry guessed had been constructed about 1000 B.C., was still perfectly smooth. Immediately under the walls they found layers of yellow and brown ash, the ruins of a wood and thatch community upon which the house had been constructed.

Two days later, working from one of the new western terraces at a depth of thirteen feet below the foundation of the limestone house, they came upon a wall six feet thick. Henry was ecstatic.

"I think we've made it! This wall should be resting on primary soil!"

She shared his sense of expectancy.

"Let's figure," he continued. "We're thirty-three feet below the plateau of the mound here. Our big platform is at forty-six feet, but we may have another few feet to go. Thirty-three from forty-six is thirteen. Our wall would have to go down at least thirteen feet."

"Could it?"

"I am going to have to tear down this beautiful house to find out."

"Oh, I'm sorry. Is there no other way to get at it?"

"None. But if the wall does go down to primary rock, I will reverently preserve it."

They were disappointed when the wall proved to be merely the foundation of another house, still older than the smooth-stoned house of 1000 B.C., which was now destroyed.

"We've still no proof that we are down to the Trojan level," he groused when they were labeling their finds of the day. "And I've been digging for more than two months."

He got up and paced the floor of the workroom agitatedly; he had figured and refigured; read and reread all the material available.

"This last foundation, how would you date that?" she asked.

"The immediate successors of the ancient Trojans."

"Then why be disheartened if we are that close?"

He handed her a near-perfect vase with an owl's head for cleaning and cataloguing.

"You're right. We'll persevere."

They had a message from Frank Calvert that he and Mrs. Calvert were going to visit Frederick Calvert at Thymbria and would be stopping by Hissarlik to visit with the Schliemanns about noon on Sunday to see what progress had been made. Sophia worked out a menu with Yannakis and Polyxene for Sunday's dinner, a pure Greek meal which she thought would delight their guests.

Late Saturday afternoon when Henry was working with a group of seventy men, laying out still a third hundred-foot terrace, he came across the markers which divided the government's half of the mound from Frank Calvert's half. At the edge of the steep north cliff he found a deep depression in the ground. His tape measure showed it to be over a hundred feet long and seventy-six feet wide. He sent Yannakis to the house to summon Sophia. When she arrived he explained that she was gazing into a quarry, even as the Colosseum had served as a quarry for the Romans for centuries.

"You remember the Turkish cemeteries we have seen through the Troad, the marble blocks serving as tombstones?"

"Yes. You said that they were early Greek."

"That's right. The Turks came here hundreds of years ago searching for pillars and marble blocks. What they took away with them must have amounted to a whole city, the temple, city council, palaces. We have another proof of how many stone and marble cities were buried in this mount."

As dusk was falling and the workmen were preparing to leave for Renkoi and the surrounding villages, Henry noticed that on the government's side of the boundary, in what he believed to be the ruins of a temple built about 310 B.C. by Lysimachus, Alexander the Great's comrade, earth that had been pulled away from a hillside revealed a jutting marble block on which he recognized art work. He touched Sophia on the arm, then moved quickly to the workmen, crying in a hearty voice:

"It's dark now. Stones may come tumbling down. Bring your tools to the storehouse. Yannakis is ready to pay."

Sophia had not moved since Henry signaled. She bowed to each of the men as they passed, wished them a good reunion with their families. When the last man had disappeared from sight she moved to Henry's side.

"Sophia, help me. We must uncover enough of this slab to make sure what it is. I'll use a shovel to loosen the earth around it. You clear it away with your hands. There is no danger of its moving, it's locked in tight."

They worked hard and fast in the dry earth to free a good portion of the block. It was of Parian marble, triglyphs surrounding a carved metope, over six feet long, three feet high and twenty-two inches thick.

They stepped back from their discovery and impulsively reached out for each other's hand. Henry almost crushed hers in the intensity of his emotion. The metope in its center was a sculpture in high relief representing Apollo the sun god riding his four horses across the skies. Above Apollo's head could be seen the sun's disk. Henry cried:

"It's magnificent! Apollo's flowing robe and his expressive face are worthy of the best carving on the Acropolis. And the four horses wildly snorting, traversing the universe with infinite power, their anatomy is so accurately rendered I frankly confess I have never seen such a masterly work. It is the first great piece of art we have found."

He ran his hands over the carving, tenderly.

"It is in perfect condition. See the Doric columns, and how each horse has a distinct and separate posture, front hoofs high in the air as though straining to leap forward."

Sophia looked behind her in the gloaming.

"Are we on Frank Calvert's land or the government's?"

"It's close. Not more than a few yards from the quarry on Frank's side. But it's definitely on the Turkish government's land."

"May the saints forgive us, but how is it possible to cut in half a beautiful piece of sculpture? Neither half would have meaning with Apollo on one half, the horses on another . . ."

". . . and its value, from the viewpoint of ancient art, would be destroyed. It's the equivalent of cutting the Venus de Milo down the center, or splitting Michelangelo's David from his hair down through his crotch, with one leg going to each owner. Mayhem!"

Sophia's eyes sparkled.

"I have a better solution. The block is two feet thick. Instead of cutting it down the middle, vertically, with the line going straight through Apollo and the front horse, why not cut it in the width, the whole six-foot length of it, so that we keep the front half and the Turkish government gets the back?"

Henry joined Sophia's laughter. He threw his arm around her shoulder.

"Only a Greek would have thought of that solution."

She asked cautiously, "Seriously, do you think we ought to cover it for safety's sake?"

"No, the guards have already left and won't be back until Monday morning. Nobody will come into the digs until then. I want to show it to Frank Calvert tomorrow."

The Calverts arrived from Thymbria about eleven o'clock. Henry and Sophia took them immediately to see what had been accomplished since Henry arrived at the beginning of April. Frank was thunderstruck at the amount of earth Henry's crews had moved, and at the number of platforms, terraces and side galleries dug into the government's half of the land.

"But you haven't actually found any of the buildings of Troy?" he asked.

"The remains of buildings, but no acropolis, no temple, no palace . . . yet."

"It's a gigantic task."

"We haven't done much on your half but we are planning to start. Let me show you a marble quarry which the Turks, looking for tombstones, dug out of your side hundreds of years ago. Then I've got something really startling to exhibit."

Frank gazed down at the rectangular depression, said:

"I have often wondered how that hole got there. You're right, of course; now I remember seeing marble pillars and blocks as far away as Alexandria Troas, down the coast about forty miles."

Sophia slipped her hand under Mrs. Calvert's arm and guided her to the Apollo metope. Henry and Frank Calvert followed immediately behind. Henry had brought a soft cloth with which he wiped down the face of the sculpture. Mrs. Calvert was the first to speak:

"Oh, it's a beauty. I've not seen a better one, even in the museums. How old do you think it is?"

Henry and Frank discussed the matter quietly for a few moments, then agreed that it was probably Hellenic, 300 to 200 B.C.

"We have a problem," said Sophia with a short, forced laugh; "what do we do with it?"

Henry repeated to the Calverts the conversation he and Sophia had had the evening before, both serious and jocular, about how to cut the Apollo in half.

"I've a better solution," said Frank. "Why not just spirit it out of the country? The Turks don't need half of your first great art discovery."

"But how? We dare not cart it into Çanakkale . . ."

"Didn't you tell me that you have a small freighter coming to provision you?"

"Yes," Henry replied. "Captain Papaliolos of the *Taxiarchis* is due in Besika Bay in a day or two."

"Excellent!" Frank had entered into the problem as though it were a game of bowls. "How many men do you have here that you can trust?"

"My three foremen."

"And Yannakis," Sophia added; "he's the most trustworthy of all."

"Very good," said Frank. "This afternoon cover the marble with tarpaulin, rope it, borrow the stoutest farm wagon you can find in Ciplak and haul it down to the beach at Besika Bay. Leave it covered on the sand; no one will bother with it. Does your captain have a windlass on his ship?"

"An ancient drum with thick ropes and a hand crank."

"Good show!" said Frank. "You can have it aboard the *Taxiarchis* and in Piraeus before anyone here will know about it."

A silence fell. The four stood quietly. Sophia broke the tension:

"Please let us go back to the house now. We have prepared a Greek dinner for you . . . caviar canapés, *taramosalata, keftedakia,* marinated lamb brains . . ."

When the Calverts had departed Henry sent Yannakis into Ciplak to the Dramali family to strike a bargain for the use of their big farm wagon and two horses. Sophia had misgivings. She said:

"My dear, I don't want to sound righteous, but is this a wholly proper thing to do?"

"Nothing in this wicked world is wholly proper. Since we both agreed that the Apollo could not be cut in half the only alternative is to hand it over intact to the museum. Are you prepared to do that?"

"No. . . . I guess I am a little frightened as well as being a little prudish. Would we lose our permit if we got caught?"

"We're not going to get caught. Leave the mechanics to me. I will take full responsibility."

She laughed uneasily.

"I was thinking about *moral* responsibility."

Henry, Sophia and the three foremen went directly to the Apollo, carrying rolls of tarpaulin and stout rope. By the time they got the marble covered and securely tied, Yannakis had arrived with the farm wagon, backing it up to the end of the two-ton block. While he held the horses steady, the foremen used a windlass to raise the marble to the level of the wagon floor and insert the sculpture onto its bed. It was securely lashed down. Yannakis and Polyxene got on the high driver's seat. Makres and Demetriou sat on the marble and rolled cigarettes. Henry gave one last order:

"Leave it on the beach exactly where the little whaleboat was beached and you picked up our supplies last time."

On Tuesday a message arrived at the Schliemann house that the S.S. *Taxiarchis* had dropped anchor in Besika Bay. Captain Papaliolos had brought Henry the dozen ten-foot-high iron levers he had ordered. Henry rode down to the beach immediately. Yannakis again borrowed Dramali's wagon, taking the windlass from the digs with him.

No one had touched the tarpaulin-covered object. The captain's family, with Yannakis working the windlass, got the marble into the small boat and when the boat drew alongside the *Taxiarchis*, Captain Papaliolos used his own windlass to raise it to the afterdeck. During the process Yannakis loaded baskets of supplies and the ten-foot levers into the wagon.

Farewells were shouted from the beach and the ship. The captain had in his pocket a letter to Georgios Engastromenos instructing him to pick up the Apollo in Piraeus and to deposit it in the Schliemann garden by the center pool.

The captain backed out into the bay, slowly turned his freighter around and headed into the Aegean. At that moment one of the Turkish guards came down from the hill and onto the sand, whipping his donkey savagely with his heels to get more speed out of him. When he reached the wagon he spilled off the donkey's back and landed face to face with Henry.

"What are you doing?" he demanded.

"Taking our supplies home," replied Henry.

"You know I don't mean that. What have you put on the ship that I have not seen? I heard in Ciplak that you moved something big on Sunday. Is that what you are taking away? I demand to know what it is."

"There is nothing to get excited about. Just oversized crates carrying our half of the finds."

"Call the ship back! I want to see what you put on it."

"I think it is too far away," Henry said blandly, "but you may shout an order to return if you like."

The guard cupped his hands to give volume to his voice but no one on the *Taxiarchis* was listening. Henry did his best to placate the guard. His anger was soon spent. The ship was moving to the horizon leaving a trail of black smoke behind it.

That evening Henry brought out a bottle of his best French wine to celebrate. Sophia observed:

"We should do something rather quickly to put the guard in a favorable light so that he will not get into trouble with his superiors."

"A good idea," Henry replied as he inhaled the wine's bouquet. "What do you suggest?"

"Does the museum have any *pithoi* of our heroic dimensions?"

"I think not."

"You said you were going to take those giant jars out of the wall in the hill."

"Yes."

"Then why not do it tomorrow and turn over the museum's half to the guard?"

"I'll do better than that; I will send them seven and keep three for ourselves. That will show our good will." He raised his glass to her, then drank. "We must be extremely careful how we ship them, for they must go by wagon to Çanakkale, then steamer to Constantinople, and again into wagons from the docks to the museum. We must find thick cloth in which to wrap them, then build supports inside the cases to keep them steady. Their value is doubled if we take them out of the earth in perfect condition."

The next morning a crew began carefully to clear the earth behind the giant *pithoi* and gently loosen its hold on the ancient vases. Yannakis set up a workshop outside the kitchen, then went off to buy wood planking with which to construct cases eight feet tall and six feet wide. The miner, Photides, and two foremen finally contented themselves with a system of horizontal supports spaced through the narrow mouth on top, the wide belly of the middle and the narrow base.

The releasing of the *pithoi*, sawing and hammering of the boxes, the covering with substantial straw matting, fitting into the boxes, attaching of supports and final sealing of the cases comprised several days of work. It also comprised several hundred dollars of cost.

Henry grumbled. "We have to pay not only for the steamer freight to Constantinople but also for the wagons to the door of the museum."

"Yes, but those seven perfect vases will make you friends in Constantinople," consoled Sophia.

5.

She found Polyxene to be a pleasant companion. The girl became an eager housekeeper, disinfecting the Schliemann bed each night and airing their linen and blankets every morning; keeping a relentless eye out for scorpions and forty-leggers, which still managed to creep in under the doors and window joinings. She also did the family wash. Sophia taught her how to use the iron she had brought from Athens on Henry's shirts, including the starching of his collars. She also gave the sixteen-year-old an hour's lesson each day in the reading and writing of Greek.

The two girls got along well together, chatting lightheartedly in Greek while the men were away. Polyxene told stories about growing up as a Greek in Turkey. Sophia entertained with tales of the life in Athens and read to Polyxene the letters from the family about Andromache. The baby was trying new words, could walk a few steps. Sophia was relaxed about her until she heard from Katingo that she had caught cold.

"Henry, do you think I ought to go back to Athens to make sure that Andromache is all right?"

"You are worrying needlessly. Children's colds last for two or three days. Andromache would be completely well by the time your ship was passing through the Sporades."

Polyxene said she wished she too could dig. Sophia got some tools from the storeroom and the two girls opened a trench a short distance from the house. To Polyxene's delight they found terra-cotta whorls, some with interesting linear decorations, quite close to the surface. As they dug farther down, widening the trench, other articles were unearthed: a knife, a two-sided ax, some ivory carvings. Sophia showed Polyxene how to group the shards into what would end up as pots. When Polyxene had assembled her first whole pot she clapped her hands in glee.

"It's yours, Poly," said Sophia. "You may take it home with you and keep it."

Polyxene seized Sophia's hand and kissed it.

Along with the scorpions and forty-leggers they had a problem with the owls that roosted in the digs. They started "shouting," as Henry described it, with an interminable whooo . . . whooo . . . whooo . . . long before midnight and continued until first light. Close by, one particular owl sitting on a nest with two eggs had a weirdly penetrating cry. She spoiled several nights' sleep. Henry finally cried in desperation:

"The owl was Athena's favorite. I am not superstitious, but I still don't like to kill that one who is tormenting us. Why can't we move the nest into a tree in the Troad?"

Polyxene, who was clearing the supper table, said:

"Move the nest, mama owl desert the eggs, the young birds die. But so many owls. Why worry?"

Henry ordered the owl and the nest disposed of. That night they all slept soundly.

The greedy animal in mankind also surfaced. Henry paid the workmen a bonus of a quarter of a piaster, one cent, for every artifact they found and brought to him. On days when the debris was barren they started to make forgeries, scratching decorations on plain shards. The ruse worked. Henry and Sophia were too busy to examine each piece thoroughly . . . until the third night, when Sophia was cleaning and sorting the shards and saw the freshly incised cuts. She showed them to Henry:

"I know they think we're crazy; but why do they think we're stupid in the bargain?"

"Greed, my dear, the deadliest of man's sins. But I know how to put a stop to it: I'll fine them two piasters every time they try to trick us."

Since Henry could not persuade Sophia, even in the increasingly warmer weather, to gallop down to the Dardanelles with him and have a swim, he decided to build her a shower. Makres, who had constructed docks on his native island, cut a hole in the roof in one corner of the bedroom, installed a barrel with a trap door on hinges, and then built a small, closetlike enclosure so that Sophia could step in, close the door behind her and pull on a long chain that opened the trap door of the barrel. Yannakis filled it with water each morning and by the time Sophia got back from her work in the digs the sun had warmed it.

Like the Dramali house in Ciplak the year before, the Schliemann house became an infirmary, the people in the neighborhood bringing in any number of complaints, many of them serious, which neither Henry nor Sophia knew how to treat. The one thing Henry insisted upon was that the women bathe in the Hellespont or Aegean every day. At first they refused; it was against both Turkish and Turkophone tradition for women to bathe in the sea. Then, in desperation over increasing illness, and hopeful that the Schliemanns could perform miracles as they had the year before, they did actually immerse themselves. In many instances the bathing helped their general health.

A seventeen-year-old girl from Neochori whose body was covered with ulcers, with one large one over her left eye, was too weak to walk or stand. She had been brought by her father on a donkey. She was also coughing badly.

"How can we possibly help her?" cried Sophia.

The girl had been bled by the parish priest seven times in the last month. Sophia gave her a dose of castor oil. Henry ordered sea baths every day. A month later the girl walked three miles from Neochori to thank him, fell on her knees and kissed his shoes. Sophia raised her up, looked at the skin tissue covering her left eye.

"Henry, this could be cut away by an eye doctor. We could send her . . ."

". . . the nearest is in Constantinople. Her whole family would have to accompany her. There is no way. These people here don't know any more about medicine than the Achaeans did back in 1200 B.C. Or your Dr. Venizelos in Athens today," Henry added bitterly; "perhaps less. Agamemnon says to his brother Menelaus, 'The leech shall search the wound and lay thereon simples, medicines, that shall make thee cease from dark pains. . . .' When Eurypylus was wounded he asked Patroclus, 'Lead me to my black ship and cut the arrow from my thigh, and wash the black blood from it with warm water.' Patroclus did this, then 'upon it cast a bitter root; he had rubbed it between his hands, a root that slayeth pain; and the wound waxed dry, and the blood ceased.' "

Sophia ignored his reference to Dr. Venizelos; she had thought his bitterness had passed. She observed, "The women of the villages must know a good deal about their own roots, herbs, leaves, berries. . . . Don't you think?"

"Yes. All peasant peoples do. That knowledge is handed down from generation to generation. Yet these root and herb medicines are good for healing only a limited number of illnesses."

By the first week in July the temperature had risen to eighty-eight degrees. The work slowed. They also lost seven days because of rain and festivals. More hundreds of cubic yards of debris had joined the thousands already moved, and there was still no sign of the ancient buildings he coveted. He became short-tempered.

"The Renkoits and others of the Greeks are no longer giving me a full day's work. I've taken a count. The average worker lays down his tools three times each hour, takes his tobacco out of a pouch, leisurely rolls it, wets one edge to make it stick, searches his pockets for a match or borrows one, slowly lights and inhales, thereby wasting at least ten minutes out of each hour. I give them a half hour at nine to rest and smoke, and an hour and a half at noon for eating and smoking. I'm going to put an end to it."

"Won't that cause a small-scale mutiny?"

"Let it. I've suffered enough impudence from the Renkoits. They've never worked for anyone before, only for themselves, and they simply don't know the meaning of a full day's work."

At the midday rest period he announced his ban on smoking during the working hours. The seventy Renkoits hooted. Sophia understood their derisive comments and choice epithets better than Henry. She told him:

"They refuse to accept your condition. If they cannot smoke as much as they want, they won't work."

Henry was furious.

"They think that because the weather is good I won't sacrifice the hours. They'll learn better. Yannakis, pay a half day's wage to those who want to quit."

The Renkoits took their money, then stood around the edge of the dig hurling imprecations at laborers from the other villages who had accepted the order. When blasphemous words did not stop the other men, the Renkoits began pelting them with stones. Henry summoned Yannakis, said:

"Take one of the horses and tour the Turkish villages. Bring me back workmen to replace the Renkoits."

Yannakis merely bowed his head.

The Renkoits did not go home that night. They slept in their camp, determined to be there for the beginning of the next day's work. Sophia slept only in snatches, fearful of a physical attack. In the morning Henry went as usual for his swim, returning in time to see Yannakis writing down the names of one hundred and twenty new Turkish workers. The Renkoits, astonished at the man's recruiting powers, started their long trudge homeward. Henry, who was something less than euphoric about the virtues of the Turkish government and its officials, confessed to Sophia, "These men are conscientious and agreeable. They have turned my thinking around."

"I'm sorry for the Renkoits," Sophia mused; "instead of a hare they found a bear."

Makres and Demetriou began to complain that the inner walls of earth and debris were so hard they could not be picked down any further.

"Why not mine them?" asked Photides. "Make tunnels. That'll weaken their structure."

Henry approved the idea and the men worked out a plan to divide the earth walls into sixteen-foot segments so that each of them, ten feet thick, could be tackled separately. Photides built a shelter of thick logs with a plank roof so that when the warning cry of downcoming stones was heard the workmen in the trench could flee to the structure for safety.

A few mornings later Henry and Sophia were supervising separate crews when one of the earth walls which had been extensively mined collapsed with the sound of a cannon. Photides and a workman were in the shelter sharpening their tools. The collapsed earth completely buried it. Sophia, who was the closest, ran to what was now a small earthen mound. Henry was only a few steps behind her.

"I can hear moaning," she cried.

Workmen came running from all directions. They picked up shovels and pickaxes to dig out the imprisoned men. Henry stopped them.

"You may hit them and hurt them. Use your hands."

Sophia and Henry dug alongside the men. It took time, but the stout walls and roof of the shelter held, there was sufficient space to provide the men with air. They emerged unhurt. Even the pantheist Henry Schliemann crossed himself three times, right to left. Sophia said:

"I fervently thank God for His great mercy that no one of us has been hurt."

Henry came close and laid his cheek on hers.

"It's your hand on my shoulder. That is my talisman."

The accident gave Henry a bad night.

"It's a serious defeat, Sophia," he said as he thrashed about the room in his dressing robe and slippers. "We're going to have to abandon the concept of the great platform as a mechanism to push through the entire mound. We'll keep digging toward the south to join up with Photides but we'll have to go back to the trench idea of last year."

"The platform is by no means a failure, Henry. Working from it, you have uncovered a considerable part of the mount."

"Yes, but it has enabled us to touch primary soil for only a limited space. And what did we find there? A few urns, some bones of animals, pieces of pottery, a number of round terra cottas."

His methods had failed. He did not know in which direction to turn next.

"I'm frustrated, Sophia." He scratched his scalp vigorously with his blunted fingernails, as though the excitation might put new or different ideas into his head. "Everything I want is here, but how do I find it?"

"It's like all exploration," she said quietly. "One day one is in a cold wind, naked as a shorn lamb; the next day in the Garden of Eden."

The wind from Athens, too, was exceedingly cold.

Although Henry had met with oral skepticism and even ridicule about his notion of where Troy lay buried, and some accusations of being foolhardy in spending his time and money on such a fruitless hobby, there had never been a written attack against him. They now received a copy of the Athens *Newspaper of the Debates*, in which Henry had been publishing his journal, which contained a strong attack against the articles, his theories and his excavations, written by Georgios Nikolaides, a member of the Archaeological Society and consequently a man of prestige. Nikolaides was a Cretan, had taken his law degree at the University of Pisa, then turned to archaeological studies in Florence. His book *The Iliad and Its Topography*, which he first published in France and later enlarged for the Greek version, had made him an authority in the Homeric field.

Nikolaides's main thrust was that Dr. Schliemann was giving himself "unnecessary trouble," was squandering money like a profligate, was making unscientific and unscholarly claims due to the enthusiasm of the amateur who had no training in academia and hence was unqualified to publish. He was deluding the public with his fantasies, an ill service which all trained professionals deplored; for not one word that Dr. Schliemann was publishing in the *Newspaper of the Debates*, the *Levant Herald* or the periodical of the Greek Philological Society had the remotest connection with provable fact. All honest and sensible men knew that Troy could never be found by excavating earth and debris because the city had been created from the whole cloth of Homer's poetic imagination. It existed nowhere except in the pages of *The Iliad*. Dr. Schliemann should therefore cease and desist, find another, innocuous hobby in which to indulge himself and leave the serious business of archaeology to the trained authorities in the field.

Henry glared at the paper, ground his teeth with rage. Since he had yet found little more than artifacts which he could claim to be Trojan, he was vulnerable.

"I don't believe that Nikolaides has ever been in the Troad," he thundered. "He theorizes while I dig."

She had no answer.

His nerves became frazzled. He was short with the workmen, or fell into periods of dejected silence, was sometimes sharp with Sophia. She did not take it personally, she knew the dichotomy of his position: absolute certitude that here had stood Homer's Troy, and failure to find any indisputable evidence of its existence.

She reminded him that he had told her in the beginning that they would have to dig for five years to complete the job.

"Last year hardly counts," she offered. "We got started late and were able to dig for only six weeks before the rains washed us out. This is really our first year and we've been excavating for only three months. Give yourself time."

"A life sentence!" he replied grimly. "Sometimes I don't know which is the prisoner in this mount, Troy or myself."

She was a good prophet. On the third day of concentrated digging in a new trench running south from the platform they found a treasure trove: a silver hairpin, copper nails, ivory needles, plates, knives, daggers, ivory and copper rings. Bracelets of copper were found at a depth of thirty-three to fifty-two feet below the plateau. The objects they were accumulating in their baskets, black cups, hammers, axes, granite weights, wedges of transparent green stone, fine marble idols, stone quoits with a hole in the center, all were ancient, beautifully made and, except for the terra cottas, splendidly preserved.

Henry cried triumphantly, "Let's widen the trench at an angle on both sides. Perhaps we'll come upon houses and palaces."

His eyes were bright, he was shoveling out the debris of the trench and sifting it with a new conviction that he was working on primary soil. For the first time during the excavation Sophia saw him throw off his coat, loosen his necktie at the collar, roll his sleeves up to his elbows.

Their next find was a small burial ground. They unearthed two three-legged vessels on the primary rock. Before moving them he searched inside for evidence which would give a clue to their age. In one of them he was astonished to find the remains of an embryo. He called to Sophia, who was working ahead of him in the channel.

"Look, the bones of an embryo, about six months along, I would gauge."

". . . embryo . . . but how could it have survived? We've never even found human ashes in a funeral vase."

"Tonight I will send a letter to Dr. Aretaios, professor of surgery at the University of Athens, and ask his scientific opinion. I would theorize that the mother died before giving birth, was cremated, but the embryo's bones were protected by the membrane which enclosed it. I shall have the skeleton restored by a skillful surgeon."

Sophia stood beside the urn. Henry's whipped nerves had taken their toll of her own. Her reaction at seeing the tiny bones of the child who had never lived became deeply emotional, a collage of images carried her to Athens, the miscarriage of the embryo within herself, almost the age and size of this unborn child. All of the disappointment of her loss only four months before washed vividly over her. She felt dizzy, her knees grew weak. She fell into a faint at Henry's feet.

She awakened in her bed back at the house. In reply to her question about how she got there, Henry said:

"Yannakis and Photides made a litter and carried you. What happened?"

"When I saw that embryo I relived my own miscarriage."

Henry turned pale, his expression grief-stricken.

"What an insensitive, stupid man I am! Why did I not remember? I should have concealed those bones from you."

She wet her parched lips with drops of water from the glass by the bed.

"No need to blame yourself, Henry. It happened to me without my willing; some inner force felled me."

The explanation from Dr. Aretaios about the embryo was quite different from Henry's. Dr. Aretaios wrote, "The preservation of the bones of the embryo is only possible on the supposition that the mother had brought forth the child and then died, that her body was burned and the unburned embryo was put into the funeral urn with her ashes."

Henry doubled his work crews in the widening trench. Very shortly they came upon a house and then, toward the end of the same day, what seemed to be a palace. He was jubilant. He examined the blocks of hewn stones, scraping the edges with his pocket knife and sifting the cuttings into an envelope. He showed Sophia the orange-colored dust.

"Now you can see why the houses and palaces were so easily destroyed. The stones were joined together only with earth. When destruction hit the walls, everything in the house was crushed. When this pile of stones is removed we should find interesting things under them."

It was long past midnight when they stopped cleaning the silver, copper, nails, daggers, rings, and writing descriptions in their journal. She thought she would be far too aroused to sleep but remembered nothing from the time she put her head on the pillow until Henry awoke her shortly after five in the morning with a cup of coffee. He had already had his swim.

They began the removal of the hewn stones that morning. By noon the men had cleared the debris from within one spacious house and one palace. Here they found hearths, what appeared to be open courtyards, walls dividing rooms, thresholds, bones of animals, boar's tusks, small shells, horns of buffalo, ram, stag.

In the afternoon they reaped another harvest, indications of the life that had been lived within the walls. After supper they separated the good-sized splendid terra-cotta shards until they had several piles for reconstruction. Yannakis washed them, Polyxene boiled the fish glue and Sophia and Henry set to work on the kitchen table rebuilding the pots. Although there were parts missing they had the beginning outlines of new and startlingly different jars and vases: a large yellowish bowl thirteen inches high and nearly seventeen inches broad which, in addition to a handle, was adorned with three large curled ram's horns; a black vase with round bottom and small rings on either side, apparently for hanging; a curious red vessel in the form of two jugs joined to each other at the bulge, with long, perfectly upright beak-shaped mouths.

They learned something about prehistoric housekeeping. The inhabitants of this particular stratum threw their refuse on the earthen floor. When the debris rose too high they brought in earth, covered over the debris with a foot of new flooring, then raised the walls and pushed up the roof. Sophia was nonplused.

"They could have thrown everything into the gutter and let the rains wash it away."

"My dear wife, it doesn't rain in the Troad for six months out of the year."

"Then what about burning it in the fireplace?"

"Burn animal bones, sea shells? Have you tried that?"

"Very well, I won't sit in judgment on the Trojan housewives."

6.

As they broadened their trench on its way through the mound they saw evolve before their eyes, exposed on the hillock on both sides, three more settlements: walls, streets, conflicting areas of debris, built in three different eras, with different architecture, different drainageways. The second from the bottom was from a thirty-three-foot level to twenty-three feet; the third from the twenty-third to thirteenth; the fourth was thirteen to six feet from the surface of the plateau. It was obvious that their four new strata had been built with no knowledge of what lay beneath: walls crossed earlier walls at odd angles, inimical levels juxtaposed each other, small and large stone constructions followed their own courses. The same was true of the houses; they stood one above the other, sometimes running at right angles to the ones below or facing in the opposite direction: a multi-layer cake of communities covering a depth of forty-six to fifty-two feet of man-made hill, constructed over a period of two thousand years. Now the vast mound had become a giant building whose roof had blown off in an explosion, and in whose interior one saw exposed rooms, walls, corridors, doors, floors, patios.

"It staggers the imagination!" Sophia cried.

"We've got to excavate all four levels," Henry said, dazed; "but how do I dig out the next layer upward and not have the two layers on top of it fall down on our hapless heads?"

Their first important find in the city just above them were houses whose foundations were made of stones but the walls of brick. The fire which had consumed the community had effectively fired the bricks, they had withstood all shock of earthquake and conquest. Because of the protection of the brick walls the objects within them, pottery with Aryan religious symbols and brilliant red goblets Henry labeled "immense champagne glasses with two mighty handles," had been preserved almost whole. Sophia was bubbling with joy.

"Henry, no fish glue! Look at this vase: it's a pig, the funny head and nose in front and the spout and handle at the rear. It's a jewel, a museum piece!"

"Don't say that word," Henry commanded, "or that's exactly where it will end up . . . in Constantinople. We'll hide that one from the guards. Surely we're allowed to appropriate . . . misappropriate . . . one piece."

Water and funeral urns appeared in large numbers, five feet high and some of them three feet wide. Athena vases with owl's heads, breasts, navels, each with upraised arms; globular vessels with a tall neck resembling a chimney; round terra-cotta votive offerings with ingenious symbolical decorations, the holy tree of life, the sun god, shards with the *sauvastika* Henry remembered having seen in many religious artifacts: Hindu, Persian, Celt. Then came kitchen finds: dishes, *pithoi* for storing oil and wine. There were implements of war as well: copper battle-axes, lances, arrows, knives. The soldier guards became excited at these recognizable weapons, quickly jumped down into the trenches and picked out their half of the find before Henry had had a chance to subtly delineate the separation which gave him a shade of advantage.

That night, polishing their metal trophies, Henry mused:

"These too were a warlike people, even as the Trojans. Or maybe it was the perennial need to defend oneself. . . ."

As he turned he knocked off the worktable a mass of burned metal and wires which they had found that afternoon among the yellow ash of a house that had been destroyed by fire. They had thrown it casually into a basket along with the other finds, and taken it back to the house at sunset. A wire which held the packet together broke. Out tumbled a number of pieces of jewelry. They crouched on the floor above the find, their knees touching. Henry first pulled out three silver bracelets.

"Look at this treble-strand bracelet," he exclaimed. "It has an earring of six wires welded to it by the fire."

In the lamplight Sophia caught a reflection of dull yellow. She slipped her hand under the packet, drew forth a gleaming object.

"It's an earring of gold," she said softly. "See these rows of little stars on both sides. Open your hand. There, you now have in your possession the first sign of the treasure of Priam: 'Take thou store of bronze and gold,' Hector pleads with Achilles, in hopes of not being killed, 'gifts that my father and queenly mother shall give thee. . . .' Homer never mentions a gold mine in the Troad."

"No. I'm convinced there was none. But the Trojans bought talents of gold from the land caravans and had their own goldsmiths design and make gold jewelry. If we can find one earring, we can find a hundred! And bracelets of gold, cups of gold, diadems of gold. It's here, Sophia. . . ."

They slogged their way through the intense heat of late July. The men worked in clothing wet with perspiration; the sun had a biting quality that raised welts on any part of the body exposed to it. Along with the heat and brilliant glare came winds from the north, sweeping down the Dardanelles from the Black Sea and the Sea of Marmara, driving the dust into their eyes and blinding them. Sophia made herself a *yashmak* out of white cloth, cutting and sewing it so that it covered her hair and all of her face, leaving only a slit at eye level.

In August the Greek and Turkish farmers had to harvest their crops. The work force was depleted. Henry wrote to the German consul in the Gallipoli Peninsula to whom he had sent copies of his articles the year before, asking if he would recruit laborers for him. He sent a similar letter to the English consul in Constantinople, offering to pay the fare to Çanakkale. Both men responded favorably. Henry again had his hundred and fifty men digging in his four levels. It became more difficult each day to move the debris; it had to be carried increasing distances to get it out of the way. The English consul in Constantinople secured for them ten more handcarts and twenty additional wheelbarrows. The *Taxiarchis* brought other equipment.

One night Sophia was entering the costs of the ten man-carts and forty additional wheelbarrows which had just arrived, as well as the forty workmen sent to them by the German consul, men who received traveling expenses and an extra daily stipend to cover the cost of their food and rooms. She was startled and then frightened at the sums of money he was pouring out every day. She asked:

"Have you ever added up all the money you have laid out on this year's excavations?"

He looked up sharply from a group of carved ivory idols he was describing in his diary, apparently surprised at Sophia's question.

"Not in the account book itself. But I keep a rough figure in my mind."

"What do you suppose the figure is going to be for 1872?"

"I'm not concerned. What it has to cost, it costs."

She made a quick totaling up and saw that at their present rate of expenditure the year's excavations would amount to fifty thousand dollars. She gasped. It was a fortune! With the exception of the man who had given the Arsakeion to Athens, and the one for whom Eugène Piat had designed a palace on Syntagma Square, few of the rich men of Greece could claim that they had fifty thousand dollars to spend on an activity which would not bring back more money on its investment. She wanted to ask Henry if he could afford it but decided that it was not an advisable question. She gazed at the top of his head, across the table, where he was writing, in his small, intense, disciplined hand, a comparison of his ivory idols with others he had seen in the Orient. She thought: "He would bankrupt himself to discover Troy."

Walking his great platform and his trenches, examining his finds and rereading his Homer, Henry decided that the temple built by Lysimachus lay directly above the much older Trojan temple where Alexander himself had worshiped. He decided they must go back to the big temple where they had found the marble Apollo and start digging straight down through the foundations.

The two crews under Makres and Demetriou started at dawn, following Henry's markings for a new twenty-foot-wide opening. At midmorning Sophia came to Henry's side to watch progress. Suddenly he gasped. She shook him by the shoulder.

"Henry, are you ill?"

He licked his dry lips, put out his hand and pointed to a wall the crew had unearthed. It lay considerably below the foundation of Lysimachus's temple.

"It's six feet thick," he said hoarsely, "and goes down at least another ten feet from the top we are looking at."

The men began digging furiously to get to its base.

"See that quantity of similar stones lying at the foot of the wall," Henry exclaimed.

"They're huge."

"That indicates that the wall went up much higher, possibly as high as Homer claimed. And it's built in the cyclopean manner."

Sophia felt herself tremble.

"Henry, have you really done it? Have we found the wall built by Poseidon and Apollo?"

"There can be no question about it. This is the *first wall*. The bottom goes down to forty-four feet below the surface. Everything that you see from here, gazing upward, including Lysimachus's temple, was built on top of this primary wall."

They stood transfixed. Only the sound of the shovels and the thud of earth into the wheelbarrows broke into the silence.

"Congratulations," Sophia finally whispered. "You were right, and the rest of the world was wrong."

Henry held his hand to his heart.

"Now that we've got Priam's wall everything else should be findable."

In mid-August Yannakis summoned Sophia from her workbench. Henry was pacing the terrace above a deep trench.

"I've come up against the most extraordinary structure. It has the crew completely stopped. I know I am on an accurate line with Photides coming up from the south. His trench isn't that far away, but I'm not going to be able to continue. Look here. We've been digging around the north side."

She looked at a large stone structure breaching the trench.

"Isn't it a continuation of the primary wall?"

"Yes and no. It appears to be a part of the great defense wall but it projects backward a considerable number of feet. I have to find out if it also projects forward on the south side. . . ."

At that moment Photides came striding up the hill toward them, his cap off, wiping the perspiration from his forehead back through his thinning hair. He was shaking his head in puzzlement.

"Doctor, we've come to a dead end. We're blocked by the most massive pile of stones we've encountered yet in the two hundred feet of digging. I don't understand it. Would you come look?"

Sophia asked, "Does it project southward beyond the defense wall?"

"Yes, at least fifteen feet, maybe twenty."

Sophia and Henry stared at each other, wide-eyed.

"My God, Sophia!" exclaimed Henry. "We've come upon the Great Tower!"

Tears sprang to his eyes. Sophia had trouble getting the words out of her throat.

"The Trojan Tower? The one on which Priam asked Helen to identify the leaders of the Achaean forces surging toward the wall?"

Henry would no more have gone to the digs without his copy of *The Iliad* than without his trousers, vest and gold chain. He took the small-sized edition with its tiny type from the side pocket of his coat, put on his spectacles and within a moment had leafed through to the lines he wanted in Book III.

> " 'Come hither, dear child, and sit before me, that thou mayest see thy former lord and thy kinsfolk and thy people— thou art nowise to blame in my eyes; it is the gods, methinks, that are to blame who roused against me the tearful war of the Achaeans—and that thou mayest tell me who is this huge warrior, this man of Achaea so valiant and so tall. Verily there be others that are even taller by a head, but so comely a man have mine eyes never yet beheld. . . .' "

He flipped the pages to Book VI for confirmation.

" 'But to the height of Troy's topmost tower Andromache is gone; since tidings came the Trojan force was over-
matched. . . .' "

Henry and Photides brought their crews to the tower and started
them digging at an accelerated pace to uncover the north and south
sides. Henry made rapid calculations in his notebook, then explained to
Sophia:

"My estimate is that we've hit the tower at mid-point. We're going
to have to clear another twenty feet below, and perhaps another twenty
on its upward course."

"That's a lot of earth to move."

"We'll have to dump it a considerable distance away." He turned to
Yannakis. "Hire me the carts drawn by horses right away." And to
Sophia: "In the meanwhile we will work with wheelbarrows and man-
carts."

While excavating around the upper part of the tower he discovered a
depression some thirty feet long. In it he found two copper lances,
several arrowheads, a double-edged saw, copper and silver nails, great
quantities of bones. It appeared to be a trench built for the protection
of archers. It took a good many days of feverish activity under the
scorching August sun before the tower stood exposed on its north and
south sides, cutting across the whole length of Henry's master trench.
Yannakis had been able to rent only seven horse-drawn carts, but they
sped up the removal of the compacted earth. It was of a chalky nature,
composed of calcium carbonate or limestone. On the north side of the
tower there was a hillock of calcareous earth sixty-five feet broad and
sixteen feet high, presumably the earth which the Trojans had had to
remove to make their foundation excavations for the tower. When the
men had pierced the hillock, Henry found that the north side of the
tower consisted of large blocks of stones piled one upon the other; only
the upper part of the tower had been constructed of masonry. On the
south side, however, overlooking the Troad plain, the tower was solid
masonry, blocks of limestone cemented together with earth clay. It was
forty feet thick.

That night after supper Henry thrashed out his ideas and his puzzle-
ments.

"My great disappointment is that it seems our existing tower is only
twenty feet high. Does it sound logical that the enormous pile of stones
we found at the base must have fallen from the tower?"

"It does, Henry. After all, there have been a dozen settlements built
between the present top of the tower and the present top of the
plateau."

Henry picked up his pen and wrote in his diary:

For the preservation of what remains we have to thank the ruins which entirely covered the tower as it now stands. It is probable that after the destruction of Troy much more of it remained standing, and that the part which rose above the ruins of the town was destroyed by the successors of the Trojans, who possessed neither walls nor fortifications. Considering the enormous accumulation of debris, I believe that the tower once stood on the western edge of the acropolis where its situation would be most interesting and imposing; for its top would have commanded not only a view of the whole Plain of Troy, but of the sea with the islands of Tenedos, Imbros and Samothrace. There is not a more sublime situation in the area of Troy than this, *and I therefore presume that it is the "Great Tower of Ilium"* which Andromache ascended because "she had heard that the Trojans were hard pressed and the power of the Achaeans was great." After having been buried for thirty-one centuries, and after successive nations have built their houses and palaces high above its summit during thousands of years, this tower has again been brought to light, and commands a view, if not of the whole plain, at least of the northern part and of the Hellespont. May this sacred and sublime monument of Greek heroism forever attract the eyes of those who sail through the Hellespont! May it become a place to which the inquiring youth of all future generations shall make pilgrimage and fan their enthusiasm for knowledge, and above all for the noble language and literature of Greece!

The following day brought another discovery at a depth of forty-two feet: the remains of a house on native rock with the skeleton of a woman in it. The skull was in an especially good state of preservation. The mouth was somewhat protruding, and showed good but astonishingly small teeth. It was the first adult skeleton they had found. Henry was elated.

"At last we've found a Trojan!"

His enthusiasm was infectious.

"If only these bones could speak, what a tale they would have to tell!"

"Why are they so yellow?" asked Sophia.

"The lady was overtaken by fire and burned alive. We'll take her back to Athens and reconstruct her."

"Which half are you giving to the museum?"

"The guards are superstitious. They don't want any part of skeletons. She is all ours."

When Sophia used her fingertips to brush away the layer of ash from the sides of the bones, she made several other discoveries: a finger ring, three earrings and a dress pin of gold. Two of the earrings were primitive, consisting of simple gold wire, as was the third earring, which, however, was much more finely wrought and ended in a leaf formed of six gold wires of equal thickness. The finger ring was made of three gold wires.

Henry held the jewelry in his hands and examined it carefully; his face was flushed with pleasure.

"If only the Trojans had built tombs the way the Egyptians did, and buried their kings with all their valuable possessions. What treasures we could take out to show the world!"

"We'll just have to make do, Henry. The Great Tower and the defense wall are more important."

Marsh fever struck in a virulent form in mid-August. The workmen went down in increasing numbers; first ten, then twenty, then thirty. There was not enough quinine to medicate them all. Henry increased his own and Sophia's dosage and gave the normal dose of four grains to Yannakis and Polyxene, as well as the three indispensable foremen. Polyxene became ill, then Yannakis, then all three of the foremen. By the third week Henry had barely a skeleton crew at the dig. Then he and Sophia developed chills and fever. Their cases were mild compared to the others. Polyxene was suffering paroxysms and the foremen could not get out of their beds without being seized with uncontrollable shaking. Henry fed them all large doses of quinine until he ran out completely.

"Dear one, I'm afraid we're going to have to close up shop," he told Sophia. "I had hoped to continue for at least another month, and every day now should bring important discoveries, but I think we would be wise to get out of the Troad. This malaria is going to get worse rather than better. I must make one trip to Çanakkale. There is a photographer I want to bring out so that we can take back to Athens a full picture of the excavations. The land surveyor to whom I wrote in Constantinople should also be in Çanakkale by now. He agreed to come and draw accurate engineering maps of the site."

He was away for two days, returning with the German photographer Siebrecht and a Greek land surveyor by the name of Sisilas. He worked with them for several days getting all the maps and pictures he wanted.

"I know what my eye saw and what the camera was pointed at," he told Sophia. "Now all we can do is pray that the negatives come out well. I felt sorry for Siebrecht, working in that naked sun all day with his head inside a black cloth."

She had done most of the packing.

"When do we leave?"

They looked at each other, lean and worn again despite the new house and ample provisions.

"There's a ship sailing from Constantinople to Piraeus in five days. I've reserved our cabin and space for Makres and Demetriou. Frank Calvert was delighted with his half of our finds, though he did not want everything. He and Mrs. Calvert and the children each picked their favorite piece. We'll take the balance back to Athens."

Henry hired a caretaker. Yannakis stacked their thousands of dollars' worth of shovels, levers, windlasses, wheelbarrows, pickaxes in the kitchen and the foremen's sleeping quarters. Henry arranged for him to be paid a monthly salary from the bank in Çanakkale, in return for which he was to visit the site, check over the equipment once a week, and do whatever repairs were needed. He would also have the camp and houses ready by the turn of the year when the Schliemanns were scheduled to return. He promised to scour the Troad for the best hundred and fifty men he could find.

Four days later Henry and Sophia stood at the gate to the dig while Henry paid off the men, thanked them and asked them to return the following January. They had no sooner reached the door of the house than there was a tremendous clap of thunder and then, after four months without a drop of rain, a cloudburst.

They had closed out the works at exactly the right moment. There would be mud in the digs for weeks.

The next morning Henry woke Sophia at first light and asked her to accompany him to the tower. She was to bring his journal, pen and ink and a bottle of French wine. By the time they reached the defense wall the sun was flaming over the Ida Mountains and lighting the fast-moving waters of the Dardanelles. He took her hand and led her up the mound of earth next to the tower so that they could stand on top of the tower itself. Pulling himself up to his full height, Henry opened his journal and, writing and proclaiming to Sophia and to the entire world, cried:

"I flatter myself with the hope that, as a reward for my enormous expenses and all my privations, annoyances and sufferings in this wilderness, but above all for my important discoveries, the civilized world will acknowledge my right to rechristen this sacred locality. In the name of the divine Homer I baptize it with that name of immortal renown which fills the heart of everyone with joy and enthusiasm. I give it the name of 'TROY' and I call the acropolis, where I am writing these lines, by the name of the 'Pergamus of Troy.'"

Sophia slipped her hand into his, smiled at him, her red lips parted, her dark eyes beautiful with love and fulfillment.

"Amen," she whispered.

BOOK FIVE

TROY?

1.

SEPTEMBER is a divine month in Athens. A light breeze moves down from the north Aegean carrying with it a salty promise of autumnal coolness under a beneficent sun that warms without burning and rides like Apollo in his chariot across flawless blue skies.

The maid, the little nanny and Andromache were in the house to welcome the Schliemanns home. Everything was scrubbed and shining for their return. It took Sophia and Henry only a few days to shake off the last effects of their malaria: home is where the body heals. Andromache, now seventeen months old, was walking, her chubby legs slightly bowed; she greeted her parents with a gurgling monologue.

They spent much of their day in the garden; the trees had grown, the palms revived, wisteria covered the trellises of the back wall with cool greenness; the fount was filled with fresh water and gave the garden the feel of moisture, the doves were cooing softly in their cote. The vines they had trained on three sides of the octagonal teahouse sheltered them from the noon sun when Sophia had their dinner served out of doors.

Henry had a platform built for their beautiful, purloined Apollo metope, placing it alongside the fount so that Sophia could see it when she read or played with Andromache in the teahouse. Since there was little work space left in the house he also built a covered shed on the far side of the garden and installed long worktables for the cleaning and repairing of the hundreds of pots, vases, idols, cups, hammers, axes, plates they had accumulated.

They worked in the cool of the early morning hours in the garden shed, preparing the finds for exhibition to their Athenian friends. At ten Henry walked down to the Fair Greece to read the foreign newspapers over several cups of coffee. Sophia went into her kitchen to prepare dinner with the foods she herself had bought at dawn from the street vendors, supplemented by the maid's purchases at the Central Market. It was a joy to be reunited with the traditional adage, "The culinary art is as important as any of the other arts, and a more consistent bringer of pleasure."

Now she happily set about cooking an octopus in red wine sauce, discarding the ink sac, sautéing the onions in olive oil until golden and then adding a bay leaf; or a *stefado* of lean beef flavored with tomato paste, clove of garlic, wine vinegar, walnut halves. Her cheeks were red from the hot stove, the room was infused with delicious smells.

Henry returned promptly at one-thirty for dinner. There were no Engastromenoses present in these early weeks. After the one celebration dinner on their first Sunday at home, when the entire clan had gathered, Sophia suggested gently that Henry needed quiet and privacy in order to dispatch his neglected business affairs. After their nap, during which all of Athens lay somnolent below them, they cut across the city to the bay at Phaleron and the new baths. Henry had engaged their favorite driver, Ioannes Maltezos, and his double carriage on a full-time basis. He insisted that Andromache accompany them.

"I'm going to teach her how to swim. This is the time to begin."

To Sophia's surprise the child took to the water, untiring in her pleasure at having her father show her how to move her arms and legs.

By eight in the evening they were at their regular table at one of the Dardanelles cafés, the Yannakis or Dore. Here, while Sophia held Andromache on her lap and fed her ice cream, she and Henry received their friends and relatives in a widening circle about the marble-topped table. They were home at nine, had a light supper, then spent a tranquil hour in the garden watching the golden moon move across the darkened Athenian sky. They went to sleep early, for they were up at dawn.

Henry was writing steadily for the Greek, German, French and English newspapers, reports of the development in what he now insistently called Troy rather than the mound of Hissarlik. The Greek scholars were polite; the French academics cynical; the German philologists contemptuous; the English were enthusiastic; the Americans, who picked up their stories from the London *Times,* were entertained by the adventures of Henry and Sophia Schliemann in the wilds of Asia Minor.

The day before she had sailed to join Henry in May, Sophia had received from him an article he had written for the Athens *Newspaper of the Debates.* He had instructed her to turn it over to her cousin to correct the grammar and to have photographic copies made of the cross and *sauvastika* that would illustrate it. Georgios Engastromenos had promised to attend to it. When the article had appeared Henry turned livid. It had never been corrected and was filled with the newspaper's mistakes as well. There were not only errors in the grammar but misspellings of words which changed the meaning altogether. She had not had to read more than a few paragraphs to realize the text was completely garbled, the drawings of the cross and *sauvastika* erroneously printed, and that Henry was right to be outraged.

"The mistakes are so terribly many and of such a nature all people will laugh at me," he had cried. "I would rather cut off my right hand than see my name under such foolishness."

The error-laden article and the attack on him in the same journal by Georgios Nikolaides had put him at a disadvantage with the faculty of the University of Athens.

But not with their friends. Émile Burnouf lent them the two assistants who had first helped convert their shards into viable vases. Henry put them on a generous salary. He also engaged Louise Burnouf to come to the garden shed each morning to make drawings of their finds as they were cleaned, classified, numbered and set out on the table at the far end of the shed. Louise sat on a high stool, her soft blond hair falling to her waist, her deep blue eyes alive with excitement at the challenge Henry had set:

"Make your sketches completely accurate, for I shall want to use them in my book about Troy."

Sophia did not deny him the camaraderie of the young girl during the working hours; however, since Henry had a photographer working several days a week to get a complete record of the finds, she considered Louise's employment redundant. Madame Victoria, coming upon Louise and Henry with their heads together over one of Louise's drawings, was not as generous.

"Who is she?" she asked Sophia.

"Louise Burnouf, daughter of the director of the French Archaeological Institute. Henry has hired her as his staff artist."

"It is not proper for Henry to have so young and beautiful a girl working at his side every day. It is dangerous, as well."

"Dangerous?"

". . . all men are susceptible. . . . After all, Henry is wealthy, influential, he would be a good catch . . ."

"For a fisherman?"

". . . for an ambitious young woman who also happened to be unscrupulous. There are plenty of young men in Athens who are good artists."

Sophia's lips closed firmly above her strong chin. She was remembering the six years in which Henry had gone without a woman after he separated from Ekaterina; and of his breaking the fast only when he realized that he had to prove to himself that he had not become impotent and hence could fulfill his husbandly duties, before he proposed marriage.

"Mother, I forbid you ever to bring up this subject again."

After an absence of nearly six months during which they had received only an occasional *Newspaper of the Debates*, Henry was starved for news. His few hours daily at the Fair Greece were insufficient, so he ordered the Athens newspapers to be delivered to the house. He had instilled in Sophia an interest in the continuing world news and she too fell into the habit of reading them, though her time was limited. Henry insisted that she take a course in advanced German at the Varvakeion School and have Kyria N. Kontopoulos, an excellent teacher, come to their home several mornings a week to continue her training in French and English. Henry demanded no less of himself; he devoted several hours each day to the study of rare books which he borrowed from the National Library on the subjects of ancient art, language, mythology and religious symbols.

The Athens to which they returned resembled their dig, with open ditches in every street for the laying of lead or iron pipe to conduct water from newly completed aqueducts into private homes. Henry subscribed at once, and just in time, for in mid-September they suffered an unendurable heat wave. They could not sleep at night, even though they kept the front and back windows wide open. Henry called in a carpenter to screen in their veranda with mosquitoproof netting, which helped. So did the cold water now flowing into the house, a luxury Sophia had never known, and into the fountain in their garden.

It was a period of creative ferment and cultural vitality. Henry subscribed to each of the new journals and periodicals being introduced: the *Athenaion*, which published material on the sciences; the *Guardian of the East*, which dealt with politics; *Parthenon*, a literary journal; *Penelope*, concerned with women's fashions. The National Museum published its first volume of a catalogue of ancient coins in its possession. Henry brought home a copy for Sophia:

"You are the numismatist of the family."

She pored over the illustrations to see whether the museum had any coins like the ones she had been finding in Troy.

Henry decided they must begin to play a role in Athenian social life, a decision Sophia took to mean that he was considering Greece his permanent home. They went to Syntagma Square with Professor Koumanoudes and Xavier-John Landerer to witness the official turning on of the water in the garden fountain, to the parched Athenians a wonder to behold. When the University of Athens began its fall semester they attended the rector's opening lecture in the Great Celebration Hall. The Burnoufs invited them to the laying of the foundation stone for the French Archaeological Institute on the land donated by the Greek government at the foot of Mt. Lycabettus. Ambassador Ferry of France gave a celebration dinner to which the Schliemanns were invited. Henry persuaded Sophia to join the Association of Ladies, which was in process of founding a Workshop for Poor Women. The women were taught dressmaking, weaving, embroidery; the work was to be sold in the bazaars under the sponsorship of Queen Olga, and the women were to be paid whatever their handiwork brought.

"It is time you began to take your rightful place in Greek circles," declared Henry.

Sophia assented, going twice a week to teach embroidery, which her mother had taught her. The ladies of the Association were far older than Sophia but they accepted her and were fascinated by her stories of life in Ciplak and Hissarlik.

As one of the few Americans residing permanently in Athens, Dr. Henry Schliemann and his wife were invited to the American Embassy to participate in the wedding of the ambassador's daughter to the son of the mayor of New York City, and to attend the formal dinner following the marriage ceremony. At the dinner they met George Boker, who had been the United States minister resident to Turkey for over two years. He was an enthusiast of archaeology and had read most of Henry's papers. He asked if he might return home with them to see their finds, stayed for supper, admired the Schliemanns' terra cottas, advised them that he had not seen any of the artifacts Henry had forwarded on to the museum in Constantinople, and was dazzled by the Apollo marble with its four rearing horses.

Henry continued to contribute and pay for the publication of his articles in the Athens *Newspaper of the Debates*. He was amused when its owner bought a home just a short way down the street from them at Mousson Street 8. It was also to be used as an editorial office. Henry quipped:

"I won't have far to walk to deliver my articles or pick up my galleys, will I?"

He had signed contracts with F. A. Brockhaus in Leipzig and Maisonneuve et Cie. in Paris for the publication of his Trojan journals. Each publisher had pledged to put out two hundred sets, a small volume of his text and a much larger one containing pages of drawings and photographs of all the finds. Henry was to furnish the drawings and photographs himself, to be mounted on uniform-sized pages which would be either bound or assembled in a loose-leaf folio. To this end he searched Athens for the stoutest of white paper and located a supply with almost parchment-like strength. He confided to Sophia exuberantly:

"I'd like to publish the book by the end of 1873. It will establish us in the academic world."

They rode in their open carriage to the theater to see *Saoul* and the tragedy, *Timoleon*; to hear a recital by the Leipzig pianist Olga Dubois at the Hotel of the Foreigners. They were invited to the opening of a new hotel and restaurant near the café Fair Greece, where Sophia was astonished to learn of a service being offered to the residents of

Athens. It was called "catering"; the restaurant had a staff which went into private homes to prepare and serve dinner parties.

"The day will never come when I can't cook dinner for my own guests!" Sophia swore.

"Don't be so sure. Suppose I wanted fifty to one hundred guests. Wouldn't you like to have a crew of cooks come in?"

"Let's take our guests in smaller doses. It's pleasanter that way."

The city continued to grow at an even faster pace than Henry had predicted. There was more paving, more street lights, buildings, even a streetcar line was being considered. Still another new hotel, the New York, opened to take care of the influx of tourists from Europe, England, faraway America. Henry's land purchases quadrupled in value. At the same time, crime was increasing. Sophia rarely picked up a newspaper without reading about a burglary. A Nikolaos Karytharakes, employed at the pharmacy of G. Tzerahis, opened his boss's safe at night and stole three hundred drachmas. Twenty-five hundred drachmas were stolen from a shop on Kalamiotou Street. The police could not find these thieves, but they did arrest a looting gang at the wood shop of the merchant Kolokoures.

As the year wore on Athens became embroiled in external contests. The most insistent was the Laurium question, the right to remove the slag from the ancient silver mines. The Greek government claimed ownership but so much of the stock of the Serpieri Company, which was formed to exploit the mines, had been bought by citizens of France and Italy that their governments were threatening to go to war against Greece. There was the ongoing quarrel with Bulgaria which had created a schism with the Mother Church, first to gain its religious independence from the Phanariots in Constantinople, then to push for political independence from Turkey. They went to the cathedral to hear Archimandrite Averkios, First Secretary of the Holy Synod, read a text on the finality of the Bulgarian schism. When he had completed his formal address, he extemporized with a single line:

"All evils come down from the north."

Riding home in their carriage, Sophia asked Henry:

"What did he mean?"

"Russia. He's accusing them of whipping up the Bulgarian revolt."

The next day the Russian ambassador demanded that Archimandrite Averkios be dismissed. He was. Henry commented dryly, "That's a relief. I don't think Greece could whip France, Italy and Russia all at the same time."

Fierce internal political battles were also being waged. The ministers of the majority party resigned. King George I dissolved Parliament. New elections were called for late January 1873.

"Alas!" said Henry. "Our family can't vote. I'm an American citizen and you're a woman."

"I can't change my sex but you could change your nationality. Since you adore Greece, wouldn't you like to become a citizen?"

"No. . . . I think I'll remain an American. There are advantages for us, as you saw in Constantinople. Besides, changing my nationality a fourth time might make me appear a fickle man. By the way, there is a warning in this morning's paper that those who delay returning their books to the National Library and oblige the library's ushers to collect them at home will not be permitted to borrow books in the future. I've had my volumes for months. I'd better return them today or I'll be banned for life!"

Their work on the ancient objects they had brought home was progressing rapidly. Dr. Aretaios and an associate reassembled Henry's "Trojan" female skeleton as well as the embryo. Dr. Aretaios suggested they be protected in glass cases, which Henry immediately ordered made in a shop in the Plaka.

Now that they had completed the work of cleaning, cataloguing and sketching, Henry projected a protective roof from the back wall of the garden eight feet into the garden itself and built tables on which to show some of their heroic pieces: the seven-foot-high *pithoi*, an earthen vessel with a handle that had been used as a bell, double-edged battle-axes. They also eliminated some of the furniture from the livingroom to create more flat table space on which to display their jugs with beak-shaped mouths, the black vases in the form of hourglasses, the brilliant red goblets like champagne glasses. Henry was overjoyed at the feel of his house and garden with its fascinating displays. Sophia said:

"This is a little Schliemann Museum."

"Dear soul, that is what I meant it to be. One day we will have a big Schliemann Museum. I shall build it for the city on one of my good pieces of land. When we have completed our excavations we will give everything to our beloved Athens."

By the end of October, when all was ready, Henry invited Professor Stephanos Koumanoudes for dinner and to inspect their archaeological haul. Professor Koumanoudes, secretary of the Greek Archaeological Society, was visibly impressed. From a lifetime of experience of collecting and preserving Greek antiquities he was able to date most of the pieces that had emerged from the later Greek settlements.

"I must say that you have a variety of markings and decorations that will add a new chapter to our dictionary derived from ancient ceramics. Many of these I have never seen before. And I must congratulate you on getting down to native soil as you promised you would last January.

Is this photograph of the Great Tower and defense wall part of Homer's Troy?"

"I think so, but I can't prove it yet."

"Keep trying."

A few days later Professor Xavier-John Landerer came to dinner. He
too was impressed by the artifacts.

"I gather this is only half of what you found?"

"Yes," replied Henry. Then with a mild blush he added, "Perhaps
somewhat the better half."

Landerer asked if he might take some shards from the various strata
of Hissarlik to his laboratory at the university.

"Forgive me if I don't use the word Troy. I'm not cynical, just skepti-
cal. Let me sample these terra cottas and the chemical composition of
the varying colors of clay. Then I may be able to make some educated
guesses about their age."

That Sunday they invited John Latham, the English railroad manager,
Eugène Piat and the engineer Laurent, who despite his insobriety had
done a superb job of mapping and charting the mound for Henry's
giant platform. These three were more interested in the photographs
of the digs and the drawings of the land surveyor than in the archaeological objects. They had a technical discussion of how Henry should proceed, engineering-wise, in his further excavations.

They sent out invitations to the faculty of the University of Athens
and the Polytechnical Institute to come and see the finds and judge
for themselves their beauty and worth.

"Please let me include the teachers at the Arsakeion," pleaded Sophia.
"I want them to be proud of me."

"They will be, Sophidion."

The academicians came, first singly, then in groups. Henry was charming and patient, giving everyone a complete tour, explaining the level
at which each artifact had been found. Not all who came were friendly.
Some were suspicious, others disbelievers. A few showed open hostility.
Sophia was gratified at Henry's imperturbability. He was determined not
to take offense but to answer all questions, no matter how derogatory,
with illustrations and readings from books in his library, books about
other lands and other religions which corroborated his thinking.

Sophia was not able to tell whether her husband convinced any of
the skeptics; but she found a subtle change come over the people they
met. Where before many of them had thought that Henry Schliemann
was a millionaire fool throwing his money away on an absurd hobby,
they now had to admit, from the artifacts, from the photographs and
drawings of the many levels of the mound, that Dr. Schliemann was
indeed unearthing an ancient and complex settlement. Not Troy, of

course, since Troy was a creation of the Homeridae; but certainly an archaeological find which would justify the expenditure of such large sums of money, time and energy. When she told Henry of her observation, he replied with a half smile:

"That's sufficient accolade for the moment. By the end of next year they'll begin to say, 'It's Troy all right, though of course not Homer's Troy.' Then, in another year or two, when we have completed our excavations, they will come full circle."

2.

When the sea water cooled Sophia packed picnic lunches and they took Andromache for trips in the carriage a mile or two up in the Hymettus Mountains to the Kaisariane Monastery, which had been built in the tenth century on the site of a fifth-century basilica. They spread their blanket among centuries-old trees. Another day they went to the Monastery of Daphni with its Byzantine church of A.D. 1080 surrounded by groves of laurels. There were fine Gothic arches and beautiful battlements. Henry's favorite place for their picnics was Eleusis, where the famous mysteries, which no man had ever dared speak or write about, had been founded to perpetuate the gift of the first grain of corn by the goddess Demeter in thanks for shelter; and along with the first grain of corn, an equally important gift, the knowledge of how to till the soil.

Wherever they went, Henry carried a history book in his pocket; after they had had their picnic, and while Andromache napped, Henry would read to Sophia the origin and stormy life tales of these venerable, sacred places.

"I'm sorry Andromache is too young to profit from the lessons," Sophia commented.

"I plan to educate her exactly as I am training you. I will start when she is four or five."

With the coming of the first November rains Henry decided that he needed a trip through Germany to settle business matters and search for improved equipment for the following year's dig. No sooner had he left than Andromache developed a high fever. Sophia summoned Dr. Venizelos but he could not determine the nature of the illness. Madame Victoria suggested precautionary measures, then tried to comfort Sophia by assuring her that all children developed fevers which came and went rapidly.

"All six of you children had them."

The child remained ill for ten days. There was no symptom to sug-

gest the nature of the attack. With Henry away, the full responsibility
for Andromache was Sophia's. If anything should happen Henry would
never forgive her. She remembered his grief in Paris over the death of
his daughter Natalya and his need to assess blame and apportion guilt.
She held Andromache in her arms for almost the whole ten days; awoke
every hour of the night, prayed, wiped the child's face and hands with
a cool cloth. Her brother Spyros hardly left her side.

November 21 was the day of the Presentation of the Virgin Mary.
Sophia asked her mother to watch over Andromache, then rode quickly
past the entrance to the Acropolis and down the hill to St. Panaghitsa's
in Romvis Square. The church was heavy with incense, filled with dozens of unmarried women who were called Mary. This was their name
day. She picked up a candle, lighted it and went to a low shrine covered
by a long red satin cloth with a gold cross embroidered in the center
where there was an image of the Virgin Mary. She kissed the image
and prayed fervently for the recovery of her daughter.

Returning home, she was greeted by a happy Madame Victoria, who
cried:

"It's a miracle! While you were in the church praying, Andromache's
fever broke. Her temperature is dropping fast."

The pain around Sophia's heart fell away. She sank to her knees before her icon and murmured:

"Thank you, dear Mother of God."

When Henry returned two days later he was shocked to learn that
his daughter had been ill during most of his absence. After he had kissed
her on each cheek he turned to Sophia and said sternly:

"I am sorry about Andromache, but I am more concerned about
what you have suffered. For ten days you had our sick daughter in your
arms! But if the illness had been contagious you would have come down
yourself. Do you think that our child recovered because you sacrificed
yourself for her? I am happy that she has recovered, but I am crying
about you."

Sophia declined the reproof. She went close to him, put her mouth
up to be kissed.

"You've lost weight," he declared. "If you'll rest for a few days I'll
take you on the trip to Mt. Olympus that I promised."

Her eyes flashed with pleasure.

The following Thursday they took an Austrian ship from Piraeus to
Thessalonika, a pleasant day-and-a-half journey, most of which Sophia
spent in their spacious stateroom embroidering and reading the new
Greek translation of Molière which Henry had bought for her in
Vilperg's bookstore. In Thessalonika he rented a caïque to take them
to the small port of Skala Litochorou. She held her breath uneasily
while watching schools of fish dart by. Fortunately the sea remained

calm. From Skala Litochorou it was a three-hour horseback ride to the village near the base of Mt. Olympus, where there was a rustic inn. Henry engaged the rooms on the second floor facing the mountain. He pulled back the thick draperies, opened the shutters. There in all its majesty stood Mt. Olympus, the Mountain of the Gods. They had caught glimpses of it while riding up to the village, but most of it had been shrouded in fog. Now all was clear.

"*Panaghia mou!*" cried Sophia.

Amused, Henry said, "You are mixing your religions."

Yet he too was staggered at the glory of the mountain, which reached not merely into the skies but through them into the heavens and beyond, into an immense void of space. The mountain was of shattering proportions, a staggering immensity of stone which dwarfed everything else in the universe. They could not see to the top or embrace its breadth. It was more than a mountain, or even a mountain range. It was an impenetrable boundary cast up at the very edge of the earth.

"It makes my senses reel," she confessed.

"And my heart to pound," Henry echoed. "Now you know why Zeus and Hera, Apollo, Hermes, Hephaestus, Athena, Aphrodite, Ares, Hestia and Artemis all built their great palaces on its peak. From there they could see and control their world."

Their sittingroom was over the kitchen and had a continuation of the downstairs fireplace. Henry summoned the owner, who laid a log fire, lighted it, then sent up a bottle of *retsina* and a plate of *mezethakia*, something to whet the appetite. A table was set before the fire, with fresh linens, colorful country crockery, and then a fluffy omelet with a thick-crusted bread sliced longways through the middle and spread with hot butter and garlic.

After supper, lying warm and comfortable in bed overlooking the living vastness of Mt. Olympus as it absorbed and conquered the black skies, Henry populated for her the immortal peak.

"The most glorious palace, even more than Zeus's, is that of Hephaestus, the crippled vulcan and artist, son of Zeus and Hera. We have this picture from *The Iliad* when Thetis comes to Olympus to plead with Hephaestus to forge a new suit of armor for her son Achilles since Patroclus had gone into battle wearing Achilles's man-made armor and been slain, the armor lost.

" 'Thetis came unto the house of Hephaestus, imperishable, decked with stars, pre-eminent among the houses of immortals, wrought all of bronze, that the crook-foot god himself had built him. Him she found sweating with toil as he moved to and fro about his bellows in eager haste; for he was fashioning tripods, twenty in all, to stand around the wall of his well-builded hall, and golden wheels had he set beneath the base of each that of themselves they might enter the gathering of the gods at his wish and again return to his house, a wonder to behold. . . . And fair Charis made her [Thetis] to sit on a silver-studded chair.' "

"Beautiful!" she murmured. "I can see the palace before me shining in the darkness way up on that snow-clad peak."

Henry continued:

"Zeus's palace had a threshold of bronze. For Hera, her son Hephaestus had 'fitted strong doors to the doorposts with a secret bolt, that no other god might open. Therein she entered, and closed the bright doors. . . .' "

Henry's voice when pronouncing ancient Greek was entirely unlike his normal speaking voice, which sometimes had a tendency to be high and thin. When reading from classical Greek literature his spirit was ennobled, his voice became as strong, deep and melodious as those of the actors in the ancient dramas of Euripides or Sophocles playing before thousands in the Herodes Atticus Theater.

Sophia folded herself into her husband's arms, said softly:

"I feel as though I too were falling asleep in my chamber on Olympus."

When she awoke the next morning the sun was shining on the craggy, inscrutable face of Mt. Olympus. Henry had departed at four in the morning with a guide, riding horseback to the base of the mountain where the winding trail started. From there he would walk, hour after hour, on the steep side of Olympus. He would be able to climb a considerable distance in the one day, but he could not reach the peak. For that he would have to stay overnight in the rest cabin high among the crags and monumental timbers, and return the following night. He had told Sophia that he did not want to leave her alone, that he would join her for a late supper.

"Symbolically," he had said, "there is no top to Mt. Olympus. There are only peaks upon peaks, piled unto eternity. A man could climb all his life, yet never reach the palaces of the gods. They still exist, of course; the gods are there too, drinking wine, plucking the lyre, singing, being jealous, playing tricks on each other, contesting for power. But their ultimate peak is not attainable. The gods get there by flying from Mt. Ida, let us say. Man cannot fly. Leonardo da Vinci tried it on a hill just a mile or two from Settignano, where Michelangelo lived. All he got for his trouble was a broken leg. Doubtless it was a warning: gods fly, man walks."

The mistress of the inn brought her coffee. Reclining on a couch with the volume of Molière, her mind wandered. "We are digging at Troy not only to find Priam's immortal city but also as archaeologists to reconstruct the daily life of the Trojans. Can we do that for the life of the ancient gods?"

She picked up Henry's copy of The Iliad and in Book I came upon a stunning passage:

> The goddess, white-armed Hera, smiled, and smiling took in her hand the cup from her son. Then he poured wine for all the other gods from left to right, drawing forth sweet nectar from the bowl. And laughter unquenchable arose among the blessed gods as they saw Hephaestus puffing through the palace.
>
> Thus the whole day long till set of sun they feasted, nor did their heart lack aught of the equal feast, nor of the beauteous lyre that Apollo held, nor yet of the muses that sang, replying one to the other with sweet voices. . . .
>
> But when the bright light of the sun was set, they went each to his own house to take their rest.

When she finished the passage she turned to the back of the book where Henry had pasted in several pages of his notes on where to find the different categories of subject matter in the book: Clothing and Costume; Funeral and Burial Customs; Weapons of War. The one that intrigued her most was titled, Gods Interfering in Trojan War.

Using Henry's page references, she read again the story of how Achilles, his pride mortally wounded by Agamemnon's taking away his lovely captive, Briseis, asks his mother, Thetis, to intercede with Zeus so that the Achaeans will be beaten. Hera, who protects the Achaeans, quarrels with her brother-husband Zeus until their son Hephaestus calms them down. She sends Athena down to Odysseus to convince him that they must stay one more year and they will destroy Troy. Aphrodite, daughter of Zeus, shrouds Paris in a thick mist to protect him from Menelaus. . . .

"It's a strange life Henry and I live," Sophia mused. "We are very much a part of 1872. We argue the Laurium question and pray that it will not cause a war. Henry sends contributions to the School for Poor Children. When we pass King George and Queen Olga walking the streets of Athens unattended Henry always remarks, 'This could never happen in Europe. Greece is a democracy.' When at the opening of the new session of the Holy Synod the Minister of Ecclesiastics emphasizes the importance of the education of the clergy, I cry out in anger, 'Then why don't you bring Bishop Vimpos back from Tripolis?'

"We also live in the age of Homer, sometime around 1000 to 900 B.C.

Henry has a standing order for all the books and monographs from Germany, France, Scandinavia, England that deal with prehistory to learn whether the bard was drawing materials from his own time or depicting the years of the Trojan-Achaean War, some two hundred years before, from his own knowledge of the Troad and the accessibility of folk memory. One has to work from internal evidence: the differences, if such there were, between the religions, the idols, the worship of the gods; the weaponry, the armor, the power of the chieftains; the foods raised, the houses built, the clothing and ornaments worn; the iconography, signs and symbols on the terra cottas which Henry describes as 'the best encyclopedia of the time before written language evolved.' Henry has not caught out Homer very often."

It was on this level that they lived most intensely. All of their months of digging in Troy, the months in Athens preparing for the next year's excavations or restoring the magnificent treasures they had brought from the digs . . . these were spent in the age that had blossomed and then vanished three thousand years before! This was the time of fascination for both of them, when they lived at the height of their energy, imagination, talent, joy.

She stepped out of the tall windows to the veranda overlooking Mt. Olympus. Part of the trail upward was visible to her. She searched for Henry, climbing not so much a mountain as an ancient age of mythology.

Back in Athens Henry had business mail to answer, articles to write for the archaeological journals, plans to make for their departure in January. He was also searching for a competent artist who would be willing to live in the Troad. Sophia took Andromache in the carriage to Colonos to visit. Day by day her father was losing part of the big stomach which overhung his belt.

"Father, what is wrong?" she asked. "I've never seen you eat so little. And your laughter doesn't boom through the house the way it used to."

Georgios Engastromenos refused to take himself seriously.

"It's nothing, Sophidion, just a passing indigestion. At my age, to be losing my shape! All these years I have been giving the lie to the canard that there are no fat Greeks. My girth has been my most distinguishing possession. Everyone down the Ermou, through the reaches of Monastiraki, has saluted me when I passed. Pound by pound my identity has been evaporating. It's worse than having lost my money."

"Both are recoverable, my dear father," Sophia retorted. "Tomorrow you are going to see Dr. Skiadaresses. Perhaps he will put you on a special diet."

"Don't utter that word," cried Georgios. "The Greeks have been hungry for hundreds of years. The word 'diet' is the ugliest in our language."

Alexandros also disturbed her. He had more and more taken over the running of the drapery shop. Business was good, for he was a shrewd bargainer with a flair for sensing the coming styles of both Greek and European fabrics. Now that Georgios was not feeling well and was coming into the shop for only an hour or two a day, Alexandros was encouraging him to stay home altogether. It became evident that he was trying to force his brother Spyros out of the shop as well. Spyros confided to Sophia:

"I may have to leave soon. Alexandros has reduced me to errand-boy chores. I may have to look for another job. But what am I qualified to do? I have neither the head nor the heart for business."

Sophia's sympathy went out to her brother; he was small of face and figure, his expression vague. When she sometimes asked him during his long silences, "What are you thinking?" he would reply, "Nothing. I am just waiting to see what happens next."

That evening Henry reassured her.

"When Spyros can no longer remain in the family shop I will find something for him."

The day before the New Year the streets of Athens were full of people shopping for presents for their families. The jewelry stores were already sold out, the toy shops so full there was no more room to enter. Sophia let Henry proceed alone to Monastiraki while she returned to Koromelas's bookstore. Here she bought Michael Deffner's new collection of fairy tales, which she planned to read to Andromache. For Henry she selected the recently published *History of Greece from the Conquest of Constantinople*.

The next morning they were awakened early by a cannonade to announce the New Year. At ten they were in the cathedral for the doxology. King George and Queen Olga were present. At eleven the king received his ministers and a long line of honored male guests at the palace overlooking Syntagma Square. Henry had been pleased to receive an invitation, his first to the royal palace. At twelve the queen, wearing a national costume, received the Association of Ladies. That evening they returned to the palace, Henry in white tie and tails, Sophia in a sumptuous gown of sheer muslin, the fabric for which Alexandros had selected. The square low neck was trimmed with a wide French lace, as was the long train. There was a corsage of silk roses at the neck and one where the train joined the drape of the gown. Each lady was given a small and elegant dance card as she arrived. Sophia's was completely filled by the time the dancing started at ten o'clock with quadrilles which lasted thirty minutes each. These were followed with a polka, mazurka and waltz, which lasted for fifteen minutes each, then came the lancers, which consisted of six dances and lasted until midnight, at which time dinner was served. The dancing then continued until four in the morning, with the last cotillion.

Henry commented:

"I'm not as good on the dance floor as I am in an archaeological trench. But stamina I do have. I'll outlast those handsome young British navy officers."

Sophia chuckled, a low melodious sound.

"You said we have to take our rightful place in Greek society. As of this moment I would say that we have arrived."

He frowned.

"Don't mistake me, *chryse mou*, my golden one, I am not a social climber. It's only that I think we need this position to help us gain acceptance for our work."

For the celebration of the Epiphany, little Christmas, the Schliemanns rode out to Colonos early in the morning to join the Engastromenos family in St. Meletios's for the ceremony which would commemorate Christ's baptism in the river Jordan. The priest prayed over the water in the font, then sang the baptismal hymn before immersing the cross in the holy water. After blessing the congregation he gave to each member, both those inside the little chapel and the larger group outside, a vial of the holy water to take home. Sophia's father sprinkled a little of the water in each room of his home. Sophia put the Schliemanns' three bottles, with which to sprinkle and sanctify the rooms of her own home, into the carriage for safekeeping. While digging at Hissarlik she had fallen into a mild form of Henry's pantheism; it seemed natural in the Troad for the time in which they were living, amidst Trojans and Achaeans who had one set of gods on Mt. Olympus and Mt. Ida and another set in nature: the gods of fire, of wind, of the sun, of the sea, of the woods, of the rivers. But when she returned to Athens and to the contemporary world she reverted to her beloved Greek Orthodoxy, attending Mass on Sunday, stopping in at a church for each of the saint's days to light a candle and say a prayer for the well-being of her family. She went to confession once a year, as she was required to do, sitting across a table from the priest at St. Panaghitsa's in Athens or St. Meletios's in Colonos. Since her early quarrels with Henry, which she had confessed in full, she was rather hard pressed to think up any improprieties, let alone sins to reveal.

At midday they sat down to Madame Victoria's traditional Epiphany roast turkey stuffed with chestnuts. Dr. Skiadaresses's diet seemed to have arrested Georgios's illness. Later in the afternoon both families rode down to Piraeus. A large crowd was gathered. At a given signal the priest threw a cross into the waters to sanctify them. The young man who recovered it and came to the surface with the cross in his hand would receive the admiration of all Athens. Four young men threw themselves fully dressed into the sea. The first to emerge, with the cross held triumphantly in the air, was Alexandros.

"He was always determined to succeed," Sophia whispered to Henry.

Bishop Theokletos Vimpos came to Athens for an ecclesiastical conference a few days later. He was completely enthralled by Henry's photographs and drawings of the excavations, as well as by the hundreds of ancient artifacts.

"Faith is the dominant element in my character," he assured them. "I believe that you have found the Great Tower and the great defense wall. I believe that these lances, axes, arrows were used by the Trojans to defend themselves against the Achaeans. Henry, they say about you at the university that your greatest weakness is enthusiasm. You are accused of not taking a slow, detached, scientific attitude toward your work. You are accused of jumping to conclusions with the speed of a hummingbird reversing its flight in mid-air. That your imagination leaps and soars with the slightest possible evidence, and you weave bolts of fabric from the scantiest threads. So your critics say!"

"Those are the kindest charges I have heard from my opponents," Henry replied with a wry smile.

"But faith is contagious," Theokletos Vimpos mused, "if one has the capacity to accept enthusiasm. I believed you when you said that one day you would become an archaeologist. I believed you when you told me you wanted a Greek wife. I believed you when you told me you had fallen in love with Sophia's photograph and that she was the woman you would marry. Why then should I doubt you now?"

Vimpos's long lean face, which was growing to look more like an El Greco painting every day, was changed in composition by a warm smile that flashed like a refreshing spring rain across his dark eyes as he turned to Sophia.

"You are growing more beautiful with every spadeful of earth you dig."

Madame Victoria was not as sanguine. She took Sophia aside.

"My dear, Henry says you will be leaving again by the end of the month."

"Yes."

"I ask this not unkindly. For how many years do you intend to leave your daughter and your home for months at a time?"

"Until we have unearthed Troy!"

There was the usual stack of morning mail. Henry glanced through the envelopes quickly, selecting one postmarked at Çanakkale. It was an angry letter from Frank Calvert. He had heard a rumor that Henry had sold the Apollo metope in Europe for a large sum of money. Calvert maintained that the Apollo had been found not on Turkish government land but actually a few feet inside his own part of the hill. He did not accuse Henry of dishonesty in reporting the location of the Apollo but simply of being mistaken. He wanted his half of the sale price, after Henry had deducted the shipping costs, to be sent to him in Çanakkale.

They were sitting in the garden in brittle sunshine. Sophia looked at the Apollo, pure white marble against the pure blue sky.

"Where would Frank have heard a story like that?"

"I don't know, but rumors fly like bats: at night, and blind."

"One can see why he would be upset. He knows it was not on his land but he did provide you with the *modus operandi* for spiriting it out of the Troad."

"I will write to him immediately and tell him that I did not bring out the marble to sell in London or Paris; that it will never be for sale. That I brought it here to be a beautiful ornament for our garden."

Frank Calvert was not reassured. What now emerged was the motivation behind his first letter. His anger arose not so much over the reported sale of the Apollo but from a far deeper cause, one they found in advance galleys of an article which he was publishing in the *Levant Herald*: a blistering attack upon Henry and his work at Hissarlik. The charges were so bitter that Sophia and Henry turned to each other in amazement.

They were not long in finding the clue. *Frank Calvert had never believed Henry Schliemann would find Troy in the hill of Hissarlik.* Now, lo and behold! Henry was beginning to achieve fame through his reports to the newspapers of Europe, and especially in the London *Times*, which had congratulated him for his archaeological initiative. Henry Schliemann was becoming a hero in Great Britain while he, Frank Calvert, was unknown except in circles which still considered him a traitor to his country. This had to be galling for him. He had written an article in which he claimed that it was he, rather than Henry Schliemann, who had discovered Troy.

"In point of truth," Henry ceded, "Frank did start three shallow trenches at his end of the mound; but in his accustomed fashion he dug for only a few days and quit."

Calvert attempted to destroy Henry's credibility. He charged that if stone implements had existed in Troy Homer would have mentioned them. Therefore none of the strata Henry had cut through which contained stone implements could belong to Homer's Troy. Nor had

Homer ever mentioned flint saws or stone knives. Calvert also claimed that Henry was mistaken in his description of the house walls found in the mound; that he misstated the size of them, and the materials from which they were built. He challenged Henry's description of the size and functional purpose of his terra cottas as being erroneous and endeavored to discredit Henry's differentiation between the prehistoric ages on the mound and the later Greek settlements.

"I'm shocked," cried Henry. "I loved that man and I thought he was fond of us."

"So he is," she said musingly, "but he's grieving. Envy causes grief. But I don't understand his reasoning. First he claims that it was he instead of you who discovered Troy, then he spends the rest of the article trying to prove that, whichever one of you discovered Troy, it is not Homer's Troy. Will the article hurt us?"

Henry shook his head mournfully.

"Those who want us to be wrong will accept his charges."

He paced the garden slowly, sadly.

"One strives for scientific accuracy and someone kicks that credibility down a ravine. I will have to answer him in print of course, but we'll wait until we are back in the Troad."

"Will he revoke our right to dig on his half of the hill?"

"I don't think so. He is not a vindictive man. He won't really be happy about this outburst."

By mid-January Henry's preparations were almost completed for the 1873 expedition. He had found a young and pleasant artist, Polychronios Lempesses, who was intrigued by the challenge of setting down in India ink the continuing work in the excavations and the historical finds that would emerge. He was unmarried and had no obligations in Athens.

Yannakis, Polyxene and Photides were ready to move back to Troy the moment the Schliemanns arrived. Demetriou, the younger and better of the two foremen from the year before, regretfully could not return because of family difficulties. The second foreman, Theodorus Makres, had taken a job out of Athens and could not be located. In the end Henry hired Captain Georgios Tsirogiannes, explaining to Sophia:

"The gift of command is rarely met with except among seamen. Speaking of seamen, we've lost our Captain Papaliolos and his *Taxiarchis*. He has contracted to run between Crete and Alexandria for the rest of the year. But he has recommended an old friend, Captain Theodorou. I've seen his ship, the *Omonoia*. He will come into Besika Bay once a month with supplies and take out our finds."

3.

Their ship swung alongside the dock at Çanakkale in midafternoon. Yannakis was there with a farm wagon to pick up their crates of supplies. The two foremen Henry had brought with him from Athens, Captain Tsirogiannes and an Albanian from Salamis, helped Yannakis load the wagon and rode out with him to Hissarlik.

Henry registered at the quayside Hotel Nikolaides where they had dropped their bags two years ago before Frank Calvert invited them to stay with him.

"It's better to be on the safe side," said Henry. "I doubt that Frank will invite us to stay. But I do want to go over the material of his article point by point in a friendly way before I respond."

It was a cold, blustery last-of-January day. They were walking past the governor's house. The Calvert mansion was just ahead. Henry shook his head in puzzlement.

"This is something you just don't do to a friend. He doesn't have to believe anything I advocate about Troy, but to expose me to criticism and ridicule . . ."

Frank Calvert seemed neither surprised nor displeased when his butler ushered them into the library. He had chairs brought up in front of a crackling wood fire and offered them a brandy. Henry asked quietly why Frank had decided to put his criticism into print. Frank changed the subject.

Henry was not to be put off.

"Frank, you said in your article that the small flint saws and stone knives that I found are proof against Hissarlik being the site of Troy because Homer never mentions them . . ."

Frank rose, slowly poured himself another brandy. Mrs. Calvert came into the room, greeted Henry cordially and embraced Sophia. She wanted no part of this male foolishness.

"My dear, why don't you come into the sittingroom and have a cup of tea with me? We have lots of news to exchange."

Sophia was happy to leave what she knew was going to become an unfriendly debate. She and Mrs. Calvert exchanged news about their children and their plans for the year. About an hour later Henry came for her. He was alone and making a determined effort not to let the expression on his face bespeak his feelings. He thanked Mrs. Calvert for taking care of Sophia, politely declined her offer of a cup of tea. Frank did not come to say good-by. They walked rapidly down the freezing street to their hotel. Once through the small, dark entry and in their room, Henry exploded.

"Frank is angry. He will not listen to reason or fact. He insists that every criticism he has published is true and necessary to keep the record straight. He insists that, although he discovered Troy before I did, it cannot be Homer's Troy because we are finding no Byzantine objects and there was a continuous civilization at Hissarlik as late as the fourteenth century. He has no artifacts to prove it. He is confusing Hissarlik with Alexandria Troas."

Sophia said with a wry smile:

"That argument got you politely ejected, I gather. Did he deny us the right to dig on his half of the mound?"

"No, not yet. But the more discoveries we make, the closer he's going to get to it. I told you we were going to need this hotel room. I will have them bring up some supper."

"It would cripple us if Frank shut down his half of the hill."

"That's why I am going to have to employ more men and work faster. We're going to have to radiate in all directions from the Watch-tower. . . ."

Early the next morning they crossed the main street to the governor's house. Henry said:

"I think it would be wise if we went in and paid our respects."

Governor Achmed Pasha was a dour but polite man. He welcomed them back to the Troad, had an orderly bring in the tiny cups of sweet black coffee. Then said in a casual tone:

"Of course you know about the new law that is being passed in Constantinople?"

Startled, Henry asked:

"New law? No, I haven't heard anything. What does it refer to?"

"To all archaeological excavation. To the treasures of Turkey."

Sophia saw that Henry's face had gone ashen. He asked:

"Do you have a copy of the law in your office?"

"No, it has not been passed yet. It is being discussed."

"Do you know its provisions?"

"Yes, and they apply to you. First, a complete list of all items found while digging has to be properly prepared and forwarded to the Minister of Public Instruction. Second, nothing can be exported to a foreign country from any part of His Majesty's territory unless an official permit is obtained. Third, if some of the above-mentioned items are considered necessary for the museum, and are desired to be purchased, the museum shall have these items for a sum which it deems proper. Fourth, an export permit will be given for the finds which the museum does not wish to retain. However, nothing may be exported from His

Majesty's territory to a foreign country unless a customs tax shall be paid after the permit is issued. Lastly, if anyone should be discovered trying to smuggle archaeological finds out of the country, they shall all be confiscated."

Sophia cried:

"But that invalidates our *firman!* How can the government issue a legal license and then revoke it?"

The governor was not hostile. He responded quietly:

"Governments have the right to change their laws. When the law is changed it invalidates any previous law or license that goes against its provisions."

"But I have tens of thousands of dollars invested in these excavations," cried Henry. "I am about to spend thousands more. This is not a law I can live with."

The governor permitted himself one of his rare thin smiles.

"You don't have to, Dr. Schliemann, for the moment at least. These discussions may go on for months. The law may be written and changed a dozen times before it is promulgated. I suggest that you don't worry about it until I have an official copy on my desk."

They stumbled out of the governor's house into the cold wind, Henry glassy-eyed and trembling, Sophia with a pain in the pit of her stomach.

"What that new law will amount to," said Henry, "is total confiscation! The museum will take absolutely everything of value and pay us a few piasters. We'll be left with nothing but the shards."

They arrived at the site to find that Yannakis with two skilled craftsmen from Renkoi had completed the stone house which Sophia had designed before they left the year before. He had used blocks of stone which had been turned up in the excavations; the two workmen had hewn them so they fit into each other. Sophia had planned their bedroom and diningroom to be the same size as the ones in the wooden house but she expanded the workroom considerably so that they would have more space for the tables. She stood by one of the windows overlooking the Dardanelles and the Aegean, then turned to Yannakis, who was waiting, hat in hand, expectancy written large across his eyes.

"You've done a fine job, Yannakis. We'll be comfortable here."

He had moved their furniture in. Polyxene had made the bed, there was a log fire giving out warmth and food simmering on the stove awaiting their arrival. Photides welcomed them back to Troy. He, Captain Tsirogiannes and the Albanian had been installed in the wooden house the Schliemanns had used the year before.

Sophia put her icon on the night table. Henry smiled approvingly.

"It's amazing how you convert a strange house into a home by the simple act of setting out that icon."

"That's the major difference between your ancient Greeks, who feared their gods, and we Christians, who love ours. The Greeks and the Achaeans propitiated their gods by spilling wine on the ground and burning the fat thighs of bulls, lambs and goats so that the fragrant smoke would reach up to Mt. Ida and Mt. Olympus. We don't offer up sacrifices . . ."

"Oh yes, you do! Every Orthodox church is full of gold and silver bracelets, necklaces, rings, crosses . . ."

Sophia had the good grace to blush.

They took a quick turn around the dig, then Polyxene served them a hot supper in their new diningroom. They retired early. Henry woke her at five, saying:

"The work crews should arrive soon."

Yannakis had cleaned the tools, oiled the wheelbarrows, sharpened the shovels and pickaxes so that everything was in readiness. By six o'clock the men began coming in from half a dozen surrounding villages. Soon there were one hundred and fifty Greeks and Turks. Henry divided them into five work crews, each digging in a different area or direction: channels, trenches, terraces, clearing along the defense wall, getting down to the base of the Watchtower, which was on solid rock; digging deeper under the large temple in an attempt to find the original, smaller Trojan temple he was convinced lay beneath it. Each of the three foremen had his own crew; Henry himself took charge of the largest, which was clearing the southwest side of the tower. Sophia was in charge of a fifth group.

The Turkish government had set only one guard over them, Amin Effendi. His was a hopeless task, with five scattered work crews to watch, each of them turning up interesting objects: a brilliant red terra-cotta hippopotamus, vases and goblets, large flat plates, marble idols of the goddess Athena with the owl's head; and down at a depth of ten feet, two-ton blocks of marble carved in Doric style which Henry believed were part of Lysimachus's temple. Since there were no inscriptions on them he sent them crashing down the steep hill to the Trojan plain.

Amin Effendi was a bright young man out of the governor's office, personable and well educated. He had every intention of doing a painstaking job. Though he was not aggressive by nature, he faced up to the Schliemanns from the beginning. When they made their first finds he said:

"I'll have to have complete lists by the end of every day so that we'll have them ready when the new law goes into effect."

"My *firman* does not oblige me to do so. No one can be forced to obey a law that is not in existence."

"The governor informs me that it will be passed soon. Isn't it easier for you to make your day-by-day lists? We can do them together to avoid errors, and I'll send my copy in to the museum in Constantinople."

Sophia did her best to stay out of the discussions but sometimes she could not control her feelings.

"Amin Effendi, the museum does not want these lists yet. It is your privilege to keep an accounting, if you so desire, but that is not the way we work. We wait until we have cleaned our objects, then we describe them in our daily journal and number the artifacts to correspond to the journal entry. If and when the new law is passed I can draw up a complete and accurate list from our journal."

The young guard seemed propitiated.

"Your procedures are your own, Kyria Schliemann; however I feel it is my duty to keep my own daily lists."

Henry replied quietly, "If you insist, we'll make it possible for you. The finds made by the five separate crews will be brought to the porch of our house at dusk. You can work on them there."

"Thank you, Dr. Schliemann, but I prefer to make my entries as the materials come out of the ground."

Sophia thought, "You are going to need a race horse to keep circling this hill all day."

The choice of Captain Tsirogiannes proved to be a good one. His men were making more progress than any of the others, including Henry's. The Albanian from Salamis, however, was not making the progress required of him; his crew seemed sullen. Henry asked Sophia to work around them to see if she could pick up from their patois the cause of the slowdown. Very soon she reported:

"It's resentment against an Albanian. I gather they think he is of inferior stock and hence should not be giving orders."

"Since I cannot wave my hand over him and say, 'Once an Albanian, now a Greek,' I had better let him go. I'll cable Demetriou and offer him a bonus large enough to solve his family problems. A good foreman is more useful to me than ten workmen."

Demetriou joined them within a week.

Their evenings were more social now that they had Polychronios Lempesses working with them. Yannakis had cleaned out the storeroom and made him comfortable there. Lempesses was a spry little chap, chirpy and pleasant company as well as a skilled technician whose hand recorded accurately what his eye saw. During the first days he made lifelike drawings of the digs and the workmen, then went sketching in the Troad to capture the flavor of the countryside. He asked permission to help clean the terra cottas, the stone implements, the metal weapons, then set them before him in a row and drew them in India ink. He endeared himself to Henry and Sophia by the quality of his work.

The sea captain, Georgios Tsirogiannes, was a silent man who had no wish for company after he had commanded forty workmen all day. He went to sleep soon after supper. However Photides confessed to Sophia that since he himself was not a good sleeper he spent many hours awake with nothing to do and no one to talk to. When he saw that Polychronios Lempesses was working from dark to midnight in the workroom with Sophia and Henry, he asked permission to join them. Henry did not care for the idea but Sophia said:

"He's lonely and needs company. You say he's excellent at directing the cuts and gradings. I'm sure you want to keep him."

"By all means. He's the only semi-engineer we have."

Photides was overjoyed. Before long he became Henry's amanuensis, copying faithfully Henry's reports to be sent to the Greek newspapers. His main pleasure was in helping Sophia with washing down the terra cottas and assembling the more beautiful shards for which he cooked the fish glue in the kitchen. Henry commented:

"You have gathered an admirer. He hardly takes his eyes off you."

They had been in Troy for only two weeks when a bitter cold descended upon them, the temperature sinking to 23° Fahrenheit at night. Sophia and Henry were able to sleep well in their stone house, under the wool blankets she had brought from Athens the year before, but the foremen shivered sleeplessly through the first night and got up with colds. In the morning Photides told them that the icy north wind had blown with such violence that it penetrated the chinks in the wood house. They could not keep the oil lamps lighted, and the water was frozen in their basin. The men looked grim.

"Perhaps we ought to swap houses with them until this cold wave is over," Sophia suggested. "They will be much warmer in here."

"Yes, I think we must. Otherwise they will fall ill. I'll have Yannakis exchange the beds. We'll do all right under our blankets. Besides, we can always warm each other."

They made the exchange. The foremen slept comfortably in the stone house and Sophia and Henry survived the following nights catching bits of sleep. It was warmer down in the trenches of the excavation, but even so the men who had hats, overcoats and scarves wore them while digging.

On the morning of the fifth day the sun came out. The winds whispered away. The Troad was warm again. Yannakis and Photides brought the Schliemanns' bed back into the stone house. Photides thanked Sophia for her thoughtfulness. Since Yannakis was spending most of the day hunting for more workmen, Henry asked Sophia to take over the crying of *paidos* at the breakfast and midday rest periods. She went to each of the groups and, using her hands to funnel her voice, called the "stop work."

Their difficulties were not over. A merchant from Smyrna seduced Henry's workers by an offer of piecework, so much a licorice root dug up. The men could make fifty cents a day, whereas Henry was paying only thirty-six cents during this period of shorter winter light. More than half of the force left to gather the roots and extract the juice to be used for medicinal purposes. Almost the whole of Renkoi became employed in the task, which extended to two weeks. Yannakis tried recruiting in the other villages but there were not many workers available. Henry worried over the wasted days.

The weather became warm and clear. Henry again had his full contingent of workers. The workdays were lengthening. He raised the men's wages. He was pleased with the eleven thousand cubic yards of earth and debris which his own crew had moved from around the site of the temple. The other four crews were doing equally well in other parts of the hill. Exciting finds were brought to the surface hour by hour: a copper sickle over five inches long, their first agricultural implement; copper weapons, lances and arrowheads, long thin copper nails with round heads. Henry's crew, now digging in a trench in a northwestern direction to lay bare the Great Tower on that side, came upon two ten-foot-thick walls, one above the other, though at a variant angle. When the topmost wall was sufficiently uncovered, he called Sophia over to show her that it had been built in part of Corinthian pillars. The lower wall was remarkable because most of the massive blocks had the signature of the carver or builder, a sigma, Σ, a delta, Δ, an upsilon, Υ.

With the work proceeding fast and well, Sophia fell into a comfortable routine. She had coffee with Henry when he returned from his swim at dawn, then stayed with her crew in the excavation until work was halted for the dinner period. All of the finds of the morning were brought up to the workroom. She saw Amin Effendi writing constantly in his notebook, but she knew there were objects he did not see because he could not be in five trenches at the same time. He was not designating the half of the treasures which he would choose for the museum because he was convinced that the new law would go into effect within a matter of weeks, and then the Schliemanns would have to ship everything to Constantinople, where the museum director would decide which of the objects he wished to retain.

Although she was in perfect health, with high color in her cheeks because of the hours of work in the sun, Henry insisted that she take a nap after the midday meal and not come back until the afternoon had grown cooler. During these hours he added the supervision of her crew to his. The stone house was cool and pleasant. When Sophia awoke she visited with Polyxene, planned their dinner for the following day. They amused each other with innocent jokes about Yannakis's pride in cooking.

By the end of February Henry had a daily average of one hundred and sixty men on the mound. He was happy with the way the digging was going in uncovering the Watchtower, defense wall and the temple. He had expected to have to dig against time only on the Calvert half of the mound. Now the impending new law was a second pressure hanging over him. He threw out trenches, channels and terraces in all directions. His own group, uncovering the eastern portion of the tower, advanced rapidly because this excavation was near the southern declivity of the hill and the rubbish did not have to be carted far off. Because of this he made several innovations in his techniques, one of which was to release the special men loading wheelbarrows and let each workman fill his own, eliminating one operation.

Unwilling to gripe at the real cause of his tension, he complained that the price of Turkish wine had risen sharply:

"An *oka* of wine, two bottles, which last year cost me five cents, now costs eight cents."

"But, Henry, it is of excellent quality and you prefer it to French wines."

"It is not the wine I am complaining about, it's the raising of the price."

Another complaint was that when he began finding fragments of terra-cotta serpents whose heads were sometimes molded with horns the workmen broke off the horns and took them home with them because in the Troad there was a superstition that the horns of serpents could cure epilepsy and other diseases. One workman had taken home a vaseful of these horns the year before; now Henry tried to persuade the men that this was pure superstition. They were not convinced.

Next they began to be surrounded by villagers coming to the site of the excavations with two-wheeled carts drawn by oxen and waiting along the periphery of the excavation to haul away the stones after Henry's men brought them to the surface, claiming they wanted them to build churches and bridges. They were very large, splendidly hewn blocks, but it took too much time and labor to roll them over the side of the hill and down into the plain, so the crews engaged in what Henry described as the "terrible work" of breaking them up so that they could be more conveniently removed. The villagers stood and waited until Henry's men had broken up the blocks and hauled them away from the

work areas before loading them into their carts. Henry was furious that
they refused to help in any way. He tried every stratagem he could
think of to get them to do so.

"Those of you who help us break up the stones and move them out
of the digs will become the legal owners."

The leader of a group of Turkophones wet down the paper of his
brown, lumpy cigarette, shrugged and murmured:

"We are, anyway."

Henry attempted to be stern.

"These stones belong to me. I unearthed them at considerable expense. If you touch them, I will have you arrested."

The leader replied:

"You have permission to dig them. Once they are off the mound they
are anybody's property."

Sophia tried moral suasion. To the Christian Greeks from Yeni-shehr
she said in their patois:

"You are building a church tower in your village?"

"Yes."

"A tower to reach up to God?"

"There aren't enough stones."

"Doesn't Christianity teach you to help other people, to be charitable
and brotherly?"

"It teaches us how to build stone towers on our churches."

The villagers continued to gather and Henry's men to break up the
large blocks before dumping them away from the trenches.

He was still concentrating on the large temple and made some startling discoveries. He found four earthen pipes, twenty-two inches long
and twelve inches thick, laid together to bring water to the temple from
the upper Thymbrius, then three marble slabs covered with ancient
Greek inscriptions which spoke in their text of being set up in "The
Temple." He was overjoyed. For him "The Temple" could only mean
the Temple of Athena. No other sanctuary would be permitted to call
itself "The Temple." Another proof for him was that the building was
turned toward the rising sun and corresponded exactly with the position of the Parthenon in Athens. He had the three slabs taken to their
workroom where he scrubbed them with warm water and Sophia under-
took the translation. From it they were able to date the slabs as be-
longing to the third century B.C.

When Sophia completed the texts she looked up at Henry, puzzlement
flowing across her large, dark eyes.

"My dear, I don't mean to lessen your joy but there is no mention in
them anywhere of religious matters. They seem to be about the grant-

ing of land to certain individuals by the king. They are somewhat similar to the slabs we found in our first dig."

The balloon of Henry's enthusiasm could not be pricked by so small a pin. He replied:

"No matter. The earlier slabs made no mention of a temple. These say specifically, do they not, that they are to be hung in 'The Temple'?"

"Yes."

A disappointment was that he could not find any whole sculptures in the temple. The floor, when they finally dug down to it, consisted of large slabs of sandstone. Henry believed the statues had been destroyed by religious zeal or wantonness. If the temple had had an earthen floor the statuary would have sunk in during the centuries and been preserved. The sandstone protected them and they were still standing upright when the destroyers moved in.

Directly below the temple he found highly polished battle-axes of exquisite workmanship and wondered how it was possible for the craftsmen of those ancient times with the meager tools at their disposal to make anything of such excellent quality.

Their workroom was jammed with beautiful objects: terra-cotta vases without the owl's face but with female breasts, a large navel and with two small upright handles in the form of arms. Each day the men brought in baskets of granite quoits, diorite saws, hammers, knives. In one of the channels they came upon an immense number of wine jars that were six feet high. They were in the month of March and the days were growing longer. Polychronios Lempesses and Photides, sometimes joined by Yannakis and Polyxene, spent the hours until midnight polishing, repairing, grouping the finds. Sophia no longer did the physical work; it took her up to six hours a night to describe in detail every object found that day. Henry had sequestered a portion of the worktable as a writing desk. Each night he set down, sometimes in Greek, often in French or German, the detailed story of the day's progress. He carried a pocket compass with him so he could jot down the directions accurately when he discovered new walls.

"We must begin to get our half of the finds out of here," he confided to Sophia as they fell exhaustedly into bed.

It was Sophia's crew which discovered the first gold of the year's dig; two copper nails studded with gold ornaments. When she ran to Henry's area with the nails in her hand, a triumphant gleam came into his eyes.

"Good for you!"

But his supreme pride was the Great Watchtower. He wrote in his journal:

> It is worth a journey round the world to see this tower, whose site was at all events so high that it not only commanded a view of the plain but also of the plateau lying to the south of it.

The men working on the west side of the tower found the ruins of a very large house, which Henry decided must have belonged to a rich man because the floors of several rooms were laid with red stone slabs splendidly polished. Henry looked up at the sky and said to no one in particular, "This is the largest villa we have found yet. Can Priam's palace be far behind?"

4.

Spring came early. By the middle of March the Troad was covered with wild flowers, crocuses and purple garlic flowers. The trees were beginning to sprout new leaves, but the temperature rose so rapidly that the nearby marshes, which had been sparsely flooded because of a shortage of winter rains, began to dry up and Sophia could hear the croaking of the frogs as they began to die off. Fever struck the workmen. This time Henry had come prepared with an adequate stock of quinine. He increased the dosage taken by himself and Sophia, as well as his foremen and the artist Lempesses. Because of the longer workdays, he was again obliged to raise the workers' wages, this time to ten piasters a day, forty cents.

It was Henry who made the most remarkable find in these weeks of steady digging: a large knob or scepter handle of the purest crystal sculptured into a marvelous lion's head. When he showed his prize to Sophia at the nine o'clock break, he exclaimed:

"It's the first crystal we have come upon. There were plenty of lions in the mountains above the Troad. Homer speaks of them. He could not possibly have described so excellently the characteristics of this animal had he not had frequent opportunity of watching them."

It was the beginning of a series of startling hour-by-hour discoveries which enthralled them. Close to the lion's head they found a splendidly cut hexagon of the purest crystal; then a pyramid of black, white and blue streaked marble, the first of its kind they had unearthed. Next came a copper instrument resembling a horse's bit, copper knives, stone lances. And on top of the tower two parts of what appeared to be musical instruments, the first they had seen: an ornamented piece of ivory almost the shape of a flute, and a flat bone with a hole at one end and three at the other.

"If we keep making finds like this," Henry exulted, "we will truly be able to assemble a family portrait of the Trojan."

Henry changed the angle of his attack and opened what he described as a great cutting in front of the very door of their stone house. By the time his crew had dug down ten feet they had found several large and splendid vessels. Sophia's favorite was an elegant black vase in the shape of a soup tureen. She claimed it for herself.

"I am going to serve you *arni vrasto*, lamb broth with vegetables, in this tureen the very first night we're home on Mousson Street."

A little lower in the trench they found mixing bowls, the larger ones having four handles and standing two feet high.

"You're working in someone's kitchen," Sophia commented that evening. "All we need to find now is a lamb roasting on a spit."

From thirteen to twenty-six feet down, in addition to coming upon house walls, one with a corner joining at right angles, they unearthed a wealth of vases, each in its own curious form. Sophia marked for special attention a brilliant black vase with two breasts and two handles. She also persuaded Henry to let one of his men build storks' nests on the roofs of both the stone and wooden houses. They were plentiful in the Turkish villages, sometimes as many as a dozen of them nesting on one roof in Kalifatli. It was a beautiful sight. Henry was agreeable.

"While I was growing up in Germany it was considered good luck to have storks nest on your roof."

"Not to mention the fact that they eat all the insects and frogs in the neighborhood. I certainly hope they like the forty-leggers we're still battling."

Henry engaged the best of the Turkish carpenters, Mastro-Yannes, to build the nests the way the storks liked them. But not one stork ever nested on their roofs. Henry said grimly, "That could mean that no good luck is going to descend on our houses."

"Nonsense," retorted Sophia. "It only means that the wind gets too strong up here on the heights and the storks are afraid their nests will be blown away."

At the end of March the workers returned home to trim their vineyards. The excavation practically closed down. What little digging they could do turned up a plate of pure gold in the form of an arrowhead, a woman's skull, well preserved with neat little teeth, in an intact terracotta vase. In the same vase, human ashes, bits of bone and a copper hairpin. A high and icy north wind returned. There was no way to heat the houses. At night Sophia and Henry tried to write and copy their articles for the papers but their fingers froze around the pens. Once again they turned the stone house over to their superintendents and tried to stay warm in the wooden house by loading the fireplace with heavy logs before getting into bed. This was nearly their undoing, for the stones of the fireplace sat on the wooden floor. Henry awoke at three, smelling smoke. To his consternation he saw that several yards of the floor boards were on fire and the north wall was just catching. He picked Sophia up in her blankets, carried her to the door, kicked it open and ran with her a few yards to safety.

She awoke abruptly.

"For heaven's sake, what is hap . . ."

". . . fire, the whole room. You stay here. I'll get the men."

The foremen came running. Henry poured the contents of a bath on the north wall, which stopped the burning there. Photides, in his long underwear, beat on the floor with rough sacking. Captain Tsirogiannes and Demetriou broke up the floor, then dumped quantities of damp earth on the smoldering boards.

Sophia, still swaddled in the blanket, stood at the open door studying the damage. The north wall was blackened but intact. About a third of the floor was gone but the portion under the bed was saved. Polyxene came out with a pot of herb tea. Henry said:

"Yannakis, take my bed back to the stone house. I'll install Kyria Schliemann there, then we can all dress and, at first light, build a new floor for this house."

The cold lasted for six days.

The early April weather was glorious. One hundred and fifty men and their wheelbarrows again assembled on the site. Above the tower Henry found a house of more than eight rooms, in which they uncovered a crucible for melting copper, some of it still lying inside; molds for casting copper bars, and an enormous quantity of black, red and brown shards. One room of the house had a smooth limestone floor. Black marks on the walls of other rooms caused Henry to observe:

"The floors were of wood. When they burned they blackened the lower parts of the stone walls."

Then Easter was upon them. The Turkophones returned to their villages for the week of religious ceremonies. On Maundy Thursday Sophia was up before dawn to hang a red cloth from the bedroom facing east so that it could catch the first rays of the sun. Polyxene boiled a dozen eggs and, when they had cooled, dyed them red. Sophia baked the Easter buns of flour, olive oil and almonds. That night she opened her Bible and, kneeling before her icon, read aloud the twelve gospel passages describing the Passion. She fasted on Good Friday. Early Saturday morning she went searching for wild flowers to place before the Virgin. Later in the day she baked the Easter bread while Yannakis slaughtered the paschal lamb which he had been fattening in a pen behind the kitchen. On Sunday she lighted a candle before the Virgin and persuaded Yannakis to let Polyxene and herself cook the traditional Easter dinner.

After the holidays Sophia's crew made an important find: a five-foot altar of slate granite, the upper part in the form of a crescent on which the head and neck of the animal to be sacrificed was placed; below, a slab of green slate, apparently for carrying off the blood. It was in perfect condition.

"We'll leave it *in situ*," Henry exclaimed, "so that everyone who comes to Troy will see it intact."

Henry added more men to Sophia's crew since this seemed fertile ground. The two of them worked together. They were soon rewarded with complete skeletons of what could have been warriors; near each lay a copper helmet with a *phalos* or ridge which had contained the horsehair plumes worn by the Trojans. Beside one lay his large copper lance. Henry read from *The Iliad*:

> "'Antilochus was first to slay a warrior of the Trojans in full armor, a goodly man amid the foremost fighters, Echepolus. Him was he first to smite upon the horn of his helmet with crest of horsehair, and into his forehead drave the spear. . . .'"

At that moment the guard appeared. He agreed to leaving the altar where it was.

"Will you want one of these skeletons?" asked Sophia in a voice which indicated that she did not expect him to.

"No bones."

"Thank you," she answered. "We'll take them back to Athens."

Henry summoned the carpenter and asked him to build a plank bed large enough to hold the two skeletons. Later that afternoon they were moved gingerly onto the planking and carried to the workroom. That night while Lempesses was making his drawings of the warriors he pointed out something curious.

"The heads are large but remarkably narrow. In fact I've never sketched so narrow a head. Doctor, could it be that these heavy copper helmets compressed their bone structure?"

"I doubt it. They wore helmets only in battle. It could simply be another distinguishing feature of the early Trojan, similar to the very small teeth we found in the female skull."

Later, when Lempesses and Photides had left, Henry tried out new conjectures, hypotheses, theories on Sophia.

". . . we found the warriors just above the top of the tower. We know that Priam's palace was close to the tower, and that from the palace there ran the great paved road which led to the double Scaean Gate, the plain and the battlefield. . . . The altar and the skeletons lay to the east of the tower. The paved road and the Scaean Gate should be on the *west* side, leading out to the Troad. . . . Tomorrow we shift the crews to the *west* side."

Four days later, on April 9, they struck a road at a depth of thirty feet from their working surface. Excavating from side to side, they found that the cobblestone road was seventeen feet wide. Henry was wild with excitement. His enthusiasm spread among the workmen, for in his need to get the utmost out of each day's work he sometimes gave them bonuses when great discoveries were made. Half dazed at the intuitive accuracy with which he had made for his objective, Sophia sat on the edge of a wall watching the dirt and debris fly into wheelbarrows, and wheelbarrows fly in every direction to dump their loads.

"Which way do you clear the road, Henry," she asked, "down to the plain, or up to the palace of Priam?"

"Both ways. We'll have Photides take sixty men and dig down to the bottom, because the road must lead to the Scaean Gate at the foot of the hill. I'll take the remaining hundred men and start excavating upward. This beautifully paved street must lead to a grand building at the top of it."

It took Photides's crew nearly a week to clear a length of thirty-three feet of the cobbled road down to where it ended at the plain. They found not the slightest indication of gates! The actual gates of stout timbers would have vanished in the fire, but their anchoring holes or moorings should be intact.

That night Henry and Sophia joined the men at their supper table in the kitchen.

"There were no gates. Why?" he asked. "If I were a general commanding an army being pursued to the very walls of my fortress, I would put my double defense gates, through which the enemy could not penetrate, at the base of the hill where my soldiers and their horses and chariots could reach safety at the earliest possible moment."

The next morning Henry estimated how high up the hill he would have to go before he struck the assumed top of the road; once he was there he should also be at the location of his "grand building," which he thought of as the palace of Priam. Still working on the Turkish side of the hill, he set out for himself an area to be excavated of seventy-eight square feet. In the process he came upon three sets of city walls, built at angles which proved that the second set of builders did not know of the walls below them, and the third set had no suspicion that there were two walls beneath them. Digging through the ruins of a later Greek city, he found a vase with Egyptian hieroglyphics which gave proof of the trade between Troy and Egypt. Then he found a dish in high relief of two youths embracing and kissing each other, the figures well portrayed. At twenty feet down he came across a terra-cotta handle of a large cup; upon it was the head of an ox executed with great skill. Sophia exclaimed:

"This reminds me of Homer's 'ox-eyed, queenly Hera.'"

He moved almost seven thousand cubic yards of earth and found the ruins of two large houses, the more modern on top, the ancient one below. Both had been destroyed by fire. Both were filled with wood ashes and burnt debris. The walls of the lower house were thicker and more solidly built than the upper one; it appeared to be on a straight line with the paved road.

"The road could only have been used when this ancient house was still inhabited."

"If it ran directly out of Priam's palace . . ." Sophia added, "then can you say . . ."

"Not yet! Where is the double Scaean Gate? It should have been at the base of the hill."

"Perhaps not! We have not yet uncovered the whole road going up," Sophia said consolingly.

Misery ran rampant in his eyes.

"Even if we do," he said hoarsely, "it will be in the wrong place."

"Only from the account Homer wrote two hundred years after the war. The whole area had been rebuilt by then. He would not have actually seen the gates. Folk memory can misplace it by forty or fifty feet without committing a grave historical error."

"True. The name was known only from tradition. . . ."

It took several days to tear down the walls of the more modern structure. Then, as he worked to uncover the ancient building, built on an elevation to give it a commanding position, he came upon wall projections into which the top and bottom of a huge gate had been anchored. Two very large copper bolts lay in the center of the aperture where the halves of the stout wooden gate would have closed. He sent one of the men to summon Sophia, who was digging below him. Her crew was having difficulties clearing the road because here too there was a series of walls standing on top of the road which they had to break down and remove.

When she came flying up the hill and saw him standing with the two copper bolts in the one hand and pointing with the other to the notches in the stone wall where the gate had been hinged, she burst into tears:

"*Panaghia mou!* You have actually found Homer's double Scaean Gate!"

"One of them. We need the second."

His eyes were dancing so crazily in their sockets that he could not hold her face in focus.

Following the stone walls upward in a seventeen-foot corridor, Henry and Sophia together found the position of the second gate where it had been anchored into stone walls five feet out from the ancient build-ing, twenty feet farther up the hill from the bottom gate.

Sophia joined the group around Henry. The men were making mi-nute examinations of the top gate.

"But why is it supported on both sides by the wall leading into the ancient building?" Sophia asked. "The fighting troops, chariots and horses could not have gone through the building."

Henry was master of himself again. "This second gate would have led into a large courtyard. From here they could have dispersed to their homes, stables, barracks by several roads leading out of the courtyard into the city. Homer says:

"'Hector hasted from the house back over the same way along the well-built streets. When now he was come to the gate, as he passed through the great city, the Scaean Gate, whereby he was minded to go forth to the plain, there came running to meet him his beauteous wife, Andromache. . . .'"

That night, exhausted but triumphant, Henry paced their bedroom.

"The site of this building directly above the gate, together with its solid structure, leaves no doubt that it was the grandest building in Troy; nay, that it must have been the palace of Priam!"

"If it is Priam's palace, there should be a treasure trove under the debris and stone."

"I need to make a trip into Çanakkale to bring back Siebrecht to photograph the road and the gate markings. I'm also going to cable Monsieur Piat and ask him to send out Laurent to map our excavations and draw up plans for unearthing the rest of the acropolis."

Sophia was uneasy. "I know we're digging on Turkish government land now, but won't the rest of the acropolis extend us on to Frank Calvert's half?"

He wheeled, stared at her for a moment, frowned.

"I'll seek a reconciliation. Will you be all right for a day or two with-out me?"

"I'll ask Yannakis to lend me Polyxene for company."

Henry left before dawn for the long horseback ride into Çanakkale. Sophia rose at first light and spent the entire day directing the digging inside the palace walls. She ate midday dinner alone in her diningroom, Polyxene standing by to chat. In the evening she ate at the kitchen ta-ble with Yannakis, Polyxene, Photides, the artist and the two foremen. She waited until Polyxene had cleaned up, then the two of them re-turned to the stone house where Sophia wrote letters home and descrip-tions of material found during the day. Yannakis joined them but by eleven o'clock he was yawning.

"It's time for you to go to sleep," Sophia said.

Polyxene asked:

"Would you like me to sleep here with you tonight, with Master gone?"

"Thank you, it's not necessary. Go ahead with Yannakis."

She went to bed at midnight and fell asleep the moment she put her head on the pillow. She did not know how long she had been sleeping when she awakened with a start. Someone was in bed with her. It was too dark to see whom. Then she caught the strong smell of Photides, who hated water on his skin. For an instant she felt terror, then she started to fight, for Photides had put an arm around her and was trying to pull her closer to him. Then he started to kiss her, first on the cheeks, then on the mouth. She used her free hand to scratch his cheeks, feeling the blood on her fingers. Photides took his face away as he cursed. Sophia screamed:

"Yannakis! Yannakis! Help! Come quickly!"

Photides put a gnarled hand over her mouth to gag her. This time, instead of trying to kiss her, he made awkward movements to climb on top of her. She clawed at his eyes, causing him to cry out in pain. She too cried out:

"Yannakis! Yannakis! Help! Wake up! Help!"

Photides, cursing again, changed tactics and tried to push Sophia beneath him. She fought him with every ounce of her strength and rage. She panicked, thinking:

"My God, I'm going to be raped by this crazed man!"

At that moment the door flew open. Yannakis was in his nightshirt. Polyxene was right behind him. He caught one glimpse of Photides, picked the miner out of Sophia's bed as though he were a sack of flour, lifted him high in the air in his tremendous arms and dashed him to the floor with a terrifying force.

Photides was knocked unconscious. Yannakis picked him up again, ordered Polyxene:

"Stay with Kyria Schliemann. Take care of her." To Sophia he said, "I take this animal to my room. I sit on him and beat him until Master come home. Master say so, I kill him!"

He went out, carrying Photides. Polyxene pulled a chair up to the side of the bed, took Sophia's hand in hers, murmured tender reassurances.

Sophia began to sob, long racking sobs that churned her insides. All night long she wept. First chills shook her slender body, then fever rose to torment her further. Polyxene washed her hands and face, got a brush and gently stroked her hair. It did not soothe the dull burning inside her head. She was sick to her stomach. In the early morning hours she started retching.

"Try to sleep," Polyxene urged. "I stay right here."

After a time she fell into something more torpor than sleep but even then the nightmare came bursting through, and she jumped out of bed screaming.

Henry had started out from Çanakkale before dawn and had ridden hard. He was home before noon. He cried in anguish when he saw Sophia:

"What has happened?"

Polyxene quietly slipped out the door. Sophia flung herself into her husband's arms and wept bitterly. It was a considerable time before he could get anything out of her. When she had stumblingly told him what happened, Henry cried:

"Where is the wretch? I'll kill him!"

"No need," she whispered wearily. "Yannakis is in the process. You'll find them in his room."

He returned a short time later, trembling with rage.

"Yannakis is still sitting on the beast. He told me, 'Every time he try to get up, I beat him more.' I've sent for the Dramali farm wagon. Yannakis is roping him now. We'll take him into Çanakkale and prison. He can rot away the next ten years in some filthy cell where he belongs."

Sophia took a grip on herself, straightened out her thinking.

"No, Henry. I don't want anyone else to know. I'm ashamed enough as it is."

"You're ashamed? For what?"

"I don't want people talking about me . . . what happened. I could not live with that."

"There will be no talk! I'll see to that."

She put her cheek on his, supplicated:

"Errikaki, please. Just send him away."

He was silent for a moment, then said with sharp reluctance:

"Very well. If that's what you want. I'll send him to be hanged somewhere else."

Henry was a solid source of comfort. He left her alone as little as possible, and when he did go into the digs Polyxene stayed with her. Yannakis was stationed outside the door, looking like a block carved out of the face of Mt. Ida. At night when they went to bed Henry held her in his arms, tenderly stroking her hair and cheeks until she fell asleep. There were no more tears, but every once in a while, involuntarily, a shudder shook her frame and left her trembling.

"Time is the greatest of all sponges, *agapete mou*, it sops up unpleasant memories as though they were sea water. Then you throw the sponge away and the bad memories have vanished."

"I'll be all right in a few days. I want to get back into the excavation. I miss it."

Instead, late that afternoon, a messenger arrived from Dokos, Henry's agent in Çanakkale. He carried a cable from Madame Victoria to Sophia:

FATHER DESPERATELY ILL. PLEASE RETURN IMMEDIATELY.

All thoughts of her own tribulations vanished from her mind. She fell to her knees before the Virgin and prayed ardently that her father might be spared. She sent Yannakis to summon Henry from one of the deep cuts he was carving into the acropolis. She began packing at once. Henry was there within a few minutes. When he read the cable he kissed Sophia gently on each cheek, then gave the messenger money to hire a carriage. He also wrote out a cable for the man to send to his friend George Boker in the American Consulate to reserve them a cabin on the first ship leaving Constantinople for Piraeus.

"We'll be home in five days, four if we are fortunate," he assured her. "Your father is a strong man. We'll soon be with him to feed him medicine and love."

"No, *philtate mou*, just take me into Çanakkale and put me on the ship for Constantinople. You can't stop the work here, not with the Turkish government and Frank Calvert ready to take over."

"Only you are important."

"I'll feel better knowing you are making progress. If you want me to have company perhaps I can take Polyxene along?"

Henry turned to Yannakis, asking his permission. Yannakis puffed up with as much pride as though Henry had bestowed a medal on him.

"Poly take care of Kyria Schliemann . . . and see Athens."

When she was halfway down the gangplank at Piraeus she caught sight of Spyros's face as he gazed upward watching the passengers disembark. Immediately she knew the worst: for the unfailingly imperturbable Spyros was pale, tense and, for the first time Sophia could remember, had lines of sorrow furrowed down his cheeks.

She dug her nails into her palms. Spyros took her in his arms. "I'm sorry, dear Sophidion."

"Father is dead, isn't he?"

"Yes. He died last night."

"I never got a chance to say good-by to him."

"He knew you were on the way and tried to hold out. His last words were 'Kiss my little Sophia for me, and tell her that I have always loved her.'"

She wept softly, her head on Spyros's shoulder. After a moment she whispered:

"How does one live without a father? Papa was always there, every day of our lives, with his big laugh and his big hugs to share his joys and comfort us."

"I know. For us it was like waking up one morning to find that the Acropolis had sunk into a hole and disappeared."

"How is Mother?"

"She is making herself ill. It will be a comfort to her to have you at home. The porters are bringing down the baggage."

"What happened, Spyros?"

"He wasted away. A growth in his stomach, the doctor said."

When they reached Athens, Sophia sent Polyxene to Mousson Street. Then she and Spyros took a carriage to Colonos. Marigo opened the door of the house before Sophia could reach the knob. Then she and her mother were weeping in each other's arms. Her sister Katingo had taken Andromache home with her after Georgios's death.

Madame Victoria led Sophia into the parlor where Georgios was laid out on a low narrow bed that had been made that morning. The family had dressed him in his best suit. His head was slightly raised on a cushion and he faced eastward. Candles were burning at his head and feet. There was a lighted lamp to guide his spirit if it should return home.

Sophia kissed each member of her family. They were all dressed in black. Relatives and friends kept coming in. The priest arrived, put on his stole, burned incense and read a short prayer. Sophia, her mother, sisters and female relatives sat around the dead man, weeping. The men were obliged to stand in the next room. Every few minutes a cry went up from one of the women praising Georgios Engastromenos's virtues.

Sophia remained silent, holding her mother's hand. A coffin was brought into the parlor. Georgios was placed in it. The bier was covered with flowers. Darkness fell. An "unsleeping lamp" was lit; it would burn for forty days. Sophia and her family were also "unsleeping lamps." They remained with the coffin, speaking softly, telling stories of Georgios's goodness and kindness.

The next morning, when it was time for the funeral, two priests came to the house accompanied by the deacon. The coffin was lifted to the shoulders of four young cousins. The priests went first, holding candles. The deacon followed with the censer, burning coal and incense. Then came the coffin, followed by Madame Victoria and her children. The procession wound through the surrounding streets on its way to the church. As it passed, housewives closed their windows, merchants closed the doors of their shops.

The bier was placed in the church to face east. The family sat on chairs on both sides. At the end of the hour's funeral service, one of the priests invited the family to give "the last kiss" to the dead. Sophia kissed the icon on the coffin. She and the family moved their chairs to the open door. Friends and relatives passed by murmuring their condolences.

The coffin was placed on a funeral carriage. Sophia, her family and friends followed on foot, making the long and heartbroken pilgrimage to the main cemetery in Athens. For Sophia it was a walk from life to death, for she felt that with the passing of her father something within her had died too, her youth, an innocence perhaps. At the cemetery she watched the coffin being lowered into the grave. The priest took a shovel of earth and threw it, in the form of a cross, into the grave, along with olive oil from the church *lampion,* and the coal and incense from the censer. Sophia and her family each threw a bit of watered earth into the grave. The coffin was covered. The family surrounded the grave, eating a piece of sweet bread, careful to see that no crumb fell to the ground, and drinking a glass of wine. Friends and relatives had brought a variety of foods to the cemetery. Georgios would remain on earth for forty days before going to heaven and this food, after being blessed, would minister to his bodily needs. It was a deeply sad moment when the family had to leave the cemetery.

Sophia went home with Katingo to pick up Andromache. In the carriage she said to her older sister:

"There is a weight on my heart that feels like a bar of lead. But I must not let Andromache feel my grief. She would not understand. It would hurt her."

In the mornings Sophia and Polyxene played with Andromache. The child was as mischievous and fun-loving as ever. In the afternoons Sophia rode out to be with her mother. She wrote to Henry every day, telling him of her sorrow and of Madame Victoria's uncontrolled weeping. Her mother was unable to reconcile herself to Georgios's eternal absence. Requiems were held on the third and ninth day. Sophia joined her relatives in cutting and eating a piece of *kollyva,* a wheat cake covered with white sugar and garnished with ornaments, almonds, raisins, pieces of pomegranate; by so doing they were participating in the dead man's meal. She was aware that much of the ritual was pagan, handed down from ancient Greece to be woven into the Christian religion; and once again, as on Mt. Olympus, she had the eerie feeling of living on time levels thousands of years apart.

If the nights seemed endless, the days too were unbearably long.

There arose within her an old conflict: her loyalty to her family and her loyalty to Henry, who needed her sorely now. She wanted to return to her husband, to the Troad, to their honeycombed mountain. How long could she stay? How long *should* she stay?

Henry solved her problem.

Troy, 14 May 1873

My warmly beloved wife,

Console yourself, my dearest, with the thought that we all go, before long, the way your excellent father did. Console yourself for the good of our little daughter who has such a need for her mother. Console yourself with the thought that all your tears are not going to bring your beloved father back to life. Also, console yourself that he went away as a good and pious man, away from the constant gruesome struggles, pains and cares of this life to the life beyond, where he enjoys true happiness.

If however your grief cannot be consoled, then get into the next boat and come to me here and I will do everything in my power to lighten your heart and bring joy to your sweet eyes.

She took Andromache to her Aunt Katingo's, gathered up Polyxene, had Spyros take them back to Piraeus.

5.

Henry met her in Çanakkale. They did not call on the Calverts. Henry told her how distressing his visit to Çanakkale had been. Frank Calvert had learned about the finding of the Scaean Gate and Priam's palace. He categorically refused Henry the right to dig any further on his land. Henry's visit to the governor, a new appointee called Ibrahim Pasha, had been equally chilling: the new law controlling all finds on Turkish territory had reached final form and was about to be signed by the Sultan or the Minister of Public Instruction.

When she walked into her stone house, which now stood on the edge of Henry's latest excavation trench, she thought for a fleeting moment that the memory of Photides's attack might return. But the death of her father had absorbed and then cast away the unpleasant memory, like Henry's sea-soaked sponge. In any event she had little time to linger. With his arm about her waist, Henry took her into the workroom to show her the fine ivory and bone idols, the implements of war he had uncovered in Priam's palace. There were some of the most remarkably shaped and decorated vases in their three years of excavating.

Sophia was particularly delighted with a brilliant brown vase of Athena, with the owl's head, wearing a necklace; another with what Henry described as a pair of spectacles; a small vessel in female form, with hair down its back, gathered into a plait and falling almost to the ankles. Henry commented that it reminded him of the karyatides on the Acropolis in Athens. He then showed her a vase with considerable writing around the widening area below the neck.

"Oh, Henry, at long last! Enough writing to be deciphered. Could it be Trojan? Have you finally discovered an example of the Trojan language?"

Henry picked up the vase and held it fondly.

"It has to be! We found it at the very bottom of Priam's palace, walled in by protecting stones. We'll take it back with us under our arm." Then, realizing that he was jumping to a non-*scholastiké* conclusion, he added regretfully, "Of course there is the outside chance that it was brought in from another area by traders. . . ."

Since they were now short a foreman, Sophia spent the entire day in the digs. Henry started a new and deep cutting on the northwest side of the mountain, looking for more buildings of the acropolis. Instead he came up against a formidable wall, thirteen feet high and ten feet thick, which blocked his way into the city. It took several days to break through.

On Saturday, the last day of May, there was no dawn. The sun appeared on the horizon as swiftly as though it had been shot out of a cannon concealed behind the Ida Mountains. Sophia was already dressed in a cool, loose-fitting blue blouse and skirt of linen-cotton, and was tying her hair in a knot on top of her head when she heard the familiar hoofbeats of Henry's horse bringing him back from his daily bath in the Aegean. She pinned on her wide-brimmed hat and joined him in the kitchen house for coffee. Henry bade her a cheerful good morning, his cheeks flushed with color from the swim and the ride. It was a quarter to five; out the window they could see the workmen streaming into the digs with their shovels, pickaxes and iron bars in hand. Henry asked her to take her crew back to the new area directly by the side of the palace of King Priam where they had rediscovered the defense wall, and move southward, unearthing as far as she could.

"It's slow going, Henry, down at that thirty-foot level. The stratum of red, burned ruins is five feet thick and hard as stone."

"Make what progress you can. Monday morning I'll give you more pickaxes."

By seven in the morning her workmen were down to a softer debris and were excavating at a faster rate along a ten-foot-high wall. When

Henry came by on his frequent rounds of inspection, he asked if she had any interesting finds.

"Nothing yet. The debris was too solid. But this softer ash layer looks promising. I'll start using my rake on it."

Henry too picked up a rake, which he had learned to use with a slow, delicate movement so that he would merely touch rather than hit any submerged vase or pot. Sophia stood by, watching to see if her prediction would prove true. Henry had been raking for only a few moments when he uncovered a large copper shield like an oval tray. He crouched down, dusted off the shield, lifted one end, then quickly replaced it. He stood up, faced Sophia with eyes as large and bright as the morning's sun.

"My God, Sophia, I caught the gleam of gold under that shield, a whole pile of gold!"

Sophia glanced over her shoulder, saw that her crew, digging a number of feet away, had seen and heard nothing. She said softly:

"What shall we do?"

"Call out *paidos*, rest period."

"At seven in the morning?"

"Tell them it's my birthday. I just this moment remembered. Yannakis will pay everyone a full day's wage and they can return to their villages to celebrate for the weekend. Make certain that the guard hears you, and that he takes off with the rest."

Sophia walked down to her crew, called *paidos*, as she had for months at the breakfast and midday rest periods. Her crew was so delighted at the good news they hardly listened to her "birthday" explanation. After they had gathered their tools and left, she made the rounds of the crews working under Captain Tsirogiannes and Spyridon Demetriou, calling:

"*Paidos!* Good holiday. Everyone will be paid for the full day. We will see you at dawn, Monday morning."

Yannakis had the cash in his money belt. Sophia stood by while he paid off the men and checked them out in his little book. When the last of the men, and the guard with them, had set out in varying directions for their villages, Sophia said:

"Thank you, Yannakis. Dr. Schliemann wants you and Polyxene to have the extra day of celebration too. Wouldn't you like to visit your relatives in Renkoi?"

Yannakis's big bearded face broke into a wide-whiskered grin.

"Kyria Schliemann is good master. Poly like to see her mother. We go right away?"

"Yes. Take Captain Tsirogiannes, Lempesses and Demetriou with you. Give them each a bonus of fifty piasters to pay their expenses in Renkoi. Take the same bonus for yourself."

The giant fell to his knees. Before Sophia could count to a hundred the five hilarious vacationers were on donkeys bound for Renkoi.

The dig was quiet and motionless. They were alone.

She returned to find Henry hovering over his treasure. When she told him how thoroughly she had cleaned out Hissarlik, he threw his arms around her and cried:

"You're a genius."

"Now let's see what you've found."

Henry took off his coat and vest, loosened his collar, then removed the copper shield. Lying on top of the mass of metal were a copper cauldron and plate. Then, gleaming in all its pristine beauty, they saw a globular bottle, six inches high and five in diameter. Sophia gasped. Henry lifted it from its cache and placed it in Sophia's hands.

"It's of the purest gold," he murmured reverentially.

Next he brought forth a gold cup, after that a boat-shaped gold vessel with two large handles, exquisitely designed. Sophia sat on a rock and held each of them, wiping them clean with her underskirt.

"These too are pure gold," she said.

"No question about it." His voice was quivering. "Now I'm coming to a layer of silver: here are three vases, a goblet, a dish, all wonderfully made."

"What have we discovered, Henry?" she asked breathlessly. "A treasure trove for sure, but why is it all concentrated in this one small area?"

"Look at this long copper strap. It ends in two round nailheads. I believe it is a hasp from a chest which kept the chest closed and locked."

There followed a series of copper daggers, knives . . . and then, uttering a cry of triumph, he straightened up. In his hand he held a four-inch-long copper key.

"The key to the chest!" he cried. "The wooden chest burned; the metal survived."

"Let me try my hand," she asked.

He moved aside a few inches. Sophia leaned over, drew forth a large silver vase. They peered into its opening, their cheeks touching, and both were awe-stricken at what they saw: it was filled with incredibly beautiful gold jewelry.

"Holy Mother of God!" murmured Sophia softly.

She was still for a long moment, then moved aside two more gold goblets to find herself staring at a wealth of gold earrings, gold rings, gold buttons, gold bracelets . . .

Henry took over.

"Go up to the house as quickly as you can and bring back your red shawl. Even with no one around, we can't take a chance of this gold being seen."

It was only a couple of hundred feet. She was back quickly. Henry wrapped the gold bottle and gold cups carefully in her shawl. She took them up to the house and hid them under the bed. When she returned, he wrapped the silver vases and goblets, a handful of the gold jewelry in his coat, left her to guard the hoard.

Next he folded Sophia's shawl around the silver vase filled with gold jewelry and directed her to carry it to the house and hide it under a pillow.

In his coat he then carried off the copper axes and knives, the shield; Sophia followed with the balance of the gold jewelry, the copper hasp and key.

Once inside the house Henry backed a heavy chair against the door, pulled the curtains over the windows and asked Sophia to pull back the blankets and lay bare the white sheet on the bed. When she had done this he turned the large silver vase upside down over the center of the sheet. What they saw tumble out paralyzed them of speech or movement. . . . A gold fillet to hold back a woman's hair. Two large gold diadems, one consisting of a gold fillet twenty-two inches long from which there hung on either side seven gold chains to cover the temples. Each of the chains had eleven square leaves of gold; they were joined to one another by four gold cross chains. At the end of each of these there hung a glittering gold idol of Athena. Across the forehead there were forty-seven small gold pendants adorned with gold leaves.

The second diadem was twenty inches long and was composed of a gold chain from which were suspended on each side eight additional chains, completely covered with gold leaves. At the end of every one of the sixteen chains there hung a gold idol with the owl's head of Athena. Across the forehead, on chains four inches long, also covered with gold leaves, were more gold idols; and at the end of each, a double gold leaf.

Henry picked up the first diadem and placed it lovingly on Sophia's head. It fit perfectly.

"*Vassilissa* Schliemann. Queen Sophia. You are Helen of Troy!" he exclaimed rapturously.

She went to the mirror on her washstand to gaze at the hundreds of golden chains running through golden leaves and ending in glittering golden idols.

"I've never seen anything like this in any museum," she exclaimed.

"There is nothing anywhere like it in the world. It is pure Trojan!"

She returned to the bed where Henry was pouring out a river of gold earrings, bracelets, finger rings, literally thousands of gold buttons and studs to be used to ornament leather belts, shields, knife handles, a shower of beads of varying shapes: stars, leaves, pegs, cylinders.

Henry sat her down on the edge of the bed, put bracelets on her

TROY?   267

wrists, earrings in her ears, rings on her fingers. She was too dazed to protest.

He kneeled before her, kissed her on the lips. She could not decide whether there were stars or tears in his eyes. He was as exalted as a man who had gazed upon the face of God.

"Do you know what we have here, *chryse mou?* The final evidence to prove that we have uncovered Priam's Troy. This is the treasure of Priam! No one can conceivably dispute this evidence! Our fight has been won. We have the treasure of Priam in our hands. This gold fillet is precisely the one Andromache tears off her hair when she learns of Hector's death."

She shook her head, hearing the long gold chains of the diadem tinkle against each other.

"Henry, how did Priam's treasure chest get *outside* the defense wall? We should have found it inside the ruins of the palace."

He chuckled.

"So we would have if someone had not picked up the chest and attempted to carry it to safety. That would have been when the Achaean soldiers flooded through the gates of Troy. The box would have been too heavy for a woman to carry. It must have been a man. When he saw the Achaean soldiers pursuing him, he dropped the heavy chest to speed his flight. It fell into soft earth, became covered over, and no one has seen it . . . until our rake touched the copper shield this morning."

She nodded her head in agreement.

The gold was comparatively clean, for little dust or debris had penetrated the copper shield and protecting layers of silver and copper objects. Sophia took a hand towel and ran it over the large globular vase and boat-shaped cup, took them into the workroom and set them upon the worktable. Henry, trailing her, exclaimed:

"They are superb. What fine goldsmiths the Trojans must have had. Did you know that the stonemason and the goldsmith practiced the oldest professions of man?"

"They are surely both well represented here in Troy! Henry, how do we proceed? There are a thousand pieces of gold jewelry on our bed, and thousands more of gold buttons and beads. Shall we separate them into categories and try to list them in our journal . . . ?"

Suddenly she stopped. They looked at each other with the first realization of their situation.

"No, no! We must say nothing. Write nothing!" Henry cried. "We must concentrate on how to get this incredible treasure out of here."

"We are not going to report any part of the find?"

"We must not. The new Turkish law may already be signed. The government would confiscate the entire treasure."

He was agitated now, his eyes dark and defensive. It was hazardous to cross him at such a time, but she felt it necessary to think the matter through.

"Would you be willing to give the museum their half if the old law still applied?"

He was silent, grinding on his molars in protest.

"We could set aside the more wonderful pieces for ourselves: the round bottle, the diadems . . ." she continued.

"And destroy its entity! They would be taking away from us our proof that we are in Homer's Troy and have the oft-mentioned treasure of Priam. We must take it back in its entirety! We must have the collection mounted and exhibited in the capitals of the world: Athens, Berlin, Paris, Rome, London, New York. This collection is not only our reward for our work and dedication, it is the living, gleaming testimony that we have uncovered the royal palace!"

A considerable part of Henry's future rested in this treasure trove.

"How do you plan to get it out of here?"

"The way we did the Apollo metope."

"When is Captain Theodorou due in at Besika Bay?"

"Not for a week or more."

"How do we keep it safe until then?"

"We wipe everything down, divide the pieces roughly into categories and wrap them securely in your old clothes, then pack everything in your traveling trunk and lock it. Next we'll announce to the foremen our closing date, two weeks from now, June 14. That will be our reason for beginning to pack our personal belongings. We'll keep on digging, but each day retire more of our equipment and get it ready for shipment, as I mean to take everything home with us. Dear one, our excavations here are finished. We have succeeded. With this treasure, and the Great Watchtower, the Scaean Gate, the paved road, Priam's palace, we have established the truth of Troy!"

Sophia took off her diadem, began separating the gold objects on the sheet.

"When Adolphe Laurent arrives I will have him draw engineering maps of everything we have accomplished here so that no one in Europe can doubt any longer. Then, for future use, I'll have him make sketches for excavating the remaining part of the mountain, including Frank Calvert's half. I'm certain the Calverts and Schliemanns will become friends again one day."

They worked through the night, cleaning, grouping, wrapping the finds in several of Sophia's old suits and dresses, then carefully layered them in her trunk. It was dawn when they finished. Henry brought in his journal, scrawled some twenty pages without drawings. He was writing so hastily that Sophia, looking over his shoulder, saw many cross-outs and corrections, the first time this had ever happened in his diaries. He was nervous, uncertain, even confused. The attempt to tell that he had found a great treasure, and precisely where, without revealing the vast gold hoard, was too much for him. She put a hand on his shoulder, said:

"Anyone looking at this journal in the future is going to know exactly where and when you found King Priam's treasure! Come to bed now, we need rest. I have the trunk locked and pushed into a corner under my skirts."

He closed the diary, returned it to the workroom.

"It's Sunday," she murmured. "There is no one here to wake us."

6.

The harvest season was starting. Henry was down to sixty men.

"That suits me fine," he confided to Sophia. "All I want to do now is to expose the rest of the defense wall south to the Scaean Gate. Because there will be more and more visitors coming in to see Troy after my articles and book are published I also want to excavate further in the palace, particularly that twenty-foot room on which no buildings of a later period rest."

In order to break down the enormous block of earth separating his western and northwestern cuttings from the Great Watchtower, he was forced to tear down the wooden house in which they had lived the year before.

"I'm sad to see it go," said Sophia; "it's as though I were losing part of my home. We were happy there."

"We'll be happy as long as we are working archaeologists," he replied. "And that's what I mean for us to be for the rest of our lives."

It seemed incredible to them that anyone could have learned. At first they thought it was the fact that Henry was tapering off the operation, having Yannakis clean and oil the wheelbarrows and prepare them for shipment; the fact that the men now knew none of them would be returning after the harvest; that they had only a limited time left for this weird employment of tearing down a mountain. But a subtle change had come over the atmosphere of the digs, and over the workmen. Henry and Sophia caught furtive glances on the part of the Greeks as they walked past, inspecting the work of clearing the defense wall. Occasionally they saw the Turkish workers whispering among themselves, stopping suddenly when the Schliemanns approached. Henry perceived a sly sullenness. The guard, Amin Effendi, had become

silent in his presence, even when he was selecting the museum's half of
the more valuable finds. Nothing was said outright, no one attempted
to come near the house or took any untoward action. It was simply a
new undercurrent of suspicion or mistrust.

"Can they possibly know about our treasure?" Sophia asked Henry
late at night, in their bedroom, where they could not be overheard.
"There was not a soul on the mountain with us."

"I'm sure they do not," he replied; "but they suspect we have found
something important that we are concealing from them. They don't
know its nature or value. It's just an intuitive feeling of having been
left out."

"Perhaps they are beginning to ask themselves why we gave them
last Saturday off; they may have found out somehow that it was not
your birthday. Perhaps there has been some slight change in our own
attitude of which we are not aware. Perhaps it is just a general sadness
that comes at the end of things. . . ."

"All these possibilities exist," he admitted; "but there is only one
positive. We must leave here as quickly as possible."

"How many more days before the *Omonoia* arrives?"

"Five or six, I estimate. We must set Yannakis and Mastro-Yannes to
building boxes and crates immediately in which to take out our half of
the finds."

The carpentry began early in the morning. Adolphe Laurent and
the photographer Siebrecht arrived together with their equipment and
both went to work at once documenting the excavations. Sophia confined herself to the workroom, grouping the terra cottas, ivory and stone
pieces to be crated. They also set out several dozen wicker baskets of
varying sizes which Sophia packed with the skill she had acquired over
the past three years. Amin Effendi never left the area where the packing was being done. He checked every piece being put into the baskets
and crates, made a list of them and compared the Schliemanns' possessions with his own lists of the finds which he had sent once a week
to Constantinople. He made no accusations, nor did he attempt to
disrupt the work, but he knew that in some way he was being taken
advantage of. He further knew that there was nothing he could do
about it.

The *Omonoia* arrived on the thirteenth of June. Yannakis rented the
Dramali farm wagon and brought it to the front of the stone house. As
the guard stood by, the two foremen loaded the crates, boxes and
baskets into the wagon. Each had Amin Effendi's mark on it, put there
before he had permitted anything to be closed, including the baskets
covered with rough cloths Sophia and Polyxene had stitched together
with which to enclose them. The baskets were then tightly roped.

At the last moment Yannakis brought out two of Henry's suitcases, a smaller one of Sophia's, and then her steamer trunk. The guard made no effort to have the baggage opened. After all, it contained only the personal possessions which Dr. and Kyria Schliemann had brought with them from Athens five months before.

Henry rode down to the bay with Yannakis, watched all of his crates, baskets and luggage transported from the small boat to the *Omonoia*. The night before Sophia had written a letter to her mother for Henry to give to Captain Theodorou to deliver to the Engastromenos house in Colonos immediately on his arrival:

> We have found some interesting materials which will arrive on Captain Theodorou's ship. As soon as this letter reaches you please have Spyros and Alexandros engage two back-of-the-garden storerooms in Athens where the crates and luggage can be safely deposited until we return to claim them. The rooms should be in separate parts of the town and capable of being locked and the key taken. There should be no entrance from any other part of the house. . . .

He had also asked of her:

"Instruct your brothers that nothing they take off the ship in Piraeus is to be opened at the Customs House. If the officials refuse our request, let them seal everything with the customs stamp and hold them in storage until I arrive. But by all means they must not let the customs open anything!"

Henry bade farewell to the captain, handed him Sophia's letter with instructions that he himself must place it in the hands of Madame Victoria. The captain nodded agreement, said, "Until we meet in Athens"; and very soon the little ship was puffing its black smoke across the Aegean toward the Sporades.

That same day Henry rented two fishing caïques in the village of Kum Kale. Yannakis kept the farm wagon for the rest of the day, transporting all of the tools and other equipment to the small boats which would take them directly to Piraeus, where they would be placed in storehouses until Henry found a proper place for them.

Yannakis paid off the last of the workmen a couple of hours before dusk. They were asked to remain by the stone house overlooking the cratered hill. At Sophia's suggestion Henry had sent for the priest of Yeni-shehr to bless the excavation site. The priest did so in rather vague and confused terms. He seemed terrified at the sight before them, with its vast cuts, channels, terraces, tunnels, exposed walls and ruins of houses from a pagan time. However he caught his second wind and, turning his back on the digs, invoked heavenly blessings upon the

earthly welfare of his own community. He then said Mass. When he had
finished, Henry addressed the assembled men:

"It is a bosom-lifting feeling that in spite of these gigantic excavations nobody lost his life. That in spite of the grave dangers no one
suffered any dangerous injuries. For this too I offer thanks to God.
Kyria Schliemann and I bid you all farewell and wish you a good year."

The Mass and Henry's friendly words seemed to dissolve whatever
hostility or suspicion may have lurked in the minds of the workmen
during the past days. Each in turn murmured his good wishes and farewell. Soon they were on their donkeys, booting the little animals homeward to their villages. Laurent and Siebrecht, the painter and the
foremen left for Çanakkale.

Only Yannakis and Polyxene remained. Henry informed them that
they would be kept on salary, that they were to box and ship the remaining terra cottas and shards which they had not had time to prepare
for the Omonoia. Sophia embraced Polyxene, then said to Yannakis:

"Please catch the three wild cats that we have been feeding and who
have kept the field mice away. Also I would like two storks. Do you
think you can catch them all and ship them safely to Piraeus?"

Yannakis scratched both sides of his enormous head in perplexity.

"Kyria Schliemann, I never catched a stork. Never saw anyone else
catch one. But I try."

They slept for the last time in their stone house above the Scaean
Gate, Priam's palace, the defense wall and paved road. They were alone
for their farewells to Troy. At dawn the driver of the carriage, who had
arrived the evening before and slept in Ciplak, presented himself. He
carried the last of their bags to his carriage.

Then they made for the main road connecting Smyrna and Çanakkale. Sophia turned her head over her shoulder for a last look at the
bastion of Troy, the Troad plain, the Dardanelles flowing into the
Aegean, along with the shining silver ribbons of the Scamander and
Simois rivers. It was a June morning of such utter clarity that she felt
she could reach out and touch the islands of Imbros and Samothrace.

With an intense pang of nostalgia she realized that she was losing
her most important home, where both she and her marriage had come
of age. It was almost four years since she had been summoned from
St. Meletios's to the back garden of her family's house in Colonos to
meet a stranger with whom her Uncle Vimpos and her parents had
been proposing a marriage. She recalled her disappointment when she
was introduced to Henry Schliemann, a small, colorless, bald, middle-
aged man whose only virtue seemed to be that he had taken three separate fortunes out of Russia and California.

She recalled also the transformation that had come over him when he started to speak about Homer and Troy; his positive knowledge of where Priam's "immortal city" lay, here at Hissarlik, at the mouth of the Dardanelles; how he would unearth the mountain-fortress until he had reached the great defense walls, the king's palace, the Watchtower, the paved road leading out of the palace through the double Scaean Gate and down to the Troad battlefield.

Glancing sideways at her husband, she thought:

"He's a genius. A natural-born genius. And one of the world's heroic fighters. He went against the scholars, the historians, the philologists, none of whom believed there ever was a Troy, and he has proved them all to be wrong." They would now have to acknowledge, with all his tangible and irrefutable proofs at hand, that he had been the profoundest and most daring scholar of them all.

It hadn't been easy! She had become ill in Paris; they had quarreled about her homesickness and about the help her family so desperately needed. There was his temper, his alternate bouts of stinginess and generosity. He was an opportunist who would say almost anything to achieve his ends. There was her own youth and immaturity. There was the time when she did not think she could love him, or that the marriage could endure.

But all that had ended when they moved the first shovel and wheelbarrow onto the mountain of Hissarlik. They had worked side by side through freezing winds, burning suns, choking dust, bouts of malaria. The hardships had only increased their love and dedication to each other.

She turned to her husband to see if he too was sad to be leaving. She saw at once that Henry was thinking not backward but forward. The long road down which they were driving was not the one he saw. Instead he was traveling the longer road from Athens to the Peloponnesus: Olympia . . . Tiryns . . . Mycenae, to where he would excavate next. There was an expression on his face, as he sat against the leather back of the carriage staring directly ahead, which said:

"We are just beginning."

BOOK SIX

A BRIDGE OF DAYS

1.

S PYROS was at the dock at Piraeus to meet them. "No trouble with customs. They passed everything without opening a basket. I put the trunk in a garden storeroom on the last street up on Lycabettus. Here's the key and a receipt from the owner of the house, K. R. Papadopoulos, for a hundred and seventy drachs. I paid only one month in advance since I didn't know how long you would need it. Alexandros went in the opposite direction, rented a storeroom in Monastiraki, behind an old Turkish home, walled in like a fortress."

Henry flashed Sophia a smile of approval.

"You were right, *Vassilissa* Sophia: Cretan blood speaks a language of its own."

He turned to Spyros. "You did well. I see Ioannes Maltezos waving to us from his carriage. After we have dropped Sophia at Mousson Street you can take me to the Papadopoulos house. We don't want to be conspicuous so we'll leave the carriage several blocks away."

"Have to anyway, the hill is pretty steep for horses. There are only a handful of houses that high up."

It was midmorning when Sophia reached home. Her mother was there to greet her, as well as Marigo and Katingo. But it was Andromache who gave the official welcome, jumping into her mother's arms, crying:

"Mama, Mama home!"

The child was plump and healthy. Sophia kissed her mother, murmuring, "You are good for Andromache."

On her tour of inspection of the house, Sophia saw that Madame Victoria was also good for the house.

"Mother, you're a better housekeeper than I'll ever be."

Her mother was pleased.

Henry returned, a grin lighting his lean features.

"Everything is intact. The lock on your trunk was not tampered with. The gold looks even more beautiful than when we hid it between the folds of your clothing."

The maid also welcomed them. She and Madame Victoria had dinner cooking on the stove. But they would need a new nursemaid. Madame Victoria had one standing by, also from a Colonos family. Her name was Calypso. She was a plain girl, about eighteen, and had a nice way with Andromache. Sophia hired her. Their houseboy had been working elsewhere but would return to his old room in the semi-basement.

Before dinner Sophia took Henry out to their garden.

"I looked at it from the window but I didn't want to walk about until we could do it together."

It was a glorious June day. Their path was almost blocked by a profusion of honeysuckle, jasmine and ivy. The lemon trees, which they had planted in a row against one wall, had already dropped their flowers; the small green fruit was emerging. The mulberry tree was a mass of dark green foliage. Sophia exclaimed:

"Isn't it a delicious sight! I know that's an inappropriate word but I do not only see and smell our garden, I can taste it."

That evening, after they had put their daughter to bed, they got into comfortable night clothes and sat out on the screened veranda facing the Acropolis. It was good to be in the moon-shadow of the Parthenon again. Henry was organizing their months ahead.

"Above all, we must be careful that no one learns the whereabouts of our treasure. No one knows we have it except Minister Resident Boker in Constantinople; he had done so much for us that I felt he had a right to know about it."

"Aren't you going to bring it here?" she asked.

"Only a few pieces at a time, to photograph for our book."

Every several days Spyros would take a small suitcase to the Lycabettus storeroom, return the gold pieces that had been photographed and bring back a new batch of rings or bracelets to Mousson Street. On other days he would go with Ioannes Maltezos in his carriage to the Monastiraki storeroom and bring down a basket of terra cottas and other antiquities to be cleaned, repaired and photographed. The same photographer who had been working for months to get clear images of everything from the 1871 and 1872 excavations came whenever he was summoned and set up his camera in Henry's study. No one was allowed in the room when the gold was there, neither family nor servants. Close-mouthed Spyros did not have to be warned not to talk; the photographer was safe as well.

"By bribery," Henry confessed; "I've offered him a substantial bonus if he never utters one word about the gold."

The work went on at a feverish pace. Sophia's main job was to string together into two necklaces, one of eleven strands, the other with thirteen, the eight thousand small gold beads, four thousand to a necklace. Henry wanted a full-page photograph of the important headdresses with their hundreds of strands of golden leaves linked by fine chains, and the necklaces Sophia had strung together. Her next task was to assemble on one board the long gold earrings, each with half a dozen strands, the smaller earrings and finger rings, the decorations worn on leather belts, knife handles, scabbards. She placed on top of the collection the wide gold fillet or headband. Henry mounted the copper key to the chest at the top of the board.

Next she set up on one shelf the fourteen beautifully wrought gold and silver cups, bottles, vases. Henry cleaned the copper daggers and knives, the large vessels, swords and finally the copper cauldron and shield which had covered and protected the precious metal over the millennia. When all the gold pieces had been individually photographed, Henry decided that he wanted the entire treasure photographed on a single sheet, not only the gold but the silver finds, the copper shield and cauldron. He insisted that the reader be able to see the collection as assembled on one page. For at least a few hours he had to have the entire treasure in his home.

"When would this be safest?" he asked Sophia.

"On a religious or national holiday, when all government offices and businesses are shut down and the people are celebrating. No one will notice the steamer trunk in the carriage."

St. Peter and St. Paul's Day fell on Sunday, June 29. Everything except the churches and the coffee shops would be closed, Mousson Street deserted.

The photographer arrived just after dawn, plentifully supplied with film. Henry and Sophia grouped their eight thousand gold objects on four long shelves in the garden shed where there would be good light. The cauldron and shield were placed on the floor, the gold fitted tightly together. It took a number of hours before the photographer was satisfied that he had enough exposures to emerge with sharp images. When this was done, Henry said:

"Now I want you to take some photographs of Kyria Schliemann."

Sophia was wearing a high-necked black dress, her lustrous dark hair puffed high on her head. She had placed a beauty mark on her left cheek. First Henry took a diadem and set it carefully on her head, its long side pieces reaching her shoulders. Then he asked her to place the gold wire through her pierced ears and wear the six-stranded gold earrings which ended in golden idols, while he attached two long earrings to the high collar of her dress. He instructed the photographer to take a close-up picture so that the jewelry could be seen in the finest detail. The photographer put his black cloth over his camera and over his head, squeezed on the bulb in his right hand. He took pictures until Sophia grew weary and self-conscious, her face flushed.

"Helen of Troy was never more beautiful," Henry cried, his own face ablaze with pride.

"Or more uncomfortable. Could we have done with this now?"

"Very well, let's take each piece off, gently. We'll put them back in the trunk. Spyros can then return it to its Lycabettus home. It's all safe now, recorded for history."

It proved to be the most erroneous statement of Henry Schliemann's life.

The baskets of terra cottas and their other finds were brought one by one from the storehouse in Monastiraki. Émile Burnouf's two young archaeologists helped restore them. Henry and Sophia worked on the coppers, ivories, stones, marbles. Sophia had nimble fingers and had achieved a sureness of touch in handling the ancient artifacts. Henry then hired an amanuensis to make two copies of his Trojan journals, the one in German to go to Leipzig, the second to go to the Greek ambassador in Berlin, Alexander R. Rangabé, who had agreed to do the French translation. His larger task was to reproduce at his own expense over two hundred separate sheets of photographs for each volume, picturing the important finds.

"That is a staggering task," exclaimed Sophia, her dark eyes enormous as she gazed penetratingly at her husband, whose capacity to astonish her appeared endless. "You intend to publish two hundred sets of the text and folio in German and an equal number in French. That sounds like eighty thousand photograph pages!"

Henry laughed. "A little less, perhaps."

"How will they possibly do it?"

"I've hired an agent, a Mr. Chrysikopoulos, who will work with the photographer. I'll check through the photographs as they come along so that we can eliminate faulty prints. Brockhaus will do the glueing in Leipzig."

Henry was a pacer. He jumped up from his desk chair, strode back and forth before the windows overlooking Athens. A change of mood was evidenced by an excitement which almost physically leapt out of him to engulf her. Suddenly he crouched down before her, took her hands firmly in his.

"Sophidion, I want to tell you what I have been up to these past several days. I've been speaking with a number of members of the Parliament. I've offered one of our big corner lots plus two hundred thousand francs to build a beautiful museum to house our entire Trojan collection."

Sophia threw her arms around him.

"Oh, my beloved Henry, I'm so proud of you."

"However I'm imposing conditions: although the museum will be Greek-owned, the ownership of the collection must remain in my hands until my death."

"Whatever for?" she asked. "Do you intend to move it around . . . to other museums?"

"No, no, I won't retain the right to move anything. It's a matter of pride. The building will be named the Schliemann Museum. But the world must know that the collection belongs to me as long as I am alive."

He was not able to put down his immense sense of pride in accomplishment. It had been a driving force all during his adult life. He was generous to those around him. He had supported his own family and taken on Sophia's. He had just assured Spyros that he would have a lifetime job with him. He dealt fairly with people he employed, paying them respect as well as above-average wages. He could sometimes be unscrupulous, like having persuaded a friend in New York to perjure himself to the end that he, Henry Schliemann, could secure his American citizenship papers. Or buying a house and a small business as evidence that he intended to become a permanent resident of Indianapolis, where he applied for a divorce. His strength as well as his sometime moral weakness was that he desperately needed what he wanted, when he wanted it; the end justified the means. . . . He justified these lapses into moral obloquy on the grounds that he had to obtain a certain result in order to make heroic contributions to the world. He could not remember his terrifying outbursts of temper, let alone control or understand them.

He turned back to Sophia.

"In return for the museum and our collection I am asking for a permit from the Greek government to excavate at Olympia and Mycenae."

The *Newspaper of the Debates* began publishing the last parts of the journal from Troy. Other Athens papers featured articles about the work and reported in detail Henry's intention to turn over his finds from Troy, and later from his Greek digs, to the Greek government to be housed in a museum for which he was offering two hundred thousand francs.

The weather turned hot. They attended the theater at Phaleron to hear *The Barber of Seville*. Instead of cooking their main meal at home, they went down to the Athens Hotel, which was popular for its fine food. The city was in turmoil, with armed forces being gathered because of political unrest over the last parliamentary election; the editor of the Athens *Times* was being put into prison for publishing an article criticizing the king.

As the heat continued all those who could moved out to the countryside or went to live by the sea.

"Henry, can we afford to buy a house in Kiphissia?"

"Not just yet, Sophidion."

In the cool of an early dawn they walked into the main entrance of the Acropolis, mounting the broad marble steps. They rested in front of the Venetian tower, also called the Frankish tower, which had been built in the fourteenth century by the Venetians then occupying Greece. It covered sixteen hundred square feet of the former Propylaea, the monumental roofed gateway on the west side of the Acropolis, and consisted of large slabs of marble taken from various monuments and the Herodes Atticus Theater. It was eighty feet high, its walls were five feet thick, and it was devoid of architectural merit. It could be seen from any spot in Athens. Aside from the fact that it had been constructed by tearing down pure Greek buildings, it had become the symbol of the crowded Turkish village installed on the Acropolis. The Greek Archaeological Society had long hoped to tear it down and restore the Propylaea.

Henry looked at it with new attention.

"Perhaps we can help them one day," he mused.

Early in July they were awakened by the sound of bells ringing across Athens to announce the death of Theophilos, the archbishop.

"There will be an election for a new archbishop," Sophia said.

"Would Bishop Vimpos have a chance of being elected?" Henry asked.

They were having coffee in the small dining area off the kitchen. Sophia was wearing a loose-fitting pink negligee she had brought from Paris.

"It's not impossible. Wouldn't it be wonderful?"

The next day at 5:00 P.M. they attended the archbishop's funeral. The corpse had been dressed in his best vestments and was sitting on a throne, his hand raised in a sign of blessing. On July 11 Theokletos Vimpos arrived in Athens for the election. There had been a good deal of speculation about his chances of becoming the new archbishop. His scholarly training made him a logical successor.

When he came to visit the Schliemanns, Sophia saw that there had again been a change in him. On his last visit he had been dust-covered and dispirited; his robes, as well as his eyes and beard, threadbare. Now he was wearing new robes; his voice was bright.

"Heartiest congratulations to you both for uncovering Priam's Troy," he cried. "Henry always said he would."

Conflict streamed across Sophia's dark eyes.

"You have something to confess, my child?"

"Yes. We have done something, Henry and I, that may not have been altogether ethical."

She told him of their discovery of the treasure and how they had smuggled it out of Turkey despite the provision in their *firman* which said that half of everything they found was to be turned over to the Constantinople Museum. She also related the extenuating circumstances: the new law the Turkish government had been in process of passing.

"Are you asking me for absolution as a bishop of your Church? Or are you asking me as a blood relative to approve your actions?"

Sophia lowered her head. "Both, I guess."

"As a priest I can find God's forgiveness for you. But please don't ask me to make a moral judgment. If I approve of what you have done I must assume some of the moral obloquy. If I don't, I will be hurting one of my dearest young relatives. I suggest that you put your faith in your husband and that you let him take full responsibility for the family."

Sophia looked up, saw that the bishop's eyes were twinkling. She said with a chuckle low in her throat, "Spoken like the Delphic oracle." After a moment, "There is talk that the University of Athens favors you to be the successor."

His dark eyes, so much like her own, lighted with pleasure.

"Not yet. I am too young. In the Orthodox Church age brings authority. A white beard is preferable to a black one. As you can see, I am in mid-position, my black beard is merely streaked with gray." He laughed lightly. "Ambition on the part of a priest for advancement would be considered a sin. . . . Though of course the idea has crossed my mind once or twice."

The Archbishop of Corfu, Antonios Chariates, was elected. When Bishop Vimpos came to Mousson Street to say his farewells, he commented:

"I don't think the election was legal. It was held without a quorum of the Holy Synod; and without informing the Ministry of Ecclesiastics. I will be back for the next election if my theories are right. Perhaps the gray in my hair will have turned white by then."

Bishop Vimpos had read not only the theology of his Church but the laws of Greece concerning the Church. His judgment proved correct. The Ministry of Ecclesiastics declared the election of the Archbishop of Corfu null and void.

Their difficulties began with a letter from Yannakis. The suspicions that had surrounded them during their last two weeks in Troy had broken into the open.

Very honored Mossiou H. Schliemann,

I have need to come to Athens and stay there for a few days
and get out of the trouble and torment of the government.
Now for the second time they got me down to Dardanelles
with the *zaptie* [police]. The people think I murdered somebody, and my mother and Polyxene in tears, and my sisters.
They questioned me. "I don't know nothing" I replied. Any-
how I begged your friend Mr. Dokos if I come to need perhaps
he can help us.

Your servant, Yannakis

"Poor Yannakis," cried Sophia.

"They're trying to frighten him," exclaimed Henry, "thinking they
can get information out of him. You see how wise it was to send him
home for that weekend."

If Sophia was shocked at the attack on Yannakis, she was aghast at
Henry's next move. He wrote a long article for the *Augsburger Allgemeine Zeitung* telling the story of his discoveries during their last
month in Troy, including a detailed and graphic description of the
entire treasure of Priam.

"Henry, why are you exposing yourself this way? No one knows
about this treasure except Boker in Constantinople. Once this article
appears, the Turks will know precisely what we smuggled out."

Henry took the outburst calmly, patting her outstretched pleading
hand.

"Everyone will know in six months anyway when our book comes
out. I've already written the Prologue for the folio telling exactly how
we made the find. The public will see our photographs of all the magnificent gold pieces."

"A book is different from a newspaper, Henry. Brockhaus in Leipzig and Maisonneuve et Cie. in Paris are distinguished publishing
houses . . ."

"The *Augsburger Allgemeine Zeitung*," he interrupted, "is also a distinguished journal, publishing scientific material."

"Won't your article afford the Turkish government a means to recover the treasure? Won't your character be assaulted on the grounds
you violated your agreement? Why are you in such a hurry? By the time
your book is published, your Athens museum will be accepted; you'll
have the Greek government behind you."

"Sophidion, I'm on fire to get this information to the public so that
no one can any longer dispute the authenticity of our Troy. However
I won't let the Turkish government find out about the gold from the
article. I'm going to write to Dr. Philip Déthier, the director of the Con-

stantinople Museum, and frankly admit that we took out the gold because they were about to violate my permit by passing a new and
confiscatory law. I am going to propose a three-month joint excavation
to complete our digs at Troy. I will pay all expenses; *everything* we
find will go to Constantinople. Everyone agrees their museum is a
shambles, with little of value being shown. I am going to offer them
forty thousand francs with which to modernize the building and exhibit what we have already given them as well as everything else we will
discover. That should mollify them."

She realized that it was futile to try to stop him. He had figured out
his campaign and was satisfied that it would work. She thought, "When
the digging stops I am no longer his partner. I am now just his wife,
and as a wife I have no right to interfere or dissent. So as a good wife I
will do what all good Greek wives do: subside and assent."

The weeks following publication of the *Augsburger Allgemeine
Zeitung* article on July 26 were horrendous. The Turkish ambassador
in Berlin cabled its contents to the Minister of Public Instruction in
Constantinople, who promptly cabled the Turkish ambassador in
Athens, Essad Bey. The Turkish ambassador lodged a protest with Kalliphronas, the Greek Minister of Public Instruction. The Greek government wanted no trouble with the Turks; only recently the order of the
Big Cross had been conferred on the Sultan, which had brought about
friendly relations between the two countries. Now this good will could
be shattered. Just to enable the fish glue to boil over, Henry was accused in one of the local papers of having had all of the gold pieces
made to order in Athens!

Kalliphronas immediately took action against Henry Schliemann.
First he rejected Henry's offer to build a museum in Athens in which
to install his Trojan collection. Then he refused him a permit to excavate in Olympia, and instead granted the right to the Prussian Archaeological Society, which had also applied for it.

The Schliemanns became the least popular people in Athens. Not to
the family, of course; the first law of Greek life is the loyalty of blood.
But it was as though they had suddenly been isolated for having caught
an infectious disease. Their friends on the university faculty did not
totally abandon them. They stood by, quietly waiting for a resolution
of the case, while finding it inconvenient to visit the house on Mousson
Street.

Disregarding the fact that Sophia had warned him against the indiscretion of publishing the newspaper article, he followed her from room
to room venting his rage.

"They simply cannot treat me this way! I flatter myself that by the discovery of Troy I have a claim to the gratitude of the whole civilized world. Particularly to that of Greece!"

In an attempt to take some of the pressure off himself, Henry sent a letter to American Minister Resident Boker enclosing a conciliatory letter to Safvet Pasha, Minister of Public Instruction in Constantinople, with the same proposal he had made to Déthier: to pay all costs for a joint excavation of Troy for three months, the Turkish government to keep all antiquities found, to reconstruct their museum. The minister did not reply; instead Henry received a stiff letter from Boker:

> The difficulty of your case appears to be in the eyes of the Ottoman authorities, not so much in your having broken a law, but in your having violated a written contract, voluntarily signed by you, to divide all articles found by you with the Constantinople Museum.
>
> Although for the sake of Science it may be well that you were able to remove what you call "Priam's Treasure" safely from Turkey, yet its effect on future explorations will be, I fear, most damaging, tending to increase the jealousy of the government to such a degree that all permissions to excavate may be refused to foreigners.

2.

The heat of the August afternoons was stifling. They took the carriage down to Phaleron for a few hours to cool themselves in the sea. Their house and many others lacked water because the main supply was being used to lay the dust in the streets. In the mornings Henry locked himself in his study, writing business correspondence in an attempt to disassociate himself from his difficulties. He became so preoccupied that he forgot to congratulate his wife on their fourth anniversary, or to bring her a gift.

They went into town as little as possible. "I think we had best hide in a cave until the hurricane passes," he suggested. Besides, the streets were torn up, gas pipes being laid in the trenches. Henry was one of the first to subscribe, buying his wall fixtures from the gas company and having them installed in both the downstairs and upstairs rooms. It took the workmen a week to open the floors and walls but when Henry first turned the keys at the sides of the fixtures and applied a match they were delighted at the way the rooms blazed with light.

If Henry managed to sidetrack their difficulties, the days and weeks that went by were uneasy ones for Sophia. Away from Troy and the excitements of discovery, she now felt a full burden of guilt. She was as culpable as Henry. She had helped carry the gold into their house in Troy, had helped secrete it in her trunk, guarded it until the trunk was moved down to Besika Bay and loaded on the *Omonoia*. If Henry had not fully accepted her advice as a partner, he gave her ample credit for the find; he had included a complete report of her activities in the *Augsburger Allgemeine Zeitung* article which was now being reproduced throughout Europe. The news spread that the Ottoman Empire would sue them in the Greek courts. It was not until October that she worked up sufficient courage to urge Henry to give up half of the gold.

"Why?"

"To put an end to our misery."

"I am suffering no misery."

"I am. I'd give them half of the gold to clear my conscience."

"Déthier writes me to give the whole of it back. He promises to house it in a refurbished museum."

"Have you offered them half?"

"No."

"Why not?"

"Because they have signed their new decree into law. Once I show them the treasure they will take it all."

During the Christmas holidays the renowned Keeper of Greek and Roman Antiquities of the British Museum, Charles T. Newton, arrived in Athens as Henry's guest. They had been corresponding for several years. The object of his visit was an examination of the Trojan finds. He was enchanted with the beauty and historical value of the prehistoric terra cottas, ivories, stone idols, weaponry which he declared to be straight out of Homer. On the third day he asked gently:

"Would it be possible for me to see the gold treasure? You may trust my discretion."

Henry puzzled over this. He desperately wanted Newton to see the objects but there were dangers involved. He could not take Newton up to the storeroom on Lycabettus; the sight of two obvious foreigners in the wrong part of town would arouse suspicion. Finally he sent Spyros to the storeroom on Christmas Day when Athens was in church, with instructions to bring back the two diadems, the two necklaces of four thousand beads each and a couple of examples of the earrings and bracelets.

When Henry opened the suitcase in their livingroom with all doors and windows locked, Newton's eyes bulged.

"My word," he exclaimed, "they are exquisite. The quantity is staggering. May I hold them in my hands?"

After Newton had studied them, he said:

"This is one of the most important archaeological finds of all times. But, my two dear friends, should they be sitting in a suitcase, hidden clandestinely? Should they not be in a great museum where all the world can see them?"

Henry smiled. "You mean the British Museum?"

"Your collection would join one of the very finest."

"That is true, Mr. Newton," replied Sophia gently; "but the collection is pledged to Athens."

"Oh, I didn't mean for you to give it to us gratis. It is much too valuable for that."

"Are you suggesting a sale?" Henry asked.

"Yes. At a price you would consider fair and just. It would take me some time to raise such a large sum of money . . ."

"My dear Mr. Newton," said Sophia sternly, her lips tautly compressed, "we do not intend to sell the collection. We are going to give it to Greece just as soon as our difficulties with Turkey are resolved."

Newton turned inquiring eyes on Henry. He hesitated for a moment.

"My wife is right. We will not sell it. But we appreciate your interest."

Shortly after Charles Newton had left for London an extraordinary article appeared in the *Levant Herald*. Nassif Pasha had raided the homes of Henry's former workmen in Kalifatli and Yeni-shehr. He had found "a precious treasure of necklaces, bracelets and earrings as well as sticks of compact gold." He had confiscated the finds which the workmen had stolen, and sent the culprits to jail.

The Schliemanns stared at each other in amazement; Henry was torn between anger at having been cheated by his workmen and gratification over the proof that there had been so much gold buried in Troy that he could no longer be accused of having had his treasure made in Athens. Sophia cried:

"Henry, the museum in Constantinople now has its gold from Troy! Four *okas* of gold adds up to about eleven pounds. That's a substantial amount of treasure for their museum. The Turks should now be content."

"Never believe it, dear heart. It will only serve to whet their appetites!"

Sophia smoothed her hair back from its central part, fitting it neatly behind her ears.

"Why don't we demand our half of their gold as rightfully ours under our *firman?*"

Henry jerked his head up from the article he was rereading.

She smiled wistfully.

"That might earn us a standoff."

On January 21, 1874, the Holy Synod met again to elect an Archbishop of Athens. Bishop Vimpos came in from Tripolis. On the afternoon of his arrival a crowd of some fifty people, many of them students from the university, gathered in front of the meeting hall, shouting:

"Theo Vimpos for archbishop! Theo Vimpos for archbishop!"

Eight policemen were sent to break up the demonstration. The news swept across Athens. The citizens could not remember such a scene having taken place before. The Synod fell into quarrels. No one was elected.

The next day, Parliament having reconvened, there was a dance at the royal palace. The Schliemanns were not invited.

Trojan Antiquities was published at the end of January 1874. It was a large, handsome volume. Champing with impatience, Henry had spent his time making friends for the book. He took a full set of photographs and advance galleys to Professor Kastorches of the Archaeological Department of the University of Athens. Euthymios Kastorches, fifty-nine years old, had studied history and archaeology in Germany. He became a full professor at the university in 1858 and was the man who, in 1850, had persuaded the Minister of Public Instruction to revive the Archaeological Society of which he was still a member. Kastorches was so impressed by what he saw that he asked permission to study the actual finds. Henry invited him for Sunday dinner. Kastorches spent hours attempting to date the artifacts.

"I suppose I won't see the gold until all the furor dies down."

"At the earliest possible moment," Henry promised.

Prime Minister William Gladstone of England had written *Studies on Homer and the Homeric Age* a number of years before and had become an authority in the field. Henry sent him a copy of *Ithaca, the Peloponnesus and Troy* as well as the *Augsburger Allgemeine Zeitung* article. It was Gladstone's firm belief that the Trojans had spoken Greek, with which Henry agreed. He received a cordial and heartening reply:

> The facts which you appear to have established are of the highest importance to primitive history, and I may take even a selfish pleasure in them when I contemplate their bearing on my own interpretations of the Homeric text.

This was offset by an article in the prestigious British *Academy* by the Oxford scholar, Max Müller, based on Henry's account in the *Augsburger Allgemeine Zeitung*. A major portion of Müller's well-mannered attack was the refutation of Henry's claim that the thousands of owl-faced idols he had found were representations of the Greek goddess Athena. Müller did not consider there was enough proof to support the theory. He also wrote that it was impossible for Henry Schliemann to have found the treasure of Priam in Troy because it would have been picked up as booty by the Achaeans and carried off.

The reception of *Trojan Antiquities*, they soon saw, followed much the same pattern. Émile Burnouf wrote a splendid piece for the *Revue des Deux Mondes*, the French Academy acknowledging Henry's discoveries. The German scholars were what Henry described as "murderous." He was accused of having committed unforgivable sins against archaeology by pulling down walls, buildings, temples . . . of having made wild guesses and postulated absurd theories in one chapter which he renounced in the next . . . of being confused, inconsistent . . . worse, he was a fraud: all of the gold articles pictured in his book had been bought in the bazaars of Constantinople and other Near East cities!

Sophia did not escape the cruelty. She was ridiculed by two young Germans in Rome who evoked "great laughter" after reading Henry's report of how he had "thanked Providence for rewarding his faith, and his wife for saving the treasure in her shawl." One of the twenty-two-year-olds attended a soiree in women's clothing, carrying a bulky red shawl. Upon being introduced as "Madame Schliemann," the youth opened the shawl and dumped a pile of old kitchen pots at the feet of the assemblage. The prank was a hilarious success.

Henry comforted her.

"It's pure envy, coating their mouths like dried fever blisters"; but he was not the kind of man to take the abuse sitting down, except for the endless hours he remained at his desk writing counterarticles to every newspaper and learned journal that attacked him for "imaginative guesses," "leaps into the stratosphere of conjecture." He set up a network in each important city in Europe and England to supply him with articles about his book, good and bad, so that he could answer them himself, paint his own portrait and that of the Troy he knew and loved.

"Indefatigable," Sophia mused as she watched him work the same twenty hours a day that he had at Troy.

And in effect wasn't she continuing to work by his side, under the most primitive conditions of academic warfare? Suffering intense cold, biting north winds, blasts of scorching heat, deadly scorpions . . . until Henry's discoveries should be accepted for their inherent worth, and he was treated not as an impostor trying to fob off a Stone Age village at the mouth of the Dardanelles as Homer's apocryphal Troy, but as a reputable scientist and archaeologist, indeed, the father of modern archaeology!

Turkish Ambassador Essad Bey hired three Greek lawyers to draw up the proper papers in the name of the Constantinople Museum. The lawyers applied for a writ which would sequester and entail the Schliemann house and furnishings to be held against any judgment made in favor of the museum. Henry engaged two lawyers of high reputation in Athens, Lucas Halkokondyles and Leonidas Delegeorges, to defend him.

On Candlemas Day they returned from church to find their furniture askew and their chests of drawers standing partially open.

"Someone has searched our belongings!" Henry cried in exasperation. "They've been keeping watch, hoping to find a time when we would all be out together!"

"Henry, has anyone a legal right to do this?"

"Certainly not. It's a criminal act. I shall report it to the Minister of Justice and the chief of police. We're going to find out who 'they' were!"

Even as the intruders had found no gold, Henry was unable to track them down. The chief of police denied the idea that any of his men would break into a private home. The Minister of Justice said no court order had been issued, hence no one in the Greek government would entertain such an idea. The lawyers for Ambassador Essad Bey categorically denied any such infraction of international law on the part of the Turks.

"I'm going to petition the customs at Piraeus to be allowed to take all my antiquities out of Greece," said Henry sternly.

It was as though he had struck her across the face.

"You promised me that everything would remain here and be given to the Greek government!"

"I'm not going to move anything. I just want the official right to do so in case I see that the Turks will get court approval to confiscate."

It took a number of days, but the customs officials received word from Athens not to put any obstacles in his way. Henry kept the official papers close at hand.

In Turkey, Yannakis was arrested again and put in jail as a traitor to his country. The government guard, Amin Effendi, was fired and threatened with punishment. Henry wrote a strong letter to the Turkish Minister of Public Instruction claiming that "no one ever watched over my excavations more relentlessly." Amin Effendi did not get his government job back, but neither was he arrested or tried for "serious dereliction of duty."

Henry grew restive. He had the feeling of himself being a prisoner. Sophia had learned to read the signs; when he could no longer control a situation he took to travel. She wondered where he would be off to: London, Berlin, Paris? He surprised her by saying:

"I think we'll take a trip down to Mycenae. There's a ship leaving Piraeus for Nauplion Monday morning at six."

She studied his face. He had lost weight in the last months and looked gaunt, with high bone ridges and hollow cheeks. Yet there was no diminution of his physical powers.

"I want to look the ground over and show it to you. I'm applying for a permit to dig there."

"Haven't they already turned us down?"

"Not really. They took Olympia away from us and gave it to the Prussians. Mycenae was left in limbo. Kalliphronas retired from the Ministry of Public Instruction two days ago; he was sixty-nine. That may have removed one obstacle. I will submit my application to the new minister this afternoon."

When he returned Sophia asked how he had made out.

Ioannes Valassopoulos had taken Kalliphronas's place. Henry had not met him before.

"He filed my application, nothing more. I asked if it would be all right if we went down for a few days to look over the area and make some general observations. . . . He said visitors were welcome but I could not excavate." He shrugged. "It's beautiful country around the Bay of Argos. You'll enjoy it."

They took the steamer from Piraeus the following Monday. Their packing was light except for Pausanias's *Guide to Greece* and Aeschylus's *Oresteia*. It seemed to Sophia that Henry appeared hurried.

"Is there a reason? Are the Turks threatening to serve papers on you?"

"Not yet." His grin was on the weak side. "I just want to get off before the new minister rejects my permit. That gives me more latitude for action."

Since it was the middle of February, Sophia feared the worst from the sea . . . and got it. Then the waters grew calm and she recovered, enjoying the islands of Hydra and Spetsae as their steamer came close enough to see the small protected harbors, the mountains rising immediately behind with the solidness of a stone wall. Their ship now swung into the Bay of Argos, heading north for the jewellike Nauplion with its tiny island fortress just offshore.

Nauplion was a favorite vacation spot for Athenians. The Olympus was a comfortable hotel with rooms overlooking the sea, and a diningroom that specialized in fish *plaki*: sea bass, halibut, haddock caught at dawn and baked in fillets. It was a cool night. They called for extra blankets and another lamp. Sophia's icon on the table beside the bed instantly converted the strange room to a familiar one. Henry read to her from the books he had bought over the years in London on the subject of Mycenae. He explained how curious it was that from the time Pausanias wrote his *Guide to Greece* in the second century A.D., in which he had told a good deal about Mycenae, until a quiver of four books had been written about Mycenae between 1810 and 1834, almost nothing had been published on the subject. During that span of years four Englishmen, peripatetic travelers always, had come to Argos, described and sketched the impregnable fortress at Mycenae and its sister fortress at Tiryns. Since then, for the past forty years, no one had bothered to set down in print anything about the former capital and the overpowering Mycenaean civilization.

"Our journal will make a thoroughgoing book, once we have our permit and start to dig. Listen to what Dodwell writes in *Tour Through Greece*, published in 1819. 'There is no place in Greece where a regular and extensive plan of excavation might be prosecuted with more probable advantage, or where remains of greater interest and a higher antiquity might be brought to light. . . .'"

In an aside he murmured:

"He was speaking to me. It took me fifty-five years to get the message."

"I hope the new minister gets the message," she replied sleepily.

3.

Henry had ordered a double carriage for six o'clock the following morning, shortly after sunrise. He had already had his swim in the bay. The first part of their leisurely drive to Mycenae was through green country, albeit marshy from the winter rains. This fertile part of the plain produced some of the best grass to be found in Greece, causing Homer to sing throughout *The Iliad* the praises of "horse-breeding" and "horse-nourishing" Argos. One mile out of Nauplion they passed the cyclopean walls of the mighty Tiryns, placed on its strategic elevation to command the Bay of Argos and repulse any attempted invasion by sea. Tiryns had been ruled over by Diomedes, who had played an important role in the siege of Troy until wounded in battle. The proximity of two such formidable contemporary fortresses had puzzled ancient as well as modern historians until they had come to the conclusion that Tiryns was an ally of Mycenae, a smaller settlement and fortress owing its allegiance to Agamemnon.

Sophia wondered out loud, as the horses clop-clopped their way past the incredibly mammoth blocks of stone that formed the outer walls, how men could have raised enormous block upon block without modern hoists or cranes.

"The same way the Egyptians did in building their pyramids. I don't know the answer to that one either."

Gazing backward at the mound, covered by earth and debris much as Hissarlik had been, Sophia asked:

"Has anyone tried to excavate Tiryns?"

"Only our French translator, the Greek ambassador at Berlin. He dug for a day and quit. I intend to excavate here . . . but it's far down on my list."

They drove into the thriving town of Argos, capital and chief market place for the area. They introduced themselves to the prefect, who received them with the customary formal courtesy.

"We simply want to go on record as making our way to Mycenae for about a week."

"You do not intend to excavate, Mr. Schliemann?"

"No. I have come to make soundings in order to ascertain what the accumulation of rubbish amounts to in the different areas."

"If you confine yourself to soundings I think there would be no objections, particularly since you have reported your intentions to me."

They moved into the northern part of the Plain of Argos. The countryside changed drastically, for here the land was dry and barren; in the background was a range of cloud-piercing, stony mountains which cut off their rain. Not so the area considerably higher up to which their carriage pulled them slowly on the rocky slope off the main road; for all around the gaggle of houses of Charvati, the small community at the foot of Mycenae, were green fields, orchards, vineyards; a fertile pocket. Its eight houses were huddled as close together as neighbors gossiping over a backyard fence.

The driver stopped in front of the most attractive of the houses, two stories with a sloping slate roof, two big windows on the bottom floor, the indispensable french doors and grillwork balcony. On either side of the house was a tall pepper tree, the masculine one on the right, the feminine on the left. In the area behind the house they could see a small pond with geese, turkeys, chickens, a dovecote.

Henry knocked on the front door, was received, remained only a few moments. He emerged with a broad smile on his face.

"Our reputation has preceded us. They know about our excavations at Troy and are delighted to learn that we may dig here. They are cleaning out the two top rooms for us; we'll have the upstairs for ourselves. Family name is Dases."

They were as comfortable as though the house had been a hotel. They not only had two rooms filled with sunlight and air from the large windows but also inherited a four-generation family, spirited and hospitable. The house and lands on which the Dases family raised hay, grapes, figs, almonds, oranges, and in a vegetable patch melons, tomatoes, string beans, onions, lettuce, had come down from their great-grandparents. They also raised sheep, had a flock of goats, assorted horses, donkeys, dogs . . .

Sophia and Henry were presented first to the Dases grandparents. The parents who ran the house and farm, Demetrios and Ioanna Dases, were in their mid-forties. They had half a dozen children with names out of Homer: Ajax, Diomedes, Agamemnon. Two of the daughters had already borne children. In Charvati few sons ever moved out of a house; they brought their wives into the family enclosure and raised their children there, each generation taking over when the parents grew old.

Basins of warm water were brought up so that Sophia and Henry could wash their hands and faces. Sophia inspected the rooms; the one large bed was built of cypress, the mattress stuffed with goat and sheep wool. The second room had a couple of narrow cots, chairs and a table which Henry said would suffice for their books and journal.

The kitchen was the communal room of the family, the only gathering place except for an outside porch. All of the women of the family participated in the preparation of the food, though it was clear that Ioanna was the major-domo. Sophia felt at home here; it reminded her of the early years when Madame Victoria taught her three daughters how to cook in the kitchen of the flat above the drapery shop on Romvis Square. Ioanna invited Sophia to join in; one of the daughters tied an apron around her full-skirted wool dress. She found herself laughing and helping to prepare the stuffed tomatoes *laderes*. Each of the women wore a white shirt under a sleeveless dress which was ankle-length and made of linen woven at home.

The men sat around, their rough rattan chairs tipped against the wall, smoking and chatting. Demetrios asked:

"Dr. Schliemann, will you dig in Mycenae as you did at Troy?"

"I do not have a permit from the government."

The man threw up his hands in a contemptuous gesture, his expression saying, "The government! Why bother with them?"

"I must co-operate. Everything I find I have promised to turn over to Greece."

"When you have this . . . paper . . . what do you hope to find?"

"The palace of Agamemnon."

"Agreed. It is there. At the top of the mountain somewhere."

"Also the royal tombs."

Demetrios was so startled he almost let his chair slide from under him.

"Of whom?"

"Those of the party returning from the sack of Troy, the ones murdered by Clytemnestra and Aegisthus: Agamemnon, his charioteer Eurymedon, Cassandra, her twins . . ."

"Everyone has searched for those," Demetrios exclaimed, "even the last Turkish governor of the Peloponnesus, Veli Pasha, who broke into that tomb by the Lion Gate, toward the end of the Turkish occupation. For hundreds of years people have looked, even my great-grandfather! Agamemnon's tomb and the others would be filled with gold; no one here believes they exist."

"Ah, but they do. Pausanias said so in his *Guide to Greece*."

Dases shrugged. "Dr. Schliemann, you are a finder. One newspaper said you have a divining rod, a dowser, that finds water under a dry surface. What is in Mycenae to find, you will find. The royal tombs . . . no."

Henry asked that two horses be saddled for them. He and Sophia rode up the rocky road past the other houses; soon they were on a wagon-width trail through the fields. A series of three vast mountains, running from north to south, loomed before them. The chief one was Mt. Euboea with craggy outcroppings of rugged stone forming miniature mountains of their own. Seen against the sky-enveloping Mt. Euboea, the citadel of Mycenae looked like a modest hill, not much taller than Hissarlik. But standing at its base, Mycenae appeared an awesome fortress.

The bend swung sharply to their left, going uphill more steeply. Sophia exclaimed, "What is that?"

"The Treasury or Tomb of Atreus."

She studied the structure with wonder. The *dromos*, or wide passageway, had been filled with stones, earth and debris but it had been sufficiently cleared by Turkish Veli Pasha, who had hoped to loot the tomb of its riches, to enable Sophia to see the finely hewn stone gate, the fourteen-foot-long double lintel, and above it the deep, open triangle used for giant sculptures as well as to take the burden of weight off the lintel. The stone-block walls on either side of the triangle, as well as those of the *dromos* leading to the gate, were monumental in size and in a good state of preservation.

"This tomb is built into the hill, isn't it?" she asked.

"More properly, dug out of the hill. When the architects had the space they needed they built stone-block tombs called 'beehives' because of their conical shape. This Treasury of Atreus is said to be as great a structure as the pyramids of Egypt."

Another hundred yards up the trail Henry stopped both horses. For the first time she saw the full citadel of Mycenae. They were standing above a gorge running high with winter rains and melted snow. Beyond was an open low-lying rocky area. Towering above it was the cyclopean western defense wall of the acropolis of Mycenae.

"*Panaghia mou!*" Sophia murmured under her breath. "Those blocks of stone are bigger than the ones at Tiryns that we saw this morning."

"Yes. They are the most massive in this part of the world. Called after the Cyclopes, the one-eyed giants who worked in Hephaestus's forge making thunderbolts for Zeus."

"On top of Mt. Olympus. I can see the Cyclopes working Hephaestus's bellows."

"There are some other things I would like you to see just as clearly. Because when you do you will help me find the royal tombs. In the time of Agamemnon there was a bridge over this gorge. Just beyond this ravine lay the town, its buildings going up to the base of the great defense wall. I don't know how many in number, there is no record, but it was a good-sized settlement extending to the ridge behind us. That's why the bridge. The community also ran down the plain we have just passed, but not too far because it all had to be walled in. Not a huge wall, all they needed was a slight one because at the first sign of alarm the inhabitants could rush into the citadel by one of its two gates. Inside the cyclopean wall they were safe, for they had their own water, the spring of Perseia, and at the rear of the acropolis there was a fertile valley unapproachable by attackers, from which they could gather their food."

"The same situation as at Troy."

He patted her on the shoulder.

"Like it, but more invulnerable. The main entrance is just around that curve."

As they moved upward she studied the whole of Mycenae. The millennia had covered most of it with earth but she could still see, beyond the exposed high defense wall, the suggestions of terraces, cuttings which might originally have been roads or trails to the top where Henry said there had been a temple and the magnificent palace of Atreus and his son Agamemnon. When Agamemnon's young son Orestes had returned as a man to kill his mother and her paramour for their murder of his father, and had assumed his rightful command of the Mycenaean Empire, he also occupied the palace, and his son after him. But that mighty empire had been exhausted by the Trojan War and was toppled by the Dorians who, flooding in from the north at the end of the twelfth century B.C., from Epirus and Macedonia, conquered all of the Peloponnesus and most of the Greek mainland. The family that produced Atreus, Agamemnon and Orestes had ruled for hundreds of years. According to Thucydides, Mycenae fell just eighty years after the burning of Troy. That had been the end of the Mycenaean civilization.

They rounded the curve in the narrow trail. There in full view was the Lion Gate. It was beautiful, as thrilling a sight as she had ever seen. Huge pillars, each of a single piece of stone, stood upright on either side, ten feet apart, supporting a massive lintel carved from a single mammoth block, its ends extending past the uprights anchored from above by stone blocks as stupendous as those in the cyclopean wall. Above the lintel, standing on their own base, were two headless lions, each with its front paws on the raised base of an altar which supported a pillar, religious or heraldic, said to be a sacred pillar of the House of Atreus.

"Henry, they are so lifelike. But did someone steal the heads?"

"Not until some of the stone blocks from above came tumbling down. Earthquake probably. Took the lions' heads with them."

The road leading to the gate, and the gate itself, had been filled with stones and earth over the centuries. The lintel now stood only three or four feet above the ground.

"How high was this lintel originally?" Sophia asked.

"As a guess, about twelve feet, maybe more. It had to admit the kings in chariots."

They crawled on their hands and knees through a small aperture and were inside the citadel, a clearing now used for grazing. Straight ahead and to their right was level rocky ground ending at the defense wall. To their left and towering above them, the mountain was carved into a fortress.

"Let's start up from here," Henry suggested. "We'll chart a course through the boulders and brush."

It was a long rough climb but the view from the top was superb. The afternoon was clear; they could see all the way down the Argos plain, with the sea eight or nine miles away at Nauplion sparkling green-blue on the horizon. Henry led her to the edge of a cliff looking into a deep dark canyon which separated Mycenae from the neighboring mountain. On the side of the cliff were sections of protecting walls. Henry stretched his arm across the lower town and ravine to the road they had climbed.

"Look straight ahead to where I'm pointing, the ridge above the road. Can you see the Treasury of Atreus? Atreus built it there so that he could sit in the outside court of his palace and look at it."

"You mean we're actually standing in Atreus's outer court?"

He grinned. "That would be too easy. But it's somewhere on this promontory. So is the bathtub in which one ancient author says Clytemnestra and Aegisthus murdered Agamemnon, enveloping him in an enormous fish net she had been weaving for ten years for that purpose. Pausanias says he was killed at a banquet."

They zigzagged down the mountain, Henry going immediately in front of her to keep her from stumbling. When they reached the inner side of the Lion Gate once again Sophia asked:

"Where will you start your soundings?"

"About a hundred yards south of here, on a straight line."

He took a well-thumbed copy of Pausanias out of his side pocket and read aloud:

> "Amongst other remains of the wall is the gate, on which stand lions. They are said to be the work of the Cyclopes. . . . In the ruins of Mycenae is the fountain called Perseia and the subterranean buildings of Atreus and his children, in which they stored their treasures. . . . There is the tomb of Agamemnon and that of his charioteer Eurymedon, and of Electra. Teledamus and Pelops were buried in the same sepulchre, for it is said that Cassandra bore these twins, and that, while as yet infants, they were slaughtered by Aegisthus together with their parents. Clytemnestra and Aegisthus were buried at a little distance from the wall, because they were thought unworthy to have their tombs inside of it, where Agamemnon reposed and those who were killed together with him."

"It seems clear enough. Why haven't the tombs been found?"

"Because for hundreds of years readers have thought that Pausanias means the wall enclosing the lower town. But that wall had already crumbled and disappeared by the time he visited here in the second century A.D., so he could not have been referring to the lower wall. He was referring to these cyclopean walls closing in the heart of the citadel. Therefore we will search inside these walls, where no one has dug."

All of their troubles and anxieties, housed in Athens, were left behind, forgotten; the world's insinuation of disrespect non-existent. It was almost as though they were starting a new life, freshly awakened to the inspiring challenge with which they had started their married life high on the hill at Hissarlik.

They stood with eyes blazing, cheeks flushed from the climb down.

"Dedicated men make time stand still the way Joshua made the sun stand still," she thought. Aloud she said:

"You read Homer right. Perhaps you are reading Pausanias right too."

They returned to the Dases house before dusk, in time for Henry to share an *ouzo* with the men of the family. There were some fifteen members seated around the circular table, with Sophia and Henry sharing the place of honor with the grandparents. The conversation was friendly and spirited. Henry asked Demetrios:

"Could I get two men to help me dig for the next few days?"

"Of course. Myself and one of my sons."

"We'll start at first light."

"Then you do intend to excavate?"

"No. Just to make some soundings."

It appeared that the hundred residents of Charvati were all inter-related, for the occupants of the other houses came to call, wishing to meet and welcome the Daseses' guests. Babies had been left at home with younger children but most of the adults came, murmuring:

"*Kalos orisate,* we welcome you."

As with the neighbors at Aulis, they had a scrubbed and best-dress look, a compliment to the guests.

At eight o'clock Henry found his hosts.

"If you would forgive us, Madame Schliemann and I will retire. It's been a long day and I still want to read Aeschylus's *Agamemnon* to her."

Ioanna Dases said supplicatingly:

"Dr. Schliemann, could you not read it to all of us? We women do not know how to read. We know the story; it comes from father to son, but none of us have heard the play as it was written."

Henry read by firelight. The intertwined families sat on benches brought from the porch. As Sophia scanned the rows of quiet eager faces her memories went back to the night in Aulis when Henry had read the *Iphigenia in Aulis* sitting before a similar fireplace.

Henry must have been remembering too, for he placed the book face down on his lap.

"The first thing you must recall before we get to the murder of Agamemnon is that Clytemnestra had provocation. In a raid Agamemnon killed her husband and dashed her infant to death at her feet. As the conqueror he then married Clytemnestra, and later tricked her into bringing their own beloved young daughter, Iphigenia, to Aulis on the pretext that she was to marry Achilles. Actually he intended to sacrifice the girl to the goddess Artemis so that she would send the winds, permitting his vast fleet from all the kingdoms of Achaea to leave their harbor and set sail for Troy. In spite of Clytemnestra's and Iphigenia's tearful pleas, Agamemnon ran his knife across his daughter's throat."

There were tears in the eyes of the women, young and old. Henry continued:

"Clytemnestra plotted his murder from that moment on. Not long after Agamemnon's departure she took a paramour who ruled with her, Aegisthus, Agamemnon's cousin. Aegisthus too had a motive for his act: his older brothers had been murdered by Agamemnon's father.

"In order to insure their knowledge of the time of Agamemnon's return from Troy, Clytemnestra sent her household soldiers to establish a system of beacon fires that started from Mt. Ida, skipped to Lemnos, Athos, Messapion, Asopus, beyond the Saronic gulf to Mycenae. When these beacon lights tell Clytemnestra and Aegisthus that Troy has fallen, the plotters are ready for Agamemnon's arrival."

He read quietly. The kitchenful of people sat riveted and silent. When he reached the climactic scene, Henry heightened the pitch of his reading.

> "Much have I said before to serve necessity,
> but I will take no shame now to unsay it all.
> How else could I, arming hate against hateful men
> disguised in seeming tenderness, fence high the nets
> of ruin beyond overleaping? Thus to me
> the conflict born of ancient bitterness is not
> a thing new thought upon, but pondered deep in time.
> I stand now where I struck him down. The thing is done.
> Thus have I wrought, and I will not deny it now.
> That he might not escape nor beat aside his death,
> as fishermen cast their huge circling nets I spread
> deadly abundance of rich robes, and caught him fast.
> I struck him twice. In two great cries of agony
> he buckled at the knees and fell. When he was down
> I struck him the third blow, in thanks and reverence
> to Zeus the lord of dead men underneath the ground."

One by one the Dases family and kinfolk came to Henry to thank him. Then the Schliemanns climbed the stairs and closed the door to their bedroom.

The winter sun had stumbled up the east slope of Mt. Euboea and spent most of its strength in the effort, for it was cool when Henry, Sophia, Demetrios and his son Ajax made the sharp turn toward the Lion Gate. Demetrios braked his wagon alongside the tremendous east wall leading to the lions. Ajax jammed stones behind the wheels before unloading the tools. Henry had rejected the family wheelbarrow because:

"I'm not supposed to be excavating, therefore I can't move any soil. I intend to dig sampling shafts. Not wide or deep, only enough to get a purchase on the different kinds of earth or rock we will encounter."

They crawled through the Lion Gate into the legend-rich acropolis of Mycenae, whence the Achaean Empire had been ruled. Henry took out his compass.

"We'll start straight south from the Lion Gate. Let's try half a dozen shafts here on the first western and southwestern terraces."

Demetrios and Ajax began digging twenty feet apart, adhering to Henry's request to keep the shafts small in dimension. He went back and forth between the two, sifting the earth and making notes on its composition. Sometimes he was content to go down only four or five feet, at others eight or ten.

They dug and refilled several shafts during the morning. There were few finds. At eleven a younger Dases son arrived on a donkey with a pannier of bread, cheese, olives, hard-boiled eggs, wine. Late in the afternoon they struck, within a hundred yards of the Lion Gate, two cyclopean house walls. Henry was pleased.

"This is encouraging. Let us stop for the day. Please fill in the shafts."

Riding down the hill in the wagon, the setting sun throwing a glow of firelight against the acropolis, Sophia exclaimed:

"Think how beautiful and imposing this must have been during the reigns of Atreus and Agamemnon. Silver chariots, powerful horses from the Argolid, the Mycenaean soldiers in their copper and brass armor, plumes flying from their headdress, swords in their belts, long lances under their arms, gold ornaments on their wrist straps . . ."

"Gone," said Demetrios sadly; "nothing now but stones and terraces and shepherds grazing their sheep."

The next day they dug a dozen shafts, continuing southward, and found nothing but an unsculptured slab which Henry judged had been a tombstone. The third and fourth days, during which they sank a total of thirty-four holes, taught them something about the various strata of earth beneath; it was mostly fill, and contained only some shards of female idols and terra-cotta cows, some small pieces of round uncarved stone.

It was still pitch-black on the fifth morning when they were awakened by the noise of a carriage coming up the hill, a sharp knock on the front door, then the sound of excited voices below.

"We had better dress," Henry said; "something has happened."

It had indeed, as they learned when they went down the stairs. In the midst of the family was a red-eyed young man, talking almost in a shout.

"What is it, Demetrios?" Henry asked.

"This is Ioannes, my nephew from Argos. He works in the prefecture. Yesterday afternoon the prefect received a telegram from the Minister of Public Instruction in Athens informing him that Dr. Henry Schliemann was excavating at Mycenae and that the prefect must prevent him from putting a spade in the earth. Ioannes thought you would want to know before the prefect sends his officers. . . ."

Henry gripped the man's arm.

"You did well to warn me and to bring the carriage. We will leave at once."

Henry left a generous sum on the kitchen sideboard. Ioannes loaded the suitcases into the carriage. Demetrios said:

"When you return with your permit for a long stay, you will come here to us?"

"Of course. And you shall be my foreman."

"I accept. Go now. If officers arrive, we know nothing."

Ioannes drove them to their hotel in Nauplion, assuring them that he could return to Argos unseen. They shook hands, Henry leaving a sum in Ioannes's palm, then made themselves comfortable in the suite they had occupied before going out to Mycenae. They took a walk along the sea, had supper in their room. They were about to retire when there was a knock on the door. Henry opened it. An officer was standing there. In full uniform.

"Dr. Schliemann?"

"Yes."

"I am the chief of police in Nauplion, Leonidas Leonardos. Please understand that I come here as a visitor. I know that you are an American citizen and I should not like to cause an international incident."

"You are more than welcome."

At that moment Sophia entered the room. The chief of police stared at her, then exclaimed:

"Sophia Engastromenos! You are Mrs. Schliemann?"

"Yes. I remember you. You used to visit us on Romvis Square."

"Certainly so! I knew your father."

"Come sit down. It is good to see you again. Please share our coffee and *glyko*."

The officer accepted the plate of cherry candy. It was apparent that he was embarrassed.

"Would you like to see what we have taken from Mycenae?"

". . . yes. I have a telegram ordering me to search your luggage."

She brought out a small wicker basket, took off the lid, exposed the few potsherds of the cows and idols, the round pieces of stone.

The man turned to Henry, apologetically.

"Those fragments are nothing. I will draft a report on this card. Then we can both sign it."

He wrote:

> As such objects are to be found on the site of all ancient cities, and as this hard substance was stone rather than marble and cannot be of any interest, I handed them all over to Mr. Schliemann, who adds his signature to mine on this document.

The chief of police signed the note, handed it to Henry for his signature. He then told Sophia how delightful it was to see her.

4.

Back in Athens they went immediately to the office of the Minister of Public Instruction. He refused to see them, sending word that they were to report to Panaghiotes Eustratiades, General Inspector of Antiquities, who had published frequent articles in the *Archaeological Newspaper* and had been elected a member of the Academy of Sciences of Berlin and of the Archaeological Institute of Rome. It was he who had signed the contract with the Prussians for the excavations at Olympia.

He greeted the Schliemanns glacially. Henry jumped with both feet into what was more explanation than apology.

"Curator Eustratiades, I reported to the prefect of Argos on my way to Mycenae that I did not yet have my permit and was merely going to survey . . ."

The curator broke in, angrily.

"Apparently you believe the Greeks do not respect their laws and you are free to make fun of them."

"Please believe me, I have no such thoughts. Whoever informed you that I was excavating at Mycenae was mistaken. I was merely studying the terrain . . . a few shallow holes to gauge the texture of the earth there against the day when I will have my permit."

"That day will be long in coming!"

Henry paled, fell silent before the curator's wrath. Sophia said quietly, "With respect, Mr. Curator, our soundings were little more than an experiment. We did no harm."

"Did you put a spade into the ground?"

"Yes."

"Then you broke the law."

Henry had been searching in his throat to find his lost voice.

"We came here to apologize for doing something that caused you difficulties. I regret that. I will not put a spade into Greek soil again until you issue me an official permit. Please be so generous as to accept my apology. It is a sincere and honest one."

Henry's apology honed a few metal shavings off the edge of the curator's outrage.

"Very well. At least you were respectful enough to come to my office immediately upon your return and acknowledge my authority."

"I have the small basket of potsherds in the carriage. Would you like me to have my driver deliver them to your department?"

"No! We cannot accept legally what was illegally taken from our earth. Do with them what you will."

Sophia and Henry thanked him for receiving them. He accepted their offer to shake hands, his cold fingers darting off theirs with the motion of a bird in flight. They walked to a nearby café. Sophia said over a cup of tea:

"I'm afraid we've hurt ourselves."

"I know." He was filled with remorse. "It was a mistake. I should have stayed away from Mycenae until the permit came through. But you know how restless I get, how . . . *driven* . . . when I'm not able to dig."

"No need to flagellate yourself. What is done is done."

As a direct result of his confrontation with Curator Eustratiades and the knowledge that the Mycenae permit would now be hard come by, Henry redoubled his efforts to persuade the Turkish government to allow him to complete his excavations at Troy. Dr. Philip Déthier replied from Constantinople, a letter dated March 21, 1874, in which he made a counterproposal which his Mecklenburg wife helped him compose in German:

> I am making a proposition to you: let bygones be bygones, give back your collection to us and we shall house it in a brand-new *Schliemann Museum* in Constantinople that we shall build for you. Thus, "Fortuna" will be linked timelessly with your fame, and you shall be remembered always with thankfulness and your work will find its happy conclusion.

"We're falling over each other trying to see who will pay for a new museum," Henry commented with an unamused laugh; "that will give you an idea of the value of our Trojan treasure."

"Henry, I'm frightened. Think of the charges against you, the months in court, the talk in Athens. Wouldn't it be wiser just to send them their half through our Greek ambassador?"

He came to where she was sitting in a big parlor chair, took from her hands the pillowcase she was embroidering, and kneeled before her.

"Dear one, I know it would be easier on you. But I beg you to believe that this collection must be kept intact to preserve its value and meaning. The Greek courts will not take the treasure from us to return it to the Turks even though considerable pressure may be put upon them."

Émile and Louise Burnouf came on Sunday afternoon to visit and assemble the shards from Mycenae. Their work finished, Sophia had hot chocolate and almond tortes brought out to the garden teahouse. Burnouf asked after Henry's problem with the Turkish government.

"Dr. Déthier, the director of the Constantinople Museum, is being sent to Athens to persuade me out of the treasure. If he cannot do that, the three Greek lawyers chosen by the Turkish ambassador here are going to apply to the president of the Court of First Instance to get a judgment against me."

"That's alarming," said Burnouf.

"If things look bad would it be possible to transfer everything to the French Archaeological Institute? The institute is an adjunct of the French Embassy and hence considered French soil. The police could not enter, even if the court decided against me."

"You're welcome to bring the treasure into the institute. We'll keep it for you as long as you like."

Louise tilted her chin upward and said with her most devastating smile:

"Dr. Schliemann, when you make this first step with the treasure and put it on French soil, symbolically speaking, why not put it on French soil in reality?"

Henry was silent.

"Father and I have discussed this. Where would the treasure be safer or more brilliantly displayed than in the Louvre in Paris? Give Father permission; he will secure an acceptance from the director of the Louvre and the treasure will be on display in the world's greatest museum."

Sophia fixed Louise with a hard stare.

"That will be enough of that nonsense, Louise. My husband has already given his word that the treasure will remain in Athens. That is where it is going to stay as long as I have a voice in this matter."

At the end of March Philip Déthier arrived and sent Henry a note starting with "My Dear Friend," asking if he might come to visit. He arrived at noon the following day, accompanied by Mr. Mishaak, First Secretary of the Turkish Embassy. Déthier was limping from a leg malaise but he was in good humor, stroked back his glossy pomaded hair with a tight gesture of both hands and launched into a detailed exposition of the Turkish government's case. Mishaak sat on the edge of a chair in a corner of the livingroom.

Déthier was an educated man, fond of interlarding his talk with moral precepts out of the Bible. He had come with a persuasive offer: not only would the Turkish government build a Schliemann Museum at its own expense, but Henry would have his *firman* renewed and could dig anywhere he wanted in the Sultan's realm.

Henry asked:

"You have already put into effect your new law that all those who excavate must present their finds to the museum for examination?"

"Yes. It was signed into law earlier this year."

"It empowers the government to buy in at a nominal price any part of the excavator's half?"

"Yes. But we intend to be fair."

"Then except for men who are searching for lost cities such as Troy, I think the Turkish government is going to have to do its own excavating in the years to come."

Déthier did not comment but instead rose and began examining the terra cottas in the livingroom: the jugs with beak-shaped mouths, the black vases in the form of hourglasses, the brilliant red goblets resembling champagne glasses. When he had completed his tour he stood in front of Henry.

"You took the best of everything."

"No, only our half. Frequently your guards had first choice."

"But you outwitted them."

"There is a little larceny in all of us, Dr. Déthier. But if you prefer our pieces to yours, you have only yourself to blame. You sent us guards who had little training . . ."

Sophia wanted to avoid a quarrel.

"Gentlemen, shall we have coffee in the garden? The flowers have blossomed early this year. There are masses of color."

They had no sooner emerged from the house and started down the gravel path than Déthier saw the marble metope of Apollo riding his four fiery steeds. He hobbled up to the heroic sculpture, examined it with the eyes of a connoisseur.

"Turkish?"

"Greek."

"Obviously. But found on Turkish soil?"

"Yes."

"Which half did we get?"

"There was no way. The sculpture would have been destroyed."

"This was the huge crate you shipped out of Besika Bay in your Greek freighter. The one our guard came a few moments too late to stop."

"We compensated for it immediately," Sophia protested; "by shipping you seven of our ten giant *pithoi*."

"Admitted. And they arrived in good condition, thanks to your expert packing." He turned to Henry. "We also appreciate your skill and perseverance in excavating. In this issue of the *Quarterly Review* I have acknowledged that Hissarlik was the site of Troy."

"I thank you for that."

"I had read about this Apollo in your book. No matter. What matters now is the gold. We must have our half. With the publication of your book, the Turkish government feels that it has been shamed before the world. Their dignity must be restored."

"I am willing to go to great lengths to do that. I have already offered to dig for you for three months this summer. In that three months, which will cost me fifty thousand dollars, we will dig up enough great objects to fill your museum . . . after I have paid to have it remodeled to suit your needs. Have you ever heard of a more generous offer?"

"Never. If not for the treasure I would jump to accept it. But the Sultan wants his share of the gold jewelry. My hands are tied."

"The gold of Priam must never be divided. Besides, you already have a large quantity of Trojan gold recovered from my workmen."

"That is your last word?"

"Yes. Except that I want us to remain friends."

"It cannot be. I will see you next in court where we will be adversaries. Good day, Dr. Schliemann. Good day, Madame Schliemann."

He limped out of the garden, trailed by the First Secretary. Henry was not disturbed. Sophia was. Controversy gave her a stomachache.

"I married the wrong man for a quiet peaceful existence. Henry will always live at the center of a storm. If he does not create it he attracts it the way pollen attracts bees."

Philip Déthier translated into Greek Henry's account of his findings at Troy in 1873. The lawyers employed by the Ottoman government drew up an appeal to the president of the Greek Court of First Instance to which they attached the list of the gold objects and a request that the president confiscate the treasure. One of Henry's lawyers, Halkokondyles, secured a copy of the brief and brought it to Mousson Street. Henry was startled by the appeal for confiscation.

"What does this mean?" he demanded of his lawyer.

Halkokondyles was a soft-spoken man whose thick glasses rarely obscured a legal point.

"They asked for 'a writ for the seizure of goods to prevent their sale or destruction,' as provided in a treaty between Turkey and Greece."

The petition was filed on April 3. On April 6 the three-judge court heard the lawyers for both sides. Henry was not summoned. One Athens newspaper commented:

"The president should have ordered the summoning of Mr. Schliemann to give him a chance to plead for his own case. This is an injustice done to Mr. Schliemann."

Two days later Henry and Sophia were notified that the judgment of the court would be read at 5:00 P.M. They dressed, took their carriage down to the court, seated themselves at the rear of the room. The president summed up from the opinion:

"The Court of First Instance turns down the petition of the lawyers of the Ottoman government as vague. According to civil proceedings, when one files such a petition about things which he claims to be his own, he must describe or at least name them one by one, otherwise the petition is vague and unacceptable. In this case, the applicants referred to the German edition where Mr. Schliemann had described his discoveries. The court considers this description incomplete. However the court would consider a more complete list if counsel wishes to submit it."

"Vague and unacceptable!" crowed Henry, opening a bottle of brandy with which to celebrate. "Sophidion, have you ever heard more beautiful words?"

"Not recently. Is it all over, then?"

"Not if I know Déthier. His lawyers will now assemble and attempt to draw up a detailed list of the gold. If the Court of First Instance should rule against us next time, we are in trouble. There will be no way to protect ourselves. Our hiding place could be discovered. We had better move the trunk into the French Archaeological Institute."

Sophia felt her hackles rise.

"I don't like it, Henry. The gold is perfectly safe where it is now. Once it gets into the hands of Burnouf and that daughter of his, we may never get it back."

"Come now, Sophia. I will cover the lock with my sealing wax to make sure that no one tampers with it."

"Tampering is not what is on my mind. The Burnoufs are going to do everything in their power to get the gold for the Louvre."

"He makes a very logical case for putting the treasure, whole and complete, in a great museum in the 'Mother of Cities.' Many more people will see it there . . ."

Her eyelids flared.

"You have no right to let him persuade you. You have given me your word that the treasure will belong to the Greek people."

He put his arm about her, tried to quiet her.

"You are worrying needlessly. All I am trying to do now is to put the find where no one can touch it. I am going to do it this afternoon."

That Sunday, April 14, 1874, Marigo married Demetrios Georgiades, a professor of mathematics at a girls' high school. Henry served as best man. Sophia withdrew the four-thousand-dollar dowry Henry had deposited in the National Bank of Greece and presented the money to the couple. It was a joyous day for the family; for a few hours Sophia was able to put out of her mind all of her anxieties.

A few days later Henry announced:

"The Burnoufs have invited us for dinner tomorrow."

"I don't want to go."

"Why not? They are good friends."

"They have an ulterior motive."

"Please don't cause trouble."

She could not refuse. She dressed the following morning with a sense of dread. Her instincts told her that there was going to be a row.

She was right. Émile Burnouf, over an apéritif in his livingroom, said in a confident tone:

"I have written to the director of the Louvre and reported our conversations. In a cable I received from him yesterday he expressed his pleasure at the idea that the treasure of Priam might come to the Louvre. He is conferring today with our Minister Fortou to get his approval for the acceptance."

Sophia trembled with rage. She cried:

"You had no right to do that!"

Burnouf replied gently, "I had every right, my dear Mrs. Schliemann."

"Who gave you that right?"

"Your good husband. Who else?"

She turned to Henry, her dark eyes blazing like live coals.

"Have you been arranging all this behind my back . . . ?"

"You're jumping to conclusions, *philtate mou*. I have made no offer to the Louvre. I have merely discussed with Émile whether the treasure is safe here or if it would be better to take it out of Greece."

She turned her fury back on Burnouf.

"Then how dare you tell the director that the treasure of Priam is available to him?"

Louise came to Sophia's side.

"Father didn't say that, Mrs. Schliemann. It's a matter of proper procedure. Before an offer can be made to us we have to know officially that it will be accepted."

"Us? Who are us? France? The director of the Louvre? The Prime Minister?"

Louise's blue eyes did not blink or darken in color.

"I consider myself a good and loyal friend. What we have been doing is in your best interest . . ."

She knew she was in too high a state of anger to speak in polite terms. It was her need to have the treasure remain in her homeland rather than the aggressiveness of the Burnoufs that aroused her. For almost a year now she had lived with the fear that the gold might be stolen out of the Lycabettus storeroom, or that the Ottoman government would somehow seize it. And now Henry was intimating that it might go to France.

"I am perfectly capable of taking care of my own best interest."

"Madame Schliemann, I don't think you should speak so harshly to Louise," Burnouf said, coming between them. "The responsibility is mine."

"Yours!" Her voice was ice cold now. "You are doing everything you can to wheedle the treasure out of us. Your motive is a selfish one. You have been unpopular as director. You think if you can pull off this coup your status will be restored in Paris. But I won't allow it! Henry, please take me home."

She trembled all the way up the hill. Henry kept a withdrawn silence. Once in the house he followed her upstairs, asked her to come into their little sittingroom and closed the door behind her.

"Sophia, I've never seen you behave this way. It may be true that Émile is serving his own best interests. There are advantages to him. But there are equally advantages to us."

"Name one!"

"The permanent security of the gold. The Turks are never going to stop trying to get possession of it. One day they'll find a court which will sustain them."

"I don't believe that, nor do your attorneys."

"Sophia, you sadden me. Why are you behaving as though you were my enemy instead of my friend?"

". . . enemy! For trying to keep for Athens what is rightly hers?"

"No, Sophidion. It is not rightly hers. It is ours, and the world's. . . . It's too late. I've made up my mind."

She stared at him for a long moment.

"To do what?"

"To give the treasure of Priam to the Louvre. I'm writing to Minister Fortou today saying that I will present my Trojan collection to their museum. I will also hand over a copy of my letter to French Ambassador Marquis de Gabriac. I have his assurance that I will receive a telegram from Paris within a week. Then the ambassador can take possession of the collection on behalf of France."

Tears came to her eyes. She was defeated. She rose and left the room.

It was a strange week. Sophia did not again raise the question of the gold, the Burnoufs or the Louvre. Nor did Henry. They spoke to each other only when necessary, quietly, almost formally. When Henry's lawyers came to the house she absented herself from the meetings. She did not accompany him for his daily swims at New Phaleron. She concerned herself with housewifely duties. She did not feel that there was a quarrel between herself and her husband, but rather that she had been demoted from an equal to that of the normal posture for a Greek wife who had no voice in the external affairs of the family. First at seventeen and now at twenty-two she was caught between loyalty to her husband and loyalty to her family, for Athens was her family, and Greece and the early Achaeans were family as well.

It was a bad week for Henry too; he could never tolerate waiting and now it was compounded by uncertainties about the future. An intuitive calm told Sophia that at the end of the week Henry had not received his cablegram of acceptance of the collection from Paris. Nor was he any happier on the eighth, ninth or tenth day. Rather he grew more withdrawn, wearing his spectacles even when not reading or writing. They did not discuss the fact that on April 29 the attorneys for the Constantinople Museum had filed an amended, lengthier brief.

It took Henry twelve days of waiting before he cracked. He returned for dinner at his usually prompt one-thirty, but with a different expression on his face. Even the way he walked and squared back his shoulders was different. He carried a bouquet of roses, carnations and irises for Sophia and leaned over to peck her on the cheek, a formidable task he had not dared venture since the Burnouf dinner.

"Sophidion, could we talk?"

"It is the privilege of a husband to talk at his wife."

"I am not attempting to exercise my privileges."

She asked the maid to transfer the setting from the family dining area to the formal diningroom. Henry did not begin speaking at once. Instead he devoured his beef broth with pasta. Sophia did not touch hers, sitting with hands folded in her lap. When he had finished, Henry looked up and smiled broadly.

"Delicious! I was starved. First time I've had any appetite in twelve days."

"When you have a great deal on your mind, it's hard to put a great deal in your stomach."

"An old Cretan saw, if I ever heard one. *Chryse mou*, first I must tell you what I did this morning. I cabled Minister Fortou in Paris that my offer was revoked. Then I delivered a letter to Ambassador de Gabriac informing him that since he had not fulfilled our agreement the gold treasure was no longer available to the Louvre. My last move this morning was to inform Burnouf that I was going to remove our treasure from the French Archaeological Institute. . . ."

Sophia did not react.

"My dear, I have done you an injustice. Not in what I attempted to do, because the treasure *must* remain safe, but in the arbitrary manner in which I carried on conversations with Burnouf and de Gabriac without your knowledge; I made the decision to give the treasure to the Louvre without your agreement. In fact, knowing how disappointed you would be. That is no way to treat a confrere, a full partner. The gold is half yours. You helped find it and helped us to bring it home." Having gotten that off his chest, he reached to the core of the dilemma. "I should have known that France would not accept a gift the Ottoman Empire is suing to recover. The French would not be receptive to a quarrel between France and Turkey."

"What do you intend to do now?"

"Make amends. First to my long-suffering Greek wife, whom I adore. . . . I put two hundred thousand francs in escrow for the museum we have offered to build in Athens to house our whole collection. I know they turned us down once, but times change, ministers and curators change. I will release the news publicly that I regard it as a matter of honor that the collection remain here permanently and that I shall build a museum for its exhibition."

A tiny smile played about the corners of her mouth. She admitted that neither the Greek government nor the Department of Antiquities had exactly courted them. They talked animatedly for an hour as though Henry had been abroad. Afterward they took their nap in each other's arms, dressed Andromache and rode down to New Phaleron where they swam together and laughed like a family reunited after a long separation.

5.

On May 1 they again went to court to hear the pleading of the Turkish petition. This time they walked, in order to see the doors and balconies of the Athens houses wreathed with May Day flowers. They listened to both sides present what the newspapers later described as "long discourses."

"What puzzles me," Sophia whispered, "is how they could find additional material for their list. They have nowhere to go except your book, and they used that for their first writ."

The three judges agreed.

The Constantinople Museum's case was again dismissed. Dr. Philip

Déthier was recalled to Constantinople. Ambassador Essad Bey wrote to the Greek Minister of Foreign Affairs pointing out Article 24 of the 1855 treaty between Greece and Turkey and asked what assurances the government could give to Turkey against such decisions of the Greek courts.

On May 11 the Ottoman advocates filed a petition in the Court of Appeals against the decision of the Court of First Instance. Their case was strengthened by an article in a British newspaper: at the end of April, Charles Newton had given a talk on the Trojan finds to the Royal Society of Antiquaries in London. He was discreet about the gold collection, saying nothing that was not already in Henry's book. However the treasure became a subject of debate in the English Parliament, and Lord Stanhope asked whether a proposal would be made for the purchase of part of the Schliemann collection. Benjamin Disraeli replied that he was "not prepared to propose such a thing." The exchange was reported in the London *Times,* and within a matter of days had drenched Athens like a winter rain.

"How could such a thing happen?" Sophia wailed.

"Certainly not through our friend Newton."

"He might have said that he had discussed the purchase with us."

"The wind has ears. I will now have to buy space in the important newspapers setting forth a categorical denial that I ever contemplated selling the gold."

On the sixteenth of May the case was heard before a panel of five judges of the Court of Appeals, the president in the center and two judges on either side of him. From the beginning Sophia and Henry sensed that the atmosphere in this courtroom was different from that of the Court of First Instance. The Ottoman government's attorneys had secured a copy of the London *Times* and read into the record the news of the discussion in the British Parliament about the possibility of purchasing a part of the Trojan collection. They had also accumulated copies of the telegrams and letters from Henry to French Ambassador de Gabriac and to Minister Fortou in Paris. They maintained that the Greek courts had every right and obligation under their treaty with Turkey to "seize goods in order to prevent their sale or destruction; foreigners are not excepted from this rule."

During the afternoon session Henry's lawyers put up a spirited defense of his right to preserve his ownership of the treasure. They read into the evidence the story from the *Newspaper of the Debates* that the Constantinople Museum already had a large portion of gold discovered at Troy, half of which belonged to the Schliemanns since it had been stolen by their own workmen. They countered the article of the London *Times* with Henry's sworn testimony that Mr. Newton of the

British Museum, while visiting in Athens, had asked if he might consider selling the treasure to the British, and Henry's assertion that the treasure would never be for sale. They had no way to deny that Henry had offered the treasure to the Louvre, but alleged that that action could not be deemed a "sale or destruction" of the goods. They then built up the case against a Greek court giving a verdict against an American citizen in favor of a foreign country. This, claimed the lawyers, would be not only illegal but unconstitutional; therefore the Court of Appeals had no jurisdiction to overthrow the two decisions of the Court of First Instance.

Later in the afternoon the president of the court announced that he and the other four judges would take the two briefs into conference. They would have a decision within a week.

The next day the Holy Synod passed over Theokletos Vimpos, electing as Archbishop of Athens Prokopios, Archbishop of Messenia, adjacent to Vimpos's diocese at Tripolis.

Bishop Vimpos came to Mousson Street for a last visit. It was a sad gathering. In the year that had passed since Athens had lost its archbishop, Bishop Vimpos had begun to believe that he could become the successor. As for the Schliemanns, the excitement of the excavation, the finds, and the anticipation of the world's acclaim for Henry's discovery of Homer's Troy were thoroughly drained. The pleasure of finding the treasure was being lost in the fight to keep it.

They attempted to fill the week of waiting with activities which would give them little opportunity to worry. They attended the afternoon concerts in Syntagma and Omonoia squares, went to hear one of Athens's new favorites, the violinist Robbio, and another day to watch Greek actors do the comedy *The Frogs*.

After six days they were back in the Court of Appeals with their attorneys. The president read aloud the decision of the five judges. The concluding paragraph came as a clap of thunder:

"The Court of Appeals orders the seizure of the entire gold treasure in the possession of Mr. Heinrich Schliemann; and its return to the Constantinople Museum."

The Schliemanns were stunned.

The entire gold treasure to be seized . . . returned to Turkey!

They sat in the back of their carriage blind-eyed and silent, sick at heart. Their minds had not allowed the possibility of such a catastrophe. The attorneys for the Constantinople Museum had succeeded beyond their wildest hopes.

They would of course exercise their right of appeal. Their lawyers, crestfallen but doing their best to look indignant, insisted that the Court of Appeals' decision was illegal and would be thrown out by the Areopagus, the highest court in Greece, and that the chances for the decision to be annulled were good.

Henry gave Sophia a hard glance over one shoulder.

"They thought our chances in the Court of Appeals were excellent too. And see what happened. It's that cursed article in the London *Times* that did us in."

Under her breath Sophia murmured, ". . . or the offer to the Louvre. . . ."

Once home, she said, "Why not take off your hat and coat and cool yourself in the garden? I'll have Calypso bring us a lemonade. Isn't it wonderful that an ice factory has opened in Athens? I bought some this morning from their street cart."

While their chunks of ice tinkled in the lemonade glasses, Sophia asked the question that was foremost in both their minds.

"What can we do if the Areopagus refuses to send the case back to a lower court for retrial?"

"I'll tell you what we won't do! We won't turn over the treasure to anyone. We'll manage to get it to England or the United States, as Minister Resident Boker advised me to do at the beginning."

Tears welled in Sophia's eyes.

The next morning two bailiffs arrived with a "search and seizure" order signed by the president of the Court of Appeals. They searched the house thoroughly, and then the garden sheds. Henry dogged their footsteps. He said not one word to the bailiffs but his unspoken imprecations filled the air with spume. When they could find no gold they left as silently as they had entered. Henry slammed the door behind them.

Anxiety crawled over their minds with the feel of ants crawling over their hands; their only comfort was that the Athenian press was saying that the Court of Appeals had made a political rather than a legal decision. The weather turned warm and so they drove out along the sea to bathe and picnic on the beach.

Within five days their attorneys had drawn up their appeal to the Areopagus. This highest court sent word that they would review the case but that their docket was already full for the remainder of the term. They could not hear the evidence until the fall.

"I had hoped that we could be easy through the summer," said Sophia dolefully.

"However, now that the Areopagus has accepted our appeal, the Turks will not be allowed to seize the treasure. I am thinking of taking a quick trip through northern Greece and the Peloponnesus in August. If I do, you can rent that house in Kiphissia you are so fond of and invite your family to vacation with you."

They were in the garden. The lemon trees were bearing, the flowering shrubs coming into deep spring color. She could tell by the excited way in which he was walking along the paths and moving his hands that he was in the process of gestation.

"Sophia, I have had an idea these past few days. It seems to me that the Greek people, if not the government, are behind us in our troubles with the Turks. I would like to do something in return."

"Like what?"

"Come, let us walk up to the Acropolis."

They came into the main entrance of the Acropolis, mounted the broad steps. Henry steered her to the fourteenth-century Venetian tower.

"I am going to ask permission of the government to tear it down . . . at my expense."

She threw her arms about his neck and kissed him impulsively.

"That's the best idea you have had since we left Troy! It would be a service the Greek people would never forget."

Henry was distressed to learn that he would have to go for his permission to the Minister of Public Instruction, Valassopoulos, and the General Inspector of Antiquities, Eustratiades. However his suggestion was warmly received by both men, who gave him their permission in writing. The sole stricture was that the marbles and stones of the tower be carefully preserved so that they could be restored to the Propylaea and the Herodes Atticus Theater.

Henry bought the wood for the scaffolding, hired his two foremen, Demetriou and Captain Tsirogiannes, and was preparing to engage a skilled work crew when King George ordered the ministers to rescind their permission. Henry sat in his study and wrote a letter to King George:

> I have asked permission from the Ministers to tear down the Venetian tower because it is a shame. It covers the most beautiful parts of the Propylaea and contains hundreds of inscriptions from the flowering of the Hellenic times. My suggestion was accepted with joy by the entire Greek population . . . to have the Propylaea freed from the ugly appendage. I had already bought the wood for the scaffolding when I was horrified to find out from the Minister of Public Instruction that I would no longer be permitted to work anywhere in Greece for the public welfare.
>
> There must be a misunderstanding of which I am not aware. Perhaps I have done something in which I have incurred your displeasure.

I ask you in all humility how I could have come into disfavor with you. All I ask is the right to remove the Venetian monstrosity from the Acropolis.

The letter was effective. The king did not reply directly but instructed the Minister of Public Instruction to allow Dr. Henry Schliemann to provide the funds for the tearing down of the tower. However the work was to be done by the Greek Archaeological Society . . . without the active participation of Henry Schliemann!

Sophia did her best to console him.

"I know you will miss the activity and the adventure of directing the work, but you have accomplished the end you sought. The ugly tower will be gone and the stones saved to be put back in their proper places. The public will be just as grateful to you."

On July 4 the Archaeological Society addressed a letter of thanks to Henry for the thirteen thousand drachmas, twenty-six hundred dollars, he had given them for the demolition of the tower.

For Sophia it was a warm lazy drifting summer without calendar or clock. Time was a fluid instead of a solid. They often spent the day by the sea, taking a picnic basket with them. The new bathing costumes were calf length and the daily newspaper deplored the fact that one "sees the disgusting sight of some women of the lowest classes bathing half naked, with men looking at them from all sides."

They had a tacit agreement not to discuss the upcoming trial or any other aspect of their work, and adopted a new regime. After a full day's outing they retired early to the veranda roofed by thousands of brilliant stars in the clear night sky. Henry got into one of the cool nightshirts he had had made in Paris and remained with her as long as she was awake, chatting, reading aloud. The moment she fell asleep he got up, went to his study. Each day brought quantities of mail from around the world as well as articles from newspapers and learned journals, both praising and attacking him. He answered all with letter-articles as long as the originals. When Sophia was awakened by the cauldronlike sun coming over the Acropolis in the morning, he was already stirring about.

Toward the end of July Sophia and Andromache waved good-by to him as he boarded the S.S. Byzantium. He had leased the house in Kiphissia which Sophia had admired each time they passed it in their carriage. There were tall shade trees and the quietly flowing river along one side of the property. The house had two bedrooms in one wing, a bedroom, water closet and kitchen in the other; and in the center a large combined parlor and diningroom. In front there was a covered veranda, and at the rear, glass doors which led to a back yard overlooking the river, and an enormous climbing vine. Sophia moved her entourage to the charming village, her mother, her brothers. Madame Victoria soon filled the house with the sweet odors of baking. She was happiest when she had Sophia to herself, with the redoubtable Dr. Schliemann some hundred or more miles away. Her sister Katingo brought her children out frequently to play with Andromache. Sophia commented to Katingo:

"It's wonderful how cut off from the world I feel out here, listening to the wind in the trees at night and the river moving past me, but still always there. I have been able to put our troubles with the courts of Athens out of mind. I live for every present moment and don't think about the future."

Though the street to the square in Kiphissia was torn up, she took Andromache in to see the king and queen walking under the plane trees.

Cards and letters from Henry reached her almost daily. He had revisited Aulis; moved on to Lamia, the terminal point of the new railroad; spent a couple of days at Thermopylae reading Herodotus; then moved on to Delphi, describing to Sophia the awe-inspiring mountain into which a thousand years of religious history had been carved. He climbed Mt. Parnassos, poked into the ruins of Orchomenos, where he intended to dig one day . . .

August went by quickly. On the twenty-second the little town celebrated the queen's twenty-third birthday. Sophia was now twenty-two.

Henry was home by early September. Sophia and Andromache moved back to Mousson Street. The heat was intense, but Syntagma Square was crowded again with Athenians returned from their summer vacations. An ordinance was passed that heavy transportation carriages could no longer use the central streets. Carriage drivers were not to beat their horses. There was a blossoming of new Greek newspapers, and a new French weekly, *Le Petit Journal d'Athènes*. The French theater began its new season with *Mignon*.

There were almost two weeks of sessions with their lawyers before the Areopagus convened on September 15. The contestants were heard by the judges, who then took the matter under advisement.

"How long will we have to wait for a decision?" Henry demanded.

"Not long," he was told. "Put the matter out of your mind."

Early fall brought a new series of vitriolic attacks. Déthier, back from the Troad, announced that the building discovered by Henry was not Priam's palace but a farm of Trojan peasants. The cruelest and most ironic attack, however, emanated from an Athenian, Spyridon Komnos, former librarian of the National Library, who accused Henry of forging his Trojan antiquities, of fraud in the digging up of pottery from various

places and representing his collection as having been discovered at Hissarlik. It was published in the Greek newspaper *Athenaion* during the
time they were waiting for the judgment of the Areopagus as to whether
the Trojan treasure must be returned to the Turks! The French Institute in Paris, in their official journal, also joined the attack. A
belittling article appeared in a Cologne, Germany, newspaper. A total
repudiation of the finds and theories was launched by Virlet d'Aoust,
"ancient member" of the 1830 expedition to the Peloponnesus. Frank
Calvert, who had taken his brother's place as the United States consul
in Çanakkale, further dismembered the finds in the English *Athenaeum*.

Along with the frustration of the contradictory charges, Henry was
griped by the attacks of writers who were willing to admit that the
Schliemanns had unearthed "a Troy" or at least a fascinating culture
out of prehistory, but that it had been nothing more than a "lucky accident." He had stumbled onto the dig with the luck of the beginner
and the amateur. It could never happen again in a thousand years!
Every time Henry saw the phrase "blind luck," he was furious.

". . . luck . . . luck!" he cried to Sophia. "The favorite word of the
envious and the spiteful . . . and the incompetent. It explains why
somebody else has accomplished something while they did not. It is a
one-word rationale to justify their having done nothing with their lives.
It brings everyone else down to their own level of lassitude. . . .
Luck . . . ! It . . ."

Sophia put her hand gently across his mouth.

It was war!

He was on guard and counterattacking by day and night. Sophia
never did know when he slept. He answered the Cologne article in
German, the charges in the *Journal Officiel* in French, the Turkish accusations in Turkish, and was planning to answer Calvert's second attack in English. Sophia observed that, outraged as he was when he first
read the tirades, roaming the house and garden uttering imprecations
with gestures denoting raped innocence, the bouts of fury lasted a
short time. He then went to his desk and wrote denials, repudiations,
pages justifying his claims by quoting from the opinion of Charles Newton before the Royal Society of Antiquaries and his published monograph in the *Academy*; from the views of classical scholar Professor
Gomperz of Vienna, who had deciphered some of the inscriptions and
declared them to be pure Greek with ancient Cyprian characters; while
Max Müller's article for the *Academy* gave reproductions of the Trojan
letters and their relationship to the Cyprian language.

He was a hero only in England. His *Trojan Antiquities* was being
translated into English and would be published by Mr. John Murray.
They had retitled the book *Troy and Its Remains*, found a good trans-

lator, Dora Schmitz, and secured the editorial services of an eminent classicist, Professor Philip Smith, to make the necessary revisions. Philip Smith wrote a generous Preface, ending with the line:

> The name of Troy can no longer be withheld from the "splendid ruins" of the great and wealthy city which stood upon its traditional site—a city which has been sacked by enemies and burnt with fire.

Best of all was an invitation from the prestigious Royal Society of Antiquaries to lecture before their group on June 24, 1875; Prime Minister William Gladstone had generously offered to make the introduction, which assured Henry a respectful reception. *Troy and Its Remains* would be released about the same date. Henry's spirits soared.

"Sophia, after our English stay it would be a good time to tour the Continent: Holland, Hungary, Denmark, Sweden, Austria, Germany, where you will meet my family. Now the museums will fascinate you because of the relation of their exhibits to our own finds at Troy."

Her eyes lighted with pleasure.

"I'd like to take Andromache with us. And Calypso to care for her while we are busy."

Henry was in an expansive mood.

"Granted. We'll also invite Spyros to Paris to spend a week with us there."

Before the end of September the seven judges of the Areopagus rendered their decision. They had confined themselves to the judicial errors that had been made rather than to the essence of the case, and on these grounds annulled the decision of the Court of Appeals.

The attorneys for the Constantinople Museum filed new briefs with the Court of First Instance. This time round the court decided that Henry Schliemann had violated one of the clauses of his contract, and ordered an appraisal of the Trojan treasure by three experts and the payment by Henry Schliemann to the Ottoman government of half of their worth.

The Ottoman government refused to accept the decision. They went back to the Court of Appeals demanding total confiscation of the gold.

On October 10 the Court of Appeals turned down the Ottoman brief, and on November 21 the three experts appointed by the Court of First Instance, having been refused permission by Henry to see the actual gold, made an estimate of its worth from Henry's book. They arrived at a sum of drachmas for the gold, plus a sum of drachmas for the Apollo, a total of something over four thousand dollars.

Henry promptly agreed to pay his half share to the Turkish government. That put an end to the lawsuits.

It was over!

6.

Winter was coming; in the streets, under the light of small lanterns, the vendors were selling hot chestnuts; there were short torrential rains. But in the Schliemann home there was jubilation. Sophia sent their young errand boy and their carriage driver with invitations to dinner to all those who had supported Henry during his trial, even though they had not found it expedient to visit Mousson Street. She was so elated to have the burden lifted off the family chest, she even included Louise Burnouf.

Although the decision was received by the Turkish government without severe criticism, they regarded it merely as a conciliatory gesture on the part of the Greek court toward the Sultan. It was apparent they were unwilling to accept the two-thousand-dollar monetary judgment as a satisfactory settlement. Henry was informed by the Turkish Embassy's First Secretary that the government was sending Photiades Bey to Athens as their new ambassador to work out a more just and amiable disposition of the case.

"They know what I want," Henry told Sophia, "a renewal of my *firman*. They know how anxious I am to complete the digs at Troy, and they know I am willing to give something valuable in order to have the *firman* renewed. I offered them eight thousand dollars with which to refurbish their museum. I'm hoping they will consider that a fair bargain."

"If they did," replied Sophia, "why would they send Photiades Bey to us? They need only remind you of your pledge."

"That promise was made while the case was in the courts and the whole treasure at stake. Now I am obliged to pay only the two thousand dollars required of me by the Court of First Instance."

Sophia put her hands on her husband's shoulders, her eyes rested fully on his.

"Let us receive Photiades Bey in our home as a friend. You know what the people of Crete say about saving face: it's more important than saving food."

To their surprise and Henry's consternation it took until April 1875 to get their affairs settled with the Turkish government. This was not the fault of Photiades Bey or of Safvet Pasha, Minister of Public Instruction, who was satisfied with Henry's offer of eight thousand dollars in addition to the fine. The problem was caused by Dr. Philip Déthier, whose position in Turkey had been seriously undermined by his recall to Constantinople.

During the almost five months of negotiation, their impatience was absorbed by the hours they spent on the Acropolis watching the workmen loosen and then lower the ancient stones of the Venetian tower as delicately as though they were jewels.

Henry made the arrangements for their European journey. Their rooms at the Charing Cross Hotel in London were comfortable; friends had sent flowers which the maid put in tall vases in the parlor. Sophia liked London. The May weather was cool but pleasant. Her English was slightly accented . . .

". . . but then," she commented, "so is that of most Englishmen!"

Henry and his long-time associates at Schröder's took Sophia on a sightseeing tour of Westminster Abbey, Buckingham Palace, the Tower of London, the bazaar in Petticoat Lane, the bridges over the Thames. How young and underbuilt was Athens by comparison. She was surprised at the numbers of men and women in the streets, the somber clothing and constant rainwear and umbrellas, the absence of sidewalk cafés. Charles Newton returned their hospitality by taking them through the museum's treasures, then gave a luncheon in their honor. Sophia was delighted by the beauty of the Elgin Marbles, then became indignant that they had been removed from the Parthenon and their rightful Greek home. She managed to forget her displeasure the next day when Mr. Gladstone set aside places for them in the public gallery in the House of Commons where she witnessed a spirited debate among the members. At the afternoon recess he took them out to the sun-filled terrace overlooking the Thames where she met several members of the Cabinet over tea and strawberries served with clotted cream.

A fever which had begun to bother her in Athens and on shipboard had vanished in the enchantment of her first visit to England. On the fifth morning she awoke with alternating chills and heat to see rain streaming across the curtained windows of their bedroom. Her head ached, her skin was irritable. Henry summoned a Dr. Farré, recommended as "the first doctor of England." Dr. Farré called it a *febricula*, which Henry had him translate into "remittent fever. We'll just have to let it run its course."

"Surely you have some recommendations?"

"I suggest you take Mrs. Schliemann to Brighton. The warm baths there are most relaxing. The sea, the sun and rest . . . Nature has a way of curing its own upsets."

Through the kind offices of Schröder, Henry located a pleasant house for rent at 151 King's Road in Brighton. A maid came with the house, a Miss Stely. Henry saw that Sophia, Andromache and Calypso were comfortably installed with an abundance of fruits, vegetables, groceries . . . and an order for six London newspapers to be delivered to Sophia daily so she could collect any articles about him. When he kissed her good-by, before catching his train for London, she said fondly:

"I know that women are not allowed into the Society's lectures so I wouldn't have been able to hear you even if I were in London. At the moment that you will be speaking I will make libations as Priam did when starting his voyage to see Achilles at the Achaean camp to ransom the body of Hector."

The hot steam baths helped considerably. Soon she was able to accompany Andromache and Calypso to the beach and take sea baths as well.

Henry's lecture to the Royal Society of Antiquaries on June 24 at Burlington House was a solid success. Six journalists attended. She clipped the stories for Henry. The picture she liked best was in the *Illustrated London News*. It showed Dr. Schliemann in a frock coat, white tie, low shirt collar which made his neck appear longer, pince-nez glasses, reading at a table on which stood two tall lamps and surrounded by a sea of the most important scholars and men of letters in England. She knew that it had to be the most gratifying moment in Henry's life.

The cure was working while Henry was making friends with the scholars at Oxford and Cambridge. The man he admired most was Max Müller, who had come around to a position of strong support for Henry's work. A warm friendship developed. On the weekends he came to Brighton to swim and relax while they rescheduled their travels to take care of several lectures that had been offered to him because of his enthusiastic reception at Burlington House.

In late July they moved on to Paris and had a reunion with Spyros at the Hotel Louvois. Then Sophia's fever returned. When she felt too weak to get out of bed Henry grew anxious and sent Spyros to find the Greek doctor who five years before had accurately assessed Sophia's stomach troubles and advised Henry to take his wife home to Greece. He observed:

"There is a problem connected with this kind of fever; it is recurring. No one knows why. It's not serious. A couple of weeks of rest and it will disappear, eventually for good."

"A couple of weeks!" Henry got out his travel itinerary and showed the doctor their departure date and fast-moving schedule through six countries. The doctor observed dryly:

"Then you're either going to postpone your journey or leave Kyria Schliemann in Paris. She is in no condition to undertake a tour."

Henry was miserable, Sophia unhappy.

"You've been looking forward to this trip," she pleaded, "and now you have important lectures scheduled. Go by yourself. I'll be all right here with Spyros and Calypso to watch over me."

"You're certain you won't mind?"

". . . I'll mind. But I don't want to deprive you of your travels. Keep it to five weeks. That's as long as I want to be in Paris without my husband."

"I'll be back in five weeks to the day. Here are twenty-five hundred francs. I don't think you'll need more than half of it but I want you to have it for contingencies."

Within a week the fever was gone and she was out of bed. Spyros engaged a carriage to take her riding in the Bois de Boulogne each afternoon, stopping in a cool spot to let Andromache play on the grass. She returned several times to the circus she had enjoyed so thoroughly on her first trip. Eugène Piat was in Paris; he took her to the Opéra Comique. A friend of Henry's invited her to the theater to see a fashionable comedy. She read for hours stretched out comfortably on a chaise. In writing to Henry she alternated between French and English, which prompted him to reply: "You write much better English than French."

Henry wrote frequently. In Leyden he had "rushed into the museum which he examined with the greatest curiosity in detail." From The Hague he wrote of having dinner at the palace with Queen Sophie of Holland. Then came a paragraph that so shocked her that she had to read it several times to believe her eyes. Henry had asked her to send him the hotel bill each week so that he could check it carefully. When he received her letter enclosing the first bill he wrote in ancient Greek:

> My dear, from the enclosed account you see that for *each* lunch they charge you 7 francs, and never less than 5½ francs. Please *avoid* such *shame* and have your lunch *outside*, because there with no difficulty you can have an excellent lunch for 1½ or 2 francs. Leave it to fools and madmen to eat lunch at 7 francs and eat yours with 1½ or 2 francs. Take your morning coffee at the hotel, because this is not expensive, also you will always have *dinner* there, but at all cost avoid this destructive lunch which anyhow is a terrible swindle. Hoping to hear from you with nothing but good and happy news, I embrace you my darling wife,
>
> Schliemann

She sat with her mouth open, unbelieving. Then spent the next hour trying to fathom this incredible man.

"He offers land and a museum to the Greek government, which cost him at least fifty thousand dollars. He offers to pay all costs for a joint excavation in Turkey which would cost another fifty thousand dollars. He voluntarily gives the Turkish government eight thousand dollars to refurbish their museum. Yet he objects to having his wife eat her midday meal in the diningroom of the Hotel Louvois because it would cost between five and seven francs, when she can go outside and have lunch for the equivalent of thirty or forty cents."

How strange were the workings of the human mind!

"Can it be in the difference between when I'm working at his side as a partner, and being merely an appendage when apart? Is it the difference between what he considers important and unimportant? Or is it a quality of miserliness over inconsequential sums? In any event I will continue to have lunch right here in the hotel. The food is excellent and we are beautifully cared for."

They all went to the Gare du Nord to welcome him the first week of September and carry him to the Hotel Louvois by carriage.

He never mentioned the fact that Madame Schliemann's bills proved that she had taken her lunches in the Hotel Louvois for the entire five weeks, or that the five hundred dollars he had left her had vanished and he had had to send her more money.

Sophia asked herself, "Is he wise enough not to bring up the issue, or has he simply forgotten his earlier impulse?"

After six years of marriage she still did not know; but she had won her own War of Independence. She chuckled to herself:

"I can now wear the medal my father won in his War of Independence for Greece."

Back at the hotel, Henry was bitterly disappointed that there was no permit from either Greece or Turkey awaiting him. He chafed at the continuing delays.

"I'm simply not alive when I'm not excavating," he exclaimed over supper in the parlor of their suite. "You think I am possessed. I do not deny it. I must start to dig again soon."

"But where, Henry?"

"I have had a note from Signor Fiorelli, the director-general of a museum in Rome. He urges me to dig at Albano, south of Rome. To see if I can find pottery or other objects of human industry below a thick layer of volcanic rock."

She knew this was a stopgap. Watching the euphoria of his European tour disappear, she decided to return to Athens the better to solicit the Turkish ambassador as well as Georgios Milesses, their own new

Minister of Public Instruction with whom she had a family acquaintance.

They took ship from Marseilles. Henry disembarked at Naples. From the first of his letters she sensed how disappointed and chagrined he was. In Albano the farmer who leased him a vineyard in which to dig deceived him by showing him Etruscan and Roman vases supposedly found under the lava. When Henry reached native soil he found no sign of human life. He had been gulled.

By the middle of October he was in Palermo, Sicily. An official encouraged him to dig near Marsala, on a small island known as Pantelleria. She received a cablegram:

> I AM LIVING HERE IN THE MIDST OF SO MUCH FILTH AND MISERY
> THAT I CANNOT ASK YOU TO JOIN ME.

In Pantelleria he found a thin crust of earth with nothing under it. He moved on to Segesta, then to Taormina, Syracuse . . . distraught. He had to dig somewhere . . . anywhere.

His troubled letters and apparent misery spurred her to make more determined efforts in Athens. She went to see their attorney, Delegeorges. He advised against again approaching the Turks at that time; Turkey was having internal problems. She visited their friends at the university and the ministry, urging them to use their influence on Georgios Milesses.

It was not until late in November, with Henry complaining, "It is not possible to find any antiquities here that the museums don't already possess. I want to stay in the prehistoric epoch," that a letter was forwarded to him from Rashid Pasha, Minister of Foreign Affairs in Constantinople, saying that a new *firman* was being discussed in a friendly way. Henry packed and took the first ship out of Naples for Piraeus.

It was close to the holiday season when he received a second letter from Rashid Pasha that seemed to contain a signal that all opposition had been put down and if he would come to Constantinople he could secure his *firman*. Sophia was reluctant to let him go away for the New Year and Epiphany, but he was too excited to be stopped. Nor did she want to be responsible for having held him back if the permit should not be forthcoming. Henry knew that the holidays were sacred to her and did not suggest that she accompany him, but rather that she be prepared to come for a three-month stay once he had the permit in his hands. To this Sophia agreed. He bought gifts for everyone and left.

His letters from Constantinople were grim.

I am still encountering the very greatest difficulties. I don't think I would ever be able to surmount them were it not for the universal interest my discovery of Troy has excited, and for the great enthusiasm the foreign ambassadors in Constantinople feel for Homer and his Ilium. . . .

A week later he was still writing that his *firman* was expected any day. He was comfortably settled in the Hotel de Byzance and had joined the company of "learned and very distinguished foreigners." At table some seven or eight languages were used interchangeably, which Henry found a delight. He did, however, miss his friend George Boker, who had been sent to Russia as the American envoy extraordinary and minister plenipotentiary.

It was a number of weeks later before he asked her to come by ship to Constantinople, to bring her old clothes and be ready for a three-month dig. She decided to leave at the beginning of February, and made her reservation. Henry was delighted. He told her how eager his companions at table were to meet her, that she would find there "more mental enjoyment and more amusement than you ever before enjoyed."

Then she too received a signal, from the Greek Minister of Public Instruction, which made her feel that she was as close to getting the Greek permit as Henry was to getting the Turkish one. She cabled her regrets. Henry was disappointed, but there was little he could say since he still did not have the *firman*.

When Henry left he had taken part of his equipment on the ship with him. Spyros was to send on the balance when Henry needed it. Henry and his friends among the foreign diplomats in Constantinople worked indefatigably but it was not until May 5 that he actually held the long-sought *firman* in his hands. Sophia smiled when she saw the terms in which he had cabled her the good news:

ODYSSEUS HAS NOT SUFFERED SO MUCH IN HIS TEN-YEAR JOURNEY TRYING TO GET HOME FROM TROY THAN I HAVE SUFFERED IN CONSTANTINOPLE DURING THESE MONTHS.

However she was not to join him in Troy for a few weeks because, as Yannakis had written, their old house was no good any more. The peasants had broken the doors and windows; the tiles had been taken off the roof so that the rains had poured inside and ruined everything. The digs themselves were in need of repair; the walls had fallen down, there were ten feet of mud in the excavations. The Scamander River had flooded the Troad three times, leaving six feet of water from the base of Troy to the sea. Even with good workmen, Henry wrote, it would take them weeks to build a livable stone house on the site of the old one and erect the other wooden buildings. He would send her word when Troy was once again livable.

He never did send the word. Once he reached Hissarlik he encountered nothing but aggravation and delay. Yannakis was not permitted to work at Troy; the poor giant was literally afraid for his life. The same governor of the district was still in Çanakkale, but his attitude toward Henry had changed. Henry could hire only Turks now, no Turkophones. That seriously cut down the labor supply. He was assigned a guard, Isset Effendi, whose instructions were so severe they were almost brutalizing. He dogged Henry's footsteps by day and night, never allowing him a moment of privacy. When Henry finally got the mud out of his trenches, which was a back-breaking task, and began to find a few interesting objects around Priam's palace, he was denied the right to photograph them. Nor was he allowed to make drawings of the structure of walls or cobbled streets.

The final blow came when Governor Ibrahim Pasha rode out to the digs to check on what Henry was doing. Henry's *firman* gave him six hundred acres of land adjacent to the excavation on which he had the right to build whatever houses and sheds he required for himself, his workers and equipment. Governor Ibrahim Pasha studied Henry's simple buildings, took a copy of the *firman* out of his coat pocket, found what he was looking for and said sharply:

"Dr. Schliemann, you are violating the terms of your *firman*."

"What do you mean? I have done nothing, removed nothing . . ."

"You are obliged to cover these six hundred acres with houses and magazines of stone and wood."

"Cover the entire six hundred acres! But whatever for? It would be a whole city. I have no further need of buildings."

"The permit does not discuss your needs. It states explicitly that you must cover the whole of the six hundred acres."

"Governor Ibrahim Pasha, that interpretation is ridiculous. How could I possibly cover whole fields? And why would anybody in the Sultan's government be foolish enough to make such a stipulation?"

"I know nothing about all this. I have to interpret the agreement strictly or I will be in trouble with Constantinople. You are to do no more excavating until you have covered the six hundred acres with wood and stone buildings."

Henry knew he was defeated. He could go back to Constantinople and request a letter from the Minister of Public Instruction stating specifically that he did not have to cover the entire six hundred acres or any given number of acres. But he knew how slowly the mills ground in the Turkish government. To make matters worse, his one strong friend,

Rashid Pasha, Minister of Foreign Affairs, had been murdered. Safvet Pasha had been moved up to be Minister of Foreign Affairs; there would be a new man as Minister of Public Instruction. Perhaps a stranger to Henry, perhaps even hostile. He was confident that he could get the *firman* clarified on the ridiculous issue, but how many more weeks, or months, would it take? And then, what would he return to? Opposition, obstructionism, lack of workers, denial of all rights to make scientific recordings of his finds.

It was hopeless. He had been mistaken in thinking that he could go back to Troy to complete his work. He had wasted months waiting in the hotel in Constantinople, separated from his wife and daughter, his home and intimate business affairs. He had wasted two months at the digs and done very little except remove the mud that had washed down into his trenches and terraces over the past three years.

He ordered the equipment crated and shipped back to Piraeus, cabled Sophia that he was returning for good.

He boarded the ship to Greece, depressed.

Sophia was at Piraeus to meet him. She stood on the dock waving a piece of paper in the air triumphantly, her face wreathed in the broadest smile he had ever seen.

"Our permit to dig at Mycenae," she cried the moment he was within earshot. "We can start excavating there immediately."

BOOK SEVEN

MYCENAE!

1.

NAUPLION'S chief of police, Leonidas Leonardos, was at the dock
to meet them, his medals colorful in the lengthening sunset of
a July day.

"We've looked forward to this moment for two long years," cried
Henry. "May I introduce my three professor friends: Dr. Euthymios
Kastorches was born here in the Peloponnesus and is now professor of
Greek archaeology at the University of Athens. Dr. Spyridon Phindikles is professor of philology at the university and vice-president of the
Archaeological Society. Dr. Ioannes Papadakes is professor of mathematics and astronomy at the university, and has been its rector. They
have been kind enough to come along for a week's inspection of Tiryns
and Mycenae."

Leonidas Leonardos bowed low at each introduction of the prestigious scholars.

"I have inspected the rooms you reserved at the Hotel Olympus. You
have the same suite where I had the pleasure of visiting you in 1874."

They walked the short distance to the hotel, followed by porters. The
luggage had been roped and slung over their shoulders, one bag in
front, the other behind. The manager had set up a table for them in
the rear garden where they had supper under an immense plane tree.
The presence of the professors in the Argolid as his guests buoyed Henry's spirits. Their co-operation at Tiryns for several days while he sank
some experimental shafts, and then their tour of inspection at Mycenae,
implied University of Athens interest in his excavations.

When Sophia awakened at dawn Henry had already returned from
his swim in the bay. His chest and arms were glowing with color where
he dried them vigorously with a rough towel.

"Time to get up, love. The carriages are waiting, our picnic dinner has
been prepared in the kitchen."

For good luck, Sophia put on the one-piece dress with long sleeves and
wide skirt that she had worn at Troy during their last rewarding weeks.
She also carried a scarf and her widest-brimmed hat and gloves against
the summer sun. She, Henry and the three professors were on their way
by sunrise. It was only a mile from Nauplion to Tiryns. Shortly, they
were all standing beneath the cyclopean walls, a sight which staggered

the senses. The blocks of stone were so colossal, the walls themselves so impossible to build, that one could not believe they stood there.

"I can see the walls," Sophia murmured, "but I cannot assimilate them."

They turned off the main road and walked a short distance along the south base of the flat rocky plateau of Tiryns. The drivers took their food and cool drinks up to the interior galleries that had been cut in the twenty-five- to fifty-foot-thick walls to serve as communication lines leading to the armories, food storage and towers, with six windowlike openings for the archers. They themselves entered on the eastern side through a wide ramp supported by a wall of cyclopean masonry. On the right of the majestic gate was a tower which Henry estimated to be forty feet high and the professors claimed could be the oldest tower built in Greece.

Demetrios Dases was there to greet them. Weeks before Henry had shipped his Troy equipment to him. The hundreds of pickaxes, shovels, crowbars were now at Mycenae, with only sufficient tools here for the four-day survey. Demetrios had brought ten workmen from Charvati. Henry assigned two workmen to each of his party, and to Sophia as well. Each selected his location. Professor Kastorches and Sophia chose to dig on the higher level of the citadel; the other two professors on the lower. Henry took Demetrios and the remaining two workmen to lay out the dimensions of a broad trench diagonally across the highest part of the citadel.

Sophia and Professor Kastorches found two sets of house walls, made of small stones joined with earth. On the lower acropolis the two groups found a large fragment of a painted Hera idol with female breasts and uplifted arms resembling cow horns. They also sifted out masses of painted potsherds. The sun had mounted with a knifelike intensity but it was cool in the arched passageways where they ate their dinner. In the thirteen shafts on the upper level, and three on the lower, they found the terra cottas they were looking for. In the evenings, after the professors had had their swim, they assembled in the Schliemanns' sittingroom where Sophia had laid out the day's finds: tripods, large vases with perforated handles, small jugs, pots, dishes and cups, some made on the potter's wheel, some primitive.

After five days the caravan moved to Mycenae. Henry made arrangements for the pottery finds to be packed in baskets and shipped back to the Archaeological Society on the same ship the three professors would take after the tour of Mycenae. Demetrios informed Henry that he had sixty workmen ready for the signal to start the digging. Henry staked out the dig following Pausanias's clue as to where the royal tombs might lie. All three professors extended sincere wishes of good fortune.

When they had gone Henry said wistfully:

"I wish we could have persuaded one of them to remain on as the Archaeological Society's overseer instead of that young Mr. Stamatakes they're sending us to stand guard. I had two discussions with him in Athens and he smiled only once. I find that frightening."

The Dases family greeted them warmly. For two and a half years they had been waiting for the Schliemanns to return. Their rooms were ready; the men had put up new wooden shutters against the fierce summer sun. The random-length plank floors had been scraped and polished. Sophia had brought along a crate of sheets, pillowcases, towels, blankets against the anticipated cold of October and November. She had also brought a supply of soap and other toiletries to last for three to four months. They would dig until the heavy rains of November drove them out.

Henry had written to Demetrios to build nightstands for either side of the bed, and to curtain off a corner of the bedroom to be used as a clothes closet. While they had brought with them mainly their oldest clothing for the rough work ahead, they had also put into their luggage a couple of good dresses and an extra suit for church and visits to Argos and Nauplion. Sophia opened her suitcase, placed her icon on her nightstand and offered a prayer to the Virgin Mary to keep them well during their Mycenae stay, and to enable Henry to fulfill a reasonable portion of his high hopes.

Henry had sent a draft from the National Bank of Greece to its bank in Argos so the Dases family would have the cash on hand to buy the things they would need. He also sent a sketch of the shower bath at Hissarlik. It was to be out of doors, with only enough roof to hold the tilted water barrel with its release chain. But how to find another Yannakis? Their problem would be simpler here, since Demetrios would be paid a lump sum each Saturday night for the number of cubic meters of earth which that part of the crew he had contracted for had moved. However they would need a check-in list for the workmen from other villages who would have to be paid in cash during the week as well as on Saturday.

Henry settled on the middle Dases son, Nikolaos, just turned sixteen, a bright-eyed golden-skinned gangling boy who had attended several sessions of school at Argos and had continued to teach himself by reading whenever he could lay his hands on a book. Henry gave him a notebook and explained Yannakis's name-check method. Nikolaos was also to be in charge of the water supply for the workers. Barrels had to be filled at the nearest spring, loaded onto two-wheel horse carts and moved uphill in a continuous supply to the shadeless throat-parching acropolis. The men sweltering under the early August sun would empty the barrels as quickly as they were taken off the carts.

The workers earned two and a half drachmas a day, fifty cents, the foreman five drachmas. Henry paid Nikolaos a dollar a day. The Dases family was delighted; Nikolaos would now have the money to stay in Nauplion the following year and attend a higher school. The wages were larger than Henry had paid in the Troad, but the people of the Argolid lived on a higher economic plane than those in the Troad.

When the Schliemanns had settled in they were informed that Panaghiotes Stamatakes, the Archaeological Society's watchdog, had moved into a house across the road, choosing it because it was the only one that had an enclosed storehouse at the back. He had installed a lock on the door to which he would have the only key. The storehouse would serve as the depository for all finds from the excavation. With the permission of the Dases family, Sophia and Henry invited Stamatakes to dinner. He declined. The next day, August 8, 1876, was a religious holiday, the feast of St. Panteleemon. The villagers gathered at their tiny chapel where a visiting priest held one of his several services of the day. The Schliemanns attended with the Dases family; Stamatakes did not appear. The villagers were offended. They commented:

"He thinks he's too good for a peasant chapel and a country priest."

The family with whom he was staying said, "He keeps himself to himself. Eats his meals in his room."

"Maybe he's just shy," Henry suggested. "Unaccustomed to meeting strangers. I think we should try again."

They again invited him to dinner. Stamatakes again declined.

After the sun had spent its heat they climbed up to the Treasury of Atreus. The exquisite beehive architecture gave Sophia a sense of the perfectibility of man and his talents. An inner calm and tranquillity came over her, the effect that every great work of art has on the human spirit.

Stamatakes remained holed up in his room the entire holiday. At dusk Henry asked, "Do you think I ought to pay him a courtesy call? We are going to be working together for months and I should like us to be friends."

Sophia replied sternly, "Definitely not! As the younger man, it was his duty to pay his respects to you. He has already shown signs of arrogance. Greek men have more than enough pride . . . because of what their ancestors accomplished! No need to further puff up our Mr. Stamatakes."

"Very well. You're my authority on the character of the Greeks," Henry replied with an amused smile.

The next morning they were up before dawn, had coffee, got onto their mules and rode up the sharply curving hill to the Lion Gate. Demetrios had spent the Monday before the holiday in transporting Henry's heavy equipment onto the acropolis plateau where the agora had stood: the pickaxes, shovels, iron levers. There was a sheepherder's trail that led up from the road through a narrow break in the wall. Demetrios's men used this footpath to bring in the equipment. The sixty men were as colorful as the Turks and Turkophones of Hissarlik. Over their trousers they wore a thick skirt, a *kelembia*, white or beige in color, pleated at the waist; all clothing was made of a cloth called *drili* which the women wove at home and then dyed.

Henry apportioned the crews and marked out a trench moving in a southerly direction, starting forty feet from the Lion Gate, to open an area about a hundred feet square. He gave Demetrios forty workmen, took ten for himself at the Lion Gate. When he had started his men clearing debris from the entrance, Sophia asked:

"Could we walk over to that other treasury? The one with its top caved in?"

On their last trip, despite the overgrowth of weeds and foliage, they had been able to peer down into its darkness.

"Why are you interested in that particular treasury? It lies outside the cyclopean walls by at least four hundred feet. It is not one of the royal tombs we are searching for."

"I'll tell you when we get there."

They scrambled down the pitted slope covered with rocks and dry brush, then made their way up the mound ahead of them. By lying on their stomachs and pushing back the weeds and brush lodged in the cracks of soil between the rocks they were able to clear a space about three feet round. From the sunlight that sifted into the pitch-black interior they could approximate the depth of the beehive treasury.

"It's going to be a major task to free this formation from its three-thousand-year grave," Henry observed; "even more difficult to locate and clear out will be its *dromos*, its entranceway. But it would be a magnificent addition to archaeology."

A smile came over Sophia's soap-scrubbed face. Her dark eyes were alive with anticipation.

"I would like to undertake this dig myself. I mean, quite independent of your work in the acropolis. If I could free this treasury and it proved to be even half as beautiful as the Treasury of Atreus, I would feel that I had truly made a contribution."

". . . with no help from your aging husband."

"One small bit. Tomorrow morning, come up here and help me get my sightings. I'll make do with whatever you can spare, men and equipment both."

When they returned to the Lion Gate they found that Stamatakes had arrived. He was arguing with Henry's crew, ordering them to stop work. Like Henry, he was dressed in the same clothes he wore at his desk in Athens: white shirt, dark tie, dark suit, vest. He was slim, with perfect white teeth and superb posture. He held his head aloof on his neck as though he were looking beyond the dirty, dusty work of a dig to the orderly beauty of the National Library in Athens, where man's wisdom was contained in books . . . with no need to sink a pickax and shovel into debris.

The Schliemanns greeted him cheerfully.

"Good morning, Mr. Stamatakes."

Stamatakes bowed formally in reply, said nothing.

"I hope you are comfortable in your lodgings," said Sophia.

"Primitive."

"Oh. I'm sorry. We did invite you both days to come and have dinner with us. The Dases family would have welcomed you. Their women are good cooks."

Stamatakes lowered his eyes to theirs as they stood side by side at the Lion Gate, their heads above the massive lintel.

"I think I should advise you at once," he said coldly, "that I have no intention of entering into a social relationship with you. I am here as the government ephor of antiquities and representative of the Greek Archaeological Society; there will be no exchanges between us except on matters of the excavation and the finds. In that way I can hew rigidly to the letter of my instructions."

Sophia and Henry gazed at each other, eyebrows lifted. It was Georgios Sarkis, their first guard at Hissarlik, all over again; a man unhappy to be there. Henry said harshly:

"Very well, but stay out from under our feet or you'll get those long shinbones of yours thoroughly skinned."

Stamatakes thrust out his underlip, said in a drawl, "I have nothing more to say to you except to issue you your orders."

"You're not issuing orders to me or anybody else! Your job here is to collect our finds and ship them back to Athens, nothing more."

Stamatakes pulled his lips back over the beautiful white teeth.

"I am to be shown any important find *in situ* before it is removed. You may not dig in more than two places at a time; and they are to be close enough together so that I can observe everything going on. You may dig in only specified areas, which I will mark out for you . . ."

"*Fick dich Selbst*," screamed Henry in German, knowing that Sophia would not understand the words.

"That is physically impossible," retorted Stamatakes.

Henry's men had resumed their work of sinking pickaxes and shovels into the three-thousand-year accumulation of stones, earth and debris at the entrance of the Lion Gate. Stamatakes turned to them and cried:

"No, no! You can't touch this approach road!"

"Why not?" Henry demanded.

"Because we have to preserve this height—we don't know how many feet above the original road we are—in order to ease our job of raising these cyclopean stones back into the parallel walls leading to the gate."

"I intend to clear an access space in the middle of the road only as wide as the gate itself. All the stones and debris at both sides will be left *in situ* to give us a higher platform from which to raise the huge blocks."

Mollified, Stamatakes said more quietly, "Well thought out."

"Thank you." Turning to the workmen, he said, "Please resume your digging. When your basket is filled, take it to the horse cart and dump the earth and stones in it."

By dawn of the next morning Demetrios had assembled sixty-three workmen. Henry put twelve at the Lion Gate, Demetrios took forty-three, which left a crew of eight for Sophia. She and Henry took her eight men to the nearby buried treasury.

"Now, Henry, let's stand at the top, next to the cave-in. From which direction do you gauge the *dromos* will most probably lead into the beehive?"

Henry studied the terrain, took out his compass, made some calculations in a notebook.

"You plan to dig a trench across the entrance passage?"

"Yes. As close to the triangle above the lintel as I can get. Once I have located the top of that triangle I will know from the figures on the Treasury of Atreus approximately how many feet I will have to dig down to the lintel, and then how much farther down it will be from the bottom of the lintel to the threshold into the tomb."

"Very well, start your trench on the south side of the mound."

"I will. But why?"

"Look at the surrounding topography. Two of the directions would be taking you uphill. The third would be farthest away from the acropolis. An entrance on the south side would be the strategic one."

"I understand. Knowing the dimensions of the Treasury of Atreus, can you gauge how far from this caved-in top I must go to hit the *dromos*?"

"Approximately. Start your trench forty feet from here. I'm going out a little bit to make sure you don't hit the side of the entrance itself. Your trench, when you get deep enough, should not be more than two or three feet from the triangle. At what you consider the right depth change your direction and head back at a right angle toward the treasury."

None of her experiences with her Hissarlik crew, which had resented being given orders by a woman, were repeated at Mycenae. Her workers were from Charvati, they had come into the Dases house on the first evening to welcome the Schliemanns to their village and had listened with pleasure to Henry's reading of *Agamemnon*. Henry had said to them:

"This treasury is going to be Kyria Schliemann's excavation. She will direct the work. Please do your best for her."

She sighted and then measured the distance Henry had indicated, told her eight men to start digging at the designated spot. She established the width of the trench by piling up small stones on either side of the submerged *dromos*, and gave them their southerly direction by laying out a line of mounded stones in lieu of the pegs and cord used at Hissarlik.

Any hope she had of making fast progress was soon dashed. The men found the soil hard and full of large blocks. During the long workday the diggers were able to penetrate only a few inches deep in the twenty-five-foot trench she needed to traverse the *dromos* and block walls lining the passage to the tomb.

She had not been working long when Stamatakes came on the double from the Lion Gate. He cried:

"You may not excavate this treasury!"

"Why not?"

"Neither you nor anyone else may remove this heavy blanket of earth. It is the force which is keeping the stones of the beehive securely locked together. Remove their impounding force and the entire stone structure may fall in."

"What makes you think I intend to tear down this entire hill? All I plan to do is to locate the *dromos*, clear it, find the entrance and then clear out the inside of the treasury itself, making it available for everyone to see, as the Treasury of Atreus is available. Isn't that what archaeology is about?"

"Kyria Schliemann, I spent years at the university making myself an expert. Why don't you let me be the authority on archaeology around here?"

"So I will . . . when I see the first set of calluses on your hands from wielding a pickax or a shovel."

"Ha! You resent the academician. You are being a snob because you happened to have dug at Hissarlik."

" 'Happened to have dug'! We excavated at Hissarlik because my husband had the genius to know that it was the site of Homer's Troy."

Stamatakes waved this away with a dismissing gesture of his arm. "I have little appetite for this contretemps, Kyria Schliemann. I will make a formal entry in my notebook that I have categorically ordered you to leave this treasury alone. I shall also cable the notation to Athens this evening."

"I'm sure the ride into Argos will do you good. In the meanwhile I am going to try to locate and clear the *dromos*. You're not afraid the clearing of the entrance passage will endanger the treasury?"

He turned and walked back toward the Lion Gate. Sophia sent one of her workmen to summon Henry. He observed:

"There's only one way to control Stamatakes, short of dropping him down this opening. I'll cable the Society this evening and ask them to send us an engineer of their choice, at my expense, who can examine the various structures and give us official sanction to go ahead."

Henry was having a problem outside the gate with the immensity of the stone blocks, some of them off the top of the inside cyclopean wall. He believed they had been cast down by the Mycenaeans themselves in their defense against the attacking Argives who had finally conquered Mycenae in 468 B.C. The debris he was digging through, he determined, was not the result of successive habitations as it had been in Troy, but rather had washed down from the upper terraces. It gave him little trouble but the huge stones could not be moved with the equipment he had at hand. He realized that he would have to bring out lifting machinery and the men to operate it. For the moment he contented himself with having his crew of twelve men rope the boulders and drag them inch by inch out of the way of the entrance to the Lion Gate, letting them lie against the massive outside cyclopean central walls.

By the end of the day neither he nor Sophia had found anything but a few scattered shards. Stamatakes, however, did not find these fragments unimportant. He gathered the tiniest bits in his basket and took them down to his storeroom in Charvati.

The third day was more rewarding. Demetrios's crew working inside the gate came upon the calcined remnants of a large dwelling house. His men dug down to expose the remaining walls. When Henry inspected the ruins he found that the house had been destroyed by a fire of such intensity that even the cyclopean wall which formed the rear of the house had been blackened. In the debris the workers found fine potsherds decorated with archaic designs in red, yellow and brown; a pottery cow's head with horns; most startling, an enormous iron key with four teeth.

"It could be the key to the Lion Gate!" Henry exclaimed.

Stamatakes, who was gobbling up the artifacts the instant they came out of the ground, said under his breath, "There he goes again, our 'enthusiast.' One key, and he is already opening the heavy wooden doors of the gate."

Henry was too busy to be bothered. In the debris he was finding coins, Hellenic and Macedonian terra cottas and fluted vases. Henry asked:

"Mr. Stamatakes, you have been trained in classical history. When do the historians say Mycenae ceased to be inhabited?"

"In 468 B.C. when the Argives conquered the bastion."

"But look here, we have just dug up Hellenic vases and Macedonian coins which are about two hundred years later."

Stamatakes stared at the coins and artifacts. Henry continued:

"There had to be later settlements. I would think both Hellenic and later Macedonian, from about 300 to 100 B.C. We know the place was desolate when Pausanias came through in A.D. 170. But these relics would indicate another couple of hundred years of life on this rock."

There was a faint gleam of respect in Stamatakes's eyes.

"Hellenic, yes. You've found enough pottery to indicate that. But Macedonian, no."

Henry subsided. He believed the fluted vases and terra-cotta figures corresponded with pieces from the Macedonian age he had seen in museums. But no need to push Stamatakes too far or too fast.

2.

The sun was scorching. There was dust, dirt, glare and not a blade of grass. The Bay of Nauplion was too far away for Henry's predawn swim. He missed it sorely. Dusk did not come until 9:00 P.M. Since they started work at five in the morning that meant a sixteen-hour workday with no one leaving the mound except for illness, of which there was little. It was a longer workday than they had experienced in Troy, but Sophia stood up to it well, fully clothed against the sting of the sun. Water was in short supply this late in the summer, with the creeks and wells dried up. However Ioanna Dases saved for the Schliemanns a few inches of the precious liquid for their nightly showers, after which Sophia put on a cool dress and Henry consented to shed his jacket before descending to the outdoor porch for a dinner of cold potato soup, chicken and a cold artichoke.

Henry and Sophia slipped comfortably into the family life of the Dases household. Since they were bringing work to every male over sixteen in this and the surrounding villages they were highly regarded as provisioners for a prosperous cash year ahead. Underlying the gratitude, which rarely bred affection, was the feeling in Charvati of mutual respect, which did breed affection. Henry and Sophia were good employers; they gave the men their instructions politely. The workmen, independent villagers and farmers, would not have liked needling or curt orders.

"There's only one disappointment," Henry observed to Sophia while they were sitting in the shade of an olive tree in the Dases garden; "it's our host, Demetrios. It was apparent from the beginning in Tiryns. He simply does not know how to co-ordinate the ongoing work, or make the best use of our tools. He is not only slowing us down, but he cannot come out as a contractor. I pay him one drachma for every meter of earth he moves. He has moved five hundred meters so far. This will earn him enough for his workmen but he will have little left over for himself. He will grow discouraged."

"Why not pay him a bonus at the end of the week, equal to what he expected to earn for himself? Are there workmen who appear faster or brighter than the others? Find a diplomatic way to break up Demetrios's crew and give the new group a different foreman."

"That's indicated. I'll assure Demetrios that his take will be as large. That should assuage any hurt feelings."

The one with the hardest lot was Panaghiotes Stamatakes. He had made it clear that he was dissatisfied with his accommodations as well as the food served. It was said that he considered himself superior to the people of Argolis. The workmen overheard his daily quarrels with Henry and Sophia, watched his attempts to close down the work at the Lion Gate and Sophia's treasury. Word spread that he was an obstructionist whose main objective appeared to be the limiting of the excavation . . . and consequently their sparse supply of outside cash. That made Stamatakes not only disliked but virtually an outcast. When he tried to give orders to the workmen, even when they were not against the Schliemanns, they turned a deaf ear. That was not to say that Stamatakes was about to lose his power of speech. He was at the Schliemanns all day long, protesting every aspect of their work as dangerous and unscientific.

It took a week before they made any important discoveries. Henry's was first, a small chamber immediately to the east of the Lion Gate, inside the acropolis. It was an ancient doorkeeper's post, four and a half feet high, the ceiling consisting of one huge slab of stone. The men cleared it out by the lunch hour, when Henry proudly displayed it to Sophia.

Demetrios's crew next uncovered several unmarked stone slabs five feet tall and three feet wide standing straight up in the earth, next to each other in a row, like a stone fence. They were heavy, difficult to move out of the ground, some eleven feet below the surface of the plateau, and once they had been taken out, what to do with them? Henry had found nothing like this at Troy; what was their purpose, their function?

When he showed them to Sophia, he said:

"They are probably without significance. I doubt that Stamatakes would want these plain slabs brought down to his storeroom. Better to leave them *in situ* until the whole of the acropolis is excavated. Then perhaps their meaning will emerge."

Sophia made her discovery the following day. The members of her crew were working toward one another from opposite sides of the trench, moving in an arch over the side walls of the *dromos*. After they had dug several feet deep, Sophia directed the men to turn and excavate in the direction of the treasury, where she hoped to find the top of the triangle. After digging several feet there was a cry from the workmen:

"Kyria Schliemann, it's here! We have found it."

She was only a few feet away, watching two workmen dump their debris over the side of the hill. She slid down into the trench, scrambled to its center, reached up and ran her fingers over the apex of the stone triangle which was used in all beehive constructions to lessen the weight on the lintel, as well as to house decorative or religious sculptures, such as the lions in the Lion Gate. Henry's projection of where she would find the main entrance of the treasury had been accurate. She marveled at his intuition, that divining rod which led him to Priam's palace, the treasure, the Scaean Gate, the paved road out to the Troad.

"It's a special gift," she thought.

Henry suppressed any desire to exult in his own omniscience.

"Well done, Sophidion. It took you only eight days to cut through this stone-packed earth. I'll send some more men over to you from Demetrios's crew. Go straight down now, and release as much of the triangle as you can. Then turn around and go backward on the entrance path. As you do, you will uncover more of the side walls of the *dromos*. Spill the earth over the downhill side, until you come to the end of the walls and reach the native soil of the long passage."

"*Doule sas,* your slave!"

During the next few days the crew working on the acropolis turned up a diorite ax, heads of Hera idols, thousands of fragments of beautifully decorated archaic vases painted with flowers, animals and birds in strange combinations: a horse with the head of a stork and the horns of a gazelle. They found goblets of white clay resembling those at a fifty-foot depth at Troy; others resembling the Bordeaux wineglasses of Troy.

Stamatakes shepherded every fragment into a series of baskets which the workmen took up to the Lion Gate where they were transferred to a horse cart and taken into Charvati under his eagle eye, and then locked in his storehouse.

"I've had enough of this nonsense," Henry told Sophia after dinner that night. "I have the right to see these objects and describe them in my journal. I'm going over to his house right now. . . ."

Sophia gave him a peck on the cheek. He kissed her eyelids.

"Go to sleep. You've been digging away at that *dromos* since five this morning."

She started for the stairs, turned.

"Do me one favor. Don't murder each other."

She did not hear Henry come in, nor did she awaken until he shook her shoulder at half past four.

"What time did you get back?" she asked with a yawn.

"At two."

"How did it go?"

"Badly, at first. He claimed I had no right to inspect the finds or describe them until they had been turned over to the Archaeological Society. I showed him my permit which says that I shall have the right of examination and description of all objects I bring to light. He insisted that clause meant 'examine and describe' in Athens. I stood my ground and he finally agreed. We worked for four hours. Actually, he became co-operative, sometimes wiping incrustations off objects I could not see clearly enough to describe."

"Glory to the Holy Virgin! But you have had only two and a half hours' sleep. You can't do that and work out in that broiling sun for sixteen hours."

"I'll sleep at home this winter. I told Stamatakes we would have to work every night until we caught up. He replied, 'It will be at the expense of my health!' "

Sophia felt a pang of pity for Stamatakes.

"He's doing a job he doesn't like, in a place he doesn't want to be," she said quietly. "You can't expect him to keep up with a man who is going to excavate Mycenae so thoroughly that in the years to come his name will be identified with Atreus, Agamemnon, Clytemnestra, Aegisthus. Stamatakes is working in August 1876. You're working in 1200 B.C. Think of the unfair advantage that gives you over that poor lad!"

Henry continued to uncover uprights of unpolished white stone. He now assumed they were tombstones. He had not yet dug deep enough to know what the tombs contained or whether they were there at all. It was on August 19 that he made his first momentous discovery, though he was puzzled and confused about its nature. Some twenty to thirty feet south of the cyclopean house his men uncovered two large undoubtable tombstones carved with bas-reliefs. They stood a foot apart on a line from north to south. Henry summoned Sophia, as he had at Troy when he came upon a major find. Stamatakes stood off at a distance, his expression saying, "I'm not worried, those slabs are too large for you to steal."

"What have you come upon, Henry, a cemetery?" Sophia asked.

"Perhaps. But is it the one we are looking for . . . ?"

The northernmost tombstone was of a soft calcareous stone, four feet high and six inches thick. The top was cracked and broken, but the bottom half was so well preserved that Henry could trace a carved hunting scene with a hunter standing in a chariot holding the reins in one hand and a broad sword in the other.

"Look, Sophidion, how the outstretched legs of the horse show his great speed. Here is his dog chasing a flying deer. These decorations must have symbolic significance: the ovals, spirals, this row of letters behind the chariot . . ."

". . . letters? Do we have our first evidence of the Mycenaean language?"

"Too early to tell. They may be nothing more than ornamentation."

The second of what Henry called "sepulchral stelae" was only one foot away, six feet high and in a much better state of preservation. The upper half was also filled with linear decorations; on the bottom half was carved a warrior in a seated position. In his left hand he held an unsheathed sword, in the right, a lance so long that it ended at the stallion's head. At the head of the horse stood a second, naked, warrior, who held in his hand a double-edged sword.

"My dear, this stone gives us a unique and precious specimen of the Homeric chariot. It does not form a semicircle as we were led to imagine from the sculptures of classical antiquity, or from the ancient chariot that is preserved in the Munich Museum. It is quadrangular in form, and the chariot-box is fastened onto it just as *The Iliad* says: 'When she had thus spoken swift-footed Iris departed; but the king bade his sons make ready the light-running mule wagon, and bind the wicker box thereon.' These stelae are the first clues we've had that we are approaching Agamemnon's Mycenae. The sculptured slabs should be of the same epoch as the lions over the gate."

Panaghiotes Stamatakes was completely unpredictable. When Henry asked for permission to take to the Dases house certain interesting finds, Stamatakes agreed in a pleasant manner, although he obliged Henry to sign a receipt for every piece he took home with him. However the very next day, when he found that Sophia had split her crew, one half digging straight down to the lintel at the base of the broad triangle, the other digging and carrying out the solid fill of earth which had totally covered the *dromos*, he flew into a rage. As the crews progressed, the façade of the treasury, made of handsomely hewn stones, began to emerge into the same shimmering heat waves and clear dry air it had known when the master masons constructed it thousands of years before. Stamatakes cried:

"Stop! Stop all work immediately!"

The workmen leaned on their shovels.

"Whatever are you screaming about, Mr. Stamatakes?" asked Sophia.

"I'm not screaming. I'm just ordering in the simplest possible terms that no more earth be removed from this façade. I'll have to insist that the men bring back the earth they have dumped, and cover those stones again."

Sophia was shocked. She forgot that only a few days before she had felt sorry for the hapless young man.

"Mr. Stamatakes, have you had too much sun? You know that the archaeologist's job is to uncover, to free the antiquities, not to cover them."

Stamatakes shouted in a voice so loud that even Henry's crews working on the acropolis could hear.

"You an archaeologist? Don't make me laugh. You're just a Greek housewife who has lost her bearings and forgotten her proper place in life!"

"And you are a perfect Greek gentleman and scholar."

"I am immune to your insults. Look at these wall-stones you have exposed. They cannot stand this sudden exposure after being buried under damp soil for thousands of years. They will crumble and fall away."

"Oh, come, Stamatakes," she said, shaking her head angrily, "look at the façade of the Treasury of Atreus. It has not crumbled since Veli Pasha exposed it more than fifty years ago."

Stamatakes's tanned skin grew white under the 120° Mycenaean sun.

"Kyria Schliemann," he said coldly, "I've done my best to be polite to you. I order you to cover this wall to its very top. I will summon an engineer to examine the masonry binding the stones."

"I have already examined the masonry. Though it is only earth it has set as solid as cement."

"*You* have examined the masonry! What presumption . . ."

He was now beyond control. Sophia could no longer follow what he said. The tirade lasted for about ten minutes. She did not attempt to stop him. Henry had heard the shouting from the inside of the Lion Gate; he made his way across the rubbled field, arriving in time to hear the last part of the outburst. Stamatakes was exhausted and panting for breath.

Sophia addressed her husband, making no effort to keep Stamatakes from hearing:

"I think I had better go back to Charvati and write a letter to the Greek Archaeological Society asking that this man be recalled. When I tell them about his senseless obstructionism, the rudeness he has heaped upon my head, I'm sure this wretch will get his wish and spend the rest of the summer at the seashore."

"I approve," said Henry quietly. "I'll take your crew up on the acropolis to work with me. There is a horse cart standing idle. The driver will take you home. We'll stop work on the treasury until the engineer I have requested arrives, or we hear from the Society."

He now turned to Stamatakes and said in an undertone as lethal as the edge of a fine-honed dagger:

"If you ever go within ten feet of my wife again I will cut your balls off!"

Stamatakes was a man of conviction who had through some inexplicable twist of fate found himself in a broiling inferno with a couple of Tatars on his well-manicured hands. He tangled with Henry the following morning when he saw Henry's crew digging away the thick crust outside the Lion Gate in an attempt to lower the debris level and establish a better road for the horse carts. Henry was carefully avoiding the cyclopean walls. Stamatakes cried:

"You may not move another shovelful of earth. You will weaken the support near the gate, and the two lions may fall and be smashed!"

"I am watching every massive block. There has been no more movement in these past two weeks than there has been since the fall of Mycenae."

Stamatakes ignored him.

"I shut down the work at the treasury yesterday, and I am shutting you down this very moment. You've said you plan to discover the royal tombs. Why don't you get on with your folly? Once you have taken the whole of the acropolis down to native soil, then perhaps we can all leave this God-forsaken spot."

Henry was silent for a considerable time. He was beginning to understand the real difference between the academician with his romantic and theoretical interests, his timid turning of the pages of books, and the archaeologist who dug in the field, with its discomfort and disappointment, its need for courageous decision, its tremendous excitement of discovery.

"If I refuse to follow your instructions?" he asked.

"I will promptly telegraph the Archaeological Society to have your permit revoked. That would cut *your* balls off!"

Henry did not believe that Stamatakes could do this, but the permit and the dig were too vital for him to take the chance.

"Very well. I'll confine the work to digging inside the acropolis until an engineer arrives."

Sophia included this second work stoppage in her complaint to Athens.

With the work on the treasury and Lion Gate closed down, Henry started a second trench two hundred feet southwest of the gate. He now had a full complement of one hundred and twenty-five workmen. The largest of the crews came upon the walls of a massive building with many rooms. The more distant crew came upon a situation which Henry had faced many times in Troy: a wall superimposed on top of another wall. After close examination Henry decided that the top wall was part of a Roman fortification. This structure, in Henry's book of history, was a recent one and did not interest him. There was a possibility that the wall beneath it was sufficiently ancient to belong to the Mycenaean settlement. Since he was excavating to discover the prehistory of Mycenae, it was the bottom wall that was valuable to him.

"What shall I do, Doctor?" asked one of the foremen. "Work around it or tear it down?"

"Tear it down."

Stamatakes scrambled down the side of the hill.

"Don't touch one single stone."

The workmen stopped, looked to Henry for their orders. Henry said calmly:

"It's of little importance. A *nouveau arrivé*, one of the last."

"It's of no importance to you!" Stamatakes cried. "You destroy everything in your path. But all antiquities are valuable to archaeologists. I forbid you to touch these walls."

Henry shrugged. He turned to his men:

"Dig around the walls."

The next morning Stamatakes overslept. By the time he reached the digs Henry's crew had pulled down the Roman wall and exposed the lower one. Henry left Sophia to supervise the excavations while he worked with the other half of his crew, who were excavating beyond the large house they had uncovered, searching for other buildings.

Stamatakes stared at the rocks of the destroyed Roman wall. When he spoke to Sophia his voice was without inflection.

"Kyria Schliemann, I expressly forbade your husband to tear down that wall."

Sophia replied in an equally quiet voice:

"Mr. Stamatakes, my husband is a learned man. The Roman wall was interfering with the progress of his work. You are not an experienced man. Dr. Schliemann is also an excitable man; he will terminate the excavation if you block him at every point."

"Your husband would demolish everything in order to lay bare the Mycenaean walls. He looks upon Greek or Roman vases with disgust. He treats me as if I were a barbarian. I too will cable to the Minister of Public Instruction and suggest that if he is not satisfied with me I be recalled."

Stamatakes went into Argos to send his telegram to Athens.

The following day, Sunday, the prefect of Argos arrived in the village of Charvati. He had a telegram with him from the Minister of Public Instruction which he showed to Stamatakes:

GO YOURSELF AT ONCE TO MYCENAE AND TELL STAMATAKES THAT HE MUST NOT PERMIT ANY WALLS WHATEVER TO BE PULLED DOWN, FROM WHATEVER PERIOD THEY DATE. ALSO EXCAVATIONS MUST NOT BE MADE IN SEVERAL PLACES AT ONCE, IN ORDER TO MAKE RELIABLE SUPERVISION POSSIBLE. THE NUMBER OF WORK- MEN MUST BE LIMITED. THE EPHOR IS RESPONSIBLE FOR ANY IN- FRINGEMENT OF THESE PROVISIONS.

The prefect summoned Henry and Sophia to the house of the mayor of Charvati, Panaghiotes Nesos. He informed the Schliemanns of the content of the telegram, then asked them all to go with him up to the citadel and tell him what work was to be done. Henry rejected the suggestion. He was trembling with ill-suppressed anger.

"I do not acknowledge Stamatakes's reading of the document I signed. No one has this matter so much at heart as I, and no one is so anxious about the excavation as I. To no one is it so sacred. No one else has been troubled about its protection and preservation or invested his time and money in it. This is the end. I shall shut down the entire dig."

Henry and Sophia ate no supper that night. They went up to their rooms despondent. The office was hot from the penetration of the setting sun. Henry paced the floor erratically. Sophia put on a cool nightgown, then slumped in a chair watching him. It took some time, but he stopped and, wheeling about the room, stood directly in front of her.

"I guess I have to make it up with Stamatakes . . ."

"Yes, you must."

"We can't abandon the excavation in which we are uncovering such wonderful things. . . ."

"I agree with you."

"Then what shall I do?"

"Swallow your pride, go across the road, reconcile with him."

"I will do it. Early tomorrow morning I will ride into Argos and inform the prefect that the work will go on."

3.

Continuing his work on the acropolis, Henry unearthed another dozen upright stone slabs relating to each other on a wide curving line. By now a pattern had begun to emerge, an inside row of uprights standing three feet in front of the back row within the curve. Scattered around the tall uprights were three-foot tablets, also unadorned, which apparently related to the uprights.

"There was a circular structure here," Henry said; "I think that in the next few weeks, as we find more of the uprights, they may constitute a closed circle."

The same day he uncovered two more sculptured sepulchral stelae which were so certainly tombstones as to throw doubt on the curving line of uprights. The additional tombstones were in a direct line with the two he had found earlier. Measuring them, he found them to be approximately four feet wide and over four feet tall. On the first there was the carving of a man in a chariot drawn by a horse, of which he held the reins. Another man stood before the horse, appearing to oppose its progress; he held in his hand a long lance which he seemed to thrust into the body of the man in the chariot. Both men were naked.

The second stone was found some ten feet farther south. This had a broad border on the right and left; the remaining space was divided into three vertical compartments of equal size which reached down to more than half the height of the stone. The side compartments contained a broad waving pattern like the coils of a serpent.

At dawn the next day, a Sunday, Henry excused himself from church services and went by horseback into Nauplion. He had developed a tapeworm, or so the Dases family said when they heard the symptoms: abdominal discomfort similar to an acute appendicitis; spasms and cramping, loss of appetite, some nausea. Henry's lifetime philosophy about illness was, "Ignore it, and it will go away." This time he was hopeful of finding some medicine in a Nauplion pharmacy that would expel the parasitic creature.

He also intended to visit a painter whose name and address he had secured, who might be willing to do at Mycenae what Polychronios Lempesses had done at Troy. Perikles Komnenos and Henry quickly agreed on salary. Komnenos would stay at the dig at least a month if his services were needed. He packed a painting kit with materials, threw a few articles of clothing into a canvas bag and returned with Henry to Charvati. Henry had not, however, found any medicine to cure his tapeworm.

On Monday morning Perikles Komnenos took his materials up to the dig and began painting copies of the four tombstones, not only the chariots, horses, hunters and warriors, but also the linear designs.

Sophia received a reply to her letter to Athens. It was from their friend Professor Euthymios Kastorches, who had been their companion for the week at Tiryns. It was with great sorrow that he had received her letter and it was difficult to judge from afar whether Stamatakes was right or not. As, however, he was the representative of the government and they had not another to send, he begged "my lady Sophia to have the patience to humor the man for the sake of science and of Greece. He is an unavoidable evil." Kastorches had also written to Stamatakes.

She hoped that his letter would urge Stamatakes to give the Schliemanns more latitude in their work. With Henry's assent she took her crew up to the entrance wall of the treasury. While lowering the level and hauling off the earth and debris she found ancient painted pottery with geometrical patterns, rude terra-cotta idols of Hera in the female and cow forms.

Stamatakes did not stop her. Instead he watched her workmen closely and gathered the terra cottas into his baskets. Sophia now had thirty workmen. This enabled her to unearth the triangle and the facing of the treasury down to the stone lintel, as well as dig out the enormous amount of earth with which the one-hundred-and-twenty-foot-long *dromos* had been covered.

Henry did not resume work at the Lion Gate. Instead he had his crew concentrated on a newly discovered wall made up of small stones, and apparently of considerable depth, circular, similar to the curve of the stone slabs of which he had by now unearthed close to fifty. The relationship of the curved ancient wall to the curved ancient uprights was inexplicable despite the fact that part of the uprights were found on top of the curving wall. They appeared to make up about a third part of a full circle.

Perikles Komnenos, when he had finished painting the tombstones, turned his attention to the vases, terra cottas, idols, weaponry and figures of animals. To lessen the work hours of Stamatakes, both Henry and Sophia left the digs in charge of their foremen about two hours before quitting time and went with Stamatakes to his storehouse in the village, taking Komnenos with them. For a short while they were able to relive the happy evenings at Hissarlik when they had cleaned, sketched, described and numbered each artifact for Henry's journal. They returned to the Dases house for dinner, after which they went up to their office and Henry began writing his articles for the London *Times*. Sophia copied each page of the article as Henry finished it so that they could have a complete record on hand. For her own part she began a series for the Athens *Ephimeris*, a daily paper which had expressed an interest in some articles. Henry too sent telegrams to the *Ephimeris*.

Then at the foot of the first sculptured tombstone Henry unearthed black ashes. Among them was a large button of wood covered with a thick leaf of gold on which was engraved a circle, a triangle and three knives. He cried to Sophia:

"Our first gold of Mycenae. . . ."

Sophia turned the button over in her hands as he went on.

"Remember when we found the first gold in Troy, the gold earring in the midst of that lump of burned metal? We were so excited we hardly slept that night. I am strongly tempted to pocket this gold button but I shall restrain myself."

As he dug under the feet of the tombstones he began to find gray ash. At first he assumed that the ashes were from the cremation of human bodies; however he found only animal bones among them and decided they were the result of religious sacrifices.

He continued to uncover more sculptured stelae, the most interesting of which represented a naked boy who had been standing on a chariot although that part of the stone had been broken off. The boy held the reins in his left hand, his right hand was stretched straight ahead of him. Henry was both elated and unsettled. He had never seen figures or ornamentation such as these in Greek sculpture.

"I think they may be unique," he suggested to Sophia; "but this time I am not going to be accused of amateur enthusiasm. We are going to let the Archaeological Society make the decision."

He was having equally good results in the large cyclopean house on the north of his second trench where he was excavating seventeen feet below the plateau. He found ashes of wood and animal matter intermixed with bones, largely of swine, and thousands of fragments of painted archaic vases, molds for casting jewelry, a treasure of bronze objects including knives, wheels, lances, double-edged hatchets, hairpins; gems of steatite, onyx and agate decorated with intaglios of animals, the most beautiful of which was of red onyx showing an antelope authentically carved from nature.

By now he had cleared enough of the small stone wall and additional stone uprights to be certain that they would constitute a full circle. He also came to understand that, since the acropolis had originally sloped sharply downhill from the Lion Gate, the circular wall had been built up and the area filled with earth. One of the purposes was undoubtedly to make it possible for the unsculptured slabs to stand level and upright.

Sitting in the upstairs office making her entries in the cost journal, Sophia noted that they had already invested twenty thousand dollars in the dig. She put down her pencil and turned to Henry.

"Henry, about that cemetery circle . . . Can the royal tombs be below where you are digging? So close to the Lion Gate?"

"My interpretation of Pausanias is that he actually saw the royal tombs," he replied pensively. "He could not have seen the tombstones we have unearthed because I assume they were already covered by some twelve to fourteen feet of earth and debris washed down from the mountainside. It follows that if Pausanias did not see our tombstones, then they could not have been any part of the royal tombs."

In the first third of September Sophia and her crew uncovered the complete facing of the treasury straight down to the lintel. Her work was expedited by the two horse carts Henry provided her which moved out the debris of the *dromos* at a quickening pace. Now her task was to dig straight down to the native earth so that they could locate the threshold. By this time they had cleared away enough of the debris to learn that their treasury would be nearly as large as the Treasury of Atreus, the entrance road as long and as wide.

Henry studied her progress.

"As long as the treasuries served as storehouses for the wealth of the early kings the entrances must have been accessible to the royal family. The question arises, when were the *dromos* and the gate hidden under these tremendous masses of debris? When the king died did they bury him along with his treasure? Or had they disbursed it? Were they tomb treasuries?"

"It would help to know whose tomb it was," replied Sophia. "Some of the painted geometric patterns I am finding resemble the Attic vases which are considered the most ancient terra cottas in Greece. Doesn't that mean that the *dromos* must have been filled and hidden in remote antiquity?"

By the time she had the lintel completely exposed and had measured the triangle, which was better than six feet wide at its base and more than ten feet tall, she found on the lintel and the jutting stone above evidence of decorations which would have adorned the entrance. It was her hope that, once her men had cleared the entrance and she could get into the beehive itself, she would come upon these ancient sculptures.

As they approached mid-September the sun was relentless; a tempest blew dust into their eyes, severely inflaming them. Sophia adopted the Turkish *yashmak*, which gave her face moderate protection. Henry, who was suffering more each day from his growing tapeworm, found relief in hyperbole. In the notes for his planned book on Mycenae, he wrote:

"In spite of these annoyances, nothing more interesting can be imagined than the excavation of a prehistoric city of immortal glory, where nearly every object, even to the fragments of pottery, reveals a new page of history."

The blessed truce with Stamatakes which had existed since the exchange of letters blew up when Sophia came across three rows of stone steps extending across the width of her *dromos*. Henry guessed they were the steps of a Hellenic villa.

"Henry, I'm going to have to remove these steps if we are going to clear out the entrance approach."

"Of course. Have the stones carefully piled so we can check their age and workmanship."

Stamatakes came flying, the old expression of fury on his face. He shouted:

"You workmen! Stop all of your digging! Stand aside from these steps. They are an antiquity. They must be preserved."

Sophia had no desire for another shouting match. She said quietly:

"Mr. Stamatakes, how do you suggest that we preserve these steps? They must be removed if we are to open up the *dromos*."

His eyes flashed.

"I will take them out. I will preserve them. I will tunnel under them and at the proper moment remove them intact so that we can place them elsewhere."

"Stamatakes, there is no way to tunnel under those rows of stone. They will fall in on you. Why not let Kyria Schliemann remove them and have the workmen set them up in proper order in another spot?"

"Absolutely no! In order for Kyria Schliemann's men to move these steps they will have to break them up. That will destroy their value. I will move them whole. You saw my instructions. I am to preserve all ancient monuments."

He walked away. After a reflective pause Sophia asked:

"What do we do now?"

"Yesterday your mother wrote that Andromache had a cold. You said you wished you could go back to Athens for a few days to take care of the child . . ."

"I said I would feel more comfortable if I were there with Andromache . . ."

". . . I will take you into Nauplion this afternoon. You can catch tomorrow's boat back to Piraeus. In Athens please find time to go to see the Minister of Public Instruction and our friend Kastorches at the Archaeological Society. Have Stamatakes released, since he thinks he is in prison here anyway. And in the name of God, anybody's god, get them to send us an engineer!"

August spreads a wool blanket of heat over dusty Athens; by September the sun covering had been reduced to a linen sheet. As her carriage pulled up the hill beneath the Parthenon she breathed in the fragrant air, so reviving after the heat and glare of Mycenae. Turning into familiar Mousson Street, her mind went back to her several returns from Troy. Was a pattern emerging for the rest of her life? After Troy, Mycenae; after Mycenae, Tiryns; after Tiryns, Orchomenos. After Orchomenos . . . where?

Madame Victoria had been slowed down by rheumatism but she had watched lovingly over Andromache. The five-year-old child still had a remnant of fever. After their happy reunion, Spyros confided:

"It's not the cold that bothers her. Andromache has been very sad from longing for you."

Sophia was crushed by the implication that she had been neglecting her daughter. Yet did not a wife have to choose sometimes between her duty to her husband and to her child? When the cold had completely disappeared, she took Andromache into her own bed to sleep at night, which Andromache adored.

"Mama, you won't go back to Mycenae, will you?"

"Yes, dear, I must, though only for a few weeks, until the rains come. But next year we'll take you with us. There are plenty of Dases children for you to play with."

Andromache clapped her hands with delight.

At the first opportunity Sophia went to see Dr. Skiadaresses, who gave her a prescription of oleoresin of aspidium for Henry's tapeworm, to be followed by castor oil. She had the prescription filled and sent Spyros to Piraeus so that it would be on the next ship for Nauplion. A couple of days later she received a telegram:

TAPEWORM GONE. ALL FORTY FEET OF IT. FEELING BETTER.

Sophia found Athens greatly exercised over the situation in the Greek districts still under the Turks, especially Thessaly. Bands of Circassians, who were fleeing the Russians, were settling in these northern areas and were reported to be killing and violating the Greek residents. Demonstrations were organized in which angry cries were heard:

"Prepare for war!"

Spyros and her younger brother Panaghiotes, almost ready to enter the university, took her to a late afternoon protest meeting on the Pnyx, where they joined eight thousand Athenians to listen to university professors exhort the crowd to a fever pitch of patriotism against the Turks. Through her mind flitted the irreverent thought that Henry would never be able to return to Troy to finish his work. Yet as she read the newspapers, which she had not seen for many weeks, she realized that there would be no war; Turkey was already engaged in a civil war, with its districts of Bosnia and Herzegovina in revolt against the Sultan.

She caught up with the family news as well, learned that Panaghiotes had decided to study archaeology so that he could work with his brother-in-law. Spyros went over Henry's account books with her, and she extended Henry's invitation to him to come back with her to Mycenae and serve as foreman of one of the crews.

She discovered that her articles in *Ephimeris* had been well received. Her manner was more restrained than Henry's; she did no theorizing or projecting of ideas which classical scholars could quarrel with. It was the first time that a woman had written about an archaeological excavation; the Greek men forgave her only because she was married to Dr. Henry Schliemann. She sent a note to Georgios Milesses, Minister of Public Instruction and an acquaintance of the Engastromenos family. Milesses answered by return messenger, saying he would be happy to receive her the following morning at ten.

She dressed with special care, wearing a rose taffeta suit dress with its blouse and trim at the bottom of the ankle-length skirt of white satin. The white satin of the slim neckband set off the deep Argolid tan of her smooth rose and olive skin, yet made her appear sedate and older than her twenty-four years.

Georgios Milesses was a plain-looking, plain-spoken man who had served for years in the Parliament as a deputy of the district of Kranidion in the Peloponnesus. He had visited Mycenae a number of times and could visualize the Lion Gate, the citadel within the cyclopean walls, the terraced mountain above.

"I understand you are having difficulties with Ephor Stamatakes," he said in a voice which took no sides.

"Yes. I wish to speak in moderate terms about Ephor Stamatakes, yet at the same time make it clear that life at Mycenae has been a series of crises and impasses. The highly productive work at the Lion Gate and the treasury . . ."

". . . I have long hoped to see them excavated!"

". . . is at a standstill. If only we could have an older and more experienced man who would not constantly be frightened at our making a mistake which might cost him his job."

Georgios Milesses wheeled about in his chair with his back to his guest. When he faced Sophia again his plainness of feature was enlivened by a sheen of authority.

"Ephor Stamatakes did a good job of supervising the building of the museum at Sparta. As one of our three new inspectors of archaeology, his supervision of the excavations at Delos was satisfactory. He has ap-

parently been guilty of overzealousness, even as your husband has sometimes been guilty of overimpetuousness."

"Then there is no chance of having him replaced?" Her voice was
freighted with distress.

"I think you would be unhappy later if you injured this earnest young
man's career. However if you will give me a few moments I will write
to Ephor Stamatakes, asking him to use more restraint in dealing with
you. I will also ask him to have more confidence in Dr. Schliemann's
archaeological judgment."

The next morning she went to visit Euthymios Kastorches, a member of the council of the Archaeological Society. For this visit she wore
a pretty silk dress trimmed with laces. Here she changed her angle of
attack: foreshortening the story of her difficulties with Stamatakes and
stressing their need for an engineer who would give them a professional
view of what they might and might not safely excavate.

"I agree, Kyria Schliemann, that that is the proper solution. An engineer friend of mine, Charilaos Souïdas, has just returned from his summer home in Corfu. I will persuade him to take the next ship out of
Piraeus for Nauplion."

The tears of gratitude in her eyes were more than enough thanks for
Euthymios Kastorches.

A few days later she received a telegram from Henry:

THE ENGINEER CHARILAOS SOUÏDAS TO MY JOY FOUND THE WALLS
OF THE TREASURY SOLID ENOUGH AND IS OF THE OPINION THAT
THE LION GATE CAN BE CLEARED. BRAVO TO YOU FROM AN ADOR-
ING HUSBAND.

Two days later a second telegram arrived:

ARGOS SEPT. 30, 1876
NO EXCAVATION IS TO CONTINUE WITHOUT YOUR SUPERVISION. I
EXPECT YOU BY ALL MEANS IN NAUPLION NEXT MONDAY OR ELSE
I DIE. SCHLIEMANN

She read it a second time, then burst into laughter.

She prepared to leave for Nauplion, albeit slowly, for she was reluctant to part from Andromache so soon. It proved to be good fortune
that she procrastinated, for she received yet another telegram:

REMAIN IN ATHENS. THE OTTOMAN GOVERNMENT HAS REQUESTED
THAT I RETURN TO TROY TO EXPLAIN THE EXCAVATIONS TO HIS MAJ-
ESTY DOM PEDRO OF BRAZIL.

Henry's trip to Troy gave Sophia another three weeks to be with her
daughter. Henry was back in Athens on October 21 to report on his

visit and to take her back to Mycenae. The dig at Troy had been totally neglected since his last frustrating attempt to clear out the trenches and channels; nevertheless His Majesty Dom Pedro had been fascinated by the excavations, following Henry's tour with a copy of Homer in his hand. The Turkish government had appeared to be grateful.

Sophia assured Andromache that she and Henry would be home soon. Spyros packed to return with them.

4.

The rains started the day after their return. By dawn the area was drenched. Henry took Sophia to Stamatakes's house to show her his finds during her weeks of absence. Stamatakes, who had been refreshed by the three-week reprieve, preceded them across the back yard and opened the locked door. It was dark and musty inside.

Henry was proudest of a vase fragment on which six fully armed warriors were setting out on a military expedition. They wore coats of mail that reached from the neck to below the hips.

"This should be an accurate portrait of the fighting men Agamemnon took with him to Troy."

When they emerged from the storehouse the rain had lightened considerably. Henry suggested they put on their heavy boots and ask one of the Dases boys to drive them up to the dig in the family wagon.

They stopped along the road and walked across the field to the treasury. Henry guided her to the beginning of the *dromos*. Instantly she saw that he had cleared a path as wide as the entrance gate itself, and dug down some eight feet.

"I see you got Stamatakes's permission to remove the steps."

"Not on your life. He was positive he could tunnel under them but once he made his tunnel they fell in. I had them hauled to one side."

He estimated they had another ten feet to go before striking the native earth of the *dromos*. He had also cleared out a portion of the thirteen-foot-thick entrance tunnel.

"I wanted *you* to make the breakthrough into the beehive itself; after all, this is your special excavation. Spyros can help you clear out the rest. You should be the first to enter the treasury."

"It will be an exciting moment for me," she confessed. "Has there been anyone inside since it was covered over?"

"Only if Veli Pasha or an earlier tomb robber lowered himself on a rope," replied Henry.

They recrossed the field, got into the Dases wagon and rode up to the Lion Gate. Henry had reduced the level of the roadway and cleared a six-foot-wide opening through the gate entrance. However he had not yet reached the threshold. On either side of the gate stood a tremendous block of debris, untouched, *in situ*. When Sophia asked why he had not moved more of this material he replied with annoyance:

"The Greek Archaeological Society forced me to leave it this way. They have promised to send a second engineer who will secure the two lions with cramp irons."

He linked his arm through hers and for the first time they walked together through the gate into the citadel, the flat area of which he considered to be the agora, not in the sense of it being a market place but rather a meeting place built upon an ancient cemetery.

"Pausanias writes that in Megara they built it so 'in order that they might have the tomb of the heroes within the place for council.'"

He had dug down some twelve feet in this agora at what looked like promising spots. He also had his first clue as to the function of the upright stone slabs.

"I know from Sophocles's *Oedipus Tyrannus* that some agoras were circular: 'Artemis who sits on the Agora's glorious circular seat.' Euripides speaks of the 'circle of the agora' in his play *Orestes*. I have found several of these sets of stone blocks, one in front of the other, with a cross slab between. That's what leads me to believe they may have been used as benches for the council."

He took her for a closer inspection of the four sites he had been digging: two areas marked by sculptured tombstones, the other two containing unsculptured slabs.

"Under these stones there should be tombs. I will work this area."

He showed her through what he now believed to be the royal palace, seven exposed chambers, the largest of which was thirteen by eighteen feet. Having been taken to the top of the mountain on their earliest visit and envisioned the outside court where Atreus liked to sit and look across to his Treasury, Sophia had doubts about this collection of rooms being the palace of Atreus and Agamemnon. She said nothing; she had known Henry to change his mind, sometimes in the middle of an entry in his journal. After all, he was groping in the darkness of prehistory for understandings few men had attempted before.

They returned to the Dases house to get into dry clothing. There was a telegram awaiting them; Emperor Dom Pedro and his entourage would arrive on Sunday morning for a visit to the excavation. They would be coming from Corinth.

"If the royal party is going to be here for most of Sunday, it would be proper for us to provide their dinner," commented Sophia.

"But there is no room in Charvati large enough to hold such a party," said Henry. "Why don't we do something unheard of . . . clean out the

Treasury of Atreus, set up tables there and serve the dinner by candle-light?"

She clapped her hands with delight the way Andromache did.

"Bizarre! And from what you have told me about the Emperor it will be an unforgettable experience for him. You can clear out the Treasury. I will draw up the menu and ask the Dases women to prepare the dinner."

Henry promptly sent one of the Dases boys into Argos to post a tele-gram to Bishop Theokletos Vimpos, inviting him to come to Mycenae to say Mass and have dinner with Emperor Dom Pedro. It was a half day's ride but Henry was so confident that Vimpos would come that he engaged quarters for him at the mayor's house in Charvati.

Bishop Vimpos arrived on Saturday. Henry and Sophia took him up the hill to the Treasury of Atreus. He was fascinated by the architecture, the twenty-foot-wide entrance to the opening which soared to a height of eighteen feet and was topped by two huge slabs of skillfully cut and polished stone. They took him into the main chamber, fifty feet high and fifty feet wide. The only light filtered in from the open gateway. Henry explained:

"This dome is built of well-wrought blocks of hard breccia placed in regular layers and joined with the greatest precision without any bind-ing material. From the fourth course of stones upward you will see in each stone two bored holes, and in many of them remnants of bronze nails. These nails had broad flat heads and can have had no other pur-pose than to retain the bronze plates with which the whole interior was once decorated. Homer says:

> "'Like the sun or the moonbeam in bright splendor, so beamed the high palace of the magnanimous Alcinous; for the brazen walls extended from the threshold of the gate to the innermost part of the building; their entablature was of blue steel.'"

Vimpos drew in a long breath, let it out, exclaimed:

"It's magnificent! But why do you show me this before your own findings?"

Henry chuckled. "Time for that later. I had two motives in bringing you here. First to tell you that this is where you will be having dinner with Emperor Dom Pedro of Brazil tomorrow. Second, to ask whether it would be possible for you to hold Mass here tomorrow morning when the Emperor arrives. The entire village is of course determined to be present and our chapel in Charvati is too tiny to hold but a fraction of them."

Bishop Vimpos's eyes roamed to a dark chamber on his right, entirely

cut out of rock. It was pitch-black, the floor covered with four feet of
the detritus of bats' dung. Henry had dug through some of this and
found a large bowl, two feet deep, and near it a calcareous stone monument. He suspected that the side chamber had been used for religious
sacrifices. He did not mention this.

"You want me to hold Mass in a treasury or tomb inhabited by ancient gods?"

"If it is possible."

"Oh, it is possible. I have altar cloth, special candles, wine chalice,
incense burner and the bowl for the holy water. But would it be fitting
or proper?"

Henry and Sophia remained silent.

"What was the religion of Mycenae?"

"Polytheism."

"I wrote you a letter after I had finished your *Trojan Antiquities* urging you to pay less attention to pagan gods and more to Christianity."

"I chose not to remember that letter. It was not worthy of our friendship."

Vimpos blushed.

"I accept the rebuke. I shall make up for it by saying Mass here tomorrow morning. Christ is mightier than Zeus. Tomorrow I shall sanctify this pagan tomb and convert it into a cathedral."

Dom Pedro and his party arrived at midmorning. The prefect of
Argos and the police chief of Nauplion were not far behind. The Schliemanns were pleased to find as the official guide for the Emperor their
old friend Stephanos Koumanoudes, the philologist from the university
and secretary of the Archaeological Society who had saved so many of
the antiquities in Athens: the Dionysus Theater, the Stoa of Attalus.
Dom Pedro had the heroic head and barrel chest of a Roman senator.
His bountiful white full-face beard was as soft as silk; he had a full stand
of slightly darker white hair. His was the visage of a nobleman, thanks
to the wide-spaced, compassionately expressive dark eyes.

Now fifty, Dom Pedro had been crowned Emperor of Brazil when
only fifteen. He had become known in South America for his "conscientious and enlightened rule." He had prohibited the slave trade in 1850
and five years before had emancipated all slaves in Brazil. He brought
about public improvements, fostered education, was an earnest patron
of the arts and sciences. What endeared him most to Henry was that
he knew Homer by heart, had studied Henry's book on Troy and had
himself requested of the Turkish government that Dr. Schliemann show
him the excavations there. Like Henry, he was an enthusiast; he loved
to come up with ideas, opinions, theories . . . particularly about
archaeology.

Dom Pedro and his friends were taken to the Treasury of Atreus in carriages which Henry had ordered from Argos. The entire village followed on foot, winding up the curving road as though on a pilgrimage. Bishop Vimpos was standing behind an improvised altar; a candle on either end gleamed on the purple altar cloth. The Treasury was beautiful in the flickering light. Henry led the Brazilians to a position immediately in front of the altar. The Schliemanns, Spyros, Stamatakes and Koumanoudes took their places behind them, along with the prefect of Argos and Police Chief Leonardos. Next in order were the mayor and then the Schliemanns' hosts, the Dases family. Soon the beehive chamber was filled with a hundred Charvatians and their neighbors from the surrounding villages. Those who could not get in stood in the *dromos*.

Bishop Vimpos, his thin face grave, said Mass. The aroma of Orthodox incense began to filter through the Treasury. The congregation was too crowded to kneel but he took no notice of this. He was intent upon converting the pagan temple into a Greek Orthodox shrine. His sermon was mercifully brief:

"There is but one God, and Jesus is His Son."

After ardently blessing the parishioners as though to make up for any qualm about whether he had banished Zeus, Hera and Apollo, the bishop and his congregation filed out. While Henry and Sophia gave Dom Pedro a tour of Sophia's treasury, the Lion Gate, the stelae and carved tombstone area of the agora, the Dases family set up long planks on wooden horses in the center of the dome and covered them with the best tablecloth, silver and glassware the village could supply. Candles were placed at regular intervals. They decorated the whole with autumnal flowers. At two o'clock Sophia seated the party with proper protocol, each finding the place card she had filled out the night before. The candles were lighted. Emperor Dom Pedro turned to Sophia and murmured:

"I feel as though I am about to dine with the ages!"

Bishop Vimpos blessed the assemblage and gave thanks for the food about to be partaken. *Ouzo* was served to the men, bottles of Argolid wine opened, glasses filled. The women of Charvati had prepared a feast of Greek dishes: *dolmadakia*, stuffed mussels, pickled squid, dried salted smelts, eggplant dip with *keftedakia*. There was barbecued lamb, broiled chicken, liver in casserole, a fresh ham *macaronada*, *moussaka*; and for dessert, rolled *baklava*, *trigona* with blanched almonds and thick black coffee.

Emperor Dom Pedro rose, toasted King George and Queen Olga, Bishop Vimpos, his guide Professor Koumanoudes, the women of Charvati who had cooked and served the dinner, his hosts, Dr. and Kyria Schliemann:

"Who have afforded me one of the most memorable days of my life."

Henry squeezed Sophia's hand under the table. They glanced up to find Stamatakes staring at them, his eyes full of wonder.

Only a few weeks remained before the steady rains and shortening workday. Henry planned to close down the digs in mid-November. Since he had less than three weeks left and only seventy-seven workmen, he put a small crew at the Lion Gate, hoping to dig down to the threshold, gave Sophia and Spyros some men and two horse carts for the treasury, and put the rest of his crew within the double row of upright slabs in the agora. He was not convinced that the royal tombs lay here, but it was his best chance . . . his only chance. He also found the opportunity to spirit away a few potsherds to send to Max Müller in London.

Henry and Stamatakes had agreed that, since he was going to excavate extensively here, the four sculptured tombstones should be removed to Charvati. Henry had been digging around them; now that they were gone he was able to broaden the area of excavation.

His first important find came at three feet below the level at which the tombstones had stood: two stone slabs lying on top of each other with a third slab jutting off at a sharp angle. On top of the horizontal slab was part of a human jaw with three teeth intact.

Rain held them up much of the following week, though Henry persisted upon working through the mud until he had reached the natural rock base of the mound. He received a distinct but encouraging shock: a section of the large solid rock had been cut into and dug out, some ten by twenty feet. Why would this rock have been hollowed out . . . except to create a tomb? The area was difficult to dig in because it held the rain water. Nevertheless he made a grinding kind of progress downward, finding more large slabs of stone lying flat upon each other.

At the same time Sophia had her own small triumph. Her men, digging to the threshold of the treasury gate, quickly removed the earth lying loosely under the lintel and in the gateway. When a great amount of this debris had been shoveled into the horse cart, her entire crew stopped work and stood around her in a circle as she made her entrance into the treasury itself. It was suffused with a soft light coming from the opening above. As a woman and as an archaeologist, she found it a thrilling moment. Since she did not believe that Veli Pasha had lowered himself into the vault, she would have been the first human being to stand inside the treasury since it had been sealed. It was a unique and emotional experience, so gratifying that she was never to forget it.

She beckoned to her crew, who came in with their pickaxes and shovels and began clearing out the central area. If the treasury had not been looted there should be important artifacts to be found. She combed the shallow shovels of earth before they were dumped into baskets en route to the horse carts. The finds were not spectacular but they were encouraging, the most interesting of which was a fragment of blue marble ornamented with fish-spine designs.

One of the Romaïdes brothers from a photography shop in Athens arrived, began photographing all of the work in progress and the objects taken out of the earth. Henry felt he also needed an engineer to draw archaeological plans of the excavation. Police Chief Leonardos recommended an army lieutenant who had some leisure time. Henry rode into Nauplion Friday, November 3, to interview him. It drizzled on the ride to town. The two men hit it off at once. Vasilios Drosinos was bright and apparently well trained for his job. He had read many of Henry's articles in the *Newspaper of the Debates* and had been fascinated by the discoveries at Troy. He accepted Henry's invitation at once.

The following day, Saturday, Henry's men worked their way down to the threshold of the Lion Gate. His crew now totaled one hundred men. Just inside the threshold they found a bronze or copper seal ring. On it were carved two young ladies who Sophia said were of "marvelous beauty."

"What pleases me," added Henry, "is their simple and beautiful coiffures. And their gestures . . . they are sitting close to each other, looking in opposite directions. . . ."

Also near the Lion Gate they unearthed transparent red stones perforated so as to form necklaces, idols in all shapes, a splendidly painted tripod, a small silver ring, a cylindrically formed lump of lead which Henry believed to have been a weight, and a golden earring made of thick gold wires which was very much like the earrings they had brought home from Troy.

On the eight-foot-wide threshold stone they saw grooves made by chariot wheels as they came in and out of the acropolis.

"Though I am not convinced these are the markings of chariot wheels; they could get chariots through the Lion Gate all right, but then where would they go? The mountain is too steep for them; and I doubt if there was space enough between the edge of the agora and the interior cyclopean wall for them to pass."

On Monday Vasilios Drosinos arrived. The lieutenant went to work immediately with his surveying instruments.

The sun came out, the mud dried and the digging accelerated. Henry returned to the rock tomb site. Nineteen feet into the debris they found a second wood button plated with gold. They came upon pottery, handmade and monochrome black or red. The lustrous surface was as fine as the best they had discovered at the lowest city of Troy.

During the next two days he found twelve more gold buttons; several leaves of gold; many bones, human intermixed with swine; a large ax, and more monochrome prehistoric vases. He had to stop excavating at the north side of the tomb because there had been built upon it some of the double row of stone uprights.

"I can't excavate under them without destroying them," he said to Drosinos.

"You're right. Best to leave them *in situ*."

"I feel that this tomb has been plundered and things thrown back in a hodgepodge manner. That's probably why we find handmade and wheel-made pottery thrown in together. Or else when this wall of slabs was built above the tomb everything in it was exhumed and later replaced."

Again the rain fell. Henry sent Sophia back to the Dases house while he made his way to the first discovered crypt. Water was already collecting at the base; soon it would be a morass of mud. He was disappointed. He was convinced that it was a tomb and there were bodies at the bottom of it.

The moment the rain stopped he began excavating a new area above the solid rock, marked by unsculptured five-foot tombstones. This area was twenty feet east of the first tomb. By noon of the next day, Saturday, they had reached the stone walls of a second tomb, filled with an unmixed natural earth. Dark rain clouds rolled over them, and the men were sloshing around in the mud. Henry observed to Sophia:

"It's futile to try to go on. We'll end the dig tomorrow, and go into Nauplion on Monday morning."

"That makes sense. We can start again in the early spring."

In order to lay out the following year's work, he wanted to establish two more tomb sites, or large apertures, which had been cut into the rock base. He started half a dozen men digging at a site where he had also discovered unmarked tombstones. A second crew blocked off the area of darker soil which appeared to have been brought in from elsewhere. Henry had high hopes that this would eventually lead him to a fourth tomb and that this vast rocky area ringed with uprights was indeed a necropolis.

He urged the workmen to dig at an increased speed, offering a bonus for the Sunday job. His men responded, bringing out fragments of tombstones and painted pottery. By late afternoon they were down thirteen feet below the top of the rock, a total of twenty-five feet below the plateau of the agora. The problem was hauling out the debris. Lieutenant Drosinos threw together rough ladders with rungs of tree branches and attached shoulder straps to the baskets so that the men could carry them to the top and dump them into the horse carts after being sifted for finds.

Two feet farther down in this second tomb site they struck a new phenomenon, a layer of pebbles which was not natural to the terrain. Henry ordered the men to leave aside their picks and shovels and to use their hands and small knives to determine the outer edges of the pebble bed. It turned out to be five feet long and three feet wide. Sophia came down to see what the excitement was about. Lieutenant Drosinos asked:

"What do you suppose its purpose was, this strata of pebbles? It is certainly handmade."

Henry mused for a while.

"There's no way to tell until we remove it. Men, please move this pebble bed aside, but only with your fingers, slowly and carefully."

When the pebbles had been finger-raked to all four sides there appeared a thin layer of black ash. Sophia saw a first flash of bright metal. Instinctively she moved ash over the metal to cover it, rose and said in an aside to Henry:

"*Paidos.* It's getting late and dark. Dismiss the men . . ."

He caught the urgency in her voice.

"And tell them to return tomorrow?"

"Yes."

"Very well. Should we summon Stamatakes?"

"It would be wisest."

"Lieutenant Drosinos, would you please ask Mr. Stamatakes to come here."

When the two of them were alone at the bottom of the tomb, twenty-seven feet below the surface of the agora, in deepening gloom and darkness, Henry murmured:

"What do we have?"

She gestured for him to drop to his knees beside her. Slowly, gently they brushed aside the layer of ash; and there before their astonished eyes lay a tremendous gold leaf. Still brushing ash with their fingertips, they uncovered a mass of gold leaves. Removing them one by one, they saw that they had been used to cover the rib cage of a corpse. Breathing hard but saying no word, they removed the gold leaf at the head of the body and found the remains of a skull. Brushing aside ash from the skull, they found still another batch of gold leaves, thicker than the rest and bound together by a silver wire. The body was lying with its head to the east, feet to the west. Sophia had a flash of recognition; that was the way her father had been laid out in his coffin.

In a voice so hoarse that she could hardly recognize it, Sophia heard Henry say:

"We have found our first royal tomb! Our first royal corpse!"

Sophia was quivering. They still had plenty of room within this tomb to find other bodies . . . At that moment Stamatakes came tumbling down the tree-branch ladder, took a look at the gold leaves and the corpse, whistled in incredulity. Henry maintained his command of the situation.

"We'll have to move all this gold out tonight."

Stamatakes agreed.

"We'll need a soft cloth in which to carry it. Lieutenant Drosinos, would you get us one?"

In the near darkness Henry began removing the gold leaves from the corpse. Lieutenant Drosinos returned with a piece of woolen material. When all of the leaves had been assembled, Henry asked Drosinos to tie the cloth with a piece of rope. He then turned the informal bag over to Stamatakes.

"Let's all of us ride down to your storeroom. I want each leaf numbered. Then I want a receipt for the total."

Stamatakes agreed. Henry asked that a guard be posted at the tomb for the night.

"I have no guard."

"I'll ask Demetrios and Ajax to do it for me."

By the time they reached the Dases house, dinner was over. Ioanna had kept two pots on the stove for them. They ate with difficulty. Demetrios and Ajax asked no questions, mounted their donkeys, each with a shotgun. Henry had not told them what they would be guarding, but they knew it had to be important. Both men carried blankets against the November cold.

Henry and Sophia talked far into the night. Their mood of hope, expectancy, was too high to allow for sleep. There was no possibility of their returning to Athens. It was almost dawn before Sophia dozed off. As far as she could tell, Henry did not sleep at all.

They were back at the tomb at first light. So was Stamatakes. Immediately they found more gold, which they had not been able to see in the dark: five splendid crosses, each formed by the joining of four gold leaves; four circular strands of gold and many more single leaves. All of these Sophia described in her notebook, as did Stamatakes, who took possession, but not before giving Sophia a receipt.

Henry set his crew to excavating toward the natural rock walls of the tomb on all four sides. By eleven in the morning they had reached dimensions of twelve by twenty-one feet; the walls were lined with a wainscot of small quarry stones some ten feet high, and were lightly blackened by fire. But that was all he did learn, for a driving rain forced them out of the crypt. Sophia spent most of the day with the Dases women, sewing together pieces of tarpaulin to make a cover for the tomb which would keep the rain out. At dusk Demetrios and Ajax took it up to the acropolis, fastening it down on all four sides with rows of heavy stones.

The rain continued all day Tuesday, with Henry pacing their upstairs rooms like a caged tiger, bringing down on the head of the god of rain every imprecation he could think of in eighteen languages. Sophia did what she could to quiet him but he could not contain his impatience.

Wednesday the sun came out, partially drying Mycenae. The covering tarp had helped to keep a lot of the water out of the excavation. Henry used as many men as he could fit into the small area of the rock to dig down on each side of the pebble bed where they had found their first corpse. For the first couple of feet he allowed them to use their hand picks and shovels, but cautiously. The moment they reached two more pebble beds, lying side by side, Henry sent the workmen above to dig at the other sites. The Schliemanns and Lieutenant Drosinos carefully moved the gravel aside. Working on their hands and knees, Henry and Sophia sifted through the ashes until they exposed two more half-burned skeletons covered with gold. Henry gasped. Sophia had an eerie feeling. She was crouching in the dark, cold, wet tomb, frightened at the sight of these kings who had been buried in this rock chamber some three thousand years before. Did she have a right to expose them after all these millennia? Was she an intruder? A grave robber? There was said to be a curse which fell on the heads of those who disturbed the dead.

Around each skull there were five diadems of solid gold, nineteen inches long and four inches broad in the center, held within a frame of copper wire to give them solidity. They were different in form from the two they had found in Troy, which had a series of hanging chains. As they sifted through the ashes they turned up nine more gold crosses. Then came articles similar to the ones they had found in Troy: weapons in the form of obsidian and bronze knives; fragments of a large silver vase with a mouth of copper which was thickly plated with gold and ornamented with intaglio work; a silver cup; many fragments of exquisitely ornamented handmade and wheel-made pottery; quantities of terra-cotta tripods. For Henry the most important objects were two two-horned Hera idols. He exclaimed:

"This proves that the goddess was already worshiped in this shape in times of remote antiquity, to which this sepulcher belongs."

Sophia heard Stamatakes murmur under his breath:

"It proves no such thing. Why don't you stick to your artifacts and leave theories to those of us who are trained to understand the boundaries within which one is allowed to theorize?"

Henry was busy elsewhere and had not heard the condescending remarks. Sophia gave Stamatakes a withering glance.

The bones and skulls of the three corpses had been preserved, only
the flesh having been burned by the small fire set on a bottom layer of
similar pebbles. But when Henry tried to remove the skeletons he found
that they had suffered so badly from the moisture that they crumbled
at his touch. He brought out as much of the bones as he could, even as
he had the three skeletons he had found at Troy.

On the ride back to Charvati, Henry ruminated:

"In Troy they cremated Hector and Patroclus, saving only their
bones from the fire. Here in Mycenae they appear to have put the royal
corpses between two layers of pebbles and burned only enough wood
to consume the clothes and the flesh, perhaps as a purifying process."

Stamatakes had not been listening. He announced:

"I am going to cable Athens tonight for several government clerks to
help catalogue the finds. Also, I'm going to ask for a detachment of
soldiers to guard the treasures. We must not let anything be stolen."

Henry replied sweetly, "I trust you were not thinking of Kyria Schliemann and myself, *Mister* Stamatakes."

5.

They were in a high state of excitement. Henry spent most of the
night writing articles for the London *Times*. Sophia continued her
series for the *Ephimeris*. When she did go to bed she had nightmares in
which she was trapped in the bottom of a dank tomb and could not
get out. The partial skulls of long-departed kings took on flesh again
and glared at her.

"Who are you? Why have you disturbed my rest?"

The Dases house was in a state of turmoil. Although no one of
Charvati had seen any of the gold, everyone knew that ancient skeletons had been brought out of the tomb. Folk memory had taught them
that if the tombs of the Mycenaean monarchs should ever be found,
they would be filled with the richest gold treasures the world had yet
known. They had seen Stamatakes come into Charvati hugging a bag to
his chest. As with the people of the Troad, after Henry and Sophia had
discovered the treasure of Priam, the Charvatians knew that the first gold
of Mycenae had been delivered into the hands of their guests, Dr. and
Kyria Schliemann.

When Spyros finished clearing out the middle portion of the treasury, which Sophia and Henry had been forced to believe had indeed
been plundered, Romaïdes, the photographer, took pictures of Sophia

in her shiny black hat, warm wool jacket with frogged buttons, and long wool skirt, standing in front of the enormous entrance below the hollowed-out triangular niche, her crew grouped inside the center of the beehive, the sunlight streaming down on them. The moment the photograph was published the beehive became known as "Mrs. Schliemann's Treasury." Some time later it was given the official title of the Tomb of Clytemnestra.

Despite the continuing bad weather, Henry could not desist.

He set a crew to excavating for a third tomb. It proved difficult because the two unsculptured tombstones resting above it were secured deep in the earth by enormous square blocks. At three feet below their base Henry came upon two large slabs lying horizontally, and five feet below that three more slabs, slabs which Henry now believed had been used to cover over the tomb . . . or to mark it.

"It shows the veneration with which all of these tombs were regarded. Though the original tombstones had been covered with soil, the precise spot of the graves was so well known, they were marked by new slabs."

The men dug through enormous amounts of debris in the direction of the mouth of the rock-walled opening. Thirty feet of earth was removed in baskets and taken to the surface. They came across skeletons of a number of men without trappings of any kind. They were sunk in debris full of knives and fragments of vases, and were so decomposed they could not be gotten out at all.

"They may have been the king's bodyguards," Henry observed. "We know that in some Mediterranean countries the king's bodyguards were buried with him, as well as his attendants and household servants."

At one point they came upon an overhanging rock. Henry had offered the men a drink-penny for all objects, even the most trifling, they came upon. Because so many artifacts lay below the rock, which had a dangerous crack in it, two of the workmen kept returning to the spot for more finds. Henry, watching them, saw the crack widen. He lunged in, dragged the men a little distance when suddenly it fell with a thundering crash. All three were knocked down by the splinters of rock and the force of the fall. Sophia ran to Henry, helped him up, brushed the dirt from his clothes.

"It's all right, my dear. I'm not hurt. Neither are the men. Shades of Troy!"

Then came an infuriating two days of such intense rain that they could not go out at all. Henry asked Stamatakes's permission to sketch, photograph and describe the gold-ornamented pieces for their journal. Stamatakes was adamant.

"I have a guard in front of that padlock twenty-four hours a day. His instructions are to let no one in, not even if I say he may."

On the next dry day Henry found the mouth of the third tomb nine feet below the disjointed skeletons. It was a full week after he had completed excavating the second tomb before he finally came to the layer of river pebbles and under it a layer of fine clay. Like the other tombs, grooves had been cut into the rock walls ten to sixteen feet high, and the sides lined with small quarry stones. Sophia, Spyros, Lieutenant Drosinos helped him clear away the two strata. There, with eyes wide and mouths open, they came upon three bodies "smothered with gold," some of it showing signs of smoke and fire, some of it fused. Their emotions went skittering through their minds and soft viscera like March winds.

Henry, working on his knees, examined the skeletons carefully. He looked across the bodies at Sophia, who was kneeling on the other side, and exclaimed:

"I believe these three skeletons are women because of the smallness of the bones, the smallness of the teeth. This must have been an old woman because her teeth are worn and very irregular. We could genuinely call this a funeral pyre because the bodies are burned. You can see signs of the fire and smoke to which they were exposed on the side walls."

They began collecting dozens and then hundreds of two-and-a-half-to three-inch round, thick plates of gold with repoussé decorations. By the time they had finished assembling the plates they found to their amazement that they had seven hundred of them. They had taken them from above and below the bodies as well as all around them. Henry cried:

"A good part of them must have been strewn all over the bottom of this sepulcher before the funeral pyres were dressed. The rest of them must have been laid on the bodies after the fires had died down."

It was a shallow crypt, only four feet deep into the rock. They had dug out the entire area and there was light from the cool November sun overhead. As they brushed the ash from one round plate after another they were staggered by the variety of decorations: flowers, butterflies, leaf patterns, an octopus or cuttlefish with eight arms in spiral form; broad waving bands resembling the serpents on the tombstone.

Sophia made the next find: three sections of a necklace which had become unstrung. All three were done in intaglio, the first of Hercules killing the Nemean Lion; the second of two warriors battling; the third showing a kneeling lion whose forefeet were placed over a rocky hillside. They seemed older than the goldsmith's work they had found at Troy.

"I've never heard mention of gold being mined in the Argolid," Sophia said; "where do these incredible quantities of gold come from?"

"Perhaps as they came to Troy, in trade throughout the Aegean and Mediterranean. This jewelry could have been brought in already decorated, or the Mycenaeans, who doubtless had their own goldsmiths, could have traded for gold bars. See what I've just uncovered: ten gold grasshoppers, or crickets, on gold chains."

They dug and sifted for hours, working on their hands and knees on either side of the funeral pyres, watched, cold-eyed, by Stamatakes. Every few moments there would be an exclamation of joy or astonishment as they brought forth gold griffins, hearts, crouching lions, stags with three-branched horns, globular ornaments, finely wrought brooches, ornaments showing two women with pigeons on their heads, cuttlefish, a gold griffin, flying. Sophia exclaimed:

"Most of these ornaments are perforated, Henry, either to string together or attach to clothing."

Henry had not heard her, he was breathing hard. At the head of one of the three bodies he had just unearthed a magnificent crown of gold. It had suffered from the funeral fire which had blackened it but was the most superb object they had yet found. Two feet long, it had thirty-six large leaves attached to it and was covered with shieldlike ornaments, the decorations standing in low relief.

"This is one of the most beautiful examples of the goldsmith's art I have ever seen," Henry whispered to her. "Come here by my side. There is a small hole at either end of the crown and some thin gold wire by which it was fastened. Let me see how it looks on you before Stamatakes claims it."

She knelt beside him while he adjusted the crown so that the thirty-six leaves stood upright on her head.

"It is more beautiful than the diadems we found in Troy. I am going to insist that I be allowed to photograph you in this crown when we get down to the storehouse."

Stamatakes had overheard. He said, "There will be no photographs of the gold until we take all this treasure back to Athens."

Henry shot him a deadly look, Sophia returned to her own fingertip digging. Hers was the next find, a second gold diadem. She cried out:

"Henry, there is still part of the skull inside. Should I separate it from the skull?"

"Leave it alone," Stamatakes ordered, "that decision belongs to the Archaeological Society."

They spent the entire day in what Henry described as "the greatest gold cache in the world." One after another they found five more diadems. They had to brush away the fine black ash still sticking to the

gold. A few moments later Sophia unearthed two others, decorated with
vertical rows of spirals. This brought the total to nine.

"This has to be a tomb of queens," Sophia gasped, almost stunned
at what they were turning up.

"One queen. These bodies were all buried at the same time. The
others were doubtless princesses. And it was not Clytemnestra: the
Mycenaeans buried her outside the walls because she was unworthy of
being buried in the acropolis. Then how far back do we go? To Atreus
. . . Pelops . . . ?"

In the ashes Henry next found two large gold stars, double crosses
held together by a gold pin. Searching along one of the bodies, he came
upon a gold brooch on which a woman stood with extended arms, her
face in profile. He wiped the brooch clean and handed it to Sophia, who
studied it intently.

"She is Grecian, no question of that. Look at this long nose which
comes straight out from her forehead. These big eyes . . ."

". . . almost as large as yours," said Henry with a smile.

Sophia looked up sharply to see that Stamatakes was carefully putting the finds into a cloth bag and was not watching her. She whispered
to Henry:

"She also has a most ample bosom . . . and don't go making any further comparisons!"

They continued their sifting of the ashes in a growing state of emotional turmoil at the enormity of the treasure: gold earrings, necklaces,
six bracelets, two pairs of scales, a child's mask with cutouts for the eyes.
The mask was crumpled but as Henry held it in one hand he commented:

"This means that a child must have been cremated in this tomb.
Pausanias says that was the tradition of the day. It could be a child who
died shortly after his mother. But there is no evidence of the little one."

Sophia dug out two scepters, which again indicated that this was a
royal tomb; the silver staffs were gold-plated, the handles of rock
crystal. Then in rapid succession she found a lady's comb of gold with
bone teeth; gold and amber beads; gold breastpins; a gold goblet decorated with fish; a gold box whose lid still fit perfectly. At the same
time Henry was sifting from the ash a lovely globular gold vase with a
handle on each side, and three more gold vessels fitted with lids; an
unornamented silver vase, then a silver vessel and goblet.

Their last find of the day was a puzzling one. Near the head of each
of the three bodies was a copper-plated box, four by ten inches in size,
filled with a block of wood. Henry said tentatively:

"I could make a conjecture: these were head pillows for the dead.
Even as were the pillows of alabaster the Egyptians used."

Stamatakes, overwhelmed by the enormity of the treasure at which he was looking, began to panic at his own responsibility in the excavation. Suppose the gold should disappear? He and he alone would be held accountable. It would be a fatal blemish on his record. Breathing hard and leaning with his back against the wall of the third tomb—he had yet to put his fingers in the ground—he made his decision. Crouching alongside Henry, he announced:

"Dr. Schliemann, all of your work in this tomb will have to stop."

Henry looked astonished.

"Stop? How could we conceivably stop with all this gold emerging from antiquity?"

". . . precisely the point. What we see before our eyes has inestimable value. We must give this gold every protection. I can't go on until the governor of the province is present."

"That's nonsense! Between us we can protect and preserve every particle of gold dust. My permit says nothing about a governor being present."

"I know that. It's an order I am issuing to you as ephor of antiquities."

"We are not obliged to take orders from you. If you want the governor at hand for your own protection, go get him."

Stamatakes scrambled up the ladder and reluctantly left the site to send a telegram to Nauplion and to Athens, again asking for soldiers.

It was no longer possible to keep from Charvati the fact that gold jewelry of great worth had been found in the tombs. There were too many workmen around to see, to catch snatches of conversation. Aside from these confirmations, they had only to look at the expression on the Schliemann faces: the glowing pride, the ecstasy of fulfillment. The admiration, the reverence felt for Henry and Sophia by the Dases family and Charvati, for having understood and having accomplished what no other had throughout their history, was deeper than the tombs. Demetrios Dases, a proud and independent man, bowing as though to his master, said:

"I was wrong. So were we all. We said there were no royal tombs on the acropolis. I might have discouraged you . . ."

"No, Demetrios, you were right. You said, 'What there is to find, Dr. Schliemann will find.' "

They tackled a fourth area the following day. It was unmarked by tombstones but the soil was darker than the rest of the agora. Here also Sophia's crew had earlier unearthed a round altar constructed of cyclopean stones twenty feet below the surface of the mound. Henry had not wanted her to proceed until he had completed his work on the third tomb. Now he brought a large crew to the area, where he carefully dismantled the six-foot-round and four-foot-high altar so that it could be reassembled in Athens. Once the workmen had hauled away the blocks Henry had his men start excavating the darker soil.

The calendar read November 25. Miraculously, the steady rains held off, though in another two weeks Mycenae would be deluged. Spurring his work crew to dig as rapidly as possible, Henry found the top of his fourth tomb only six feet below where Sophia's altar had stood. By locating the four stone walls he saw that this was the largest tomb yet, twenty-four feet long and eighteen feet wide. The altar had been sitting in the very center.

The work of excavating went rapidly for the first five feet. When Henry surmised that they were coming close to the upper layer of pebbles, he, Sophia and Spyros took over the task, cutting the earth away carefully with their knives, an exceedingly painful task as they worked on their knees in the cold, wet earth.

Their patience was rewarded. They came upon the three-inch layer of pebbles which they cleared away without difficulty; next there was a four-inch layer of white clay. Again there were grooves cut into the rock wall of the tomb, almost ten feet high, and the sides were lined with quarry stones covered with pieces of schist, a crystalline slate, held together with white clay and slightly blackened. The exposed wall slanted markedly inward. Once the layer of white clay had been laboriously removed they found two bodies. There was evidence of the same small fire, wood, and clothing ash with one crucial difference: each face was covered with a large gold mask. One mask had been very much injured in the funeral fire and by the heavy weight of the stones and debris. Henry cleaned it with his handkerchief, but a good deal of ash still stuck to the gold. He then held it up for Sophia's scrutiny.

"Study it for some moments, Sophidion, you can get a tolerable idea of the features. See here, the large oval, youthful face with the high forehead, the long Grecian nose, the small mouth with thin lips. The eyes are shut but see how well marked the hairs of the eyelashes and eyebrows are."

The second mask showed a different character, leading them to wonder whether these masks were not actual portraits made of the dead kings by their goldsmiths after the ruler's death. It appeared so to Sophia, for this second mask as she held it in both hands to examine it minutely had a round face, blown-out cheeks, a short forehead and a nose which struck off at an oblique angle from the hollow between the eyes. This monarch, she observed, had a small mouth with inordinately thick lips. His eyes were shut as in the first mask, the eyelashes and eyebrows strongly evident.

They put the two masks carefully aside. Within seconds, Stamatakes had scooped them up and put them into his woolen bag. Henry, Sophia and Spyros continued with tense excitement, removing dirt and ash from the bodies with their knives, uncovering five large bronze vessels, four of them filled with earth and ash. The fifth was literally a gold mine; out of it they took one hundred buttons covered with intaglio-worked gold plate. After a moment of exultation they went back to their digging and very quickly uncovered an extraordinarily large silver cow's head from which sprang two curving horns of gold plate, their insides filled with half-rotted wood. On its forehead there was an ornamented gold sun two inches in diameter. Flushed with pleasure, Henry exclaimed:

"There can be no doubt that this cow's head was intended to represent Hera, the patron deity of Mycenae."

They stopped only briefly for their midday meal. Upon descending once again the depth of thirty-three feet to the bottom of the tomb, they unearthed a pile of twenty bronze swords and many lances. Gold from the inlay work on the wooden sheaths of the swords was lying on the ground. In the midst of the swords they found a number of round gold plates with the same intaglio work they had removed from their first corpse in the second tomb.

During the rest of the afternoon they dug out bronze vessels, silver vases and gold vases. Scattered between them was an enormous number of small gold leaves. Spyros was overjoyed when he discovered a completely new phenomenon, a massive gold belt consisting of pure metal.

It was not Stamatakes's desire for the presence of the governor of the province at the digs but rather the Archaeological Society in Athens which stopped Henry and Sophia. That evening when they returned to the Dases house there was a telegram from the Society saying that Professor Spyridon Phindikles was leaving the next day for Mycenae, and that Dr. Schliemann was to suspend activities until his arrival. The sting of losing two days' work this late in the year was eased considerably for Henry because it was his friend Professor Phindikles, who had spent the first week of this expedition with the Schliemanns at Tiryns and had visited Mycenae with them for one day, who was coming.

Stamatakes was reassured by the news that his superior would arrive and take over full responsibility. He was also assured that soldiers were on the way to protect the tombs and the gold. Because much of his anxiety had subsided, he allowed Henry and Sophia to work in the storeroom all day Sunday, and for a full day on Monday. They annotated much of the descriptive material they needed for Henry's book on Mycenae during these two days of uninterrupted study and commentary.

Before they went to work in the storeroom on Monday morning Henry wrote an article for the London *Times* in which he said that, despite the fact that he had uncovered only two bodies thus far in the fourth tomb, this was "the tomb which the tradition of the ancients designated as the tomb of the King of Men, Agamemnon, Cassandra, Eurymedon and their companions."

6.

Professor Spyridon Phindikles arrived so early Tuesday morning that he must have left Nauplion before dawn. Henry took him at once to the storehouse and showed him the treasure that had been collected so far. Phindikles was stunned, his eyes glazed as he handled one by one the hundreds of gold ornaments, masks, diadems.

"You have indeed hit the royal tombs," he murmured.

Delighted with the professor's reaction, Henry replied, "Let us go up to the dig immediately. I am convinced there are more bodies in that fourth tomb. I want you to see them covered with gold from head to foot. It is an incredible experience!"

As they rode up the hill Henry took a sidewise glance at his friend, recalling his career. Phindikles had studied at the University of Athens and then taken postgraduate work in Germany. After serving as a high school teacher, he was appointed professor of Greek philology at the university, and had served for many years as vice-president of the Greek Archaeological Society. Despite their liking and respect for each other, the two men were at polar extremes on their attitude toward science. Henry was constantly accused of publishing too quickly, of being obliged to contradict himself with succeeding reports. Phindikles, though he was a man of considerable courage in all other aspects of his life, was too timid to release the scientific materials he had accumulated. At the age of fifty-six he had published nothing and had already asked a colleague to destroy all of his notes at the time of his death. He admired Henry Schliemann for his audacity even though he was convinced there were pitfalls as deep as any royal tomb in publishing opinions, theories, even educated guesses before the scientific finds had been counterchecked half a dozen times.

On the way Professor Phindikles stopped to inspect Sophia's *dromos* and treasury which had been nothing more than a dirt-covered mound when he saw it in August. He congratulated her warmly on her accomplishment. In August, too, the underlying roadbed to the Lion Gate had been covered by ten feet of earth, boulders and cyclopean blocks. He was generous in his compliments to Henry for freeing the splendid monument.

They went down to the floor of the fourth tomb. Professor Phindikles examined the two skeletons which Henry had not attempted to remove.

"They are out of prehistory, that seems certain," he observed. "What makes you so sure there are other corpses in this tomb?"

"As you can see, we have reached this lowest level in only one third of the floor space."

Henry summoned Demetrios and Ajax and two more of their family members. They came down the ladder with their shovels and baskets. Henry cautioned them to work lightly in removing the earth. With a stick he drew a line indicating approximately where they should come across a new top layer of pebbles. The digging and hauling away took a couple of hours; when the Dases men's shovels brought up the first few pebbles, Henry relieved them. Professor Phindikles joined in the clearing away of the last thin layer of dirt revealing the pebble bed.

"The corpses, if such there be, will lie under this bed of pebbles and on top of another. I had not heard of this method of cremation before, but the two layers of pebbles apparently afford the proper amount of ventilation so that the flesh and clothing are destroyed but the skeletons and treasures are left largely unburned."

There were three more separate funeral pyres. When the top layer of pebbles of each had been cleared away, they found three corpses lying with their heads to the east and feet to the west. When Phindikles saw the heads covered with gold masks he cried out in astonishment. Then they saw the breasts covered with large gold breastplates, a magnificent gold crown decorated with rosettes and rows of shieldlike circles, a massive gold bracelet with flowers soldered onto it.

"Big enough to fit on the loins of an ordinary man," Henry said reverently.

Phindikles held it in his hands with disbelief. There were two large gold signet rings, one with a portrait of a hunter with his chariot drawn by two stallions, the other showing a battle scene in which one warrior seemed to be vanquishing the other three.

Sophia, Spyros, Henry and now Dr. Phindikles crouched around the sides of the freshly discovered bodies. They had little space in which to work because the slanting quarry stone wall, rising nine feet high here, considerably diminished the size of the sepulcher at the bottom. At midday Sophia asked Ajax to bring some food down to the bottom of the tomb, with water and a cloth with which they might wash their hands. She persuaded the men to stop work for a few moments. They sat on the bottom of the tomb, backs to the walls, drinking wine, eating bread, cheese and olives, while passing the masks, crowns, bracelets from one to the other, commenting on the quality and approximate age of the workmanship. Henry, who had been studying the third mask, observed:

"The wrinkles to the right and left above the mouth, and the expression of the very large mouth with thin lips, can leave no doubt that we have here the portrait of a man of advanced age."

Phindikles observed that the faces represented by the masks were totally different from the idolized statues of gods and heroes. Henry put his hand fondly around Sophia's shoulder in the damp cold of the tomb and replied with considerable satisfaction:

"It was Kyria Schliemann who first suggested that each of these masks was a likeness of the deceased whose face it covered."

"They almost have to be portraits," Phindikles agreed.

They worked for several more hours uncovering nine gold vessels, the first a monumental two-handled goblet, two furrowed gold goblets each encircled by nine parallel furrows, a finely shaped wine flagon with a large handle, the whole flagon covered with a network of interwoven linear ornamentation. The others were decorated with broad bands representing knife blades; a goblet had a handle fastened to it with gold nails. Henry held this last one up for examination.

"I found a goblet of exactly this shape at Troy at a depth of fifty feet in the most ancient of the four prehistoric cities, but it was of terra cotta."

Sophia, who was working close to the wall and digging under the third skeleton, sifted through the ash to a massive gold goblet. It was encircled by a row of fourteen rosettes. Even the edges of the handles were ornamented. Phindikles hefted it up and down in his hand, judging that it weighed four pounds troy. He commented, with his face ablaze with joy:

"It is one of the most splendid jewels of your Mycenaean treasure."

Henry, who was digging through the bottom layer of pebbles to the middle corpse, next came upon another sizable goblet, with horizontal handles and decorated with two gold pigeons. Henry turned to Phindikles, his face pale.

"Don't you agree that this goblet nearly fits the description of Nestor's goblet in *The Iliad*:

"She placed beside them a splendid goblet, which the old man
had brought with him from home; it was studded with golden
pins; it had four handles, on each of which pecked two golden
pigeons; the goblet had two bottoms."

They worked through the afternoon, all four of them finding objects, including Spyros, who dug out a beautifully shaped silver flagon with a long vertical handle. Each in turn held aloft a trophy, exclaiming over it: three shoulder belts of gold decorated with rows of rosettes; one hundred large and small beads of amber. As Henry passed a handful of the beads around he observed:

"All these beads must have been strung in necklaces, even as were the thousands of gold beads we found in the treasure of Priam. Professor Phindikles, wouldn't you say that their presence in the tombs among such prodigious treasures of gold ornaments seems to prove that amber was very precious and was considered as an important ornament in the time of the Mycenaean kings?"

Tentatively, Spyridon Phindikles said in his undidactic tone:

"It would appear so. Let us refer to the books in the National Library when we get back to Athens."

Work began early the following morning. Henry was intrigued by finding three miniature buildings of gold in repoussé work. After examining them he passed them to Sophia, and she passed them along to Professor Phindikles. All three chipped in with fragmented observations:

". . . too small for a dwelling house, surely. Do you suppose they were intended to represent temples?" ". . . look, this building has two pigeons perched on the roof." ". . . it also has columns very like the column between the two lions at the Lion Gate!"

For the first time Stamatakes got down on his knees and began digging through the ashes, pebbles and underlying earth. Now there were five of them feverishly making discoveries: four gold diadems, a small delicately ornamented gold belt; heavy gold pins used either as breast- or hairpins; a solid gold lion cub; a gold star formed by three double leaves of gold soldered together in the center; gold finger rings, two small battle-axes of thin gold plate; a copper fork with three curved prongs; alabaster vases, handsomely fashioned bone lids of jars; a hollow animal which seemed to have served as a vase, with feet of a buffalo . . .

Time sped by as they kept their fingers and hands working in the earth and pebbles, smudges of soil on their foreheads and faces as they wiped an occasional bit of perspiration despite the cold, the knees of their trousers pale with clay, Sophia's skirt streaked with earth.

In the closing hours of the afternoon when the light was failing, they came upon buttons of wood in the form of crosses plated with gold; a hundred small gold flowers; more than a hundred pieces of round gold plate; another hundred shieldlike pieces of decorated gold. There appeared before their dazed and unbelieving eyes silver goblets,

bowls, vases; a wooden comb with a curved gold handle; some fifty cuttlefish obviously cast in the same mold; obsidian arrowheads; sixty
boars' teeth which had been used to decorate the helmets of these long-
dead monarchs. This time it was Professor Phindikles who quoted *The
Iliad*:

> "And on his brows a leathern headpiece placed
> Well wrought within, with numerous straps secured,
> And on the outside, with wild boar's gleaming tusks
> Profusely garnished, scattered here and there
> By skillful hand."

At the very last they came upon bronze swords, lances, long knives,
an alabaster sword handle adorned with large flat gold nailheads.
Henry observed that they had found similar alabaster knobs at Troy
but that he had not known that they were sword handles. Sophia
added:

"I remember, Henry, you fancied that they had served as handles to
house doors or walking sticks."

And finally they unearthed thirty copper vessels, copper tripods such
as *The Iliad* and *The Odyssey* represented as prizes in the games, and
as darkness overtook them at the bottom of the tomb, a large quantity
of oyster shells, some of which had never been opened.

Henry commented:

"As in the funeral customs of ancient Egypt, food was supplied for
the deceased. And all this broken pottery by which we have been surrounded might indicate a custom which you still have in Greece of
breaking vases filled with water on the tombs of departed friends."

Stamatakes had said when they were excavating the third tomb that
some of the gold finds were so thin that the edges would break off if
they were placed in sacks. He had asked one of the Charvati carpenters
to make a series of shallow boxes. All during the day, as the masks,
diadems, bracelets, ornaments had been brought forth, he had arranged them in the boxes, attaching the lids and handing them up the
ladder to one of his assistants, who placed it alongside the others in
the horse cart which was being guarded by four soldiers who had arrived
from Athens.

Now, with the day's work done, they carried the remaining boxes up
the ladder. They all walked behind the cart. When they reached
Stamatakes's storehouse, the soldiers helped to carry the treasure inside.
Stamatakes closed the door behind them, lighted two lamps. They were
all exhausted and at the same time exhilarated as they took the lids
off the boxes and stood gripping one another's hands, ravished by the
beauty of the ancient gold jewels as they gleamed in the lamplight.

There was so much work to be done here! Each piece had to be photographed, catalogued, described. Yet there was no time to do any of it, only time enough to hold the many marvelous pieces in their hands and study them. There was a knock on the door. Stamatakes admitted Ioanna Dases and her older daughter carrying covered plates of hot food, as well as a bottle of *ouzo*. They were wearing short dark woolen overcoats against the cold. The men drank the licorice-tasting liquor, then fell to eating ravenously. When they had finished they held a council of war. How to protect the gold? How to get it all back to Athens safely? Stamatakes, who had been a student of Professor Phindikles at the university, and whose manner had changed from the bellicose to obsequity, said politely:

"Professor Phindikles, don't you think you ought to take all of this gold with you when you return? I will fasten down each of these boxes securely, and you can take our guard of soldiers, who will see it safely on board ship."

"I agree. I will cable the Society to have a guard at the dock at Piraeus to escort the treasure to the National Bank."

Sophia saw Henry swallow hard, a half-frustrated smile lifting one corner of his mouth. She could read his thoughts:

"I am the one who discovered the tombs. I am the one who excavated them and found the remains of the ancient kings. I am the one who brought forth from the earth what is probably the most magnificent treasure ever taken out of an earlier civilization. Yet suddenly I am no one. I am not even included in the discussion. They will do with this monumental collection whatever they want. I will not be consulted in Athens either. All of this I have found; I have poured forth tremendous amounts of brains, energy and money. Yet already I am an outsider. There is no further need of me."

After they crossed the road toward the Dases house they could see a number of fires which the soldiers on the acropolis had set at their guard posts in order to keep warm during the night. Henry was awestruck, his mind reeling back through history. He said, more to himself than to his companions:

"For the first time since its capture by the Argives in 468 B.C., and so for the first time during 2,344 years, the acropolis of Mycenae has a garrison whose watch fires, seen by night throughout the whole Plain of Argos, carry back the mind to the watch kept for Agamemnon's return from Troy, and the signal which warned Clytemnestra and her paramour of his approach. . . ."

They went upstairs and said good night as Professor Phindikles retired to the second of the Schliemanns' rooms, which they had afforded him for his stay. Sophia went to bed; but Henry got out paper and ink,

grasped the narrow nightstand between his knees and wrote out a
telegram for King George I:

> With extreme joy I announce to Your Majesty that I have
> discovered the tombs which tradition, echoed by Pausanias,
> has designated as the sepulchers of Agamemnon, Cassandra,
> Eurymedon and all their companions who were killed while
> partaking of a banquet with Clytemnestra and her lover Ae-
> gisthus. They were surrounded with a double circle of stone
> slabs. . . . I found in the tombs immense treasures and ar-
> chaic objects of pure gold.
>
> These treasures by themselves are sufficient to fill a great
> museum, which will be the most wonderful in the world, and
> will attract to Greece for centuries thousands of strangers
> from every land.
>
> Because I work only for the pure love of science I naturally
> have no claim to these treasures. I give them with a lively en-
> thusiasm and intact to Greece. May God grant that these
> treasures may become the cornerstone of an immense national
> wealth.

Henry shook Sophia gently by the shoulder. She had just drifted
into a dreamless sleep. He handed her the telegram, asking her to read
it.

"I simply feel we must not be anonymous . . . displaced. We'll have
difficulties enough when we get back to Athens and attempt to establish the historicity of our tombs. There will be the same volley of gun-
fire we're still suffering about Troy and the treasure of Priam. That's
why I think we ought to make a frontal attack."

Sophia rubbed her eyes, read the telegram. She handed the sheet of
paper back to Henry with a nod of approval.

"I approve. As they say in Crete, never turn your back on an adversary."

7.

The next morning, November 30, Henry moved to the fifth area in
the rock that was demarcated by the tombstone of the carved serpent's
coils. Sophia's crew had already excavated into more than twenty feet
of earth. At this depth they had found two unsculptured stelae. Three
feet below that the men arrived at the opening to the rock tomb itself. The following morning, Henry, Sophia, Spyros, Phindikles and
Stamatakes with a few of Demetrios's faster workers cleared the whole

area of the tomb, twelve feet long and ten feet wide. To their surprise the rock dugout was only two feet deep, by far the shallowest tomb they had found.

When they had put aside the top layer of pebbles there were the remains of only one skeleton covered by masses of ashes. Henry removed a gold diadem from the skull. They examined the shieldlike circles, flowers and wheels in rotation, and in between the series of etched spirals. When Henry tried to raise the skull it disintegrated in his hands. On one side of the body they dug out a lance head, two small bronze swords and two bronze knives. Sophia, working on the opposite side, found a gold drinking cup ornamented with horizontal bands and strokes resembling fish spines. Aside from a great many shards of handmade pottery intermixed with wheel-made pottery, their last find was a fragmented green vase of Egyptian porcelain. Several hours of searching revealed nothing more.

"It's a disappointment after the fourth tomb and its riches," Henry mused. "What we have to do now is to go back to that first tomb which we abandoned when it became rain-filled."

Spyros's crew had begun digging there the afternoon before. With twenty men hand-picked by Demetrios, Henry resumed the excavation. They were already down more than twenty feet from the surface of the agora. From his previous experience Henry assumed he would have to go another ten feet. The air was clear and bright, the rain water had evaporated; his crew was able to move rapidly, digging out the earth within an area of twelve by twenty-two feet, carting off the semidried debris in baskets. It was only an hour before the noon meal and rest that they located the actual sides of the tomb, lined with cyclopean stone. It became narrower and narrower as they worked their way downward to a second wall of schist reinforced with clay which projected into the tomb on all four sides.

When they reached the layer of pebbles closest to the base and removed it, they found their first body, which lay on the south side, feet to the west. It appeared to be a male of considerable size; the body had been squeezed into a space of only five and a half feet. But when they gazed at the head there was an indrawing of breath bespeaking awe. They were gazing upon the most beautiful mask in all of the tombs. The features were Hellenic, the nose straight and narrow, the eyes large with lifelike eyelids; a heroic mouth with well-proportioned lips; a superb beard which left the chin clean; gracefully carved eyebrows and a luxuriant mustache which turned upward at each end.

"It is the face of a monarch," Henry exclaimed. "The greatest of them all . . ."

Spyridon Phindikles looked at Henry quizzically.

"It has to be Agamemnon! There can be no doubt!" exclaimed Henry. "Look at the authority, the power, the superb gift of command. I am certain that we have at long last come upon the body of Agamemnon!"

Professor Phindikles was noncommittal.

Sophia said quietly:

"My dear Henry, you have already reported to the London *Times* and King George that the fourth tomb contained the bodies of Agamemnon and his companions."

"That is the nature of archaeology. Each day of digging brings new finds and upsets the theories of the day before," he replied blandly.

In this narrow tomb bottom, in the quiet tone he would have used to one of his students, Professor Phindikles reprimanded Henry.

"My dear Dr. Schliemann, the first law of science is that you withhold judgment until all of the evidence is in."

Henry felt neither hurt nor admonished.

"Perfectly true, Professor Phindikles. But that is not my nature. It is also not the nature of my work. I want the world to experience our excavations and discoveries as they happen, hour by hour, day by day. If I make assumptions as I go along it is because I conceived of that method as being at the core of my work. When later evidence proves that I have been in error, I admit it quite honestly and go on to what I believe to be the next true assumption. In this way people see not only our every find but learn our every thought. That is the only way I can make my excavations a total experience for the public."

Professor Phindikles patted Henry on the shoulder in paternal and affectionate fashion.

"Well said, Dr. Schliemann. Each of us must express himself according to the demands of his own character."

They went back to work. Unfortunately "Agamemnon's" skull crumbled upon being exposed to the air. Henry cursed under his breath. In the meanwhile Sophia and Phindikles were examining "Agamemnon's" remarkable breastplate, almost two feet long and over a foot broad, of pure gold. Two protruding shieldlike bosses represented "Agamemnon's" breasts; the remainder of the breastplate was profusely ornamented with repoussé spirals. When the two men gingerly removed the breastplate they found little of the skeleton left. What they assumed to be an arm bone had attached to it a broad gold ribbon richly ornamented. From both sides of the body they took out fifteen bronze swords; ten were found at "Agamemnon's" feet. Many of the swords were of extreme size, such as the "King of Men" would have carried. They also found bronze knives, lances, parts of gilded swords. Moving rapidly in the cramped quarters, they unearthed a mine of amber beads, cylinders of gold plate, gold leaves whole or in fragments, broken silver vases and silver tongs; an alabaster vase whose mouthpiece was of bronze plated with gold; inside this vase were handfuls of round gold buttons.

They now moved to the funeral pyre slightly to the north. To their chagrin they found that this body had been plundered. There was no layer of pebbles or clay on top of it and the ashes had been mulled around. The body was without gold ornaments. Henry exclaimed:

"Now I know why I found those twelve gold buttons and leaves when we dug down toward this tomb earlier. Grave robbers dug a narrow shaft straight down, hit this middle body, gathered up all the gold they could get their hands on and fled."

Sophia asked, "When did all this take place?"

Because the shaft had contained the same compacted debris as the rest of the area, the men arrived at the conclusion that the grave robbing had taken place before the capture of Mycenae by the Argives.

On the following morning, December 1, they made the most extraordinary find. It was at the north end. The small crew began removing the remaining earth and soon came to the first layer of pebbles. Once again Henry sent the workmen above ground while he, Sophia and Professor Phindikles cleared away the ash-strewn and fire-blackened pebbles with their hands. Here they found the third skeleton. The mask over the face had been so badly crushed that no clear portrait of the face was discernible. But when Henry removed the mask and the breastplate the explorers stood stunned. For here were a preserved head and torso, with a face that was almost palpitatingly alive as it stared up at them through closed eyelids. They saw first the broad, bald forehead; a vacant area where there must have been a short nose; and a thin-lipped mouth which disclosed a complete set of thirty-two white and perfect teeth. The body had been laid out in such a compressed space that the shoulders were hunched up around the chin and the back of the head. The rib cage was in good condition though all flesh between the ribs and the backbone had vanished, leaving the backbone pressed up against the ribs. The hipbones lay in their proper place but the body from the groin down was gone.

It was a good face, strong, characterful and, certainly during life, a handsome one. When Henry could catch his breath he said in an aside to Sophia:

"This face is very much like the picture which my imagination formed of Agamemnon long ago."

"Now, Henry," Sophia admonished sternly, "you cannot have three Agamemnons. You have to make up your mind which one was commander of the Achaean forces."

"I know," he said ruefully. "That magnificent mask on that first figure is surely the portrait of Agamemnon. However we found no face under the mask. So now what I'm stuck with is the mask of one man, about whom I had dreamed, and the face of another. It's a problem I will have to wrestle with."

They began inspecting the layer of gold and gold treasures which surrounded the body. The breastplate was mighty but plain, sixteen inches long and ten broad. To the right of the body they uncovered two bronze swords. The handle of one of the swords was thickly plated with gold. Henry did not have to move more than one foot before he found eleven more bronze swords, gold plates, more than a hundred gold buttons. Sophia uncovered in her area twelve more gold plates, one of which showed a lion chasing a stag. Very soon there surfaced a mammoth gold drinking cup.

Henry turned to Professor Phindikles.

"It's simply a miracle that this mortal corpse has remained almost intact since antiquity. I am afraid to touch it for fear the whole figure will break up as the others have. Would you by any chance know anything about embalming?"

Professor Phindikles said, "To give it permanent hardness? Unfortunately, no. I doubt if anyone else in the Argolid does."

"Then the least I can do," said Henry, "is to send for our painter in Nauplion and have him come out immediately to do a portrait. Then we will have preserved the image for posterity."

Henry climbed out of the tomb, took a note pad out of his pocket, scrawled a telegram to Perikles Komnenos urging him to come at once.

By the time Henry climbed back down into the tomb it was already growing dark. Professor Phindikles suggested:

"Don't you think it would be better to wait until morning before we do any more exploring down here? We don't want to accidentally injure these earthly remains."

"Will it be safe to leave the tomb in this condition?" Sophia asked. "There must be a tremendous number of gold objects buried beneath the ash and dirt."

Henry agreed with Sophia. He suggested that they work by candlelight. Professor Phindikles exercised his gentle authority.

"The soldiers will keep everyone out."

Henry and Sophia yielded. He called for Stamatakes to come and get the last boxes of the precious metal, jewelry, breastplate and mask. They called for ropes to be lowered, the boxes were tied longways and across; and then he shouted for the trove to be hauled up. Stamatakes, waiting at the mouth of the tomb, untied the ropes, covered the boxes with a coarse cloth and took them to the horse cart where he placed them alongside the others, covering them with a blanket. The fiercest-looking of the soldiers had been selected to stand guard at this horse cart all day, though the precaution was unnecessary. The Argolids would have dreaded stealing anything from a more than three-thousand-year-old tomb; it would have brought a curse down upon them, even as the people of the Troad believed that if they worked on a saint's day "the saint will strike us!"

The next morning they rode up to the acropolis in the Dases horse cart. They began sifting through the earth of the tomb and were soon rewarded with the discovery of a thick gold goblet ornamented with three lions running at tremendous speed. They found two more gold goblets and a smaller drinking cup. Scattered through the debris and apparently not related to any one skeleton were silver goblets and a large silver vase. Sophia, scratching through the dirt with a small pocket knife, turned up an alabaster drinking cup. Phindikles came upon a cache of gold plates like double eagles leaning against each other, their heads turned in opposite directions.

Perikles Komnenos arrived on horseback late in the morning, his saddlebags filled with sketching pad, canvas, brushes and oil paints. Henry took him down into the tomb at once. When Komnenos said that he wanted to make crayon sketches first, Henry replied:

"Art is your profession, not mine. Do what you must to bring out a faithful portrait. We are going to have to try to move this body out of here in a day or two."

The others climbed out of the tomb and had their food-rest period, sitting on undecorated stelae in the December sun, as thin as some of the gold straps and bands they had found. They were not alone. The day before some of the workmen had caught a glimpse of the "mortal corpse"; they had been fascinated by what they saw. Word had spread quickly among the other workmen, all of whom had gathered around the mouth of the tomb. When Henry saw the almost paralyzed astonishment on their faces, he had commented to Sophia:

"The whole of the Argolid is going to know about this discovery. Word will spread tonight and tomorrow morning like wildfire."

By midmorning the people of the surrounding villages were streaming in, arriving on horseback, donkey, in farm wagons, on foot. They craned down into the tomb to catch a glimpse of this ancient man still so vividly alive and present. By midafternoon carriages began arriving from Argos. Demetrios and Spyros remained down in the tomb. The soldiers threw a rope cordon around to keep people at a proper distance, and also to keep them from falling in. After each new group arrived they were lost in silence and wonderment; then their words and questions poured forth, joining those of the several hundred now on the acropolis.

Henry, Sophia and Professor Phindikles circulated among the crowd
asking people if they knew anything about embalming, or if not, could
they name someone who did.

Late in the afternoon, still working on their hands and knees and
with a great deal of care, Henry and Sophia turned up shieldlike dishes,
the top fragment of a silver vase with a gold mouthpiece and handle,
hundreds more of gold buttons, and highly decorated broad golden
ribbons whose purpose they could not guess. In the closing hours they
unearthed gold ornaments for greaves; pieces of carved bone and ivory
which appeared to have been knife handles; deeper down, large copper
vessels, a quadrangular wooden box, two sides of which were carved to
represent a lion and a dog. The wood was as moist as a wet sponge and
Henry felt that it would dissolve before they could get it to the surface.
Instead it hardened the moment it was taken out of the tomb. Intermixed with all the ash and dirt were shards of pottery and, as in the
smaller tomb, evidences of food, particularly oysters.

Sophia found it an eerie experience to be working all day in the presence of this almost living man. This long-dead monarch, whatever his
name may have been, seemed to be watching her even when she was
working with her back to him. When she turned in his direction she
could not keep her eyes off the animated, expressive face. The king
seemed to be talking to her. She did not know what he was saying, she
did not recognize the language, but in these two days, far more strongly
than she had ever felt it before, she knew that she was again living intensely on the two time levels of her husband's life and her own: the
Year of Our Lord 1876; and the year of his lordship who had survived
the crushing impact of more than three millennia. She was sensitive to
the life he had lived, though her actual knowledge was limited to what
she and Henry had unearthed at Troy, and here at Mycenae. The king
did not frighten her; though his face was powerful in structure it was
not menacing. She felt she could have been happy as a subject of this
monarch as he ruled over the vast and beautiful Mycenaean civilization, lived comfortably in this acropolis. After all, was she not married
to a man who was a monarch in his own world? The spectacular treasure
of these tombs had been Henry Schliemann's accomplishment and his
alone. Through him, for the first time, the world would know how the
Mycenaeans had lived and died; perhaps even some of their innermost
secrets. She had one bold wish she did not confide even to Henry: that
Homer could have been beside them during these revealing days; so
much of what he had written about the Mycenaeans had come to life
to prove the authenticity of *The Iliad* and *The Odyssey*.

Darkness came early now on this second day of December. The
crowds dispersed. Henry and his little group remained around the tomb

until the soldiers had lighted half a dozen campfires and pledged not to move more than a couple of feet away during the entire night.

The following day, December 3, there were a full thousand Argolids collected from all over the province, eager to see the unbelievable phenomenon: one of their remote ancestors who had returned to them. The soldiery was still keeping its barricade against anyone attempting to climb down into the tomb. While Henry was standing on top of the agora chatting with the police chief of Nauplion and the prefect of Argos, a middle-aged, bald-headed man wearing thick spectacles and a blue half smock walked up to them. He was carrying a tightly lashed bundle in his hand.

"Mr. Prefect, would you be so kind as to introduce me to Dr. Schliemann. I have a suggestion to make to him."

The prefect turned to Henry and said, "This is our pharmacist from Argos, Spyridon Nikolaou."

A glint came into Henry's eyes.

"I hope your suggestion is the one I have been waiting for."

"Yes, Dr. Schliemann, I believe it is. A dozen of my friends have come into my pharmacy to tell me that you are searching for someone who knows about embalming. I have read the material on the Egyptian embalmers; they preserved bodies by injecting spices. On two occasions I was called to Nauplion to preserve the bodies of sailors so they could be taken home for burial. I used alcohol in which I had dissolved gum sandarac. The alcohol preserves the resin as a varnish. Apparently the method works because I had letters from the sailors' families thanking me."

"You are most welcome," Henry exclaimed. "This is what I have been hoping for. Come with me."

Henry led the pharmacist down the ladder. Nikolaou examined the corpse carefully, then took out the ingredients from his kit.

"You understand I can only apply my solution to the parts that are exposed."

"Preserve for us everything that your brush can touch. Then we'll get a sheet of iron or plank under him and move him out intact."

The pharmacist poured a quantity of alcohol into his bowl, opened his pouch of gum sandarac, mixed the resinlike matter into the alcohol. He looked up at Henry with all the pride of a professional.

"Dr. Schliemann, I suggest that I begin on this broad forehead and work my way down over his face, mouth, teeth, chin, rib cage . . ."

"Yes, yes," said Henry impatiently, "you are the expert."

To the painter Komnenos, who resented this intrusion upon his work, Henry said in a solacing tone:

"You have done just fine. It is an accurate portrait both in structure and in color. . . ."

". . . haven't finished yet!"

"I know. No conscientious artist ever finishes. But please give Spyridon Nikolaou an hour or two to preserve the remains. You can continue your painting while we find a way to remove our ancient friend in one piece."

The throngs jammed against the soldiers' barricade, demanding the right to watch the process. Sophia was afraid they might break through, fall the thirty-three feet to the bottom. She asked Leonidas Leonardos and the prefect to please warn the people, but the murmuring protest at not being able to see the cadaver being given a coat of resin did not die away.

Spyridon Nikolaou began his work slowly with a narrow brush and worked steadily for two hours. When he finished he straightened up, tried to flick the stains off his smock.

"There, Dr. Schliemann, I believe your old friend will remain intact. He is not embalmed but he is certainly in a state of preservation. You have my word that you can take him back to Athens."

Professor Phindikles, who had come down the ladder to watch the process, congratulated the pharmacist in the name of the Greek Archaeological Society. To Henry's utter amazement the professor took out his wallet, asked the man what his charge would be, and paid him in cash. Henry said:

"Professor, you astonish me! This is the first time in all of my years of digging that anyone has paid one drachma of my cost."

Professor Phindikles beamed.

"I have been authorized by the Society to pay such costs. I will also pay for the removal of our monarch from the tomb and the cost of shipping him back to Athens."

The pharmacist shook hands all around, climbed the ladder and acknowledged the applause of the crowd. Sophia rejoined the men at the bottom of the tomb.

"I've measured the body," said Henry; "now I'll ride into Argos with the prefect and find an iron plate big enough to slip under him."

They dropped Sophia at the Dases house. Henry continued into Argos with the prefect. Together they went to the town blacksmith and had several narrow sheets of iron plate welded together. The litter was ready by nightfall. Henry returned with the iron plate lashed to the back of the carriage. Demetrios and Ajax unloaded it and leaned it against the horse cart, which would take it up to the acropolis the next morning.

It was another sleepless night. Henry talked straight through until dawn. Sophia could hear only part of what appeared to be an autobiographical reminiscence in which he went back to the beginnings of his first boyhood interest in Troy and Mycenae, then worked his way forward in great and loving detail through the staggering results of the past days.

They dressed at first light. The members of the Dases household were already up. There was hot coffee on the kitchen table. Demetrios and Ajax had already loaded the iron plate onto the cart. Henry, Sophia and Professor Phindikles rode donkeys up to the Lion Gate.

It took half a dozen workmen to lower the plate gingerly into the tomb. They tried to dig out the layer of pebbles below the skeleton but they had been mashed into the soft rock of the floor by the weight that had been pressing upon them over the ages. Henry and the professor commanded the job from either side of the now hardened mummy. But every effort to insert the plate so that they could lift the body from its long-time bed failed. After several hours of trying, Professor Phindikles said:

"Dr. Schliemann, we're just going to have to think of something else."

Henry shook his head in despair.

"I know. I've been trying to figure out an alternative method. Suppose we cut a small trench into the rock all around the body, then make a horizontal incision? We could cut out a slab about two inches thick, then lift slab, pebbles and body together."

"And insert the iron?"

"No. We will then need a plank box to hold him intact as we lift him out. We will have to get some wood planks nailed together to put underneath the rock, then build a box around the figure."

Two of the Dases men went into the village to get the planking. In the meanwhile Henry's crew began laboriously to cut through the rock beneath the pebble bed with only their shovels and knives to work with. The process took several hours. Demetrios returned, the men lowered the planks to the bottom of the tomb. One by one they were set in place and the verticals nailed to the bottom planks until a four-sided box had been created.

As large a crowd as had assembled the day before was on hand to watch as Henry's crew lowered strong ropes; they were slipped under the box and tied securely to avoid slippage. Henry, Sophia and Professor Phindikles scrambled up the ladder. It took over a dozen men to pull up the heavy treasure with a kind of chanting grunt. It came up inch by inch, smoothly. After a considerable time, during which Henry held Sophia's hand in his so tightly that she felt the bones were being crushed, the heavy cargo reached the surface, was pulled to one side and laid reverentially on the topsoil of the agora.

There was no keeping back the crowd now. Every person had to have a look at the face. There was no danger; the people were patient, filing past the corpse as though he were the king of Greece who had died only the day before and was lying in state in the cathedral in Athens. There was a numb yet eloquent silence.

The last of the Argolids had passed in review. Henry directed his men to load the funeral box onto the horse cart. The crew protested, crying:

"Dr. Schliemann, let us carry him into Charvati on our shoulders. It will be the greatest honor of our lives."

Six men on each side raised the box onto their shoulders. Two more walked in front and still another two behind. Henry and Sophia walked immediately behind the casket. Professor Phindikles and Spyros came next. Behind them came Stamatakes flanked on either side by Leonidas Leonardos and the prefect of Argos.

It was a royal procession. Night began to fall as the pallbearers moved through the Lion Gate and down the curving road to Charvati. By the time they reached the village it was dark; but the village was ablaze with torches held high in the air by the farmers of the neighborhood, who escorted the procession to its resting place in the storehouse.

While the storehouse door was being opened, Ioanna Dases linked her arm through Sophia's. Sophia was surprised to see that there were tears in the older woman's eyes. She asked:

"Ioanna, why are you crying?"

"I feel bad for the poor man. All these thousands of years he has been safe. No one could hurt him down there in the tomb. He had privacy. What will happen to him now?"

Sophia put her arm around her friend's shoulder, said consolingly:

"Why, Ioanna, he will be immortalized! He will live forever in Athens in a great archaeological museum. People will come from all over the world to kneel before him and to pledge their allegiance!"

BOOK EIGHT

IT TAKES TIME TO MATURE

1.

THE Athens newspapers had carried word of the arrival of the Schliemann party from Mycenae and had described some of their remarkable finds. A group of friends were on the dock to greet them. All watched as the boxes of gold were moved off the ship to a subterranean vault in the National Bank of Greece near Omonoia Square.

Sophia and Henry entered the house on Mousson Street with a sense of triumph. Sophia slipped back into the role of mother and housewife. Andromache was at her side the entire day, enchanted at the promise that she would be going to Mycenae in the spring. Henry inspected his trunks of Trojan treasures in their rear garden storehouses and found them in order. The house was a happy domicile . . . until Henry ran into what he called "planned obstructionism" in his desire to have the gold treasures photographed so that he could take the pictures to London where engravings would be made for John Murray's publication.

He went first for permission to the president of the Greek Archaeological Society, Philippos Ioannou. Ioannou did not so much deny Henry the permission as put him off. Henry next went to the Minister of Public Instruction, Georgios Milesses, who advised:

"Be patient. We must wait until Stamatakes returns."

Henry flushed, said with a touch of sarcasm:

"What is the power of a watchman over the treasures he was guarding?"

"The Archaeological Society insists."

Henry next went to his friend Stephanos Koumanoudes, who had brought Emperor Dom Pedro to Mycenae. He explained how much time would be required to get the two hundred photographs he needed; and what a meticulous job he wanted to do, since *Mycenae* was to be published in New York, Paris and Leipzig, each of the firms using the same engravings.

"My dear friend, I understand your impatience. However the Archaeological Society has decided that they want to be present, as a Committee of the Whole, when the boxes are first opened."

Henry had no one else to turn to. He had not heard from King George I, which meant that he could not intrude upon the palace. Since he could not fume publicly, the house shook with his hard-footed pacing and his denouncement of the authorities.

"It was *I* who discovered the treasures! It was *I* who paid the costs. It was *I* who made this gift of incalculable value to the Greek people!"

Sophia's efforts to mollify him, as each day's delay upset him more, succeeded in small measure but at large cost to her nerves. Early one morning she donned a black and white wool dress decorated with dark gray laces and went to see Euthymios Kastorches. He had secured them the engineer who had approved their continuing to dig at the Lion Gate and the treasury.

"All I ask is that you set the date for the Society meeting at the earliest possible moment. It would be a kindness to me."

Kastorches's dark eyes brooded over the problem for several moments.

"The Archaeological Society has voted not to visit the National Bank until next year. I will do my best to get the date set early. I know that will be an intolerable wait for your volcanic husband, another three weeks, but there are intermediate steps I can take that will solace him."

The following noon Henry received a note inviting the Schliemanns to come to the office of the Minister of Public Instruction on December 14, where one box of finds: some of the more valuable Hera idols, the key to the Lion Gate, the incised seal ring with the two women of the beautiful hairdos and fragments of the warrior vase was to be shown.

When they returned home from this meeting they found an invitation from King George to visit him at the palace the next day. Professor Phindikles had assured the king that Henry Schliemann had not exaggerated, that the gold treasure was probably the single greatest collection discovered anywhere in the world.

The next day they dressed in the same well-tailored but conservative outfits they had worn the year before when Mr. Gladstone took them to tea on the Terrace of the House of Commons. They left their carriage in front of the great door of the palace, went through the big hall and were shown into the office of the chamberlain. He took them along a corridor to the audience room next to the king's private study. The chamberlain formally announced Dr. and Kyria Schliemann. The king received them warmly. He was dressed in his dark blue admiral's uniform which had two rows of gold buttons on the jacket and a high collar embroidered with gold thread. George I, elected to succeed King Otho, who had been deposed by the military, had been king for thirteen years now, yet he was only thirty-one years old.

Henry and Sophia were invited to sit in armchairs facing the king. Sophia remained very still while Henry graphically related their adventures in finding the tombs and bringing out the treasures. When he had finished, King George said:

"I congratulate you. You may be sure I am eager to see the gold. I understand the Archaeological Society is opening the chests the first of the year."

On the way down the palace steps, flushed with pleasure and reassurance by the king's enthusiasm, Sophia murmured:

"So an early January date is now set, thanks to our friend Kastorches."

He smiled at her, gratitude mixed into his relief.

"You have done well, Sophidion."

"You should use the next two weeks to write the final article you planned for the London *Times*, and rewrite those parts of your journal you wanted to expand."

He gave her a quizzical glance.

"And be quiet about it, you mean? Restore peace to Mousson Street? It shall be done."

Henry rose at dawn to write the London *Times* article and to put into book form the informal entries from his journal. At ten he walked down to the Fair Greece for coffee and to read the European and English newspapers. He was at home promptly at one-thirty; after their nap he took Sophia and Andromache for a carriage ride into the country. Having agreed to rescue Yannakis, Polyxene and their son Hector, who were living in poverty and disgrace in Renkoi, he sent them passage money to take ship to Piraeus. Sophia furnished the semi-basement as an apartment where they would be able to enjoy some of the privacy of family life. The Turkophones were overjoyed to be free again and reunited with the Schliemanns. There were tears in the giant's eyes when he fell on one knee, kissed Sophia's hand, murmured reverentially:

"*Doulos sas.*"

Polyxene embraced Sophia as a long-lost sister. Henry put Yannakis in charge of the gardens and whatever repairs needed doing in the house. He begged Henry to deposit his wage in a bank each month; there was a farm outside of Renkoi he wanted to buy.

January dawned clear but with the crisp bite of winter. They rode down to St. Panaghitsa's for the service, then over to the National Bank. Members of the Archaeological Society had begun to assemble in the director's office. Several of the members' wives belonged to the Association of Ladies. They greeted Sophia heartily, took pride in the articles she had written for the *Ephimeris*, but particularly for her excavation which had freed the imposing "Treasury of Mrs. Schliemann."

President Philippos Ioannou led the way down to the basement vault, in front of which stood an armed guard. The director of the bank and the president of the Society inserted their keys. The heavy door swung open.

Ephor Stamatakes was the last to enter. He had returned to Athens four days after Henry and Sophia had seen the king, with another thirteen trunks of Henry's finds. They too had been locked in the bank vault. The boxes of gold weighed only thirty pounds; the other finds, including the tombstones, decorated stelae and arrowheads of stone, weighed six thousand.

The basement vault of stone and cement was large, cool, burglar-proof; a custodian lighted several gas lamps. President Ioannou asked Henry which of his boxes of treasure he wished to have opened. Henry indicated the one he knew contained the most staggering crowns, masks, breastplates, goblets. Stamatakes, who had sealed the box in Charvati, came forward, "as though he had discovered the royal tombs himself," Sophia thought. He ignored the Schliemanns, whom he had not seen or spoken to since his return, pried the lid from the box. He was about to lift out the first of the gold masks when Henry intervened.

"Mr. Stamatakes, I placed these treasures in the box; I shall take them out."

Stamatakes retreated to the far end of the room. Henry first brought forth several of the gold diadems found among the skulls of the second tomb. There was an awed silence, then a sharp intaking of breath, voices exclaiming, ". . . exquisite." . . . "I've never seen anything more beautiful." . . . "Unbelievable." . . . "We cannot equal such workmanship today."

Henry described the different tomb structures, the beds of pebbles, the skeletons, and then the royal gold itself. He displayed the hundreds of gold plates with repoussé decorations, the crown of gold with its thirty-six leaves, the two large gold masks from the fourth tomb, "Nestor's goblet" decorated with two gold pigeons . . . the incredibly beautiful mask of Agamemnon, with its powerful nose, trimmed mustache, narrow face and chin beard.

The audience was stunned. Then the assemblage burst into applause. There were cries of "Bravo! Bravo!" President Ioannou, who had not permitted anyone to touch the gold, including himself, said:

"Dr. Schliemann, my heartfelt congratulations. Not only to you and Kyria Schliemann, but to us, the Greek people; and to all the world which will share this magnificent treasure with us. In my travels to the most famous museums I have never seen anything to compare with your discoveries. You have enriched all of mankind!"

He turned to his members, saw the approval on their faces. "You may begin your photographing tomorrow."

2.

January of 1877 was a month of intensive work. Henry spent most of the day at the bank, setting up the gold pieces at their best possible angles; grouping the smaller pieces, earrings, ornamented leaves, bracelets, necklaces into attractive compositions. He wanted all the important finds in the pages of his forthcoming book.

His task was made simpler because John Murray was paying to have the photographs converted into engravings. Each morning the Romaïdes brothers would bring Henry the developed negatives of the material shot the day before. When the film was not as clean in its detail as Henry desired, they would redo it.

There was an aspect of the work in the basement vault that was not so readily solved. Henry was irritated that he had to work under the close supervision of a committee of five: Stamatakes, two members of the Archaeological Society, the General Inspector of Antiquities, the vice-president of the National Bank. Not all five were present throughout Henry's ten-hour workday; the vice-president was sometimes called upstairs on a bank matter, the others had additional duties in the city. But there seemed to be a general agreement among the committee that at least three of them had to be present at all times. They kept careful lists of everything Henry took out of the boxes, and at closing time checked to make sure that every object had been returned.

"They think I am going to steal part of the treasure," Henry growled to Sophia. "If I had intended to do so, I could have done it more easily in Mycenae."

"It's because we smuggled the treasure of Priam out of Turkey," she mourned. "They have not forgotten."

Sophia observed that something good always arrived on the scene coupled to something unfortunate. Henry was relieved of Stamatakes's omnipresence when the Society sent him to Mycenae to make tests for future excavations and to build a guardhouse on the acropolis; but Henry was informed that during Stamatakes's absence he would be allowed to photograph only the clay, bronze and stone artifacts.

On January 20, Henry received a telegram from Lieutenant Drosinos, whom he had sent to Mycenae to draw some additional plans. Drosinos believed he had stumbled across a new grave site outside the small retaining wall of the agora. He suggested that Henry come at once.

"I don't think it's possible," Henry declared. "I won't drop everything and rush down."

On January 26, King George and Queen Olga came to the basement room accompanied by the Duke and Duchess of Edinburgh. Henry set forth the finest of the gold masks and diadems. The royal couple was enchanted. That night a message awaited him at home: Ephor Stamatakes had excavated the grave site Lieutenant Drosinos had cabled them about and found a cache of gold: four vases, each decorated with the head of a dog, bottles, rings engraved with palm trees and luxuriously dressed women, heads of bulls, necklaces . . .

Henry's face went ashen. He began to shake as though in a seizure. He stumbled a few steps and collapsed into a chair.

"What have I allowed to happen?" he moaned, bent over from the waist and holding his face in his hands. "I should have gone to Mycenae the moment Drosinos's telegram arrived. Of all the people in the world to stumble onto a grave, Stamatakes would be my last choice. Mycenae was ours. Now we will have to share it with that insufferable . . ."

Sophia tried to find words of comfort.

"My dear, you're exaggerating. Mycenae is ours: the opening of the Lion Gate, the treasury, the royal tombs . . . ours, all ours. Your book will prove it."

Henry raised his head, exposing bloodshot eyes. He appeared to have aged twenty years.

"He has been improbable all along. Now he will be impossible."

"There's one thing he can't do," she cried. "He cannot publish anything about his finds! Your permit gives you the exclusive rights to everything found in Mycenae."

The tic along his left jawbone quieted.

"Yes, we can keep him from writing; but he can also keep us from describing his pieces in our book. What a fool I was! I was within a few feet of that cache, right next to the large house I excavated outside the grave circle. Why didn't I make that little extra effort?"

"Errikaki, stop flagellating yourself."

When he left the house she found herself emotionally spent; for the first time in almost two years her insides were in turmoil.

A few days later they received a letter from Drosinos telling what had happened. When he went to Mycenae on January 20 to draw the additional plans for Henry, he noticed that outside the grave circle there appeared to be an area similar to the graves already discovered. He warned the soldier on duty, Panopoulos, to protect the site against visitors and cabled Henry his belief. When he returned to Nauplion he found Stamatakes waiting for him. He told Stamatakes that he had alerted the watchman about the possibility of another grave site, and had cabled the information to Henry. Stamatakes proceeded to Mycenae and immediately excavated the site. Lieutenant Drosinos was sending a copy of his letter to the newspaper *Stoa*.

At the end of January, on the same day that Lieutenant Drosinos's letter appeared in the *Stoa*, Stamatakes returned from Mycenae and took the new treasure to the basement vault of the National Bank. Outraged at Drosinos's published letter, he wrote a counter-article which appeared in the *Ephimeris* of February 2. In it he stated that when he went to Drosinos's house to study the latest drawings of Mycenae, Drosinos told him that he had seen the signs of a grave outside the grave-circle wall. Stamatakes had informed him that it was impossible to find a grave outside this smaller wall. Nothing more had been said about the matter. Drosinos had not drawn Stamatakes's attention to any particular spot. Stamatakes had found his gold in the ruins of a building. He had found animal bones, not human, therefore it was not a grave. His discovery of the cache had been solely his own doing.

Henry and Sophia followed the quarrel in the press. On February 7, Drosinos counterattacked with the categorical statement that nothing Stamatakes said in his article was true. Two days later Stamatakes retaliated with a blistering paragraph:

> It is not true that Drosinos drew my attention to anything. He wrote all this to be pleasant to Henry Schliemann and draw money from him. Henry Schliemann is afraid that my recent discoveries might be published by someone else and he is eager to include them in his book, from which he expects great financial profits.

The Archaeological Society and government officials with whom Stamatakes worked believed his version. Lieutenant Drosinos found himself in serious trouble: it was learned that he had not asked permission of his superior to go to Mycenae to work for Henry. On instructions from Athens he was demoted in rank and fined a month's salary.

"It is my obligation to keep Lieutenant Drosinos from such severe punishment," Henry insisted. "After all, he was without an assignment and had the spare time."

"Everyone who works for us is penalized," said Sophia with a note of sadness in her voice.

It took considerable doing but Henry persevered, pleading Drosinos's case with the Minister of Public Instruction, the officers of the Archaeological Society, anyone who might have influence with the Greek government. He succeeded in having Drosinos retain his title of lieutenant but could not get the fine rescinded. He sent the man an equivalent sum.

Henry had no sooner rescued Drosinos than another friend, the chief of police of Nauplion, was discharged and then threatened with a jail term. Leonidas Leonardos was accused of having received a one-thousand-franc tip from Emperor Dom Pedro for guarding the Emperor during his stay at Nauplion, and of having lied to his men, claiming that the Emperor had given him only the forty francs which he had shared with his officers. Leonardos wrote to Henry swearing that he had received only forty francs, eight dollars. Henry promptly wrote to the Prime Minister asking him to pardon Leonardos. The Prime Minister did not respond. Henry wrote again, swearing that Leonardos was a totally honest man who would not cheat his men. The truth of the matter appeared to be that Leonardos and the mayor of Nauplion had quarreled. The mayor had spread the story. When the Prime Minister still remained silent, Henry wrote to Emperor Dom Pedro, who was traveling in Cairo, asking, "in the name of sacred truth and humanity," how much Leonardos had received, forty francs or more?

The Emperor cabled the moment he received the letter, testifying that he had given the sum of forty francs and nothing more. The Prime Minister studied the cablegram long enough to have read it five times. He then apologized to Henry for not having answered his letters, and sent instructions to Nauplion ordering Leonardos returned to his post.

Henry's first desire was to see the new gold pieces. From Stamatakes's brief listing of them in his telegram to the Archaeological Society they did not sound like his own findings. Since Stamatakes insisted that he had found the cache inside the ruins of an old house, and not in a grave, Henry was certain the gold had belonged to a private family. This lessened its importance. Still, he would have to include photographs in his Mycenae book if it was to be complete.

Ephor Stamatakes had a modest office in one of the government-rented buildings in the center of town. He said, "Come in," when Henry knocked on the door, then gazed at him without recognition. Henry asked if they could go together to the National Bank and see the gold and other artifacts Stamatakes had brought back with him. Stamatakes replied in a flat tone:

"I am not yet ready to open the boxes."

"May I ask when you intend to do so?"

"I don't know. Not for some time. I have reports to write. I will open the boxes when the members of the Greek Archaeological Society and the university can be present."

"But you know that I will have to include this cache in my book on Mycenae?"

Stamatakes stared up from his office chair.

"You are no friend of mine, Mr. Schliemann. You fought for Lieutenant Drosinos, who called me a liar in the public prints."

"He is a good engineer. What purpose would it have served to ruin his army career?"

"The purpose of truth!" Harshly. "But you have never been interested in truth. You are interested only in yourself, whatever fame and fortune you can extract from your two lucky strikes at Hissarlik and Mycenae."

Again Henry trudged the government offices. He was never outrightly denied permission to see Stamatakes's finds, but he was told delays were inevitable. He remained polite with the important men with whom he was pleading but at home he poured out his hatred for Stamatakes, "that government clerk"; his anger and anguish at being passed from office to office and friend to friend with no helping hand.

The General Inspector of Antiquities had no great fondness for Henry; it was to Eustratiades that Henry and Sophia had had to report three years before, after their first exploratory trip to Mycenae, when Henry had been accused of having contempt for Greek law. Yet now Eustratiades was the one who instructed Stamatakes to meet him and the Schliemanns at the National Bank on the afternoon of February 18, at which time he was to permit Dr. Schliemann to photograph the find. Some degree of calm returned to Henry's excitable mind.

"*Combustible* would be a more proper word," said Sophia.

Even while photographing at a furious clip Henry began planning a permanent home for his collections from Troy and Mycenae. He told Sophia, while they chatted over supper:

"I'm going back to my original plan, the one that was discarded when the lawsuits began. I'm going to offer a big corner lot near the university and the same forty thousand dollars to build a museum which the architect, Ziller, has agreed to design."

"Only one is yours, Henry. The Mycenae finds belong to Greece."

"Don't quibble! Can't you picture how breath-taking the Schliemann Museum will be, with our gold, gems, vases, stelae . . . ? People will come from all over the world."

She held her tongue. Henry still did not understand the Greek character. Yet he had realized, if only for a moment in Charvati, when Phindikles and Stamatakes had discussed the handling of the treasure, leaving him out of the discussion, that they had no further need for his services. The members of the Archaeological Society and the departments of the government that handled antiquities had all graduated from the University of Athens, had the same training, the same values inculcated into them. They were a homogeneous group into which Henry could not fit. He was a foreigner, an eccentric, an "enthusiast." They would reject him.

And so it happened. The Prime Minister, the Minister of Public Instruction, the president of the Archaeological Society all thanked him for his generous offer; but they had already begun building their own monumental national museum which would house all the antiquities found in Greece, those already in hand, those to come from Olympia, Delphi . . .

Henry felt humiliated, turned sullen. Then, after a few days, he came up with a second idea. He went to the proper officials and asked if he might begin to design and build glass cases and display shelves for an early exhibition of the Mycenae treasure. They said they were in no hurry to exhibit: there was a great deal of work left to be done in restoring a number of the pieces, putting together the potsherds, drawing up a catalogue.

Sophia winced when he related these happenings. She had known he was going to be hurt again when he told her about this plan to pressure the Society into the fastest possible exhibition.

Henry had endless resilience.

"I am sure they are unable to think of an exhibition this year because they have no suitable place to stage it. I will scour the city and find the best possible hall."

It took him several days of walking the streets to find that there was no space at the university, no appropriate government building they could use. Then he stumbled across a pleasant building in the otherwise unfinished Polytechnical School. He spoke to the rector, agreed to pay a substantial rent, gained the permission. But when he brought this news to the Archaeological Society they were not impressed.

"Dr. Schliemann, we have already told you that we are not interested in exhibiting this year. And possibly not next year. We want to think out everything in advance so that the display will be immaculate."

Frustrated, he poured out his woes to his wife, who had been successfully concealing her own frustration.

"Henry, this is hard for me to say about my fellow Greeks. It is going to sound cruel. But they will be content to wait for several years, until you will no longer be associated with the excavation, so that it can be a wholly Athenian exhibition, *their* exhibition, owing nothing to Dr. Henry Schliemann."

Henry stared at her for a long time, as though she had struck him in the face. Tears came into his eyes.

"Very well, since I am unwanted here I shall negotiate with the South Kensington Museum in London to show our treasure of Priam. Prime

Minister Gladstone encouraged me to do so and he informs me that they will be delighted to have the exhibition."

His decision enabled him to recover his poise. Sophia was happy for her husband, sad for herself. Once the treasure left Athens it might never return!

A telegram from London elated Henry. He read it to her several times, wanting her to savor his joy. He had been invited to lecture at the Royal Archaeological Institute of Great Britain and Ireland in May, at which time they would both be given diplomas and be made honorary members.

"Two diplomas!" cried Sophia with a smile. "Henry, it will be like graduating from the university together!"

Henry let it be known that he did not care to excavate at Mycenae any more.

"After the royal tombs, the unearthing of the palace would be an anticlimax for me. Nor do I want to dig any more in Greece. I want us to resume our work in Troy."

"Troy! What more do you hope to find there?"

"I want to uncover the rest of Priam's palace. We failed to finish the job because we had to get the gold out. I want to lay bare the whole of the third, or burned city, also the entire circuit of the defense wall. There may be more layers in Troy than we ever dreamed of, possibly as many as seven. I want to excavate all of them. There are years of work to be done there, and now that I have more experience I can be more scientific in my methods."

Sophia sighed. She could not take Andromache to Troy. There were no schools, no doctors. Henry did have his *firman*, but it was good for only one more year, until May 5, 1878, and he had already accepted the invitation of the Royal Archaeological Institute!

3.

Germany's academic scholars, the most respected in the world, did not wait for his book on Mycenae to be published to deprecate the royal tombs and golden treasure. They used his articles in the London *Times* as a basis to continue their artillery fire.

Dr. Ernst Curtius, author of a renowned book on the Peloponnesus and the history of Greece, a former professor at the University of Berlin, was the archaeologist who had succeeded in getting Olympia for the Prussian government, and was in charge of the excavation there. Henry had met him in Berlin in 1871. The two men had corresponded and, despite the fact that Curtius believed that Troy had been built at Bounarbashi, became good acquaintances.

Dr. Curtius had been given the right to examine the Mycenae gold at the National Bank. He wrote to his wife:

> The gold is of such incredible thinness that the hero Agamemnon must have been but a beggarly prince. These graves in the acropolis resemble nothing in classical antiquity.

Mrs. Curtius wrote an article for a German newspaper centered around her husband's letter. It was an attack on Henry's theories about Mycenae, and also the worth of the finds. Curtius's opinion would be accepted throughout the German-speaking world and was likely to be picked up by the press of other countries.

The attack made Henry furious. He retaliated by pointing out that "the German government has also found the excavations at Olympia disappointing. If they do not find anything worth speaking of at Olympia, it is because they work like ignorant fools, without order or system, and throw all the rubbish within fifty yards of the site they excavate. With one third of the money they have spent I would have done wonders. . . . They are too *learned* to make excavations."

A second attack came from Ernst Boetticher, a German army captain turned scholar. At a conference in Berlin, after the Schliemanns' first dig at Hissarlik, Captain Boetticher had made a speech asserting that there never had been a Troy and that Homer was a group name covering several hundred years of poets and bards. Henry had risen to his feet and told the assemblage that Captain Boetticher knew nothing about the interior evidence of *The Iliad* and *The Odyssey*, which proved that Homer was indeed one man, the first immortal poet. The indiscretion earned him a lifetime enemy. Boetticher published articles and finally a book declaring Hissarlik merely a fire necropolis, a burial mound where the dead had been cremated. He also accused Henry of destroying the cross walls of the furnaces and of publishing falsified plans in his book on Troy.

Captain Boetticher now had the Mycenae materials to work on. He accused Henry of fraud, of salting the holes in the rock and, quoting Professor Curtius's description of the gold as "of incredible thinness," charged that Henry had made it thin to keep his costs down!

A third attack called Henry Schliemann a spendthrift and irresponsible fool, squandering his fortune to gain an expensive notoriety. Henry was forced into the position of revealing a sufficient amount of his assets to prove that the fifty thousand dollars a year he spent on excavations came out of income rather than capital, with enough income left over to support his family.

"I guess I lulled myself into a state of false security," Sophia said, trying to keep her stomach quiet. "That there were people who never believed there was an actual Troy, and hence refused to accept your claims about it even after an abundance of proof, *that* I can understand. But history has always known there were royal tombs at Mycenae, and that royal tombs of that era were filled with treasures. They know our Greek government supervised the dig. Why would Curtius talk down the exquisite gold masks, diadems, goblets . . . ?"

Henry had turned from being angry to being glum.

"I would never have believed Curtius to be so mean-spirited as to direct his wife to attack our finds. It is envy and spite. Now the Greek Archaeological Society will say, 'Schliemann brings us thirty pounds of gold treasure; and along with it, double that amount of trouble.' "

Sophia did not think of herself as a weak reed. She had a strong body, one that had endured vicious weather in the Troad, thrived under the primitive living conditions of Ciplak and Hissarlik. The fifteen-hour workday at Mycenae, sometimes in icy wind and rain, at others in skin-blistering sun, had not defeated her. Nor did she consider herself weak of will. She could accomplish what was asked of her, or fight what she believed to be wrongheaded.

"Strong of body and will," she mourned. "But alas! not of nervous system."

Controversy, ridicule, sledge-hammer attacks on the integrity of Henry or herself, deprecatory allusions to them as "lacking ability," ". . . untrained," "false and fraudulent at every step of the way," "barnacles on the bottom of the great ship of science," "pretenders, braggarts, unqualified to consort with academia" . . . All these attacks, published for the world to see, shook her with the force of twelve-foot waves pounding the superstructure of a small Greek freighter. Henry's blistering published counterattacks served as a catharsis for him. This means of escape was not in her character. She could not step forth into the public arena and do battle. Henry was busy completing his hundreds of photographs for *Mycenae* and writing a concluding chapter on the finds of "a government clerk by the name of Stamatakes." She herself had little to do: Yannakis took care of the house, Polyxene was there to care for Andromache, her young cook from the Plaka was excellent.

She fell into a state of lassitude. She had no appetite, was unable to yield to Henry's blandishments that she "eat a good meal and drink a glass of wine." She slept poorly, lost weight. When one day Henry found her in bed on his return for the midday dinner, he became seriously concerned. He drew a chair up to the bed, took her hand in his, kissed it.

"My dear child, you must not let our present difficulties get you down. We will be in England in a few weeks, where we are admired. These wretched attacks will vanish like chimney smoke. It is the work of the jealous scholar, the closed, established circle! To the public, in all countries, we are heroes, revered, leading the most exciting and adventurous lives. You are famous, Kyria Schliemann! That should be solace and vindication for you."

She managed a fleeting smile.

"I know, Errikaki. I don't want to be affected this way. Just give me time. I'll be back on my feet again . . . excavating in Troy."

Henry decided to leave for London on March 18, sailing from Piraeus, but Sophia knew several days in advance that she could not make it. Biliary attacks kept her in bed. She forced herself to get up and spend some hours with Katingo, who was still frail after problems encountered at the birth of her fourth child. Andromache, now almost six, was shedding her baby teeth and enduring pain and fever as the new ones cut their way through her gums. More serious was Madame Victoria's condition, for she had suffered what Dr. Skiadaresses described as "a mild heart attack. But it would be wise not to tell your mother. Just keep her inactive for a few weeks." Sophia installed her mother in the adjoining bedroom.

Charles Newton of the British Museum paid her a surprise visit at the end of March. His crisp clipped mustache and short strands of hair were graying, but his light blue eyes were as young and cheerful as ever. Sophia was pleased to see him again. They sat together on the satin divan.

"Madame Schliemann, I have just come from the gold. Marvelous! Unbelievable! Ernst Curtius is completely wrong. These are ancient objects, very close to the time of Agamemnon. I'm taking Curtius to the National Bank with me tomorrow."

Sophia thanked him, then murmured, "For the Germans Henry can do nothing right. For the English he can do nothing wrong."

Newton patted her hand in a paternal fashion.

"My dear Madame Schliemann, we are all born with two sets of prejudices: we love our country but resent it when one of our countrymen rises above us."

Two days later she received a visit from Professor Ernst Curtius. Curtius, whom Sophia had never met, had a leonine head and a mop of white hair that seemed to spurt in tufts rather than single strands, rolling backward to cover his ears and neck. He had a magnificently wide-set and penetrating pair of eyes.

"Kyria Schliemann, I am anxious that there should be no misunderstanding about the article attacking your husband's finds in Mycenae which was written by Frau Curtius based on a comment in one of my letters to her. I have often asked my wife to write such articles during the years when I traveled through Greece gathering materials for my *History of Greece*. But this article was a mistake."

She spoke with some asperity.

"The article itself, or your judgment?"

"Both. I judged the treasure too quickly and, I can perceive it now, with a touch of envy. Your good friend, Charles Newton, spent three hours at the National Bank with me yesterday morning going over the gold masks, diadems, breastplates. I was wrong. They are indeed ancient. Not at all thin, as I complained, but as solid a gold and craftsmanship as I have seen. Since I want not even a shadow of ill feeling to exist between your husband and myself, I ask you to send him this letter of apology and retraction."

Sophia took the slim envelope from his hand, then said quietly:

"Could you not also retract in the same newspaper where Frau Curtius published the attack?"

"No, Kyria Schliemann, I cannot do that . . . it would put my wife in a bad light and bring criticism down upon her. I understand that Dr. Schliemann's book on Mycenae will soon be ready for publication. I will review it in the German archaeological journals. There I can make a more telling retribution among our scholars."

Sophia felt as though a sack of beans had been lifted from her back. She thanked Curtius, poured him a cup of tea, said, "Let me tell you a little about our excavations in the royal tombs. . . ."

Good news grows in clusters, like bunches of grapes in the summer sun. Sophia awakened a few mornings later to find that several of the Athenian newspapers announced the enthusiastic reception given Henry for a speech he had delivered before the Royal Society of Antiquaries in London. One of the Greek papers said:

"We must confess the Greek failure to recognize the man's worth."

A few days later she received a copy of the *London Illustrated News* which contained an article about "Mrs. Schliemann's Treasury," and her work in uncovering it.

> As the dome of this monument had long been broken, it was well enough known; but now thanks to Mrs. Schliemann the whole of it has been excavated and exposed to view. While her husband was busy within the walls of the Acropolis, she undertook the exploration of the relic of the past. . . .

Sophia read the article with a catch in her throat. If her bouts were caused by the stress of living with Henry Schliemann, there were extraordinary compensations. She ardently wanted him beside her now.

One night, early in May, sleepless and feeling lonesome, she got out of bed, went to Henry's desk in his study and wrote him a poem in ancient Greek:

> O, superior being, your ardor will destroy you;
> Don't you pity your little daughter and poor wife
> Who want to be with you?
> Are all the praises of the British preferable to me?

The next morning she read her poem in the truth-telling sunlight. She realized that the answer, at least partially, was "Yes." Henry's invitations to lecture before the learned societies of Great Britain had now risen to ten. He needed at least a month more of work with his publisher, John Murray, and with Cooper and Whymper, England's best engravers, who were preparing the plates to be used in the book on Mycenae.

Andromache's teeth had finally broken through; the fever was gone. Katingo had recovered from her postnatal problems. Madame Victoria was up and around, unaware that she had suffered a heart attack. Sophia had Dr. Skiadaresses find a nurse to watch over her mother. This accomplished, she donned her "Amalia," the Greek national costume: shoe-length skirt of blue silk with red dots, white blouse of light cotton cloth, short jacket and fez of red velvet. She then took ship to Marseilles with her little entourage of Andromache, Polyxene and Spyros, and after that the train to Paris, where Henry had promised to welcome her and escort her across the English Channel.

They had a happy reunion at the Hotel Louvois. A couple of days later they reached the house which Henry had rented at 15 Keppel Street, near the British Museum, and found an official document awaiting them. The president of the Royal Archaeological Institute of Great Britain and Ireland, Lord Talbot de Malahide, had won a unanimous vote from his membership that:

> Mrs. Schliemann be invited to honor the Institute by her presence on an early occasion at a special meeting in these rooms at 5 P.M. and that she be requested to read a paper upon such a subject as may be agreeable to her.

At the same time she would receive her diploma and honorary membership in the Royal Archaeological Institute, one of the most prestigious in Great Britain. Henry was delighted. Sophia was overcome.

"Henry, I have never spoken in public! What would I say?"

He laughed away her stage fright.

"Anything you want to say: about your Greek heritage, your excavations at Troy and Mycenae . . ."

"In Greek or English?"

"English. Then everyone will understand you. Why not write it in Greek? When you have expressed yourself to your own satisfaction, we'll translate it into English. Max Müller will polish it for you. You have three full weeks. The speech need be only twenty minutes long."

Their rented house was comfortable, if gloomy. The livingroom was painted a dark brown; the diningroom walls were a dark varnish-colored wallpaper. Their bedroom window was draped, as were the downstairs rooms, with curtains and heavy blue velvet hangings supported by brass rings on a thick mahogany pole. Neither light nor air could penetrate. All of the rooms were impossibly overcrowded: a grand piano, tables, couches, chairs, jardinières, screens, pots of ferns, palms, chiffoniers of carved walnut inlaid with ivory, massive sideboards for the china, bowls of wax fruit.

"I don't see how people get through this maze of furniture in the dark," Sophia observed. "Henry, you must do one thing for me: take down the draperies, open the windows, let in some light and air."

"We'll probably need a crowbar to get the windows open. The English think fresh air is bad for the lungs."

The weather for the rest of May was ideal: a warming sun, the air clear and sparkling. Breakfast was served to Sophia in bed by a cook who had come with the house; a robust English meal of porridge, eggs and bacon, toast, marmalade and tea.

"Henry, how can I possibly eat all this? I have nothing but a cup of coffee in the morning."

"Pretend you are an Englishwoman. You could use a little flesh around your hips. Then I'll be more comfortable too."

To her surprise she finished her breakfast each morning. There was no trace of the illness that had dogged her footsteps in Athens. She had no responsibilities, the cook shopped for the food, worked with Henry on the menus. After breakfast she put on her dressing gown and slippers and went to the desk Henry had moved between the east and south windows of the library. Here she wrote for several hours in the sunshine, sorting out her ideas for a first draft.

It was a happy time. Henry had three more speeches to prepare: for the Athenaeum Club, the Royal Institute of Great Britain and the Royal Historical Society. Since there was some overlapping of membership between the august bodies, he fastidiously avoided repetition. That meant intensive bouts of writing. From eight until eleven they worked together in the companionship she so much enjoyed. Then they went to luncheon in the home or garden of one of the many

friends Henry had made during his frequent stays in London. Sophia's
ear became attuned to the sound of English. Henry said:

"When you have finished your paper, I'll ask Philip Smith to re-
hearse it with you so that your delivery will be unaccented."

By June 8, Henry, Sophia, Max Müller and Philip Smith were well content with her speech and her manner of delivery. They arrived by carriage at 16 New Burlington Street West at five minutes after 5:00 P.M.,
as had been requested. She walked up the sweeping staircase escorted
by officers of the Institute and was then officially greeted by the president, Lord Talbot de Malahide, and by William Gladstone, no longer
Prime Minister but still a leader of his party in Parliament. They
escorted her to the dais.

Quiet fell when she entered. The hundreds of members and guests in
the great hall had not been prepared for her youth—she was only
twenty-five—or her classical Greek beauty. Lord Malahide introduced
her with friendly wit. There were a number of women in the audience,
beautifully groomed and gowned. So was Sophia; Henry had taken her
to the most fashionable couturier in London, who designed a long,
loose-fitting printed silk dress with hat to match. The only jewelry she
wore was her wedding ring and the coral necklace Henry had given her
a few days after their first meeting in the garden in Colonos. Gazing
at the hall of faces, all turned up to her in respect and anticipation—
few if any women had been invited to speak before this body—she felt
at ease. It had been a long and rocky uphill climb, their eight years of
marriage, but now she was at the crest; below her was spread a glorious
panorama.

Lord Malahide presented her with a bouquet of flowers representing
the Greek national colors. During the introduction Sophia recognized,
in the front rows, Charles Newton; Dr. Hieronymus Myriantheus,
Archimandrite of the Greek community; Ioannes Gennadius, Greek
chargé d'affaires in London, who was renowned for spending almost
his entire salary on old and rare books about the history of Greece
and Turkey; a number of people who had entertained them, the Duke
of Argyle, Lord Houghton, Robert Browning; their publisher, John
Murray; and a number of professors from Oxford and Cambridge.

The genteel applause that had been going on during her reverie now
stopped. She launched with confidence into her discourse. Max Müller
had been wise enough to leave in a few of her more colorful twists of
the English language. Philip Smith had taught her to give full value to
each syllable; but he had not quite extinguished her accent, which her
listeners found piquant.

She started off with a eulogy of her own people:

"At a time when the rest of the world was still living in the darkness of night, my ancestors, the ancient Greeks, had in science and arts reached such a pitch of perfection as can never be surpassed by man. Our political institutions, our statesmen, our orators, our philosophers and our poets have in all posterior ages been objects of wonder and admiration to the world at large. . . ."

She went into a brief history of Greece from the time of Agamemnon, Achilles, Odysseus to Pericles, Solon and Plato. After that she spoke of their own work.

"Alexander the Great never slept without having under his pillow a copy of Homer. To Dr. Schliemann's and my admiration for Homer are we indebted for the discoveries of Troy and to Pausanias for the five royal tombs of Mycenae with their treasures. . . . The part I have taken in the discoveries is but small. In Mycenae I excavated the large treasury close to the Lion Gate. . . . Though I found no treasures there, yet this exploration has been of some importance to science because I found there a mass of most interesting pottery which shows us the remote antiquity in which the treasury was shut up."

She described the opening of the royal tombs at Mycenae, their miraculous treasures still intact. The audience sat spellbound. Henry was bursting with excitement and pride. He was Pygmalion. He had taken a seventeen-year-old Greek gymnasium graduate, educated her and made her known everywhere.

The fascinating story finished, Sophia thanked England for its generous assistance, without which Greece could not have attained her independence from Turkey, concluding with "an appeal to the English ladies to teach their children the sonorous language of my ancestors so that they may be able to read Homer and our other immortal classics in the original."

She looked up from her paper, turned the full gaze of her large brown eyes on the audience:

"I terminate in warmly thanking you for the indulgence with which you have listened to an enthusiast for Homer."

She received a standing ovation. That night there was a banquet for the Schliemanns given by the Lord Mayor and attended by members of all ten of the scientific and literary groups to whom Henry had spoken. From that moment on until their departure at the end of June, they were entertained in the great houses of London: luncheons, garden parties, dinners. Sophia loved every minute of it.

"No wonder you adore it all," Henry said to her after they had returned from a formal ball given for them by Lord Acton. "You are petted, coddled, admired and surrounded by affection."

"I must confess it is nice," she murmured while Henry unhooked the back of her wine-red gown. "Why can't some part of this happen to us in Athens? Why is our work acclaimed here, while we meet little but rejection and mistrust at home?"

"I cannot refrain from admitting candidly to you that my love for England and the English people, but particularly for London and the Londoners, is growing hourly more and more intense. Mr. Ioannes Gennadius rejoices at the idea of our fixing our permanent residence in London because he is of the opinion that with our enthusiasm for ancient and modern Greece we could be of immense advantage to his and your country. . . ."

He paused for a moment, kissed a corner of her mouth gently, then asked:

"Why should we not live where we are wanted?"

But first he needed a rest, confessing that he was tired after the long series of lectures and parties. "Tired" was a word she could not remember his having used; it so startled her that she put up no objection to a stay in Paris. Henry had arranged with his agent for a three-month lease on a full-floor apartment at 20 Rue de Tilsitt, an apartment building which he owned on the Étoile of the Champs Élysées.

4.

Paris was hot in July, the city half deserted. Henry hired a handsome carriage drawn by matching bays and they went for picnics in the cool of the Bois de Boulogne, taking Andromache with them. Often they made the longer trip to the forest of Fontainebleau where they stayed overnight at a comfortable little inn in the woods, having their evening meal in a cool garden with a brook murmuring melodiously as it drifted past.

It was five years since her miscarriage. Dr. Venizelos, hearing her expression of regret, explained:

"Patience, my dear Kyria Schliemann. Nature has its own cycles and its designs for normal carrying. When you do conceive, you will know that it is her signal to you that all is well."

Now, in her complete sense of well-being, she conceived again. She said nothing to Henry, not wanting to expose him to disappointment.

Sections of galley proof of the Mycenae book reached Henry every few days. He was astonished at the number of errors in the English text; he was also dissatisfied with the engravings which pictured his finds. He wrote long letters to John Murray in London telling why the engravings had to come out sharper and clearer. His French publisher, Hachette, insisted that Henry pay the full costs of the book. Henry now considered himself a professional writer; it wounded his vanity to think that he had to subsidize his own work. But what frustrated him more was that his discussions with the South Kensington Museum for the display of his Trojan finds had bogged down.

By mid-August he could no longer contain himself.

"Sophidion, I must go back to London to work with Philip Smith on the galleys and with Cooper and Whymper on the engravings. They *must* come out right. I must also secure a set for Hachette's French edition, and I should meet with the directors of the South Kensington Museum to get my exhibition back on the tracks."

Sophia did not want to be left in Paris without her husband; by the same token she knew that he must get his work done. Besides, her objections would do her no good!

"Very well, my dear, but please accomplish everything quickly."

Two days after Henry left she went to the little drawer in the breakfront where he kept cash for their immediate needs. She was astonished to find only four hundred francs. She opened an adjoining drawer where Henry kept his unpaid bills. Adding them up, she found that, in his preoccupation and haste to get away, there were two thousand francs of unpaid accounts. During the next few days she dispensed the eighty dollars he had left to bill collectors who came to the front door. It was also time to replenish their food supply, pay the wages of the servants and put in their coal. She sent Henry a cable asking how he expected her to pay their bills.

She received no answer to her cable. Perhaps he was visiting in the country, or with Max Müller at Oxford. . . . She then sent him a barrage of letters:

> . . . I am ashamed that, while I am Schliemann's wife, I do not have money to pay for our clothing or the coal. I will not die for lack of money, but please tell me if it is fair even to have to talk about this matter?

These two sentences got under Henry's skin. He wrote:

> I understand my mistake about money. I am enclosing a check. It should last you until I return in mid-September.

Sophia looked at the check and gasped. The sum was so small it would barely cover their food. Tears of vexation came to her eyes.

"Oh, that miserly streak when we are apart. Very well. I shall eat the honors he has brought me!"

By mid-September she began to feel achy. She went to see two doctors, one French, Dr. Chatillon; the other Greek, Dr. Damaskenos. Both confirmed that she was pregnant. Only then did she allow herself the thrill of knowing she would have a second child. The following day

Henry returned from London. She told him the news. He exclaimed his joy, danced her around the tightly packed gold-brocaded Louis XIV furniture.

"I shall have my son," he cried. "My Greek son!"

Whereupon he went out on a buying spree, bringing home a lusciously soft sable wrap which he draped around her shoulders.

"To keep you warm in winter," he said exultantly. "It is beautiful on you."

Sophia stroked the soft rich skins, unable to believe her eyes or gain control of her spinning senses.

Henry had brought back good news from London: the galleys and engravings were now in fine shape. His exhibition at the South Kensington Museum was to open at the end of December and remain on display for at least six months. The museum had agreed to defray all expenses of the shipment from Athens to London. He would have to return to Athens soon to crate the forty-odd boxes of the treasure of Priam and the hundreds of other finds from Troy. Gladstone had, after some hesitation, agreed to write an introduction to *Mycenae*; this would be of enormous help throughout the English-speaking world.

Their first week together was delightful. They went twice to the Opéra Comique. Henry took Andromache to the circus which Sophia had so much loved when she was a bride in Paris in 1869. During the last week of the month the weather turned, the skies became gray, rain began to fall. With the cold, Sophia developed pains in her legs and back similar to the ones she had suffered five years before which presaged her miscarriage.

Henry became alarmed, sent Spyros to bring Dr. Damaskenos. The doctor, who was aware of the history of Sophia's miscarriage, saw no cause for alarm.

"Then I can return to Athens?"

Henry had a watery mist in his eyes.

"Dearest one, we don't dare! It's a long train trip to Marseilles . . . the sea gets rough this time of year . . . if you were to become terribly seasick . . ."

She turned to the doctor, her lips and chin set in a determined stance.

"Dr. Damaskenos, you said I was healthy and that I will have a normal pregnancy. What harm can a few days of travel do me?"

Dr. Damaskenos shook his head no.

"I'm obliged to agree with your husband, Kyria Schliemann. It's too risky. If anything happened and you lost the child you would never forgive yourself."

She insisted that Dr. Chatillon be brought to the apartment. He was of the same opinion as Dr. Damaskenos. Defeated, Sophia said with a heavy heart, "Who am I to fight my husband and two doctors?"

At the last moment Henry asked if he could take Spyros back to Athens to help pack the gold. He wanted no one else to see or touch it. Spyros went gray at the idea of leaving Sophia alone in a foreign city. Sophia replied:

"If you take Spyros, I come along, whether I live or die on the trip. You have Yannakis at home to pack the boxes for you."

At the mention of Yannakis's name, Polyxene, who was in the room with Andromache, burst into tears, fell to her knees before Sophia.

"Kyria Schliemann, I beg you, let me go home to my husband and child. It has been months . . . I am so lonesome for them . . ."

Sophia stood silent for a moment, then put a hand under the younger girl's arm and helped her up.

"Yes, Poly, go home to your family. I should be the first to understand how dead the days can be when you are separated from those you love."

Henry found a young French nursemaid to replace Polyxene. He named her Hecuba, after his habit of giving people who worked for him names out of Greek mythology. He also left a fair sum of money. It was a good thing he did. Two days after Henry's departure, his agent called to inform Madame Schliemann that she had to be out of the apartment on the last day of the month as it had been leased to another family.

". . . out of the apartment?" Sophia gasped. "That's not possible. Surely my husband renewed the lease?"

"No, madame." The agent was apologetic but firm. "Your arrangement was for three months, July, August and September. When your husband did not renew I had to seek new tenants. They move in on October 1."

Sophia sank into a chair, gazed at the agent wide-eyed.

"How can you put me out of an apartment my husband owns?"

"My job is to see that every one of Dr. Schliemann's hundreds of apartments are occupied all year round. If he had said just one word . . ."

Sophia turned to her brother.

"Spyros, what do we do?"

"We move. Tomorrow." He turned to the agent. "You handle other properties. Perhaps you have some suggestions for us."

"I have a two-story house available on Boulevard Haussmann. I could take you there now, if you wish. Madame Schliemann would find it agreeable."

Spyros reported back to Sophia that the house was clean and spacious, far less cluttered than their present apartment. When Sophia

nodded her agreement he hired a small moving van, packed their belongings, moved them the following morning. He bristled with happiness that he had stepped into a crisis and handled it well. Not so
Sophia. The landlord demanded that she pay the first month's rent in
cash. She then paid the salaries of the servants and bought wood for
the fireplace. This used up the last of the money Henry had left her.

"I am so mad," she told Spyros. "I feel like a hellion. I wish I had
Doctor Henry Schliemann in front of me this very moment. I would spit
right in his eye!"

Spyros laughed so hard he fell off a chair onto the Turkish rug. After
a while Sophia began to laugh too.

"Only the best when he is here. Poverty when he is away. Have you
ever heard of such a ridiculous man? I'm not even going to give him
the satisfaction of knowing what has happened to us. We shall slowly
starve to death with dignity. When Henry returns he can bury us all
together in a mass grave the way they did those bodyguards in front of
the third royal tomb at Mycenae."

"It is better to remember Mother's Cretan proverb," Spyros said with
a grin. " 'Who has his hope in God never goes to bed hungry; and if he
does, sleep feeds him.' "

If Henry had a preternatural gift for finding cities that were fig-
ments of a poet's imagination, and royal tombs which had never been
documented, he had no intuitive perception of his wife's plight. He
wrote her long affectionate letters telling her that all was going well in
Athens: the treasure of Priam, the finest *pithoi*, Athena idols, whorls,
terra-cotta vessels had been securely boxed and shipped to London.

Most important, the gold of Mycenae was finally exhibited on October
18 at the Polytechnical School, the place he had made arrangements to
rent seven months before. He had been momentarily crestfallen
when the Archaeological Society attended to all of the details without
consulting him, but when he attended the opening and was cordially
greeted by important members of the Society, government and the university, he saw that the exhibition had been superbly mounted. The
Society had had made wooden display tables standing waist high on
graceful, carved legs, and large enough to comprise thirteen shallow
compartments. One compartment displayed two gold masks, another
rows of daggers, a third, gold bracelets . . . At the end of the table
there were lined up fifteen gold cups and vases. Other tables displayed
the gold breastplates, diadems, gold belt, ornamental lions, griffins.
Watching each table was an armed guard. While the visitors were
not permitted to touch the individual objects, the women, wearing
their prettiest hats, puffed shoulder jackets and floor-length skirts, the
men in their Sunday attire, holding their hats in their hands, were able

to lean over the tables to see each of the objects and its masterly design. Several of the men, Henry noticed, used magnifying glasses to study the details.

The king and queen visited the exhibition and invited Henry back to the palace for dinner. The Athenian newspapers gave him his proper due. Staggered by the incredible treasure from prehistory, they congratulated him in the highest terms. In the days that followed, strangers stopped him in the streets to thank him. During the opening hours, between one and four, lines formed in the courtyard of the Polytechnic School with people waiting their turn to enter.

Henry managed to return to his family on the last day of October. His face flushed with shame over his failure to renew the lease and the fact that her supply of cash had been exhausted within two days of his departure.

"Why didn't you cable me? How did you live?"

"By begging," replied Sophia acerbically. "Andromache and I got tin cups and walked down the Rue de Rivoli with signs on our chests reading *Please help the starving Henry Schliemann family.*"

"I deserved that!" he groaned. "But it will never happen again. I'll go down to the bank immediately and sign a form ordering them to pay you whatever sum you need on the first and fifteenth of each month. Now could you all get dressed? I'm taking the family to dinner. We'll make up for lost time."

"Not all in one evening, we won't," Sophia replied tartly, knowing these would be her last words of reproach. "Our stomachs have shrunk."

He remained only two days, then left for Germany. He was having considerable trouble with his right ear. He had suffered intermittent pain for a year, sometimes extremely severe. Now the ear was inflamed. Along with the pain there was a diminution of hearing.

"I went to a doctor in Athens. He recommended that I stop my sea baths. But I could never do that; it is better that I keep my whole body healthy than favor one troublesome spot."

"It's more than a troublesome spot, Henry," she said with concern. "You love talking to people too much to allow yourself to grow deaf."

"Then you approve of my going to see Dr. Von Troeltsch in Würzburg? He is said to be one of the finest ear specialists in Europe?"

He returned in mid-November, the inflammation gone, the pain reduced. Dr. Von Troeltsch had prescribed syringe bathing of the ear every night with a solution containing laudanum. He was not to seabathe over the winter, not in any sea! Sophia too had recurrent pains, in her legs and back. They made an agreement not to talk about their ills but to enjoy their time together before Henry had to leave for

London to supervise the unpacking of the crates and the mounting of the exhibition at the South Kensington Museum.

A copy of *Mycenae* reached them from John Murray. It was a big, handsomely published book with a long and laudatory preface by the Right Honorable William E. Gladstone, M.P. It contained five hundred and fifty vignettes, many of them actual size, of the important gold finds, as well as many of the double axes, ivories, buttons, Hera idols, vases of alabaster. There were seven full-page plates, four in color; thirteen of the decorated terra cottas, and eight engineering plans, including a topographical map of the entire acropolis area, the circular agora with its five sepulchers and the plans of Sophia's Treasury. The volume was bound in brown leather, with the Lion Gate re-created on the front cover in gold. A frontispiece showed "The Treasury close to the Lion Gate. Excavated by Mrs. Schliemann." The American edition, published by Scribner, Armstrong & Company, was using on its front binding an engraving of Sophia standing in the cleared *dromos*, before the gate, lintel, triangle and view of the interior of Mrs. Schliemann's Treasury, outlined in gold.

Henry had kept secret the fact that *Mycenae* was going into the world with Sophia Schliemann and her Treasury as what the Greeks called its *telesma*, talisman. She kissed him warmly.

"That was generous of you, *philtate mou*."

He smiled wryly, ducked a shoulder in deprecation.

"God moves in mysterious ways His miracles to perform."

5.

Henry was off again. She tried to reconcile herself to the cold and overcast of the Paris winter. Spyros managed the house, checked the bills, made the payments. She found a pleasant young woman to tutor Andromache, then spent most of her days in an upstairs sittingroom since both doctors warned her to avoid the stairs. She had occasional visitors; some of Henry's long-time French friends, sometimes a Greek friend, Mrs. Christake or Mrs. Delighianne. The Burnoufs were in Paris and came to talk about "the hot Greek sun and the floating islands of the Aegean." Once she went to the theater but had had to climb a flight of stairs, and in the middle of the performance suffered a moment of panic. She must not lose this child!

Herself marooned in the upstairs of the house, and Spyros speaking not a word of French, their affairs started to go bad. The servants began to steal. Since they knew she was helpless, they grew increasingly lazy. Her complaints drew impertinent replies or bland denials. It took a number of days to replace them, always at a higher wage. In the interim she and Andromache took over the kitchen and did the cooking. Spyros's face bore an expression of severity that reminded her of Madame Victoria.

"You are on your feet too much. The doctor warned you against that."

Henry's letters from London were filled with joy at the way their exhibition was shaping up. Then came a sharp letter of reproach. Why was she asking for more money than he had instructed the bank to pay her? Was she being extravagant, or merely careless? While it was true that her bills were higher than they should have been, she felt trapped. She replied:

> My dear, why do you make so many remarks to me on the expenditures? I don't know what to do. I count every franc and spend it unwillingly. . . .

She explained why the cost of running the house had risen so considerably. He wrote her a conciliatory note: when he had reproved her he had had severe pain in his right ear. It was growing worse. She was to remain quiet. When he returned at Christmas, he would take over the management of the house. . . .

Next her mother became ill again. Was it another heart attack? Katingo and Marigo would not tell her. Sophia wrote, asking her mother if she would like to come to Paris and live with the family. Madame Victoria replied that she would dearly love to come but her doctor had told her she would not be able to travel for a month or two.

At the end of November Sophia received an agitated letter from Henry. He was in a deep state of shock and gloom. Ephor Stamatakes, excavating at Mycenae, had discovered a sixth tomb! Close to the five Henry had unearthed! The tomb contained two burned skeletons and a haul of gold objects. There was no way to take credit away from Stamatakes this time. No one had led him to the grave; he had found it himself. It was small comfort to Henry that Stamatakes would have found nothing if Henry had not discovered the royal grave circle. He cried:

"Our *Mycenae* is just out and already it is incomplete. That blasted government clerk has done us in."

Next, his ear had become so inflamed and painful that he had had to go back to Germany and Dr. Von Troeltsch, missing the opening of the Trojan exhibit at the South Kensington Museum.

He barely made it back to Paris for Epiphany, spent the time primarily grousing about Stamatakes and his sixth grave, then took off for Athens. Sophia read with trepidation of his ground-breaking ceremony for the new palacelike home he intended to build on his large property on Panepistimiou Street just down from the royal palace. Some time ago he had hired Ernst Ziller, the most famous architect in Athens, to work on the design for this baronial mansion, or "Palace of Troy" as he more frequently referred to it, then had become concerned that the Greeks would consider him a parvenu and showoff and told Ziller that the building would have to wait a few years. Ziller had submitted a bill for the work at hand. Henry paid so small a fraction of it that the architect had felt obliged to sue. Henry realized his mistake and paid the fee in full. In the flush of his Greek official acceptance, the absence of animosity now that they had the treasure from Mycenae on display under their own aegis, he had Ziller complete the plans for Iliou Melathron, the name he had selected for the three-story, twenty-five-room building with a grand ballroom and several salons on the first floor. The building would take two years to build. Sophia could not accept the enormousness of the home but now felt cheated that she had not shared in the ceremony.

The birth of their son on March 16, 1878, wiped out all their disappointments. Henry had always intended to name a Greek son Odysseus. Because of the discovery of the royal tombs he changed his mind and named the boy Agamemnon, King of Men. It was a normal, easy birth; both Sophia and the boy were in fine condition. Madame Victoria had arrived in February to keep Sophia company during her last heavy-laden weeks; for Sophia, the presence of her bustling mother, who took over the kitchen and prepared their favorite Greek dishes, was a godsend.

Henry exclaimed:

"I know it sounds oriental of me, but I rejoice that the Schliemann name will now be perpetuated." He leaned over the bed to kiss Sophia on the forehead, said, "You have given me the greatest gift of all: a son. What gift can I give you in return?"

It took Sophia only minutes to make her decision.

"That lovely little house in Kiphissia."

"It's yours. I'll cable my agent in Athens today. We can spend the summer there introducing Agamemnon to the river and the trees."

He would not allow Sophia to travel back to Greece until May when she could have a pleasant passage. Once back home, Sophia took over the Kiphissia house, furnishing it sparsely in the Greek tradition. Henry neither helped nor interfered; he considered it Sophia's summer home. He was building his own Palace of Troy, sending all over Europe and England for catalogues of furniture, candelabra, tiles, iron grillwork, carpets, Haviland china.

He ordered his iron for beams and grillwork from Germany, where he also had his carpets woven. From England he bought cement, glass panels and mirrors. The mosaic tiles for the floors he ordered from

Italy; he created the Roman designs himself and hired a group of Italians from Leghorn to lay them. His bricks would come from Argos; and although wood was scarce in Greece, he considered no other kind for his paneling. He also drew sketches for the murals in the main rooms and searched Greek classical literature for pertinent quotations with which to adorn his walls.

Ernst Ziller was in their Mousson Street home every morning now, working with Henry on the details. He frequently stayed for midday dinner. Henry supervised work on the site during the afternoons. Once a week when King George and Queen Olga visited their horses at the royal stables they would cross Panepistimiou Street and observe the progress on the structure.

Sophia had met Ziller casually seven years before when Henry first hired the architect to draw plans for his Iliou Melathron. Gazing at the man across her diningroom table, she ruminated that Ziller was a man of the utmost seriousness about his work without the humorlessness of deadly intent. He was dapper, clean shaven except for a rollicking mustache which ended in rolled tips. He had a fine stand of black hair which turned silver in the Greek sunlight, and a strong, handsome face dominated by deep-set dark eyes. He considered architecture one of the fine arts; to make his point to the Greek people he wore a wide flaring collar and a flowing bow tie of the kind favored by the bohemian painters of Paris. By combining ancient Greek architecture with Renaissance rhythm and decoration he had become Athens' favorite.

Henry Schliemann's stricture to Ziller had been:

"I have lived all my life in small-sized houses; now I want spaciousness. I also want a large marble outside staircase leading to the main floor and a terrace on the roof."

Ziller had replied:

"The exterior design should be German-Hellenic. We'll keep it simple and elegant, even though massive in form. We'll use random-length granite blocks for a base but compensate with five tall, wide arches on each of the first and second floors facing the street. This will keep the structure light enough to fly and should get us the most handsome building in Athens."

Henry had rubbed his hands with ill-suppressed excitement. Sophia felt a sense of bleakness. For their first home on Mousson Street, which from the very beginning Henry had considered only temporary, he had let her help choose the district, the house, the furnishings. But this palace was to be Henry Schliemann's monument to himself. She asked herself:

"Is this selfish of me? Should I not be rejoicing that he is at long last getting the Medici palace he has so well earned?"

In any event she would be a good Greek wife, admire his monument, live in it and, God help her, manage it when he was away.

When Henry was out of the room for a moment, she asked quietly:

"Mr. Ziller, what is it that drives a man to build one of the largest palaces in Greece?"

Ziller's dark eyes lightened as he gazed at Sophia.

"Great men should build great mansions."

"As a home or as a testimonial?"

Ziller did not trim the edges of truth with a cookie cutter.

"Both. It's possible to live comfortably in a palace. Not easy, but possible. If one has the taste for it."

"I don't."

"So I gather, Kyria Schliemann. You will be a reigning queen in Iliou Melathron."

"I have no desire to be a reigning queen."

However she knew that this palace would mean that Henry would permanently reside in Athens. Although they had been happy in London and Henry had said, "Why should we not live where we are wanted?" she needed her home to be in Greece. It was not merely that she loved the land of her birth, she felt an extension of it, of the Greek earth and sea, that the veins and arteries running from her brain through her body did not end at her feet but went deep into the soil and the Aegean to draw their sustenance. As for Henry, the larger he built his Iliou Melathron, the more heroic its conception, the more of himself he poured into it, the more he would not want to leave it. She was relieved to see that he had been willing to keep it just a bit smaller than the royal palace. She knew how much constraint her husband had had to impose upon himself to achieve this gesture of good taste. He would love his extraordinary home with a passion; it would give him the stature in Greece for which he longed and had never quite been able to grasp in his two digging hands.

As for herself, she would have to grow up to this magnificent home. Henry would invite the world of important people to come to it and stay as his guests. That was why he had designed the extra bedrooms on the second floor. When his itching feet were not scratching themselves on the roads, railroads and ships radiating in every direction from Athens, she would have to be the gracious hostess. Several times in the past, when he was away, he had sent her distinguished guests with detailed instructions on how to entertain them. She had a vision now of herself standing at the top of his marble staircase for the next twenty or thirty years welcoming strangers from all compass points of the earth. Henry Schliemann would own Iliou Melathron; Iliou Melathron would own her! Fortunately summer came round once a year. She smiled inwardly at the thought of her little house in Kiphissia with its majestic trees and burbling stream.

6.

Henry's drive, now that *Mycenae* was published in England, Germany and the United States, with the French translation imminent, was to secure a renewal of his *firman* to excavate further in Troy. When he learned that it would not be issued until September at the earliest, he grew restless, went back to Paris on business, to Germany for an ear treatment, then to London to confer with Sir Austen Layard, the British ambassador to Turkey. After stopping off in Athens for a few days to admire and play with his son, he dashed off to Ithaca for a month in an attempt to locate the palace of Odysseus. Rumors floated between the two Dardanelles cafés that Henry Schliemann was content anywhere except at home with his wife and children. The gossip troubled Sophia. How to explain to a curious world that the peripatetic Henry Schliemann had wandered the world for almost all of his fifty-six years, that he was only truly tied down when he was excavating!

The *firman* arrived. Henry announced that he would dig for only two months, until the rains came. Since there was no comfortable building at Hissarlik, it would be better for her to remain at home with the children.

Sophia stopped feeling sorry for herself when her brother Spyros became seriously ill. He lost weight, had a chronic fever, headache, an inability to identify. The doctors could not determine the cause. Shortly after he had a first attack of hemiplegia, a stroke on the left side; the left part of his mouth turned downward, his left arm and leg were weak. The doctors knew something catastrophic had taken place, a tumor or a hemorrhage, but they had no way to relieve or to cure him. Sophia was inconsolable. Poor Spyros, first he had been an unnecessary third wheel in his family's drapery shop, then for years he had served as her protector. Though he was only in his early thirties, it might be too late now for him to do anything on his own.

Henry returned from Troy in early December. He felt that he had made progress during his two months there. Yannakis had been allowed to return to his service and had restored a number of buildings on the northwest slope of Hissarlik: a storehouse for the antiquities, with the Turkish official, Kadry Bey, retaining the only key; a wooden house for the ten guards Henry employed to protect the digs against the brigands roaming the Troad. He had also constructed barracks for overseers, servants and visitors; a shed to store his equipment, a small diningroom,

stables. Yannakis was independent now and demanded sixty dollars a
month because he felt that he was indispensable. He brought in his
brother from Renkoi to manage a bread and wine shop. They sold on
credit but Yannakis could not lose; he was the paymaster and deducted what was owed him from each man's wage. From being dis-
graced and poverty-stricken, Yannakis now accumulated the money
needed to buy the farm he wanted.

Henry was pleased with the finds. He was allowed to keep only a
third and Kadry Bey maintained a sharp eye on the division to see
that he did not get the best third. Nor for that matter did Henry try to
outwit the Turkish official; he was anxious to keep this permit on a
permanent basis. Among the treasures were vessels containing gold
beads, earrings, plates, bars. It was gratifying that as a result of his
books, articles, controversies Troy had become well known. Visitors
came from all over the world. Henry gave each a thorough tour of the
excavations; they left as converts. The most frequent visitors were off
the British naval ships anchored in Besika Bay. Frank Calvert had been
pardoned by Queen Victoria: the story was that Frank's young
daughter had brought flowers to the Sultan of Turkey when his yacht
was tied up at Çanakkale and begged him to intercede for her father
when he met with Queen Victoria for a conference. Frank had become
a new man. He rode out to Hissarlik to congratulate Henry on his
Mycenae treasures.

"Nor will there be any more disputations about who discovered
Troy," he declared to Henry. "You did!"

The two men embraced. Frank told of his hopes of excavating at
Hanaï Tepeh.

"I'll bring along some equipment and several of my best diggers,"
Henry volunteered.

Back in Athens Henry was wonderful with the children. He tutored
Andromache for two hours a day in German and French. From the moment of Agamemnon's birth the little one had been obliged to sleep
with a copy of Homer under his pillow. Henry had read a hundred lines
of The Iliad to the infant after his first bath. Bishop Vimpos had come
in from Tripolis to perform the baptism shortly before Henry left for
Troy; the godfather was Ioannes Soutsos, who had been the Greek ambassador to St. Petersburg during the years Theokletos Vimpos and
Henry Schliemann had lived there. The three men enjoyed their reunion
in Athens. Henry insisted that both children have dinner at the table
with him. Though the weather was cold, he and Sophia bundled up the
children and took them for rides into the countryside. Most important
for Sophia, who had begun to fear that Henry had grown indifferent to
her, was that he was once again an ardent lover.

Henry acquired a new love to add to his renewed love for his wife: Dr. Rudolf Virchow, internationally famous medical scientist, professor of pathological anatomy at the University of Berlin, leader of the German school that dominated world medicine during the second half of the nineteenth century. That was only half of Virchow's life; he had also been elected to the Berlin Municipal Council and to the Prussian Diet. He founded political parties, scientific reviews, was a radical innovator who published a steady stream of monographs and books on anatomy, anthropology, archaeology.

Neither Henry nor Sophia had ever met Virchow, though Henry had corresponded with him and invited him to come out to Troy in 1872 or 1873 at Henry's expense because Virchow was fascinated by prehistory. The doctor had been too occupied to come. Henry invited him again in the spring of 1879. To Henry's delight he accepted. Sophia's belief that Virchow was making the trip because of interest in Troy was soon dispelled. Henry had written to Virchow about his difficulties with his Trojan treasures, which had been at the South Kensington Museum for a year. The museum was asking that he remove the collection, for they sorely needed the exhibition space.

"Why don't you bring it back to Athens where it belongs?" asked Sophia.

". . . no . . . I'm not ready to bring it back yet. Perhaps I can arrange to show it elsewhere; the Louvre, or in St. Petersburg . . ."

"But you will eventually bring it home?"

Henry evaded the question.

In January a letter arrived from Virchow:

"It is sad that you, not unjustifiably, feel at heart somewhat estranged from your own country. . . . But you should not forget that public opinion has always been entirely on your side in spite of the difficulties which the classical experts have caused you."

By the end of February 1879, Émile Burnouf, now living in Paris, had agreed to come out to Troy as archaeological adviser and overseer. Louise was not to accompany her father. But neither was Sophia to be there.

"Sophia, my dear, we have no house. I sleep in one of the nine compartments of the barracks occupied by my foremen and visitors. The nearest woman is in Ciplak. The toilet facilities are primitive. Yannakis is too busy to do any more than cook my Sunday supper, with no proper stove such as you brought out in 1872. Polyxene is never there; there is no place for her. When we are working full blast there will be one hundred and fifty men living at the camp. That would be too dangerous for you. It isn't as though we were going back to Mycenae, where you would be safe and comfortable with the Dases women. The Troad is now a battlefield between the brigands and the villagers. They plunder, murder, rape . . . If they heard there was a beautiful young woman in our camp I'd have to employ a hundred gendarmes instead of ten. Even then, I would worry about you night and day. Stay at home, my love, with our little ones, where you are safe and well cared for. Watch over the construction of our beautiful new home. I'll be back by the end of June, then we'll have the entire summer together. We can spend a month in your house in Kiphissia and rent a house at Kastella for August so we can have our thirty sea baths. . . ."

Sophia was crestfallen, but Henry had demolished her arguments one by one. She would have to remain here on Mousson Street.

Dr. Rudolf Virchow came to Athens en route to Troy. Sophia invited him to dinner, curious to see what manner of man this was who had so completely enchanted Henry; and to get a gauge on her adversary for the possession of the Trojan treasures. She saw at once that her imaginings were far off the mark. Rudolf Virchow was not the aggressive, bristling, predatory creature she had feared; rather, he was soft-spoken, gentle, with a profound admiration for Henry's talent and accomplishments.

She studied him across the diningroom table while he enjoyed her island shrimp and fish *plaki*. Though less than three months older than Henry, he seemed years older. Known affectionately in Berlin as *der kleine Doktor*, he was short, his face wrinkled and parchmentlike. His small eyes, covered by spectacles, were at once penetrating and kind. He wore a mustache and beard which came down the narrow strip of his chin bone, ending in a strong round beard of such substantiality that one knew he would not endure fools gladly. He was, from his thinning grizzled hair to his tiny feet, a rebel, not only in medicine and politics but in the newly demarcated area of public health. Bismarck, who ruled the German Empire, hated him so profoundly that he once challenged Virchow to a duel. Virchow's amusement over the incident gave Berlin one of its few chances to laugh at its Iron Chancellor. Like Henry, Virchow inhaled languages as though they were fresh air: Latin, Greek, Hebrew, Arabic, English, French, Italian, Dutch. In the year in which Sophia and Henry had been married, 1869, he founded the first German Anthropological Society as well as the Berlin Society of Anthropology, Ethnology and Prehistory, at the same time practicing medicine and carrying on his duties as a member of the City Council of Berlin. Like so many little men, he was blessed with good health, needed only a few hours of sleep, managed to find vacation time to bowl, swim and climb mountains.

They conversed in German during dinner and afterward in Henry's study.

"I have never met a medical scientist before," she told him. "I'd like to know about your research. Henry is sometimes accused of making hasty judgments, of substituting surmise for demonstrable fact."

Virchow smiled gently.

"That's true, sometimes he does. But his guesses are important as starting points for speculations about the life of early peoples. Even his mistakes are valuable; they drive him and other archaeologists to prove that he is wrong, and to dig deeper for the truth."

"You are kind to say so. . . ."

"Frau Schliemann," Virchow interrupted, "my task is so much easier than Dr. Schliemann's. We invented a whole science of pathological anatomy, but we had the human body under our eyes, corpses to dissect. Our surgery is slowly teaching us what goes wrong with certain parts of the body. We make our mistakes too, usually at the patient's expense; and some of our wild guesses and speculative theories have been more wrong than Dr. Schliemann's ever could be! That is the nature of science; at the beginning one knows nothing. But if we explore and dare to postulate our new ideas, at the end of our lives we will come out with a body of knowledge, no matter how modest."

"I am so eager to get back to the digs," she confided.

Dr. Virchow was no more able to persuade Henry to summon his wife than he had been to persuade the Prussian Diet to institute reforms for the lower-income groups of the country. Henry wrote to her:

> You say you want to come to Troy. Now in spite of all my wishes, I cannot advise you to do this and anyhow I am very busy at this time. Every morning I go on horseback to the distant tombs, the ones they call "heroic," and about noon I am back at Hissarlik to supervise the excavations where I have many workers employed. So I would not be able to exchange any more than two words with you. And also the days are so cloudy here, a real wintertime and very severe too.

As a complete non sequitur he added:

> Next time you see Dr. Virchow, speak French to him. Your French is better than his.

The children were her solace. She took them for a long walk each morning. Andromache, now a sturdy eight years old, loved to push Agamemnon in the pram Henry had imported from England. In the afternoons she and Katingo or Marigo exchanged visits so that their children could play while the sisters chatted. Sometimes she invited Panaghiotes to midday dinner. The following year he would enter the University of Athens to study archaeology. Spyros's left side was still paralyzed. He spent most of the time in bed, getting up to hobble around when she was with him.

"He cared for me for so many years," she thought; "now it's my turn to care for him."

A few weeks later Madame Victoria had a second heart attack, this one serious. Dr. Skiadaresses prescribed complete bed rest, a special diet, no worries or aggravations. Madame Victoria refused to have a nurse.

"Why do I need a nurse when I have a favorite daughter to watch over me?"

Sophia brought her brother and her mother in from Colonos. The house on Mousson Street was turned into a private hospital, with Spyros in one bedroom, her mother in another. Sophia moved the two children into her own room, putting a small cot on either side of her *matrimoniale*. She engaged a couple, experienced domestics, to occupy the semi-basement apartment they had prepared for Yannakis and Polyxene. Since Spyros was no longer able to keep the books she had to take them over, though she had never considered herself a good business-woman. She also spent several hours each day on Panepistimiou Street at the mansion. It was in a sufficiently advanced stage for her to see its proportions; the very size of it staggered her each time it came into view. Henry had engaged a foreman who checked the materials pouring in and paid the workmen but he wanted Sophia to supervise the day-by-day progress.

"How can I?" she demanded. "There must be a hundred workmen crawling over the building: German carpenters, Italian stonemasons and tile setters, French plasterers, Greek plumbers . . ."

By the end of May Henry had been gone for three full months. She found herself worn to a frazzle. There was simply no escape from her routine or her responsibilities, she had even to forgo the simplest pleasures: a band concert in Syntagma Square or a matinee at the Boukoura Theater. She gave no dinner parties; few friends included her when Henry was away.

"A woman alone," she thought, "is the most unwanted creature in the world!"

She did not permit herself to fall ill. There were no stomach spasms, no internal disorders, no revolt of her nervous system. Her strongest feeling was of being neglected.

In mid-May Dr. Rudolf Virchow returned from Troy. He was bronzed from his month in the Troad gathering specimens of its flora and fauna, excavating at the heroic tumuli in the plain, making long horseback journeys with Henry and Burnouf as far as the top of Mt. Ida. Most of his enthusiasm was centered around Henry's two discoveries of gold, one on the north side of the hill on a fallen house wall, the second at a depth of thirty-three feet, near where Henry and Sophia had found the treasure of Priam six years before. Virchow described the gold discs, similar to those of Mycenae; a breast ornament consisting of many chains with gold idols at the end, gold earrings, bracelets, beads, head-bands. The museum in Constantinople would now have the gold denied to them by the Athenian courts.

Yet the greatest fulfillment for Virchow was observing how Henry brought to light and freed the entire wall surrounding Troy; and how he had excavated the ruins of the three upper cities horizontally until he had reached the recognizable calcined debris of the third or burned city: Homer's Troy.

"I'm happy for Henry's sake," Sophia said; "but I'm envious. Henry married me to help him find Troy. Quite frankly, I now feel left out."

"From what I have seen of your mother and brother, you have been under considerable strain."

Tears came to Sophia's eyes. The sympathy in Virchow's voice un-corked the bottle of her loneliness, her longing to be with Henry, her fears that he would continue to excavate and make great discoveries and long journeys without her.

To divert her, Virchow told her stories of how he had replaced Henry as the medical doctor in the Troad.

"I cannot sufficiently praise your husband, who never grew impatient of acting as interpreter, explaining my prescriptions with the greatest care."

The next day he returned with a letter he had written to Henry for which he wanted Sophia's approval, since she had revealed her personal feelings to him in confidence.

Sophia read:

> Your wife . . . is longing for your return and now fears you may leave her once more in the course of the summer. My ad-vice is that you make up your mind to devote a little more time to her. She obviously feels neglected, and as she is surrounded by several ill members of her family, she does not get the neces-sary distraction. She obviously lacks pleasant amusements. By the great position in which she has been placed and by your training, she has come to make higher claims on life. . . .

7.

Henry returned to Athens early in June. He was thoroughly pleased with himself. Dr. Virchow had taught him a great deal about what he called "scientific poise and caution." Although he had bitterly resented the criticism of other archaeologists and classical scholars over his methods, he had nonetheless taken their scoldings to heart. He told Sophia:

"Having brought down to one level the whole space I intended to explore, I began excavating house by house, gradually proceeding with this work in the direction of the northern slope. In this manner I was able to excavate all the houses of the third city without injuring their walls."

He had conceived a new book to be called *Ilios* which would not only bring the Trojan excavations up to date, with the new maps and plans drawn by Burnouf, but also make the change from the highly personal day-by-day journal form of *Troy and Its Remains*, with its ongoing mistakes in judgment, to an objective and scientific relating of everything found during the digs at Hissarlik.

They were having late afternoon coffee in the teahouse of their neglected garden.

"From now on I'll take you on every possible dig. The next place I'd like to excavate is Orchomenos. There are only three towns which Homer quotes as being proverbially rich in gold: Troy, Mycenae and Orchomenos."

Sophia perked up at the news even though they would not start out until the following year; he needed time at home to write *Ilios* and prepare the fifteen hundred engravings of the important new finds.

"Give me two or three weeks to answer my correspondence, take care of some business matters and make sure Iliou Melathron is being built properly. Then we're off for a month to Kissingen in Bavaria to take the waters. We'll include the children; it will be splendid. In the meanwhile we are going to enjoy Athens; we'll go to the concerts and theaters and restaurants. You've been cooped up far too long."

As so often in the past, Sophia had meant to be angry with him when he returned; or at least resentful. She could not accomplish it; when Henry was contrite, he was prodigal with his love, attention, solicitude for her well-being. He even provided the money with which her mother could buy a small house in Athens. This news yielded a miraculous cure for Madame Victoria. She was soon on her feet. It took her only a few days to find the home she wanted. Henry moved her and Spyros into the house, installed a maid and cook to care for them.

"Thank you, my dear, this will lessen my burden. . . ."

"Having an eccentric old husband is burden enough!"

They were relieved of another burden a few days later when Lieutenant Vasilios Drosinos knocked on the front door of Mousson Street to notify the Schliemanns that the engineering corps had transferred him to Athens, that the army had little work for him to do, and could he be of some service?

"Can you!" Henry exploded. "My present foreman is not working out and the architect must go away for some months. How would you like to become engineer and foreman of Iliou Melathron? This time we get permission from your supervisors."

Drosinos was put in charge of all construction, became paymaster, inspected and paid for materials as they arrived, supervised everyone from the Italian mosaic setters to the French and Bavarian muralists, the English glaziers.

"It's good to have him back in the family," Sophia commented. "Yannakis is successful now, Frank Calvert is our friend again, Drosinos is making more to support his wife and children. That grandmother's tale about what dire things happened to people who opened royal tombs is mythology."

They spent the month of July in Kissingen. Sophia never knew whether it was the waters or her husband's solicitude but by the end of the month she had regained her lost pounds and felt radiant. When it was time to return to Athens, Henry asked permission to go to Paris and work with Burnouf on the new maps for the projected *Ilios*. Sophia went to the house in Kiphissia, inviting her sisters to visit.

When Henry returned she moved back to Mousson Street. He installed himself in his office, surrounded by hundreds of pages of his Trojan diaries and running commentary. He drove himself so hard that by November he had finished chapters on topography, ethnology, geography, religion and the controversy over the site. Wanting to expand the scope of the book, he besieged scholars to contribute chapters. Many agreed. "I want the general public to enjoy this volume," he explained. The only time he left his study was to go down to the mansion.

Life was pleasant. Andromache was entered in the primary school of the Arsakeion and doing well; Agamemnon was building a large vocabulary for a boy not quite two years old. Madame Victoria was moving about Athens freely and Spyros had recovered sufficiently to walk the streets with the aid of a cane. Henry remembered their tenth anniversary in time to buy Sophia an armful of sentimental gifts.

The only undercurrent of tension was the treasure of Priam. In 1876 Charles Newton declined Henry's offer to lend the collection to the British Museum, sending it instead to the South Kensington Museum. Now, in 1880, so world-famous had it become that Newton suggested Henry name a price, for he was certain Gladstone could get Parliament to buy it for the British Museum. While in the Troad the year before, Henry had corresponded with Baron Nicolai Bogoschewsky in St. Petersburg, whom he had known during his years in the Russian capital, exploring the possibility of selling the treasure to the Hermitage.

"Why Russia?" Sophia asked, flabbergasted.

"Because I lived for twenty years of my life in St. Petersburg. I made my first fortune there."

"That's the first I've heard of that sentiment!"

She shook her head in disbelief. First he had offered the treasure to the Louvre for free, while declaring that Greece was the land he adored. Next he refused Newton the opportunity to buy it for the British Museum but shortly after offered it to the Russians for the Hermitage. She knew that he had also corresponded with responsible people in the United States because the new Metropolitan Museum in New York was scheduled to open. And she was sure that Dr. Virchow had done an effective job while in the Troad to have Henry present the treasures to the museum in Berlin. . . .

"The German people have libeled me for seven years," Henry commented, "but now they have come round. My books are highly appreciated by them. Besides, in getting old my attachment for my mother country increases. I will offer it free to Berlin. All the same I will make heavy demands on the Kaiser. . . ."

"Precisely what is it you are after, Henry?" she asked.

"Recognition . . . acknowledgment of the value of my contribution as an archaeologist."

"Then why not offer it again to the Greek government? Our National Museum will be completed in a few years. If you combine the Trojan collection with the Mycenae finds, they would make the greatest single archaeological exhibit in the world."

He did not respond.

What she felt was not anger but pain. How did one reason with a man who was behaving like a whirling dervish among the museums of the world? Like a young girl trying to make the most out of her one and only virginity.

Because of the multiplicity of his negotiations, she felt safe.

The following months were spent in translating and securing publication of *Ilios* in several countries. In April Harper's accepted it for the United States, offering a ten per cent royalty. When Henry completed his translation from English into German he took the manuscript to Leipzig where Brockhaus promised that the German edition would come out early in 1881. The English edition, now in the process of being bound, would be the first to appear. His French publisher turned him down because of the losses incurred with *Mycenae*. Since Henry had covered the losses, he did not know why they were so upset. Undaunted, he went searching for another French publisher.

At the same time they moved into the not quite finished Iliou Melathron. Henry explained that he wanted to be on hand to supervise the muralists. There was no way to change his mind. It was a wrench for her to see the last of their personal possessions being loaded on a wagon and hauled away from Mousson Street. She had spent ten years of her married life in this house. Andromache had been born here. They had brought their first finds from Troy to this garden. Though there had been difficulties and bad times, they had been happy with their work and progress. Henry was going to lease the house; it was difficult for her to think of strangers living in the intimacy of her first home.

In July their permit to dig at Orchomenos came through. Henry kept his word; they would excavate together. Troy, Mycenae and Orchomenos: all "proverbially rich in gold." Henry would complete their work on this fabled trilogy. He arranged for his excavating equipment to be put in order.

Sophia spent half of July in Kiphissia, the other half in a rented house in Kastella so the children could play on the beach and in the sea; Henry had already taught Agamemnon to swim. The social event of their summer was the engagement of her brother Alexandros to eighteen-year-old Anastasia Pavlidou, whose parents gave a bounteous party in celebration. In August she and Henry went to Karlsbad to take the waters. After a few weeks he left for Leipzig to work with the German publisher of *Ilios*. When Sophia returned to Athens she found their new home almost completed. The two museum rooms on the street level which Henry had set aside for his archaeological treasures needed only exhibition shelves. The three servants' rooms had been furnished almost sumptuously, and included a bathroom. Sophia had wanted to buy the fixtures for the large kitchen, also on this ground floor, but Henry had bought the equipment himself. She had to acknowledge that he had done a good job, importing the best stoves, porcelain sinks and washbins.

The main floor, which one entered by the marble outside staircase, had no furnishings, but hundreds of boxes stood in the backyard bearing addresses from every country in Europe, including much of the furniture from Henry's apartment in Paris. It was from Paris that he also imported his bathtubs and hot water heaters; from Maison Chevalier came tall, elaborately decorated wardrobes, sofas, richly carved and decorated tables and upholstered chairs. For the enormous ballroom, its ceiling and walls covered with highly colored birds and plants of the Troad, he had secured a gross of cane-bottom chairs.

An inside staircase led to the top floor where Henry had built himself a library. In it she found the ponderous, elaborately carved desk and great chairs which he had ordered. His books, brought from Paris and Mousson Street, were in crates and wicker baskets; Henry insisted that he had to put every title in its proper place on the shelves himself. He also had Sophia order a large number of titles from Brockhaus while he ordered from the catalogues of English and French publishers. The library was situated directly above the ballroom and was only a little smaller, so that one had a sense of spaciousness and air even after the three rows of light-colored but substantial shelves had been installed, on top of which he meant to place a number of his Trojan vases. The adjoining winter study on the south side of the library would catch the sun; the north study, reached from the opposite end of the library, would be cool during the hot months.

Across the hall from the library and overlooking Athens was the master bedroom. One end of it had been set aside for Sophia's boudoir. When she entered it she felt a stab of dismay. Henry had furnished it as though it were a man's dressingroom, or perhaps a soldier's from ancient Sparta. There was nothing soft or feminine anywhere in color or texture. A stiff and narrow chair sat in front of a dark wood dressing table with drawers for her cosmetics. There was a small mirror.

"I won't stand for it," she vowed. "This one tiny spot in this castle is going to be mine, and I will furnish it as I want."

She would also see to it that the children's rooms were warm and friendly.

Henry returned toward the end of October. The workmen opened the crates in the garden and moved the furniture into the house. No one of the rooms was to have curtains or draperies. Since no one could see in, the side rooms faced their garden, the front ones on Panepistimiou Street paralleled a gallery set behind the two stories of elegant arches, Henry did not deem them necessary.

"Priam had no curtains in his palace. Everything in this house has to be clear-sighted."

"I will have curtains in my boudoir," Sophia announced. "Henry, I have the impression that in the back of your mind you are attempting to re-create the palace of Priam!"

"Only in part," he replied sotto voce. "If I had really been trying, I would not have let Ziller use the German-Hellenic architecture. I would have used the classical Greek of the university and the National Library."

He then installed twenty-four larger-than-life-sized marble figures of the ancient gods and goddesses along the four sides of the roof.

8.

Bavarian painters adorned the walls and ceilings of the salons of Iliou Melathron with designs sketched by Henry, one ceiling mural depicting the marble metope of Apollo the sun god driving his four magnificent steeds across the heavens. The marble metope itself he placed on the lintel of the major entrance door, toward the top of the marble staircase. Then, on November 13, 1880, they left for their new dig. Despite the fact that Homer's description of Orchomenos portended a prosperous and powerful settlement, little had been published about it. Henry had only vague information when he set the date for their excavation.

Orchomenos was founded, according to legend, by Minyas the ancestor of the Argonauts. The acropolis originally lay on the east side of the great Lake Kopaïs, where cyclopean walls had been built. Since the lake had no drainage, floods and malaria fever drove the early settlers high onto Mt. Akontion on the west side of the lake where, according to Strabo the historian, they built a new acropolis and a treasury.

They left Panepistimiou Street at seven in the morning by carriage, took Piraeus Street through olive groves past Daphni and Eleusis, rode along the Aegean, which was kicking up whitecaps, and stayed the night at Thevai, the site of ancient Kadmeia. The next morning they drove to Levadeia, a good-sized town in Boeotia, some sixty miles north of Athens and only a few miles from Orchomenos. Here they moved in with the family of police officer Georgios Loukides, who counseled them on the best way to assemble a work crew.

At dawn the next day they rode horseback to Orchomenos and, with a few workmen, began to sink shafts in varying locations of the early town. They found little, only a few pieces of ancient vases.

The following day, while Henry was wandering over the top of the mountain looking for a possible excavation site for the palace of Minyas, Sophia discovered a treasury. Like the treasury she had excavated at Mycenae, this one was also covered by centuries of earth and debris. Here too the top of the beehive had fallen in. Lying flat on her belly and enclosing the light, she could see the huge stones which had formed its apex lying piled on top of each other on the bottom of the structure.

She summoned Henry. They decided that she would locate the *dromos* and work toward the gate. He would start digging from above until he had moved enough earth to uncover at least half of the gate.

To her keen disappointment there was no *dromos*. It had been utterly destroyed except for the presence of one distinguishing marker by the demarch of the neighboring village of Skripou, who had used the beautiful stone blocks to build a chapel.

They remained at Orchomenos for a month, traveling by horseback from Levadeia at dawn each morning, returning at dusk. Henry managed to assemble one hundred workmen; they had enormous difficulty in removing the huge fallen stones. As they cleared out an increasing amount of space they found a number of bronze nails.

"These nails could have no other use than to hold the bronze slabs which covered the interior of the walls," Henry observed.

Sophia's most important discovery, on the right side of the beehive, was a door and a corridor at the end of which appeared a second opening. It was closed by a slab richly decorated with reliefs and sculpted flowers. At first she thought it to be the door to an adjoining grave; it proved, however, to be one of the higher wall stones which had fallen down and blocked the entrance to a second room.

"Henry, do you think we can get some equipment in Levadeia to move this slab? I'd like to see the inside room before the rains stop us."

"Too late, my dear, the rain clouds are massing thick and black. We'll return in March."

They reached Athens on December 9. Henry found a letter awaiting him from the South Kensington Museum insisting that he remove his collection. The Museum of Science and Art in Edinburgh was asking if they might have it.

"Are you willing?" Sophia asked.

"No."

"Why not?"

"I want it shown in a great European capital."

"Has Athens been admitted into Europe yet?"

"I think not; it's still eastern Mediterranean."

"Henry, I urge you to bring the treasure home. The display shelves have already been put up in our exhibition rooms."

He gazed at her noncommittally, then set his workmen to opening newly arrived Parisian crates and setting out gold-leaf chairs, chaises, tables, breakfronts. They had cluttered the apartment in Paris; here the pieces seemed lost in the vastness of the high-ceilinged ballroom, three salons, diningroom.

Daily letters arrived from Dr. Virchow. From the bits and pieces that escaped Henry, Sophia gathered that the Berlin Museum was rejecting not Henry's collection but his conditions. In his offering letter to Kaiser Wilhelm he had demanded that he become an honorary citizen of Berlin; that he be allowed to present the collection to the German people rather than to the Kaiser and the German government. The museum must bear his name, or at the least his name must be included in the title. He was to have the right to set up the exhibition and supervise its installation. He was to be given the order of *Pour le mérite*, the highest private order the Kaiser could bestow. Finally, he wanted to be elected a member of the prestigious Berlin Academy.

Dr. Virchow persuaded him to drop his demands for the citation and membership in the Berlin Academy. Even he, Virchow, had not been elected. The Ethnographical Museum which was in process of construction in Berlin, where Henry's treasures would most likely be installed, could not bear his name. Henry must in fact give the collection "to the German people in perpetual possession and inalienable custody under the control of the Prussian administration, on condition that it should be arranged by Schliemann himself in a befitting manner in the new Ethnographical Museum, in rooms which for all time must bear the name of Schliemann."

Henry rewrote his offering letter, accepting Virchow's conditions. Virchow replied immediately assuring Henry that Berlin would accept his new offer even if he, Virchow, had to work on it for months. He would have to gain the co-operation of Bismarck but he was accustomed to sitting for hours in Bismarck's outer office waiting to fight for a cause in which he believed.

When Sophia came into the library Henry handed her the last exchange of letters between Virchow and himself. His face was expressionless.

Sophia read the two letters, feeling dry and brittle. There was no need to say anything. She turned, walked out of the library, went to her boudoir, locked the door and threw herself down on the chaise longue.

Lost, irretrievably lost to Greece, their beautiful treasures of Troy . . . lost to an alien land. She was filled with despair. The satisfying work she had done, the honors bestowed upon her in London, in Berlin with the illustrated *Frauen Zeitung's* cover picture of her, her hard-won position in Athens as an archaeologist, all were as ash in her mouth. In the seven years since the treasure of Priam had reached Athens what had she had from it but trouble and grief? She broke down in body-racking sobs.

The following morning Henry left for London to crate the treasure. Neither one said good-by.

He did not return for Christmas; he had not yet completed the packing of the forty crates that were to be shipped to Berlin. But Bishop Vimpos arrived in Athens for the holidays. His cheeks were sallow, his eyes sunken. He blessed the new house, then Sophia took him on a guided tour of Iliou Melathron and its newly planted gardens inside the three-foot encompassing cement wall, its spacious area at the rear profuse with fruit trees and flowering shrubs. Vimpos was stunned by the massiveness of the structure, overwhelmed by the murals and quotations from the classics covering almost every wall and ceiling. When they returned to the more intimate family salon he made only one comment:

"Blessed are the meek, for they shall inherit the earth."

Then he asked quietly:

"What is troubling you, Sophidion?"

She told him about Henry's gift of the Trojan treasures to Germany. He studied her face, made the sign of the cross three times in the air above her head.

"There is only one way to stay alive, dear child. That is to absorb our defeats. Find the strength to submit to God's will. You ought to have learned that by now, though you are only twenty-eight." He sighed deeply. "I am twenty years older than you and have had more time to learn that lesson."

He put his arm around her shoulders.

"No use to quarrel with Henry. There is no stopping a man possessed. He has done what he had to do. Stand by his side. Feel sympathy, even joy, for this poor stricken man who is compensating for the meanness of his youth by bringing jewels to those who rejected him. Take joy in your own accomplishment. Act out your own courage, your love for him. We must help the defenseless. It is the combination of wisdom and resignation that sustains a good marriage and a good life."

Henry returned from London at the end of the first week in January. The boxes containing the treasure of Priam had been shipped to the vault of the Reichsbank in Berlin. He talked about their return to Orchomenos; announced that he had set the date of February 11 for the official opening of Iliou Melathron and had compiled a guest list of two hundred, including his family in Germany.

"Can you be ready that soon? The Parisian chandeliers aren't in yet, the carpets arrived but we didn't want to lay them until you got home . . ."

He was standing by his desk in the library. He pulled her toward him, kissed her gently on each corner of the mouth. It was their fondest moment since he had arrived home. Somehow he sensed their travail was over.

"Don't worry, little one. I'll take care of everything. I'll write out the menu, hire the chefs, waiters, the orchestra for our first dancing party in the ballroom. You will be the most beautiful hostess in Greece. You will stand at the head of the marble staircase with me and inside our glorious foyer and receive the great and the noble."

"Because I am ornamental," she twitted.

"Yes. And because you are also one of the best excavators of treasuries and royal tombs in the world."

At the end of January Henry received a formal letter from Kaiser Wilhelm accepting the archaeological finds from Troy in the name of the German people. His face was flushed with pride. Sophia congratulated her husband. Then she too received word from Berlin: a telegram from Crown Prince Frederick thanking her for "the precious gift of Trojan antiquities presented by your famous husband."

Sophia was taken by surprise. Her lips trembled.

"Why is the Crown Prince thanking me?" she asked.

Henry was delighted.

"It's a tribute to you personally. The royal family knows that you are the codiscoverer of the gold treasure, and of Troy, that you are deserving of half the credit!"

Sophia stared at Henry in amazement. Would she never wear out her capacity for astonishment over her husband's character? He had completely forgotten that he had gone against her wishes in giving the treasures to Germany. He truly believed that the disposition of the Trojan finds was a joint decision. Unless she brought up the matter, and she had not the slightest intention of doing so, he would go through the rest of his life convinced that she had wanted the fruit of their venture at Troy to go to Berlin!

The following weeks were hectic. Henry got the superb chandeliers hung in the ballroom, salons and diningroom; the exquisitely carved marble fireplaces with tall mirrors above them installed in each of the first-floor rooms. He erected on top of the street-side cement wall a tall wrought-iron fence made in England, elaborately patterned with long looping whorls resembling filigree work and two winged griffins resting on a row of *sauvastikas* like the ones he had found at Troy. He then supervised the installation of the huge double iron gate, also of filigree work and griffins which, when closed, converted Iliou Melathron into an impregnable fortress. The Italian artisans finished their year of work laying the mosaic floor which, like the walls and ceiling, were designed by Henry with the flowers and birds of the Troad. Andromache named the social rooms Flora and Fauna.

The first night they went to bed in the new house Sophia had seen Henry put a copy of *The Iliad* under his pillow.

"The bard will sing to me all night long," he declared.

She forgave his foolishness because, inscribed above the molding of their bedroom door, Henry had had the muralist paint his edited verse from *The Iliad*:

> Whoever is good and has his mind in the right place
> loves his own woman and takes care of her.

For their private bathroom, Henry had gone to the bawdy comic poet Eubulus:

> Next, Thebes I came to, where they dine all night
> And day as well, and every house in sight
> Boasts its own privy—to full man a boon
> As great as any known beneath the moon.

He had restrained himself in the diningroom. There were only three inscriptions. She imagined that he had done this purposely so as not to interfere with the digestion. On the western wall, in the frame of an ancient building with an arched roof and painted in white letters against a blue background, was a passage from *The Odyssey*:

> For myself I declare that there is no greater fulfillment of delight than when joy possesses a whole people, and banqueters in the halls listen to a minstrel as they sit in order due, and by them tables are laden with bread and meat, and the cupbearer draws wine from the bowl and bears it round and pours it into the cups. This seems to my mind the fairest thing there is.

The library was Henry's favorite room in the house. It was a carpenter's masterpiece, for it had seven separate doors, each beautifully fitted; three led out to a covered portico with mosaic floor where Henry could walk while he read or thought through a problem. Another led to a large upper hall from which he could enter their bedroom. Above the main door from the large hallway he had painted in gold:

Study is everything.

Above the door leading to the north study was inscribed the motto that had been above the door of Plato's Academy:

All who do not study geometry, remain outside.

Above the other doors and on the walls were quotations from Homer, Lucian, old Greek sayings such as "Lack of education is grievous." One of the verses from Homer had a line missing! Henry was furious. The myriad quotations caused Sophia to quip:

"You don't really need all these books; you can just sit back in your chair and read the walls."

Henry did not take offense because she had been gracious enough not to comment on the several misspellings in his quotations. No one of the workmen had been able to read ancient Greek! He sat behind his dark mahogany desk with its carved feet in the form of lions. At the end of each arm of his throne chair there were carved owls, symbols of his favorite goddess, Athena.

"Don't you love the frescoes and inscriptions?" he asked.

"As the discoverer of Troy, you could do no other. I have the feeling that I am back in the Arsakeion in my white blouse and navy-blue skirt."

The ballroom was Henry's chef d'oeuvre. High on the walls was a running frieze of nude cupidlike children reading Homer or Pausanias, excavating and discovering the treasures of Troy and Mycenae. Interspersed with these putti was a figure of his son, two-year-old Agamemnon, resting on a rock with his arms folded and gazing out at a landscape, presumably the Troad. Another figure was a mild caricature of Henry himself watching the dancers through horn-rimmed spectacles.

"Henry, you're too vain to be left out of the Palace of Troy completely," cried Sophia, amused, "yet you have the modesty to laugh at yourself . . . a little!"

"Would you like to be represented among the putti?"

"Thank you, no. I'll stay down on the floor and dance."

Henry had had ten inscriptions beautifully inscribed on the four walls, five from Hesiod's *Works and Days*, two from *The Iliad*; two were epigrams, one, an Olympian ode from Pindar.

There were few areas of the Palace of Troy which Henry had left undecorated. The corridors, hallways, stairwells, all bore their burden of golden wisdom, and in the very center of the building on Panepistimiou, where the passers-by on this main street of Athens could see it, was incised and lettered in gold in the broad strip of marble which separated the upper and lower sets of arches and columns:

ΙΛΙΟΥ ΜΕΛΑΘΡΟΝ

9.

The house was a blaze of light; it seemed to illuminate all of Athens. The candelabra with their hundreds of tall virginal candles, the Parisian chandeliers, countless wall brackets, all were alive with light. There were high torches in every nook and cranny of the spacious gardens. Boys carrying torches cried the liveried drivers of the carriages arriving in both directions along Panepistimiou Street through the spacious gates where two footmen helped the women guests in their elaborate ball gowns, the men in their traditional tails and white tie, to alight. Pages escorted them up the marble staircase and through the tall bronze grill-work double front door. A series of maids in long black uniforms covered by full-length starched ruffle-trimmed white aprons took both the men's and women's wraps. Few stopped to read the aphorism Henry had inscribed above the door:

> For if you add only a little to a little and do this often
> soon that little will become great.

As each couple entered the ballroom a uniformed butler announced their names and titles in a voice which filled the "salon for evening parties." Henry and Sophia stood together toward the rear of the ballroom and welcomed their guests. Sophia wore a rose-pink gown adorned with vertical rows of violets and green leaves. Following the French fashion, the gown was sleeveless, with a square décolletage and a two-foot train, tight at the waist to show off her slender figure. She wore her hair caught up high on her head and adorned with the same violets and green leaves. Henry had had a three-tier gold necklace made for her, remarkably similar to the necklace from the treasure of Priam.

Waiters in dark green uniforms passed trays of champagne in the elegant Waterford glasses Henry had imported from England. There was little conversation from nine-thirty when the first guests arrived until ten, when the Prime Minister made his entrance, but a quiet hum filled the room, for everyone was fascinated to see who had been invited and who had accepted the near royal summons.

Everyone had accepted except King George I and Queen Olga, who were away! The entire Cabinet, a number of the better-known members of Parliament, a considerable sector of the University of Athens faculty as well as the Archaeological Society, including Panaghiotes Stamatakes; the diplomatic corps, wearing their medals and honors; the Archbishop of Athens; the governors of the National Bank of Greece; important merchants; Bishop Vimpos and Sophia's family, her mother, sisters with their husbands, Alexandros with his fiancée, Spyros, Panaghiotes; two of Henry's sisters with their husbands came from Germany. Down from Lamia came Lieutenant Drosinos and up from Nauplion Police Chief Leonidas Leonardos.

Kaisares's twenty-piece orchestra, stationed inside the doorway of a smaller salon, began playing a quadrille, followed it with a fifteen-minute polka, a mazurka, a waltz, then lancers which lasted until midnight. The ladies were provided with decorated notebooks in which the men reserved dances. Butlers passed trays of *mezethakia*: caviar, sardine and anchovy canapés; *toursi* to sustain the two hundred whirling dancers.

At midnight the music stopped and an informal supper was served as the guests sat or stood about the ballroom commenting on the Pompeian rust-orange frescoes, reading the inscriptions Henry had had painted around the huge room. The longest inscription was the most appropriate and came from Homer:

> Therein furthermore the famed god of the two strong arms cunningly wrought a dancing floor like unto that which in wide Knossos Daedalus fashioned of old for fair-tressed Ariadne. There were youths dancing and maidens of the price of many cattle, holding their hands upon the wrists one of the other. . . .

A retinue of maids and butlers came up the stairs from the kitchen, so close together and so numerous they looked like a line of ants. The waiters carried the trays of French champagne. The maids carried *keftedakia*, Greek sausages, fried mussels, *kalamaria*, broiled shrimp, stuffed grape leaves; chicken pilaf, *shish kebab*. Then came sweets: apricot chocolate custard cake, crème torte, golden nut meringue, *baklava*, Greek coffee.

At one o'clock Kaisares raised his baton and the dancing continued until three in the morning. The departing guests paid the Schliemanns the highest of compliments.

Alexandros was married at Anastasia's family church. The only cloud on the horizon was that he might soon be conscripted in a war against Turkey. Panaghiotes was already in the army, stationed in Athens and attending the university at the same time. The Schliemanns entertained often, for Iliou Melathron received its guests with grace and beauty. On March 9, Henry gave a dinner in honor of the Count and Countess of Waldenburg. The German ambassador to Greece, J. M. von Radowitz, was on hand, as was most of the diplomatic corps. Toasting his guests in German, Henry made the observation, frequently seen in print, that the Germans were the true descendants of the Greeks! Sophia's cheeks flushed. She rose to give her toast in French:

"Ladies and gentlemen, allow me to drink to the health of all the representatives of the great powers who honor us tonight. I do not indulge in politics, but I will refute my husband, who just said that Germans are the true descendants of the Greeks. No! Modern Greeks are the descendants of the ancient Greeks!"

When the last of the guests had departed, Henry threw his arm around Sophia's shoulders.

"Madame Ambassadress, I'm not sure that was an entirely proper speech. But you were right!"

A few days later they were invited to accompany the official Greek Archaeological Society party to Olympia where the German Archaeological Institute had uncovered enough to indicate the majestic beauties of the Temple of Zeus, giant sculptures of the gods, Phidias's workshop, the agora, palaestra, the stadium, at least its starting and ending points, with the foot holes for the runners, and to establish the ancient plan of the city. Henry fumed. He had so much wanted to excavate Olympia!

There was no railway connecting Athens with Patras and Olympia. To travel by carriage would have taken a full twenty-four hours, with at least two nights of rest in modest hostelries. Instead they took ship from Piraeus to Kalamaki, a three-hour sail, crossed the isthmus at Corinth and took another ship around the northern tip of the Peloponnesus, past Patras to the port of Katakolon. From here it was a three-hour carriage ride inland to Olympia. It was also a twenty-four-hour journey, but with a night's sleep on board the second vessel.

After their guided tour by the German directorium, a young man separated himself from the others and introduced himself as Wilhelm Dörpfeld. He explained that he had been working at the dig as an architect for six years. Dörpfeld was tall, clean shaven except for a modest mustache, not good-looking but with a pleasant face and a cool but at the same time ingratiating manner. He had read everything Henry had written; understood the difficulties he had encountered in Troy, where the terrain to be excavated resembled what he called in Italian a *mille folie*, a thousand-layered cake.

He asked Henry why he had never visited the German Archaeological Institute in Athens. The young men there had admired and appreciated Henry's dogged courage and vast skills, he asserted, even if the older scholars had not. No one in the world could touch him! He had rescued archaeology from being unknown and uninteresting, dealing with dead stones, and transmuted it into an exciting science.

"We all know you are the father of modern archaeology," he concluded.

Sophia studied the young man's face to see if he were flattering Henry and, if so, for what purpose. But there was not the slightest hint of insincerity; it was the admiration of a younger man for an older one who had paved the way into the future and done so with tools fashioned by his own hand.

Dörpfeld came from a line of twelfth-century German peasants. His father began as a schoolteacher and became a well-known educator. One of his ancestors had been a blacksmith, and Wilhelm Dörpfeld had the sturdy shoulders, chest, hips and tree-trunk legs of this ancestor. After his architectural training he had gone to work in the office of Frederick Adler, his professor at the Technical School, who was making the preliminary plans for the excavations at Olympia. Ernst Curtius, the man who had attacked the quality of the gold masks at Mycenae, was to be in charge and, liking the talented young man, invited him to come to Olympia as an assistant to the field architect.

"That day was the turning point of my life," he told the Schliemanns. "I no longer wanted to design new buildings. I wanted to dig up old ones, the cities, fortresses and temples of prehistoric times. By the same token I will always remain an architect; when one has found the ruins of ancient structures, perhaps only a floor or a foot or two of wall, it is necessary from the scientific point of view to map them accurately, and from that base re-create them as they were in the glory of their long-gone age."

Sophia looked at Henry, met his gaze, saw that he had had the same reaction. This was the young architect-scientist they had needed! She thought:

"You don't know it, young man, but you have just become Dr. Schliemann's first assistant when he returns to Troy."

The next day they received a telegram from Alexandros. Spyros had suffered another paralytic stroke and died almost at once. They were delaying the funeral until Sophia and Henry could return to Athens.

Sophia wept in Henry's arms. Poor Spyros, to be gone so young.

"I understand your grief," Henry responded soothingly. "Perhaps he is gone because he had so insecure a grip on life. Do you remember when I first asked him, 'What do you want to become?' and he replied, 'Nothing. I already am'?"

They packed and made arrangements for the fastest possible journey home.

Several days later they gathered at the family plot in the First Cemetery. Georgios Engastromenos's bones had been removed three years after his burial, gathered into a small box and put to one side of the family grave. Now it was Spyros's coffin that was lowered into it. The priest murmured, "*Eonía i mními*, may your memory be eternal," took a shovel of earth and threw it in the form of a cross into the grave, along with the olive oil from the church *lampion*, the coal and incense from the censer. Sophia and her family each threw a bit of scattered earth onto the coffin. Friends and relatives had brought the sustenance which would minister to Spyros's bodily needs during the forty days he would remain on earth before going to heaven.

Sophia remembered Bishop Vimpos saying that life is a journey from the cradle to the grave; that we all follow the same route, be it longer or shorter. Only one thing was required: that, along the way, we love.

Her heart heavy within her, she murmured:

"May your memory be eternal, my poor unborn brother."

They went back to Orchomenos in March, taking as their guests A. H. Sayce, the renowned English Assyriologist, and Panaghiotes Eustratiades, General Inspector of Greek Antiquities. All four stayed with Georgios Loukides, the police officer. Shortly after dawn they were in the treasury clearing out a quantity of carefully dressed square marble blocks, as well as cornices which probably belonged to a small sanctuary within the beehive. Sophia and Eustratiades, with a crew of workmen, removed the twenty-five feet of earth filling the second room, which had been cut straight into the natural rock, as had the royal tombs of Mycenae. The tomb had been plundered in antiquity but the four ceiling stones, which were decorated with the same spirals and rosettes they

had found on the tombstones in Mycenae, were so important archaeolog-
ically that Eustratiades decided to transfer them to Athens.

Back home, two weeks later, Henry wrote a monograph about their
finds. When Sophia read it she saw that he had failed to mention her
work on the treasury. She said nothing about the omission.

"Would you like me to translate your report into Greek?"

"By all means. And write an introduction telling about your own
participation in the dig. Koromelas will publish it for us."

10.

There was no railroad connection between Athens and Berlin. Sophia,
Henry and the two children took ship from Piraeus to Brindisi, where
they boarded a train and traveled up the length of Italy, then changed
to the German railroad system. Dr. Rudolf and Frau Virchow were at
the railroad station in Berlin to meet them, accompanied by one of their
six children, Adele, about Sophia's age. They had two spacious carriages
waiting, and a wagon for the trunks and other luggage. Their four-room
suite at the Tiergarten Hotel was on the top floor with windows
overlooking the six-hundred-acre park and its several sparkling lakes.
Rudolf Virchow seemed to Sophia even slighter than she had remembered him. While two stiffly starched maids served coffee and cake, Virchow took charge:

"I have checked the box of gold treasure in the vault of the Reichsbank. Your six seals attached at the South Kensington Museum are
untouched. I will meet you at the bank at nine in the morning. From
there we can walk over to the Museum of Industrial Art, which only
recently opened. They have set several rooms aside for your approval.
Immediately next door is the museum where the treasures will ultimately come to roost; but they still have five years of construction."

Frau Rose Virchow had engaged a young governess for Andromache
and Agamemnon who would take them for walks, rowing in the Tiergarten and to the zoological gardens. The children had never seen a zoo
and became wildly excited at the idea of tigers, leopards, elephants and
hundreds of foreign birds.

Sophia could not tell whether she liked Berlin or was overwhelmed by
it. Compared to Athens, which had had difficulties growing to a popula-
tion of one hundred thousand, Berlin was a great city, with its million
inhabitants and a vitality so palpable as to reach out and grasp her. The
streets were wide, immaculately clean; every few blocks there was an
open plaza with shade trees and frequently a covered bandstand. There
were dozens of new buildings going up, all of four or five stories, each

with distinct decorations, and built so solidly of brick, stone and cement
that it could last an eternity.

That evening the Virchows gave a dinner in honor of the Schliemanns, inviting doctors, university scientists and members of the Berlin
Society of Anthropology, Ernst Curtius and young Dörpfeld. The
Schliemanns were congratulated on their work in both Troy and Mycenae. Conspicuous by his absence was Captain Boetticher, who had
made every effort to block the acceptance by Germany of the Trojan
treasures on the grounds that they were not worthy of being shown in
Berlin. For the first time the Schliemanns learned to what lengths Virchow had gone to gain this acceptance.

Many invitations were extended to them. Sophia was grateful that
Henry had insisted she learn German. She understood what was being
said around her, was able to read the Berlin newspapers, and was astonished to have one doctor who was her partner at a dinner party say to
her:

"Were you born in Germany and taken to Greece as a child?"

Sophia gave him her pleasantest smile.

"You are a flatterer, my dear Doctor. I have an accent in English,
French and German. I can hear it when I speak. However I accept your
compliment."

Henry spent a good deal of time in the museum directing carpenters
and placing the four thousand objects of his collection on the freshly
varnished shelves and tables made to his measurements. The iron cases
which were to contain the gold were still not completed. Wilhelm
Dörpfeld helped wherever he could. Both Henry and Sophia became
fond of him. He was warm in his enthusiasm for archaeology, yet quiet
in discussing people or the problems of the day. Often he was invited
to dinner parties because it became known that he was going out to
Troy with Henry as soon as the Turkish government renewed his firman. Henry made it plain to his archaeological friends why he needed
Dörpfeld: as an architect, he had the scientific training which had not
been available to Henry.

Adele Virchow showed Sophia the spacious Lustgarten, took her
through the royal palace, across a bridge over the Spree and then along
Unter den Linden, the most famous promenade in Berlin, stopping
for a coffee at an outside cafe next to the Cafe Bauer with its raised
porch and iron railing. Sophia attended the Royal Opera House to
hear Wagner's *Tristan und Isolde*. It was the first complete Wagne-
rian opera she had heard. The power and furor of the music flailed
the heart out of her chest. She was astonished at how long the performance lasted, over four hours, with the audience staving off mal-

nutrition by eating frankfurters and sandwiches, accompanied by tall
steins of beer, during the frequent intermissions. She thought:

"The Germans are a resolute people. If they can sit still and adore
every note of Wagner for over four hours, they can conquer the world.
Apparently they think so too. I have never seen so many monuments to
war victories in my life."

There were other differences for her between the structured Germany
and her beloved free-flowing Greece. Berlin was rigidly stratified so-
cially and even more rigidly controlled by the Kaiser, the Iron Chancellor and the ruling aristocracy of the component states. No one would
ever see the Kaiser and the Kaiserin walking down the streets in easy
fashion, unguarded, as King George and Queen Olga did. She came to
understand why the German scholars had attacked Henry so bitterly.

July 7 arrived. Henry's three sisters had come to Berlin for the ceremonies. At Henry's request Bishop Vimpos was also invited. Their
suite at the Tiergarten Hotel was lavishly filled with flowers. At one
o'clock Mayor Forckenbeck of Berlin arrived with members of the City
Council, the diminutive Virchow in the lead, the expression on his face
one of triumph. The Council had voted to make Dr. Heinrich Schliemann an honorary citizen of Berlin. This honor had been accorded only
twice before, to Chancellor Bismarck and Field Marshal von Moltke. In
a throaty official voice the mayor read the full proclamation. With the
fall of his last laudatory syllable the waiters streamed into the room
carrying trays of champagne. Others brought platters of small open-
faced ham, cheese and herring sandwiches.

That evening there was a banquet in the *Festsaal* of the Rathaus. The
city hall was an imposing brick edifice with terra-cotta and granite facing. The news of the granting of the honorary citizenship had been
widely disseminated in the Berlin newspapers. Henry was recognized
on the streets. But no more so than Sophia, for only the previous September there had been that beautiful drawing of her on the front page
of the *Frauen Zeitung*, which was widely read by the women of Berlin.

Sophia and Henry were met at the foot of the stairs by the Mayor,
the City Council, the Minister of State, the president of the German
Geographical Society, Professor Schöne, who was the director of the
royal museums; and the director of the German Archives. The rest of
the several hundred formally attired guests were waiting in the small
Hall of Legends, dignitaries from the government, heads of the departments at the university and members of Berlin's learned societies. After
French champagne, caviar, oysters, pâté and salt pretzels everyone entered through carved oaken doors into the *Festsaal*, which was over one

hundred feet in length, almost sixty feet wide and extended upward three stories.

"Even bigger than Iliou Melathron," Sophia whispered to Henry wickedly.

Sophia and Henry were seated at the head table. She was too filled with emotion to taste more than a few mouthfuls of the dinner. The Germans had conquered the French in the war of 1870, but the French had conquered the German palate. Each French dish was served with a different French wine.

The front cover of the menu carried a picture of Henry sitting on Priam's throne, a pickax in his right hand and in his left a miniature goddess Nike offering him an olive branch. A bear at his feet represented the town of Berlin. The writing on the cover was in Greek, a compliment to Sophia's heritage.

Mayor Forckenbeck rose. The guests came to attention. Dr. Rudolf Virchow was introduced. His voice rang out over the *Festsaal*.

"I wish to find in my vocabulary the most spirited words of welcome to the newest honorary citizen of Berlin, and to his good wife. It gives me the utmost pleasure that Dr. Schliemann, who has been out of his native Germany for forty years, was reawakened by a love of the fatherland. Out of this reawakened love came Dr. Schliemann's decision to give us the rich results of his discoveries and to make Berlin the guardian of his treasures. These remarkable treasures shall reside for all time in our city as a monument to Dr. Schliemann's devotion to science."

The audience rose to its feet to give Henry a round of applause. Sophia kept her eyes on her husband as he responded, his face bright, tranquil, confident. The grocery clerk who had slept under the counter at Herr Theodor Hückstaedt's store had come full circle.

"I am greatly appreciative of this remarkable honor bestowed upon me. I wish to express my heartfelt thanks to the Mayor, the City Council and to all residents of Berlin. Frankly, it was because of my dear and esteemed friend, Professor Rudolf Virchow, that I gave my finds to Germany where they shall remain forever. I could speak eloquently to you about the joy of discovery in archaeology, as you all well know. But it gives me even more satisfaction and sense of fulfillment that my wife and I have been able to make this contribution to Germany."

After the applause had died down, Professor Schöne, head of the royal museums, rose to his feet.

"I have been specially honored by the Mayor and the City Council of Berlin to give a toast to Frau Dr. Sophia Schliemann."

With this he turned to Sophia, raised his glass and said quite formally:

"Frau Dr. Sophia, I have the pleasure to announce that you too are now an honorary citizen of Berlin."

The richly illustrated citation which had been handed by the Mayor to Henry, and which he had held in his hands while making his own response, was now passed down the table to Sophia. She knew even before she glanced at the diploma that it contained only the name of Herr Dr. Heinrich Schliemann, that the name of Frau Dr. Sophia would not be found there. It did not matter; she saw only the glow on Henry's face and the happiness in his eyes at this total reward.

She rose, held the citation across the lace overlay of her black velvet gown. In answer to the applause from the great men of Berlin she replied in her mildly accented German:

"I accept this honor in my husband's name. He is the one who had the vision and the courage to go against the world and open for all times new vistas of prehistory. If I have been allowed to share in some modest way in his work, that is out of the goodness of his heart. That I have been able to participate in this magnificent adventure and help bring my husband's work to heights rarely afforded to any one individual on this earth means that my life too has been fulfilled. I may shed a quiet tear because the treasure is forever lost to my beloved Athens. But if it had to go anywhere, Herr Dr. Schliemann and Herr Dr. Virchow are right in saying that it should come to the country of my husband's birth. I thank God for all the goodness that has come to me during the twelve years of my marriage; and I close with feelings of deepest gratitude to Kaiser Wilhelm, the Crown Prince, Chancellor Bismarck, Herr Dr. Virchow and all the wonderful men of science and the humanities who have made this glorious night come true."

She looked down the head table to where Bishop Vimpos was beaming at her, touched two fingers to her lips, turned them a little and blew him an almost imperceptible kiss.

BOOK NINE

WHAT IS BETWEEN MAN AND GOD?

1.

Sophia was thirty on January 1, 1882, Henry was sixty on January 6. They gave themselves a joint party at Iliou Melathron to celebrate. At this point he was exactly twice her age.

"How do you feel at thirty?"

"Mature. How do you feel at sixty?"

"Somewhere along the line I picked up the idea that when a man reaches sixty he is old."

"Do you in fact feel old?"

"No. But sometimes the idea is stronger than the fact."

For Sophia time ceased to be fragmented, splintered into hours, days, weeks. It flowed past as effortlessly as the stream at the bottom of her garden in Kiphissia. In the past all clocks and calendars had stood before her as geologically stratified as Mt. Ida. Now she believed with the women of the Troad that "time is like the Simois and Scamander rivers; it flows at its own rate of speed." The mature age of thirty provided her with a frame of reference. She was able to put passing events into perspective.

Henry was eager to go out to Troy, not to find additional treasure, though everything turned up by the shovel would be welcomed; but rather to settle doubts that had grown in his mind since the publication of *Ilios* in 1880. They were seated before a log fire in his library. He laid out the focal point of his skepticism for Sophia.

"I no longer find it possible to believe that Homer, so true to nature, with almost the fidelity of an eyewitness, could have represented Ilium as 'great,' 'elegant,' 'flourishing and well inhabited,' 'well-built city with large streets,' had it been in reality only a very little town. The Troy we unearthed within the fortification walls was a small area."

She nodded in agreement.

"Had Troy been merely a small fortified borough such as the ruins of our third city indicate, a few hundred men might have taken it easily in a few days, and the Trojan War with its ten-year siege would have had only the slenderest foundation."

"I understand."

"I find it impossible to think that the catastrophe of a little town would have been taken up by the bards; that the legend of the event could have survived in folk memory, or come down to Homer to be magnified by him to gigantic proportions. . . ."

He paced the library, a fair-sized walk.

"Somewhere along the line we have made a mistake. I have to find out what it was."

He planned his next dig. Iliou Melathron became a battalion headquarters before a major attack. Two of their guest rooms were occupied by Wilhelm Dörpfeld and a younger architect from Vienna, Joseph Höfler, who came highly recommended. Henry selected three overseers, two of whom had won praise for their work at Olympia. He chose a personal servant whom he named Oedipus and a female cook whom he called Jocasté. Then into the garden came a string of wagons bringing a hundred large iron shovels and wheelbarrows, fifty large hoes, forty iron crowbars, twenty man carts and an equal number of horse carts. The children loved every minute of the excitement, demanding to know when they could go to Troy to dig. Sophia watched gratefully as the last of the tools, crates and provisions moved out the gate on their way to Piraeus and quiet replaced the turmoil.

Henry left in mid-February. Sophia would join him in early June when the good weather set in, and take Andromache with her. His first letters were filled with outrage. Although he had found his buildings and equipment safe—he had left a Turkish overseer at the camp after his 1879 dig—and had only to roof the buildings with waterproof felt, their work was paralyzed by the Turkish official Beder Eddin Effendi, who had categorically refused to allow Dörpfeld and Höfler to make any drawings on the grounds that they were spies trying to map the fort at Kum Kale, five miles away. This had come about because Dörpfeld insisted on using a surveying instrument to take his measurements. Heavily restricted in their own work, the two architects turned to helping Henry clear out three newly discovered gates, lateral and cross walls, the substructures of buildings.

When Sophia and Andromache reached Troy it was a bustling camp with a hundred and fifty workmen. Henry had fixed up two rooms of his own barrack for them; the diningroom was of rude planks but Yannakis and Polyxene had gathered wild flowers with which to decorate the table. Polyxene took the eleven-year-old Andromache under her wing.

After her first dinner Sophia sat back contentedly.

"You're living well, Errikaki; Chicago corned beef, ox tongue, good English cheese, peaches. Where does all this come from?"

"Our friends at Schröder & Company in London."

After his swim in the Aegean the following morning, Henry, Dörpfeld and Höfler took Sophia for a tour of the newest excavations. As they moved about the multiple-terraced Troy Sophia saw that the workmen had brought to light foundations of Hellenic or Roman edifices in the part of Hissarlik which Henry had not previously excavated. He had expected to find on this northern slope more metopes like the beautiful Apollo metope they had found there in 1872, but the twenty-five laborers who worked for nearly two months came up with only a marble female head of a late Macedonian period. He had explored the large theater immediately to the east of the acropolis, emptied the Hellenic well, the mouth of which they had brought to light in the autumn of 1871. He had also dug a trench two hundred and forty feet long across the eastern slope of the acropolis in order to ascertain how far the citadels of the earliest prehistoric cities extended in that direction. On the acropolis they unearthed two edifices, probably temples, from the burned city. Both temples had been destroyed in a fearful catastrophe, together with all the other buildings of what they now called the second settlement.

During the noon rest hour Henry confided to Sophia:

"My key mistake was that when I was here in 1879 I did not rightly distinguish between a second and third settlement. All of my doubts during the last year arose from the fact that my third city was too small to be Homer's Troy. Those walls of large blocks were the foundations of a second Troy. Where I went wrong was in making a judgment about the layer of calcined ruins you saw lying immediately upon the walls of large blocks. I thought that the debris of burned brick represented the remains of a later Troy built upon the walls of the second Troy. Dörpfeld and Höfler have now convinced me that these remains are brick walls which were added to the stone foundations of the earlier city.

"The second Troy is the burned city and it is considerably larger than the third settlement. We will walk around the total area. You will see that it is large enough to contain an entire acropolis, temples, palaces, government buildings. This is the Troy that Homer wrote about."

"With no more than a thousand people living within these walls?"

"Homer did not intend for us to think so. The mass of Trojans lived outside the acropolis and palace grounds, down on the plain, precisely as they did at Mycenae. We can't estimate how many there were, but they would have made a numerous war force."

"We thought that the largest building we found in what you now call the third, smaller, Troy was the palace of Priam. What happens to the palace . . . and to the treasure?"

Henry was only a little disconcerted.

"The large building which we called the palace definitely does belong to the third settlement. It just is not Priam's palace, which has to be in the second settlement, the one the Achaeans burned. We have not found it yet. However the treasure can still be Priam's. By excavating down to the foundations of the second settlement we found a tower of the second city precisely where we found the treasure in the debris."

Sophia felt a sense of personal loss. They had lived for years with the belief that they had unearthed the authentic palace of Priam. She was relieved that the treasure was indeed found in Priam's Troy. Another thought hit her. What about the authenticity of their double Scaean Gate?

He shook his head sadly.

"The one we have been calling the Scaean Gate is not the Scaean Gate. Homer was right after all. We conjecture that the Scaean Gate must have been down on the plain, not forty feet above it as we rationalized. I am now convinced that it is in the defense wall of the lower city, where the mass of people lived, and was not a gate leading into the acropolis."

"Henry, think of all the published material. Are you going to have to retract?"

Henry displayed no anguish.

"Virchow told you in Athens that that is the nature of science. We must dare to explore, always seek new, corrected ideas. I am not embarrassed at getting closer to the truth. I am exhilarated by it."

Sophia and Andromache had been at Troy for only a few weeks, Andromache roaming the fields with Polyxene, Sophia tramping the ongoing digs, when the marshes of the Troad dried up, the frogs died and malaria struck Henry's camp. Henry provided liberal doses of quinine to his family and staff but the workmen began coming down with fever and staying off the job. He received a stern letter from Rudolf Virchow:

> Send Frau Sophia and Andromache home. Your wife knows how great my affection for her is, and she will, I hope, bear me no grudge for this. . . .

"Virchow is right," Henry observed. "I won't be able to dig here longer than July. In the morning I will have Yannakis drive you into Çanakkale."

Henry brought a recurring bout of malaria back to Athens with him. It did not prevent him from attempting to change the Turkish government's mind about Dörpfeld's surveying of Troy. For his next book, *Troja*, which would bring the story of the excavation up to date, he needed full-scale, accurate maps not only of Hissarlik but of the entire Troad. He wrote to Chancellor Bismarck asking him to intercede. When J. M. von Radowitz, a skilled diplomat, was appointed German ambas-

sador to the Sultan he took up the issue at once and was able to allay the
fears of the Turks. Dörpfeld was dispatched to undertake the architectural maps. Henry spent his weeks in his library writing on his book and
having photographs made of the recent finds. Sophia divided her time
between Kiphissia and Athens.

At the turn of 1883 Dörpfeld brought in the first scientific plan of
the acropolis. He had concentrated on the second city, clearly demarcat-
ing the various stages of Priam's Troy: the towers, defense walls, gates,
house walls, streets. In order to establish a complete picture of the
mount of Hissarlik he also mapped the first and oldest city, what was
left of it, as well as the newly discerned third Troy which had been built
upon the burned Troy of Priam. Henry, Dörpfeld and Höfler created
a map delineating in different colors the numerous layers of Troy. By
May Henry was happy to have the manuscript completed in English as
well as German.

But he had developed a series of mysterious illnesses which he refused to discuss with Sophia. She knew that both ears were now inflamed
because he had continued his sea bathing over the winter. He planned
to work on *Troja* with Brockhaus in Leipzig, then see his doctor in
Würzburg and afterward visit his family at Ankershagen. This time he
did not want to travel alone. Sophia and both children must accompany
him. They would also visit Paris, London and the Isle of Wight.

Toward the middle of June he was to appear in Queens College, Oxford, where he would become an honorary fellow of that prestigious in-
stitution. He was at last to have an authentic degree from a great
university. Sophia had developed an instinct for detecting Henry's fic-
tion, or backward-projected fantasy, from the core of reality. In his autobiography at the beginning of *Ilios* he had claimed that the eight pages
he had submitted to the University of Rostock was "a dissertation written in ancient Greek," a task which few of the most learned scholars
would have attempted. In actuality he had written it in modern French.
In his excavating, in the books he published about his work, he was
scrupulously honest, trustworthy. In his private life he was an epic poet
whose personal odyssey was based more on invention than memory. He
had the talent to rewrite the past, to make its strands fit harmoniously
into the present fabric of his life. He did not lie, he re-created, he took
an eraser to the blackboard of his younger years, wiped out the gritty
chalk marks of actuality and, with a firm, bold hand, wrote a more lyri-
cal version of his past.

"Ah well," she mused, "everyone should have the privilege of rewrit-
ing his youth."

2.

Sophia enjoyed the company of Andromache and Agamemnon. They were bright and beautiful children. Henry, having applied for permission to excavate at Tiryns, was content to spend the balance of the year in his library sending *Ilios* to press in French, *Troja* in English and German. He became godfather of Alexandros's first child, providing the baby's wardrobe and silver cross, spent hours talking archaeology to Panaghiotes, who was doing well at the university. Sad news arrived from the Troad. Yannakis had fallen into the Scamander River and drowned. Sophia and Henry wrote consoling letters to Polyxene; Henry assured her that a monthly payment would continue to reach her.

The permit to excavate at Tiryns, sister citadel to Mycenae, was not forthcoming. Though Panaghiotes Stamatakes had become General Inspector of Antiquities, neither Sophia nor Henry blamed him for the delay; the unfortunate man, only thirty-six, had contracted a serious illness shortly after being appointed to the post he had so long coveted. In early February of 1884 Demetrios Voulpiotes, the Minister of Public Instruction, managed to gain Stamatakes's consent. Henry sailed for Nauplion on March 15 with his wheelbarrows, shovels, pickaxes. Tiryns was a natural choice for his next dig. The excavations could round out the picture of the Mycenaean civilization.

Sophia remained at Iliou Melathron with Wilhelm Dörpfeld and his blue-eyed, flaxen-haired wife as house guests. Dörpfeld was one year younger than Sophia; his wife younger still. He was to join Henry at Tiryns at the end of March, taking Panaghiotes with him; Sophia and Frau Dörpfeld would join them at the Hotel des Étrangers in Nauplion in April.

Henry started digging with sixty Albanians whom he recruited in Nauplion and the farm area around Tiryns; and fifteen men from Charvati who had worked for him at Mycenae. Stamatakes appointed as Henry's ephor a young man by the name of Philios. Stamatakes was too ill to be thinking of vengeance, but he had given Ephor Philios such stern instructions that Henry wrote to Sophia that it was like being back in Mycenae during the early months of their running battle with him. Philios would not let Henry examine the morning's finds during the dinner hour for fear some of them might disappear; he telegraphed to his superior in Athens:

SCHLIEMANN HAS CREWS DIGGING IN FOUR SEPARATE PLACES AT THE SAME TIME. I CANNOT POSSIBLY SUPERVISE FOUR EXCAVATIONS WHICH ARE DISTANT FROM EACH OTHER.

As had happened in Mycenae, Ephor Philios managed to shut down the dig. Again, as in Mycenae, Henry telegraphed Sophia to visit the Minister of Public Instruction and get Ephor Philios under control. Their friend Voulpiotes was entirely sympathetic.

It was the middle of April when Sophia arrived in Nauplion with Frau Dörpfeld and a French painter by the name of Gilliéron, whom Henry had asked her to employ for the copying of the superb potteries and wall paintings they were finding, including a fresco of bull tamers or dancers. The following morning Sophia awakened at 3:45 A.M. She dressed quickly in the full skirt and sturdy shoes that had become her digging uniform. Since there were marshes between Nauplion and Tiryns, she joined Henry in swallowing four grains of quinine. They crossed the waterfront street to the sea where a boatman arrived promptly at four o'clock. He took them from the quay out to the open sea where Henry dove off the little caïque and swam for ten minutes. After he had dressed they went to the Agamemnon Café to have a cup of black coffee, then got into the carriage which was waiting for them. In twenty-five minutes they were at Tiryns, before sunrise, sending the carriage back for the Dörpfelds.

The four breakfasted together at 8:00 A.M. while the workmen were resting, sitting on the floor of the old palace of Tiryns, which Henry had uncovered on the highest part of the hill, surrounded by a double wall. Because the cyclopean walls were still intact it had been a simple matter for Dörpfeld to draw a sketch of the settlement. Henry's workmen had unearthed, under only three to five feet of debris, the very big, old palace with its mosaic floor of small stones. Parts of the palace wall were still standing. In the digging process they found vases and idols similar to the ones found at Mycenae, confirming that the two citadels were contemporaneous.

Henry and Dörpfeld made stunning discoveries. In the palace itself there were numerous bases of pillars still *in situ*. The huge stone doorsills still lay in the doorway. They had cleared the great ramp on the east side, released the gigantic defense tower, dug the earth and debris out of a high walled approach, found a tremendous folding gate. In dimension and grandeur the approach road and the gate resembled those at Mycenae. Their most thrilling find, which they were still excavating, was the megaron; supported by four pillars, it was a room thirty-six feet long and thirty feet wide, with a large circle in its center for the hearth. Adjoining it were an antechamber, vestibule and large paved courtyard; nearby was a bathroom similar to the one rumored to be in the still uncovered palace of Mycenae. This "hall of the men" was so similar in construction to the two buildings in Troy which Henry had identified as temples that he now realized he had in fact been unearthing part of the royal palace in Troy. They had to have been constructed at approximately the same period in prehistory.

When he closed down the digs he returned to Athens to spend his time writing the early chapters of *Tiryns*. On New Year's Day of 1885 Sophia invited the family to lunch at Iliou Melathron. Her mother was coming from her house on foot, accompanied by Panaghiotes. As they crossed Syntagma Square she was shaken by a series of sharp pains in the chest. Panaghiotes summoned a nearby carriage. Madame Victoria managed to get up the marble staircase, then collapsed on the threshold. Sophia and Henry came running. Panaghiotes and a manservant carried her upstairs to a bedroom. Madame Victoria kissed Sophia on the cheek several times, murmured:

". . . my dearest daughter, you have been good to me. . . . I came to wish you Happy New Year and happy birthday. Now I must say . . . good-by. . . ."

She turned her head slightly to where Henry was kneeling by her side.

". . . my dear son . . . I am dying. Let me kiss you good-by."

She kissed Henry on the cheek six times, so faintly he could barely feel her lips. Then she closed her eyes and became silent. By the time the doctor arrived she was dead.

Once again Sophia and the family gathered at the Engastromenos plot where the priest intoned "*Eonía i mními.*"

Sophia felt numb. As her mother's coffin was covered with earth she murmured, "May your memory be eternal." In the carriage on the way home she said to Henry in a voice dry and hoarse:

"Both my parents are gone. I am now the older generation."

Back at Iliou Melathron Henry gave her a thimbleful of brandy to help dissipate her feeling of hollowness. A few days later she found him in the library drawing a sketch for a magnificent mausoleum. An upper section resembled a miniature Greek temple with four columns and a pediment; between the door of the lower massive walk-in tomb and the delicate temple above was a frieze of Henry and his workmen excavating at Troy.

"What in the world is that?" she asked.

"It's a sketch I'm giving to Ziller," Henry replied, "so that he can design a noble sepulcher. After we're dead I want us to be housed together eternally."

"Thank you for the lovely sentiment, my dear, but I prefer to live in the same house with you *alive*."

"I am now sixty-three, and this capricious body of mine is racked with all manner of strange illnesses. Frankly, I don't want my bones removed from my grave three years after I'm dead. Nor yours either. I will leave

Ziller's plan in my will along with fifty thousand drachmas to build the structure."

In March Panaghiotes Stamatakes died. Henry and Sophia attended the funeral. Memories of their early clashes seeped away; with Stamatakes dead, Henry wrote kindly about him in his book on Tiryns.

Early in 1885 Henry sent the eminently capable Dörpfeld back to Tiryns. He worked so fast and so well that he was able to contribute maps and plans for the palace on the acropolis and the middle fortress, which apparently contained lodgings for the servants; as well as the lower citadel, which yielded up storerooms, stalls for the horses and rooms for the retainers. They discovered fragments of wall paintings in the women's hall decorated with human figures as well as geometric designs. The women's dwelling had a separate court and numerous chambers, almost precisely as Homer had described the quarters of Penelope in *The Odyssey*.

Henry spent scattered weeks at Tiryns, leaving most of the supervision to Dörpfeld. Sophia was puzzled by this until she happened upon what appeared to be an unfinished letter Henry had left on a chair in the library:

> . . . But I am fatigued and have an immense desire to withdraw from excavations and to pass the rest of my life quietly. I feel I cannot stand any longer this tremendous work. Besides wherever I hitherto put the spade into the ground, I always discovered new worlds for archaeology at Troy, Mycenae, Orchomenos, Tiryns—each of them have brought to light wonders. But fortune is a capricious woman; perhaps she would now turn me her back; perhaps I should henceforward only find fiascoes! I ought to imitate Rossini, who stopped after having composed a few but splendid operas, which can never be excelled. When I retire from excavating and book writing, I shall be able to travel again. . . .

She was crushed. She had seen that his strength was waning, that illnesses were taking their toll. What she had not realized was that the greatest joy of his life, excavating, had been exhausted. It took several days to reconcile herself to the fact that Henry was willing to spend his remaining years defending work already accomplished, rather than start new digs and new controversies.

In the spring he was notified that Queen Victoria would present him with the Gold Medal for Art and Science. He went to London in May. Sophia and the children joined him at the Hotel du Pavillon Impérial in Boulogne-sur-Mer in France. They enjoyed a three-week vacation on the beach before leaving for Switzerland where Andromache was to attend a private school. They toured Switzerland, moved into a hotel at St. Moritz, then went on to Lausanne where the school was located, and where they would stay during the school year. Sophia's brother Panaghiotes had graduated from the university and been named ephor to the excavations of the French Archaeological Institute in Boeotia. When his dig closed down in September he came to visit them and brought the news that Henry had been elected a member of the German Archaeological Institute in Athens. Henry was delighted.

"I'll have to build them a first-rate institute to match the French. The house they're renting now on Academias Street is grossly inadequate. I'll charge them a modest rental."

He became restless, made trips into Germany and France, then went off to Constantinople where, through some process Sophia never did discover, he bought from the Imperial Museum the two thirds of his finds at Troy during the 1878 and 1879 excavations. He had the crates shipped back to Iliou Melathron and installed the collection in his own museum. By the first of the year 1886 Sophia became tired of being alone in Lausanne, gathered up her children and took them back to Athens.

Tiryns appeared in England, Germany, France and the United States late in 1885 and early in 1886. Two chapters were contributed by Dörpfeld. The book was widely read by Henry's loyal public but in the spring of 1886 controversy arose in London over a series of attacks in the *Times* accusing Dr. Schliemann of "mistaking rude medieval masonry for masonry of the heroic age" and of confusing Byzantine ruins with prehistoric ruins. The attacks on his integrity, which included his work at Troy and Mycenae, were so fierce and unexpected that he decided to go to London to defend himself. He took Dörpfeld with him to buttress his arguments.

The issues were discussed at a special July meeting of the Hellenic Society. Before a packed hall, Dr. Schliemann was confronted by W. J. Stillman, a *Times* correspondent, one of the *Times* editors, and an architect by the name of F. C. Penrose who had visited Tiryns and studied the excavations. Henry and Dörpfeld replied forcefully, backing their arguments with photographs, maps, drawings and artifacts from Troy, Mycenae and Tiryns. Henry had been defended in the *Times* by Max Müller and Arthur Evans, the future excavator of Knossos.

A few days later Henry received a letter from the secretary of the Hellenic Society which read:

> I have been looking carefully through my notes of the debate and I really cannot find any important point that was not answered at the time either by Dr. Dörpfeld or yourself. . . .

I am sure that the universal opinion here among all who are really competent to judge was that, so far as the high antiquity of the palace at Tiryns is concerned, the case of your opponents utterly and completely broke down. . . .

However the argument was not finally settled until Penrose accepted Henry's invitation to return with him and Dörpfeld, as Henry's guest, to Tiryns. The three men spent several days at the digs going over the evidence. In the end Penrose "handsomely conceded all points at issue."

Henry fulfilled the promise of his unfinished letter "to travel again." He took off for Egypt twice, the first time in 1887, the second in 1888 with his beloved friend Rudolf Virchow. They went up the Nile as far as Luxor. Between the two trips he commissioned Ziller and Dörpfeld to design a building for the German Archaeological Institute on a large lot on Pinakoton Street and, when the building was completed in the summer of 1888, took them in as tenants.

His victory over the English critics of the Tiryns discoveries in London in 1886 had done nothing to silence Captain Ernst Boetticher's continuing attacks from Berlin on Hissarlik as a fire necropolis and nothing more. Henry decided to use the same tactics on Boetticher that he had on Penrose and invited the man to Troy. Boetticher finally accepted in December of 1889. Henry also invited, as impartial witnesses, Professor Niemann of the Academy of Fine Arts in Vienna and a Major Steffen who had published well-known maps and plans of Mycenae. Days were spent in a detailed study of Troy, Dörpfeld stepping in when he saw that Henry was tiring. The two witnesses, Niemann and Steffen, were convinced of the veracity and fidelity of Henry's findings. Captain Boetticher was unmoved. Hissarlik was a fire necropolis and he told his public so in newly published articles. During the coming year his theory gained wider acceptance. Henry fumed. Sophia, trying to raise her two children in love and peace, decided that every pioneer was an opener of tombs.

"I was wrong; the old grandmother's tale is right," she told Henry. "If you disturb long-dead monarchs . . . long-dead ideas, they put a curse on you and make your life intolerable."

"Not mine!" cried Henry, his face ashen. "I'm going to stage an international conference. I'm going to invite to Troy the director of the Berlin Museum, the professor of archaeology at Heidelberg, the director of the Constantinople Museum, the director of the American School of Classical Studies in Athens . . ."

He invited them all and they accepted, a distinguished group of eight authorities including his friend Frank Calvert. This time he triumphed. The international conference agreed that there were no traces pointing to a necropolis or to the burning of corpses; that the second layer contained ruins of buildings, the most important of which resembled the palaces of Tiryns and Mycenae. Captain Boetticher's voice was stilled, though others would continue to whisper that Troy was located at Bounarbashi, not Hissarlik.

"This contest will never end," Sophia decided. "We will live with it the rest of our days."

3.

Henry's doctors in Germany had been speaking for several years about the advisability of an operation on both ears. It was not until the beginning of November that he left for Halle to consult with a Dr. Hermann Schwartz who was reputed to be an authority on ear surgery. Sophia rarely accompanied Henry to Germany for his ear treatments but surgery was a different matter.

"I will come with you, *agapete mou*, in case Dr. Schwartz decides to operate."

"Thank you, Sophidion, but it would be better if you remained here. Dr. Schwartz tells me that if he operates on both ears I will be completely deaf for at least three weeks; and that it will be necessary for me to stay in Halle for a month after the operation. The weather is cold there this time of the year, snow, fog, damp. If I can't hear you, if I am in pain, it would only make matters worse. I will write to you. . . ."

Within a few days Sophia learned that Dr. Schwartz had declared the operation on both ears to be urgent. Henry moved from the Hamburg Hotel to the private home of a widow, Frau Dr. Mathilde Goetz, who had four sons of university age. She would not only receive his visitors but be his nurse while he was convalescing. His next letter, giving the details of the operation, was frightening: Dr. Schwartz had taken out of the right ear three ossified growths. The left ear proved an even more serious problem, for the ossification rested on the fine bone of the cranium. Dr. Schwartz had had to remove and then sew back the outside wing of Henry's ear. The operation was complicated by profuse bleeding. Henry awakened feeling nauseous from the chloroform, his head swathed in bandages and his hospital bed surrounded by Dr. Schwartz and his assistants, who were anxiously awaiting his return to consciousness.

She must not come to Halle! Although he was miserable at being alone, no company would do him any good. Both ears were swollen; his acoustic ducts were closed, he could not hear a single sound. He had moved back into Frau Goetz's house, but it was so bitterly cold that

he was not permitted to go out. He could not wash, could not shave
. . . was not fit company for man or beast, with terrible pain in both
ears that kept him awake all night.

Each letter grew worse. His left ear was now filled with pus; the pain
was excruciating, the cold intense. In the morning the windowpanes
were full of ice despite the fact that he had kept the stove going during
the night. Would she postpone their Christmas tree until he got back?
He did not think he could make it for Christmas. But please send him
the copies of the *Academy* and *Athenaeum* as they reached the house.

Dr. Schwartz examined Henry's ears, assured him that the pain would
cease, that he would enjoy sharp hearing and very shortly be able to
leave Halle. All he would have to do would be to wear a bandage over
his ears, not expose them to the cold. Henry made plans to go to Leipzig to see his publisher, then to Berlin and Paris. However with the coming of December the pain in his left ear increased. Dr. Schwartz applied
opium to sedate it. Henry still could not hear a sound. . . .

His next letter came from Paris. He had scolded her for not writing to
him often enough but he was delighted when he reached the Grand
Hotel to find six letters which had been accumulating there. His left ear
had healed but when he left Halle he had forgotten to put cotton wool
into it. He caught cold and was obliged to see an ear specialist in Paris.
. . . He would soon be leaving for Naples where he wanted to spend
two days inspecting the new archaeological uncoverings at Pompeii.

In Naples he put up at the Grand Hotel; the proprietor was an old
friend. His left ear was again giving him tremendous pain. A Dr. Cozzolini gave him an injection. The drug helped but the doctor recommended that he not travel back to Athens for a few days. The following
day he visited the Pompeian excavations with Dr. Cozzolini. He ate
alone in the hotel diningroom on Christmas Eve and had breakfast in
the coffee room the next morning.

Then the details filtering through to her became almost incomprehensible. On Christmas Day he left the hotel about ten in the morning,
apparently to get another injection. He never reached the doctor's office. On a street near Piazza della Santa Carità he fell unconscious to the
pavement. When he came to and the men who had gathered around
him asked what was wrong, he was unable to speak. The police carried
him to the nearest hospital but no one found the wallet, filled with
gold pieces, which was buried deep inside a coat pocket. The hospital
would not admit him because he could provide no identification. Having no other choice, the police carried him to the station house
where fortunately they found Dr. Cozzolini's card in a vest pocket.
They summoned the doctor who, shocked at what had happened, identified the semiconscious man as the famous Dr. Henry Schliemann. Dr.

Cozzolini ordered a comfortable carriage, took Henry back to the Grand Hotel where he fed him some broth and had him carried upstairs to his bed.

A well-known German surgeon living in Naples, Dr. von Schoen, was summoned. He made an incision in Henry's left ear, cleaned it, but feared another operation might be needed in order to probe more deeply. Henry was unable to speak the entire night. The proprietor of the hotel stayed with him, feeding him broth and coffee.

The next morning, the day after Christmas, Dr. Cozzolini, Dr. von Schoen and six of their associates assembled to discuss the feasibility of a trepanation of Henry's cranium. While the discussion was going on in the next room, Henry quietly slipped out of what little consciousness he had been able to retain.

The ongoing developments reached Sophia in a series of telegrams. As soon as she learned that Henry had fallen unconscious on the street she packed her bags to leave Athens. It was Friday, there was no steamship sailing for Brindisi until the following day. In the early evening the final telegram arrived. Her husband was dead.

Dörpfeld and her brother Panaghiotes persuaded Sophia to let them take the Saturday ship to Brindisi to bring Henry's body back to Athens.

She sat in the library at Henry's desk racked with pity and sorrow, not only because Henry was gone: she was not taken totally by surprise, he had been ailing for a considerable time, his grip on his many affairs had become less focused; but that he had died in a hotel bed far from home, with none of his family to hold his hand and kiss him good-by. Guilt came next: she should have gone to Halle with him in the first place, certainly after she had learned the seriousness of his operation. But how often in their twenty-one years of marriage had she gone against his explicit wishes? He had not wanted her to come. . . .

She should have insisted that he come directly home from Halle to be nursed back to health in the warmer climate of Athens, surrounded by his beautiful possessions, by his wife, grown daughter and Greek son, instead of traveling to Berlin to see Virchow, to Paris to see other friends, and then to Naples to see Pompeii . . . all directly in character. She had never had a way to control him. No one had!

She shuddered as she pictured him being rejected by a hospital where his life might have been saved, because no one could identify him. Not identify Dr. Henry Schliemann, one of the most famous men in the world! Even now cablegrams of condolence were pouring in from everywhere; newspapers were running long stories of his bizarre yet creative life, the magnificent contribution he had made to the science of archaeology, to the knowledge of prehistory.

Henry Schliemann, dead just before his sixty-ninth birthday, had run his life span. He had fulfilled himself. Homer's Troy, Pausanias's royal tombs at Mycenae, the treasury at Orchomenos, the palace at Tiryns . . .

It was all in the past now.

In a few days Dörpfeld and Panaghiotes would bring him back home, the last of his many journeys. When his will was opened she would appropriate the fifty thousand drachmas for the building of his sepulcher. A Protestant chaplain would conduct the funeral service. As soon as the sepulcher was ready, Henry's body would be laid to rest there . . . forever.

She stretched her arms across his desk, lowered her head onto them. Loneliness flooded her being.

She was alone at the age of thirty-eight. Mistress of the grandiose Iliou Melathron, which she would have to manage herself. Andromache was nineteen, interested in a student at the university. It was probable that she would marry soon and leave. Agamemnon was only twelve. He would be a solace to her.

She knew the content of the will Henry had drawn on January 10, 1889. He had provided generously for his Russian family; there were gifts to his sisters, to Virchow and Dörpfeld. Andromache and Agamemnon were left valuable real estate. Despite the fact that he had obliged her father to accompany him to a notary public in Athens, where Georgios Engastromenos had had to sign a paper to the effect that his seventeen-year-old daughter would have no hold on his estate, Henry had left her Iliou Melathron and all of its contents, a building in Berlin and considerable other assets including the ownership of the new German Archaeological Institute building. She would be comfortable. She could maintain Iliou Melathron in the fashion Henry wanted, follow his instruction to receive everyone who came to his Palace of Troy, to offer them hospitality and show them their Trojan collection in the two museum rooms. When she was tired there was always the house in Kiphissia to which she could escape.

She rose from the desk, left the library and went downstairs. She walked slowly through the ballroom, stood beneath Henry's portrait in the frieze above, was surrounded by the quotations he had selected from the Greek classics he adored, heard his voice reading the passages to her over the years. Memories flooded over her like the waves of the Aegean Sea. Theokletos Vimpos had made a good marriage for her, guided her through its stormy episodes.

She would never love again; never marry again. She would remain in Athens as Kyria Sophia Schliemann, provide Dörpfeld with funds to continue the digging at Troy, defend the character and life work of her husband against the Captain Boettichers of Germany, the Stillmans and Penroses of England and all others who would attempt to belittle him. She was young, she was well, she would live a great many years. The fact of a long widowhood had been implicit from the beginning. She had no quarrel with her fate.

She walked up the stairs to her boudoir, sank to her knees before the Virgin Mary, prayed for the soul of Henry Schliemann, that his memory might be eternal.

AUTHOR'S NOTE

One of the problems encountered in writing this book was the fact that two different calendars were in use during the time. Henry Schliemann and the rest of Europe used the Gregorian calendar, as we do today. Greece was still using the Julian calendar, twelve days behind the Gregorian calendar. Sophia Schliemann seems to date her letters in the old style, the date the Greek newspapers also used. The dates used in Henry's books, diaries and letters are according to the new calendar. As a result there are some seeming contradictions as to when certain events took place. Greece did not officially adopt the Gregorian calendar until March 1, 1923.

Letter from Henry to Sophia dated November 26, 1889:

> Dearest, I gave you the money for your household accounts until the last cent to keep you going until the 1st of December, and I showed you the letter to the Ionian Bank by which I opened an account for you as from the 1st of December of the *new* calendar. By Jupiter, you simply *cannot* have forgotten all that!

Those readers hoping to see the treasure of Priam in Berlin will be disappointed. It has disappeared. When the Russian army was approaching Berlin toward the end of World War II the curators of the Berlin Museum for Early History bundled up the gold, some say in four separate packets, and hid it or buried it. To this day not a single gold bead has surfaced. There are numerous conjectures as to what happened: its hiding place was lost; it was bombed, melted down, confiscated . . . stolen. There is still a faint hope that it will reappear one day, unharmed and intact.

ACKNOWLEDGMENTS

I wish to express my appreciation to the Greek and Turkish governments for their wholehearted help and co-operation with every aspect of this book. In both countries the Ministers of Culture and Education made available archival materials, charted my travels, opened the doors of their universities, libraries, museums, gave me access to their archaeological sites.

In Athens I am indebted to the American School of Classical Studies, the French Archaeological Institute, the German Archaeological Institute, the British School of Archaeology, the National Library and the National Museum for considerable help in the research. I am also indebted to Mary Castriotis, Peter Delatolas, Constantinos Doxiadis, George Kournoutos, Konet Kryiazis, Professor and Mrs. Sp. Marinatos, Takis Muzenidis, Phrosso Mylof, Panos Nicalopolos, John Sideris, Alex Skeferi, Eberhard Slenczka, Stathis Stikas, Loukia Voudouris, Helen (Mrs. Alan) Wace.

In Turkey I am indebted to Erol Akçal, Ilhan Akşit, Tulay Alpertunga, Ambassador Pierluigi Alvera, Dr. Necati Dolunay, Nuri Eren, Üstün Ete, Lisa French, Sayin Geneal Cemal Gökar, Celik Gülersoy, Talat Halman, Hamit Kartal, Turgut Koyuncuoğlu, Professor Tahsin Özgüç, Eleanor Özkaptan, Admiral Cemal Suer.

In California I am indebted to Suzanna Ewing, Dr. and Mrs. Milton Heifetz, Dr. Emil Krahulic, Helen Lambros, Cornelius Leondes, Gloria Luchenbill, Dr. Constantin von Dziembowski, Mary von Sternberg.

I wish to thank Dr. Milton O. Gustafson of the National Archives and Records Service, Washington, D.C., and the Eli Lilly Company of Indianapolis for their helpfulness.

Finally, I want to express my deep gratitude to Ken McCormick for his thirty-five years as my friend, counselor and editor at Doubleday.

SELECT BIBLIOGRAPHY

BOOKS WRITTEN BY HENRY SCHLIEMANN

La Chine et le Japon au temps présent, 1867.
Ithaque, le Péloponnèse, Troie, 1869.
Antiquités Troyennes, 1874.
Atlas des Antiquités Troyennes, 1874.
Troy and Its Remains, 1874.
Mycenae, 1878.
Ilios: City and Country of the Trojans, 1880.
Orchomenos. Bericht über meine Ausgrabungen im Böotischen Orchomenos, 1881.
Reise in der Troas im Mai 1881, 1881.
Troja: Results of the Latest Researches, 1884.
Tiryns: The Prehistoric Palace of the King of Tiryns, 1885.

BOOKS WRITTEN ABOUT HENRY SCHLIEMANN

Arnold Brackman, *The Dream of Troy*, 1974.
Marjorie Braymer, *The Walls of Windy Troy*, 1960.
Eli Lilly, ed., *Schliemann in Indianapolis*, 1961.
Emil Ludwig, *Schliemann. The Story of a Gold-seeker*, trans. D. F. Tait, 1931.
Ernst Meyer, ed., *Briefe von Heinrich Schliemann*, 1936.
——, *Heinrich Schliemann—Briefwechsel*, Vol. I (1842–75), 1953; Vol. II (1876–90), 1958.
Robert Payne, *The Gold of Troy*, 1959.
Lynn and Gray Poole, *One Passion, Two Loves*, 1966.
Carl Schuchhardt, *Schliemann's Excavations*, trans. E. Sellers, 1891.
Shirley H. Weber, ed., *Schliemann's First Visit to America 1850–1851*, 1942.

BOOKS ON ARCHAEOLOGY

Ekren Akurgal, *Ancient Civilizations and Ruins of Turkey*, trans. John Whybrow and Mollie Emre, 1969.
Carl W. Blegen, *Troy*, Vol. I, Pts. 1 and 2, 1950; Vol. IV, Pts. 1 and 2, 1958.
——, *Troy and the Trojans*, 1963.

Marcel Brion, *The World of Archaeology*, trans. Miriam and Lionel Kochan, 1961.
C. W. Ceram, *Gods, Graves and Scholars*, trans. E. B. Garside, 1951.
——, *A Picture History of Archaeology*, trans. Richard and Clara Winston, 1957.
Leonard Cottrell, *The Bull of Minos*, 1958.
——, *The Land of Shinar*, 1965.
L. Sprague and Catherine C. de Camp, *Ancient Ruins and Archaeology*, 1946.
Leo Deuel, ed., *The Treasures of Time*, 1961.
Walter Leaf, *Troy: A Study in Homeric Geography*, 1912.
Paul MacKendrick, *The Greek Stone Speaks*, 1962.
George E. Mylonas, *Mycenae and the Mycenaean Age*, 1966.
William St. Clair, *Lord Elgin and the Marbles*, 1967.
Frank H. Stubbings, *Prehistoric Greece*, The World of Archaeology Series, ed. Peter Gelling, 1972.
Chrestos Tsountas and J. Irving Manatt, introduction by Dr. Dörpfeld, *The Mycenaean Age*, 1969.
Alan J. B. Wace, *Mycenae: An Archaeological History and Guide*, 1949.
Jean Zafiropulo, *Mead and Wine*, trans. Peter Green, 1966.
Erich Zehren, *The Crescent and the Bull*, trans. James Cleugh, 1962.

HISTORY

Stringfellow Barr, *The Will of Zeus*, 1961.
A. R. Burn, *Minoans, Philistines, and Greeks*, 1968.
John Cambell and Philip Sherrard, *Modern Greece*, 1968.
I. E. S. Edwards, ed., *Cambridge Ancient History*, 3rd ed., Vol. III, Pt. 1, 1973.
George Grote, *History of Greece*, 10 vols., 1888.
H. R. Hall, *The Ancient History of the Near East*, 1913.
J. M. Todd, *The Ancient World*, 1938.

CULTURE AND CIVILIZATION

Carl Bluemel, *Greek Sculptors at Work*, trans. Lydia Holland, 1955.
Richard and Eva Blum, *The Dangerous Hour*, 1970.
C. M. Bowra, *The Greek Experience*, 1957.
Lewis Richard Farnell, *Greek Hero Cults and Ideas of Immortality*, 1921.
Theodor Gomperz, *The Greek Thinkers*, Vol. I, trans. Laurie Magnus, 1901; Vol. II, trans. G. G. Berry, 1905; Vol. III, trans. G. G. Berry, 1905; Vol. IV, trans. G. G. Berry, 1912.
Edith Hamilton, *The Echo of Greece*, 1957.
Jacquetta Hawkes, *Dawn of the Gods*, 1968.
Sinclair Hood, *The Home of the Heroes*, Library of the Early Civilizations, ed. Stuart Piggott, 1967.

Werner Jaeger, *Paideia: the Ideals of Greek Culture*, Vol. I, trans. Gilbert Highet, 1945.

C. Kerényi, *The Religion of the Greeks and Romans*, trans. Christopher Holme, 1962.

H. D. F. Kitto, *The Greeks*, 1951.

R. W. Livingston, ed., *The Legacy of Greece*, 1923.

——, *The Mission of Greece*, 1928.

Seton Lloyd, *Early Highland Peoples of Anatolia*, Library of the Early Civilizations, ed. Stuart Piggott, 1967.

Friedrich Matz, *Crete and Early Greece*, Art of the World Series, trans. Ann E. Keep, 1962.

James Mellaart, *Earliest Civilizations of the Near East*, Library of the Early Civilizations, ed. Stuart Piggott, 1965.

Martin P. Nilsson, *Homer and Mycenae*, 1933.

——, *Greek Folk Religion*, 1961.

Gisela M. A. Richter, *A Handbook of Greek Art*, 1959.

Chester G. Starr, *The Ancient Greeks*, 1971.

Alan J. B. Wace, *Greece Untrodden*, 1964.

John Winckelmann, *History of Ancient Art*, 2 vols., trans. C. Henry Lodge, 1880.

Arthur M. Young, *Troy and Her Legend*, 1948.

W. Zschietzschmann, ed., *Hellas and Rome*, 1959.

LITERATURE

Aeschylus, *Prometheus Bound and Other Plays*, Penguin Classics, ed. E. V. Rieu, trans. Philip Vellacott, 1961.

Thomas W. Allen, *Homer: The Origins and the Transmission*, 1924.

J. B. Bury, *The Ancient Greek Historians*, 1958.

H. Munro Chadwick, *The Heroic Age*, 1926.

Euripides, *Alcestis, Hippolytus, Iphigenia in Tauris*, Penguin Classics, ed. E. V. Rieu, trans. Philip Vellacott, 1953.

Robert Fitzgerald, ed., *The Aeneid of Virgil*, trans. John Dryden, 1964.

Francis R. B. Godolphin, ed., *The Greek Historians*, 2 vols., 1942.

David Grene and Richmond Lattimore, eds., *The Complete Greek Tragedies*, 4 vols., 1959.

Herodotus, *The Histories*, Penguin Classics, ed. E. V. Rieu, trans. Aubrey de Sélincourt, 1954.

Hesiod, *The Homeric Hymns and Homerica*, Loeb Classical Library, ed. E. H. Warmington, trans. H. G. Evelyn-White, 1914.

Homer, *The Iliad*, trans. Alexander Pope, 1943.

——, *The Iliad*, Loeb Classical Library, ed. E. H. Warmington, 2 vols., trans. A. T. Murray, 1924.

——, *The Iliad*, Modern Library College Edition, trans. Andrew Lang, Walter Leaf, Ernest Myers, 1950.

——, *The Odyssey*, trans. Alexander Pope, 1942.

——, *The Odyssey*, Loeb Classical Library, ed. T. E. Page, 2 vols., trans. A. T. Murray, 1919.

——, *The Odyssey*, Penguin Classics, ed. and trans. E. V. Rieu, 1946.

H. D. F. Kitto, *Greek Tragedy*, 1939.

Walter Leaf, *Homer and History*, 1915.

James H. Mantinband, *Dictionary of Greek Literature*, 1966.

Mark P. O. Morford and Robert J. Lenardon, *Classical Mythology*, 1971.

Denys Page, *History and the Homeric Iliad*, Sather Classical Lectures, Vol. 31, 1959.

Pausanias, *Guide to Greece*, Penguin Classics, eds. Betty Radice and Robert Baldick, 2 vols., trans. Peter Levi, 1971.

Pindar, *The Odes*, Penguin Classics, eds. Betty Radice and Robert Baldick, trans. C. M. Bowra, 1969.

John A. Scott, *The Unity of Homer*, Sather Classical Lectures, 1965.

Sophocles, *Electra and Other Plays*, Penguin Classics, ed. E. V. Rieu, trans. E. F. Watling, 1953.

George Steiner and Robert Fagles, eds., *Homer*, 1962.

Thucydides, *The Peloponnesian War*, Penguin Classics, ed. E. V. Rieu, trans. Rex Warner, 1954.

Alan J. B. Wace and Frank H. Stubbings, eds., *A Companion to Homer*, 1962.

T. B. L. Webster, *From Mycenae to Homer*, 1958.

GREECE

Hachette World Guides, *Greece*, 1964.

The Art of Greek Cookery, St. Paul's Greek Orthodox Church, 1961.

E. D. Clarke, *Travels in Europe, Asia and Africa*, Vol. III, 1817.

E. Dodwell, *Tour Through Greece*, 1819.

——, *View and Descriptions of Cyclopean or Pelasgic Remains*, 1834.

W. Gell, *The Itinerary of Greece*, 1810.

William Leake, *Travels in the Morea*, Vol. II, 1830.

John Travlos, *Neo-Classical Architecture in Greece*, 1967.

Timothy Ware, *The Orthodox Church*, 1963.

OTHER TITLES

Oxford Classical Dictionary, 2nd ed., eds. N. G. L. Hammond and H. H. Scullard, 1970.

Erwin H. Ackerknecht, *Rudolf Virchow*, 1953.

Peter Goessler, *Wilhelm Dörpfeld*, 1951.

ARTICLES, PAMPHLETS AND MONOGRAPHS

Ilhan Akşit, *Guide to Troy*.

Franz George Brustgi, *Heinrich Schliemann*, 1971.

William M. Calder III, "Schliemann on Schliemann: A Study in the Use of Sources," *Greek, Roman and Byzantine Studies*, Vol. 13, 1972.

Frank Calvert, "Contributions to the Ancient Geography of the Troad," *Archaeological Journal*, 1860.

M. S. F. Hood, "Schliemann's Mycenae Albums," *Archaeology*, Vol. 13, No. 1, 1960.

Ernst Meyer, "Schliemann's Letters to Max Müller in Oxford," *Journal of Hellenic Studies*, Vol. 82, 1962.

William G. Niederland, "An Analytic Inquiry into the Life and Work of Heinrich Schliemann," reprinted from *Drives, Affects, Behavior*, Vol. 2, 1965.

George St. Korres, *The Inscriptions of "Iliou Melathron,"* 1974.

——, *Henry Schliemann's Last Will*, 1974.

Henry Schliemann, *The Site of the Homeric Troy*, 1875.

Helen Wace, Elizabeth Wace French, Charles Williams, *Mycenae Guide*, 1971.

NEWSPAPERS

Academy, Athenaeum, Ephimeris, Manchester *Guardian, Levant Herald,* London *Times, Newspaper of the Debates.*

A complete bibliography on Henry Schliemann, in Greek, has been compiled by Professor George St. Korres, Jr., of the University of Athens and was published in 1974.